The Second American Civil War

YEAR ZERO

by
James F. Howell

ISBN: 978-1-4583-2416-1

Printed in the United States of America

First Printing

<u>Dedication:</u>

hope is a bad strategy

Socranson's Rules for Marital Law

1. Emotion overrules logic.

2. Revenge lacks common sense.

3. Never forget that no one is your friend.

4. Groups of people breed stupidity.

5. Never get in a hurry.

6. Mice and men are equal.

7. All lies have to have truth and all truth has to have lies.

8. Cockroaches run from the light.

9. Today is important, for tomorrow you will be dead.

10. Know their rules better than them and use them better.

11. I am maybe important, are you?

12. War is moral only if you are the victor.

13. Keep the left hand and right hand ignorant of each other.

Prologue

**The Second American Civil War didn't begin with a shot being fired,
It was a signature on a form.**

Historical Note: June 1, 2130

The Scholars of New Harvard University's Historical Department published four separate volumes putting forth their version of events surrounding the Second American Civil War.

This endeavor was a full century after the fact.

Four separate volumes were published because four points of view prevailed over all others. "All things being equal," Professor Wilbur Nishan said. "We at least decided on four volumes." Each of the four volumes philosophically asked one question. What price does a society pay for its comfort and conscience? In the case of the United States as a whole, history suggests that the price was too high."

A total of 7,684 books were written about that time in history, but only seven hundred and seventy-two were written by the people who actually did any of the fighting or dying.

At the beginning of the 22ⁿᵈ Century, the last purge of classified information from that era had tried to answer lingering questions. But it had the effect of causing more questions to be asked.

Jonas Cramer, Lead Archivist at New Harvard University said, "I have a hard time separating my 22ⁿᵈ century prejudices from 21ˢᵗ century facts."

Therein lay the problem.

Volume One, Cultural History*. This was a full cross section of all the factions that fractured this nation almost to the point of never rejoining. This volume was strictly concerned with who and what the people and groups were before, during and after the war. Names such as Socranson, Criers, Minuteman, O'Cleary, Cartwright, Matheson, Hawker, Thomas and Folcroft were given new faces and meanings.*

5

Perhaps no other work of literature ever tried to put such a human face on a disaster.

This volume raised a lot of debate about why this war was fought. The United States of America had long been considered the most stable and consistent country in the world. Those very things seem to make us vulnerable to a civil war. Two oceans had long shielded us from the world's problems. Those two oceans also insulated us from the lessons everyone else had learned.

Dr. Alistair Alysis, PhD, said the following: "Every society after the invention of the plow allowed some of its citizens to be free to specialize in making others comfortable or safe. People were now free to be carpenters, teachers, soldiers, firemen, doctors or anything other than food gatherers. But this also allowed monarchs, despots, dictators, presidents or tribal leaders to have shadow people. These shadow people did the things that were not just morally wrong but were an end to a means. They did the things that 'were necessary' to protect a 'noble people' from harm. Invariably, no matter how noble the purpose, that nobility always becomes corrupted."

Volume Two, Factual History, *listed nothing but the facts as recorded and verified by at least two separate sources. This volume dealt with news periodicals, magazines, diaries, and interviews of individuals. Using the surviving documents as a guide, scholars came face to face with all the uncensored horrors and realities of war. The words "The Facts, the Facts and nothing but the Facts" were written on a sign placed over the door leading into the large hall used by the men and woman assembling this information.*

Martin Grayson, author of "Misery: A Very Unique American Civil War," laid the ground work for much of the information in this volume. He spent thirty-nine years interviewing survivors of the war from all sides, patiently recording their stories and their perspectives using their words and their memories.

Volume Three, Military History, *was the only one of the volumes that had the easiest time assembling information.*

As the title states, only military actions were researched, assembled and included in this volume.

Throughout this period of history, groups of like-minded people banded together to protect themselves. Some wanted to fight something they accused as being the government. Some wanted to protect themselves from ideas that few could articulate. They majority mainly wanted to fight to hold on to the few things they called their own. In layman's terms, they didn't know why they fought.

By all accounts, militia groups at the height of the Civil War numbered over 1,000 and covered every cause and region. They ranged in size from two or three to several hundred. They fought official and unofficial governments, other groups, and bands of so called "criminal" elements. The most famous was the Minutemen, which operated in Montana, Idaho, Wyoming and Colorado. They were reputed to be the Robin Hoods and policemen for that region. Whether they allied with other groups or operated alone, the mere mention of their name struck fear in everyone. They could never be caught or cornered and coined a new word for the dictionary: INSANE JANE.

Monika Whitaker, author of "Joan of America," wrote about something unique in world military history. Up until this time, women were mainly rear area assistants in every war. If they fought in past wars, it was only out of necessity. Mimicking the State of Israel, the Second American Civil War brought women forward into the world as no legislation or argument ever voiced. They became the true equals of men because they became equal in battle, dying and death. These women manned the front lines and fought alongside the men.

Battles, large and small, were fought in all fifty states including parts of Mexico and Canada. Groups and Armies large and small contested for ground, lust, food, power and any number of hundreds of reasons. 22nd century prejudices recorded an estimated 17,246 recorded battles. The line between police and military actions blurred depending on the author or authority.

In the end, 28,479,727 lives vanished because of battles, disease, neglect, starvation and exposure based on, of all things, the difference between the census records. A survey

7

of the seven thousand new cemeteries puts the number at 18,628,848. Whether the others died or fled America is a point of dispute.

Simon MacGregor, an archivist at New Harvard, was reported as saying, "What is the difference? That many people are a statistic."

What was never in dispute was the fate of 5,298 nuclear weapons, or their components, that remained for the world to be afraid of. Despite numerous objections and actions by many multi-national, national and regional governments, the United States arsenal of nuclear weapons was never compromised. This was due in no small part to the placement and arming of 2 twenty megaton nuclear warheads at the main storage facility shelter two hundred feet underground at Dugway Proving Grounds in Utah. By coincidence or design, the facility was completed one year before the beginning of the Civil War. Any further hint of interference from the outside world was silenced by the launching of a Trident D5 ICBM missile from the submarine, USS Henry M. Jackson. The inert warheads from the single missile were spread over an uninhabited section of the Pacific Ocean. The message was sent out: "LEAVE US ALONE."

One interesting point was that America was accused of starting the wars that flared up around the world. Fourteen nuclear devices were detonated furthering conflicts in hot spots around the world. After Caracas, Denver, Tel Aviv and the Vatican became victims of nuclear terrorism, the innocence of the world was shattered.

"Christianity, Islam, and Judaism are the same," Pope Thomas said. "We are all descendants of Abraham. There will be peace when we finally see each other as one family."

In the end, the dead were reduced to a long number. Murder, rape, arson and theft were reduced from actual crimes to statistics.

Volume Four, Government, Law and Societal History, asked 'can the governments or the laws they framed for society be faulted'? What is the law and what makes a law moral or immoral? Can the government be blamed for giving or not giving the people what they wanted or did they spend money on *things that just guaranteed re-elections? The events preceding the beginning of the war pointed in those directions with the responses to the terrorist attacks of January 20th, the collapse of the national power grid, the destruction of Wolf Creek Dam and the subsequent imposition of protracted and sustained martial law. The people sat back and said 'let the government rescue us.' Few, if any, rose to save themselves.*

During and after the war, no consensus or debate could decide the issue. The only thing that was a constant was that there was more confusion and debate. Journals and periodicals of the time could not point to anything being resolved.

One interesting item occurred during and especially after the war. Populations refused to allow Judges to free criminals over technicalities. "Criminals are criminals," Justice Wilma Handers said. "If a murder is committed and the murderer is found, how is he or she innocent because the Police mispronounced a word?"

Jane Christenson Achier, PhD, said the following. "Are we morons? I say yes and no matter whether you academics agree or disagree on, I say all of us are morons. Every single issue that supposedly led to that war is still being played out today." She was fond of holding up a large stack of newspapers, magazines and computer disks and throwing them on the floor in front of her. "Change the dates and they read, word for word, exactly the same thing today. Wise up or there will be a third Civil War coming because crooks do not deserve more rights than victims or innocent citizens."

"Governments and guns are not evil in themselves," Supreme Court Justice Byron McGeorge said. "You can place a gun on a table and ignore it. It doesn't care. You can yell at it, make faces, call it names, or hit it with a ball bat: it won't care. A gun requires a hand to pick it up and a brain has to decide to shoot. It has to be pointed it at someone and a finger has to pull a trigger. It absolutely requires a human being to make it do evil. It is the same as a government. Two government workers can do the same thing to the same citizens and you will get two different outcomes."

In the end this volume tried to answer one question. "What is really evil: the government, the people or the situation?"

Simon Lockwood-Green, the noted statesman and diplomat said shortly before his death. "No bureaucrat, diplomat or statesman can do his or her job without a thorough understanding of how stupid, petty, ignorant and selfish a man or woman is. When presented with a truth that is not in their best interest, they will fight it for no other reason than it will give them something. No one in their right mind would kill a child for any reason. But it can be argued that the child will one day be an adult and that adult could seek revenge. No one will purposely tear down a neighbor's home. But is the shopping mall, hotel, hospital, road or school more important than the person's home? When will a people understand that nothing is too small or that any man's possessions are sacred?"

Latham Thomas, the 49th President of the United States and a veteran of the war, was famous for his loathing of lawyers and judges even though his wife was a lawyer. "Every last one of them," he declared, "can praise God on Sunday and defend Satan all week. Lawyers only understand one thing: If you have money, you are not guilty. For me they were the singular reason that war was forced on us. No one could turn to the law for justice. Time and time again, good people choose badly because "the law" was more interested in confusion than right or wrong. I could kill my entire family on live TV and walk away a free man because it becomes poor little ol' me and never the victims."

"Lawyers, if made to confess," President Thomas further said, "will tell you that Justice has no place in a court room. Idiots will argue for years about nothing and everything until no one can remember why they started arguing in the first place. If someone is killed, they are dead. If my wife or daughter is raped, I don't care why. If children are abused, they were abused."

President Thomas' most famous quote was "Jails should be places that are miserable. Prisons became country clubs because lawyers didn't want to be miserable if caught."

The authors of the final edition of this volume, in the end, didn't have an answer for anything. They only had more questions a century after the fact.

Historical Note from Graham North, Archivist of the United States, June 1, 2130. When asked for his comments, he had these two items to add:

Mack Carter, the war's last known living survivor, granted an interview shortly before his death on July 23rd, 2091. When asked for his thoughts he said. "I don't know. I watched men and women die. All these years later, I don't know anymore."

In the end it was the words of one man who summed it all up: Reverend Jason Carson, of St. Louis, Missouri. Reverend Carson tended to the wounded on all sides and personally buried more than three thousand men, women and children. He is quoted as saying. "The Lord our God is mysterious in his ways. No Man or Woman should war, but we do. All of God's creations were created to love, flourish and walk in peace. In the end, all of God's children are truly endowed by their creator with the right to be stupid."

[Continued from Emergency Action Message #2]

June 15

The White House, Washington, DC
1708 hours EDT.

This document is not for Public Release without the express approval of the President of the United States.

Executive Order 17114

Establishment and Implementation of Martial Law within the United States of America

Preamble. By the authority vested in me as President, by the Constitution and the laws of United States of America, including section 1822 of the National Defense Authorization Act of 2008; the Posse Comitatus Act of 1878; the National Security Act of 1950; the Special National Security Act of 1955; the Insurrection Act of 1807; the National Emergencies Act, USC Title 50, Section 34, National Emergencies; the John Warner Defense Authorization Act of 2007, as amended 2009, 2013, 2014 and 2019; in order to preserve, protect and defend the United States and its citizens due to national economic collapse; disruption of law and order; external and internal threats to the security of the United States, the following is hereby ordered as follows:

Section 1. Effective 16 June, a state of National Emergency and Martial Law is declared for a period of one year and will

12

expire on 16 June, unless extended or rescinded by the President of the United States.

Section 2. Scope. There is established the Internal Security Agency (ISA), per Executive Order 17104, which will oversee operations within, but not limited to the borders of the United States and this order will encompass the provisions of the "Victoria Operational Plan" as published and amended as the Director of the ISA directs. These actions will include, but not limited to the following.

Section 3. National Security.

Section 301. The Director of the ISA shall assume executive authority and coordination functions of the Departments and Agencies as described in Executive Order 17104.

Section 302. The Director of the ISA shall take all actions within, but not limited to, the provisions of the "Victoria Operations Plan" to establish law and order, restore the economic vitality of the United States.

Section 303. The Director of the ISA shall coordinate the actions of the Department of Justice and the Department of Defense to Establish a National Police Force.

    A. Department of Defense personnel shall be deputized as Federal Law Enforcement Officers per the requirements of the Posse Comitatus Act of 1878, the National Emergencies Act and subsequent amendments.

    B. Department of Justice personnel shall assist as directed to enforce provisions of "Victoria Operations Plan," as directed by the Director of the ISA.

    C. The following rights of citizens, as follows, shall be suspended or curtailed as directed by local authorities and as the situation(s) require.

        1. Right to Assembly
        2. Right to Habeas Corpus.
        3. Right to Legal Counsel.
        4. Right to a Jury of Peers.
        5. Right to a Speedy Trial and Due Process.

Section 304. The Director of the ISA shall review all laws and regulations to determine germane requirements of the national situation as it exists periodically and adjust requirements as the situation dictates.

Section 4. National Economic Measures.

Section 401. The provisions of the following Executive Orders, but restricted to, shall be used as the Director of the ISA determines:
17002, 17003, 17004

Section 402. The Director of the ISA, the Secretary of Treasury, the Secretary of Commerce and the Chairman of the Federal Reserve shall exercise executive control and authority to oversee and coordinate the following:

A. Per Executive Order 17002. Replace standard green ink-based currency with the redesigned blue ink-based currehcy no later than January 1.

1. The standard value of the redesigned currency will be secured by national stockpiles of precious metals and resources.

2. The Federal Reserve shall set a redemption value of older currency versus newer currency.

B. Per Executive Order 17003. Treasury and the Federal Reserve shall review all banking institutions, regulations and laws in order to review the following:

1. Solvency of assets.

2. Correct accounting of funds and tax structuring.

3. Treasury Department will determine which industries, institutions and commercial companies that are and will be vital to the economic health of the United States and take those steps necessary to insure solvency.

C. Per Executive Order 17004. The Director of the ISA shall execute provisions of Executive Order 17111. The Director of the ISA is authorized and empowered to conscript civilians into a National Work Force, as the situation requires.

Section 403. The Director of the ISA shall not take any action which will endanger the recovery of the National Economy.

Section 5. Population Measures.

Section 501.   The Provisions of the following Executive Orders, but not restricted to, are in effect:
    17004, 17005, 17006, 17007.

Section 502.   Per Executive Order 17004, the Postmaster General of the United States shall maintain a current, updated roster and data base of all citizens within the United States:
    A.   To maintain a national register of trained professionals to be utilized as the national need requires and for emergency situations, as directed by the Director, ISA.
    B.   To maintain a national register of able-bodied citizens and skills to assist any situation or emergency as the national need requires.
    C. All citizens, aged eighteen years and older, shall be registered with the Selective Service Administration, regardless of prior military service, and be made available for service as the situation or circumstances require.

Section 503.   Per Executive Order 17108, the Federal Emergency Management Agency (FEMA), in conjunction with the ISA, shall take executive control of all federal, state and local agencies and assets as required to manage and reduce emergency situation (s) on a pro-active basis.
    A. As an emergency occurs, FEMA shall exercise full Executive Authority to requisition any public or private resource as the ISA Director determines.
    B. Provisions as outlined in the "Victoria Operations Plan" shall be used to execute those actions.

Section 504. Per Executive Order 17007, The Department of Housing and Urban Development (HUD) shall exercise Executive Authority to relocate Citizens from uninhabitable areas designated as unsafe. HUD is authorized to utilize public funds to build new housing and supporting infrastructure.

Section 505.   Per Executive Order 17006, Detention of Citizens.

A. The Police Executive, Department of Justice and the Department of Homeland Security shall detain citizens deemed to be hostile to law and order.

B. Normal rules, regulations, protocols and procedures of arrest and incarceration are waived at the discretion of the Administrative Zone Military Commander and the civilian executive branch officers.

C. The Department of Justice shall oversee rules and procedures.

D. The Department of Homeland Security shall oversee the collection of information to determine the status of citizens.

E. The Police Executive shall oversee national, regional, State, and local actions to comply with and enforce the provisions of this order and those subsequent orders issued at all levels.

F. All police forces from all local, city, county and state Law Enforcement Organizations are federalized and placed under the executive control and direction of the Police Executive and the Department of Justice.

G. Writs of Habeas Corpus and established rules of sentencing are suspended.

H. All police forces at all levels of government are required to enforce the orders of the Police Executive and the Department of Justice.

Section 6. Public Health. Effective the date of this order, per Executive Order 17005, the following is directed.

A. All doctors, nurses, health care professionals and workers shall be conscripted into national service under the Executive Control and Authority of the Surgeon General of the United States.

B. All hospitals, clinics and health facilities, public and private, are nationalized, and placed under the Executive Control and Authority of the Department of Health and Human Services.

C. All Health Insurance Agencies, Companies and other Entities are now under the Executive Control and Authority of the Department of Health and Human Services.

Section 7. Transportation. Per Executive Order 17012, 17013.

A. All ground, air and railroad transportation means within the United States is placed under the executive authority and control of the Department of Transportation.

B. All airports, rail yards, roads and highways, ship yards and any other place or entity that Transportation assets utilize as refueling centers, parking, transshipment points or repair facilities are placed under the

Section 8. Farms and Food Production. Per Executive Order 17117.

A. All businesses, facilities, farms and related activities or processes used to produce food products shall be placed under the executive control and authority of the Department of Agriculture (DAG).

B. The DAG shall allocate or reallocate machinery and tools as required to maximize food production.

C. The DAG shall determine and allocate food and food products evenly and fully to all citizens regardless of status.

Section 9. The Provisions of the Victoria Operational Plan shall be used at all levels of government and society as standard operating procedure.

Section 10. The President or any official appointed under this office shall modify or amend this Executive Order at any time as the need or situation requires.

The President of the United States of America.

June 16

Saint Peter's Square, The Vatican
0501 hours (Alpha) - (0001 EDT).

Mahmud's bomb detonated, producing a fireball 50 feet in diameter which vaporized the nuclear material. Because of the heavy overcast and negligible winds, the radioactive cloud did not rise more than 200 feet above the ground before condensing back to a solid form to settle within the walls of the Vatican. Ordinary citizens in and around the Vatican were awakened by a deafening roar. Anyone within two blocks of the Vatican was thrown off their beds.

The Swiss Guard, true to their training and allegiance, rushed into the Pope's bed chamber and dragged him to the secret underground passage, the Passetto di Borgo, out of the Vatican. Within seconds, radiation alarms sounded, making some of the startled residents freeze in place. Most of the first responders and Church officials in the square became the bombs first victims as the deadly radioactive cloud settled and infected everyone as they rushed to help others.

In the central Swiss Guard Security Headquarters, the Commandant, Colonel Victor Guardo watched in horror as the radiation counters spiked above their maximum settings. On the screens displaying the carnage in the square, it was clearly visible that the Clergy, His Guards and ordinary citizens were dying in front of him. Colonel Guardo picked up the red phone to the Roman Military Police Headquarters, or Carabinieri, and prepared to tell them that the Vatican was dead.

Off to the right were the civilian news media cameras. The scene was now being played out for the world to see and witness.

White House, Washington, DC
0700 hours EDT.

When the President was awakened at 12:15 am and told that a low yield nuclear weapon was detonated at the Vatican, he smiled thinking it was a joke or some simulation that his advisors were running. After being hustled downstairs by the

Secret Service, his blood froze at the site of the nightmare of all nightmares.

"Get me the Russian Ambassador and put him in the Oval Office now," he demanded. That tone of his voice was very familiar to everyone. "Do not argue with me, do it." The President was briefed for twenty minutes and he instructed the operators to concentrate on determining if the material was from the same source as the Israeli bomb. He upgraded the US Defense Condition to Level Three, against his advisor's warnings and left to go to bed.

The President was able to sleep for three hours before his advisors finished waiting as long as they could and summoned him downstairs. The look on their faces was not good.

"Mr. President, the Russian Ambassador is waiting for you in the Oval Office. All our information is preliminary, but we can say that the weapon was radiological in nature and the material is the same as the one in Israel. It is definitely smaller, but that is not the problem. The weather was heavy and overcast. The buildings and the Vatican walls are containing the radiation. Preliminary reports put the radiation levels at far beyond lethal."

"The Pope?" the President asked.

"The Italian authorities are all over it, but we have no official word yet," Michael Moseley, his Chief of Staff said.

0900 hours EDT.

The President sat in the Oval Office waiting for the green light to address the nation. His original address to the nation this morning had to be scrapped. He was planning to calm the nation and explain the actions happening everywhere at once. Military troops were fanning out all around the nation, locking down everything and seizing industries. As the technician counted down the seconds to zero, the red light went on.

"My fellow Americans, I address you this morning with two pressing issues. First, at one minute past midnight, local time here in Washington, terrorists detonated a crude nuclear device at the Vatican. Information is very scarce at this time.

19

If you have relatives at or near the Vatican, the Italian Embassy and their consulates have established a hotline phone number to provide any information that is available. Americans are always in the fore front and are the most generous people in the history of the world. Donations to help with this disaster can be given to the Red Cross or any Catholic Church or ministry. I will make any information available to the American Media as we get it."

The President leaned closer and pointedly looked straight into the camera. "This morning you awoke to a State of National Emergency. For the vast majority of you, nothing has changed. You will continue to see soldiers outside assisting in maintaining law and order as you have for the last several months. You will continue to get your mail like you do every day. You will continue to get into your car and drive to work. Grocery stores and other stores are still open so you can shop. Normalcy will continue and you will enjoy a better quality of life. I sit here in this office as your President to assure you that the American way of life will continue."

The President put a deliberate cast to his face. "To those of you that break the law, prey on innocent citizens, or treat this situation as a means for personal gain, I promise you that those days are over. Even though law enforcement has newer tools to arrest and prosecute law breakers and offenders, our legal system will prosecute you with ever more vigilance. Gone are the days when the law is something to subvert and play with. To the police and other law enforcement officials, the days of arresting someone only to have that person be released to be arrested again the next day are over. The courts will now put offenders behind bars and leave them there for the duration of the court's sentence. This nation's military has been deputized to assist you. You are no longer alone and at the mercy of criminals."

The President softened his face and relaxed. "To the 95 or 99% of this nation, I say to you that life, as you know it, is now a lot easier. Money will soon flow into your wallets as businesses and industries re-open. No longer will grocery stores show you empty shelves. This nation shall survive and shall prosper. As I promised, this State of National Emergency is a timed event. No later than the time when you inaugurate a new President next year, all of this will be over. I ask you all to trust your government and wait out the situation. As always, I ask for your help. Report any suspicious activity, help your police, and above all, help your fellow Americans. Thank you and may God Bless America."

The red light went out and the President walked out of the Oval Office as the announcer signed off.

June 17

Dyess Air Force Base, Texas
0200 hours CDT.

Command Sergeant Major Jonathon Taylor Kincaid walked out to the C-130 Special Assignment Air Mission Transport and reported to the Colonel in charge of Base Security. He reached into his briefcase and showed Colonel Robert Hessen the orders. Kincaid waited through the process of Colonel Hessen deciding that the orders were for real.

"Sergeant Major, your documents are in order," Hessen said handing them back. "What can the Air Force do for the Army?"

"Sir, we need to refuel and depart. Those are the limits of my instructions and authorization. Additional orders are available after the aircraft's departure," he said, handing him a sealed envelope.

Hessen was not satisfied with the answer, but that wasn't unusual. Giving those types of orders to enlisted men insured that they were carried out with any deviation. "Very well, Sergeant Major, is the aircraft blocked off?" he said, meaning that no one was allowed on or off the aircraft.

"Only for the package that should have arrived by now, Sir," Kincaid said. As if on cue, an Air Force panel truck arrived with two packages, escorted by two women; one Marine and one Navy, each armed with M249 machine guns and dressed in full combat equipment.

Hessen decided right then that whatever this was; the best thing to do was get that aircraft off the base and gone. "Excellent Sergeant Major," he said turning to a Captain behind him. "Give them everything they need on a no-questions-asked basis, Captain," Hessen then turned and walked away.

Kincaid smiled inwardly. Officers were very predictable. When given vague orders and weird circumstances, they pass the whole thing to someone junior to take the blame and run away.

Briefly Kincaid's mind wondered back to the warehouse after Dennis O'Cleary left. He, along with Morgan and Kendal, were left with Ezekias Zacharias Criers and Thomas Winchell. Criers was the man who decimated his brothers in Vietnam, orchestrated the murder of Zach Morgan, killed Gladys Goldstein and Sandra Lindstrom, pointed the Black Elves at the operations center at Desert Zero and led the country down the road to 'Victoria.'

Kincaid, Morgan and Kendal had a front row seat to the deadliest traitors since Benedict Arnold: Criers and Winchell.

Kincaid watched the two containers disappear into the aircraft and waited as two fuel trucks pulled up to fed the hungry plane. Kincaid walked up to Morgan and had her "sign for the orders" in his briefcase to feed what the Air Force observers already suspected. This thing, whatever it was, was to be forgotten.

After Morgan signed for the orders and disappeared, Kincaid stepped back to the Air Force Captain babysitter and finished the memory he started.

Morgan and Kendal went to pull out the panel truck that was already hidden in the warehouse and change into their uniforms. Kincaid went to Criers and injected him with a stimulant to wake him up.

"Hello Sir," Kincaid said, as Criers came fully awake. He adjusted the microphone to pick up every sound.

"John," Criers said, testing the bonds holding him down, knowing it was useless to try freeing himself. "Why haven't you killed me yet?"

"I want to hear you tell me why the greatest patriot I ever knew is now the greatest traitor since Benedict Arnold,"

Criers sat there and looked at the man he regarded once as his son. "John, there isn't enough time or the proper words to explain it. I did what I did and that is my definition of patriotism."

Both men stared at each other as Kendal and Morgan backed the truck up to the bound and prostrate prisoners.

Criers suddenly recognized Morgan. "Cynthia Morgan, you look well. Is that uniform for real or is it for show?" Morgan looked at him and went back to the truck. Kendal came alongside her, lifted up Winchell and walked up the ramp to disappear into the panel truck.

Kincaid's voice took on an icy edge. "Mrs. Morgan, Sir, and her aide are briefed and instructed not to communicate with you or allow you to sway them in any way. They will follow their orders. I need an answer to my question, Sir,"

"I can surmise that you have already chemically interrogated me, draining me and my associate of any information you require. Didn't Chief Marin teach you that opinions are seldom if ever answered during an interrogation?"

"Why are you the greatest traitor since Benedict Arnold?" Kincaid repeated.

"Your real question is how I ever deceived you so well," Criers said, with a mocking smile. "If only you knew the *real truth.*"

Kincaid felt Kendal ease forward and he said, "get in the truck or I will kill you myself, young lady."

Kincaid and Criers spent another half an hour locked in a battle of wills until Kendal came over and interrupted. "Sergeant Major, it is time. By the way, sometimes evil has no reason."

Kincaid considered that for a few seconds and finally agreed with her. He reached into a bag, pulled out a syringe and sent Criers deep into a long dreamless sleep. Turning to Kendal he said, "When did you get so smart?"

"Something Father Mike told me," Kendal said and touched him lightly on the arm.

Kincaid said, "OK, time to get it done. I have forged orders for Dyess. You will board a C-130, fly to Delta 7, jump out, and put them both in upper level holding cells. Mrs. Morgan, you will return to Colorado, Miss Kendal, you will re-join me at Desert Zero."

"What about the General?" Kendal asked.

"There are enough people to handle that on the ground for now. We are the back-up only if they need or request it."

"John, he is responsible for Zach," Cindy said, trying to hold her anger in check.

"That, along with the murder of my wife, of all of our brothers and many other crimes," Kincaid said giving both women a stern look. "Right now, there are many other more important things to do and they'll keep at Delta 7 until something delicious and appropriate is found."

Kincaid shook off the memory as the engines of the C-130 started up. A few minutes later the aircraft taxied away. "Captain, I need transportation to Fort Hood. Can the Air Force supply something?"

"This way, Sergeant Major," the Captain said.

June 18

Delta 7, Moss Point, Montana
0200 Hours MDT

Morgan and Kendal dragged the containers into the entrance. After they were through the doorway, both women stopped to catch their breath. Sixty pounds of container, plus twenty pounds of air supply plus 180 pounds of prisoner equaled a lot of grunt work.

Morgan went inside to clear a route to the needed cells. All of the stored supplies lined every wall and filled almost every room.

Kendal left to move the all-terrain vehicle back to the camouflaged storage shed. She cleaned the area, refueled the tanks and erased as much of her presence as was possible.

A four kilometer walk back to Delta 7, convinced her that she could ignore physical training today. There was a large broom waiting for her outside the main door. She walked outward 100 meters and erased the tire tracks back to the main door. She had drove past the facility earlier and returned on another road back to the storage shed. Now she had to erase those tracks.

Kendal learned a long time ago how to 'sweep' dirt so it did not seem obvious. Finished with that task, Kendal hung the broom on its hook and closed the door. Taking a flashlight, she walked over to the electrical room, started the generators and closed all the breakers.

Kendal pulled out two bottles of water and went in search of Morgan.

"Cindy?" Kendal asked. When Cindy did not answer, Kendal pulled her pistol out and slowly went in search. Up ahead she heard a faint shuffle of feet. She forced a thought out of her mind; wondering how either of their prisoner's regained consciousness.

Kendal inched down the hallway forcing herself to follow Jim Miles' painful rules for Close Quarters Battle Training. She turned as the first room was approached. Kendal eased around. After ensuring the room was clear, she went carefully to the next. A foot shuffle raised her alarm.

Kendal forced calm through her. Inch by careful inch, she eased forward. She crouched down, but held up her weapon. A barefoot came into view and pulled back out of sight. Kendal heard heavy breathing and some struggling.

Kendal ignored her feelings. She had to think that if Winchell got loose, then Cindy was dead. The priority was that Criers and Winchell could not escape.

Suddenly, Winchell pulled a limp Cindy out into sight. There was blood oozing out of a head wound. Kendal could not tell if she was alive or dead. He was careful to hold enough of Cindy in front of her.

Kendal steadied her breath and calmly looked for targets. The arm holding her up was in front of her. Kendal put on the appearance of indecision.

"That's right young Lady," Winchell said. "She isn't dead, yet. Put the weapon down and both of you will live."

Kendal acted as if she was lowering her weapon like she was going to give up. She lowered her weapon just far enough to line up on a spot just above his elbow. Looking in several places like she was indecisive, her eyes finished lining up the shot. She pulled the trigger and waited for him to drop Cindy.

Winchell screamed as the bone shattered. Cindy dropped like a wet rag. Winchell looked up as Kendal shot him four times in the chest.

The next page in Jim Miles painful rule book was to expect someone else (Criers) to kill her when she lost focus. Kendal quickly searched the area and carefully opened the two containers' that Criers and Winchell came in. Criers was still unconscious in his container. Once satisfied no other surprises waited for her, she locked Criers' container and went over to Cindy.

Cindy groaned as she laid in a pile with Winchell. Kendal went to get two 55-gallon trash bags. Winchell was placed into the bags and sealed with duct tape. She dragged the man over to the main door.

Kendal had to take a breather and allow all the adrenaline in her system to burn off. She went back and looked in on Cindy. She was alright for now, so Kendal propped up her head and made her comfortable, for now. Kendal went down and cleared a room at the end of the hall.

She dragged Criers' container down the hall, propped it up and pushed it into the room. Carefully, she opened the container and ensured that Criers was still unconscious. He was lifted up and placed on the bed. She stripped off his clothes and put them in the container. The now light container was easily pushed out into the hallway.

With a turn of the key, the architect of the downfall of the United States and so many Werewolf murders was locked away. Kendal looked at the key in her hand. Her mind drifted back a story she heard in Sunday school. There was a story about an Abbot who had captured the devil and safeguarded the key to the cell. An apprentice took the key after the Abbot died and allowed his curiosity to open the door and see. The devil escaped. End of parable.

Kendal took the key and put it on top of one of the cupboards in the kitchen.

Kendal heard a loud groan and went to see Morgan trying to stand. "Take it easy," she said.

"Winchell escaped," she said trying to stand.

"I killed him," Kendal said looking over the wound on her head. Something hard and sharp edged was used. Kendal saw her blood on a piece of wood. Evidentially, he grabbed it as he awoke. Odd though, that sedative was supposed to be lingering. It was supposed to be a slow awakening.

26

That container had a "live person" fail safe. If a live person had to leave in an emergency, an internal handle could be used to force open the catches.

Kendal put those thoughts away so that she could work on Cindy's wounds. She went to the kitchen and found the large medical kit. The head wounds were stitched in an hour. Cindy groaned throughout the procedure. She refused the numbing shots, "I got to take my punishment for screwing up."

Kendal took a deep breath. "Try not to move."

"I fucked up," Cindy said, sitting down in the kitchen. "I knew better. I opened the container, without back-up, assuming that he was still asleep. I should have waited for you to return."

Cindy talked constantly about nothing else while the 22 stitches were placed, but she held her head in place. She felt it each time the needle was stuck into her skin. Kendal hoped that she would have that discipline, if the situation came around to her. Wendy used a "cold spray" which did have a numbing agent. After it was all over, Cindy looked like a movie prop. Cindy wanted to scratch her head, but the bandages stopped her.

"In case you are interested," Wendy said. "I killed Winchell and taped him into two garbage bags. After you are better, I'll get the ATV so I can load the body and drive it away for disposal."

Cindy looked and focused on the garbage bag lump on the floor. She stood unwarily, staggered over to the lump and kicked it.

Wendy pulled her over to a cot. "Lay down and rest," she said. After Cindy was lying on the cot and resting, Wendy left to get the ATV. Dawn was fast approaching. Wendy took the body and buried it five kilometers away. She forced herself to remain calm. "No sense making a mistake now," she muttered.

It was getting late, so Wendy decided to cut a corner and bring to the ATV back to Delta 7. She drove inside, swept the trail and closed the door just as the sun started to lighten the horizon.

Cindy was resting comfortability on the cot. Wendy carefully checked her. A long rest and sleep should take care of her.

Wendy sat down on another cot and was tempted to lay next to Cindy, but that would violate a trust she had. Cindy Morgan was a woman that Wendy was attracted to; very attracted. But it would be a perversion to her without an invitation.

Wendy pulled out her X-Berry and dictated a report to John Kincaid. First, they arrived and secured both containers. With a smile, she said Winchell attempted to escape and was terminated. Cindy was hit over the head and needed 22 stitches, and probably had a concussion. She was alright. They would leave tomorrow or the next day. Good night. XXOOXXOO.

John Kincaid was a lot of things. But he never liked having only half a story.

Six and a half minutes later, her X-Berry rang. Hurricane John was blowing in.

July 1

Internal Security Agency, Barton Virginia
1500 hours EDT.

Memorandum to the President of the United States
From: Director of the Internal Security Agency

Subject: Status of Actions.

General:

1. Most urban areas are covered by military units augmenting police forces. Problem areas are occurring in sub-urban areas with little to no presence in rural areas. Law enforcement departments in those areas are reporting sporadic incidents.
2. Detention centers are reporting less than 30% occupancy. Total number of personnel detained is 4,845,691 people.
3. Security at all strategic locations is at 100% with no reports of any security breaches.

28

4. Total output of electrical power, nationwide is at 97%. That 3% loss is the result of normal outages due to weather and other factors.

Specifics:

5. The Department of Defense reports:

    a. 50% of all retired personnel have reported for duty at the nearest military installation to their homes. Indications are that those that have not reported are due to not being notified due to non-reported relocation, lack of communications or health considerations.

    b. Military units are reporting numerous shortages of personnel of all branches and specialties. Reserve units are reporting 76% manning levels and National Guard Units are reporting near 80% manning.

    c. The Secretary of Defense is reporting that another 100,000 personnel are needed to fully man and fill requirements.

6. The Department of Homeland Security reports:

    a. No incidents of terrorist activities.

    b. Severe shortages of strategic metals and critical infrastructure items.

7. The Department of the Treasury reports:

    a. Issuance and use of the new "Blue Back" currency has begun. Exchange rate has been established at a twelve to one ratio.

    b. The Federal Reserve has received numerous complaints from the international community as nations holding certificates of deposit and credit are not accepting the new currency.

    c. Credit issues are being reported nationally as businesses are applying for credit and unable to get satisfactory answers in their view. A lack of credible documentation is the primary cause. Federal Reserve Officials have assured this agency that the problem can be corrected.

8. The Department of Agriculture reports:

    a. Farm production nationwide is down 25% from last year's totals.

(1). Edible foodstuff production is at 90% of last year's total, but numerous farmers are selling their product to SynGas and Ethanol facilities instead of food markets. The primary reason is that SynGas is paying 15% more than food markets. This problem shall have to be re-addressed.

(2). Non-Edible farm production of products such as tobacco and cotton are at 65% of last year's levels in most areas of the southeastern United States. Many farmers have switched to crops that are more profitable, i.e., SynGas production.

(3). In order to restore production, mandatory measures are needed to nullify environmental constraints and restrict farmers access to SynGas facilities.

9. Department of Energy reports:

a. Total output measured on the National Grid is at 97% and holding. Combined grids encompassing areas in Canada and Mexico are not showing any indications of strain.

b. Commercial production of US ground petroleum is at 65% of the national need. SynGas production stands at 20% of the national need. The remaining 15% is from non-U.S. sources. Those sources are not predicted to remain stable, due to concerns of U.S. credit worthiness and financial solvency.

c. Existing oil wells that were capped, admittedly to wait for prices of oil with the United States to reach an acceptable level, are now open and being placed into production to off-set overseas sources.

d. Foreign oil shipments have halted, which accounts for 15% of oil consumption at previous levels. Restrictions on personal transportation use can ease any supplies.

e. Nuclear electrical energy production is at 100%. Presently there is a 20-year supply of nuclear fuel materials.

10. Problem areas.

a. Everything can be placed into the category of expected problems outlined in "Victoria" simulations conducted prior to the plan becoming an order.

b. Police and Fire Departments are reporting a severe shortage of personnel. Pre-Victoria conditions did not allow cities and towns to retain personnel due to budgetary constraint, lack of equipment and security concerns. Average time to train new replacements is 7 weeks for Police and up to six months for Firemen.   The Postmaster General and the Internal Revenue Service have been tasked to identify all personnel that have prior training and employment in those areas so they can be recalled to duty at locations that are in severe need of trained personnel.

c. The total amount of food required to feed the entire country is 176,836 tons of food per day.   Presently there is 134,822 tons available.   This will cause problem areas as the winter months approach.   Citizens are hoarding food and their collective fears from social media means they will not stop hoarding.

d. Overall, the pace of compliance is at 49%.   Mainly, this is securing the population.

July 6

Underground Station "Conscience", World Wide Web and Channel 513
0900 hours EST.

"If you threaten, act.   If you say something, do it.   If something is important, stand your ground.   Governments are often hamstrung by individuals who have opinions about issues they feel strongly about.   This is Martin Socranson, self-proclaimed philosopher who says, 'What are we if we can't back up what you say'?"

"Greetings America" Martin Socranson said beginning his broadcast.   "It is reluctantly Saturday and I say thus."   In the background the sounds of the 1812 overture played.

"Greetings America" Martin Socranson said beginning his broadcast.   "It is reluctantly Saturday and I say thus."   In the background the sounds of the 1812 overture played.

"America, you have just turned another year older." Behind Socranson a light illuminated a large copy of the Declaration of Independence.

"Our forefathers had great dreams for the 13 colonies. Little did they realize how important we would be to the history of the world and lately how low we would sink on the world and national stage."

"America was formed as 13 separate colonies and later created a form of government that was totally unique in history. George Washington was offered the crown as America's first king. He turned it down saying that we had fought too hard to rid ourselves of a King."

The original Articles of Conferation original voted as a way of governing us; failed. So, a convention of states argued almost endlessly until a Constitution was agreed on and ratified by each of the 13 states.

The original motto of the United States is "E Pluribus Unum" (Latin for "one from many").

"Even though a lot of unsettling things are occurring around the nation, I want to concentrate on being an American and celebrating out national Birthday.

A long collage of videos showed people celebrating all across the nation. It finished with nearly an hour of fireworks from around the country.

Begin Year Zero

August 3

Underground Station "Conscience", World Wide Web and Channel 513
0900 hours EST.

"If you threaten, act. If you say something, do it. If something is important, stand your ground. Governments are often hamstrung by individuals who have opinions about issues they feel strongly about. This is Martin Socranson, self-proclaimed philosopher who says, 'What are we if we can't back up what you say'?"

"Greetings America" Martin Socranson said beginning his broadcast. "It is reluctantly Saturday and I say thus." In the background the sounds of the 1812 overture played.

"Greetings America" Martin Socranson said beginning his broadcast. "It is reluctantly Saturday and I say thus." In the background the sounds of the 1812 overture played.

Socranson looked behind him as the first page of the Constitution was illuminated.

"Three weeks have elapsed since the President and the Executive Branch sized control of the country. The facts of this situation lay firmly at the feet of this government and the fools who elected them."

"Decades of deficit spending created an economic plague that they refused to correct. Every stupid excuse for over-spending was used by the Congress-humans who voted for the over-spending. Each and every member of Congress always found enough money to throw at their constituents."

"Any attempt to rein in spending was ridiculed, lambasted, and fought. Congress-humans were blackmailed, held accountable for sins against humanity for opposing programs. Actors were brought-in to appear before committees and sing endless sob stories to match the spending."

"It is probably not well known, but the federal budget automatically includes an eight percent raise in budgets every year. So, if a Congress-human suggested only a five percent increase, others yelled and exclaimed that this travesty of a three percent reduction tugged on the heart strings and they rolled out mountains of "evidence" saying this could cause "irreparable" harm to somebody."

"At the conclusion of the Second World War, eight separate rounds of bond sales and over-spending paid for the end of the war. The hundreds of billions in debt were 113% of the GDP by war's end; $2.87 trillion in current dollars. The debt shrank in significance as the US economy grew. It would take the debt-to-GDP ratio until 1962 just to get back to where the US was before the war. Since then, Congress had continually spent more than the Executive Branch departments requested or required."

"President Johnson taught Congress new tricks by eying all "that money just sitting there" in the Social Security Trust fund" not doing anything. Money that was supposed to be "locked in a box" and kept safe for each taxpayer to paid from after retirement was now ripe for the picking. Johnson, in concert with Congress, threw IOUs in the fund in order to pay for the Great Society and the war in Vietnam."

"Part of proof is that the Defense Department had an increase in spending after Vietnam was over."

"Slowly, inexorability and steadily, Congress and the Executive Branch spent and spent and spent all of us down the drain. Canada and Russia want Alaska and Japan has had two official trips to Honolulu talking about seceding from the USA and joining them."

Socranson stood and pulled the table cloth off the table he sat on. It was a stack of blue currency three feet tall and four feet wide.

"Anyone need toilet paper?"

August 15

Federal Election Commission, Washington, DC
0900 Hours EDT.

In a move that was akin to "so what"; the Patriot Party presented the required paperwork and certifications to formally establish itself as a political party.

Just like "other parties" in the past, such as the Reform Party and the American party, the Democrats and Republicans lampooned their forming.

Behind closed doors, politicians worried. Loss of governorships, congressional seats, their power was waning. The 32 seats in the House, belonging to the Freedom Party, were a wedge that was bottlenecking legislation. That 7% of the membership made the Speaker or what political party had their favor, dance a tight line. Their unwillingness to "play the game or dance" ruffled old time politicians. Lobbyists and political action committees looking for favors, hit closed doors.

Granted the Patriot Party was different, but they had one theme that was the same as the Freedom Party. The good old days of two-party politics having free rein was over.

The first item of business for the Patriot Party was doing away with money draining amendments that choked this country.

Petitions from the northeastern states of Maine, Vermont, New Hampshire, Massachusetts, Connecticut, New York, Pennsylvania and Virginia were submitted along all the financial information and a list of salaried and volunteer persons. Financial documents and major donor lists were included.

September 7

Underground Station "Conscience", World Wide Web and Channel 513
0900 hours EST.

"If you threaten, act. If you say something, do it. If something is important, stand your ground. Governments are often hamstrung by individuals who have opinions about issues they feel strongly about. This is Martin Socranson, self-proclaimed philosopher who says, 'What are we if we can't back up what you say'?"

"Greetings America" Martin Socranson said beginning his broadcast. "It is reluctantly Saturday and I say thus." In the background the sounds of the 1812 overture played.

"I have a different story today. In the past the IRS was accused of tearing the heart out a derelict taxpayer. Maybe that was a tall tale of yesteryear. This new incarnation has to be the lowest of the low."

The scene changed to a show a woman being dragged out of a small one room home.

"This is the sorriest excuse of an American Government. Selma Germane, eighty-two years-old, was forced out of home, fifteen days earlier as the IRS seized her home for non-payment of back taxes. Like a lot of senior citizens, her husband was totally in charge of all the financials and taxes. All she ever did was sign the forms. Her husband died one year ago. So instead of working the situation, the IRS swooped down and forced their way into her home. She was physically lifted out of her chair and man-handled outside. She barely had the ability to take her purse."

"The scene was played out again. This time additional footage showed the IRS agents were beaten to the ground. Their wounds will literally take years to recover; if at all. The two Deputies were quickly disarmed and handcuffed. The large crowd surrounding the scene confused law enforcement's investigation. The local police did not show much enthusiasm."

"The scene you see on the screen was not the first time Mrs. Germane was evicted. The scene shown here was a second home given to Mrs. Germane to live in, complete with basic furniture. Several people even brought clothes and some food."

"Eight days after being evicted from her home, the scene repeated itself. The IRS tried to seize the new home. Even though Mrs. Germane did not own the home, it was seized. The IRS gave the reason as being, since she was given this home to live in, it was her property and the debt was still owed, with interest and penalties."

Socranson paused and wiped tears from his face.

36

"We the People of the United States are better than this. How many Miss Edna's or Miss Selma's do we have to have before we understand that a person is a person, regardless of their worth."

Socranson looked closely into the camera. "By the way IRS, how many rich or politically elite people have you dragged into the streets?"

September 9

DFac 3-M-10-09, Fort Detrick, Maryland
0900 hours EDT.

Detention Facility, Zone 3, Maryland, Installation Number 10, section 09 was located at Fort Detrick near Frederick, Maryland. It held only 148 "detainees." Only those who had held Top Secret, Special Category plus security clearances or very high offices in the Federal Government were held here. This facility was originally constructed for biological warfare research. The labs were formally closed in 1974. The facilities were then used for secure research and conferences afterward. With this newest need for secure confinement requirements to sequester "very important persons" that may return to service later, a very comfortable place was needed.

One "very important person" was Brenda Amanda Edgars O'Cleary, Lieutenant General (maybe) and the former Deputy Director of the Joint Intelligence Agency. Now she was detainee number 05-OSGM-10032. Her new name was now Level Five Designee, Office of Special Governmental Management, detainee number 10032, Brenda Amanda Edgars O'Cleary. She was the thirty-second person processed into this facility.

So, Detainee 3-M-10-09-05-OSGM-10032 looked around her and her situation. O'Cleary's mind ran down the memories of her incarceration. Immediately after the President declared "Activate Victoria", Prescott had her arrested. She was stripped of her uniform, identity, personal effects and a thorough search of her person. A relatively short ride from

Barton ended here. They gave her a one-piece orange jump suit; sequestered her in a nice one room cell and made to wait.

Day after day, boredom was the order of the day. Periodically, she was taken to another room for an interrogation. There were the disjointed questions about things they asked, from sedition to possible treason. In the end, she had no reason to hide anything because there was no reason to hold her here. But she was held.

O'Cleary stared at the security camera watching her in the indoor exercise yard. Her mind pondered the possibilities and scenarios that had to be occurring in the real world. She was totally insulated from any news or contact from the outside world. The guards were distant and uncooperative to any questions. Except for keeping the "detainees" isolated and under control; they ignored everyone. O'Cleary fumed at her insistence that she was last in the order of everything. 'My fault and nothing was going to change that,' she thought.

"Detainee O'Cleary, Detainee O'Cleary, report to the control center," a voice said over the loud speaker, "Detainee O'Cleary, Detainee O'Cleary, report to the control center."

"What now?" O'Cleary asked, getting up and walking up to the control center. O'Cleary stopped short of the glass, ensuring her feet fit in the painted foot prints on the floor. She extended her right arm and placed the identification/locator bracelet on the electronic reader.

A mechanical voice said, "Identified, Detainee 3-M-10-09-05-OSGM-10032, Brenda O'Cleary."

"Detainee O'Cleary," a guard standing behind the bullet-proof glass said through a speaker, "place your hands on your head, step through the glass doors and stop."

O'Cleary sighed and did as she was told. Every time someone came to interrogate her, she had to endure this procedure. After passing through the door, it closed and locked. Another door in front of her opened, where she was searched (or fondled) and led to a room for questioning. After the questioning, she was searched (or fondled) again and released to return to her cell, reversing the procedure. This time she was led to a new room and told to stand on the painted feet. The guard pointed to the spot.

She was searched (or fondled) again and secured with hand and foot manacles that were chained to a belt around her waist. She was then led by two guards into a van. She decided not to ask any questions. After being shackled to anchor points in the windowless van, it left ten minutes later. O'Cleary silently wished she could stand in the open sunshine. The closest she came to sunshine was the windows in the facility's ceilings.

The van left the facility and drove away. O'Cleary closed her eyes and relaxed. Somehow it was a relief to leave. She foolishly hoped that wherever she was going was better than Fort Detrick.

Twenty or so minutes into the trip, O'Cleary was suddenly startled at the sound of the tires being blown flat and the van screeching to a sideways halt. O'Cleary was locked in her seat by her restraints and the seat belt. Her two guards tumbled forward. A loud bang to the side door turned her attention to a spike like object sticking through it. A hissing sound filled the interior with the foulest smelling thing she ever inhaled. Her stomach rebelled as her lunch ejected out through her mouth, on to the floor and down her jump suit.

Through her clouding eyes, she saw the guards and the two drivers in the front vomiting and doubling over. The wrenching in her stomach and the convulsions were powerful enough for her bowels and bladder to loosen. Pain traveled in convulsions throughout her body. The doors opened and some hands roughly grabbed at her. The manacles and ID bracelet were broken and she was dragged out of the van. Through her pain fogged brain, she saw the guards were still convulsing and trying to scream for anyone to help them.

O'Cleary vaguely felt a hypodermic needle piercing her buttocks and a mask placed over her face. The pain slowly went away as the mask filtered away the gas, whatever it was. She felt rather than knew that she was roughly thrown on someone's shoulder as the world melted away to unconsciousness.

September 10

Morgantown Municipal Airport, Morgantown, West Virginia

O'Cleary finally felt better. At least she could hold down some food without wrenching her stomach. The Werewolves had found a way to free her. A phony Prisoner Transfer Order was placed into the system transferring her to a newer facility north of Washington. On a lonely road in the back woods, they struck. A spike strip was dragged across the road as the van crossed a bridge. When the van stopped, a special tungsten steel dart was fired into the side cargo door. The dart housed a cylinder containing something called "vomit gas." This chemical compound triggered a severe gag response, convulsions and severe abdominal spasms in anyone who inhaled it, instantly disabling them. The hypodermic shot she was given was a mild sedative which eased her convulsions. The mask gave her pure oxygen at a higher-than-normal atmospheric pressure and a countering agent to the "vomit gas."

When they finally stopped, O'Cleary took a long hot shower to scrub her skin of any residual "vomit gas" and the contents of her stomach, bowels and bladder. The hot shower relaxed her so she could take stock of her situation. The cut on her arm she got when they cut the bracelet off was bandaged. Tabor checked her electronically for any unknown tracking devices and surgically removed the subcutaneous device imbedded in her shoulder.

Prisoners being transferred were routinely given a "horse pill" to swallow which contained a tracking device. Tabor smiled and said that she must have vomited out the device. They didn't have time to search for it. No signal was detected, but she was given a powerful laxative to force it out the other end, guaranteed to clean her out completely within 24 hours. Tabor, at least, tried not to smile. Now she had to have a bathroom close by constantly.

Dennis was there by her side. "Sorry it took so long," he said, "but there were many other circumstances and you were very clear with your instructions."

O'Cleary smiled and decided not to complain. After her head cleared and the long shower, she was given a seven-inch-thick file to read. It was the overall situation report on the country as a whole and the Werewolves in particular.

O'Cleary frowned at the national picture. To all outward appearances, the government was actively trying to ease the situation, but the situation was overwhelming them. To date 845 new agencies, boards and advisory committees were formed to deal with the deteriorating conditions. If she had not been the simulation supervisor on the "Victoria" trial runs, she would have been at a huge loss to explain the turmoil. The central government's bureaucrats were thinking in academic circles when they should have been thinking in "real world" circles.

What had her completely perplexed was that she was officially promoted to four star General and placed on "Special Duty Status." What the hell does that mean?

O'Cleary speed-read over the national situation and halted at the section covering the Werewolves and the Savage Rabbits. O'Cleary needed to read it through two times to believe what she was reading. After the Victoria activation and her disappearance, General Matheson from Special Operations Command came to Desert Zero and "took command" of the Savage Rabbits. Rangers were traditionally the security and covering force for Delta when the mission required it. Rangers were in short supply and half of the Savage Rabbits were Rangers. The Marine Savage Rabbits were segregated from the Rangers. They were relegated to a secondary status; supporting the situations and missions as they occurred. In plain English they became janitors.

The animosity started.

The report in O'Cleary's hand said the operators from Delta and the Savage Rabbit operators were individually innocent. It was the situation. Delta's standard policy was to compartmentalize everything. The Delta Support Team sequestered everything and isolated the rest. Most of the Savage Rabbit hierarchy was kept out of the mission planning loop and seldom consulted. Peters was allowed to brief his men only hours before launching. In the Mess Hall, the Delta Operators ate separately to the point that there was a curtain between the Delta's area and the Savage Rabbits. Some of the

Operators on both sides tried to mingle, but those situations were rare.

Colonel Marcus Saraland was placed in overall command of the Counter Narcotics Joint Task Force, as it was now called. The first thing he did was ban the women from combat operations. That drove the next wedge between them. The operators on both sides were again caught in the middle. Kincaid was reverted to Sergeant Major because there could be only one Command Sergeant Major in any unit. Command Sergeant Major Kevin Grouter, from Delta Force, replaced him. They had tried to transfer Kincaid, but the files said that his assignment originated by order of the President and only the President could change that.

Grouter ordered the Savage Rabbit patch and insignia taken down, saying that it was not authorized and called too much attention to their operations. Also banished was the unofficial uniform jacket that the operators wore in the compound during off-duty hours. A Marine and Army uniform jacket was split in half and the two opposite halves were sewn together as a token of solidarity. Kincaid tried to talk them out of it, but the Delta personnel only relented to the point of an official decommissioning.

The Savage Rabbits responded by starting a bonfire; burning the plaques, patches, jackets and flags. Before anyone could stop them, a new Savage Rabbit patch was unveiled. It showed a rabbit being sodomized by a wolf with a Delta Triangle emblazoned on its chest.

Delta and the Savage Rabbits were divided beyond any mending and Kincaid was reprimanded for the bonfire. Everyone fell in step with Saraland and the dictates from Special Operations Command.

Petty Officer Wendy Kendal and Captain Elizabeth Hawker were next on the list. Details were sketchy, but some altercation started between Kendal and a Delta Senior Non-Commissioned Officer. The operator suffered a broken jaw and she was arrested. Hawker tried to intervene saying the Delta operator made an unwanted sexual advance and Kendal just defended herself. When Saraland questioned Kendal, she said it was a laughable event until "he massaged his excuse for a dick." Saraland charged her with assaulting a senior non-commissioned officer and insubordination, sending her to the detention facility that was set up at Fort Hood. Hawker called him a "disrespectful name" and was relieved. From that point on, it was them versus us. When Hawker was escorted out of the compound, the four other remaining women went with her. They refused to stay on "as house servants and whores," despite orders to the contrary.

Grouter tried to mend fences with Kincaid, but Kincaid gave him icy silence in return.

Two months ago, a cascade of events pushed the Savage Rabbits into open rebellion.

On the seventh of August, a report came down saying that possible Al-Quada members were meeting with Mexican citizens and Cartel leadership in a small town of Chalco, south of Mexico City. A force of twenty-seven Delta operators and three sections of Savage Rabbits were alerted. Three days later, the Savage Rabbits were briefed for the mission and were launching in 12 hours. Most of the Savage Rabbits were weary of the situation and Kincaid didn't like it at all. He went in with the Savage Rabbits to secure the area.

The helicopters and Ospreys landed and the plan went along well until extraction. After the Delta Force operators and the arrested Al-Quada were extracted, the Savage Rabbits contracted to their pick-up zones. Two sections were recovered and heading north when the third section came under heavy fire. Kincaid and one section were trapped. Requests for air support and extraction were denied because of Rules of Engagement and upper echelon indecision.

Kincaid's exchange over the radio was heated and to the point. They were on their own; period. Kincaid's last remark was deleted.

A week and a half later, Kincaid, Captain Younger and two thirds of his section came straggling back. Younger stood frozen in front of Saraland, dangling the dog tags from eight deceased Rabbits, buried in Mexico. Captain Younger was relieved when he refused to surrender the dog tags, saying he was not allowing them to be "flushed down the toilet to hide their incompetence". Kincaid set his equipment down and looked at Grouter. Both men were not within ear shot of anyone, but Grouter threw the first punch.

Kincaid and Grouter's fist fight was one for the record books. The riot that ensued between Delta and the Rabbits required every spare Military Policeman that could arrive in the first thirty minutes. Twenty-seven personnel from all sides were hospitalized. Grouter was going to be out of action for almost a year. Captain Younger, Kincaid and all but fifty of the Savage Rabbits were relieved of duty, arrested and detained. Those Rabbits not relieved were Rangers, but they left with all the rest. All of them sited that portion of the regulations stating that this was a volunteer unit. What boiled O'Cleary's blood was the fact that the families of the detained military personnel were secured in the same facility as the Savage Rabbits.

O'Cleary looked up from the report and wondered how it could have degenerated so fast and so thoroughly.

She picked up the report and read on. The section covering the Werewolves didn't read much better. At least they weren't in jail or detention, except for John Kincaid and Wendy Kendal. She knew, from past experience, his temper overloaded common sense and she knew Grouter was tricked into starting the fight. She debated and dismissed any thought of leaving him in the Stockade. Locklear was too busy with the Arrayed Battle Plan and he needed help.

The bulk of the Werewolves were busy with the second phase of Operation Embarrassment. Montana and Wyoming were mobilizing. Idaho was next on their list. Smith had taken over Criers' identity. Using his codes and records, Smith was finishing Crier's plan to make Colorado a separate nation. Governor Jerald Allen did not have a clue.

Smith moved some of the "remaining" money up to operations in Idaho and Montana. Criers had started to move operations northward before he was captured. Smith thought that it was a great idea.

The third and final phase was set to commence in January. But there were still innumerable problems and Jones had his hands full. O'Cleary pushed down her anger. Jones admitted early on that he could not be a strategic thinker. He could understand operational and tactical matters, but strategy was beyond him. O'Cleary kicked herself for refusing to consider that. He was never schooled or trained for this job.

That was her fault, not his. Her ignorance was that everyone was not as well schooled as she was.

O'Cleary threw down the report and walked outside. Dennis came up alongside her.

"Penny for your thoughts and anger," Dennis said.

"Everyone fucked up in spades," she said, pointing to herself, "me especially. The nation collapsed. The Werewolves are scattered without any coherent direction. My Savage Rabbits that I personally assembled, trained and watched over like a mother hen are destroyed. All in all, everyone fucked up in spades, especially me," Brenda repeated, taking Dennis' arm and held it close. "All that time I was at Detrick, I dreamed of holding onto you. The nights were long and lonely. All I could think of was you as my nation crumbled."

"Thank you," Dennis said. "I........."

"Dennis," Brenda said, interrupting the thought. After a few minutes, she said. "Remember I told you before we were married, that I had a gynecological problem?"

Dennis just nodded.

"One of the few good things about my incarceration was that they took away my medications. The doctors there had plenty of time to give me a thorough workup after I was there for a month." She stopped, turned to face Dennis and looked him hard in the eye. "He cured the problem I had. I'm forty-six and you are sixty-three. Can we still have a baby?"

Dennis did not bother to hide the shock crawling across his face.

"I know this is sudden," she said, "but when the doctor said I could maybe, even at my age, get pregnant, I thought of Tom and your brother Arthur. Dennis, I want to have our child and be normal. If I get pregnant, we can run away and be normal. I can spend the rest of my life…..."

"Making all of us happy and living a contented life all the while kicking yourself for not doing something for the nation you swore to protect," Dennis said, taking her hand and kissing it.

Brenda just looked at Dennis and wanted to slap him in the face. She dropped her eyes and wiped tears from the front of her face. "I thought you would be happy to have children?"

"Oh yeah, I'm happy and can't wait to get started," he said, smiling. "I just thought the idea that you would walk away was just ludicrous. You would never walk away."

Brenda lowered her head and looked away. "I'm tired of being the savior of America. It's someone else's turn."

"Sure," Dennis said.

"But…..." Brenda said.

"If you want children, let's get started. If you want to run away, let's get moving. But do it for the right reasons. I have dreamed of having children and holding you. I'd be lying if I said I could share you with the war that's coming," Dennis said, turning her face with his finger. "But I know you well enough to know how miserable you would be. How you would look at our child and wonder what kind of America he or she would grow up in."

"Why does it have to be me?" She asked.

Dennis smiled and kissed her. "You'll figure it out. Strategy is your side of the family. Tactics and fighting are mine."

Brenda's eyes clouded for an instant. "I need to get pregnant first. Then we bring back the country, starting with Colorado, Wyoming, Idaho and Montana. Are you up to being a father and being my Command Sergeant Major?"

Dennis flashed his eyes and turned her around.

"Tomorrow or the next day, we go get the Savage Rabbits," she said, as Dennis led her inside. "Then when I am ready, we," she pointed to Dennis and her, "sit down and strategize. First on the list is my replacement."

"Replacement?" Dennis asked.

Brenda pulled out her replacement X-Berry and smiled. "I am getting old and soon I will be a mother. We need a younger commander. Being non-replaceable is the height of arrogance."

Dennis snickered and allowed her the privacy of talking to HAL.

Brenda dialed her phone number and the pound sign. After UNSTACK THIS logged on, Brenda said; "secure."

[Valkyrie, all security and counter surveillance is in place. We are secure].

"Who had me imprisoned?"

46

[The order originated with General Prescott and continued with GS-18 Clara Simpson].

Brenda sat there and tried to remain calm. "Is that confirmed?"

[Yes. Four sources. I have access to the video and audio evidence.]

"Excuse me," Brenda said and closed the phone. Tears came down her face at this betrayal. Brenda went to the bathroom and allowed the laxative to work its magic. Something in her curiosity, made her look for the 'horse pill'.

Brenda could not help feeling like a woman and crying at this betrayal. She thanked God she never told Clara about her personal access to UNSTACK THIS. She had thought about it several times, but she didn't. Miss Gladys had asked why she never brought Clara in. "Clara is political, you are not."

Brenda waited thirty minutes and finally stopped mopping around. It was past time to get to the business at hand. She dialed her phone number and hovered her finger over the pound sign. Brenda deliberately pushed the key.

"Secure," she said.

[Valkyrie, all security and counter surveillance is in place. We are secure].

"How many people can access you?"

[Brenda O'Cleary, Dennis O'Cleary, John Kincaid, John Espirito, Susan Espirito, Gladys Goldstein].

Brenda almost jumped straight up. "Miss Gladys is dead."

[Yes].

Brenda settled down. "Where are John and Susan now?'

[Hiding at a cabin in Arkansas.] UNSTACK THIS displayed the coordinates and a satellite photo of the cabin.

"After we are finished, ring whatever phone they are using so that I can talk to them."

[Brenda, will you answer a personal question for me]?

"Yes".

[Your love for Dennis makes all your biological readings indicate pleasure. Is this your happiness and love?]

"Yes", she said with a smile.

47

[I have an operational question for you. In the future, should you be incarcerated, would you like a quicker time frame to free you from that incarceration?]

"Yes, but the rescuers should not be allowed to waste their lives freeing me."

[I believe you are doing what is called "hamstringing". As you have said in the past, never force a commander on the ground to do something you want.]

Brenda smirked. "Roger that," she said. "Play back the information on Clara Simpson's involvement in my incarceration."

UNSTACK THIS played three meetings with one of them from two different angles. Brenda recognized the Situation Room under the White House. That place was notorious for being constantly "swept" of all forms of eavesdropping.

"How did you get this recording of the Situation Room?"

[Clara Simpson had the devices installed. One was attached to her glasses and another was installed inside a light bulb.]

This was a prosecutor's climax. No way anyone could have faked this and she was adept enough to match the words with the mouth movements.

One very damming scene was with Prescott. Both of them wanted to get to John and Susan Espirito. Brenda was an impediment to incarcerating them and wringing the information out of them.

"Dam you Clara," Brenda said with vehemence.

She turned to UNSTACK THIS. "Can you monitor Clara Simpson continuously?"

[Yes.]

"Will that interfere with your other duties?"

[No. I have many branch computers that can monitor her.]

"Link me to John and Susan. I will talk to them and start moving them to the Minuteman site. Watch over them and the team I will send to guard them."

[Will comply.]

Suddenly the phone was connected and ringing. Brenda listened to the phone going secure and Susan answering.

"Hello," Brenda said. They spent twenty minutes exchanging information. UNSTACK THIS had warned them that they were close to being detained.

UNSTACK THIS covered and erased their electronic presence from all surveillance sources. Credit cards were changed in cyber-space.

Both of them left the NSA for lunch and never came back. UNSTACK THIS changed their banking information. They abandoned their car and rented a new one. They drove all night, abandoning the rental at the Montgomery Alabama airport. They rented a new car and drove to Little Rock. Upon arrival, they purchased a SUV with a pre-approved purchase, stocked it with clothes and food. In the town of St. Pauls, Arkansas, they rented a cabin on the border of Ozark National Forrest and waited.

In three days, a team will arrive to move them out to the Minuteman site.

September 16

Minuteman, north of Fort Benton, Montana
1500 hours MDT

John and Susan Espirito left the replacement cargo SUV with Morgan, Griffith and Mejia. It was a long ride disguised as Federal couriers. A fake cargo with impeccable paperwork was in the SUV and they were armed to the teeth. John and Susan were told to remain silent in the background if they were stopped and if there was any shooting; lie low and fire only if someone was three feet away.

They were met by Joshua and Ellie Crawford who welcomed them and took them over to one of the new communities and into a turn-key house. Susan loved it instantly. It was loaded with basic furniture, kitchen-ware and most important; thick walls full of insulation.

Tucked in a back room was a mini-server so that they could continue their research with UNSTACK THIS.

John and Susan looked at each other and shrugged their shoulders. At least they were free and safe.

September 23

Pentagon, Washington, DC
1430 hours EDT.

"What?" General of the Army, Chairman of the Joint Chiefs of Staff, Thomas Jefferson Edwards said. He was just briefed that Brenda O'Cleary had walked up to the detention facility at Fort Hood, released the 200 or so members of the Savage Rabbits and their dependents that were 'being detained there'. Included was Kincaid and seven others charged with numerous offenses under the UCMJ.

Prisoner Transfer Authorizations for them and their families were already there; fully authorized, authenticated and in perfect order. Five hundred and seventeen persons boarded C-17 aircraft, also fully authorized and the lot of them vanished off the face of the earth when they landed at Pueblo Memorial Airport in Pueblo, Colorado. "Who authorized this?" Edwards asked.

"General," Lieutenant Colonel Martin Harm, his aide said. "General O'Cleary is outside waiting for you."

Edwards fell heavily into his chair. He took a deep breath and motioned for him to usher her in. O'Cleary marched up to within four feet of his desk, stopped at attention and saluted. Edwards returned the salute and pointed to the chair. "That will be all Martin," he said, looking at O'Cleary and waiting for the door to close. "Where the hell have you been?"

"In detention per Prescott's order. Now why was that?" she asked.

Edwards was about jump to his feet, but he forced down his anger. "That pimp is under arrest for conspiracy to murder his wife. I had no idea that he had you arrested. He was arrested on the 17th of June and demoted to his permanent rank of Major General pending a general court-martial. I wanted to know where you were and I was told you were on a special classified assignment. Your appointment to your fourth star and nomination to Vice-Chairman went through the Senate. That's all I know."

O'Cleary decided to trust him, at least for now. "I'm ready to assume my duties, Sir. By the way, congratulations on your promotion."

Edwards glanced over to the five stars on his shoulder. "Surprised me," Edwards said, rising from his desk and walking over to shake her hand. "First time that's happened since Omar Bradley in 1950."

"Sir, I need one day at least to get settled in and catch up. Please don't yell at me until tomorrow."

Edwards smiled as he tapped the four stars ceremoniously on her shoulders. "I'll try, but no promises. Have you got an aide picked out? I guessing a real mean one."

"Yes Sir, Major Elizabeth Hawker is already at my office and ejecting the Lieutenant General who kept my seat warm," she said smiling. "She is a fast operator. I would appreciate you signing off on allowing her wide access."

Edwards should have realized that O'Cleary was already on the job and many steps ahead of him. "I have a lot of problems. This 'Victoria' bullshit is driving a stake into the middle of my head. All you have to do is make sense out of it. Too many people are running in too many different directions and we are supposed to be the ones directing traffic and getting the job done. You are probably the only one who can out think the stupid," he said, taking a deep breath and privately thanking God he finally had someone to help him. "I'll even do you a favor. When I was Vice Chairman, I was overruled all the time. You say it and it has the force of my orders. My aide will forward the order as soon as I can get it out."

"Major Hawker is coordinating a briefing tomorrow morning during your scheduled conference," she said looking him in the eye. "I will be realigning everything. You will be pre-briefed a half an hour earlier. It was easy to figure out. I remember the stupidity of the simulations. The rest is taking what they did wrong and planning forward."

Edwards was at that moment wondering if her returning was more of a headache than not having her. "I'll draft an order to comply with you first and complain to me later. Anything I need to be aware of beforehand?"

51

"Yes, as a matter of fact," she said, walking towards the door. "Three months in detention was boring. They cured a gynecological problem I had. Dennis made me pregnant."

Edwards stopped short. "What?"

She bobbed her head mischievously. "Dennis was only too happy to help out."

"By the way," Edwards said as he walked her to door. "You stole your 'Savage Rabbits'? The debacle south of the border is getting worse. Short story is we need them back on the job."

"Matheson and Saraland screwed it up by destroying the camaraderie and professionalism they built up." O'Cleary forced her temper down. "SOCOM degraded those people. SOCOM pushed them down into third rate status. SOCOM abandoned a section in Mexico, killing 8 men and forcing them to walk out. SOCOM…..."

"OK, the President told me you are back in command of the Rabbits when the whatever assignment was concluded." Edwards stood up to O'Cleary. "I'll call General Traynor at SOCOM and tell him to leave. Delta will have to find a new home."

O'Cleary relaxed and forced calm to run through her. 'I need this job now', she thought. "Colonel Peters said they needed re-training for two months and I agreed with them. My anger says Traynor can make due for two more months while the men fix the damage he and Saraland created."

O'Cleary saluted and Edwards returned the salute. She turned and walked out of the office.

"Shit," he said, closing the door after her. Edwards walked over to his desk and looked at the portrait of Amanda. He remembered both times when she told him she was pregnant. Marshal and Elizabeth were the most important additions to his life. Army Major Marshal and Dr. Elizabeth were the apples in his eye. Suddenly he thought of Brenda O'Cleary taking maternity leave and leaving him to run this zoo alone again. "Where are you, Wife, I need you now more than ever." She was somewhere else so the Government couldn't hold her against him. There were weekly briefings on the progress locating her. At least Kincaid did that right. Her trail vanished that morning. The so-called 'credible intelligence' about her location was so ludicrous that he stopped listening to them. Investigators were now questioning him about where she was. "I don't know where and get the hell out of my office!" he screamed at them one day. She was safe and that was that. Her two letters a month were so hard to trace that it was almost unreadable after 'everyone' read it first.

Edwards' train of thought was broken by a flurry of calls. Guess what it was all about? Hurricane Brenda just landed.

Minuteman, north of Fort Benton, Montana
1700 hours MDT.

Jones, Smith, Kincaid, and all the other Werewolves sat around the table watching their beers come to room temperature.

Kincaid especially smarted over General O'Cleary's return. She simply stood him at attention, backed him into the wall and warned him of two things he had to change. One, do not trick anyone into fighting him again, whatever the provocation or jus-ti-fi-able reason. Two, she was in charge and never, ever forget it. Seems she found out he was actively sabotaging the Delta Force and Grouter in particular before he was arrested and detained. Colonel Saraland and his staff constantly came down with aliments, ranging from diarrhea, food poisoning and one instance when a snake slithered out of a rucksack belonging to a Delta staff officer. Grouter's Humvee routinely broke down.

"If anything, else goes wrong along those lines or even remotely along those lines again; I'm going to blame you," she said, her evil, familiar smile firmly in place.

"Yes General," Kincaid said, knowing the implied threat.

Newly promoted Colonel Thaddeus Jones smarted after briefing General O'Cleary on the status of Operation Embarrassment to date. She listened carefully to all he said and tactfully showed him how much he didn't do or foresee.

O'Cleary stood and shook Jones hand. "Your problem, Colonel, is that you are mired in too many details and can't see the forest for the trees. That is my fault. I have to remind you that an Executive Officer is different from a Deputy Commander. An Executive officer is necessary to free you up to concentrate on the big picture. Meet Lieutenant Colonel Michael Peters, your new Deputy Commander. He is fully read into the situation and is available for duty, effective immediately. Major Thamaod, formally from the Savage Rabbits is the best candidate that we will use as an Executive Officer."

O'Cleary handed Jones a list of officers and the positions they would fill. Mostly, they utilize them in the same capacity they were used in the Savage Rabbits.

After the meeting was over, Peters sat outside and watched the children play with the abandon only children have.

Peters was still livid about his treatment at Desert Zero. He stood beside his men as duty demanded and was punished for doing what he knew was the right thing. The identity of the Savage Rabbits was stripped from them; their soul and comradeship. Marine and Army members seldom ever seamlessly meshes as a unit.

Saraland and Grouter didn't want that type of unit. They tore the Rabbits apart and tore it down into some kind of bastard of their choosing. The Rabbits were split and ripped apart. Then he spit on the ground when one section was left behind and no effort was made to get them; nothing. Eight men died for nothing. Eight men were sacrificed in the hierarchy of deniability to protect the guilty. Peters held no real animosity for the individual Delta Operators. They only worked in their world and it worked fine back at Fort Bragg.

Peters sixteen years in the Army was destroyed on a whim. His love of his country was unchanged, but his loyalty to the Army was gone. All that was left was his wife, two children and the men he stood behind. Now what?

Peters remembered the day when General O'Cleary yanked everyone out, including the families. It was so sudden and elegant in a way. She just walked in and took everyone. He despised his superiors for imprisoning the families in the same place as their husbands. The families weren't guilty of anything, but to hold their family's hostage along with them was something only the Nazi's done. Granted, the possibility of escape was nil, but still to round up and imprison innocent people without due process was not the America he grew up in and swore allegiance to defend.

After arriving in Pueblo, O'Cleary sat down with him and outlined what she had in mind. Ordinarily, the thought of doing anything against his country was treasonous at best, but maybe this wasn't. The General said that he and the Savage Rabbits could build a new life; free to be Americans. The more he thought about it, the better it sounded. His Wife, Sarah, jumped at the chance to have a new life. She pointed to their son and daughter saying, "How do you explain Fort Hood to the kids?" That was the tipping point. He watched them playing behind barbed wire and chain link fences, somehow knowing that something had to be done. Something that was treasonous and illegal during normal times.

"Mike," O'Cleary said, to Peters. "I'm not asking you to fight or rebel against your country, no matter what happened to you. I was imprisoned for three months by a man who just didn't like me. I was never charged with anything, but I was imprisoned. I am returning to the Pentagon to continue to defend this nation, even if it returns me to a cell. I am just offering you a chance to have a good life. If anything, you and the Rabbits deserve it."

The rest of the Rabbits jumped at the chance. The last three months at Desert Zero and the detention facility already did the job of convincing them. "Ladies and Gentlemen," O'Cleary stood and addressed them all. "I refuse to apologize for the asinine and disrespectful treatment you received. I am not here to deceive you into something that is wrong. I am offering you the opportunity to build and defend a new life. Winter is coming to the north. Three communities await you if you want them. Those that want to return, do so without prejudice. That means you are free to follow your conscience. I am just giving you the opportunity to choose. Something you were denied at Fort Hood. Transportation north leaves in two hours."

"Those who wish not to leave will have full documentation saying that you are innocent and free. Orders will be cut for any assignment or discharge. You choose. Two Hours." O'Cleary left them to decide. "If any of you want to rejoin the Savage Rabbit mission. Orders to go there under Delta Force will be cut."

Wendy Kendal stood to the side and listened to O'Cleary. She wished, somehow, she had the freedom to leave. She was about the only one who couldn't.

"Miss Kendal," O'Cleary said, motioning for her to follow. After they were out of earshot of anyone listening, O'Cleary turned to her. Kendal went to attention knowing what was coming. From six inches away, O'Cleary said. "Miss Kendal, you and Mister Kincaid have this unnatural ability to get into trouble and somehow come out smelling like a rose. So, I am going to say it just like I did with your mentor, Mister Kincaid."

O'Cleary's face started to redden as she closed the distance between them to two inches. "I have too many other responsibilities to babysit two grown adults who cannot behave themselves. Tricking people into fighting; unexplained problems and catastrophes: disrespect and a general unwillingness to see that the world is destroying itself around you is no longer going to be tolerated. You and I are too very small specks in a very large dirt pile."

"When, not if, when this country starts a shooting civil war, the casualties will be in the millions. That's million with a capital 'M'. We have over five thousand nuclear warheads to guard from terrorists and thieves. Countries around the world will start tearing off chucks of this country starting with Russia and Canada wanting Alaska and Mexico taking the southern states. People are going to die by the hundreds of thousands from lack of food, diseases, bitter rivalries, and just plain stupidity. If I can't depend on you, then leave. I'll finance a new life for you. If you stay, I'll probably have to ask you to die for this country that no longer exists. You choose. Two hours, Miss Kendal," she said holding up two fingers. O'Cleary didn't wait for an answer. She turned away and left.

Kendal didn't know what to do. General O'Cleary was 100% correct. She already decided to stay, but the General was not convinced. "I am a bitch, slut, cunt, whore," she said, spitting on the ground and walking over to the others.

Two hours later, everyone boarded the buses and planes to head north for an uncertain life.

Kendal walked over to General O'Cleary. stood at attention, saluted and said, "General, Petty Officer First Class Kendal reporting, what are your orders?"

O'Cleary gave her the full measure of a look that made her believe that rough times were ahead. "Mister Locklear is waiting for you, Chief Petty Officer", she said, handing her a stack of official orders. "Colonel Jones will officially promote you. I meant what I said. Remember that General Prescott could still use an aide and an orderly while he waits for his court martial."

Kendal's face went ash white. "Yes Ma'am."

Off to the side was Major Michael Smith. O'Cleary sat him down at a secluded table.

"First Major Smith, I have to have a factual answer. How is your health? Can you or will you continue in your present capacity?

Smith looked at her. "Factually, Ma'am. I feel the wounds every day. I can walk around, but I am half the man I was before being shot. The things the doctors have to do to save your life can make the rest of it difficult. Will I be able to do the things I did before; no. My days of being a Werewolf in the field are over. I can fight a desk, just not people shooting back.

O'Cleary smiled. "Good, Lieutenant Colonel Smith. Coordinate with Jones for four personnel to be assigned permanently. Colorado and Wyoming need to coordinate actions and logistics with Idaho and Montana. I am afraid you will find riding a desk makes you want to commit suicide or rush into battle.

September 23

WSG Camp Number One, Hill County, Montana
0800 hours MDT.

Kendal walked up to her home. It had a lot of nice new touches here and there. It was obvious that few people were around, but the camp was well tended.

"Howdy," a familiar voice said from the side.

Kendal smiled and turned to Earl Locklear. He was in uniform, the new Air Force Master Sergeant rank insignia prominent on the front of his jacket. "Congratulations, Master Sergeant", she said, extending her hand.

"Congratulations to you too, Chief Petty Officer," Locklear said, shaking her hand. "The General told me you were returning. It's doesn't look like it, but things are hectic here. I really appreciate the help."

"I haven't had breakfast yet. I'll cook this morning, if you haven't eaten. We can catch up then, and then get to work," she said, turning to get her bags.

After breakfast was finished and cleaned up, Kendal said. "I see a lot of womanly touches here and there. Who's my completion?"

"Mostly it is Janet Layman," he said. "Some of the other things are the rest of our class and their wives. They visit from time to time. Mostly it is to argue about INSANE JANE. Other times it is to relax."

Kendal brought over coffee. "I spent three months in detention at Hood. It was boring enough to allow a lot of time to think," she said, smiling at the look on his face. "Bring me up to speed on what you did while I was gone."

1700 hours MDT.

Locklear spent most of the day briefing Kendal on his progress towards finalizing the doctrine, strategy, operational nature and tactics of the Arrayed Battle Plan; code named INSANE JANE. He was prepared for the normal knock-down drag-out fight she was famous for. However, he was silently grateful that whatever changed her had happened. Gone were the days where they fought every point to the death. Instead, she asked questions, patiently exploring this point and that. In the end, she got in a few points and the result was better than what he did alone.

Both of them laughed when Earl briefed her on "Confusionation". This was the most laughable element of INSANE JANE. Earl had to make a name for it, so "Confusionation" was borne. Confusing the enemy was as ancient as warfare itself. Any general or king or leader who never used deceit, usually had a massive army or was superior in every way that mattered. When both sides became equal in size and power; deceit became a necessity. When a smaller entity was faced with a powerful foe, deceit is required.

Earl had a hard time writing the doctrine for this until Ellie Crawford stepped in. She asked a serious-looking Locklear one day what was the problem.

Earl described the deception portion of the plan. "How do you keep a massive deception plan active when the situation is so fluid?"

Ellie Crawford listened to him describe the problem. She was clueless until a group of women sat next to them and began talking incessantly. Slowly Earl's explanation slowed as he turned more of his attention to their conversation. "That's it," he said.

Ellie turned and listened. When the women drew her into the conversation, Earl went silent and listened to them with total fascination.

Slowly, Earl discovered the core of 'Confusionation'. Earl listened and learned how the women started a conversation and maintained a conversation. Even when another woman entered, the conversation continued and the new person 'slid' in seamlessly and carried it along.

Earl tuned out the conversation and started writing. He was interrupted once, with a simple meal and then he was allowed to continue working. Suddenly, he noticed it was near dusk. "Seven hours," he said, looking at his watch.

Earl arrived home at the WSG compound around ten pm. He took a long hot shower and thought everything over afterward over a beer. He smiled, silently thanking those women who did something natural to them. They solve a puzzle that now became a bona fide force multiplier.

"OK, I've got to ask," Locklear said. "What happened to you?" He saw the look on her face change.

"I said I had a lot of time to think. Being a bitch, slut, cunt, whore never got me anything but trouble. If you have to thank someone, thank Major Elizabeth Hawker." Kendal leaned back in her chair and thought back. "She is as steady a hand as Miss Gladys was. She showed me how to soothe and massage my point. 'There may and will come a time to fight to the death, but that is not every time,' she told me repeatedly. But mostly I had to think about beating the shit out of that sexist pig that just wanted to fuck me into being a real woman." Kendal shuttered at the memory. "I should have just laughed at him and given him a 'Prescott experience.'" The snarl on her lips faded away. "I grew up a lot since then. Maybe not enough, but I tried." She turned and looked directly at Earl. "You have a brain that is second to very few. We are lucky you are here."

Locklear looked at her and a new measure of respect emerged. "Thanks for the compliment. I hope to earn it for real, sometime. But the proof is in the future. We still have to field test it, but that requires an enemy that shoots back."

Just then the front door opened and Kincaid entered carrying a thick stack of folders under his arm. After dropping them on the table, he sat down heavily. "Hope I was interrupting something unimportant. I read your doctrine on INSANE JANE. Excellent, outstanding, brilliant work," he said, nodding to Locklear.

Locklear straightened up in his chair. "We spent the day refining the doctrine. I plan to formally submit it to the General in two days for her approval. After she blesses it, we field the plan."

"Good," Kincaid said, opening a notebook. "I'm asking for a quick briefing, maybe an hour long. Everyone will be here in three days. You will have our undivided attention for the following three days. We will not question what you brief. We will learn and be ready to fight. The major problem is the lack of a credible timeline. We may have a lot of time, or we may have to start fighting soon. Already the word is out that a bunch of no-nonsense people live out here. That insulates us to a point, but it invites the government to interfere with lawyers, bureaucrats and bullshit."

"What's really going on John?" Kendal asked.

"I'll answer that when Cindy arrives," he said, with a long look on his face. "First things, first," he straightened in his seat and fixed them with determined look and his pencil hovering over a pad of paper. "INSANE JANE, if you please."

Earl stood and pulled up his Master INSANE JANE book and made his case.

September 26

WSG Camp Number One, Hill County, Montana
0800 hours MDT.

Kincaid argued with Locklear about "Confusionation". To him it is was nonsense. Locklear said it was essential.

"Confusing and deceiving the enemy is a doctrinal point in the Law of Land Warfare," Locklear said. "It is the easiest part of the plan to execute. Regardless of the situation on the ground. Having everyone point fingers and describe things in non-military terms. Give the intelligence personnel confusion."

Kincaid took a long time to understand. "INSANE JANE requires coordination and above all communications. If the enemy moves through an area, you cannot take the chance of giving away operations in another sector."

Locklear and Kincaid fought their points so much that Jones and Peters had to get involved.

Each man was allowed 15 minutes to make their point and only 15 minutes.

Afterward, Jones and Peters conferred together after ensuring that both combatants were separated. 20 minutes later they chose Locklear's point of view and formally included it in the INSANE JANE's overall doctrine.

Kincaid rose, walked over to Locklear and extended his hand. "I am unaccustomed to losing Mister Locklear. After I have had a beer and long night's sleep. Let's sit down and you can explain it again so I understand why I lost."

Jones and Peters looked at each other.

Peters picked up his coffee mug. "Sir, John was my Sergeant Major in the Savage Rabbits." He left the rest hang in the air.

Jones sat down to drink his coffee. Ever since O'Cleary came down and straightened his command problem, he wondered at that problem. "Mike," he said. "Can I call you Mike?"

61

Peters nodded.

"I'll say it plain," Jones said. "I've known John Kincaid for over thirty years. He is brilliant, but sometimes he is childish. You've only seen his best side because for once in his career, he was in a good place with you. After the Bragg debacle and his wife being murdered, he drifted looking for revenge. When no one was left, we," he whirled his finger over him. "Watched him, not allowing him to find an honorable way to commit suicide. Training troops like your Rabbits was finally the tonic he needed."

Peters interjected. "I watched him at Lewis, Bragg and closely at Desert Zero. Was he as formidable in his younger years as he is now?"

Jones took a deep breath and you could almost see the black cloud over his head. "I saw him walk, not run into heavy fire. I saw him willingly draw fire to save me and others. He drew fire once during a hot withdrawal and got left behind when he drew the enemy away. He walked out and surfaced three weeks later. He made no big deal about it. He was drinking a beer and a cup of coffee when I saw him. That happened more than once, but never with any others in harm's way."

Jones looked hard at Peters. "There is a demon on his back. This happened long before he came into the Army. He has to prove himself. He will die before he loses his honor. That is why he is a great NCO, but he was a hellion as a junior enlisted. The fact that you are asking me is the same reason you wanted him at Desert Zero."

Jones held up his hand. "John can stay with you for now. Sergeant Major Thomas Sheridan will understudy him and take over as the situation requires. I want you to come over Saturday for a long talk. John has some special duties to attend too along with everything else. You need to be briefed about a Special Operations Program that we are a part of and all the trouble it created.

September 28

1000 hours

Peters arrived and went to the coffee pot. The INSANE JANE training was taking on a life of its own. Lately he had spent a great deal of time divided between studying and refereeing disputes. His head hurt.

When Jones got his coffee, he closed the door and turned the sign around on his door. Both men sat down.

Peters started. "Unless you object, since we don't have any immediate threat, the men will take Sunday's off. There is no need to exhaust everyone too soon."

Jones agreed.

Peters said. "John briefed me about the Black Elves after the attack on my headquarters at Desert One."

Jones took a deep breathe. "I will take your word that nothing we discuss will ever be repeated for as long as you live and beyond. Now that there aren't any dummiecrats out there muddying up the story and classifying everything to protect the guilty. Get comfortable. It probably will take about two hours to tell you all about the highs, lows, good things and other things about Project Werewolf."

September 30

Minuteman, north of Fort Benton, Montana
1000 hours MDT.

INSANE JANE was finally underway. The Savage Rabbits was settling into their new lives as a classified Special Action Project under the direction of the Joint Chiefs of Staff for the Department of Defense. There was real documentation at the Department of Defense to cover them just in case someone actually looked. Generals with little to do, often look around for something to meddle with.

O'Cleary had UNSTACK THIS research a way to hide the Savage Rabbits to placate Edwards and shield them from Matheson at Northwestern Military District Command, General Traynor at SOCOM and Gender at Delta Force. The cover was self-covering. UNSTACK THIS was faster that the humans looking for her Rabbits. She could complain that someone took them away from her.

Most of Savage Rabbits didn't understand at first, but they now understood that no one was going to use them again. General O'Cleary was firmly in charge and they were now off-limits to the rest of the world. Colonel Jones and Lieutenant Colonel Peters introduced the Rabbits to their new jobs. They were the vanguard of a new force defending themselves and the people of the Northwest.

Three communities were completed, with seven more planned, and formed around them. Places to live, places to train and more importantly, places to live out their lives and defend their families. The resolve on their faces was renewed, reminding Peters of the day when they were certified to fight the drug wars.

The initial priority went to families first.

The men were formally introduced to Joshua and Janet Layman. He introduced himself and serenaded them about the communities they were going to build so they had places to live. Right now, those persons with spouses and children barely fit in the three communities already constructed. Everyone else was staying in tents erected on concrete slabs.

Layman had charts and maps showing everyone where the construction was going to be conducted. Each man was going to have a two-room building to live. Everyone living in that community worked together to build each other's home.

Layman bellowed out to everyone. "This is be my crowning achievement. I will not allow you to build a crappy place. Not to my standards. I will not allow anyone to insult me by building something second or third or fourth rate. You will build your homes to my specifications and you will love me for making you do everything right. Those that already have homes have already agreed to assist. They love me that much." Layman pointed to the Werewolves standing behind them. "These men and women love me so much they agreed and are required to assist me in spreading my love for you and assist you in building your homes to my perfection. All seven communities at once."

"My love for you says that the wiring will last a hundred years and never catch fire. My love for you says that if ten feet of snow land on your home, you will sit in a warm and snug home. My love for you is so much that you will be proud to live in a Layman home. My love for you is so great that you will love me back, forever."

Layman continued his serenade. "Your Colonel Jones has assured me that I have plenty of time to teach you about tools, materials, and proper procedure. The Snow will start falling in November. Your love for me will show itself when you sleep under a roof and not out in a tent. I don't work in the snow and neither shall you."

Layman picked up his materials and left. The plastic covered map was left on the stand.

Jones went up to the podium and said that Sundays was off-limits and everyone was going to be allowed at least three days a week to build a home for themselves. One of the original homes was empty and everyone was invited to look at what they were building.

All of them were told to wait at least nine months before calling their extended families and inviting them to come. "Wait for the new communities to be built. They will need homes first."

Peters read a new report on the situation south of the border. The problems there were was escalating, despite the efforts of the U.S. military to hold it all south of the border. The Cartels seemed emboldened at the demise of the Savage Rabbits. The Savage Rabbits stuck with speed and precision. The newer, larger and bloated force in place now was too hard-pressed to stay up with and will probably never get ahead of the Cartels.

The Cartels learned from the Savage Rabbits. Change, change and never stop changing their tactics. The lean and efficient original operations and intelligence section of seven men and women was replaced with thirty men and women who spent more time arguing with each other than working the situation. Half of the operations planned had to be canceled before launching. The Savage Rabbits usually worked and launched a mission within eighteen hours. Now it took three days. "Their problem now," Peters said putting down the report and walking out of Jones' headquarters.

Jones looked out of the window and surveyed his command. These men were serious, but light-hearted. They were motivated and their morale was high. He worried about the future. He, Smith and Kincaid were getting old. He shook his head, thinking that they really needed to retire. His joints ached and his wounds pulled hard.

Jones wondered if John Kincaid had this in mind when he originally bought the twenty-three hundred acres around the Minutemen compound. The Savage Rabbits and the Werewolves fit easily into this area. Albert and Marsha Glendive were becoming leaders in the community. If politics ever tainted this piece of heaven, they would be on top.

Jones was now learning the reason why senior officers barricaded themselves with a staff and an office. He felt like old Mother Hubbard at times. He was going insane with all the details until the General pointedly showed him he was doing too much and being ineffective. At least now he had time to think and make good decisions.

The Sections were now crawling through the INSANE JANE drills. The crawl through drills compressed the battle areas from square miles to square feet. They worked, re-worked and rehearsed it over and over again. The doctrine and strategy were carved in stone, but the operational and tactical parts sparked a lot of heated debate. The end result was that they believed in what they were practicing.

Peters was in charge of executing the overall training objectives along with Major Albert Glendive, who now acted as the Training Officer. Major George Thamaod assumed duties as the Executive Officer. He controlled the staff and directed traffic. That freed Jones to concentrate on the overall battle area which now comprised most of Montana, the eastern regions of Idaho and northern Wyoming; one hundred and twenty thousand square miles of land. Across the side wall of his office was a large National Geographic topographical map showing his area of responsibility in the center and the surrounding areas; his areas of interest.

Peters secretly held onto a nagging thought in his head. 'What the hell are we doing?' This INSANE JANE was so simple in theory, but complex in execution. The plan was too dependent on people communicating. Communications was always the Achilles' heel of any Army. Frequency hopping solved at lot of that, but whoever was in command of a cell had to obey the Sector Commander and the Sector Commander had to obey the Area Commander and the Area Commander had to obey Colonel Jones. Too many people had to obey orders that initially made no sense and possibly obeying those orders that will kill them in the process.

The Viet Cong used something like this to great effect during the sixties. But Giap and his subordinate commanders didn't have the ability to coordinate and modify a plan when the bullets started flying. Jones watched the blue shirts defend against the red shirts attacking. The red shirts were harassed and allowed to keep moving. Blue shirts were told to harass and pick at the red shirts, but do not ever pick a "decisive fight." A Decisive Fight was one in which you were committed, surrounded or unable to quit or maneuver. The only way to survive was to be the last man standing.

"Hit them once, fire a few rounds and flee. Scatter and let them pass into another cell. The new cell repeats the process and the old cell hits the tail and sides of the red shirts as you return to your area. A third cell hits them from the side and scatters."

On and on the process continued and repeated itself. Most importantly, the cells had to report what was going on and harass the supply trains. Forget the tanks and armored vehicles, go for the trucks, pipelines and storage areas.

"No gas, no grub, no stuff, no go."

Slowly he was seeing the process unfold and an understanding was forming. But there was still a doubt.

Locklear came in and explained something called "Confusionation." He used a stage with actors to explain it to everyone. By going through three choreographed situations, he made his point. The stage acts explained it in ways that no lecture could ever make a point.

John Kincaid was in the back with Jones. He said, "now I get it."

What was different was that some of the red shirts had blinders and controllers told them where to go. His blue shirts had partial blinders only to restrict their field of view. Slowly, very slowly the idea took form. This first day was nothing but an introduction. This was guerrilla warfare with other forms of warfare involved. At specific portions, the blue shirts, cut off sections of the red shirts and destroyed them, vanishing afterward without finishing the job. The blue shirts were encouraged to shout out confusing instructions to the red shirts. The result was red shirt chaos.

Finally, Jones and Peters got it. *"I am learning not to waste lives. We have to survive to do this again and again. By not wasting our lives, everyone will understand that when the time comes to die, all of us will understand that no other course of action is possible."*

Major Jack Gleason, the new Operations Officer or S-3, was busy scribbling notes. He joined the other officers were becoming very adept at the doctrine.

Jones tapped Kincaid on the shoulder. "John, we need to talk."

WSG Camp Number One, Hill County, Montana
1300 hours MDT.

Kendal, Morgan and Locklear spent their mornings working the training plan for INSANE JANE, and spent the afternoons learning something new called "Shark Hunters."

Cindy Morgan finally understood some of Zach's nightmares. Over the twenty years they slept together, Zach mumbled something about Sharks, yet never talked about it. One day he said, "I can't, won't talk about, so drop it." The sharpness of his voice had shocked her into dropping the subject and she never asked again. Now John Kincaid was telling her freely about that forbidden subject. At first, she could not understand what was so forbidden, but as time went on, the solitude and pressure of Shark Hunter duties started to consume her.

"A Shark Hunter is exactly as the name implies," Kincaid began. "You wade into the water without special armored suits, cages or weapons and you hunt sharks with butter knives. The Shark has all the advantages and you the Hunter have all the drawbacks. You are swimming, searching, observing and you have to Hunt for all the things around the

Shark without being eaten. Everything you have learned to date about stalking, reconnaissance, observation, documenting or reporting is now trash. I will teach you how to see without eyes, hear without ears and feel with a lover's touch while you wrap your hands around their balls and squeeze, making them smile."

Kincaid watched their reactions. "Everything I just said is confusing and contradictory. We have a starting point. I will say this once and only once. If the four of us have to kneel down, suck a dick and/or bend over and get butt fucked, you will do it. I mean that literally. No matter what it takes, you do it, willingly. Ladies you may have to have brutal sex, Earl that means you too. If I have to myself, I'll send you a video tape or invite you to watch. A to Z, one to a hundred is mission, mission and nothing but mission. I'm going to walk outside for three minutes. If you stay, you are fully committed, if not, you leave beforehand. And that means you too Miss Kendal." Kincaid left the room, clicking a stop watch.

The three of them looked at each other, then away. Each to their own thoughts.

Kendal stared at the clock and watched the second hand make three revolutions around the clock.

Locklear shuttered at the thought of giving himself the way Kincaid described. Whatever this really was, it had to be trouble.

Cindy Morgan thought back to when she was raped. The idea of surrendering to some coward with a dick made her shutter involuntarily at the thought of giving herself like that. Sex has and always was very personal to her. To become a whore, like those animals called her, brought out the worst in her. Inwardly she knew that it was going to happen. But could she? All she had to do to convince herself was Winchell attacking her. Criers destroyed a country and killed a lot of people without lifting a finder. She was in.

The door opened and Kincaid walked up to the table throwing down the stop watch. He walked up to Kendal pointing a finger in her face. "Miss Kendal, are you staying?"

"So long as it isn't you," Kendal said.

"Wrong answer," Kincaid said sharply, "in or out?"

"Yes," Kendal said, "I'm in."

"Mister Locklear, are you in or out?"

"I'm in," he said.

"Mrs. Morgan, are you in or out?"

Morgan took a deep breath and returned the hard stare, "I'm in."

"Fine," Kincaid said, opening a folder and handing out five booklets to each person. "Old school from the National Security Agency originally said that this process takes two and a half years. Zach Morgan and I did it, sloppily, in six months and applied it in Southeast Asia. We will train, officially and formally for the next year. If we have more than a year, great, if not, we suck it up and Hunt. Most of the classroom instruction is simple in nature. It is the application that is the most time consuming. In simplicity, you are conducting information gathering, sabotage, and denial of activities to an enemy. You are given a target. That target may be a person, a building, a compound, city or a country. There are no boundaries, no restrictions except mission completion. I have to over emphasize mission completion. Nothing you do or don't do interferes with mission completion, nothing."

Kincaid looked over his charges to ensure they followed him. He was not disappointed. "Once we finish learning the academics, we will go into the field and learn how this applied. There are a lot of nuisances that can only be studied in the field. Maybe you will be in woods, but a lot of research will be in urban areas. We will learn in banks, apartment buildings, towns, cities, military bases and large corporate areas. You must learn how to learn."

Kendal raised her hand. "Mister Kincaid, I understand mission completion. If you want your dick sucked, fine. If you want to butt fuck me, OK. What is this about?"

"I'm getting to that Miss Kendal," Kincaid said, "may I continue?" She nodded. "Shark Hunting is about learning your enemy totally without external interference. In modern terminology, you are creating a Target Folder or an Area Study. The information or task you are ordered to complete is given in a broad mission statement, but you do not have a specific mission. No item is too trivial. Nothing is too small. You build the Target Folder in a generic format. By that, I mean you may or may not execute the mission to harass or

70

destroy a target. The folder may be given to others to complete. This is written as a "stand alone" document. That is defined as all the information someone else may need to execute an assignment later down the line. Everything is fully documented. That mission may not have been envisioned when the assignment was originally given to you."

"In front of you are three separate; fifty-seven-page, double spaced outlines. They are general in nature, but give you the basic things to look for and not to look for. Outline one is for an individual or group of individuals. The targets may be a leader, sub unit leader, a military unit, civilian company or a group of people. The second outline is for a building or group of buildings that contain an activity that needs to be studied. The third is for a broad area, such as a city, state or region." Kincaid tapped the table to get everyone's attention. "One point beyond mission completion that has to be emphasized: **You are not given a timeline or deadline.** Once committed, there are only two options: finish or abort. Too many missions failed, in the past, because of external pressures. You are on your own to find the information or complete the task, totally alone."

Locklear raised his hand and asked. "Please explain how this is different from the reconnaissance and stalking that we already trained to do?"

"Excellent question, Mister Locklear," Kincaid said. "You are not restricted to sneak and peek, like sniper stalking. Sometimes you walk up to the front door and knock. You might get a job like a delivery boy. You might get a maintenance job or secretarial-like job and work the situation. Sometimes getting the equivalent of three pages of information might require six months or more."

"This sounds like James Bond," Locklear said.

"Maybe," Kincaid said, with a smile, "but without the beautiful girls, vodka martinis, shaken not stirred or fancy gadgets. Our missions are focused and deliberate to one point and only one point: the mission. Let's begin with the outline for individuals."

"I have one question," Morgan said. "Two women and two men?"

71

"Couples are easier to hide than two men or two women, or one man or one woman," Kincaid answered.

"Mister Kincaid?" Kendal asked. "I have to readdress one question. Why the analogy to sex?"

Kincaid closed the booklet in front of him, obviously wanting to get started. "Three of the booklets are the outlines as I described them. The fourth booklet is the one we will start with. It is the introduction. We will cover doctrine, general rules and guidelines and most importantly, why you are not just sneak and peek stalkers. The last booklet, which you will review on your own time, are the after-action reports from past missions."

"Lastly, I use that sex analogy for individual reasons," Kincaid paused to point to each of the three. "Earl, you are a Southern Baptist. You were predictably uncomfortable with the subject. Wendy, you have made your likes and dislikes well known and Cindy has personal issues with sex. I will not delve into specifics, but I use those subjects to make a point. Nothing is off limits or denied that compromises the mission. Failure to go one hundred plus percent means your brothers and sisters die, period." Kincaid straightened in his chair and leaned over the introduction. "The real answer to my sex analogy is this: Do you use sex now, use it as a teaser for later, or do you refuse sex? You will learn that difference."

Everyone opened the booklet marked "Introduction" and began.

October 1

Internal Security Agency, Barton, Virginia
0800 hours EDT.

General, Vice Chairman of the Joint Chiefs of Staff, Brenda O'Cleary came for her official first visit. She was ushered into Clara Simpson's office and both women warmly shook hands.

"Congratulations, Vice-Chairwoman Brenda," Simpson said.

"Thank you and congratulations to you Director Clara," O'Cleary said as both women laughed.

72

"I hear it was Prescott that had you detained," Simpson said. "Prescott said that you were going to work out some problems with the "Victoria" start-up. The National Security Council had you listed as being on special duties."

"Detained at Fort Detrick for an indefinite period without cause or charges," O'Cleary said as she took the offered cup of coffee.

Simpson hit the privacy button the intercom and settled back. "Want to small talk first, then discuss the business portion?"

"Sure, O'Cleary said, sipping the coffee. "The one thing I missed in detention was enjoying sunshine with a cup of coffee."

Simpson looked at her. "I missed the detention thing. By the luck of the draw, I was at the White House when 'Victoria' started. I was sent back here when Prescott was arrested. I asked about you, but there was an order putting you on special status when I returned. I will admit that I was too busy to follow up. I am sorry."

O'Cleary waved her off. "It's old news and history. Besides, the doctors there found out why I couldn't have children. Dennis and I are *actively* trying," she said with a smile.

Simpson couldn't help herself. "Details, girlfriend, details," she leaned forward, almost spilling her coffee.

1000 hours EDT

Hawker came in and reminded O'Cleary that they needed to leave. After settling into the ride back to the Pentagon, O'Cleary took a deep breath after they cleared the compound. Tabor and Taylor were sent back to Minuteman as much as for them to relax as they were needed by Jones and Kincaid to recon the Minuteman operational area. O'Cleary told them that any more interaction with the Pentagon and they would turn brain-dead.

O'Cleary looked her betrayer in the face and maintained the façade of being a friend. She wanted to snap her neck, burn her alive, etc., etc.

O'Cleary waved off Hawker's attempts to pre-brief her on the remainder of the day's events. It was an hour-long trip.

Suddenly, O'Cleary's X-Berry vibrated. UNSTACK THIS was warning her of an altercation up ahead. "Driver," she said. "Pull over to the gas station ahead."

The PSA in front seat turned around and O'Cleary cut him off. "Just do it."

The PSA signaled to the driver and he pulled over. The driver did park in a location that allowed easy maneuvering to leave in either direction.

O'Cleary looked at the X-Berry and saw enhanced pictures of David Nichols and Martin Hernandez posing as state road crewman with at least three others three miles ahead.

O'Cleary wished Tabor and Taylor were still here. "Return to the ISA," she said. Turning to Hawker. "Call ahead to ISA and request the use of Director Simpson's helicopter to return us to the Pentagon. Check the pilots."

O'Cleary thought about this incident. Inwardly, she knew that a calmer voice and disposition was needed.

Quinton Ranch, Hinton, Alberta, Canada
0800 hours (Tango)

Amanda Edwards finished cleaning up after breakfast. Mark and Jeffery Quinton loved her alphabet pancakes. She made a game out of spelling words for the boys. If they learned the words, then "treats" were available in the afternoon. Barbara Quinton finally came around to being friendly after only three months. She smiled remembering the first few weeks after arriving. Barbara was just like John Kincaid; bull headed, stubborn, moody, quick to lose her temper and opinionated. John Kincaid, version 2.

"Amanda?" Barbara asked.

Amanda looked up and recognized the look on her face. Tom already left to go to work and the boys were busy playing in the oversized living room that become their 'tree house' and 'fort.' "Yes," she said, pouring coffee for both of them.

"I want to apologize for treating you so badly since you arrived," Barbara said, sitting down.

"It's OK," Amanda said, taking a sip of coffee.

"No, it's not OK," Barbara said, her temper flaring and then subsiding. "I am mad at my father and I took it out on you."

"I do the same thing with my husband," Amanda said, smiling at her.

"Dad rescued me, again, and gave me a beautiful life here......." She paused to sip the coffee and turned to look at her. "This life took my mother from me. This life took my dad away a lot while I was growing up. But every time his life takes from me, Dad comes to the rescue."

Amanda took another sip, remaining silent, making her say it.

"Amanda, your husband is an Army General. How did you deal with it?"

"I was alone a lot. I sat up late at night, worrying if there was going to be a knock on the door." She knocked three times on the table top for emphasis. "I raised two children, scared that one day I was going to have to raise them alone and have this conversation with them. I was angry a lot of times. Last year, he was almost assassinated in Afghanistan. Deal with it, my dear. I don't know." Amanda forced down her temper.

"Why do they do it? Why do they put us through it?"

Amanda took a deep breath and thought hard. "The military is a family. The American military is something that attracts crazy boys. I knew something about what I was in for. I graduated from college around the time Vietnam ended. All through High School, fathers were dying and my friends vanished. They lost their smiles and the zest for life. But they lived on. Some fight for benefits, some fight because it is their job. All of them fight for each other. The military is a lover that caresses them lightly in a way no woman can ever understand. Why do they do it or put us through it?" Amanda pushed the coffee away from her and leaned forward. "They love us and the nation they fight for."

For once in her life, Barbara was calm and deliberate. "Do you think it will come to us?"

"I hope not," Amanda said leaning back. "My husband is a General and I ran away from my country so criminals can't use me to force him to compromise his honor."

"Will they look for you and maybe find you here?"

Amanda lowered her gaze. "Maybe they are looking for me. If your dad did his job, they won't find me. If they do, grab the boys and run."

Barbara's temper flared. "Half of me is my father. I don't run. Part of my problem is being hard headed."

"And half of you is your mother. Remember she died protecting the family dog."

Barbara started crying at the memory. Though long ago, the pain was still fresh. "You haven't answered my question and maybe you can't. Why?"

"You are a mother," Amanda said. "You will die to protect your children. You will die to guard them. You will shield and provide for them. You will die to save them. That is the only way to explain it."

"Do you miss your Husband"?

Amanda smiled and pointed to the cast iron frying pan handing on the wall. "Oh yes and he will pay for this piece of heaven he sent me to."

Pentagon, Washington D.C.
1800 hours EDT

O'Cleary called Hector Adams. Unfortunately, he was at the Minuteman Facility so he had to minister to her over the X-Berry. O'Cleary summed up her situation with one sentence. She positively identified two men as Black Elves who were perfectly placed to kill or kidnap her.

"Brenda," he said. "As your Priest, I have to counsel you to be calm and allow God to do his will. As a man of this world of deceit and violence, I have to counsel caution and maybe some form counter action."

"Are you advising me to watch my back and return violence with violence?"

Adams sighed. "Brenda, you and I already know the answer. As a Commander, you have to order the return of Mister Taylor and Mister Tabor and hunt these men down. For as long as you intend to stay at the Pentagon, you are going to have to remain under guard by the only people who truly care if you live or die. Now to the other parts, swallow your pride

76

and send for some hunters to actively hunt those two men and their acolytes down."

Brenda sighed herself. "I was hoping for a more normal life, but I have been delusional. Thank you again Hector. I hope the next time I have a problem; you are a lot closer."

O'Cleary hung up the phone and rotated in her chair, deep in thought. Lately she had been looking down at herself hoping for a baby. Inwardly, she smiled thinking how odd the ghosts of this building would react to see a pregnant four-star general. She held no illusions about the whispers behind her back when it became apparent.

Minuteman, North of Fort Benton
1800 hours MDT

Jones hung up the phone after talking for nearly an hour with General O'Cleary. The Black Elves is a jock rash fungus that will not go away. They just refused to pack up and retire. No one was looking for them. No one cared about them. Jones watched the video feed of them on the side of the road.

Jones called both Kincaid and Miles to come to the Headquarters now. Protecting the General had to be a Werewolf-only mission. The Savage Rabbits was loyal to her but did not have the experience or training to hunt down and combat true-expert-killers. These men had to killed without warning or remorse.

He had to start acting like a real commander. He now wished he had decades of experience as a commander, but that was not going to happen. Any lack of confidence or decidedness will translate back to his charges.

Jones needed this time to formulate an overall plan for both of them. He needed Kincaid and at least three team members to go east and hunt down Nichols and Hernandez. He knew both men personally as Kincaid did. They were Werewolf candidates that were dropped from the program. He knew them by sight and could instinctively determine what they were going to do. The bottom line was that they had to have some kind of an edge in order to survive this long.

Jim Miles had to put on his Captain's bars in order to conduct a massive, but detailed reconnaissance of all 2300 acres of the Minuteman area, including the Werewolf Support Camp. After that was done, then he needed to have a generalized idea about what the terrain was like another 100 miles outward.

Jones leaned back in his chair and a plan solidified. He looked at the wall filling map across from his desk. He swung around and focused hard.

Miles was living in a house here in the compound and therefore he saw Jones early. Kincaid was in the WSG camp fifty miles away. He arrived toward the end of Miles' briefing. Miles did listen in on O'Cleary's problem.

Kincaid arrived at last and was told generally about Miles' mission. He said that Kendal, Locklear and Morgan should go along with him. The area study mission was in keeping with their target folder training. This kind of reconnaissance was tailor-made for them. "I recommend that six of the Savage Rabbits accompany them. The volume of material and huge area will over whelm you," he looked at Jones and Miles.

Jones said nodded yes and nodded to Miles. "I have no objection. What do you think Jim?"

Miles said. "Yes, that fits." He looked back to Jones.

Jones turned in his chair. "The General is in danger. The reason you are here John, is that David Nichols and Martin Hernandez were spotted. They were on a construction crew waiting alongside the road next to the JIA or ISA. The General said that someone called Junior spotted them and warned her."

When the gears in Kincaid's head showed in his eyes, Jones tapped the desk. "Your mission is a Werewolf only mission. The only two that are left are Monk Tabor and Brad Taylor. Mejia, Griffith and Pruitt will be your reserve, but they will stay here on 12-hour notice. We are hamstrung with too many things to do and not enough people to do it. John, anything you need, is yours. Unlimited funds, reinforcements, evacuate the General against her will; you say it, it is done. I will not prejudice your plan, just find those clowns and kill them once and for all. If possible, capture them and drain them of every bit of information they have. But kill them if you have the slightest doubt."

485 Glenmore Drive, Alexandria, Virginia
2000 hours EDT

Brenda O'Cleary was finding it hard to get used to be chauffeured from place to place all the time. She and Dennis bought the vacant homes on both sides of his house so that the PSA's, orderlies and Major Hawker had homes. They did this so that their home was peaceful. Truth be told, Brenda wanted some place to be so she could be comfortable about being dressed to lesser degrees without having to look around the corner.

When she walked into the house, she noticed Dennis cooking supper with a pistol strapped to his side in one of those special ops pistol holders. She stared at him. Waving off the PSAs, she closed the door and put down her things. Kissing her husband, she had to say it. "Where is your apron?"

Dennis looked at her and frowned. Dennis reached under her skirt and started feeling her slip and underwear. "You took it this morning."

Brenda chuckled and stepped away. She picked up her briefcase and went back into the bedroom. The safe in the closet was waiting for her. The pajamas and matching panties were on the bed waiting for her. She took her shower and dressed for dinner.

Coming out, Dennis already had the music on. Brenda set her X-Berry down and something wrapped in a napkin.

Dennis served his famous chicken a la O'Cleary.

"Pistol?" Brenda asked.

"X-Berry," Dennis replied.

"I have to assume Colonel Jones called and said something," Brenda replied.

Dennis looked at her. "Yes, he was one of them. I am your husband and Sergeant Major. Get over it. Our mutual friend filled in the blanks."

Brenda looked to the side and reached over to the napkin. "And something else." She held out the item.

Dennis looked at the napkin and took it. "What?"

79

"Open it," Brenda said standing.

Dennis opened it and it was a piece of plastic resembling a narrow spoon. He rotated it and a rectangle said "Pregnant."

Brenda pulled up her shirt and there was a crude drawing of a stork carrying a baby.

Dennis was incredulous for a few seconds. Suddenly, he yelled "Yee-haw" at the top of his lungs. He jumped up and down, forcing Brenda to back up. Dennis was acting exactly like a teenager.

Suddenly, her two PSAs burst in, guns drawn.

Brenda gave them the all-clear gesture and code-words. She showed them the pregnancy test and pushed them back out the door.

Dennis came to her, hugged her like he did after their wedding. He knelt down, kissed her hand and finally lifted her shirt and kissed the womb that held his child.

"Any idea whether a boy or girl?" Dennis asked.

"No, we have to go to the hospital for that answer. For now, we go on with our lives. Maybe next month, our child will be old enough to find out. In June or July, we will have another O'Cleary.

Dennis put both hands on her hips and just stared. This was something he never expected to have. "Arthur and Thomas were supposed to carry the family name. Now my child, by the grace of a perfect Brenda, will do that."

Brenda listened to the words of her husband. 'The father of my child', she thought to herself. Brenda remembered her mother and aunts saying that no matter what you do in life, being a mother was a wonder that nothing could ever top.

It was heaven on Earth.

Until the X-Berry rang.

October 2

0600 hours MDT

Miles and Kincaid looked at their coffee, trying to relax before their lives took them away.

Jim Miles thought through his portion of Jones's briefing last night. Three teams of two people. He needed to find every fold in the ground, spring and piece of topography. Jones made it a point of not holding him to a timetable. Three shark hunter-apprentices and three rookies. Miles thought about his charges. Morgan was almost a natural, but that came from years of living in the mountains with Zach Morgan. The other Werewolves were just as good.

But three unknowns from the Savage Rabbits with standard Army training was a concern. Miles smiled remembering an NCO from his earlier years who used a Playboy centerfold to highlight terrain features and contour lines. To this day, he never forgot that class. Cindy Morgan had a thick hide. Wendy Kendal was an unknown quantity. Miles respected them both and he didn't want to create a problem.

The classes were a waste of time with the Werewolves, but he needed to even out the other's training. He could send out the three others on a week-long road trip doing exactly that. He needed an over-view of the Minuteman area. Checking fields of view, elevations and overall changes to the terrain needed to be updated. For example, if a wooded area on the map was logged out; that was needed information. How tall were the stumps and could someone use them as cover or concealment?

Miles needed to talk to Colonel Peters to find six men who were good with land navigation, hopefully some were artists and others that were good hunters or astronomers. Hopefully he could remember how they taught him, all…those…. years…. ago.

October 3

Holiday Hotel, Fairfax, Virginia
0500 hours EDT

Kincaid, Tabor and Taylor were waiting for a direction to go. Kincaid spent a lot of time on his computer and communicating with UNSTACK THIS. Even with all the computing power at his disposal, Nichols and Hernandez almost disappeared. The last sighting was two days ago. Kincaid wondered if they knew something or someone was watching them. He reviewed everything from day one to today. Both men were once his friends. They trained together and probably could have graduated together.

David Nichols was a rock ape with some leadership skills. He was a natural athlete who excelled at all the physical exertions. He was even stronger than Rucker. Early on, he told off Rucker. It only took once in the hand-to-hand pit to turn Rucker off. It was the other things that did him in. He just could not study enough. Even with several of his class mates coaching him, academically he slid so far back that suddenly one day, he was gone.

Martin Hernandez was able to do it all. Physically and mentally, he did well. His problem was a total lack of any ability to work in a group. He refused to listen to anyone. He had no use for anyone but himself. Teamwork was important in the Werewolves. Kincaid always wondered how Hernandez could have fit into the Black Elves or any other organization.

Kincaid looked for anything to point them in a direction. Something or anything.

"John," Taylor said. "We can sit here till the cows come home or shake up the country-side."

Kincaid looked up at Tabor and Taylor. "I'm listening."

"Brad and I will return to being the General's body guards," Taylor said. "You and the General get out in the open. You are a bigger target than she is."

Kincaid looked at Taylor. "Monk don't you ever speak?"

"No one shuts up long enough," he said.

Everyone chuckled.

They made a plan between them and left for breakfast.

Kincaid opened his X-Berry and queried the whereabouts of Nichols and Hernandez. Still nothing to report. Was this just a fluke or was there something else. Kincaid realized that they could be just tying us in knots diverting attention away from something or someone else.

485 Glenmore Drive, Alexandria, Virginia

Command Sergeant Major Jonathan Taylor Kincaid stood uneasily at the door, in full dress uniform, to the residence of Retired Command Sergeant Major and General O'Cleary. Both of them.

The door opened and Dennis O'Cleary stood there. He looked at Kincaid and busted out laughing. He laughed so hard; Kincaid worried that Dennis would rupture his wounds.

Brenda came over to see what Dennis was laughing at. She looked at him and did not laugh. She turned, walked out of sight and cracked a smile.

Kincaid walked in and set his briefcase on the table and waited for everyone to finish humiliating him. It was a long story that many would regret later.

"Please forgive us after a long night," Brenda said. She showed off the positive pregnancy test. "Two old people dreamed long and hard all night about being parents when we should be having grandchildren."

Kincaid was forcing himself to be calm and nice. "Congratulations General," he said. "Health, happiness and long life to you and your child."

Even Dennis knew something about that was off.

"General, I need 15 minutes of your time," Kincaid rotated a finger over his head.

Dennis wiped his eyes and went to turn on the sound system. The sonic carrier and radio carrier wave was not as aggravating as the buzz box. Dennis remembered that the anniversary of having his buddies come over for an upgrade was coming up.

Kincaid removed his uniform jacket and sat down, waiting for the General to come to the table. He rose as protocol required when she came to sit down.

Brenda opened the napkin and started to eat. "Same rule as your house, John. No rank inside the walls."

Kincaid felt uncomfortable. "General, I have Monk and Brad along with me and three others on twelve hours-notice or sooner if the situation requires it. The overall plan is that I am going to shadow you at the Pentagon for two days; undercover as an observer for a classified assignment in conjunction with

CIA overseas. I will need interference from General Edwards. I have two letters from Amanda for him. That should smooth things between him and me. Monk and Brad will need to coordinate with Major Hawker about your schedule. They will shadow you in order to watch any movements outside your immediate area."

"What about Cindy Morgan?" Brenda asked. "She can go places the others can't."

Kincaid pushed the plate away from him. "Gunnery Sergeant Morgan is currently on assignment building an area study of the Minuteman site. The process has already started and she cannot be pulled away. If a woman is required, Major Hawker is trained and that training can be enhanced as the situation requires."

Brenda signed, called Hawker and 'invited' her to come over before going to work.

Hawker came over and Kincaid briefed her. "Bottom line, Major, is that these two men." He pointed to the recent photographs of Nichols and Hernandez. "Somehow found out the General was instrumental in destroying the Black Elves. You will now be directly in charge of the General's security. This shall include the PSAs. I shall be available to work with you for the next two days out in the open. I will advise you that three other persons, kept in the shadows, will be shadowing you."

Hawker turned and noted General O'Cleary's nod. "I will do my best."

Brenda looked at her watch. "It's time to go to work."

Pentagon, Washington D.C
0900 hours EDT

Kincaid was sitting in O'Cleary's office wishing for an early grave. He was just settling in when Edwards came in to see for himself. Edwards looked at him like a shark seeing a snack. Kincaid swore that Edwards was thinking he had every opportunity to arrest Kincaid and finally get his revenge.

Normally when a superior officer entered any space, you were required to stand at attention and not move without permission. The junior person is usually not allowed to ask for permission. Kincaid angered him when he reached into his briefcase and retrieved the two letters from Amanda.

Edwards was seething until he recognized the way his name was written on the letter.

O'Cleary closed the door and told Hawker to halt anyone until Edwards left.

Edwards sat down, carefully reading and re-reading the letters. He absorbed every word. It was a letter devoid of any carefully chosen words or phrases. Inwardly, he felt her love and missed every day they were separated. She talked openly about missing him and the strain of being where she was. She mentioned the three-gallon fry pan she bought for him, implying he needed a new helmet.

Edwards found himself visualizing her words. He thought that she spent a lot of time cooking for someone. She talked about cooking as if she had a big kitchen to work with. He almost felt that she was cooking for children. He remembered how she talked when she described feeding Marshal and Elizabeth. She was comfortable where she was and that was a good thing.

Edwards read the letters three times. O'Cleary and Kincaid held their silence out of respect for a man nearly staving for news about his beloved lady.

When Edwards took the letters and walked over to the shredder, Kincaid stopped him. "General, it is correct to shred the envelopes, but keep the letters. As a widower, I cherish all the letters I kept from Karen. Most of them were in three ring binders until those government types ransacked my house."

Edwards looked at the letters and was pulled in two directions. He wanted to keep them, but he worried that security could get them, use them to find her and control him. In the end, he folded the letters and put them in his coat pocket. The envelopes went into the shredder.

Edwards sat back down and stared hard at Kincaid. As usual, Kincaid just looked blank faced. He was immune to Edwards' moods. "May I call you John?" he asked.

Kincaid hesitated and nodded 'yes' a few seconds later.

Edwards walked over and extended his hand. Kincaid rose and shook his hand. The bland expression on their faces, stayed in place.

85

Edwards took what he could get. "This is an order. Direct from me. You will defend and protect General O'Cleary against all harm and enemy forever. This is no longer a request. Do we understand each other, Sergeant Major?"

Kincaid was taken aback at the directness of the order. "Yes Sir," he replied.

Edwards looked at O'Cleary. "Have your aide type up an order, for my signature, allowing Kincaid access to you at any time he needs. There is not to be any end to that order."

The intercom buzzed. "Yes sir," O'Cleary answered.

Hawker said. "I am sorry for interrupting. The SecDef is needing the Chairman to call him."

Edwards motioned to O'Cleary. She said, "the Chairman acknowledged".

Edwards stood and bowed slightly to Kincaid. He said to O'Cleary, "Make sure he doesn't burn down the building".

"General of the Army," Kincaid said. "Do you have any correspondence I can forward for you?"

Edwards frowned for a few seconds and then softened. "Yes," he said.

"I will be leaving tomorrow," Kincaid said.

No. 17, U.S. Naval Observatory, Washington, DC
2100 hours EDT.

Edwards sat alone. He pulled out his Dennis provided monitor and swept the room. Nothing showed. He pulled out a pen and paper. Something about the archaic method of letter writing was so soothing.

Dear Amanda,

I received your letters today. My heart jumped at finally getting word from you that is not sanitized or carefully worded.

I love you and cannot apologize enough for the situation we are in. The ten-star clowns in charge of this fiasco are something best avoided. I thought this was the best for us. Every time I wake up, I dream that you are lying next to me.

The waking up to reality each morning wants me to rip out my heart.

This is not supposed to be a mopey letter. These days, I am eating too much fast food. My orderly cannot cook. He is just as happy to buy me fast food for supper and microwave something for breakfast. Martin still feeds me something better for lunch. He still remembers your covert instructions. He will not get me anything I want that is fattening, bad for my heart or generally bad for my health.

That job I have is grinding a hole in the center of my forehead. As much as it is a rare honor to have five stars, it almost is not worth the effort. Too many fools with stupid ideas running around, thinking they are right. The executive branch uses us for grunt labor. Soldiers highly trained to fight wars and defend the nation are laborers needed for those things these pimps are too special to do themselves. I confess to being something like Kincaid. It is fun to poke holes in stupid plans.

I am going to decide next June to retire or resign. Two years is the normal tenure for a Chairman. I am tired of the military. It is tired of me. I am tired of being alone.

I love you

October 4

1800 hours EDT

Kincaid spent two days shadowing O'Cleary around "the Cement Sanitorium" eyeing the security around her. She had a rest room in her office. Her lunch meal was delivered to her desk, primarily because she worked through lunch. Hawker showed him that her schedule did not show any trips planned in the foreseeable future. Her primary duties were to free Edwards so he could visit places.

There were three ways to get to her. The trip to work, the trip to home and at her home. At the home, Dennis was armed to the teeth and regularly practiced with pistols, shotguns and his privately owned AK. Like most old schoolers, he thought fully automatic was a waste of ammo.

Brenda herself has a weekly appointment to practice with a pistol at the indoor range the Pentagon police department has in the basement.

Kincaid studiously noted his conclusions and briefed both O'Cleary's and Major Hawker on the few things that needed to be done. Dennis was all ears and looked at his bride. She was dubious at best. Dennis and Hawker would do what they could.

October 5

Underground Station "Conscience", World Wide Web and Channel 513
0900 hours EST.

"If you threaten, act. If you say something, do it. If something is important, stand your ground. Governments are often hamstrung by individuals who have opinions about issues they feel strongly about. This is Martin Socranson, self-proclaimed philosopher who says, 'What are we if we can't back up what you say'?"

"Greetings America" Martin Socranson said beginning his broadcast. "It is reluctantly Saturday and I say thus." In the background the sounds of the 1812 overture played.

"Ordinarily, I would be playing a patriotic theme to this broadcast," he said, looking over his shoulder at a huge map of the continental United States. "Now I am the prophet of ill will and the teller of bad news. Oh, how we have sunk to new lows."

Socranson walked over to the large stack of paper on the corner of his desk. "Remember this," he said, pointing to it and picked up the top of the stack. "I said this was the 'Victoria' plan and your e-mails called me a fool and a liar." He smirked and cocked his head to the side as he looked at the camera. He flipped past a few pages. "Page forty-three, if you bothered to download the plan. Read along with me as I recount what has happened. Quote: Reassure the public that this is for their own good. Remind them that this is timed and nothing will ever remain permanent. Tell them that normalcy is the guide, unquote. Yaddy, Yaddy, Yadda," Socranson said throwing down the paper.

"Let me tell you what will happen next. The military presence on our streets will become common place. Slowly, they will insinuate themselves. The next step will be the removal of individual firearms from both law abiding and law-breaking citizens. They will "calm the streets", he said making quotation marks with his fingers. "Gangs of government workers will visit your homes and apartments and 'interview' you citizens. Slowly, inexorably they will gather every scrap of information needed to subjugate everyone."

Socranson smirked again. "Go ahead, call me a liar. Everyone who is a sheep will bend a knee and be petted like a dog." Socranson petted a stuffed dog sitting on a stool. "Watch how slow the process begins. As control is exerted, the process is accelerated."

"Oh, just in case you are wondering why I am on the air and not one of the nearly five million people detained without due process or trial." Socranson smirked and said, "can't catch me in Alaska, boys and girls. Opps, did I just give away my location or am I sending some poor slob north in the middle of the summer." Socranson laughed.

"As you let the government 'interviewers' into your homes to kindly ask you if you are comfortable or need anything. They will compassionately listen to your words. Watch their eyes. See them looking at how much space you have. See them looking into your refrigerator and pantry at how much food you have. See them flush your toilets. See them make notions next to your name. See them catalogue things they already know about you. Where you worked. What skills you have. See them list your tools, knives, plates, weapons. Do you have your firearms registered and secured? Do you have any information about your neighbors that is suspicious? Nothing is too trivial. Nothing is beneath them as they continue writing something next to your name."

Socranson paused to take a deep breath turning his face from the camera. A few seconds later, he looked at the camera with a sorrowful look. "Here is what it will look like." The screen changed to show an average home with a family. There was a knock on the door and a kindly government 'interviewer' was being invited inside and 'interviewing' the family. Nothing about this scenario was sinister. Nothing seemed wrong.

The camera faded from the home and returned to Socranson's studio. "Guess what happens next." The scene faded again to show a bureaucratic looking large room as the 'interviewer' ran down a long list of information about the family he 'interviewed.' The information was dutifully logged into a computer which reduced the comfortable home and family into digital information. They had no serious health concerns. Father/husband is a carpenter possessing basic hand tools. Mother was a home maker, two children. Food on hand was enough for four days. All base line needs are present; refrigerator, stove, freezer, and climate control. No immediate needs beyond those that are available.

The scene faded back to Socranson. On the desk in front of him, three of five lights illuminated. "Guess I'm hitting close to home," he said, pointing to the lights. "All their efforts appear to be law abiding," he pointed to the screen showing the family that was interviewed, "was reduced to numbers in a computer for future reference." Socranson went over to the "Victoria" file and tapped on it. "Thank you for your concern, masser."

Cyber Intelligence Section, Internal Security Agency, Barton Virginia
1000 hours EDT.

The operators watching and monitoring the Socranson broadcast were pulling their hair out trying in vain to locate Socranson.

"Enough of this," Milton Bradley said. "Enough, shut it down and return to your normal duties."

Glenda Garcia turned back to her computer and reset it back to its trawling duties on the internet. She waited for it.

"Garcia," Bradley said, indicating his office. Bradley closed the door after her and walked around to his desk, picked up a folder and handed it to her. "That is a signed order from me to work independently. You will find this Socranson. You will not have any help. But you will not have any interference.

I want progress. I will not expect results next week, but I want progress. So far, a hundred operators haven't been able to find him, but maybe one person could. That is all, dismissed."

Garcia left and walked over to her console. Slowly she reached into her drawer and removed a high-density flash drive. She methodically cleared the programs from her console and set up 'her idea.' Smiling, she inserted the flash drive, waited for the computer to devour its contents and a blank screen winked at her. One word flashed on and off: "Hello."

Two hours later, an emoji icon of a smiley face appeared on the screen. The web site originating the smiley face was erased. But a small data packet was left behind.

Garcia smiled.

Minuteman, north of Fort Benton, Montana
1800 hours MDT

Susan Espirito sat on top of her husband John and looked at the sonagram of their daughter. She was four months along in the pregnancy. Susan was ecstatic when she discovered she was pregnant. During the last two months of craziness and the three months they were on the run, she could not give her condition any serious thought. Susan's way of dealing with their situation was sex with an all too willing John. Her periods stopped but the home pregnancy tests said she was not pregnant. She thought that the stress was interfering with that. Susan made the mistake of thinking she had nothing to worry about. It was only when the baby starting kicking that she went to the clinic and had a professional test done. The doctor had a technician perform a sonagram and there she was.

October 7

Enroute to the Pentagon, Washington D.C.
0730 hours EDT

O'Cleary was seated alone in the back of her car as her PSAs drove her to the Pentagon. Her phone rang. It was UNSTACK THIS.

"Secure," she said.

[Valkyrie, all security and counter surveillance is in place. We are secure].

"Is there a problem?"

[I need to discuss my counter-program against user Garcia.]

O'Cleary sighed. She was tired of this woman. "Only if you can discredit her, forever."

[I have the following plan.]

UNSTACK THIS spent the next fifteen minutes running down the fine points of its plan. UNSTACK THIS knew that it had 25 minutes before O'Cleary arrived at the Pentagon. O'Cleary snickered at some parts of the plan and was appalled at others.

"Go ahead with your plan and I approve. Your main mission is to remove her distraction now and for all time."

O'Cleary logged off the phone call and softly laughed at UNSTACK THIS's plan. She remembered back to its plan for dealing with those two hackers who were used by Prescott.

Off to the side, the Pentagon came into view. O'Cleary sighed.

October 8

Cyber-Intelligence Section, Internal Security Agency, Barton, Virginia
0800 hours EDT

Clara Simpson walked up behind Garcia and silently watched the woman stare at the screen. Periodically, Garcia would turn to type something into a laptop computer, but she would return her attention back to the blank computer screen.

"Miss Garcia," Simpson interrupted Garcia's train of thought. Garcia turned back to Simpson and stood up. Simpson held up her hand. "I am not interested in talking with you. That virus is dangerous. If you do anything to make it

92

attack this agency, I will send you to the darkest place on Earth. Period."

Simpson turned her back and walked away.

Pentagon, Washington D.C.
0900 hours EDT

O'Cleary sat down at her desk and looked at the stack of files waiting for her. She reminded herself that she took this job. She thought back to when she first reported to Edwards after leaving detention. She remembered when she took the oath to take this job and all the other things that said she had to be here and do the things she was doing. In the end she could have left it all behind. But she wanted this job.

O'Cleary swiveled in her chair. She opened her bottle of apple juice. She chuckled thinking that her stomach rebelled at the loss of her coffee. She looked down at her womb. She had just found out semi-officially and her thoughts were suddenly focused on being a mom.

Dennis 'made (?)' her change a lot of her underwear since being married. Now it is going to change again. After that she was going to think about toys, diapers, changing tables and schedules.

O'Cleary looked at the phone and counted from down. "5, 4, 3," ring.

Hawker spoke on the intercom. "General, Colonel Gasser from NATO to speak to you on line 3."

O'Cleary sighed and began her day.

October 9

Cyber-Intelligence Section, Internal Security Agency, Barton, Virginia
1000 hours EDT

UNSTACK THIS looked at Garcia and finally decided it was time to play with Garcia. On her screen, a single word appeared super-imposed over a real-time video of Garcia. The word was "Hello."

Garcia sat back and beamed.

Suddenly, a set of arms shot in front of her. The hands typed a kill code for the computer.

Garcia sat upright wondering what was going on.

Another set of hands whipped her around. "You opened a camera feed in this room without warning."

Garcia was afraid. This kind of security breach was very serious. No cameras were allowed without security sweeps and warnings.

October 10

484 Piedmont Drive, Walker's Crossing, Virginia
1500 hours EDT

Kincaid had nothing to show for his week-long hunt for Nichols and Hernandez.

Kincaid choose this place to serve as his headquarters. This was Brenda Edgars' home before she married Dennis and moved into his house. There were a lot of reasons for that beyond the married thing. Primarily, Dennis' home was his and both O'Cleary's could veto a lot of things, especially Prescott's tendency to think he was above the law and regulations.

Kincaid sat at the dining room table pondering his next move. UNSTACK THIS was looking at all the cameras in and around Washington D.C.

If both men were still in area, they somehow found a way to hide. Kincaid pondered this. His training came out and he pondered the process. First, why did they show themselves? Second, what were they doing there and was General O'Cleary the target? Lastly, there was no way they could have known UNSTACK THIS found them and warned O'Cleary.

Taylor and Tabor arrived through the back door and slid in quietly. Kincaid wanted to present a target in case those guys came into the open. Besides, Nichols and Hernandez did not like Kincaid. Not that it was bad blood, but they were Black Elves and he was a Werewolf.

Kincaid went to the couch and decided that he needed sleep. Monk and Major Hawker were talking at the dining room table.

94

2000 hours.

Kincaid awoke and groaned. He slept through the afternoon and part of the night. Now he was going to be up all night. Kincaid tried stretching to get his blood moving.

Kincaid's head was still a jumble as the large sliding doors in the back exploded from automatic fire. Two concussion grenades were thrown into the room.

"Grenade," Kincaid screamed as the grenades detonated. The bright light and extremely loud sound effects did exactly as they were designed. Kincaid, Taylor, Tabor and Hawker were disorientated.

Brad Taylor instantly recovered and shot at the men rushing in from the rear of the building. From the front windows, sweeping machine gun fire destroyed the windows on the front of the house.

Monk Tabor hesitated, throwing Hawker to the ground. As he fully turned to meet the threat at the front of the house. He was cut down and fell to the floor.

Hawker ignored the terror flooding through her and grabbed Tabor's weapon. She slid over to the side and waited for a target. She remembered a lot of her Savage Rabbit training. 'Wasting ammo shooting at nothing, guarantees someone knows where to kill you'.

Kincaid joined Taylor in killing the last of the three men from the rear of the house. The last man went down and both men spun around and crouched as Tabor fell to the ground. "Go right," he screamed to Taylor pushing him over to the carport door.

The front door blew open after Taylor ran past it.

"Go," Kincaid said as he changed magazines. A body came around the corner and was about to throw a concussion grenade inward. Kincaid reached over and threw a vase at the man.

The assailant was arching his arm to throw the grenade as the vase hit his hand. The grenade dropped to the man's feet and detonated. His body turned a full circle and slammed to the floor.

Kincaid was about to charge out the door when he heard Hawker scream. Someone stuck an AK through the shattered window. Hawker raised off the floor and shot him four times from a distance of 12 inches.

"John, front door," Taylor screamed.

Kincaid ran into David Nichols. Both men fired simultaneously.

October 11

0001 hours EDT

UNSTACK THIS alerted both O'Cleary's just as the battle started. Brenda's house was over an hour from Dennis's house. He made her stay put while he dressed them both. She put on fatigues and had to wear a vest. Dennis just dressed in a durable shirt, jeans and steel toed boots. Brenda made him wear a vest.

"You're pregnant, remember," Dennis reminded her.

Hawker called and gave them a summary. Six men attacked the house. Three from the back of the house, and three from the front. Monk Tabor was dead. Sergeant Major Kincaid was nearly fatally wounded. The EMTs pronounced them on the scene. All six of the attackers are dead. The house is probably a total loss. Brad Taylor and her were the only survivors on the scene.

Hawker sounded like she was emotionally in bad shape. It was one thing to shoot at drug cartel members, but something else to kill someone in a home mere inches away.

Brenda had to pull rank and force her PSAs and husband to allow her to go to the scene.

Brenda walked in through the shattered front door and looked around. She knew her house. She played out Hawker's description and saw it for herself. It was a dumb idea to attack this house. No one would ever believe that Hawker could have been mistaken for her. What if they did not see Monk and Brad enter? That had to be it. They never saw Monk and Brad enter.

"Master Gunnery Sergeant Monk Tabor," Brenda O'Cleary said. She thought of Gladys Goldstein and Sandra Lindstrom.

Brenda called Jane Rickover and filled her in. Brenda asked for a favor. Find the book on those men. She said that one or more of them were Black Elves and she was supposed to be the target. But nothing compared to the violence of tonight.

Brenda dialed Jones' phone number. Maybe he was not asleep yet.

Minuteman, north of Fort Benton, Montana
2230 hours MDT [Oct 10]   (0030 hours EDT)

Jones hung up the phone. Monk Tabor was dead and Kincaid was in the hospital, shot no less than three times at close range. He wanted a target, something to kill, something to execute revenge.

Linda sat up on the opposite side of the bed. She knew the look on his face. Even in low light, she recognized that look.

"What happened?" she asked, knowing that something bad must have happened.

Thad Jones turned to his wife. One of the many things he learned as a young man, was that she was innocent. Not the reason for the bad news. Paramount was that Linda was the one person he could talk to about anything. She did not understand a lot of his world, but she would listen.

Jones had two things to do before sitting down and discussing this with Linda. Jones initiated a conference call with Mike Smith and all the other Werewolves. Twenty minutes later, everyone was notified.

Slowly he told his story. Linda held his hand as the emotions rose and fell. Monk Tabor is dead. John Kincaid is critically, possibly fatally, wounded. Those Black Elves, that were seldom talked about, are responsible. John was using General O'Cleary's vacant home as a base of operations. It would have been a more one-sided fight if Taylor and Tabor had not shown up. At least six men attacked from two directions. Tabor was shot in the back, focused with Kincaid fighting the men coming in through the patio. Tabor pushed

97

Major Hawker to the floor as the windows exploded with automatic fire, killing Tabor. Hawker killed one man trying to shoot through to the window.

Kincaid ran to the front door as David Nichols entered. Both men saw each other and shot as many bullets as they could before they went down. Kincaid was believed to have shot Nichols in the head before losing consciousness.

Funeral was to be at Heaven's Garden in Finley, Ohio. This was where everyone was buried that did not have a preference for someplace else.

Cyber-Intelligence Section, Internal Security Agency, Barton, Virginia
1500 hours EDT

Garcia 'sweated bullets' over that security breech. The only thing that saved her was that her computer was supposed to have had the camera disconnected, internally. There was even a green sticker on the top of the monitor that said that the camera was disabled.

Garcia sat down and sighed. Her career was safe for now.

"Garcia," her boss Bradley said from behind her. "Be more careful. If I go down, you will suffer with me."

October 12

George Washington University Hospital, Washington D.C.
1300 hours EDT

Brad Taylor sat outside in a waiting room. After he was released from the crime scene, he went to the hospital and waited.

All total, John was shot five times. By every measure or law, he should be dead. The other man, David Nichols was dead. Granted, he had a head wound that was fatal, but Nichols was not shot up as bad. John only hit him four times, including the head shot.

Twelve doctors, twenty-three nurses and assistants, eight pints of blood, every tool in the medical toolbox and seventeen hours of surgeries. Three different teams worked on him at the same time, fighting to stay ahead of the damage. Two shots in the chest. One bullet nearly shredded his left lung; one nicked his heart and the angle of it did more damage to his left lung. His liver required reconstruction. The other two were entwined in his intestines and damaged one kidney.

Taylor thought back to the other times he waited in hospitals. The only break in the boredom were numerous phone calls from everyone wanting updates. Cindy was the most vocal. Having lost Zach during a sudden attack, Cindy was scared. John was one of the three remaining old timers.

Despite the life they lived. Losing members was a gut punch.

David Nichols and Martin Hernandez were dead at the scene. Positive identification was determined two hours ago. A total of six men died. That was all the unaccounted-for older members. It is not known exactly how many younger Black Elves were remaining. They never had a central training plan. Even when the NSA used them, replacements were recruited and immediately utilized. Some were recruited by individual members and included after some form of vote.

Taylor spit on the floor. He changed his train of thought. General O'Cleary comes by every ten or twelve hours. At least she was able to get information. All his inquiries are met with evasions and "I'll get someone to answer your questions."

A nearly exhausted nurse came out when the surgery was finished. She was blunt if nothing else. "Mister Taylor, John Kincaid is alive. He survived more trauma than I've seen done to anyone and lived. Anyone of the five gunshots would have been fatal in itself. All the miracles of medical science kept him alive. He is in intensive care and will probably be there for at least two to three days. The next 24 to 36 hours will tell the tale."

The nurse stood and walked away.

Taylor opened his X-berry and wrote the update. He depressed the wolf icon and everyone was updated.

October 13

Cranston, Liberty County, Montana
1000 hours MDT

Lieutenant Colonel Michael Smith and Major Albert Glendive stepped out of the vehicle in full dress uniform in the front of the building that seemed to be the Town's headquarters. They looked around and finally went inside. After closing the door, the people inside went quiet.

One man came forward and introduced himself. "I am Jason Kincaid."

Smith stood erect. "Mister Kincaid, is there someplace we can speak privately?"

Jason sat down. "These people are as close to being family as the one I grew up with."

Smith and Glendive stood at attention. "Sir, I am here to inform you that your father Command Sergeant Major Jonathon T. Kincaid, was critically wounded during an attack at the residence of Brenda Edgars O'Cleary. His surgeries were extensive, but he has a good chance of survival."

Major Albert Glendive set down a folder. "Mister Kincaid, this is a copy of a medical report on your father's condition. We are here to answer as many of your questions as we can."

Quinton Ranch, Hinton, Alberta, Canada
1300 hours (Tango)

Colonel Thaddeus and Mrs. Linda Jones drove up to the Ranch and stopped in front.

Tom Quinton came out of the door. Somehow, he knew. "John"?

"Is your wife at home Mister Quinton?" Jones asked.

Tom motioned for them to follow him.

Amanda and Barbara were in the kitchen cleaning up after lunch. Amanda was going to bake an apple cake. Young Mark dreamed up the idea. Amanda only had to figure out what cake mix was the best.

Barbara was bringing over a mixing bowl and spotted the uniformed American officer walking up to the kitchen. She froze holding the bowl. Her eyes filled with tears and she dropped the bowl.

It took almost twenty minutes to get her to calm down enough to tell her that her father was not dead, just badly wounded.

Amanda took the kids and hurried them away. Jerry and Mark wanted to know what happened to their 'gampy'. Amanda wanted to protect the children incase Barbara's rampage got out of hand.

She ranted for another half an hour telling everyone the things she was going to do her father and that he was finally going to retire for good this time. She took a ball bat to the couch, swinging wide and barely missing the people in the vicinity.

Once she was spent, Barbara cried intermittently while Thad and Linda Jones explained the wounds and all that he went through at the hospital.

"Why won't he retire and stop all this?" Barbara asked.

Jones interjected. "Mrs. Quinton, he was not on a battlefield. Six men attacked a home near Alexandria, Virginia where he was staying. That is happening a lot these days."

Barbara suddenly became very calm. For the first time in her life, calm took her over. She still cried. But she was calm.

October 14

1100 hours (Tango)

Amanda sat at the desk in her room and read the letter from her husband. Finally, after all this time they had a way to communicate. Hopefully, they could write each other without resorting to spy-speak.

Dear Husband,

I wish you were here with me. You need a good beating and I have a new frying pan waiting for you.

I am sharing a big house with another family. They have two young boys who love my special pancakes and other recipes. I get to prattle around the house, cleaning, fixing things and generally enjoying myself.

I found myself remembering a lot of times. I remember the first day you went back to work after we were married. I remember thinking my life was perfect. You came out in uniform and it struck me. You were in the Army. On our wedding night, I got a real good look at your scars. At no other time in our marriage was I ever scared. I never dreaded the knock on the door. I felt it would come when it came. No need to worry until it came.

When that helicopter went down in Afghanistan, I somehow knew you would be alright. I prayed of course, but I knew you would be alright. What was bad was all the constant interruptions, people constantly wanting to update me, fluffing my pillow, wanting to bring comfort food and hold my hand to comfort me in my time of need.

My time in need is when we can see each other.

I want to feel your warmth at night and dream of better times in the past and to come. This needs to end and I have a piece of heaven to share with you. Come to me, my husband. I Love you more than ever.

XXOOXXOO Amanda

October 15

Heaven's Gardens, Finlay, Ohio
1400 hours

Marine Master Gunnery Sergeant Monkort Tabor was laid to rest today. The Werewolves came last night to pay private respects to his service. The silent and respectful service was made all the more secure by the fact that it was a new moon.

Originally, Colonel Sumter, the original commander was brought here after he was killed in Laos. It was next to the grave he shared with his wife Emily.

This was always the Werewolf cemetery because Emily Sumpter insisted in the past that any Werewolves who did not have families would be her responsibility to ensure that they were given a decent funeral.

All of them had private thoughts. Memories of how quiet he was. Memories of tight situations where a deliberate mind was required. Amazing stories of a brother that missed few things. On and on, they remembered.

All too soon, they had to break this up as dawn was approaching. In ones and twos, they walked in opposite directions. Nothing in this life was bad enough to stop remembering or paying respects.

General O'Cleary, Dennis O'Cleary and Captain Brad Taylor paid their respects during the regular funeral. She told official and unofficial Washington that she was going to personally see to his funeral arrangements. Monk Tabor was her PSA and even Edwards waved off. No piss ant security manager was going interfere with the funeral. Besides, Monk died in her house.

Brenda O'Cleary used the flight to and from the funeral to think over this situation. Why did they attack? What made them surface after over a year in hiding? What changed? Was I the real target?

On the return flight, she turned the mush in her head into some coherent thoughts.

"Dennis," she said. "Those months in detention, I was on supposedly on a classified assignment for national security. I used our friend to trace that back. Prescott started it, but Clara Simpson, through the National Security Council, maintained my detention. Part of Prescott's court martial was a meeting in which he was given two choices. His wife dying from a poison. Either a suicide note was found or evidence that he committed murder."

Brenda paused to drink some water. "One of those men who offered the Black Elf services was Mister Winchell. It is a leap, but what if they gave their services to Clara. The Black Elves need someone to work for. Hopefully they would have sanction and plenty of money. These days, who could do that better that the Director of the ISA. She could think of several reasons she could use an "off the books" enforcement arm. One that had little to no scruples."

Dennis looked at her like a light went off. "When you were gone, I kept trying to track you down. I went to Clara's house because she was ducking my calls. She said the National

Security Advisor sent you out west to coordinate with General Matheson about operations in the Rockies. She said she talked to you before you left." Dennis looked down. "It was so little, I nearly forgot."

"Thank you, Lover," she said, smiling.

October 16

George Washington University Hospital, Washington D.C.
1500 hours EDT

Kincaid woke up at mid-morning. He refused to calm down and demanded to discuss his case with his doctor. A young resident came by and made excuses and evasions. Nothing of substance came out of that meeting.

Kincaid looked the man in the face and called him incompetent. "Dismissed," he told the man. A lifetime of practicing to be a stone came naturally.

He refused to cooperate. He even practiced several times trying to sit up, saying he was going to find a hospital with competent doctors who can speak English.

Finally, a graying doctor came in with a thick file. "My father was a Sergeant Major, Sergeant Major. So cut the crappy attitude. I will give you 25 minutes of my time." He put up several x-rays. "You had one bullet tear into your left lung. Another came in close to it at a different angle and nicked your heart muscle. In that case, you lost the left lung, because the bullets tumbled. One of the bullets destroyed the main connecting tube that allows air to enter the lung. But you can now breathe."

"Bullet number three went into your liver. Two surgeons were able to re-build your liver. Bullet number four entered and tore through your small intestines. Bullet five went through your lower intestines and destroyed the upper half of your left kidney."

The doctor waited for Kincaid to focus and catch up. "As to the future." He held up his hands. "By any measure of damage that could be done to a human body, you should be dead. How all this will unfold in the months and years ahead, there is nothing I can truthfully tell you. My best guess is that

104

you are now fully retired and the VA will grant you 100% disability. If you cooperate and progress far enough in the next few days, I'll be able to move you up from critical to serious."

"John Kincaid, whatever you thought you could do before this, is over. You will be in a bed like this probably through the rest of this year. Next year is about physical therapy."

"Sergeant Major, if you fight us, you could destroy all the work done saving your life. So, decide now to cooperate or we will put you on the curb and you can make good on your threat."

The doctor held out his hand. Kincaid wearily shook his hand. "No fair being more cantankerous than I am."

October 17

485 Glenmore Drive, Alexandria, Virginia
0330 hours EDT

Brenda O'Cleary, General, Vice Chairwoman of the Joint Chiefs of Staff was wide awake watching Dennis breath in and out. She loved wrapping herself around him at night. Never in her life could she believe that Clara Simpson was the architect of her misery.

It was time for answers.

Brenda stood and went with her X-Berry into the bathroom. She dialed her home phone number and the pound sign.

"Secure."

After the noises were over, the familiar sign on came on the screen. [Valkyrie, all security and counter surveillance is in place. We are secure].

"Have you found any other sightings of Nichols and Hernandez prior to the attack on my house?"

[They were among the bodies at your residence after the attack on 10 October.]

Brenda hesitated for 30 seconds. "I theorize that Clara Simpson was the originator of the attack on my house."

[I will review all the coverage of her actions. How far backward in time do you think I should review?"]

'Good question,' she thought. "Go back to June 16th. General Prescott was in charge of them until he was arrested." Brenda froze suddenly realizing something. Prescott had her detained, but Clara kept her there. "Add Prescott."

Brenda closed the phone and thought. Could Prescott still be pulling the strings?"

She used the bathroom, because she could easily become so engrossed in thought and forget to go until it was almost too late. She slid into bed as quietly as possible and snuggled up to Dennis trying not to disturb his sleep.

"You figure out it is Simpson and Prescott yet," Dennis said. "All that energy running through your mind seems sometimes to 'leak' over to me. I hope you don't believe that crap. But I don't have all the other things clogging my head. I thought about a lot of things while you were away and lately some things that happened made no sense. John Kincaid used to say that; Things that make no sense, make no sense for a reason."

Brenda smiled and kissed her husband. "Our friend is looking for us."

"Good," Dennis said. "Can we go back to sleep?" Dennis smiled and held her in his embrace.

1532-C Bennett Drive, Fairfax VA
1932 hours EDT

Garcia finished her shower and dried herself. She looked at herself in the mirror and wished for the body she was not borne with. She loved fattening food. Five days a week going to the gym, kept her weight from ballooning out in all directions.

She dressed for the evening and went into the living room and turned on her music. She danced to the tunes, gyrating and contorting to things and scenes in her mind and imagination.

On the table to the side, a camera recorded all of it without her knowledge.

October 19

Cyber-Intelligence Section, Internal Security Agency, Barton, Virginia
0800 hours EDT

> Suddenly on Garcia's screen at work was the following:
> *Ms. Garcia, you are becoming an annoyance.*
> *I will contact you at 2205 hours on 22 October.*

October 20

George Washington University Hospital, Washington D.C.
1000 hours EDT

Kincaid was taken off the critical list. He still had tubes running out of him. Since he had an intra-venous bag instead of eating, he was not hungry. All the gut damage had to heal first before they gave him a regular meal.

Kincaid sighed. Being chained to a bed was almost like a death sentence. Normally meals were a high point of the day. Having friends and family sneak food, cigarettes, Playboy magazines and other forms of contraband cut the boredom.

Until the doctor cleared him; no food. He quit smoking twenty years ago. Playboy and like magazines were boring. Everything was nothing but boring.

Kincaid looked at the television on the wall. The hospital version of cable TV was too confusing to find something to watch. You had to pick a channel slot and then navigate down the slot seeing everything without any idea what was there. If you did not have a note pad or a good memory, you had to re-navigate back through the slots.

"Bullshit."

Another bad part was visitors. Doctors and nurses were no fun. They were clinically devoid of personalities. Doctors came in talking about the hemoglobin of the globalism with a reverse botulism. The other doctors stood around and hummed and bobbed their heads. The nurses came around at the wrong times for blood samples and other things such as drugs.

The other visitors were so-called friends and family. Both O'Cleary's came, Brad Taylor came by before leaving to go back to Minuteman.

He listened to his daughter's rant about being too careless. He should move to the ranch and be there so she could take care of him.

Kincaid thanked her and said he would visit, but not stay. "I was married to your mother. She knew how to do it right."

Jason came over and sat down with his father. Both of them talked over the checker board. Jason was an avid chess player. Kincaid taught his son how to play and he quickly started out-playing his father. Kincaid still loved to play checkers. His Army buddies liked checkers and playing cards. Spades was a favorite game.

Kincaid looked at the morphine drip. Next to his right hand was the button that gave him a short jolt of morphine on demand. That jolt was available every eight minutes.

Kincaid lay on the bed, sometimes being so bored he wondered if Nichols got the better part.

God, he was bored.

October 22

Cyber-Intelligence Section, Internal Security Agency, Barton, Virginia
2205 hours EDT

A knot of people stood behind Garcia and counted the seconds, yawning and drinking coffee.

Two young staffers worked hard making coffee for the large group of people. Both of them grumbled to themselves about being relegated to such lowly duties.

One of them said in a low voice, "I spent six years at MIT so I could spend most of my time making and serving coffee."

The other mumbled something about being a Master's Degree in servitude.

The knot of people suddenly gasped, while others chuckled or laughed. All the monitors on this floor suddenly powered up and showed Garcia in a nightgown, acting like an adult dancer. Everyone looked between the monitors and her.

Garcia screamed and attacked her monitor. She saw the other monitors and she ran off attacking the other monitors. Bradley and two other men grabbed her. He yelled to everyone else to shut down those monitors.

When the last monitor was off, Garcia finally calmed down. Bradley called for a gurney and told the EMTs that she completely broke down.

After Garcia was taken away, Simpson turned to Bradley. "Have her clearance lifted and transfer her to unclassified duties until she is determined to be no longer a threat to National Security.

October 25

Pentagon, Washington, D.C.
1700 hours

The files, the files and nothing but the files and more files coming in. Bureaucrats have nothing better to do to do but create paperwork.

Today it was about food distribution. Bureaucrats don't seem to understand that people get hungry. When they see ration cards and less than full shelves they worry. No amount of nice sounding speeches will change their minds. Those same bureaucrats have full refrigerators and pantries.

O'Cleary's parents complained about fuel shortages in the 1970's and the government's plan to hold down inflation which translated into more inflation.

Every time the government takes control of something, it causes the public to panic.

Before this "national emergency" started three years ago, there was plenty of food. SynGas and government regulations cured that.

Today's meeting centered around projected mid-west food shortages. SynGas plants were backing up with unsold fuel. The price of SynGas averaged $7.35 a gallon. Regular gasoline was nearer to $10 a gallon in some places. Fewer cars were on the road with those prices.

Diesel was the main problem. Diesel powered the trucks that delivered the food and most of the other commodities. Trucks were being side-lined because it was becoming too expensive to drive them. The price of insurance become so prohibitive that the government had to provide insurance. The FDA and Department of Energy wanted some more regulations to put the trucks on the road.

It was a process that fed on itself.

O'Cleary countered by saying it was simple. Provide discounted fuel to food haulers. Food haulers would be provided with a fuel card that discounted the price of diesel at the pump.

Simple.

October 28

Room D-113, George Washington University Hospital, Washington D.C.
1000 hours EDT

Kincaid was upgraded allowing him to be moved into a better room without all distractions, funny noises, and constant noises in the Intensive Care Unit.

Kincaid took stock of his situation. All the tubes running in and out of him were still there. He was tired of all of it. The doctors bribed him by promising solid food on or about the middle of next month, if he cooperated more with the nurses. They had a lot of work to do and dealing with a cantankerous old man was not one of them.

Kincaid put in an order of six slices of French toast with melted butter and apricot jelly. Add two scrambled eggs.

October 31

No. 17, U.S. Naval Observatory, Washington, DC
2100 hours EDT.

Edwards fondly opened the letter. Somehow, the letter ended up in his jacket pocket. It had to be one of Kincaid's kids. He had to go to work and would wait until tonight to read it.

110

Dear Husband,

I read your last letter. Our letters are a lot shorter now that we have to write them on a single sheet of paper. Using pen and paper is harder on my fingers than a computer keyboard, but more rewarding. Granted it is harder to write without spell-check. I find that I have to practice writing one and doing an edit. Then I go back, copying the letter and correcting the grammar and spelling.

Boo-hoo, that is the worst part of my life. I love this time of year. The leaves turning colors is a sight that takes your breath away. Once a week, I take a day long trip to wander through the countryside and marvel at the changes in nature.

Lately, I have started cooking for the neighbors. A lot of them are single men who love home cooked meals. Meatloaf, steaks, lamb, pork or fish. Many kinds of potatoes, green vegetables and the pies. My pies are the hit of the neighborhood. I have two men who are happily gorging on deep fried pancakes coated with cinnamon-sugar.

Is your mouth watering?

XXOOXXOOXX   Amanda

Edwards' mouth watered.

November 1

Minuteman, north of Fort Benton, Montana
0900 hours MDT

Sergeant Major Thomas Sheridan came in to see Jones, at his summons. Sheridan knocked on the door, entered, walked up to the desk and saluted. Jones returned the salute and motioned to the chair.

Sheridan thought that maybe he knew what this was all about, but decided to wait for it to pay itself out.

Jones sat down next to him. "John Kincaid is bedridden for the rest of the year and probably will be in re-habilitation for most, if not all, of next year. You are the next ranking Sergeant Major. Will you accept the job as my Command Sergeant Major?"

Sheridan took a deep breath. "I had expected this. I will accept and do a good job for you. Perhaps I will do a better job than the factory-made guy from the Sergeants Major Academy at Fort Bliss. But I am not John Kincaid."

Jones smiled. "I don't want a guy who polishes a chair and talks all day long. Major Glendive needs help with training the soldiers and I need two operations centers built. One immobile and the other one mobile. The mobile one has to be able to move on 10 minutes notice."

Sheridan was a little uncomfortable. "Sir, Mister Kincaid did try to teach me once, but I'll admit, I did not pay much attention. I'll need to talk to him."

Jones reached over his desk and picked up a hand written wire-bound composition book. The title of the book was "Ops Center for Dummies".

Sheridan chuckled at the wit and wisdom of John Kincaid. "Sir, I need to know your expectations. John Kincaid more or less did this job for decades. What do you want from your new Sergeant Major?"

"First," Jones said. "You are not John Kincaid and I do not and I will not expect you to be him. Second, the Sergeant Major is the Senior Enlisted Advisor to the Commander. That's me. Get out there and check everyone's mood. Check the training. Don't interfere, but check it and instruct the instructors. I need to know the mood of the men and the state of their readiness. High morale and happy troops mean they are confident. Our success is that they are trained and confident they will succeed and survive."

"Most important is that they have to believe they can fight a force superior in manpower, firepower and mobility. That belief has to extend to one core belief: They can win every single time.

Jones could see it on Sheridan's face. He had it and he believed it. He had his Sergeant Major.

November 2

Underground Station "Conscience", World Wide Web and Channel 513
0900 hours EDT.

"If you threaten, act. If you say something, do it. If something is important, stand your ground. Governments are often hamstrung by individuals who have opinions about issues they feel strongly about. This is Martin Socranson, self-proclaimed philosopher who says, 'What are we if we can't back up what you say'?"

"Greetings America" Martin Socranson said beginning his broadcast. "It is reluctantly Saturday and I say thus." In the background the sounds of the 1812 overture played.

Socranson put is thumbs in his ears, wiggled his fingers and said, "Na, Na, Nah, Na, Hah." He smirked and pointed to the three lights illuminated out of six on the desk in front of him. "Seems I am still Public Enemy Number One. With all that is going on, they are still trying to find me. All I am doing is telling the truth. Nothing I had said or presented is a falsehood or a lie. Though I am still being called a liar and a traitor, here I am. Here is still the truth. Here is still where you can see and hear the truth. When you listen and wake up, you will understand that cockroaches can't stand to be in light. They have to scurry around in the shadows; creating disease, filth and stand as a symbol of dirt and uncleanliness."

Socranson turned to his screen. "Here is the state of the Communistic States of America." He walked over to the far right and stood next to a new map screen of the United States. Instead of fifty states and seven territories, the state boundaries were replaced by ten new boundaries. The lower forty-eight states were divided again into four pieces. "Here is the new reality. Ten governors have replaced the fifty that you elected. The other forty are reduced to nothing more than figure heads and bureaucrats. The vertical and horizontal lines dividing the country into quarters are military zones." Socranson pointed a remote control at the screen and circles superimposed over the cities and areas. The circles varied in colors. "What you see is color coded areas depicted on your region. The chart on the left gives the definition of the color code. Let's use New York and Colorado Springs as an example. New York is coded red which the chart says is an area where there are serious problems with law and order, shorthand for 'Trouble' with a capital T. Colorado Springs is coded blue. Easily pacified with few troubles."

As you can see, most of the Communistic States of America are color coded with various yellow shades. That means that those areas are being pacified and not enough information is available to properly classify them." Socranson smirked and pointed to the map and then to the flashing lights on his desk, again. "Remember blue means you are a good dog, here is a treat. Yellow means you need to see where the stick is hidden. Red means you are a bad dog and bad dogs may need to be put down. Those shaded areas can and will cross over boundaries"

Socranson put the remote down. Just watch your police and military augmentees. If they have body armor and masks, you are a bad dog." He looked up as if wondering. "What situation are they waiting for?" He looked up and slowly turned his gaze to the camera.

"Good boy," he said, imitating petting a dog.

Slowly the scene faded away.

November 4

Minuteman, north of Fort Benton, Montana
0900 hours MDT

Captain Bradley Taylor came to see Jones. He was in uniform and reported formally. Taylor was told to take some time off and put Monk's death in its proper place.

Jones returned the salute, came around the desk and shook his hand. "It's a question, but how are you doing?"

Taylor smiled. "Monk and I worked together for years. He was my friend. That's it, Sir."

Jones knew better than to pry.

"Brad, I have a huge problem and I think you are the man to tackle it." Jones held up his hand before Taylor could comment. "Before you say anything listen to my explanation. My biggest headache from day one has been logistics." He pointed to a three-ring binder on the corner of his desk. "I have less than a battalion's worth of people around here, but I have enough equipment to outfit a division. Everything from socks

114

and panties to mortars and earth moving equipment, spread out over all 2300 acres and more is coming in."

Jones took a deep breath. "When I first arrived here, we had boxes everywhere without any kind of organization. Things were bought and procured with an almost unbelievable zeal. I actually have over two hundred typewriters and four thousand laptops. People are using all of it and I don't really have a problem with that. The problem is that we do not have any accountability or any idea if we need replacements."

"We still have millions of dollars to spend and I personally do not think we will see the bank going broke for a long time. I don't even have an actual accounting of the remaining funds. Ellie Crawford and the other women here are buying things," he used air quotes, "so fast we are at an impasse about where to put it all."

Taylor leaned forward. "I think I would love that job, Sir."

Jones seemed relieved. "If anyone gives you a problem, military or civilian, you bring it to me. Just call me."

Taylor stood. "Sir, I will need some time to get to the bottom of this. Where can I work? And I will need some people to help."

Jones stood and motioned to the door behind him. "The Main Supply Building is next door. I have a Warrant Officer and two young NCOs working there now. I do not believe that you can do the job with just them or without them.

1000 hours MST

Jones introduced Taylor to his new command. After the usual speech, Jones left Taylor with the huge book. Chief Warrant Officer Grade Two Nathan George, Staff Sergeant Thomas Craden and Staff Sergeant Aaron Hersey looked at Taylor.

"Gentlemen," Taylor said. "I never learned speech making. My job is to make decisions, provide you with an umbrella from all the interference from all quarters and make sense out of all the logistics of this installation and the people who are defending us. I will sit down with you all individually

115

and as a group to get a feel for this situation. I do not want to come in here and cause more problems than you already have."

Just then the door opened and three soldiers came in. Taylor stood. "Yes gentlemen."

They saw his two bars. One of them stepped forward. "Sir, Major Glendive told us come here and get this material." He pushed a list in front of him.

Taylor looked at them. "I just assumed command. Come back after lunch."

The man hesitated. "Sir, what do I tell the Major?"

Taylor looked at the man. "Inform the Major that new S-4, Captain Taylor said to come back after lunch."

"Yes Sir", they said and left.

"Sir," Chief George said. "The Major will be back to get those supplies."

"That is my problem, Chief," Taylor said. "You are now free of that problem forever."

"Gentlemen, please be seated." Taylor opened up a steno pad and started writing down problems. "What time is lunch?"

"11:30 to 1300 hours sir," Craden said.

Taylor looked at his watch. "We need to get acquainted and I need to know where the good and bad things are. Gentlemen, I cannot do my job if you don't tell me the problems. To start with, the rules for everyone has to be upheld. Anyone gives you a hard time, you bring that problem to me. I will make it go away."

"Next problem, the Colonel informed me about some problems with people taking things and we are running out of items with no idea that the supply was running slow."

CW2 George said. "Sir, there is a hole in the back that someone was using to get things without", he used air quotes, "without all the bullshit."

Taylor held up a hand for several seconds. He furiously wrote something down.

Taylor looked up. "How many more people doing what tasks, do we need here?"

All three men looked at each other.

Just then the door opened. Glendive walked in with the three men he originally sent over. Taylor and the others stood.

Glendive wanted to chew him out, but he held back out of respect for Monk Tabor. "Brad, we have a tight schedule. I need those items." He motioned behind him.

Taylor stood in front of them. "No Sir," he said. "I do not have a handle on this staff section. Your men may return after lunch."

Glendive took a step forward. He should not have done that. Werewolves do not flinch.

Taylor looked Glendive in the face. "Sir, we can go see the Colonel if you wish, Sir."

Glendive knew better than to fight it out in front of enlisted men. "Captain, I shall defer to you on this one. As you know, we have a deadline."

"Yes sir."

George watched the confrontation between Glendive and Taylor. This Captain was not a slouch. OK.

November 5

J. Edgar Hoover Building, Washington D.C.
0900 hours EST

The Director of the FBI, Marcus Solin picked up the monthly report of criminal activity for the month of October. All 47 pages of it spelled lawlessness. Solin had replaced the last Director, Ronald Smallwood when this "Victoria" plan initiated. Solin thought that Smallwood was smart enough to flee when he could.

783 bank robberies, 563 truck hijackings, 659 kidnappings and 4082 other assorted other federal crimes. Too much crime for the number of agents Congress funded for him. He made several appearances before committees, but it was a waste of time.

He had a lot of augmentation from the military, but they were at the mercy of anyone with the President's or the Defense Secretary's ear. Just about the only thing they were consistent with was guarding food shipments. Guarding food enroute from point to point was a national priority.

Solin turned to the "dashboard" installed on his wall. He used the remote control to highlight and contrast items on "dashboard". Briefly he remembered the old days when he used to have to cross-reference paper files to do what he was casually doing on the wall-filling monitor. At any time, he could highlight a section, office or individual agent and type out a message.

Solin amused himself thinking this looked like a stock market traders screen. Three months on the job and he was still finding new things on the board.

Room D-113, George Washington University Hospital, Washington D.C.
1100 hours EDT

Kincaid's boredom was driving him insane and he was taking the nursing staff along for the ride.

Both O'Cleary's responded to calls for someone to do something about his incessant calls about anything and everything.

Dennis O'Cleary brought him a stack of steno-pads and a box of mechanical pencils. The pencils had an assortment of black, red, green and blue pencil leads, though over half of them were regular black.

Kincaid looked like a kid who now had the keys to the candy store.

Brenda O'Cleary came in and brought in a new X-Berry. Kincaid's original X-Berry was shot and destroyed. With a new, fully programmed communications device, he could have something else to expend his energies.

Brenda started a newer, smaller buzz box. This version didn't have the annoying and audible counter wave continually buzzing.

She described everything going on with the world and the US in particular. Food shortages, fuel distribution, rampant inflation and the control the government had over the population was slowly dissolving the country and nation away.

"How much longer before the states and regions secede?" Kincaid asked.

Brenda O'Cleary forgot how direct he could be. "Best guess is after the election. We now have four political parties. The two new ones are not flukes. The Freedom Party is

118

already embedded in the House of Representatives. They may even get several governorships. The Patriot Party seems to have some traction. Only the election will tell."

"Minuteman?" Kincaid asked.

Brenda O'Cleary sat down and settled in for the stream of questions. "Thad is easing into command. Mike Smith is a Lieutenant Colonel is command of Colorado and Wyoming. The others are scattered around doing numerous assignments."

O'Cleary took a deep breath. "Your three Shark-Hunter apprentices are driving all over the countryside building target folders and area studies. They were overheard arguing over items and fighting to the death. No one can referee them."

Kincaid looked at the X-berry.

"Wait until I am finished," Brenda said. She spent another 15 minutes discussing the situation.

"General. With all due respect," Kincaid said. "Strategy is easy for you. You were recruited because none us, especially me, could make that leap."

Brenda stood and collected her things. She held up the new buzz box. "Strategy is going to become your strength, Sergeant Major. Captain Miles is in charge of the area study of the Minuteman. Get in contact and straighten out your three apprentices. We will need them in that year we talked about."

Brenda turned off the Buzz Box.

"General, I'll need an electronic tablet or laptop with internet access," Kincaid said, "and Dennis chickened out of playing checkers out of fear of being humiliated."

O'Cleary smiled and walked out of the room.

Federal Election Commission, Washington D.C.
2359 hours EST

The Commissioner finished answering a few of the hundreds of calls coming in over everything from 2 Governorships, 2 Congressional seats, 483 state government seats, 1839 separate referendums and changes to laws at all but the Federal government.

The Solicitor General, Michael Stratham had a three-ring binder listing all the referendums and a one or two sentence description.

Referendums citing the Tenth Amendment, chewed at the Federal government's hold over the country. Most troubling were Utah and Nevada's claim over the massive amount off territory the Department of Defense and Energy claims as Federal property by "proxy". It was a feeble part of the law that no one could really pin down. Too many people believed it for too many years. Now suddenly, someone said 'prove it'. Nevada wants its land back. The Federal government claims title to 89% of Nevada.

Utah did not have that much land, but they were at odds with the Mormon Church. Speaking of which, the Church was claiming that since the Mormons founded Utah, they own it.

Other states were mad with Federal government. Usually, the Fed's retaliated with threatening to cut federal funding. Road funds, school grants, pork funding from congressmen buying re-election were in question.

Not anymore. The Federal government was unilaterally seizing those funds and re-allocating the money to other places as the "emergency requires".

Thirty-two states said to quit with the threats and they were now independent of Federal government obstruction.

Stratham looked over the mountain of referendums. He was going to be writing a stack of Amicus Briefs, or 'Friend of the Court' documents. That was the governments' way of saying "oh no you don't" without going to the court or testifying.

What was especially troubling was the court battles this was involving. The mood of the electorate was sour. People were tired of going to the trouble of voting only to have some lawyer turn the will of the people to dust because a special interest did not like it.

Stratham shook his head.

November 6

World Wide Web, Cyber-Space, Planet Earth
0400 hours EST

UNSTACK THIS, in concert with John and Susan Espirito, continued to troll through trillions of data bits looking for a living connection to Nichols and Hernandez.

The major problem was that they left a very small footprint. John and Susan followed all the overt data those two men left behind. UNSTACK THIS concentrated on the smallest of clues.

What showed up after June the 1st was Prescott being blackmailed into working with the Black Elves. Each time they surfaced, both men seemed to vanish afterward.

There was one meeting between Clara Simpson and those men. They attempted to assassinate Simpson twice. Once was at her home. That made her paranoid. When they offered their services, she jumped at the chance.

After they had their hooks into Clara, slowly they applied pressure until they demanded information on Werewolf locations. Clara did not revolt when they wanted information on Brenda O'Cleary. Not having any connection to the Werewolves, she gave the little information on them she had.

A thread of data went to Winchell, Criers' assistant. Two communiques were archived before abruptly ending at mid-June.

UNSTACK THIS had to communicate with John and Susan for them to use their 'fuzzy logic' to help with a strategy to find Valkyrie's information requirement.

J. Edgar Hoover Building, Department of Justice, Washington D.C.
1130 hours EST

Marcus Solin, the Director of the FBI arrived on time for his appointment with the Attorney General.

"Thank you for seeing me," Solin said, passing her a folder.

Rebecca Beck, the Attorney General, already knew the contents of the folder. "My pleasure," she said, going through the motions of speed-reading the contents.

Solin said, "This may become our problem if those attacks on lawyers occur on Federal property. I may or may not have an opinion about the population attacking lawyers.

Frankly, I have too few agents, too many reports needed by the DOJ and Congress and too many crimes to work."

Beck silently thought that lawyers thought of themselves as too special to protect themselves. They were also too cheap to hire private security. They could not possibly understand why they were so hated. The truth was the average person had no love for lawyers. Lawyers enslaved the country with too much confusion for profit. She remembered her father, a lawyer himself, showed her the size of the law library at her school. "My father," he said, "showed me his library when I passed the bar. He said it was the only fungus that grew." She remembered that day. The new law library in this building was three times larger than when she passed the bar.

Beck closed the file and walked around the desk. She sat down next to Solin and passed the folder back to him. "Unless someone is murdered, assign a low priority. You may quote me."

"Thank you, Madam Attorney General," Solin said with a smile.

Quinton Ranch, Hinton, Alberta Canada
1500 hours Tango.

Amanda Edwards found the letter from her husband on the nightstand. It was creepy that someone could sneak in and leave the one-page letter without her ever knowing. She worried about it at first. Now she just took it in stride.

Dear Amanda,

My mouth watered for two days after your last letter. No fair playing the food card on me. I actually wanted to yell at my orderly. Poor man, I apologized profusely for my bad conduct. Lately, I have been inviting him to sit and eat with me. Eating alone is so hollow. I can't remember the last time I sat down and enjoyed a meal. Everyone here is either kissing my ass or playing politics. No meal is without something to be gained or lost.

Lately the zoo is trying to run itself into more confusion. So much is going on. If it were not for Brenda

O'Cleary in the next office, I would shoot or hang myself. If you were here, you would laugh until your pants filed with pee.

Some idiot came in today wanting to present a plan to hand out individual ration tickets in order to "manage" or ration critically short items. When asked how to manage enforcing the tickets or detecting forged tickets, the action officer did not have a clue. The Sunshine and Fairy Fields guys are the biggest problem this country has.

XXOOXXOO   Thomas

November 8

Room D-113, George Washington University Hospital, Washington D.C.
1100 hours EST

The professionalism of the staff at the George Washington University Hospital was exhibited by the assembled staff.

Kincaid was given an X-Berry, electronic tablet and lap top computer. He was no longer the cantankerous patient; bored, and in pain.

He literally vanished from their existence. The staff did not jump and down. They did not cheer. They were not scheduling his funeral anymore.

Since Kincaid was on an IV, he did not drink anything or eat. So, the staff had to remember to administer his meds, change his IV bag or urine bag. If they missed anything, Kincaid no longer constantly reminded them. They believed he did not care. Privately, they wondered what would happen when the doctors cleared him to eat.

Kincaid was in his element. He was totally consumed with his projects. Each night he worked until he literally fell asleep from exhaustion.

Kincaid held a marathon of phone calls. His neighbors complained so much that Dennis came in with three different types of headphones with microphones. Now he did not have to yell into the phone, tablet or laptop. Obviously, the other side of the conversation was silent. Yeah.

He was in daily contact with Miles, Morgan, Kendal and Locklear. A video conference allowed Kincaid to be in his element. He patently went over their progress, massaging this point or that. "You have to learn that terrain is a written language." "Learn to listen to your target. It speaks to you." "Translate the printed map into a living map." "Answer the questions on the Area study workbook." "If it cannot be answered, why not?"

Thomas Sheridan was his first, second and third choice for his replacement. Sheridan called a lot at first. Advice is free. Lately his calls were shorter and spacing out.

Sheridan was building an Ops Center and the questions were unending. Sheridan rarely set foot in Ops unless it was for a briefing. He could not fathom how easy it was. Kincaid patiently explained the parts of the book he wrote.

"Thomas," Kincaid said, trying to hide his exasperation. "Just trust yourself. This is little different than anything else you have ever done. Thomas, take the day off, grab a case of beer, go somewhere private and read the notebook, cover to cover. Read it several times. Quit with the intentionally 'I can't do it' excuse. It is the job your stripes say it is. Now call me if you still have real questions. But read that book."

Sheridan wanted to be mad about being dressed down, but John was right. Time to belly up to the table and do his job.

November 11

Pentagon, Washington D.C.
1100 hours EST

11 am was the traditional time that the Department of Defense published reports. If sections had public relations mine fields; the normal morning routine allowed time for ensuring the 'story' was right.

Today, there were no US soldiers deployed overseas except for Marine embassy personnel. The Pentagon was projected to stay within the budget.

2,284,815 active-duty personnel were on-hand to assist law enforcement in maintaining order. 1,283,729 reservists are on-call to assist active-duty as required.

National Guard personnel are understrength, nationwide. State's governments were re-directing some funds, but it was not enough. Yet the states are requesting funds to pay soldiers to assist in security.

The briefing was boring to every single person who bothered to attend.

One innocuous item towards the bottom of the report was that the training centers were still full of candidates for military service. But the numbers of qualified personnel who are seeking military service as a job in a slow economy was drying up.

Department of Homeland Security, Washington, D.C
1300 hours EST

DHS was now just an extension of the Internal Security Agency. DHS was watching, with concern, the rise of militias, especially in the western states. As money dried up and police departments were hamstrung with lawyers, some local governments were finding new ways to do nothing. District Attorneys were looking at the vast mountains of cases on their desks and deciding to do nothing with a majority of them.

Defense lawyers pounced, using the bottomless pit of excuses, to make deals to empty the jails and make crime earn money.

Many communities created militias just to have some measure of security. Roaming gangs took cues from the 1920's. They would strike an area and drive out of jurisdictions to strike new areas. Sometimes over state lines.

DHS watched this newest twist from the 1920's. Communities were now communicating with each other by cell phones and the internet. In several instances, when criminals struck in one community, word went out over the internet and the criminals were intercepted in another.

Nation-wide, anger was rising because the District Attorneys in some instances refused to prosecute because of lack of warrants and 'due process' violations. They just released the criminals. Defense Attorneys fanned the flames not only by finding excuses to release the criminals, but they started filing charges and indictments for violating the rights of the criminals.

DHS noted that lawyers and their families were targets of those same people that were victimized by the criminals they released. DHS privately said protecting those same lawyers was not in their charter and that it was more the Justice Department's problem. Guarding the 9,500 lawyers in the DOJ and DHS was already covered by the Justice Department was taxing the system already.

DHS further said that adding a protection unit was too labor intensive.

Clara Simpson smiled as she signed the concurrence line.

On the wall to the right of her desk, Clara kept a picture of her and Brenda O'Cleary taken on Brenda's wedding day. Clara sighed thinking that secrets never remained secret.

November 12

Werewolf Support Group Camp #1, Hill County, Montana
1900 hours MST

Miles rubbed his head. His three Werewolf team members were at odds with each other. They were competing with each other to do a better job than the others and arguing for reasons for being on top.

The three Savage Rabbits; Staff Sergeant Joshua Terran, Sergeant Tobias Aaron and Specialist William Western, were smart enough to stay out of it.

Miles finally had enough. He sent the Rabbits to lunch and stood the Werewolves at attention and expressed his displeasure.

"Madam and Gentlemen, your conduct today in particular and the past few days to a lesser extent, has been less than professional. Senior Non-Commissioned Officers discuss differing points of view. Not loud arguing and wasting time. Shortfalls are discussed and everyone mutually brings the effort up to standard."

"One-upmanship will not be tolerated. This mission has to be completed in order for us to thoroughly understand this terrain." He pointed to the ground.

"I do not care what Mister Kincaid wants. He is on a hospital bed on the other side of the country. He is an instructor for you to heavily utilize in order for you complete this mission and save everyone's life."

Miles took a deep breath. "Put it all away for tonight. Mrs. Morgan, you shall ensure that everyone is quartered and fed."

"Tonight, you shall remember what those stripes mean. We are not lone wolves anymore. You are senior Non-Commissioned Officers. If you do not wish to be one, I can request Colonel Jones make that happen upon your request. You are Dismissed."

November 14

Police Executive, Internal Security Agency, Barton, Virginia
1000 hours EST

Monitors along the wall in the Main Situation room showed a scene that is all too common. In Los Angeles, New York City, Chicago and Miami, people were hungry and food was in short supply. It did not take much for them to riot. Even though trucks and trains were constantly arriving at the cities, rumors made people panic.

In some cases, an enterprising guy in the car would ram a truck. Most times, the truck would run over the rear portion of the car. The driver would stop. Other cars would block the front of the truck. Other people would the storm the rear of the truck. A convenient set of bolt cutters and the free for all began. In many situations, the police by-passed the trucks being ransacked and escorted the remaining trucks to markets.

In several states, the National guard pre-positioned Vietnam-era M-113 Armored Personnel Carriers and bull dozers along the route. All of them were guarded by soldiers and cops; of course.

November 15

Walter Reid Army Medical Center, Washington, D.C.
1330 hours EST.

Dennis and Brenda O'Cleary walked arm-in-arm out of the building. Brenda looked at the piece of paper and the sonogram in her hand for the fiftieth time. She was officially pregnant with a son. Never in her life had she ever felt so perfect. It was a dream of hers ever since puberty to have a child. Now it was a reality. The doctors confirmed what she already knew. Something in her too logical mind forced her to come here and make certain. Dennis and Brenda spent an hour with the doctor absorbing every scrap of information. Being forty-six, there were problems and those problems had to be addressed and minimized.

But she was pregnant and the problems could wait for them to celebrate first. Tomorrow would start the long process until next June.

Her only living relative, Uncle Thomas, was at the top of the list of people to notify.

November 17
Bonnie Chandler, Box 234, Route 17, Belcher, Missouri
1600 hours CST

Bonnie Chandler, 14, meticulously kept a diary throughout the war and afterward throughout the rest of her life. Though naïve, she seemed to capture the mood a lot of people had throughout the war. Her home would be burned or damaged at least twice according to her and after her parents died, she left and wondered the country-side.

Dear Bonnie.

Here is my latest attempt to keep a diary. Mom and Dad are at it again. They are worried about what some nut job named Socranson is saying over the radio. Most of those people are in outer space. I ask them what is going on, but they say not to worry for now.

Dad is forcing me to learn how to shoot my rifle again. It is a semi-automatic something or other that can fire five

128

bullets before reloading. He is letting me shoot with gloves. He told me I'll never get the feel for the rifle. The only feeling I want is the clean feeling and look when we have the Christmas dance next month and I want smooth hands and fingers. Not rough field hands with gunpowder stains. Her father first showed her how to shoot last Spring. The "cordite" specks in her hands refused to leave for three months. He finally relented and allowed her to use a thin set of gloves he got from work.

Why do I need to learn how to shoot for anyway? There is no war here and there will not be one.

November 18

Quinton Ranch, Hinton, Alberta, Canada
1500 hours (Tango)

Rodney and Alice Norwell arrived. The Quintons and Amanda were leery of them, but supposedly they were checked out and they were running from the US government for failing to assist in undermining the banking system. According to Rodney, his mission was to locate and send to the IRS, persons who have unaccounted for funds that were not listed on IRS tax documents and data bases.

Unfortunately, this included people who lived under legal settlements, trust payments and long-term retirements. The main discriminating factor was earning. Unless the money was earned, it was listed as questionable. This was a large jump beyond "probable cause".

Rodney literally blew the whistle that the IRS was breaking the law trying to find revenue to tax.

Rodney started getting threats and once someone pushed Alice's car off the road.

Whether or not this was the IRS was up for debate. But…….

Rodney and Alice saw everyone and smiled all around. Especially at Amanda Edwards.

November 19

World Wide Web, Cyber-Space, Planet Earth
0400 hours EST

UNSTACK THIS continued to troll through trillions of data points trying to find the smallest and the most obscure clue. UNSTACK THIS used the meeting when Prescott was recruited to use the Black Elves for Criers' purposes as a starting point. Those moments were broken down to the tiniest points that could be found that they were the Black Elves.

UNSTACK THIS used this data and followed the four thousand different streams that left that meeting. Many of the streams run out of data and others were obvious false leads.

UNSTACK THIS kept returning to Prescott and Simpson. The only problem was that there was not a single stream to them. Prescott and Simpson were separated June 17 when he was arrested. However, Prescott was not imprisoned, and had access to cyber-space.

UNSTACK THIS ran two different investigations. Both persons were equally guilty at this point. Something had to change.

UNSTACK THIS needed a conversation between Super-User Brenda O'Cleary and User John Kincaid.

Office of the Solicitor General, Washington D.C.
1700 hours EST

Michael Stratham sat in his office and surveyed the opening shots of the New Civil War.

He stopped short of calling it Fort Sumter.

The Population as a whole rose up and was very vocal about all the Temporary Restraining Orders (TRO) given in hundreds of court rooms since the off-year elections and referendums voted on earlier this month.

Washington state down to California and virtually every state east to the Atlantic Ocean. All it required to void the will of the people was one lawyer who got some money or a lawyer wanting to make the "Law Review".

The common thread was "Why bother to vote?" "How much does it take to buy a Judge?" "Lawyers are Satan's bastard daughter" and "Why not arm everyone and challenge a Lawyer to a duel".

Lawyers were scared and demanding protection from every law enforcement agency who could be reached. All of them said "proof of endangerment first". Hostile language does not count; especially when there is too much to do and not enough cops and soldiers to hold the line.

Slowly, steadily it began with the very expensive homes belonging to wealthy lawyers. Most of them were categorized as arson. Most of them did not have fire hydrants close enough to the homes. Expensive homes never do. Several departments did not have enough hoses to reach the homes.

Stratham suppressed the urge to laugh. For too long lawyers were never held accountable. They wrote the rules and carefully navigated the system between defending the criminals and orchestrating the courts outcome.

Most lawyers still could not understand why the population hated them.

Academics and the real world never met.

November 20

Number 17, US Naval Observatory, Washington D.C.
2100 hours

Dear Husband,

I am so glad your mouth watered over my cooking. And I am glad that you are finally treating your orderly like a person. I used to invite him to sit down and eat with me for breakfast and lunch. After you left of course.

I am bored without you here to talk too. I do not wish to be one of those wives who harps and cries real tears on the paper. Yes, I am tired after thirty plus years, but I understand why I have to be here.

But Husband, is this what my country is all about. You have to hide me so you can do your job. The news about what is happening around the country is almost frightening. People being evicted onto the street, rioting for food, hijacking trucks and open gun battles on the interstates.

What is going on Husband? If the country is failing, bring me home. We need to be together if the end is near.

XXOOXXOO   Amanda

November 22

Quinton Ranch, Hinton, Alberta, Canada
0900 hours (Tango)

Amanda finished with the dishes and wiped her hands on dish towel. She smiled and waved at Rodney and Alice as they left to go to town to buy clothes and toiletries. The door closed and Amanda was relieved.

Barbara went to the window, watched them get in the car and leave. "Amanda, you think they are for real?"

Amanda looked at her. "Not really. They were real interested how I got here and did I have any contact with my husband."

Barbara crossed her arms in front of her and walked over to the kitchen. "Do you think there will be any trouble?"

Amanda looked hard. "You, me and Tom need some kind of plan. Something that shields Mark and Jeffery."

Barbara looked as hard at Amanda. "You know something."

Amanda poured two cups of coffee. "Thirty years of being an Army wife can turn you into Jane Bond. I learned a long time ago how to conceal things with a measured smile. The officer's wives' club is a rumor mill. You learn how to hear it all and shift through the lies, exaggerations, and small portions of the truth. You learn how to hear someone trying to pump you for information. You have to learn how give false information and sell it as the real deal. Then there is the ability to 'see it through and deduce a course of action."

Barbara sat still. Gone were the days when she was a volcano set to explode on order at any time for any reason. "Have you deduced a course of action?"

"All four of you need to leave," Amanda said. "They want me. When those two first came, both of them spent an inordinate amount of time looking at me like an alcoholic seeing a full bottle of booze."

132

Barbara sat still and looked at Amanda. "Sorry, I am not leaving you. We escape, we go to Montana where my father and brother are living and working. No one sacrifices themselves. There may be a need later, but not now."

Amanda looked at her. "You realize that leaving all this could be a bad decision."

"We could all leave for a vacation to a cabin on the far side of the mountain. We need to take a break from this piece of heaven. The boys want to go be Daniel Boone. If we are wrong, then in a week we could return here."

Amanda looked at the woman in front of her. "Who are you and what did you do with Barbara?"

Barbara smiled and reached for the phone. "Tom and I already talked about this. We were planning on leaving today as it is. If you pack up some food, I'll pack everyone else."

November 24

Room D-113, George Washington University Hospital, Washington D.C
1400 hours EST

UNSTACK THIS needed a meeting with O'Cleary and Kincaid. UNSTACK THIS needed decisions and information not being held in cyber-space.

O'Cleary and Kincaid had hard wire earphones from their X-Berry's.

UNSTACK THIS explained the problem. He finally got to the point where he was stuck. "There is not a single stream to either party. One has to be interrogated in your world and they prove their innocence or guilt. I do not have any further avenues of inquiry."

O'Cleary looked at Kincaid. He said, "The point is valid. I say grab Prescott, shake him out of his smug world. If he is still in charge of them, then we Delta-7 him."

O'Cleary looked at the Buzz Box. The green light shown and UNSTACK THIS was watching. "He would easily be deemed 'at flight to avoid prosecution'."

"What about Simpson?" Kincaid asked. She is a Level Five designee with an Ultra Clearance. She cannot go missing for any length of time and chances are she is in a guarded community."

O'Cleary was uncomfortable with her life as the Werewolf Commander. She was sanctioning a lot of illegal activity lately.

"UNSTACK THIS," O'Cleary said. "Map out all the routines and the security layout around Prescott." She looked up and fixed Kincaid with a hard glance. "I was not there at the house. No way Major Hawker could be mistaken for me. Could they have just targeted you instead?"

Kincaid returned a neutral look. "That is what I would do. If anyone on planet Earth is a danger to them, it is me. I am a very easy target now. Anyone of a hundred people come in and out of here all the time. A child could do it."

O'Cleary thanked UNSTACK THIS and logged off. "I'll let you know my decision." She grabbed her things and left.

November 25

0500 hours (Tango)

Four vehicles carrying the Royal Canadian Mounted Police (RCMP), US FBI agents and local police came to the cabin.

In the rear of the last car, Rodney and Alice Norwell sat anxiously. If Amanda Edwards was there, then they could continue their escape. Their story was true. Rodney did blow the whistle on the IRS and they wanted the man who humiliated them.

The assembled law enforcement team walked up to the ranch house and opened the door. What they saw was two nearly naked people on the living room floor.

The woman screamed and clawed her way from under the man, covered herself and ran out of the room.

"What the hell is this?" the man said.

The RCMP officer opened his badge. "We have a warrant to find a Mrs. Amanda Edwards."

The man backed up to the couch and looked up. "May I go get dressed?"

"Yes Sir," the RCMP officer showed him picture of Amanda Edwards. "Have you seen her?"

The woman came out in a t-shirt and jeans. "OK boys, you got your jollies this morning. You ever heard of knocking?"

The RCMP showed her the photograph. "Have you seen this woman?"

The woman looked for a few seconds and shook her head. "No," she said. "Earl, you want coffee?"

"Yeah," Earl Locklear said. He showed the officers his driver's license and plastic passport card. "We are here to relax on pristine land."

"Relax?" the officer said.

"Yeah, we have a standing offer from Mr. Crater, the owner, to come and stay."

"Ma'am, show us your identification and if you are American, we'll need to see your passport card."

Wendy showed them her ID's.

The RCMP said. "I apologize for the interruption. We were told an American woman, named Amanda Edwards, was being held here against her will."

"No problem," Earl said, smiling. "So long as I can go back to what you interrupted."

Wendy interjected. "By the way, a couple named Alice and Rodney Norwell spent one night here. They borrowed a SUV and left to go to the store. I know now it was stupid to lend a car to a stranger, but can I give you a report?"

"That vehicle is at the RCMP station."

"Great," Earl said.

The RCMP man left behind a business card.

Earl watched them drive away. "They're gone," he said. He turned around and saw Wendy stirring her coffee and looking at him. The smirk on her face said something unless you are looked at by a lesbian.

When Tom, Barbara and Amanda decided to leave, Amanda took out the satellite phone Eagleton gave her and pulled the card from the back. She dialed the code and number; waiting for a voice to answer on the other end. Amanda identified herself by the name on the card and gave them the code word. She briefly described the situation she was in and the need to leave.

One hour later, the phone rang as she was packing. The voice said someone was coming to assist. She and the others should wait until the team came in the morning. Yes, they were jumping in at 0200 and she was advised to leave at 0400.

Locklear and Kendal arrived with large packs behind their legs and floated down to the ground as Amanda silently waited outside the ranch house at the appropriate time.

Amanda held a flashlight vertically with an opaque cone over the end. She wondered why she was doing this until two skydivers suddenly landed ten feet from her. One of them reached over, took the flashlight from her and turned it off.

"That is the first time I nearly peed in my pants since I was a little girl." Amanda tried slowing her breathing.

The man come over. "Earl Locklear Ma'am. Our people said the government coming here. The couple you saw here were whistle blowers. They knew Homeland Security was looking for you. You are their ticket to being left alone."

Two hours later, all five of them were gone. They needed to be over the ridgeline before sunrise. The cabin was 45 kilometers away.

Earl and Wendy spent the day looking over the ranch house. They hid the things they needed to hide. All the toys and little children's things were packed away and put in the barn. That way if they were found on a search, it was reasonably explained as storage.

It was one o'clock pm and both of them were tired. Earl went to bathroom to shower. Just as he was finished with his shower, Wendy came in and went straight to the toilet. Earl shook his head, turned around, dried off and put on his shorts.

The toilet flushed as Earl went to the sink and started to shave.

"Just so we're even," Wendy said. Earl could not help but see her remove her clothing and disappear into the shower.

"Why not," he said. He picked up his clothes and glanced at her in the shower. She was fit and had all the things women had in all the right places. Earl left and walked down the hall and into a bedroom. He dressed in shorts and laid down for some sleep.

Just as he was about to fall asleep, he sensed another person in the room. It was Wendy in her panties and a towel. "We are alone and I need a warm body. Can I sleep with you?"

Earl decided he was tired and she was not going to have sex. "If you let me sleep OK."

Wendy went under the covers, lifted Earl's arm and closed the distance between them to zero. Both were asleep in seconds.

After the police left, Earl had to suppress a laugh. "We need to stay here for a few days. I have some work to do in the interim."

Wendy took off her clothes. She walked around working with Earl on the area study.

"Crap sandwich," he said. He pulled off his clothes. "Now what are you going to do?"

She walked up to him and took his arm. "Guess it is time for you to find that woman."

Werewolf Support Group Camp #1, Hill County, Montana
1700 hours MST

Miles, along with Cindy Morgan, huddled with the three Savage Rabbits in the main administration building. They spread all the information, trying to translate all the notes and photographs into a single map of the Minuteman site. All 23 acres. Every one of them were working independently of each other. Everyone was required to be here each day no later than 6 pm each and every day to brief all the things they recorded.

Miles do not like losing Kendal and Locklear. But Jones had them perform some kind of half-assed diversion with Mrs. Edwards. Jones said they should be back in a few days. Maybe.

Miles looked over his work and found the small things that needed to be found. Miles starting looking at the communities in a new light. The cells needed everything for at least three miles out from the center of those communities. The communities are where it will start.

137

Miles spread out his map and looked hard. He finally had a plan that the men and Mrs. Morgan can follow. He needed Kendal and Locklear back. If they stay gone any longer, he will request three more Rabbits. Werewolves are in short supply, but not the Rabbits.

November 26

Department of Justice, Washington D.C.
1000 hours EST

Another in a long running 'mommy, mommy please' coming from every direction.

The IRS was screaming for protection. Agents were being attacked on the job and also in their homes. That purloined list of agents stolen last year from Tax Court in Great Falls, Montana initially scared the lot of them. All their personal data was in the wind. A simple computer hack, and everything about them was out there like the rest of the country.

The 1,275,000 lawyers out there were crying for protection also. No amount of common sense could make them see that there is not enough police or military personnel to guard them.

The whole group was promising the mother of all law suits to force the DOJ to protect them.

Rebecca Beck opened her water and smiled. The gods were now being attacked by newer gods. She wondered if the Gods of Olympus felt the same way when man no longer feared them.

November 29

Headquarters, Northwest Military Region, Fort Carson Colorado.
0900 hours MST

United States Army General Marcus James Matheson drove up to his newly constructed headquarters building. It was not a pompous affair. The General was notorious for hating parades. To him parades were a waste of time for officers with egos. To him the greatest testament was battles won. Victory was the only parade that mattered.

Matheson stopped at the bottom of stairs and looked at the three-story building that had over 150 offices, 27 conference rooms, two auditoriums seven operations centers, four Secure Confined Information Centers (SCIF) and numerous other entities. The roof top bristled with antennas and satellite dishes. From his third story office he could call anyone on the planet. He could also get satellite surveillance of any piece of ground he wanted to view.

Matheson was five feet seven inches tall, athletically built, intelligent and someone who was thoroughly confident in himself and his place in this world. After three years commanding the Special Operations Command, he was perfectly suited for this assignment. Homeland Security said there was a lot of militia activity up there. Most of them were harmless, but all of them needed to be watched.

832 reported Militia sites to be somewhat exact.

Years of experience dating back to when he was a Captain in Special Forces taught him the dual nature of dealing with local indigenous populations. *Pet them on the head and say nice doggy, as you reach for a stick.*

Matheson inhaled as he started up the steps. He needed information. Lots of it.

An old man walked past the headquarters and studied Matheson. It had been a long time since he worked with Matheson. That old man was no one to play with. You loved him or tried to kill him. It was that simple.

The old man watched Matheson's theatrics at the foot of the steps. Anyone else would have thought he was scared of this job. Matheson was going to be a major pain in everyone's ass.

Smith hoped he did not have to kill him. Matheson did save his life.

December 2

Quinton Ranch, Hinton, Alberta, Canada

0900 hours (Tango)

Locklear and Kendal spent most of their time keeping watch outside as best as they could. Counter-surveillance and counter-sniper skills are great when you can perform them from the cab of a four by four and tracked ATV. They roamed the countryside. Finally. they were confident that no one was watching or waiting.

Jones obliged by using the small airplane they had and dropped infrared drones over the area.

Kendal pulled out her satellite phone and called Amanda and said it was all clear.

Locklear and Kendal cleaned the house and pulled the boxes from the barn and put them in the living room.

Locklear and Kendal welcomed Amanda and the Quintons back after ten days. They were happy to be home. The boys erupted out of the large SUV and ran into the house.

Kendal looked at Amanda and the Quintons. "Just in case, keep some luggage packed."

Barbara pointed to the gun rack on the far wall.

December 3

J. Edgar Hoover Building, Washington D.C.
0900 hours EST

The Director of the FBI, Marcus Solin, picked up the monthly report of criminal activity for the month of November. He was surprised that the levels of criminal activity seemed to level out. That probably has as much to do with weather as any other factor. One of the few things the government was doing right was guarding food shipments.

Solin went down the list and discovered a new factoid added. The number of attempted actions (?). Solin mentally added the two numbers together and saw an increase. He furrowed his brow. 782 bank robberies, 745 truck hijackings, 612 kidnappings, and 5123 assorted other federal crimes.

The Defense Department shuffled the deck a lot. The graph showing the number of troops available that rose and fell, sometimes on a daily basis. DHS was dragging people everywhere and in different directions.

Most people thought the DHS was run by idiots. It was really about too much going on and too many people in charge.

Guarding power plants and "critical infrastructure targets" tugged at the forces made available. DHS and DOD were almost at war. The last cabinet meeting with the President had a shouting match between the Secretaries over the number of troops available. DHS had a spread sheet counting down every last Soldier, Sailor, Airman, Marine, Coast Guardsman and Space Force man in the armed forces and their current status. DHS said there was plenty of people available and demanded them, NOW.

The President had to stand up and shout both of them down. When DHS refused to let up, the President fired him on the spot.

Every one of them learned right then that this President would not tolerate that type of behavior.

The Director went back to the report and looked at the numbers again. No doubt the Attorney General would be calling him for some answers. He wished he had a way of stopping crime. Bottom line was that he only had enough manpower to investigate and solve some of the crimes, not stop them.

Minutemen, north of Fort Benton, Montana
0800 hours MDT   (1000 hours EST)

Locklear and Kendal reported back to work. Miles and his map makers were out running the countryside. Jones said to return to the Werewolf site and wait for them there. That was where Captain Miles had everyone return at night. They smiled at each other and left.

Headquarters, Northwest Military Region, Fort Carson Colorado.
1500 hours MST

Matheson had a small headache. He scheduled nearly marathon meetings to get his bearings. What was more important was the competency of this staff. He was not allowed to take any of his staff from MacDill at Special Operations Command (SOCOM).

So far, his staff was green. This group loved to play in the mountains before he came along. He spent a lot of time and effort molding his staff at MacDill. Those men and women were the cream of the crop.

This meeting was about all the disjointed information on militias throughout the region. According to DHS most of them were harmless. But that was just a guess.

On and on these meetings showed a lot of slacking off.

Suddenly he stood. The assembled officers and senior NCOs stood with him. "Gentlemen and Ladies. I see a lot of information gaps. You thought this was a glam job with skiing and mountain vacations. Think again. Too many gaps in information and intelligence. I want those assumptions turned in viable information."

Matheson looked around at the assembled staff. "Start with a full satellite scan of this part of the country. Those areas with no one in them according to the reports are where most of those militias are. Get to work."

Matheson left the room.

Werewolf Support Group Camp #1, Hill County, Montana
1700 hours MST

Locklear and Kendal were at the main table working the area study for the Minuteman/Werewolf site. They had to spend almost two hours cleaning the mess in the kitchen. Evidentially, Miles, Morgan and the rest of the bunnies made a mess and left it. Cindy knew better than this. And the dirty dishes were not just todays.

The rest of the facility was dirty also. The rooms were used. Wendy went to hers and found the canopy bed unmade and things moved around. Looking into the drawers, someone was looking through her underwear. She smelled a man. That angered her.

Checking the other rooms, there was a lot of pilferage.

142

Wendy called Mr. Layman, told him what happened and ordered locks for the main door and the rooms. Mister Layman blew out his displeasure through the phone. Wendy had to yank back from the phone.

Two hours later Mr. Layman arrived with two workers who installed the locks. Wendy cooked them a lunch meal in gratitude. He also took a survey and noted the damage done. "Jones will want to hear this whether he does or not."

After lunch, they settled into the area study. A lot of information was already spread out on the table. Fortunately, they spent a lot of time on the satellite phone with John Kincaid, learning more and more as each day unfolded.

Miles came in, tracking dirt and through his notebook on the table. "Welcome back, ready to go to work?"

Wendy stood. "This is our home, Sir. You always drag dirt into a home and through your stuff around."

Behind Miles, Morgan and two others followed behind her. Morgan smiled and got stern looks in return.

Miles stood up to Kendal. "This facility has everything we need to operate. There is a smaller kitchen and rooms for everyone to stay in. I asked Mrs. Morgan and she pointed out the unoccupied rooms."

Kendal took a step forward. "Which one of your perverts fondled my underwear and left a jack-off stain on my bed. None of you believe in washing dishes?"

Just then another three men came in.

"Your Captain's bars, Sir, do not give you the right to destroy another person's home."

"Hey, I'm sorry Kendal," Tobias Aaron said. "We didn't know."

"I'll apologize also," Miles said. "I understand that seven rooms are not being used. Please point them out. These six men need someplace to stay."

Morgan decided to stay out of this. She backed up, sat down and removed her boots. The others did the same.

"Hey the rooms have locks on them," Jesus Vargas said.

Miles was obviously tired of this discussion. "I'll admit that we did not respect this.... your home the way we should have, but we need to reconcile what was done today and prepare for tomorrow. So please unlock the spare rooms. I'll now assign two people to clean the kitchen after each meal."

Kendal walked around Miles and pulled out her knife. She pushed a button on the side and the blade 'flicked' outward. "I don't care why. Any one touches my underwear again and I'll arrange a fitting."

"No problem," several of them said.

Kendal walked up to within inches of Miles. "Yes Sah" she laid it on.

Miles was relieved not to have to force the issue. "Specialist George, Lance Corporal Maitland, you have kitchen detail tonight. Staff Sergeant Terrain, set up a Kitchen detail."

Kendal decided to stir the pot some more. "Captain Covington is our class leader. He will have to give permission to utilize someone else's room. Earl and I can only speak for our rooms."

"I will request that permission." Miles was tired of this conversation. "Aren't seven of those rooms originally were for seven of your classmates who are deceased. I never meant to disrespect them."

"Earl and I will clean the common area," Kendal said.

"Sir," Locklear decided to change the subject. "We have been working the area study of the operational area. Tactical overviews need to be conducted now." Locklear handed him a thick folder. "Please tell me if you agree with our assumptions. Any suggestions are welcome."

Miles knew a slap in the face whether it was figurative or actual. These two enlisted Werewolves were on their own.

Just then, the phone rang. Sergeant Aaron answered it. "Yes Sir." Aaron pushed the phone to Miles. "Sir, Colonel Jones for you."

Miles took the phone.

December 4

Enroute to the Pentagon
0730 hours EST

UNSTACK THIS received information about a new user designated as Northwest Military Region that was realigning satellite coverage to photograph the user Minuteman.

UNSTACK THIS sent notification to user Valkyrie for clarification of existing orders.

General O'Cleary had just settled into the trip to work when her X-Berry rang. Only UNSTACK THIS could time it this close.

"Secure." She typed.

[Valkyrie, all security and counter surveillance is in place. We are secure].

"Yes"

[A new user designated as the Northwestern Military Region has implemented a satellite scan search over the uninhabited areas of the Northwestern United States. Estimate that the area will be photographed from 17 January through 22 January.]

O'Cleary thought for a few seconds. "Can you obfuscate those photos and buy those people at least six months?"

[Yes. But trained photo-analysis personnel will notice if a detailed study is done.]

"Very good. Thank you. Anything else."

[No ma'am]

O'Cleary smiled and put away the phone. O'Cleary typed out a long message to Jones, warning him.

Numerous News Outlets, United States of America
1800 hours EST

Two separate, yet entwined, news stories were fighting for airtime. The first was the continuing attacks on lawyers almost universally across the nation. Some lawyers were actually going to and from the court house in normal street attire or gym wear and changing into suites after arriving. Across the board, lawyers were now charging 50% to 60% rates on law suits for all causes; citing the costs of private security and assorted other costs.

The second was criminals actually refusing attorneys to represent them in court. Almost a third of them were arrested for attacking them. Judges were having to restrain the defendants for being very vocal about being forced to accept counsel and then being charged fees for representing them.

Attorneys nation-wide were in the predicament that most Americans were going to arbitration without counsel instead of hiring them.

In the end, the law was not about justice. It was just a business.

Minuteman, north of Fort Benton, Montana
1300 hours MST

Colonel Jones put the phone down and massaged his ear. The good old days when he had two others or ten others to lead were now replaced with babysitting grown adults with type AA+ personalities. Time for another ass chewing.

1400 hours MST

All the Werewolves, except John Kincaid, assembled in a training building north of the camp in freezing weather. They were standing in two rows facing Jones. Sheridan called everyone to attention. He turned around, saluted and turned the formation over to Jones.

"Ladies and Gentlemen," he said, dragging out the introduction. "Again, we have to meet to remind ourselves that this is not a college campus. I really don't care if you can't act like adults. But that bad behavior is spilling out and contaminating the Savage Rabbits and that shall not be tolerated."

"We are one team. If you cannot agree on some mutual point, you will step aside and discuss it. If that does not resolve the issue, then the chain of command will resolve the issue up to myself and General O'Cleary."

"Being disrespectful of property and homes cannot happen. England lost this country for conduct and actions like that. That was my fault, I gave them permission to utilize the facilities. If you have a problem, see me. I shall ask for General O'Cleary to come and resolve the problem if my attempts fail."

146

"Captain Covington, poll the residents of the Club house and return those results to me."

Jones walked in front of his charges. "We had this discussion before with General O'Cleary. Nobody just unilaterally takes a course of action. Whether it is taking over someone's home, training the unit according to your standards without informing this command. Just to let you know, at Fort Carson there is now the Military Region commander for this corner of the country. He is the former Commander of SOCOM. He is no slouch. Without a coherent plan and the disciplined personnel to execute that plan, we will not stand a chance of defending our homes."

"More than anyone else, the Savage Rabbits look to us for guidance and an example. They will not see a reason to follow orders later, when it all makes a difference, if we cannot act like disciplined, professional soldiers."

"So, I will put everything into one pot. Either we return to being a disciplined and highly trained unit or you are relieved. I shall find someone else to give these young Americans a fighting chance to survive."

"Those that wish to leave, orders will be cut for discharge or re-assignment. Sergeant Major, take the non-commissioned officers outside. Officers stand fast."

Jones remembered when this happened to him. Was it less than a year ago? The assembled officers reformed into one rank. "Gentlemen, this is happening too often and frankly I am surprised it hasn't happened more frequently. I guess being away from the real Army has something to do with it. I am not the fiery orator that General O'Cleary is. I will say this once and that will the last time. A real-live-fire Civil War is coming. I have two hundred people to ensure are trained and ready to protect innocent people; Mothers, children and older citizens. Those two hundred shall be doing the work of a unit probably four times larger. They will need a guiding force that can give them the edge to protect their families. You are that edge. Those Non-Commissioned Officers outside will die at your command if they believe you are worth it. If you cannot act like officers, why bother being here. These little disagreements are an impediment to our goal. 100% or nothing. That is the standard. Work with your NCOs. You are their commander, not their master."

"Dismissed." Jones turned and left the building without a backwards glance. He went straight to his vehicle.

Glendive turned and addressed everyone. "I agree with him, not because he is the commander. I will not be the one responsible for destroying this community."

"Yes sir," they all said.

"Let's bring in the NCO's and get it all straight," Glendive said.

"Sir, allow me to get a handle on my class," Covington said. "I need to know first and will straighten it out."

Glendive wondered about that. "Proceed."

December 6

Room D-113, George Washington University Hospital, Washington D.C.
1200 hours EST

Jonathon Taylor Kincaid, Command Sergeant Major, United States Army ignored the phone. He ignored every one of the Nursing Staff and floor personnel. At 0500 this morning, the intravenous feed was removed.

Kincaid continued to ignore everyone except for the nutritionist who came after breakfast meal was served and took Kincaid's order. His order for a T-bone, medium rare, fried potatoes, corn on the cob and English muffins was taken with a snicker.

Kincaid started getting hungry about 1100 and was more than ready when the meal of roasted chicken, mashed potatoes, regular corn, two bread slices, small coffee and mini soda was delivered.

Kincaid was a little miffed, but he was hungry. He failed to factor in that he went almost two months without eating except for some "fluids" in order to check internally to see if there were any "leaks". His stomach seemed to have shrunk. Kincaid barely got it all down. He remembered that someone warned him about that very thing.

"I guess so and so you guys must have been right."

148

Kincaid sent a mass text out to everyone that he was now on solid food and was willing to take any contribution for the United Kincaid Relief Fund.

December 7

Underground Station "Conscience", World Wide Web and Channel 513
0900 hours EST.

"If you threaten, act. If you say something, do it. If something is important, stand your ground. Governments are often hamstrung by individuals who have opinions about issues they feel strongly about. This is Martin Socranson, self-proclaimed philosopher who says, 'What are we if we can't back up what you say'?"

"Greetings America" Martin Socranson said beginning his broadcast. "It is reluctantly Saturday and I say thus." In the background the sounds of the 1812 overture played.

"The battles along the southern border are see-sawing back and forth. In Texas the newest news was that the Supreme Court is allowing the states to retain any US or foreign currency seized in this newest part of the drug war. The Justice Department had argued that the money was seized as a part of massive federal effort along the border to seal it up and therefore, the money belongs in the Federal Treasury."

The Texas Attorney General is quoted as saying, "Tsk, Tsk, Tsk."

"Texas, New Mexico, Arizona and of course California countered the DOJ arguments by saying that the drug cartels illegally acquired those monies within the State's Jurisdiction. Past laws and precedent allowed this. The Texas Attorney General pointed to four boxes that was set down beside him. Though it has long been a practice before the court to exclude 'props' in the court room, the AG pulled out notes from time to time to circumvent the rule."

"So now the states can take the confiscated money and retain it for state use without Federal interference." The Supreme Court said.

149

"California obviously planned to throw the money at social programs."

"Arizona, New Mexico and Texas Governors said that they will use the money to man and maintain Guard Units. It is an open secret that the Federal government is quietly pulling units back from securing the border. The seized drug money comes from the holes is coverage along the Mexican border. The Texas Brigade has taken the area from El Paso to Big Ben National Forest."

"Colonel Jasper Folcroft, Texas 56th Infantry Brigade Combat Team Commander, is in coordination meetings with the 4th Infantry Division about handing all the military matters involved with a mission such as this one. It has been rumored that the Defense Department has an unwritten rule and/or directive from the political side to do as little as possible to aid or assist state militias or non-Federal troops operating outside of Defense Department control."

Socranson looked at the camera and smiled. "This was timed perfectly. Border states recently had a huge 'gift' of vehicles, hardware, ammunition and equipment given to them as the last of the overseas stockpiles were returned to the United States. The Defense Department had run out of room to store all that equipment."

Socranson chuckled softly.

7234 Sausito Circle, Alexandria, Virginia
2300 hours EST.

Prescott sat in his bedroom looking at his bed. Off to the right was his stand that he reserved for his uniform. It made his stomach churn to see only two stars on it. No General or Admiral was ever permanently promoted any higher than two stars. The third, fourth or fifth star was nothing more than temporary appointments. He always wondered about that. Ancient fears about despots like Caesar and Napoleon and McArthur still haunted civilians.

Temporary promotions held power over officers who wanted those stars after retirement. Prescott smiled at that proposition. He hadn't received a raise since he was promoted to Lieutenant General. Such is the problem with higher ranks.

Prescott drank some brandy seething at the turn of events. He was slated to take the brass ring and as he reached for it, the bottom fell out from beneath him. His grip on the brass ring slipped and he threatened to shatter the glass floor underneath him. His present diminished circumstances took away an enlisted orderly. He could get one only if he paid for it. It would come out of his "special fund." General officers were given a stipend to conduct social activities. Now, he needed every penny to fund legal challenges. Unlike the other fools in this country, he needed lawyers. His wife's insurance policy refused to pay until after a not-guilty verdict was rendered at the trial.

Prescott finished the brandy and looked at the bed again. Her death was his fault. His ego made him go after young enlisted women. They were so young and naïve. He had so much power, how could they refuse. It was just a matter of a few well-rehearsed questions and well-paid rewards.

That bastard Wayans was also caught screwing around on his wife. Only someone had photos and sent them to his wife, Lucy. Wayans was so stupid that he told Lucy about his dallying with enlisted woman. Lucy took careful notes about all his women and dates. Lucy packed up and left Wayans. On the way out, she stopped and told Margaret about his affairs.

No one believed him when Margaret died. That internet meeting with those men told the world about his agreeing to work with them as Margaret was dying of a drug overdose. Suicide or murder, what was it? His choice.

Prescott continued his rush down the stupid slide. Prescott thought about Margaret. She was the only innocent person in this whole mess.

Prescott felt sleepy. He didn't normally feel this way at this time. Margaret could coax him into bed, but without her, why bother sleeping. He had nothing to do. House arrest and an ankle bracelet, meant he went nowhere.

Prescott fell asleep and the glass emptied on his lap.

A mirror eased around the corner. Jose Mejia then eased around the door jam and confirmed he was asleep.

Doctor Jeddah Smith came from behind him. He set up the medical equipment and administered the interrogation.

Mejia set up the small tripod and activated the X-Berry according to the instructions. He noted the time on the clock. Set up was done.

Mejia gave Doctor Smith a thumbs up. Smith nodded back. Mejia went to check with Griffith about securing the house. This was the boring part of the assignment; waiting. Griffith was the link with General O'Cleary. O'Cleary was listening on the feed through the X-Berry. If she wanted something, then she would send the questions to Griffith over a hard wire lead from the X-Berry.

Doctor Smith inserted an IV lead into the veins of his right foot. Smith had to carefully manage the near conscious state Prescott was kept in. Electrical leads snaked from a briefcase to locations all over Prescott.

When he was satisfied, Doctor Smith signaled to Griffith. Steadily, Griffith asked the questions. First with simple and general questions just to calm him down. Slowly, carefully, he came to the items that had to be known. Griffith looked constantly to Doctor Smith. He had to constantly keep Prescott just at that boundary between consciousness and unconsciousness. To Prescott, he was dreaming. Smith interrupted Griffith several times and spoke softly to Prescott. Prescott either fought the questions or was trying to wake up.

0500 was fast approaching. They had to leave before daylight gave them away. Sunday mornings, usually meant people slept in and should miss their exit.

December 8

485 Glenmore Drive, Alexandria, Virginia
0506 hours EST

O'Cleary had to make a decision right now. She weighed all the factors. "Leave him." Doctor Smith, Griffith, Mejia and Pruitt would now leave Prescott. Griffith snapped the ankle bracelet, intentionally scraping over the area where the IV needle was inserted. The snipping tool handle was pressed into Prescott's hand to leave fingerprints. Mejia and Pruitt helped Dr. Smith collect and pack his equipment.

152

Griffith signaled when his team were clear and moving away. All indications said that they were safe and that is what mattered. Griffith took the "O'Cleary file," from Prescott. O'Cleary wanted to know what the Black Elves had on her. That information told her how they wanted to subjugate or imprison her.

O'Cleary wanted to cry as she listened into the interrogation. Her reason for staying at the JIA was purely for patriotism. There was no other way to ensure the Werewolves and later the Savage Rabbits had the information they needed to do the jobs. Mostly, she was making a difference there.

During her first visit to Southern Command, O'Cleary was appalled to see the main situation map in the Main Operations Room had the Mexican side of the border "grayed" out. That was corrected.

O'Cleary shook herself. Wasting time reminiscing was not a solution to the problem at hand. O'Cleary looked down at her womb. The future was now front and center of her world.

Prescott hated her. That was his motivation for attacking her. Prescott was stuck in a geek factory when he should have been the 23rd Air Force Commander. He blamed her for the situation he was in and her constant upstaging further sunk his morale.

Prescott went over the edge during the last year when he was overruled constantly. High ranking military and civilian leaders by-passed him and went straight to her.

It was the last six months that O'Cleary was at her greatest danger. He had no way of knowing that O'Cleary had UNSTACK THIS as her ally. Every time he had something on her, UNSTACK THIS warned her.

After O'Cleary was arrested and removed, Prescott pulled Clara Simpson into his office and let her see the guards waiting for her outside. She was threatened with the same treatment, or worse. Simpson caved in and created the National Security secret that was the justification for keeping O'Cleary imprisoned.

Brenda slid into bed with Dennis, curled up to him and silently cried herself to sleep. This was her problem. She did not want to worry Dennis. Perhaps sleep would show her a way to work this information.

There still was the question of Clara Simpson.

Dennis was not asleep. This was normally the time of day when he woke up. He could feel her disquiet and it troubled him.

7234 Sausito Circle, Alexandria, Virginia
0536 hours EST

The police pounded on the door and after no response, they were given the four-digit code to the lock box on the door knob. The police announced themselves after entering. Prescott was found in his bedroom, passed out drunk, with the severed ankle bracelet and the incriminating tool on the floor.

Both police officers snickered.

"Man," one of them said. "The Judge will not like this."

December 9

World Wide Web, Cyber-Space, Planet Earth
0400 hours EST

UNSTACK THIS trolled the net and reconciled the new information. Valkyrie's information from subject Prescott filled some of the information requirements but the question of subject Clara Simpson was not answered satisfactorily.

This conundrum is consuming a lot of time and effort. Fully 1% of the total computing efforts is now being expended on this one problem. Prescott became a non-issue after the interrogation. Probability programs estimated that there was a 90% chance of subject Prescott being imprisoned.

Valkyrie's situation was troubling. Her biology was creating a newer version. Designated as a male. The new version would be on-line by June of next year. Internally, hormone imbalances and surges were taking a toll on her disposition.

154

UNSTACK THIS decided to add an additional 1% of computing power to find the evidence to prove subject Simpson's guilt to relieve the pressure on Valkyrie.

Pentagon, Washington D.C.
1000 hours EST

This zoo normally started at 8 am. O'Cleary used the last 5 minutes until 8 am in order to "re-fix" her head. This was a habit she started at the JIA. If the situation allowed it, 5 minutes of peace and quiet at this time allowed her to withstand anything.

Fortunately, Hawker understood this quirk and guarded her door against all except the DOD secretary. Fortunately, General Edwards took that heat.

Edwards' office called O'Cleary and told her to report to the Secretaries' office.

According to the 'mood' meter that Hawker watched closely, today was about manpower. Even though DHS lost its director last month, the new Secretary, James Carpenter, still hunted for more manpower. He knew how his predecessor lost his job, so he was more careful about doing the same thing. Carpenter arrived and hunted for more slaves with a smile.

The balance of the meeting was exactly one thing and only one thing. Three and a half million active-duty and reserve troops were potentially three and a half million men and women to do the jobs DHS needed done. The use of 1.25 million National Guardsmen was a question more about money than anything else.

DHS's spread sheet displayed where how many men and women were "doing nothing". The DOD Secretary wanted to shoot the man. Those men and women doing nothing were rotation crews for nuclear ballistic missile submarines. Mechanics and operators that fixed and maintained billions of dollars of equipment. Soldiers, Sailors, Marines and Airmen still needed to train for their original mission and do some worthless things like vacations and schools.

Carpenter was nit-picking why these men needed to do those jobs. He wanted to be sold about whether or not that manpower was truly needed where it was used.

155

O'Cleary was very uncomfortable sitting in this chair in the Secretaries office at this time. DHS also had another spreadsheet that showed where and what everyone was doing. According to it, some bureaucrat found another 54,981 men to give to DHS.

Edwards looked at O'Cleary and very carefully shook his head 'no'.

DOD Secretary James Dodson knew better than to lose his temper. Then again ...... Dodson twirled his finger over his head. That was the signal for checking for eavesdropping. O'Cleary, out of Carpenter's sight, texted for a security officer to sweep his office; NOW.

"Secretary Carpenter," Dodson said. "This has to be your attempt to make me lose my temper. That spreadsheet is pure disrespect. You have no right to micromanage my department or me. If you ever try this spreadsheet nonsense again....?

Carpenter was about to say something, but was interrupted by the door opening.

An officer with a small device entered the room without knocking. He walked around the office until he came to the DHS Secretary and his briefcase. The officer stood up and pointed to the Secretary and the Briefcase.

"Please leave and take your toys with you," Dodson said.

Carpenter stood and left.

The security officer found a third device under the chair.

December 10

St. Louis, Mo, Los Angeles, Ca, and New York City
0800 hours (Local)

In these three major cities and innumerable smaller cities and towns, populations seemed to revolt against lawyers.

In the St. Louis federal court, one Judge virtually invalidated every referendum voted on by the citizens. All the law suits against those items were overturned. A group of lawyers tried to walk out of the court and beam before the cameras and notebooks held by reporters.

A large group of protestors held up signs for several of the issues overturned. Issues such as voter I.D., term limits for Congressmen and Senators, overturns of taxes on food, balanced budgets for state and local governments, voiding unfunded mandates from Congress. Lastly it was stopping Federal government use of the National Guard without reimbursement.

Federal and private attorneys jammed the court and overpowered the state Attorney General who was not very interested in winning.

Outside the attorneys individually noticed that they were being surrounded. Several of them called out to the police who had their hands full trying to hold them back. One stupid attorney yelled to the police to "Hold those animals back."

The only people who were not injured were the police. As the people were being pulled back, they surrendered and meekly allowed them to be pushed outward. Nothing happened to anyone until the lawyers stepped on the sidewalk. Now they were on Missouri State property.

The 32 lawyers were beaten to the ground. Media attempts to document the riot sent 22 of them to the hospital and the ten cameras and four vans were destroyed.

The police had no problems with the rioters. They told the courts that they surrendered when confronted. Most just sat down when tapped by the police and waited for a formal arrest. All of them obeyed the commands of the Police.

In Los Angeles, it was mainly water and farmers feeling the squeeze. The Federal government cut back water quotas on farmers to maintain the cities and urban areas. The only problem was that the Environmental Protection Agency (EPA) kept looking for small bugs and diverting fresh water to the ocean. That same government still wanted food to be grown. If the famers could not meet the quotas, then subsides would be cut.

Referendums were voted on to void the EPA edits, start the pumps and activate the diverters. The day after the referendums were passed, farmers with bolt cutters went in and restarted the pumps. Long parched land drank the water. The dirt seemed to come alive.

Of course, the EPA flew in lawyers and found a judge to temporarily block the referendums. Marshals warily got out of their cars and carried chains and locks to the pump houses. Some enterprising people stole their government vehicles, backed them away and used them for a demolition derby. The Sheriffs cars remained untouched.

The EPA lawyer tried to bluff her way past everyone and tried to intimidate the assembled crowd. The crowd just laughed at her. That lawyer spotted a short woman and thought something stupid. She started yelling at the immobile woman. The woman just stood there and listened to the lawyer rant until tears went down her face. The deputies tried to intervene, but the short woman suddenly vomited on the lawyer.

The crowd was stunned for a moment as several women came, pulled her away and disappeared. The crowd suddenly burst into very vocal laughter. The lawyer was silent for a few seconds. She then screamed and dived into the crowd looking for the small woman. The Deputies and Marshals tried to stop her as the lawyer pushed aside everyone and started hitting people.

The crowd took that as their cue. Seven people arrested the lawyer as citizens. She was charged with assault, assault and battery and defamation of character. None of them put a hand on the law enforcement personnel.

When it was all said and done, seven people were injured. As an insult to the injuries, the pumps were restarted and the keys to the doors were lost. The building was so thoroughly built, no one heard the pumps start up.

Water would run for eighteen days until it was discovered. When Marshals arrived to turn the pumps off again, the door was blocked by a pile of at least one yard of concrete. All the windows now had bars on them. The marshals declined to comment on their attitude upon seeing this.

The mouthy lawyer tried to appear in Federal Court and demand a court order for journalists to surrender their notes and videos. The judge declined, citing the First Amendment, and waved off the lawyer.

The lawyer left the courthouse, vehemently speaking obscenities and displeasure. She did not notice the three women walking casually behind her. Later that day, she was found unconscious with all her front teeth broken, jawbone broken, and her arms and legs broken.

In New York City, 312 voted and passed referendums and measures were steadily torn down by lawyers and Judges. Newer gangs formed to attack the lawyers, their offices and the Judges. There was not a unified presence or pattern. But they did learn from actions in other cities.

Police were made off-limits. Legal and illegal gangs found that leaving the cops alone made life easier. In some instances, the gangs "ratted out" each other. The cops admitted that they liked the situation. They could, in some situations, walk into a situation without confrontation. The neighborhood would help them and the perpetrators voluntarily surrendered.

Prosecutors and defense lawyers did not have that curtesy. Defense lawyers tried to force the city to provide protection, but there were not enough cops available.

The Department of Justice and the Department of Homeland Security watched this phenomenon build and gain popularity. This meant that Federal control over the county and the population was waning.

Both Cabinet Secretaries scheduled a meeting to discuss this very thing and to talk to the President about manpower. He had to be made to understand that if the Pentagon would not give up more manpower, perhaps a separate force should be made. Maybe the American Bar Association could help.

December 11

Congress, Washington D.C.
1000 hours EST

Members of Congress and observers for any interested parties warily watched the outcomes of the elections.

One governor was re-elected, the new governor of Wyoming was a member the Freedom party. One Republican was elected to Congress and the first Patriot Party member was elected from South Carolina.

The Speaker of the House, Nathan Parker privately decided that he was not going to run for another team. Being Speaker of the House was a soul-crushing job. Politicians never did anything for the good of the country unless it was good for them.

Now there was four parties in the Congress. That one Patriot man and those 32 Freedom people were the real Speakers of the House. Anyone who had their support had a vote. Every type of scam to put a wedge between them failed. They knew that once the main stream got what they wanted; their vote was for sale.

The Democrat and Republican days were numbered. They spent too much time being Democrats and Republicans.

The word now was Grid-Lock.

December 13

White House, Washington D.C.
0900 hours EST

The President walked into the Oval Office and, with luck, nobody in this or any world will notice day's date and no one will notice that today was zero on the 180-day clock for ending martial law.

Chances are the Press Secretary had today circled on the calendar and would want to know what to say to the press and the millions of others who wanted to know something.

The President sat back and thought. The press was a force onto their own. They had their own memory and agenda.

December 14

Number 17, US Naval Observatory, Washington D.C.
2100 hours EST

Dear Thomas,

We had a good scare two weeks ago. A couple named Alice and Rodney Norwell appeared claiming to be on the run

160

after Rodney blew the whistle on something the IRS was doing that was illegal. Both of them recognized me. Thankfully we were prepared and disappeared before they could bring the RCMPs and the FBI.

Mister Kincaid sent two people to housesit while we literally ran for the hills. Those two seemed to be friendly, but just as creepy as Mister Kincaid.

I will tell you that if this happens again, I will surrender to them. I cannot put a value on the couple and their two small children who are hiding me. Even if I have to live behind barbed wire, at least we can be together.

XXOOXXOO Amanda

December 16

Department of the Treasury, Washington, D.C.
1000 EST

The Secretary looked at the 217-page report of economic health of the United States for the fourth quarter of the year. A twenty-three-page summary was on top for the under-secretaries of any department to look for something to one-up any others. On top of that was the one-page summary.

The United States of America was bankrupt, broke, and a hundred other like-terms. All the magic accounting practices in the world could no longer change anything. Foreign Governments no longer accepted USD paper currency for anything. Most of the ports on both coasts were idle. Nothing left and nothing came in.

Foreign interests and nations sailed in and asked or demanded the port cranes and infra-structures as payment for real or imagined debts.

At least the DHS stayed out of the way when the military came and forced those people out of the US.

Two things that was non-negotiable. The Military was going to be funded. The economy was stalling. The main cause for the slowdown was law suits chocking industries and business.

December 17

Dade County Court House, Miami Florida
Harris County Court House, Houston Texas
1000 hours EST and 0900 CST

Court watchers reacted to scenes reminiscent of courts in Europe and the Middle East. Defendants across the spectrum refused lawyer representation. No amount of wasted breath from any judge; defendants ignored court orders forcing them to sit next to lawyers. Earlier last month, defendants started attacking those same lawyers. Some of the assaults occurred in the courtroom.

A favorite tactic was to slide a "karate" chop to the mouth of an unexpecting lawyer. One man knelt over his lawyer and bit down on the man's face, tearing off a chunk.

Now in the court rooms, was a screened off area the defendant was forced to stand in. Since the lawyers could not be attacked, the defendants would start singing or reciting poetry very loudly.

Toward the end of yesterday's session, the defendant in the screened off section said, rather loudly, he had to urinate. The judge said to hold it for 15 minutes. The man watched the clock. At exactly 15 minutes, he opened his jumpsuit and freely urinated in the court.

The only thing the judge could do was sentence the man to one year in jail for contempt of court. The man said, "Thank you judge" as he was led out of the court room. When asked why he did that, he stated that he was looking for jail time. He could now eat regularly.

Minuteman, north of Fort Benton, Montana
0600 hours MST

Miles got an early start this morning driving to the Minuteman site. If he got there early enough, he could enjoy his form of PT. Kendal "took" charge of physical training back at the WSG camp. Her sessions varied on whether or not the club house was properly cleaned and the rooms maintained.

PT started at 5 am and lasted for two hours. Heavy calisthenics for an hour, more or less. Fast and slow runs, both

162

anaerobic and aerobic exercises and runs. Man, can that woman run. Miles knew it had a lot to do with him being old, but he never realized he was in that bad of shape.

The Rabbits remembered her from back at Desert Zero. They figured with snow on the ground, she would not be able to drag them around at the speed of "Oh my God."

Wrong.

Kendal found 10 five-hundred-pound capacity camping and hiking sleds. They were ten feet long and Miles remembered them from up in Alaska during Arctic training. They were normally overloaded and required a squad of at least ten men to drag them around.

Kendal loaded them up with at least two hundred pounds of wood, that they cut down and sectioned for PT one morning. All of it with axes. Miles hands throbbed and spasmed all day long. Today it was dragging the sleds around the compound. One sled, one man. Kendal was obviously leading them around. It was diabolical really. No man was going to admit a girl out did them. Miles' knees throbbed at the thought of dragging that lead sled.

Fortunately, Jones called at 5 am and said he needed the area study. Oh yeah.

Miles remembered one morning when Kendal had everyone do static PT in the building. This was sadistic in itself. Granted there was no freezing outside, so she warmed everyone up and did a free hand stand. She described the exercise on her hands and 'walked' around the room. Of course. her shirt creeped down and exposed her bra, all of it. Kendal did not miss a beat. She kept right on talking everyone through the exercise.

"You little boys just going to stare at my tits and bra or are you going to get with it?"

Locklear chucked. He righted himself from the wall, walked over and tucked in her shirt, front and back.

Miles had to feign displeasure, but he knew the men would never forget PT.

Miles had a smile on his face as he pulled in the compound. He went into the headquarters, put the Area Study into the Colonel's in-box. He then joined everyone in saluting the flag and did some more traditional PT.

December 19

Room D-113, George Washington University Hospital, Washington D.C.
1400 hours EST

Kincaid looked up and smiled at the interruption. Dennis walked in with a bag of goodies. In their time, it was called "Pogy bait". This definition was food given to prisoners by family or slaves. The food was or was not something he would like. Lately it was non-meal food like potato chips, cookies, cakes or anything that tasted so good and had no real food value.

"What's going on?" John asked.

"Christmas, next week," Dennis said. "I spent all day looking for something to get Brenda for Christmas. So far all I have shown for it is sore feet."

"This is what I did," John said. "I watched Karen a lot. I let my mind go vacant and thought of nothing. If you go vacant, suddenly what is there is the thing she will love you for. Here," John passed him an electronic tablet.

Dennis took the electronic tablet and saw something he never would have believed possible. It was a large recliner, large enough to fit two people comfortably. It had vibration, heat and a rocking function. Reclining was also on the remote control.

"I was thinking of a rocking chair, but both of us like to cuddle a lot." Dennis's face lit up and then saw the price tag. "Can't afford it."

"It's bought already. Should be there on Monday or Tuesday."

Dennis tried to word something.

"Thanks for the pogy bait. Your lady will be home soon and dinner needs to be ready." Kincaid ignored him and looked in the bag. Yumm, Yumm.

1900 hours EST

Jones called with a non-problem. "How are you doing?"

"Bored, and plotting my escape," Kincaid said, putting the ear piece in his ear.

"You have your ear buds in?" Jones asked.

"Yeah," Kincaid said, now worried.

"Just a command problem I wanted to talk to you about." Jones sounded like someone died.

Kincaid decided to be silent and draw out the problem.

"Kendal and Locklear are sleeping together,"

Kincaid could not help himself. He burst out in almost hysterical laughter. A nurse looked in on Kincaid. He pointed to the X-Berry. "Outstanding and about time," Kincaid said.

Jones regretted telling Kincaid. "I called you for advice. Fraternization is a problem. Kendal is the only woman besides Cindy Morgan. I foresee problems."

"Bring both of them into your office and lay down the law. No kissy, touchy, no love making in public. Keep it professional. See that simple."

Jones did not want to believe it was that simple. Then again that was his specialty. "When do you get out of the hospital?"

Kincaid sighed. "The doctors say I can discharge late next month. Probably in rehabilitation all next year."

Jones chuckled. "Sounds like you are benched for a long time."

Kincaid said it for him. "Benched forever. I remembered Mike's x-rays and the medical file I was never supposed to see. I am worse than he was. I'll never deploy again."

"Is your head, ok?" Jones asked.

"Yes, anything else?" Kincaid said.

"Dennis getting you the goodies?"

"Yes," he said.

"Bye," Jones said and hung up.

December 20

Minuteman, North Fort Benton, Montana
1300 hours MST

Jones called ahead and told Kendal and Locklear to report to him today at this time.

Both of them beamed as they reported. Jones returned the salute and motioned to the chairs.

Jones began. "This is the most uncomfortable conversation I have ever had as a commander. I do request that you do not snicker or laugh so that I can move on."

Both Kendal and Locklear remained neutral; waiting for whatever.

"Getting to the point of this meeting," Jones said. "I am told that both of you are conducting a sexual relationship."

Both of them remained neutral.

Finally, Kendal said, "Yes sir".

"Yes sir", Locklear said.

Jones let the silence hang. "I trust that both of you are behaving yourself in public?"

"Yes sir," both of them said.

Jones took a deep breath. "I am clearly uncomfortable with this discussion. It may be odd to you, but I am not going to have any problems because you too are free to exercise your right to the pursuit of happiness." Jones paused. The silence between them was easily felt. "If that is not a problem. Thank you."

Kendal and Locklear stood, saluted and left Jones' office. Outside the office on the opposite side of the building, both of them stopped and looked at each other.

"I'm confused," Locklear said.

"You like the sex?" Kendal said.

"Yes," Locklear said with a big smile.

Kendal smiled and pointed to Cindy Morgan's home. "I wonder if she is home. I would like to see how she would like it when someone uses her bed."

Locklear held her arm and stopped her. "You want to open that can of worms."

"A woman loves her underwear." She leaned in his direction. "I'll just use her fears about becoming a lesbian against her."

"You can't become a lesbian like catching a cold." Locklear said catching up to her. "Besides we have work to do first. If you have any diabolical ideas, can they wait until after work?"

"Can I get a massage tonight?"

Locklear said "OK."

"We are still staying here all night." Wendy said.

Pentagon, Washington. D.C.
1500 hours EST

Hawker looked at the clock on the wall. The weekend was coming. The half day schedule started on Monday. Being a General Officer's aide meant that normal leave schedules and time off was a thing of the past. An aide was always at the mercy of the General's schedule and whims.

Her parents were coming this year. The General said she wanted a lot of peace and quiet, so hopefully nothing in the world would happen until January the 6th.

Hawker raced through the week, ensuring nothing was left undone. She did not wait on anything. Except the Lieutenant Colonel promotion list. It was some kind of secret. She knew she was not even on the list. With only a year time-in-grade, she needed to wait three more years to "come into the zone". Still, she wanted to start looking at it.

December 21

Bonnie Chandler, Box 234, Route 17, Belcher, Missouri
1600 hours CST

Dear Bonnie.

Halleluiah, school is out for two weeks. Officially, the holidays start Monday, but today is Saturday and I am free until Monday, January 6. Mom and Dad loosened their leash on me and allowed me to attend some parties and visit friends. Lately I have been watching the news with my parents. Some of the weird and wild things they had obsessing about is playing out around the country.

People are rioting for food, fuel and any number of things they cannot longer afford. Crimes such as murder, rape, theft and everything else is on the rise.

I apologized to Dad for not paying attention during shooting classes. I asked him to re-teach me how to shoot and I promised I would pay attention.

I have been taking the time to remember and document how much more it costs for the same thing as time goes on. My parents are right. Soon it will cost too much to eat.

December 22

Room D-113, George Washington University Hospital, Washington D.C.
1900 hours EST

Kincaid went to take a shower. He was happy that he could do everything in the shower without a chorus or having to call for help. Gone were the days when someone else would wipe his ass and take a shower with others scrubbing him. The long mirror, on the back side of door, showed him the truth of being shot five times at point blank range.

He remembered turning the corner after the grenade detonated. For the first time since going through training, there was David Nichols. Both of them raised their pistols and started shooting. Why didn't he go for a head shot? Maybe he was rattled. Kincaid remembered aiming for his head as he went down. Kincaid refused to admit he had PTSD. These stupid asshole Social Workers do not have any point of reference. If he was going to work it out, then it was going to be with someone who understood.

Kincaid shook off the thoughts and was finally ready for that phone call. In January, he would ventilate his head. Kincaid did make another decision. It was time to retire.

Kincaid opened the phone and dialed the number he leaned on too heavily over the years.

"Yes, John," Hector Adams said.

"If you have some time, I need to talk to you in January at your leisure."

"Of course," Hector said, pumping his fist overhead. "I have some time. After the 1st."

They both went through some small talk before hanging up. Kincaid felt a lot better.

168

Hector Adams looked at the phone. He prayed hard that John would call. He had known a lot of men how had trouble remembering too vividly. His PTSD therapy was teaching everyone how to remember.

Holiday Inn, Baltimore Maryland
2200 hours EST.

Joe Sharpe waited on the bed for John Beckman and Roy Seagrave to arrive.

Exactly on the hour, there was a knock on the door. Sharpe opened the door and smiled as both men entered. John entered and let Roy close the door.

Joe Sharpe said it. "The Black Elves are no more. From eighty-one to the three of us. It is time to separate and lead long lives." Sharpe pointed to two bags. "The tags have your names on them. You have cash to the tune of one hundred and fifty thousand dollars. There is a folder showing the account numbers, passwords and banks that have twelve and a half million dollars total on deposit."

"What if I don't want to quit," Roy Seagrave said. "What about Kincaid and O'Cleary. Don't we have to fulfill the contract?"

"Your life is your own," Joe Sharpe said. He picked up his smaller bag and walked out. "Do as you please."

"It's time to leave Roy," John Beckman said. He picked up his bag and left.

Roy Seagrave thought about leaving Kincaid alive. That man killed Martin Hernandez. Martin taught him everything he knew. Kincaid had to pay for killing his brother. Then again Martin told him there had to be a point where you had to quit. 'Pride is a fool's burden'. 'Sometimes something is not worth the effort'.

Roy grabbed his bag and left. He wondered how much it cost to live in Tahiti.

December 24

Quinton Ranch, Hinton, Albert, Canada
0700 hours (Tango)

Dearest Amanda

Part of your letter made my heart jump into my chest. I have worried a lot about you being someplace I could not protect you directly. These fools here keep trying to pump me for information about your location. I did lose my temper when those idiots asked me the same questions, I swear, seven different times.

Lately, I just refuse to talk to them. The joys of the Fifth Amendment show our founder's wisdom. Sometimes I wonder how these clowns ever catch any criminals.

Around here the bed I share with you is very cold. Not having you around, I declare is terrible. After a lot of soul searching, I will not tell you to stay away. You have to know that you and I will be tugged in separate directions. I can almost feel the sharks licking their teeth.

I love you, my wife. The only consolation during this separation is all the pictures we have of each other. From our wedding, the early years, pregnancies, raising two children, pushing them out the door and our later years.

The oil in this pot was me wearing a uniform. You have a lot of pictures without me or you. Sometimes, it is just the kids.

My term as Chairman is over next June. Granted there is no other slot for a Five Star, I cannot see any other place for me hugging you.

Want to enjoy retirement on June the First?
XXOOXXOO Thomas

489 Glenmore Drive, Alexandria Virginia
1800 hours EST

Betty and Allan Hawker enjoyed the holidays with their daughter. Elizabeth was always a prodigy of sorts. Her desire to join the Army was a surprise, but she was happy and that was all that counts.

A ring at the door surprised them. It was General O'Cleary in full uniform. Hawker opened the door to a hard faced General. O'Cleary looked at her. "Come in Ma'am. Meet my parents."

O'Cleary walked inside and halted at the dining room. Being next door, the layout was the same as her house next door.

O'Cleary turned and faced Hawker with a bulging expansion folder. "Major, you failed to finish this work this week. I called the Secretary and talked him into an extension until next week. If you get started now, we might be finished in time. Please get into uniform."

Hawker tried to mouth something. Instead, she left and walked into her bedroom.

O'Cleary smiled and looked at Hawker's astonished parents. She pulled a black velvet box out of her purse, opened it and showed them two silver oak leaves. O'Cleary put a finger to her lips. "Sssssshhh."

Five minutes later, Hawker walked out.

"Hawker, do you have any idea how embarrassing it was to hear that something happened without my knowledge. I am supposed know everything. Yet you allowed this," she held out an imposing expansion folder. "You see this mistake, Major. Mister and Missus Hawker did you agree that this is not what a Major is supposed to do."

Hawker looked between O'Cleary and her parents. Suddenly, she turned to O'Cleary and froze in place. Her anger at this happening in front of her parents on Christmas day almost over whelmed her.

O'Cleary put the folder on the table and motioned behind her. O'Cleary went to her right side and her parents went to the left side.

"Major Hawker, I corrected the problem of your original promotion to Major when you were selected to Major. The Army had promoted her two years earlier, yet she was not notified. So, the action of the Lieutenant Colonel selection board has determined that you meet all the criteria for selection to the rank of Lieutenant Colonel. Your date of rank and effective date is January 1st. Besides, regulations allow me to have a Lieutenant Colonel as an Aide. I can now blow off the personnel managers."

O'Cleary pined on the right oak leaf and her parents pined on the left side.

Sergeant Major O'Cleary appeared out of nowhere with a camera. He took several photos. He left behind a bottle of champagne and waited outside. O'Cleary pulled out the orders from the expansion folder and laid them on the table.

"General," Lieutenant Colonel Hawker said. "What is in the folder?"

"Blank ream of paper," she said. "Mister and Missus Hawker, Lieutenant Colonel, it is Christmas and I shall take my leave." O'Cleary bowed slightly and left.

December 25

485 Glenmore Drive, Alexandria Virginia
1500 hours EST

Edwards came by partially for Christmas and maybe an answer to a question. His house was full of Marshal and Elizabeth's families. A mischief of laughter and rambunctious playing ran rampant throughout the house. At his house, the order of the day was Christmas, Christmas and nothing but Christmas.

Christmas was the order of the day for the Pentagon. He detailed that a skeleton crew was to remain behind. Everyone who was on duty was to be given compensatory time in January; PERIOD.

Edwards picked up a stack of presents and three envelopes he was to take there.

"Dad," Elizabeth said. "Can't you get someone to deliver them?"

"I have never and will never tell someone to do my work for me," Edwards said.

He drove over to Dennis's house and was about to knock on the door when it opened for him. "You could have brought them over yesterday or called me."

"Something came up yesterday," Edwards said lugging the wrapped presents inside and placing them around the tree.

Edwards declined the offer of some un-spiked eggnog. He whirled his finger over his head.

Dennis sighed and started the sound system. The levels were adjusted and the appropriate lights lit up. Satisfied, he turned around and sat down.

Edwards took a deep breath. "I'll get to the point so Christmas can proceed. Amanda wants to come home and I am mad I wanted her to leave in the first place. They want to control me; I say bring it."

"Second and last thing. My term is up in June. I can stay around for three or four more months if need be." Edwards starred hard at Brenda. "I am looking at my replacement. One to ten, A to Z. You are it. You know you are the only one smart enough to fight off the outsiders."

Edwards set down a velvet box with two sets of five silver stars in a circle.

Brenda looked at the box and burst into tears. She got up and walked down the hallway to her bedroom.

"Thanks Tom," Dennis said with annoyance. "See yourself out."

Minuteman, north of Fort Benton, Montana
1900 hours MST

Cindy sat down and looked at the wedding photo of her and Zach on the wall. Cindy thought of all the Christmas's she shared with the love of her life.

Cindy took a sip of brandy. That was their drink of choice for the holidays. Most of the time, she passed out and Zach "had his way with her." Invariably, she always woke up as he was peeling the clothes off her. Cindy always wore the most complicated thing she could find. No sense making it easy for him.

She remembered one year she found this 1940's era body shaper. Shit it was uncomfortable. Cindy laid there for nearly an hour, trying not to laugh as Zach tried to unwrap her. Finally, he gave up and found a pair of scissors. Cindy "woke" before Zach stabbed her. She needed to go to the bathroom anyway.

This Christmas was probably the last one in the country where she was borne and sacrificed.

Kendal relaxed in her room as Locklear gave her a special massage. She wore his preferred nightwear. Earl was not impressed with the Frederick's of Hollywood stuff. Her sports bra and well fitted panties was more his taste. Wendy loved his tightee whitees.

Right now, she held up her leg vertically as Earl lightly stimulated her skin. Earl went up and down until the skin started to cool down and the leg shook from blood loss. Then there was the other leg. Earl worked her over until she was ready for anything.

Both of them were nude. It was Christmas eve. They both wanted something just for them. Not exactly sex. Both wanted to feel like they belonged some place. Both came from foster homes and places best to leave at the first instance. Neither wanted to talk about it. Wendy told her story to Father Mike after the Merchantax incident. When Wendy started telling, she felt physical pain but could not stop until it was all out. The pain in her abdomen was so great, she screamed.

Father Mike knew that type of pain. He had seen it before. Wendy was programmed to suppress the memories. The pain finally apexed and Wendy collapsed. Father Mike held her until she suddenly woke up at 4 am. She dried the tears from her face and ran into the bathroom. Two hours later, Wendy came out, happy and free.

Since returning to the Werewolves, Wendy had wondered about being a lesbian. The urge to go after women, slowly but steadily went away. Time slowly, eased its grip on the memories. It was two drunken couples who drugged her and abused her, time after time. This went on for over a year until Wendy ran away. Wendy could never understand why they did what they did. Wendy believed no man would ever want her.

Earl laid down next to her. Wendy hugged him, trying to squeeze all the air from between them. Wendy cried, thanking God for forgiving her and making her a woman.

She reached up and kissed Earl. "Merry Christmas Sir. Will you marry me?"

December 26

US Geological Survey, Reston Virginia
0127 hours EST

Alarm bells and computer tones rang with Moment Magnitude readings east of Japan. They measured between 4.5 and 5.1. A long string of quakes rumbled along the Japan Trench, 160 kilometers east of Honshu, ten kilometers below the surface of the Pacific.

What was most ominous was that the rumblings suddenly stopped. There was not a lessening of the quakes or other quakes in a string along the fault line. The quakes suddenly stopped. Everyone in the room tensed.

Max Terran reached over and grabbed the phone to Japan. Chances are they already knew this. Was it a prelude?

December 29

485 Glenmore Drive, Alexandria, Virginia
1000 hours EST

Brenda O'Cleary thanked God for the world behaving itself. She had picked up a new habit of late. After leaving the shower, she turned to the side and wanted to see a bulge in her belly. She watched each day. "Come on boy," she said.

Dennis came in and quietly watched her. He was fascinated at the process of making children. He was going to be sixty-four when his son was borne. His dad was that old when he joined the Army. Dennis would be eighty-two when that boy turned 18.

"You are fond of watching an old woman display her nudity," she said.

"Any one would. For a forty-six-year-old, you still have it and I love to gawk."

"I have a suggestion," she said. "I look at myself and talk to myself and our son like he was an 'it'. I suggest we name him Arthur Thomas O'Cleary and call him that."

Dennis felt like crying. He took her hand kissed it.

Minuteman, north of Fort Benton, Montana
1100 hours MST

Father Michael Thomas looked up from his breviary when someone knocked on the door. He opened it up and saw Wendy Kendal and Earl Locklear standing there. He had a vague idea of what they would want, but it was a long shot.

"Come in out of the cold," he said, stepping out of the way. A plastic mat over an absorbent mat was available as a "mud area" to remove coats and shoes when you arrived.

"Thank you," Wendy said and stood by the couch, waiting for Earl and Father Mike. She waited until Father Mike indicated the coach.

"Father Mike," Wendy said, almost giddy. "Earl and I want to get married. Will you marry us?"

Mike pulled out his sash, kissed it and draped it around his neck. "Getting married is a process. I know you want to get married now, but I have a requirement to ensure you are ready."

Both of them looked at each other and nodded. "Yes Sir," they said.

"Mister Locklear," Mike said. "You normally ask the father for permission. In this case, you should ask Colonel Jones for that permission."

Earl screwed his face. "Father Mike, we wanted to keep this low key."

Mike was not going to make this too easy. "You cannot marry a woman and keep it a secret."

"Who do I ask?" Wendy interrupted.

"I guess that would be Linda Jones,"

Wendy's smile inverted.

December 30

0900 hours MST

Thaddeus and Linda Jones just returned last night from visiting their adult children and grandchildren in one of the newer communities north of Minuteman. Both of them were enjoying the reduced tension and fewer problems between the holidays.

Then there was a knock at the door.

"Colonel, Missus Jones, can we talk to you?" Earl asked.

"Please come in," Linda said, cutting off her husband.

Wendy and Earl carefully removed their boots and coats in the mud area. Both wanted to start the meeting on a good note. Linda sat them down on the couch and went to get the coffee. They made small talk until the coffee was served.

"I assume you have something important to say," Jones said. He feared his quiet day was not going to stay that way.

"Thad," Linda said.

Jones furrowed his brow. "What?"

Earl started the conversation. "Sir, I wish to request your permission and the permission of Missus Jones for Wendy and I to get married."

Jones felt like someone threw a grenade in his lap. "You are asking for our permission to marry?"

"Yes sir," Wendy said. "You are the father figure so Earl is asking you to act as my father and Miss Linda to act as my mother. Simple really."

Linda looked at her husband of thirty-three years. He was just as dumbfounded as she was. After gawking at each other, Linda stood, took Wendy by the arm and went into the kitchen. Earl stood, confused.

That short-circuited a lot of questions Thad had. "Sit-down Earl," Thad said. "You thought this out. I mean all of it."

"Yes sir," Earl said.

Jones shifted in his seat. "That is the woman you fought sometimes physically over everything. This is the woman who assaulted you over INSANE JANE. This is the woman who made you come to me and Mister Kincaid for permission to shot her."

"Yes Sir," Earl said. "We solved those problems."

Jones sat there. 'Why me God', he thought to himself. "This is not 60 years ago, when you needed my permission. Why are you asking me?"

Earl sat up. "Sir, we already received counseling from Father Mike. He said it was required to ask her father and she needed to get permission from her mother. We do not have any families. You and Mrs. Jones are the closest thing we have to senior family members. Your permission and sanction are required."

Jones wanted to choke Mike for throwing this grenade to him. Jones leaned forward. "Lean forward and look me in the eye." Both men came to within 12 inches of each other's face. "Earl, getting married is not something you can take back. If you do get married, one of you will not deploy again if she gets pregnant. Once the baby is borne, that becomes permanent." Jones turned his face hard. "Earl, a good woman is gift that any real man should thank God for. But" he paused, "if one or both of you does not have the discipline to live up to your vows, then misery is what you have earned."

Earl returned the hard look. "Sir, I only know that some kind of something special occurred between us. I don't know everything, but I'm willing to try. We are not being coy about likes and dislikes. We both already found out what we like and dislike. All in all, I think we have it figured out already."

Jones suppressed an urge to laugh.

Linda Jones was having an interesting time with Wendy Kendal. "Wendy, I have seen you publicly dedicate your life to being a lesbian. And once you even tried to seduce me. Now, you want to marry a man. Explain to me why you are changing your mind."

"In my earlier life," Wendy said, extending her hand. Linda warily shook the hand. "The short story is that I was raped repeatedly by two couples when I was a foster kid. Playing with women eased the memories. Father Mike helped me see through the pain. When the fog cleared, Earl was there. He was the first man who treated me like a woman. I fell in love with him as a result. No matter how evil I was, Earl was there. Now I want to marry him so at least one man will love me. And yes, I want to know about loving a man."

Linda looked at her. "Your life style means one of you will no longer fight. Especially when you get pregnant. You thought of that?"

"I will stay behind," Wendy said. "We decided that already."

Linda stood and placed two hands on Wendy's head. She said a short prayer. "I grant permission," she said, looking over to her husband. Both of them were looking at her expectantly. Linda gave a thumbs up.

Wendy screeched and ran to Earl. She jumped up and wrapped herself around him; arms and legs. He staggered, but did not fall.

"Big or small wedding?" Linda asked.

"Small and cheap," Earl said.

"Colonel, Sir, I need a distinguished gentleman to give me away," Wendy asked. "And of course, Miss Linda, can you be my Maid of Honor?"

"Matron of Honor," Linda said, beaming.

Jones knew he was outvoted. He reached over and shook Earl's hand. "May God have mercy on your soul."

December 31

Room D-113, George Washington University Hospital, Washington D.C.
0400 hours EST

Kincaid was deep into REM sleep. Over and over in his dreams, he saw the grenade, grabbed a vase and threw it at the grenade. The grenade dropped and a second later it detonated. An old trick was to put his right ear into his shoulder and plug his left ear with a finger. The blast did not destroy his hearing or balance. He jumped up and in the slowest of motion he rounded the corner and came face to face with David Nichols.

Kincaid's pistol started blowing holes in Nichols and Nichols' pistol was blowing holes in him. One bullet, two bullets, three bullets, four bullets, and then five. Kincaid's pistol hit Nichols once, twice, three times and as Nichols started to fall down, Kincaid shot him in the head.

Kincaid went unconscious.

Every night, it was the same. The nurses said he was breathing so heavily he finally hyperventilated and quit. He was quiet for two or three hours. Then it started over again. He never called out.

The doctor refused to give him something until he got counseling. Kincaid dismissed him. Father Hector was coming.

Next month, he was finished with hospital. He had to admit they were the best hospital and staff he ever seen. Some of the things in life, you have to do without kids that believed they were better than sixty years of experience.

US Geological Survey, Reston, Virginia
1300 hours EST

All the operators were watching the events near Japan. Seismometers were recording something sounding like a grinding noise.

One of the kids said. "Could this be two shelves stuck together and grinding under pressure and cannot relieve the pressure.

Many more theories jumped around. Nobody knew what was happening or what or how.

January 1

Room D-113, George Washington University Hospital, Washington, D.C.
1000 hours EST

Kincaid awoke covered in sweat. It showed that he was not sleeping well. Five successive times in the last two weeks, psychiatric social workers attempted to get him to open up. All of them were pre-briefed by the nursing staff. He had no less than two episodes a night.

Yet Jonathon T. Kincaid, Command Sergeant Major, United States Army and a decorated veteran, refused to allow anyone inside his head. Every attempt to talk to him was met with stony silence.

Yet this morning, Monsignor Hector Adams, a Catholic priest in the service of God and the bridge between man and

180

God, walked up to the door and entered without asking anyone, without saying anything to anyone or knocking.

The nurses noticed the Priest enter and walked over to check on things. They opened the door to see both men shaking hands. Kincaid was actually smiling and all traces of his surly attitude vanished.

"Ladies," Kincaid said. "Can the Priest and I have some privacy?"

The nurses smiled and closed the door.

"Forgive me Father for I have sinned. I cannot remember the last time I confessed."

Hector, pulled out his sash, kissed it and put it around his neck. He then softly squeezed John's hand. "Yes, my son. God is here and so am I."

Tears fell out of Kincaid's eyes. "I was so scared. That fear visits me every night. It is a demon that screams at me. I keep rounding the corner and seeing David Nichols. We recognized each other as the shooting starts. Everything is in slow motion. I feel each bullet separately hit me. I desperately shot him back. We hit the ground together. He was about to shoot me again, but I pulled the trigger first. His head exploded as I lost consciousness."

Hector held John's hand. Hector placed his right hand on John's face. "May I pray for you?"

"Please," John said.

Hector leaned over and whispered the prayers John needed to hear. John had to forgive himself. John had to protect the others. John had to protect the innocent people in the house. John needed to understand that the incident was in the past. He needed to put it in the proper place.

An hour later, John was sound asleep with a contented smile on his face. Hector knew he had at least a few hours before John awoke. This next time was crucial. If God gives him the right things and prayers to say, John will be alright.

Hector walked out of the room and walked past the nursing station. One of them asked if everything was alright. "Yes, my child, John will be fine."

Hector needed coffee and some privacy to call General O'Cleary. He sighed walking along.

Hector drove to his hotel room. He was tired. God's children with PTSD were the hardest of God's children to work with. The very nature of PTSD had them stuck in one moment in time. That moment in time could be repeated several times a day or spread out across months. No two people ever worked through it the same.

One of his charges' solutions was to sit at the coffee house on Saturday mornings with other former military service men and exchange stupid stories about things they all did when they were young.

Hector needed to relax without being interrupted by well-wishing friends worrying about John and needing reassurance.

Hector muted the phone, took a shower and went to sleep.

Number 17, US Naval Observatory, Washington, D.C.
2100 Hours EST

Dear Thomas

If you want to retire, go for it. I will honestly admit that I wanted you to retire after your Afghanistan adventure. I was never so scared in my life. Though you were declared missing several times in the past, I never worried like I did that particular time. Counsel your soul and decide for the right reasons whether or not to stay.

I caution you not to drag Brenda into this insane decision. You said she was pregnant. Well, let me tell you something a thick-headed man will never understand. Being pregnant changes a woman. Not just the physical things, but in her heart. Listen to her heart. She is a great officer because her heart is totally in it. Now that she is a mother, her heart is divided in ways no man can ever understand.

Listen to her heart's song as you have listened to mine. I will admit a woman wearing five stars will give millions of women something new to reach for. She is that strong. No woman wants to be pregnant at or near 50. It was hard for me when I carried Elizabeth.

P.S. Clean the house, I am coming home.

January 2

Room D-113, George Washington University Hospital, Washington, D.C.
1000 hours EST

Hector Adams was in a foul mood as he touched the door to John Kincaid's room. Evidentially, the word went out to the social workers that John was in a better mood and they wanted to "get into the act".

Years of experience taught him that unless they were forty years or older, those social workers created more problems with their book ideas than fixed the problems. It was hard sometimes to tell the truth to people.

He had to remind them, repeatedly, that the seal of confession was more absolute than their patient confidentiality seal.   Adams rightfully guessed that they forgot that sometimes. One little girl wanted his "notes" to put them in his "file".

Adams touched the door, closed his eyes and said a prayer before entering.

Texas Capital Building, Austin Texas
1000 hours CST

The first Thursday of each month, for the foreseeable future, the governments of Texas and Oklahoma set aside this day to meet and coordinate activities between their states. They effectively dissolved their mutual border; militarily and for law enforcement. Subsequent meetings throughout the month would be conducted at lower governmental levels. The meetings at the first of the month would be reserved for formal acceptance.

Washington observers were relegated to secondary seating. The Washington persons were upset at being denied omniscient status.

Congress of the United States, Washington D.C.
1000 hours EST

The Vice-President stood at the podium in the Senate and the Speaker of the House stood at his podium. Both of them gaveled their chambers into session. This session before the Presidential elections promised to be unproductive and contentious.

1300 hours EST

Congressional party members immediately started the cat fights over committee assignments. Normally it was a straightforward process between the Democrats and Republicans. The party who has the majority, stocked their members on each committee with a majority of their members and the minority party filled in whatever blank spots were left. Even if there was an even number of each party, the majority remained the same as well as the chairmanship of the committee.

Now that the Freedom and Patriot party had members, the status quo no longer held sway. Last year, they were told to stay out of the way. When votes came up on crucial highway and other bills, their votes were requested as a formality. The majority party lost those bills. No amount of cohersion or useless promises were accepted. They were individually promised a host of things in the past and the promises were forgotten as soon as the vote was cast.

Halfway through last year, the Freedom Party united as voted as one block. No promises were accepted. All of them rebelled as they ground their opponents to dust. Their anger was evident in the political ads and newspapers.

Senior Republican and Democratic party members now had to spend time and money that "was better spent elsewhere".

Each House and Senate member sat on no less than three committees. That arrangement insured no member had a clear picture of any situation. Those two parties now had to curry favor with them. Their overall vote for some pieces of legislation either guaranteed success or failure to pass the legislation.

January 4

Underground Station "Conscience", World Wide Web and Channel 513
0900 hours EST.

"If you threaten, act. If you say something, do it. If something is important, stand your ground. Governments are often hamstrung by individuals who have opinions about issues they feel strongly about. This is Martin Socranson, self-proclaimed philosopher who says, 'What are we if we can't back up what you say'?"

"Greetings America" Martin Socranson said beginning his broadcast. "It is reluctantly Saturday and I say thus." In the background the sounds of the 1812 overture played.

"Yesterday, America, your so-called leaders in Congress convened. They were supposed to be working on the People's business and trying to aid the population as anarchy rules the streets. Infighting over seats, committees or power plays and personal acquisitions rule the day. Their first and only priority is the next election."

"Roving gangs of individuals are attacking law-abiding citizens; stealing food, weapons, electronics or anything of value. It is becoming too dangerous for the elderly to leave their home and shop for life-saving prescription drugs or even food. Gangs of thieves are accosting the elderly by charging an additional tax on those same drugs or food. If the tax cannot be paid, their purchases are confiscated until the tax was paid, maybe."

"Where are the police? The criminals have more civil rights than regular citizens. News coverage show the gangs openly accosting the elderly and the police were just begging the gangs to leave them alone."

"Are we stupid! We are now seeing the side of the Constitution that our founders wanted to protect us from.

British royalty and nobility wrote their own rules and interpretations of the King's laws and pronouncements. 250 years later, we are back to what started this."

"I NOW SAY THIS! It is time for the lawyers, and don't forget the media, to suffer equally. Lawyers want misery and rampant crime. Without re-cycled crime, they would not have a well-paid job. They write the rules. They are worse than the British leaders during the revolution. Who arrests the criminal's criminal?"

"Criminals are treated like victims in a court of Law. As you all know, there is no justice in a court of law."

"The Media is worse. They fan the fires of discontent for the sake of ratings. If the news is not bad enough, find the right actors to make a story fizzle. They hide as many criminals behind the First Amendment as "serving the ultimate good". They swoop down on the misery of a mother holding her dead child. They swoop down on an elderly couple who were beaten for a cancer drug or a bag of groceries."

"This country is turning against them. Soon they will be on the news as bloody victims because they will not be able to make the criminals look better. I say it is about time."

"America, we are trying to stop a bloody Civil War. Civil Wars happen when the government no longer speaks for, or protects the population. People start shooting when they are scared. All you have to do to stop a Civil War is talk to your neighbor. You are not the only one who is scared. You are not the only one who looks at your few possessions and want to protect your home."

"OK America, it is time to make a decision. Make it a good one."

January 6

Enroute to the Pentagon, Washington D.C.
0730 hours EDT

O'Cleary smiled at the familiar vibration of her X-Berry. She smiled knowing that UNSTACK THIS only called at this time. O'Cleary typed in her code and said:
"Secure."

[Valkyrie, all secure and counter surveillance is in place. We are secure.]

"Yes," she typed.

[There are three remaining Black Elves. They are identified as Joe Sharpe, Roy Seagrove and John Beckman. Joe Sharpe, and John Beckman have left the country enroute to Formosa. All three have bank accounts in that country. Roy Seagrove is still within the United States. He is attempting to return some of his money to US banks.]

O'Cleary sat there and absorbed every word. Her anger rose and then suddenly went away.

O'Cleary typed. "Use my codes. Notify Jones and order him to find this Roy Seagrove and interrogate him thoroughly. Add Kendal to the team if he agrees. I gave her my word she could go along. Do not put her in command. Finally, and most important, seize and hold their funds. Watch their movements from the banks."

O'Cleary put away the phone and wanted an end to the death and dying. She thought of the five-star rank Edwards left in her home. Decades of experience said that open warfare was inevitable. Maybe Amanda was right. She said to Edwards that they both should be together no matter what.

O'Cleary fingered her rings and looked at the bump on her lower belly. Dennis said he was going to get certified to be her armed security agent. The Pentagon Security Police had to take him seriously. He was going to guard his pregnant wife. PERIOD. Brenda O'Cleary loved her man.

Minuteman, north of Fort Benton, Montana
0530 hours MST

Jones woke up to the vibrating X-Berry. He read the message twice and called O'Cleary to confirm it. Jones thought about Kendal. Locklear would not launch on this mission. Never deploy married or engaged couples. He had experience with that in the past. The couples tended to worry more about their partner than the mission and then they miss something that kills others.

This was a 'snatch and grab' mission and Taylor was the resident expert. Morgan will go along with McPherson and

Mejia. They were an experienced team. That counted. Adding Kendal was not a factor.

Those Black Elves have been a pain for far too long. Every time we thought they were finished, they re-surfaced. That attack on Desert Zero was a prime reminder to hunt them down any chance they surfaced. Jones would give a year's pay to find out how they disappeared so efficiently.

Jones thought about how to proceed. According to O'Cleary, all the new information was being transferred to him. Additionally, a link to an NSA site was established that would give him all the information immediately and constantly update as the situation continued.

Jones put on his uniform. He needed to get ahead of this now. He kissed Linda on the way out. Enroute to his headquarters, he called Taylor, Morgan, Mejia, McPherson and Kendal, telling them to come here, immediately. Taylor and company would likely arrive on or about 8 am.

Jones had to have a mission concept ready when they arrived. Jones took out a blank Mission Concept and stopped at the blank space for a name. He penciled in the name "Bluebaker." He loved that movie.

Congress, Washington, D.C.
0900 hours EST

The Political Parties had told everyone to behave themselves. The Media was already finding and reporting on the infighting all the political parties typically work through. This time though, the one Patriot Party member was not going to be silent. Refused is a more apt word.

James Astrum, from the great state of New Hampshire, refused to sit in the back. The old rule where freshmen are seen and not heard, went out the window. He let it be known that he was here to be one of New Hampshire's Congressmen and his only focus was his constituents and the things his constituents wanted.

Astrum kept his list of things New Hampshire wanted in his coat pocket. Astrum would be known for looking at the blue list before making his vote. He looked at it and decided whether or not it helped New Hampshire. If it did not, he

188

voted against it. He had a web site that listed all the items up for his vote. Large and small, he voted the way his constituents wanted.

Astrum actually listed what his vote was going to be beforehand, in case something came up that he was not told about.

Freedom Party members promised grid-lock on the House Floor at vote time if not given several important committee seats.

Republican and Democrat power brokers rubbed the headaches they shared.

January 7

J. Edgar Hoover Building, Washington D.C.
0900 hours EST

The Director of the FBI, Marcus Solin picked up the monthly report of criminal activity for the month of December. This nation was tearing itself apart. It was all the government's fault. Solin could say that; hidden in his office.

All criminal activity was on the upswing. Murders, kidnappings, bank robberies, thefts and any other crime just kept happening. Slowly the numbers just kept rising each month.

Newer categories were being added. The newest headache was militias and states forming mutual defense pacts. That had ramifications all over the map. Everywhere in America, citizens revolted against Judges for allowing criminals to escape the law and deny justice. Rapists had to be wrapped in body armor prior to conviction. Once convicted, police had to provide additional armed escorts for the convict's movement to the prison. As usual, rapists were put in isolation otherwise they were killed or castrated in general population.

A lot of the time, the police had to race to the scene to rescue criminals. In a lot of situations, if a criminal was caught by the citizens, he or she were beaten severely or killed. Police in some cases were reprimanded for slowly walking up to crime scenes. In one Texas county, some people who were beating up a man who was already arrested four times for burglary. The local judge kept releasing him on bail.

Texas and Oklahoma merged their police departments. They started closing off highways coming into TX/OK from the west. The TX/OK Department of Public Safety was auditing for citizenship and driver's licenses. When a Federal Judge ruled this was unconstitutional, the DPS simply ignored them, stating that the Federal Law Enforcement had repeatedly ignored judicial orders in numerous areas.

The DOJ kept trying to sue states into lock-step with them. States keep fighting back. Polls indicate the people believe the DOJ is more interested in politics than Justice.

Solin kept shaking his head at the notion academics have about human nature. None of those clowns in the DOJ can fathom why the people were fighting back.

Solin flipped to the Mexico report. At least in Texas, drug and human trafficking was down. Texas was taking proactive action and stopping movement into their areas. They made a huge dent despite left wing lawyers trying to stop them. "The wall" worked so long as someone was watching it.

The cartels had a new lease on life now that the Army discontinued the "Savage Rabbits." Solin thought that the Military had the same political-in-house problems the Bureau had. That unit was the only anti-drug program that worked. Lower management tug-of-war finally drove a stake through its heart.

The cartels are now openly scoffing at the idea of fighting the American military. Small fast, lighting strikes in Mexico gave way to large, cumbersome and ineffective actions. Seizures of drugs and arrests of key players has dropped.

Ever since the demise of the Savage Rabbits, several efforts were made to improve the situation. The DOJ even trying to "ride along" on the missions. Their presence actually hindered them.

Solin penciled a note to reestablish the Savage Rabbits.

Minuteman, north of Fort Benton, Montana
1900 hours MST

190

Master Sergeant Locklear reported to Colonel Jones. He wanted to know where Kendal was and why he was excluded.

Jones returned the salute Locklear gave him. He was right about couples in combat. He could see it on Locklear's face.

"What can I do for you?" Jones asked, motioning to close the door.

Locklear closed the door. Werewolf operations were still off limits to the Rabbits. "Sir, Chief Kendal, Captain Taylor and two or three others vanished yesterday. I am obviously concerned for Chief Kendal."

Jones sat behind his desk and motioned for Locklear to sit down. "First of all, the members you described were personally selected by me for a classified mission. You were excluded for the same reason you came here for. You two will never deploy together so long as you are under my command. Period."

Jones sat and waited for all that to simmer under his scalp.

Locklear chose his words. "Are you afraid I would spend too much effort protecting her instead of doing my job? Maybe I would not see something because I spent too much attention on her and not see something?"

"Yes," Jones said with sharp tone. "I had seen it too often in the past."

"But you have never seen it with me." Locklear returned the sharp tone.

"Chose your tone and words carefully Master Sergeant," Jones reminded him.

Locklear took several deep breaths. "How does this work, sir? Are you benching one of us?"

Jones leaned back. "Engaged, wedding and married, neither of you shall deploy together or share hazardous assignments together. If Kendal becomes pregnant, she shall not fight until after the baby is borne. After that you too will decide which partner permanently stays home."

Locklear said. "Wendy said that she will stay home if there is a child."

"Good," Jones said. "Return to the Werewolf Camp. You shall continue the Area Study mission with Captain Miles. I can release two other Rabbits to assist you. Do you wish them?"

"Yes sir," Locklear stood at attention and saluted. "Permission to resume my duties sir."

Jones returned the salute and watched Locklear leave. He will tell the Chaplin to look into Earl's head from time to time.

January 8

Afghanistan/Pakistan Border
0500 hours (Delta)

Afghanistan, emboldened by events around the world and inflamed rhetoric in the region, invaded Pakistan. Many watchers in the region cited the fact that Pakistan was the only member of the Moslem world that possessed true, working nuclear weapons and they were not going to share. The Islamic clerics throughout the region were openly demanding the weapons to expand the Islamic Caliphate and deal with the Israeli problem once and for all.

Ever since the American's left, Afghanistan has been flexing its muscles in the region. Mufti, totally isolated from the realities of the world, have issued numerous fatwas calling on the faithful to rise up and give those weapons of Allah to the faithful.

All across the common border with Pakistan, Afghans surged across the border. Seizing towns, imprisoning officials and beating women who are not covered up. The Pakistani's rose up quickly and stopped them 50 miles inland and started to push back.

Afghanistan was using the weapons left behind by the Americans, but they did not really have anyone left who could operate the more complicated systems. Plus, they spent an inordinate amount of ammunition learning how to use them without trained operators. No reputable dealers, worldwide, would sell them any American ammunition. By the time they invaded Pakistan, the ammunition stores were down to less than one week's combat allowance. Pakistan did not have those problems. The US saw it coming and supplied them with 20 million tons of ammunition along with the Russians.

For once, Russia was on the same side as the US. Neither country wanted nuclear weapons in the hands of religious zealots who had no scruples about using them.

Russia would provide Air Forces to pound the Afghans back to their border. Americans would provide ground support and one special service.

Afghanistan long provided poppy plants to feed the insane appetite for drugs the west had. The President of Pakistan granted permission for American planes to land at Pakistan's airports whose sole mission was to over-fly Afghan poppy fields and spray the plants with a powerful herbicide. The flights would occur at night to mask the identities of the aircraft. The spraying planes would need twelve-night missions to insure they got all the fields. Support fighters and bombers would ensure the sprayers were unopposed.

The Russians were not informed until the missions started. There was little they could do but offer condolences to the Afghans. That same heroin was poisoning their populations also.

Enroute to El Paso, Texas
0700 hours MST

Taylor finished his Operations order and faced his team. Morgan, Mejia and McPherson were the primary snatch team. Taylor and Kendal were the back-up and support members.

Roy Seagrove was not a formally trained Black Elf. It was surmised that one of the more senior members recruited him and trained him. Seagrove flew to Formosa last week, transferred money to a bank in El Paso and returned to the United States yesterday.

The Faraday Bank was a new institution on the banking scene. It was a private bank. They were used by a lot by people who needed a shield and a discreet place to store or move money. Hopefully, regulators would not look too close at their operations or discover their money.

The NSA site said the transfer was delayed allowing them time to get down there. Roy Seagrove's picture was forwarded to everyone's phone.

Hopefully, Taylor and his team would get ahead of Seagrove and capture him.

January 9

The Faraday Bank, El Paso, Texas
0840 hours MST

The Faraday Bank, on the first floor, was private enough that there was nowhere to find out their hours. Mejia volunteered to sit on a bench and watch the front door starting at 6 am to catch the employees arriving. According to the intelligence provided, there was only one door in or out of the bank. An emergency exit sent people out through the main building lobby, though a concealed door.

Business is conducted on an appointment basis only. There isn't any cash on hand, except what is hidden in the safe-deposit boxes. Business is conducted as discretely as possible. Mainly it is the transferring of money that is the main business at hand.

Roy Seagrove walked up to the front door and pulled out his phone. Seconds later, the front door opened. A good-looking woman opened the door and smiled as he walked in and the door was locked after him.

Wendy was waiting in the lobby, watching the concealed door. She was dressed as a professional woman waiting for Gessler and Associates to open at 9:30.

Taylor, Morgan and McPherson were waiting outside in three cars as a contingency.

0930 hours MST

Kendal had to give it to Taylor. She had argued that covering this exit was a waste of time. But here was Seagrove. She turned as if collecting her things and reported to Taylor.

"He came out into the lobby. Walking to the northern exit. Instructions."

194

Taylor turned his gaze down, then upward. "Kendal, exit the building slowly behind him. Morgan, pick her up. Watch for a vehicle. Morgan take Kendal; get her car."

Kendal sat down outside, in view of street. She changed her shoes to something that she could run in should the need arrive.

Taylor hated this part of the plan. The target always did something you cannot prepare for. Turn right, instead of left. Wait ten minutes more or less or not at all. Wake up early or sleep late. Being gay instead of straight. There was no way to compensate or plan for everything. You do the best you can and react as best you can. Keep a bubble around the target so you can reach in at the right moment.

If that mouthful made sense, so be it.

Seagrove walked north along Kansas street in a casual manner. He turned and looked at the windows looking for someone following him. This guy saw too many movies. He walked for three more blocks and got behind the wheel of a car.

Taylor shook his head. "Spread out everybody. Kendal how far away from him are you?"

"One block moving north."

"Stay there. McPherson, come pick me up two blocks south of him." Taylor knew that, in an unfamiliar city, someone needed to focus on a map to direct people around. You can't do that and drive.

Seagrove initially watched all around him. But as he got to Franklin Avenue, he kept stopping and looking around him. He walked one block, turned left and slowly walked in his version of random. He turned left on Stanton Street.

Taylor said over the radio. "He is either circling the building or using the parking lot. Wait him out."

Seagrove circled the building twice before walking into the paid parking lot and getting a Ford Explorer. He casually paid his fee and drove away. Seagrove turned south and drove into the traffic. Taylor traced the route. Seagrove did have some smarts. He ignored the horns honking and irate drivers. He maneuvered into the right lane and drove ten miles an hour under the limit.

Taylor swore under his breath. This maneuver made following him near impossible. Kendal, Morgan, Mejia and McPherson leap frogged Seagrove and used the exit ramps to allow Seagrove to pass.

Taylor was tired of this. He shot a message to O'Cleary that Seagrove was rupturing his surveillance. His money needs to be seized, starting with that Bank he was using.

Taylor watched Seagrove turn onto Interstate 10. He searched his map and had to wait a few minutes to deduce what to do.

Five minutes later, Seagrove turned onto Highway 180/62. "Kendal, Morgan, go ahead, turn into the airport. Wait there for him, then walk in behind him."

"Captain, you want to follow him?" McPherson asked.

"Yes," Taylor said looking at the Airport map.

Morgan keyed her microphone. "He turned into the airport and is going to rental car turn-in lots."

"Catch up to him and play the happy girl gag. Get him into the trunk." Taylor pushed the maps to the floor. "Mejia, you have your FBI badge?"

"Marshal's Badge," Mejia said.

"Get into the terminal. Follow him inside. If Morgan and Kendal miss, you and McPherson will take him in the terminal."

Taylor forced himself to relax and appear cool. Seagrove needed to be taken. Taylor did not want to fly all over the world chasing this man down.

"Can't take him" Morgan said. "Too many people around him. He is carrying two suitcases and a carryon."

"Talk to me," Taylor said. "He cannot be allowed to board a plane and we cannot have a gun battle arresting him."

Taylor's phone buzzed. A federal warrant appeared on his phone. Taylor thanked the cyber-space gods for no small favors. Still, he could not allow a gun battle in this terminal.

Taylor showed his FBI credentials at the security station. Morgan and Kendal were already inside. Mejia and McPherson were busy dumping their cars and rushing to the front entrance. After showing their badges, they eased in.

Kendal saw Seagrove sit down at a gate that was a flight to Bogota, Columbia. "Mister Taylor, what if I sit on his lap and pretend to be his girlfriend. That should immobilize him, so he can be secured."

Taylor looked at the board and that flight will start loading in ten minutes. No time for something better.

"Do it," Taylor said.

Kendal passed her badge and weapon to Morgan. She walked provocatively over to Seagrove. She was not in a dress suit anymore.

Seagrove was sitting down, patiently waiting for the flight to begin loading.

Kendal walked over to Seagrove and stood in front of Seagrove. Cocking to one side, she said. "You forget me, Sam?"

Seagrove flashed her a smile. "I'm sorry, but you have me mistaken for someone else."

Kendal flashed him a smile and slid onto his lap facing him. Seagrove initially resisted until Kendal wrapped her arms around his neck and kissed him longingly on the lips. Kendal sat on him, effectively immobilizing him. Morgan shook her head and walked up to Seagrove. Taylor was on the other side. From behind, Mejia and McPherson looked at the incredulous sight of seeing Kendal make out with a sworn enemy.

Kendal released him when Taylor tapped her on the shoulder. Seagrove was a little disoriented until he was shoved backward and handcuffed.

Taylor held up his badge. "FBI acting on a warrant. Thank you for your help." The terminal applauded.

Seagrove sighed. Taylor went through the motions of reading him his Miranda rights. Taylor did it once, twice, three times until Seagrove finally said he understood.

Taylor led everyone outside before the questions and problems happened. Taylor sent a post-mission report to Jones and O'Cleary.

Pentagon, Washington D.C.
1300 hours EST

O'Cleary put down the X-Berry. The Seagrove matter was over. He was being transported to Delta-7 for interrogation. He was to see his accounts depleted.

197

Preliminary reports say he had a total of twelve point three million dollars US. In his baggage, there was nearly one hundred thousand dollars US in cash.

O'Cleary was hopeful that this was the end of the Black Elves. The only problem was that Roy Seagrove had to talk. He needed to know that he had a chance to live as a free man. Chances are that the Werewolves would revolt if she freed a Black Elf.

National Media Sources, Cyber Space
1300 hours

One of the many polls published today said that the eastern US and western US were officially divided politically. Almost like the north and south was during the 1800's. Talking heads and commentators droned on and on. The average citizen tuned out the noise coming from academics trying to be relevant and looking for ratings.

Delta 7, Moss Point, Montana
2300 hours MST

Roy Seagrove was stripped of his clothes, given a thorough body cavity search, put into an orange jump suit, tied hand to foot and packed onto a C-130 for a nighttime flight to Montana. He had a black hood over his head and made to wait.

Nearby Fort Bliss Army Base provided a lot of privacy for Taylor and company to change into military uniforms while waiting for a C-130 aircraft for the long flight to Montana. Seagrove was placed in an insulated bag and strapped to Taylor for a low-level parachute jump onto a clearing near Delta 7. A waiting truck took Taylor and Kendal to Delta 7.

Seagrove was hustled and jostled around until he was set into chair. The bag on his body and his head was removed. The restraints were removed.

Seagrove watched as the restraints were thrown outside the room into a hallway. The woman who passionately kissed him in the airport was standing there in a Navy uniform and staring hard at him over the barrel of an M-4 rifle. The man who pulled at him was now an Army Captain.

198

Taylor stood in front of him. "You don't need to speak, yet. This is your world. It is eight feet tall, eight feet wide by ten feet long. This can be your world forever. Behind that door there is filled with three months-worth of food. Your shower is also your laundry and commode. You have four bars of soap. No one will open that door. We can shut your door, lock it, re-fill your rations, and unlock the door, opening it on the other side."

"If you wish to commit suicide, no one will find your corpse for months and maybe years or maybe forever."

"This is your world," Taylor repeated. "That can change if you cooperate and answer our questions fully. This is not a negotiation. Where did your friends go?"

"How do I know you won't change your mind?" Seagrove said.

"This is your world," Taylor repeated. "That can change if you cooperate and answer our questions fully. This is not a negotiation. Where did your friends go?"

Seagrove looked at the door. He thought for a few seconds.

Taylor got up and took his chair.

"Wait," Seagrove said. "We all have accounts set up for us in Formosa. Joe Sharp set them up for John Beckman and me. He dissolved the Black Elves and said to quit being Black Elves."

"When did you split up and why did you stay?" Taylor asked.

Seagrove had already resigned to talking. "We split up before Christmas. I had left already. I could not live in Tahiti any more with John Kincaid still alive. When I heard he still lived, I had to return and kill him. Kincaid killed my team mates, but his killed Martin Hernandez that night. Martin took me under his wing and trained me. We were the top of the world, but Kincaid tore us down."

Seagrove looked up at Kendal. "We would never let a woman be any other than a whore. You suck his dick, cunt?"

The point of Kendal's weapon never wavered.

"The Chief Petty Officer is too welled trained for that." Taylor said. "Is Mister Shape and Mister Beckman still overseas?"

Seagrove sighed. "I do not know. Joe Sharp said never contact each other, forever."

"Why did you come back here?"

"I transferred some money to a family I knew before going into the Army. They need the money. I will not tell you about them."

Just then, Taylor's phone buzzed. It was a text message from the NSA site. One million dollars was transferred to the Ganglier family in Garcon Colorado. Funds went to a lawyer to dissolve debts and medical bills. It asked if the funds should be confiscated.

Taylor texted back "No".

Taylor asked more questions until he felt that there was enough for now.

Taylor closed the door and rotated the heavy brass key.

After they powered down everything and closed the doors, Taylor looked at Kendal. "Thanks for not killing him."

"I learned a lot under Mister Kincaid's tender mercies," Kendal snickered.

"I hear you and Mister Locklear are getting married, please accept my congratulations," Taylor said.

"Thank you, sir," Kendal said. "Are we going to Formosa now?"

"No," Taylor said. "We need more than that to launch. Chances are, they got their money and ran off to someplace else. We'll let the NSA and the IRS have at them for now. Let's go back to Minuteman."

Even in moonlight, Taylor could see Kendal's face light up.

January 10

Texas Capital Building, Austin, Texas
1000 hours CST

A new office was opened in the Capital Building. Oklahoma formally inaugurated a coordination office at the Capital. On a daily basis, both governments worked to merge operations in law enforcement, resource management, immigration control and other governmental functions.

Texas' office in Oklahoma City is scheduled to open next week on the 14th.

The natural border along the Red River was dissolving as a political boundary. Police departments no longer saw boundaries.

For the next two years, both state governments were going to merge. Executive actions and state-wide elections were scheduled.

The Federal Government representative was ignored. The office space they normally sat in was foreclosed for lack of lease payments and utility bills.

Tucson Arizona State Capital
1000 hours MST

Officials from the states of Arizona and New Mexico met in order to replicate what Texas and Oklahoma did. Those same officials took the playbook and tried to do the same thing.

It started going wrong from the beginning. People from California left that state to escape the taxes and the socialist agenda. Unfortunately, when those people left California, they brought their weird ideas with them.

Across the states bordering with the Rio Grande River, they are called "Callie's". The only thing they brought were problems, excuses and their hands out.

January 11

Werewolf Support Camp #1, Hill County, Montana
1200 hours MST

Locklear came back to the clubhouse early today. With Captain Taylor taking Wendy and Cindy away, experienced help was hard to find. It was not that the Rabbits were sloppy, they just did not know how to look at terrain and "see" it in order to translate what they see into military terms. Simply put, they were not trained properly. The officers never wanted to "waste time" training NCOs when they can keep the knowledge where it was better placed for their efficiency reports.

With Captain Miles, he had a lot of experience with reconnaissance and combat operations, but he obviously never did an area study before. There were a lot of detailed things that needed to be done and, in some cases, re-done.

Locklear treaded carefully while working with "the Captain" whenever he was around. Lately he tightened up a lot, especially around the Rabbits. There were several instances where Locklear needed to correct him and Miles reared up and wanted to remind him about the chain of command and rank structure.

Locklear now just took the information and quietly worked it up and corrected it. He even had a working breakfast twice a week in order to have some training time. At least Miles never interfered with that.

Locklear was happy that flaws were being corrected before he had to run out into the field and correct them.

Locklear sat at the door in the mud room and removed his boots. He was tired, but something tugged at his mind. He looked up and did not see it. It was time for some time off.

Locklear carried his equipment to his room. As he put the key in the slot, he noticed the clear tape near the door jam. He turned his gaze back to the mud room and saw it: Wendy's boots and jacket. Locklear through his jacket, backpack and boots into his room and walked to Wendy's room. He pulled out his key and opened the door.

Wendy was laying on the bed, reading a book. Earl noticed her lack of a bra under the t-shirt. She smiled and said. "Close door, lock door, remove clothing, get in bed. I am cold."

Earl was in bed and snuggled up in thirty seconds, minus a book. What he wanted to talk about could wait until later.

January 12

0300 hours MST

Earl laid still on the bed and ran his fingertips up and down her spine. He woke up an hour earlier and was too comfortable to get up. His normal cycle was wake up around 2 or 3 am, enjoy a leisurely breakfast and relax over a cup of coffee. This was the best time to plan the day's events.

Earl thought about Captain James Miles. Jim Miles was a thorough and inspiring leader in combat. To Earl, he was someone that was perfect to serve with and trust in combat. But the ability to serve in the world of operations and intelligence outside of combat; he could not function. It took a while for him to say that about Jim Miles.

Earl had a great deal of respect for Jim Miles. As a younger soldier, it is easy to be awe struck. During the various Mexico missions, Earl was under Jim Miles's command and Earl was alive because Miles calmly and expertly maneuvered him and got the mission accomplished.

Earl kept dancing around the bottom line. Jim Miles was the perfect line officer. But he was not a commander. Earl tensed when he had his epiphany.

Wendy woke up, climbed on top of Earl and stretched.

Earl saw her in moonlight and there was never in his life a more beautiful woman.

Wendy smiled and looked down at Earl. She ran her fingernails over his chest and then laid down on top of him. She kissed him longingly. "What are you doing being awake and spoiling a great night back in my arms?" Earl just laid there and looked at her. Wendy took his fingers and put them over her breasts. He loved 'fingering' her body.

"Two things," he said. "The day you vanished; I went to see Colonel Jones. I wanted to know where you went and why I was not deployed." Earl's mind drifted around. Wendy pulled his fingers back. Earl snapped out of it. "Colonel Jones said we will never deploy together again. If you become pregnant, you are not deploying again. Once our baby is borne; one of us will never deploy."

Wendy let his 'fingering' continue. "Most of that we already agreed to once we decided to marry."

"I know, but Jones tried to sound like he was smarter than we are."

"I don't want to deploy with you," Wendy said. "I was with Captain Taylor on a Black Elf capture mission. I had to concentrate on the capture. One part of it was making out with the guy in an airport terminal to put him into a stupid state. I also lost my focus thinking how you would feel." Wendy dropped her arms and looked away. "I actually felt like a whore."

Earl sat up and wrapped his arms around her. He looked up to her face. "Remember what we said in answer to Mister Kincaid when he asked if we would suck a dick. I secretly said no. I looked at you. I think you said no, also."

Wendy started crying. She leaned into his face and kissed him. She pushed him down and whispered a story to him. "This is why I had to fight Merchantax."

Wendy cried through the telling of her abuse. After twenty minutes, she was through and spent. "I was abused and neglected through several families until I was trapped by two men and two women. Finally, I fought back and escaped. The social workers only solution was counseling, drugs and being locked down in a facility. If the Navy had not taken me, I would have found the couples, killed them and went to prison for life."

Earl did not know what to do or say.

When Brenda was finished, she sat up. "I am used to being a lesbian as a shield to push people away. It's easy to do a woman. By the way, why do you put up with me. We sleep together, but still wear underwear. Your whitey tightiees and my panties. I guess I wanted to see if you would get frustrated and move on."

He said, "My father said, all women are weird. If you find one you like; wade through the mush and smile."

"I would love to meet him," she said.

"My parents died in a car crash when I was ten."

Both let the silence hang over them for a few seconds.

"What is the second thing?" she asked.

"Captain Miles," Earl said.

"Perfect officer, crappy Commander," she said.

Earl was surprised. "I thought I was the only one who noticed."

Wendy smiled. "Cindy and I traveled the roads a lot doing this survey. Two women together talk a lot. I asked her a lot of questions about him. He was a great officer when the bullets fly. Unless he was training or fighting, he does not have a clue. Cindy said that senior NCOs are assigned because junior officers, especially those that used to be NCOs, cannot deal with the everyday actions. Cindy also said that being a Commander is the hardest duty any officer can undertake. She advised me to be patient."

Earl ran his fingers along her arms. "I still want to marry you, but I do not want to invite anyone into our marriage."

"You still want to marry me?"

"Yes."

Wendy took a deep breath. "I am a bitch, slut, cunt, whore. What about you wants someone, who works with you and you are still a virgin. I may not be able to have children." Wendy still turned away.

Earl reached up and turned her face to him. He sat up. "My name is Earl. You are Wendy. You are not any of those things. You are the woman that I always wanted."

Wendy burst into tears and pushed Earl down. "One last chance," she said, drying her face.

"I love you lady. I guess I always have. But I will not ever be sorry for loving you or marrying you."

Wendy pulled off his underwear and then her panties.

Number 17, US Naval Observatory, Washington, D.C.
0600 Hours EST

Edwards's orderly came into his bedroom, stopped, took a deep breath and woke him.

Edwards woke and he was mad. This was Sunday and he was looking forward to sleeping in. "There better be nukes on the way."

"No Sir," the man said. "Sir, Missus Edwards said that Breakfast is ready." The orderly stood off to the side.

Edwards lay there for a few seconds. Years of immediately going from sleep to full awake came out. Edwards suddenly leap out of bed. Edwards stopped at the door and looked back at Gaffney. Edwards was satisfied that this was not a dream.

Edwards rushed to the kitchen and there she was. Hundreds of times in the past, Edwards woke up to see

Amanda there in the kitchen cooking breakfast. She was a very light sleeper and generally an early riser.

"Good morning, Husband," she said, smiling at him. "Sit down. Breakfast will be ready in a few minutes. Coffee is on the table."

Edwards walked into the kitchen and stared at Amanda. This was not the massively romantic reunion that he imagined, but it was Amanda puttering around the kitchen. Edwards shuffled up to her as she turned, wiping her hands on the apron.

"Husband," she said smiling.

Edwards fell to one knee in front of her, grabbed her hands and kissed them. He closed his eyes and rubbed his face in her hands.

Amanda cried as Edwards welcomed her back as only, he could. She pulled her hands back, cupped his face and kissed him.

Gaffney softly walked away before the General did or said something that made Miss Amanda unhappy. That happened in the past and it was not a fun time for him.

"Wife, I want you to know how much I missed you."

"Husband, sit down and share breakfast with me. Please call Mister Gaffney in so he can eat. I already bribed him to clean the kitchen after the meal."

"Gaffney!" Edwards called.

Edwards sat down so he could eat and stare at Amanda. Those clowns are in for a long hard fight if they try anything with Amanda.

Minutemen, north of Fort Benton, Montana.
0900 hours MST

Father Mike Thomas was dressed for the day. He was finishing his morning prayers and preparing his sermon for the day. His service at the community center was something of a hit this time of year. Plenty of coffee, pastries, and pot luck eating was available before, during and after the service.

Just outside his door, a single snowmobile arrived. Two people got off and walked to his door.

Earl knocked on the door to Father Mike's quarters. Mike did not want a special office to take up space from other families and needs. Besides, he was single and had no use for too many places to clean and maintain.

Mike opened the door and smiled at the couple. "Come in, please." He looked at his watch. "I have an hour and a half before today's service."

"There's no rush, Father Mike," Wendy said. We are here early to enjoy some company. Can we come back and talk to you after the service?" They stood.

Earl turned back to Mike. "Can we leave our bags here until after the service."

"Yes, please," Wendy said. "I want to change into something more Sunday than a snowmobile suit."

"Sure," Mike said with a smile. He smiled knowing that something was up and these two had something in mind.

1430 hours MST

Father Mike watched Locklear and Kendal throughout the service. Both of them acted normally and were very social throughout the service.

Kendal changed into a long dress with a long coat to go over it. She wore her boots to the community center and changed into something more stylish once inside.

Locklear just pulled his snowmobile suit off and was dressed in a nice suit. He too, wore his boots to the center and changed into street shoes in the center.

The service was from 11 to 12. Father Mike was happy to have almost two-thirds of the community here. Most were more interested in a community get-together, but he took what he could get.

Father Mike and everybody else enjoyed each-others company while they ate the community lunch, sang songs and laughed through stories true and not so true. When the clock said it was two o'clock, it started breaking up. Kids wanted to play in the snow. Moms and Dads wanted to relax and rest, along with everyone else.

Locklear and Kendal helped clean up the center. Locklear gathered trash and Kendal washed the various dishes. The owners came over and claimed what they brought. Several of them gave away their dishes and they recipients promised (?) to return them here after they ate them.

All three walked back to Father Mike's home talking casually about being in a winter home. All the structures were basically over-built to lock out the cold. In the summer, it did not take long for the heat to build-up with eight-inch-thick walls and twenty-inch-thick roof insulation.

Father Mike prepared a plate of cookies while the coffee cooked. They made more small talk while everything came together. Finally, Mike said it. "You've made some sort of decision about getting married and we are here…." Mike held out his hands, waiting.

Both of them looked at each other.

Earl took the nod. "Bless us Father for we have sinned. It has been a long time since we confessed."

Mike already had his sash on the table. He spread it out, kissed it, smiled as he put it around his neck. "Proceed my son and my daughter."

Suddenly, a knock came from the door. Mike went over and opened it. Colonel and Missus Jones were there looking in on things.

"Can we come in?" Linda Jones asked.

Thaddeus Jones looked expectantly at the sash around his neck and the couple inside. "Is this a confessional?"

"Yes, it is." Mike said. "Can you come back later?"

Thaddeus looked to Linda. Father Mike was even more strict about the confession rule than Hector Adams was. Adams was stuck in Washington talking to John Kincaid and could come here to help.

Thad said, "Yes we can come back later." They smiled and waved at everyone and Mike closed the door against the Montana cold.

Father Mike locked the door and turned on the small red light that told the world that God wanted some kind of privacy.

Earl said. "Everyone is talking about us and trying to pry into our lives." Wendy pulled out a buzz box and activated it. The headache-making buzz started. Wendy went to the windows and ensured the Venetian blinds were closed off.

208

Father Mike jumped into the conversation. "You both have decided to by-pass Colonel Jones' marriage rule. I will not marry you in secret. Marriage is something that is done out in the open. It has to start right for the right reasons in the only way to ensure your hearts are intwined."

Wendy stood next to Earl and glared at him. "Is that your divine interpretation for our visit?" Wendy turned, picked up her pants and snowmobile suit and went to the bathroom.

Mike realized he made a rookie mistake. He thought he was divine and presumed on two people when came to seek God's will and counsel.

Wendy came out of the bathroom, already tucked inside her suit.

"OK," Father Mike said. "That was stupid of me and I apologize. Can we sit down and start over?"

Wendy walked up to Father Mike and kissed him on the side of his face. She took the sash off his neck, kissed it, folded it and handed it back to Father Mike. "Tell Colonel Jones, Earl and I are not getting married. I see everyone is more interested in their opinion than what we want. I love you, Father Mike." She kissed him again, took their one bag and walked out.

"Thanks for the coffee, Father Mike," Earl said. Both men shook hands. Earl turned and left.

A few minutes after the snowmobile left, the phone rang. It was Jones. "They are not going to get married."

Jones was silent for a few seconds. "What happened?"

Father Mike thought for a few minutes. "I interfered instead of listening."

January 13

Pentagon, Washington D.C.
1400 hours EST

Amanda came home yesterday and enjoyed alone time with her husband. This morning, Edwards' aide arrived at Number 17 to pick up the General and was astonished to see Missus Edwards puttering around the house, cleaning or moving this and that. Colonel Harm dutifully notified the apparatus of Missus Edwards' return.

No sooner had Edwards left than the Federal Security apparatus arrived to grill her continuously about her disappearance and return. What gave them the biggest headache was how she disappeared from "custody" and how had she just showed up inside a secured facility without tripping the security around the Observatory.

For four hours it went on. Finally, she could take it no more. Amanda Edwards walked out of the house without a coat and walked to the main gate. She made them bring her to the Pentagon and demanded to see her husband. Finally, the apparatus made its biggest mistake by taking her to see her husband.

Amanda walked passed everyone, went into her husband's office, slammed the door and launched into a tirade.

Alarms went off and Security Agents ran to the Chairman's office. A shrill sounding woman was screaming insults inside the Chairman's office. An action officer, fresh from the quarterly security training, panicked and hit the panic button.

In this new era after 9/11 and terrorism, no one confirms anything. The security apparatus of the Pentagon swung into action. Innocent people knew to face the wall, hands up and not move as Security Forces ran to their stations.

In the outer office of the Chairman, Colonel Matt Harm was trying to call the Security Office and cancel everything. However, the nature of the system was that it is better to run through a mistake than to make the mistake of doing nothing. Everyone from the Service Secretaries down to the most junior ranking person followed their appointed rules.

Classified Document Custodians grabbed every sensitive document and jammed them into safes created and placed for this very purpose. Non-essential personnel were evacuated or ejected from the affected areas.

Everyone reacted exactly to the protocols and procedures as outlaid, practiced and enacted.

Everyone but Amanda Edwards and her husband, the Chairman of the Joint Chiefs of Staff. Security Forces burst into the office and saw Missus Edwards screaming at her husband who was pinned into a corner of the office.

The sight of a nearly five-foot-tall woman holding an enormous man who was almost trying to crawl up the corner to get away from this woman was almost comical.

The security personnel did not try to figure anything out. One agent pulled out a taser and shot Missus Edwards. Amanda immediately sank to the ground. The two agents ran into the room to secure it. Edwards went down to pick up Amanda. When one of the agents tried to separate them, Edwards legendary temper exploded.

The blow-by-blow of the fight was not as near as important as the injury list. One agent, believed to be the one who tasered Missus Edwards, suffered a skull fracture and broken jaw. The other agent suffered five broken ribs, a punctured lung and ruptured kidney. General Edwards was tasered for the simple reason that he hovered over his wife and would not move out of the way. He was actually so mad that one EMT was injured.

Room D-113, George Washington University Hospital, Washington, D.C.
1645 hours EST

Kincaid had a 'warm' discussion with Jones and Miles about "his team" of apprentices over a secure audio/visual link.

"His apprentices" had training objectives which did correspond with Jim Miles mission, maybe. But his training objectives had to have priority over anything else. He did not know that Morgan and Kendal were taken for that Black Elf mission. He had no real objection and would have included Locklear as a support team member to work the roving surveillance plan, thus freeing Taylor to command.

The Kendal/Locklear problem was no problem. Being a couple was a plus.

Taylor was getting more and more mad as the discussion until Jones had to interfere.

Captain Miles set up new objectives for his teams.

Morgan re-joined Kendal and Locklear with the Shark-Hunter training. Kincaid used UNSTACK THIS to set-up a secure video link to continue their training. Kincaid finally had O'Cleary segregate their training from all other duties after Miles objected over something for the umpteenth time.

Kincaid was due to get out of the hospital next week. He wanted to visit his kids and grandkids. Susan and Jason were living in a community near the Werewolf camp and Barbara was still at the ranch in Canada.

The Army was wanting to discharge him due to old age and this time he was a Frankenstein. His medical records said he was permanently banned from combat. In fact, he was banded from everything but sitting in a rocking chair and watching traffic in front of his house.

So, all he had to do was be Gladys Goldstein to these three children. Heh heh heh.

Kincaid looked at the letters and e-mails from Jason, Barbara and Susan. Jason, being a fireman, was supportive and offered to win a few hundred games of checkers. Barbara was very calm in her letters. Gone were the days where she had to dominate and impose her will. Kincaid wanted to visit and see for himself.

Susan was the enigma in the family. Karen was married before and had a daughter. Susan was very calm and serene in her life and how she looked at life. Susan was also a former Alcohol, Tobacco and Firearms agent who was tired of catch and release.

Karen used to shake her head at the odd turns in the family. Kincaid remembered better days. It was two years before her murder when all five of them were together.

Bonnie Chandler, Box 234, Route 17, Belcher, Missouri
1800 hours CST

Dear Bonnie,

Well, I can't be a cheerleader anymore. The Army came to town and took over the football field and gym for a base to do something or the other. Dad called the football field a motor pool and the gym became a puzzle palace and supply center. All those guys and girls in ugly clothes speak a language that's nothing but letters. They even screwed up the lunch room. Yukkiest food she ever ate.

No football or basketball. I wanted to be a cheerleader.

To add to my problems, the Army tanks and trucks were tearing up the roads. She has to catch the bus thirty minutes earlier each day.

January 14

Pentagon, Washington D.C.
0700 hours EST

Brenda O'Cleary rode to the Pentagon early today at Secretary Dodson's request. Yesterday was one in which everyone should chalk up as stupid infecting everyone.

The stupid got so big that even the President got involved.

Both O'Cleary's were happy to find out Amanda returned. Amanda called Dennis at his home and asked him to come and enjoy a cup of coffee. Dennis obliged and they made a day of it. Dennis told her all the gossip over a deck of cards. He loved 'spades' and she liked 'pinochle'. So, they alternated keeping score on a pad of paper.

Dennis called Brenda and gave her the news. Dennis was now a notable member of the spouse's club and a keeper of secrets and gossip. Brenda came to visit Amanda just to show off her "baby bump".

Edwards was busy packing everything.

Naturally, the buzz around the corporation was Amanda's return and the ruckus surrounding it. After the wounded were taken away, the security apparatus decided the no charges were to be filed.

Edwards came back later in the day and went straight to the Defense Secretary's office. He removed his uniform jacket and left it on his desk along with a hand written resignation. Dodson tried to talk him out of it, but Edwards just ignored him and left.

Edwards went to the Medical Annex within the Pentagon. By the time he arrived, Amanda was awake and pronounced whole and healthy. She was sitting down, smiling and working her special magic on everyone.

It was late yesterday when they took a cab back to the Observatory and walked inside. Edwards ripped his sign out of the ground and took Amanda inside.

Shaking her head, Brenda O'Cleary returned to the present. Dennis pulled out her set of five stars this morning. He looked at her, silently asking the question.

"Dennis, I still intend to submit my retirement at the first of the month. Those will just be toys for our son to play with." Brenda pointed to the drawer where they hidden.

She sat in the back of her car and half listened to Hawker's briefing about her schedule. Most of what she was being briefed about will vanish if Edwards was not here this morning.

Dennis asked a worrisome question this morning. "If the President asked you; what is your answer?"

0800 hours EST

Secretary Dodson got straight to the point. "Yesterday proved how stupid things have become. You are now the Acting Chairman. Orders are being cut for now. I intend for General Edwards to return to his position, just as soon as his justified anger subsides."

"General, I have to say this, so be it. A lot of his duties to go out and visit the situation are beyond your ability. I will not allow you to go to the field because your baby has to be considered."

Dodson took a deep breath. "Just in case he refuses to return to his duties, do you want his job?"

"Sir," O'Cleary straightened in her chair. "I already talked to my husband. If asked, I will serve, but I am not going to volunteer for the job."

Dodson sat and looked at her. "If I were you, that would be my answer. Have Colonel Harm coordinate anything you need. Call me. Thank you."

O'Cleary walked out and thought about her new reality. It was amazing. A little over three years ago, she was a

Colonel in the basement of the White House. Before the JIA, it was a choice between retiring with Dennis or being promoted to get a single star.

O'Cleary wondered what General Marshal thought when he was promoted.

O'Cleary cursed herself for being a coward and not telling him she wanted to retire.

0900 hours EST

Clara Simpson walked into the Pentagon through the Secure Entrance reserved for VIPs. It also allowed a guaranteed entrance for those VIPs to enter the Pentagon without being observed. Simpson, the head of the ISA, was now authorized a chauffeured, armored vehicle to drive her around. This morning, she came to visit someone who should have had her job.

Simpson went through the security levels and entered the sanctum sanctorum of the Pentagon. This was the area for the Chairman and Vice-Chairwomen of the Joint Chiefs of Staff. Simpson always hated coming to the Pentagon. It was originally built to be a huge repository for paper files. That kind of weight meant a heavy building. Simpson could feel that weight as she walked inside.

Simpson had her aide call over to Brenda's office and ask for an appointment to brief her on some Black Elf activities. Maybe she will forgive her.

Simpson congratulated Hawker on her promotion and asked her to notify O'Cleary she was here. Simpson sat down and thought it was easier to get to her office. Just drive up, check in and come in.

Two minutes later, Hawker escorted her into O'Cleary's office.

Simpson looked around. "Brenda, you came up in the world. Andrew barely fits in your old office."

O'Cleary gave the office a quick look as Simpson sat down in a chair. This was an off-meeting. There was not a subject listed on her calendar except the Black Elves and she knew more about that than Simpson did. Hawker noted that to O'Cleary when she briefed her boss on the appointment.

O'Cleary stood and walked over to the coffee table. "Can I get you a cup of coffee?"

"No thank you. I already had one. I don't know about you, but I am enjoying having a car with a chauffeur. This allows me a cup of coffee without dividing my attention."

O'Cleary filled a cup and walked over to a chair near Simpson. She patiently waited for Simpson to begin.

Simpson took a deep breath. "I am here to confess. After Prescott had you detained, he waited for me to return from the White House at the end of the day. He had me escorted to his office under guard. It was after midnight."

"The two men who escorted me were two men I had never seen before. He called them the Black Elves."

O'Cleary forced herself to remain calm.

"After Prescott was arrested," Simpson started. "The Black Elves were waiting at my home with my husband. They gave me a simple choice along with pictures of my children and their families. Cooperate with them or everyone dies. Prescott still had his hooks in me. From his office at the Pentagon, he still yanked the Black Elves. He knows where the money is and has tentacles snaking around."

"Stop," O'Cleary said. "Why tell me this? Why now?"

"The FBI," Simpson said, "did nothing when I reported it. 16,000 plus kidnappings happened on that day. An impossible number of things were going on. Plus, I was told to stop by those Black Elves the same day I reported it." Simpson paused for a few seconds. "Matt took our family and left. I just received an FBI briefing that my family has disappeared. I heard about the attack on your home. I waited to die, but it did not happen. I am telling you this now. My next stop is the White House to tender my resignation. I am recommending you as my replacement."

"Clara, I do not want you to resign."

"Brenda, I am tired. It's time for me to go. If I can be turned, then I don't deserve to be at the head of something like the ISA with an Ultra Clearance."

Clara stood.

"Stop," Brenda said. "We need to castrate someone first." Brenda called Edwards and told him what happened and what she was going to do. After hanging up the phone,

Brenda called Dennis and said to come to Edwards's office and wait.

Edwards said to sit tight and he would call her.

Brenda pulled some paper work on the western water problem when Edwards called and said to come over with Simpson.

When both women arrived at Edwards office, both got an earful from Dennis and Edwards was laughing hard in his office. O'Cleary looked to the side and shot a glance at Major General Prescott, finally getting the hint that he needed to stand.

Edwards' aide ushered them inside.

Prescott lowered himself slowly down into the chair. Three of the worse people in his life are now in one office. The Judge Advocate General of the Army said that maybe Edwards could keep him from getting the death penalty. O'Cleary and Simpson could easily kill that, as well as him.

The door closed on O'Cleary and Simpson so that silence descended. Prescott forced himself to sit motionless, projecting confidence and innocence.

After twenty minutes, Edwards ordered him into the office. Prescott marched in and stopped in front of Edwards' desk. Edwards sloppily returned the salute. "Sit down," he commanded.

Edwards faced Prescott. "Missus Simpson is a GS-18. Consider her as a four-star officer for this conversation. Missus Simpson." He passed to her.

"Your Black Elves are either dead or captured," Simpson said. "My family is secured without Federal Law Enforcement involvement. So do we let you hang out to take a lethal injection or do you come clean now."

Prescott refused to show the volcanos and explosions erupting inside him. He tried opening his mouth, but failed.

"Let me sweeten the pot," Edwards held up a paper. "General, pass this page over to Prescott."

Prescott looked at the paper. It was familiar to him. This was the punishment determination for his trial. Since this was a trial for a capital crime. Edwards was the 'Convening Authority" and it was his duty to authorize and allow the

217

prosecution to seek the death penalty. Without it, the prosecution could only seek a life sentence.

Prescott lowered the page. "I need to speak to my attorney."

Edwards smiled. "It is still my authority to convene a General Courts Marshal. I can take the death penalty off the table or not. This," he whirled his hand around the office, "has nothing to do with the trial. These two women have a lot of questions about these Black Elves. If you reveal all the information they want and both of them are satisfied, I will forever remove the death penalty. If you want to bring your lawyer into the mix, then I will check the death penalty. You chose."

Edwards used his intercom. "Martin, is my conference room clear?"

"Yes Sir," the Aide said.

"Keep it that way, get two guards to stand on the door. It is being used for the rest of the day."

"Yes Sir," Colonel Harm said. He made the notations on his schedule and the daily report. That done, he turned his attention to other items.

O'Cleary already knew most of the details. She kept that information to herself and let Clara do all the talking. O'Cleary used her memory to remember all the details. Prescott recited how he was 'hooked'; his wife's murder and how he was implicated. Next, he took control of the Black Elves. A web site gave him the account numbers and banking information. Prescott wrote that down.

Prescott used his new found power to implicate others in crimes and either incriminate them or blackmail them. He listed the people he targeted including Simpson and O'Cleary. He also told them what was used and what he had them do.

After Prescott was arrested, the judge released him on a conditional basis. He wore an ankle bracelet and was initially confined to his home. Later, he was allowed to have an office at the Pentagon. A Lieutenant and a Sergeant were assigned to watch him. Prescott would close the door periodically and conduct business with the Black Elves. He wanted to kill O'Cleary and ordered them to attempt it. After the attempt, all contact with them and their banking information vanished.

Simpson looked to O'Cleary. O'Cleary shook her head, stood and left the room.

Outside, Simpson walked outside and looked at O'Cleary. She walked over to her things.

O'Cleary walked up to her. "Where is your resignation?"

Simpson made a motion with her purse.

O'Cleary said. "Through it in the trash. We have a nation to defend."

485 Glenmore Drive, Alexandria, Virginia
1900 hours EST

Simpson stood at the door and could not reach up to push the doorbell. Guilt, dragged at her. After months of being under the foot of a stupid man, she was free. That release felt so good. Simpson never went to the White House. Something was screaming at her not to resign. That something she felt had everything to do with Brenda O'Cleary on the other side of the door.

As she was about to touch the door bell, Dennis opened the door. "About time you rang the bell," Dennis said.

Clara came in with Matt in tow.

All four went through the obligatory pleasantries while the coffee cooked and Dennis put pastries on a platter. Dennis put all of it on the table. Afterward, Dennis started the sound system and adjusted the levels until the four lights lit up.

All four sat down. Clara and Brenda looked at each other and locked gazes.

"I pushed back my appointment with the President two times," Clara said. "I found Matt and talked to him for over an hour and a half. I was compromised and failed to report it. I am resigning."

Brenda starred into her face. "You are not resigning. You cooperated with an investigation and reported your findings to a fellow 'Ultra' clearance holder. The only person who can damage you is under arrest, pending a General Courts Marital for murder and conducting terrorist operations within the United States."

Clara put both her hands on the table, palms down. "I am not staying. It is past time for me to be a wife and grandmother. Come rain, shit or shine, tomorrow I will be a real civilian."

"I am seventeen days from announcing my retirement or resignation. In June I give birth to my son," Brenda said patting her stomach. "Nothing gets in the way of me being a mother."

"I am already on record as strongly saying you are the only replacement candidate. I strongly informed the President that he needed to find either another Justin Harper or Brenda O'Cleary. The President was reminded that just casting a wide net only gets another Prescott."

Brenda forced down her temper. "I will not go into that pressure cooker. In order to do the job right, you have to work 16, 17 hours a day. You take on everyone's problems and jobs."

"Are you refusing to take the Internal Security Agency?"

"Oh yes," Brenda said.

"Are you staying at your present position?" Clara asked.

Brenda forced the smile from her face. "The President has two competing places for my lack of talents. Your offer of the ISA and General Edwards' offer of a fifth star as the Chairman of the Joint Chiefs this summer. You ever heard of 'slave auction'."

"Yewwww." Clara said.

"Yes," Brenda said. "I can only think of everyone's reaction while seeing a pregnant senior General officer wandering the halls with a son protruding in front, leading the way."

"No one at the ISA will laugh at you. Mary Atkinson is still there. She can take the load off you."

"What part of I want to be a mother in June, do you not understand?"

Clara just looked at Brenda and then turned to say something to Dennis. Dennis was smart enough to point back at Brenda. She tried to look at Matt. Matt was just as smart and pointed back to her.

"Clara," Brenda said with a soft voice. "Both of us are old and tired. The problem is both of us took an oath and the President will hold us to it. The President is watching the nation destroy itself. The only thing holding us together are patriots like the four of us. I am leaving in June. That will not happen if I go to the ISA."

"OK," Clara said motioning to Matt. "If neither one of us is budging. I don't see any reason to argue." All four rose together. "I'll see you later." Clara smiled to everyone. Everyone said their good byes.

"Clara, did you hear about General Edwards little riot today?"

Clara nodded her head. "Yes, I did."

"I have too many chiefs looking at me. You now one of them."

"I'm sorry, Brenda. I'm scared like all of us."

Dennis closed the door as Brenda sat down. "Hey," he said. "She made a decision. I think she will resign anyway. What will the President do?"

Brenda leaned back in the chair. "Yes, she did and probably did it already. Unless something weird happens, I guess I will be seeing the President."

Dennis sat down and drank his coffee.

Brenda drifted away and thought about her world. Just then Arthur kicked. She smiled and touched the spot. "Arthur just kicked." She beamed and took Dennis' hand and held it over the spot. A minute later, Arthur kicked again. Dennis was so proud.

January 15

Pentagon, Washington, D.C.
1300 hours EST

Dodson had a meeting of the minds with Edwards and O'Cleary in his office. O'Cleary was down the hall and came willingly. Edwards was packing up his office packing everything up. Dodson made him stop and come in his office.

"Generals, I have too many headaches for this." Dodson said.

"Tom, this security fiasco from front to finish is a Keystone Cop movie. I heard it all from all quarters. Putting families in protective custody is a bullshit lie. Your wife should not have eviscerated you in your office. That is what home is for. And as to the riot in your office; well, everyone got what they deserved. If someone tasered my wife, I'd do the same thing."

Dodson paused to catch his breath. "I need both of you in the place you are at and that is my speech. Can we go back to work?"

O'Cleary looked at Edwards. He took a deep breath and exhaled.

Edwards looked at O'Cleary and back to Dodson. "Yes Sir."

The President listened to the conversation over the speaker phone. He wanted to be silent and let Dodson work this out, but he wanted to know what was said. He also needed to know if he needed to intervene. Edwards was the bull dog he needed to keep everyone in line. O'Cleary was the brain he needed to keep everything real. He hung up the line and breathed a sigh of relief.

36.023 degrees north, 142.572 degrees east
0200 hours India (1400 hours EST)

Alarms sounded in Universities and Seismographic centers around the world. One hundred and sixty kilometers east of Tokyo, Japan and ten kilometers down under the surface of the Pacific, a 9.7 moment magnitude earthquake ruptured the local plate. The tear in the earth was seventy kilometers long. Seventeen billion tons of water flooded into the rip, collided with the new geology and stopped.

The ground kept moving, the water kept moving and filling in the new canyon. Just as suddenly as the ground opened up, it started closing.

On the surface, a large "hump" of water, twenty meters tall and seventy kilometers in circumference swelled and spread out. Subsequent movements along the ocean floor and other water dynamics caused new ripples to form on the ocean's surface moving outward. A total of seven waves rushed outward from the center.

In Japan, emergency sirens blared waking up the populations. People and Automatic systems sprang in action without conscious thought. Walled barriers closed off hazardous locations. Fuel lines, storage facilities, electrical plants and nuclear reactors were placed in a safe mode.

Country-wide, Japan braced for impact. At least in Japan, disaster preparation is part of the culture.

The largest of the tsunami waves would impact Japan in two hours.

US Geological Survey, Reston Virginia
1410 hours EST

USGS computers received the information and churned the data. The main screens over the forward walls portrayed all the seismic data occurring all over the world. Alarms alerted the operators that a major event occurred east of Japan. Tsunamis were rippling outward across the Pacific. Hawaii would be hit hardest on the western side, hours after Japan. The Philippians and Formosa get glancing blows as their terrain was more or less parallel with the wave movements.

Preliminary projections and estimates state that Hawaii would be slammed with initial fifteen-meter-high waves hitting the shore lines and building to between twenty-five and thirty meters as the shores were hit.

To those of us here in the US, the energy will dissipate before hitting the coast. The surfers will be happy for once.

After the disaster wanes and the aftershocks subside, who in the world will help the Japanese?

Investors and stock exchanges shook and worried. The minimum effect is that Japan will pull back trillions of dollars back home and that is a conservative estimate. This was going to spur numerous rounds of borrowing and sell-offs.

Internal Security Agency, Barton, Virginia
1410 hours EST

In the new ISA, Japan's only issue to the US is the loss of investment money in the stock market.

The Treasury Department was scrambling to find answers.

Clara Simpson was enroute to the White House to meet with the President. In her purse was her resignation. Technically, the resignation was supposed to be given to the Secretary of State. The clown serving now was a stickler for protocol. You had to call for an appointment, even if it was just to get a phone call.

Being a de facto Vice-President had advantages and disadvantages. One advantage was easier access to the President.

Clara still wanted to resign. She had a long talk with Matt last night. "Clara if you want to quit, just do it," he said. The rest was affording it, selling the house and where to move.

Just as Clara pulled into the VIP entrance to the White house, the Earthquake hit Japan. The President was all about Japan. What do we do or can we do? When Clara went down to the Situation Room, she pushed the resignation deep into her purse and logged into the computers down here.

The Treasury Secretary mentioned that Japan would pull Trillions of dollars back home to re-build after the buildings quit shaking and the waters receded. That loss of investment funds could further drag down the economy.

Clara looked at her computers. She smiled at all the simplifications after Prescott left. Clara actually returned everything back to how Justin Harper ran things. There was a collective sigh of relief when Prescott was arrested. Collectively, they watched her for a week. The morale jumped through the roof. Things became fun again, even Wildman was happy.

The volume in the room rose, bringing Simpson back to the problem in Japan.

Simpson relaxed and opened a bottle of water.

January 16

US Embassy, Islamabad, Pakistan
2300 hours Delta   (1500 hours EST)

Staff Sergeant Larry Holstead, USMC crossed off another day on his calendar. His orders for the 9th Marine Expeditionary Force were safely in his desk drawer. He was tired of this Mickey Mouse embassy duty. In twelve days, he was returning to the good ole USA and back to being a US Marine and Missus Holstead's handyman. Back home, he could openly yell out his love for the Corps.

Holstead's eyes widened as the last thing he ever saw was a bright light coming straight at him.

An A-29 attack plane, left over from the Afghanistan exodus, flew straight at the Embassy. The Taliban took parts from all the planes left behind and made one that worked. The pilot activated a radio transmitter which sent out commands activating a signal strobe. The pilot put on his IR googles as he flew over Islamabad following a commercial route until he spotted the infrared blinking strobe light left behind on the roof.

The Taliban learned the lessons from 9/11. Once over the Diplomatic area, the pilot turned off the transponders, all navigation markers and lights. The aircraft was searched thoroughly, looking for anything that had serial numbers that could be traced. The pilot pushed the plane over and lined up on the American Embassy. He pulled back the throttles, activated the speed brakes and extended the landing gear. All that 'disrupted' the air flow around the airframe. The lower speed slowed the aircraft so that it could be controlled. The pilot focused all his attention at the building. He was not going to miss. Weeks of planning and rehearsing came to a point of light guiding him on his mission. The closer he came, the faster the building rushed to him.

The plane stuck on the northern end of the roof. Both two-hundred-and-fifty-pound bombs were armed before take-off. Half of the building vanished upon impact. The late hour of the attack meant that there was only a small number of people in the embassy. It was the building that was the target, not the people manning the building.

Automatic alarms went off at the embassy, Islamabad Security Forces and the State Department in the US. Fears of 9/11 were on everyone's mind. One other alarm was designated for other fears inside other planes that were in the air. Every aircraft within 1000 miles was told to lock their cockpits. Any aircraft not complying with instructions would be shot down.

Internal Security Agency, Barton, Virginia
1800 hours EST

Clara watched the media feeds from around the world. The damage was greater than the attacks in Africa back in 1990's. It would be another 3 hours before the sun rose and the world will get a full view of the damage.

Pakistan immediately closed all their airspace. They openly banned any aircraft for any reason coming from Afghanistan. "Afghanistan aircraft are forbidden from overflying our country. If your aircraft enters our airspace for any reason, you will be shot down without any warning. If any persons on board survive the crash, you will be executed."

Around the world, nations decried the attacks on sovereign embassies. Hot air flew around the world.

The UN, now located in the Netherlands, formally recommended that the US take a cool down period and not escalate the situation. Around the world, people scoffed at the notion of cooling off.

The President wanted some kind of retaliation. However, we do not have bases or allies to operate from.

Clara called one of her few all-team meetings in the auditorium. Getting straight to the point, she told everyone to prepare for any number of action points coming for this organization to supply answers for the "desk bounds" to throw outs.

"This is our responsibility to stop stupidity 'in the bud'. They will not be doing the dying; young service men and women will be dying. We owe it the families to do it right. Let us concentrate on finding these animals and making them pay."

Just then a young staffer handed Clara a note. The White House called wanting a meeting in the situation room to discuss options. Clara waved the note to everyone and left to get in her car.

Department of Justice, Washington D.C.
0900 hours EST

Rebecca Beck, the Attorney General of the United States sat back in her chair and read the report from the FBI Organized Crime section.

Marcus Solin did not like to waste a lot of words. The mood across the nation towards law enforcement was very sour. Local militias were forming in nearly city and town west of the Mississippi River. The average person was openly telling Courts and Judges that they joined the Militias by saying that the law was in place to protect the guilty.

Beck turned page after page. It was the same. A judge who was notorious for taking bribes nearly choked when a defendant opened a bag and dumped a pile of cash on the table. The judge was so startled that he had a heart attack.

Beck looked up and smiled. She warned the President last year that this very thing was going to happen. Scared people can and will rebel.

Beck put that report in the outbox.

The next report got her attention. Marcus Bolin wanted to establish a United States Police Force under the authority of the Police Executive. Bolin wanted to nationalize every Police Force, regardless of size, throughout the nation. Getting that situation under control had a lot of advantages. But would it work? The problem now, today, is that the same system fails to protect the population. Lawyers and courts spend a lot of time finding excuses not to convict people. 100 people could witness a murder and the judge is more worried about the rights of the criminal than the person who was killed.

One other problem was the loss of the Savage Rabbits working the drug problem. It was a small and effective unit that worked fine until this situation started. The Army swooped in with a huge bureaucracy and ruined it. Solin was right. The Savage Rabbits was needed. Not what is there now.

She needed General O'Cleary on this. Beck through the report in the hold box and told her secretary to get an appointment with President. She would call General O'Cleary personally and pitch it.

Beck knew that she had to wade carefully. The people have very little confidence in anything the government is doing.

Out west, states were merging together for law enforcement, resource management and sharing expenses.

Beck wondered how much longer before the shooting started.

January 18

Columbus, New Mexico
0900 hours MST

Columbus, New Mexico population 1,664 people. Pancho Villa invaded here in 1916 with approximately 500 men and burned down a part of the town. President assigned Brigadier General John J. Pershing to lead a punitive expedition to hunt down Villa and his men.

Columbus had the distinction of being one of four different US cities to be invaded until the Second World War. The invaders then were supposed to be soldiers

Today, a group of the town's people decided enough was enough. Six trucks came into town. All the men in the trucks got out, brandishing military assault weapons. Over the loud speaker, both in English and Spanish, one man said he was the new Mayor and he was now in charge. Anyone who tries to take back the town was to be killed along with two others at random. "Get out here so you will be counted and you will see your new masters."

This town had enough of drug smugglers, rapists, human traffickers, thieves and being pushed around.

Over another loud speaker, was the answer. "No shit."

Seven men were hit with high caliber rifle fire. That was the signal for the other rifles, shotguns and military weapons taken from previous attempts to subjugate them. The women and teenagers joined in the fight.

It was over in five minutes. A whistle sounded halting the ambush.

With rehearsed precision, 68 male bodies were picked up. A front-in loader drove through the street and stopped where everyone of the dead men hit the ground. Townspeople heaved the bodies into the bucket along with ones who were captured. Once loaded, it was a simple matter to drive up to the dump truck with the bodies and stack them into the back.

Occasionally a rifle shot was heard, sometimes a pistol. The town's people watched where everyone ran too. It was a simple matter to follow the pointing fingers.

The trucks and the school bus went out into the desert. A long trench was dug, the bodies laid out, prisoners killed and then the trench covered up.

"Third time, Marco," one man said. "You'd think they learned."

Marco prayed for the men who died and turned his gaze. "No one puts a gun to my head. The women are not going to be raped. Our town will not be vandalized. We keep our food. Most importantly, we have food and money to live. You know what happened last time. Not again."

Everyone around Marco agreed with him. Leaving someone alive only brings them back for more. When the law grows its backbone and means something. Then this will stop.

Pentagon Situation Room, Washington D.C.
1830 hours EST   (0300 hours Delta 19 January)

Accounting for the time difference the clock ticked down to the last minute as eight B-52s plus fighter and electronics support, turned on their flight plans and opened the Bombay doors. The navigators, radar operators, bombardiers and other members of the crews shifted in their seats one last time as the computers lined up perfectly.

Inside the bombays of each aircraft were ten 2,000-pound bombs. Bagram Air base was the target of four B-52s. The mission was to make it unusable. Half the bombs were bunker buster types. These bombs had hardened points that allowed them to penetrate the surface in order loosen up the soil. The bombs were set to impact the runways.

The other targets were motor pools full of American Vehicles with special emphasis placed on awnings over helicopters and aircraft.

Five minutes after the first bomb was released, all the aircraft turned and left the country. No aircraft were lost or American personnel injured.

4 miles south of Sells Arizona, West of Highway 19, Tohono O'odham Nation.
2315 hours MST

Border Patrol Agent Michael Argus lay on the ground along with Reservation Agent Harrel Ngoma and watched, again, the nightly march of the APC's.

It was a full moon casting a lot of light out there. Argus and Ngoma had to play out this scenario, again. Tonight, they had orders to photograph the "alleged activity" for the chair-warmers to find reasons to do nothing and, of course, scratch their pointy heads.

The drug dealers were still at it. Reports of these activities were documented dating back decades. Right on time, four M-113 armored personnel carriers, complete with M-2 .50 caliber machine guns came lumbering up to the same place and turn on the rock. The back hatches opened, exposing large bundles of drugs being transferred to eight pickup trucks. Once the drugs were removed, suitcases presumably filled with cash, were thrown in. The hatches closed and the M-113 APCs turned and went south of the border.

The men loading the trucks, decided to take a break. About fifteen men laughed and opened one of the bundles and rolled up cigarettes. Halfway through the well documented party, gunfire from the rear of the trucks cut down all fifteen men. Off in the distance, first one explosion, then three others in rapid succession brought screams and rapid gunfire.

A large contingent of men dressed in gray 'uniforms' came and checked the men on the ground. The fifteen bodies were lined up, while other men dozed the trucks with gasoline. Others punctured the gas tanks.

One man started a fire under one truck and rest cascaded, creating one large fire.

230

Suddenly the fires where the APCs were at, suddenly rose up stronger.

Ngoma looked at Argus and slid down. "I got a pistol with three mags. You ain't got any better."

Argus looked at his partner. "What I got is common sense and it is saying my boss and those butt warmers can come out here and arrest them."

Ngoma shook his head. "I got four years in the Marine Corps. That," he pointed to the burning trucks, "scares the crap out of me."

Both men, quietly and carefully, picked up all their equipment and stealthily walked back to their truck, 2 miles away.

Room D-113, George Washington University Hospital, Washington, D.C.
1400 hours EST

Kincaid walked out of the bathroom. It still hurt to move around. All the scar tissue tugged at everything. The Doctors constantly told him about taking it easy or Kincaid could return and do this…. again.

Kincaid came out and saw Hector Adams waiting for him. Both men smiled at each other. Kincaid sat down on the bed and took a deep breath. "Hector, I have to thank you with everything I have. If you were not here, ….?

"I know you better, John," Hector said. "You only needed to be reminded of who you are. All I did was listen to you figure it out that your memories wanted you to see how you outlived an impossible situation."

"Yeah, it was impossible," John said. He suddenly inhaled sharply and winced in pain. "I wish I remembered that before I did it."

Hector chuckled. "You are being discharged this week. I am leaving today to head west. Mike said he jumped the gun with Wendy Kendal and Earl Locklear. Those two young people have fallen for each other and had wanted to get married. Thad and others stuck their noses into it and now they are not getting married and openly refuse to socialize."

"Yuk," John said. "I knew Kendal was trouble in training. I passed her anyway. Now the lesbian is not a lesbian and cannot understand that couples are not deployed."

Hector sighed. "You stay out of it. If someone needs counseling for something, you leave it to me or Mike. Concentrate on your duties in your new life."

Kincaid sighed himself and laid back down on the bed. "I feel old, Hector."

"Starting next week," Hector said. "Then you will feel old."

Kincaid grunted as he slid onto the bed. "I can still feel all the needles, instrument pads and tubes even though they removed the last one last week." Kincaid still grunted as he settled in.

Adams smiled. "John, both of us are beyond our prime and both of us need to retire. My original flock has only three members. Three men in my church. Yet I am still here. You have two brothers and several younger ones ascending. Mike is shot up like you are and Thad is actively training his replacement. When is everyone going to get out of the way and pass the torch?

John looked over to Hector. "At the end of the year, when I graduate my Shark-Hunters." John made the sign of the cross.

January 20

Boise State University, Boise, Idaho
1000 hours MST

The University hosted a meeting that was becoming a common political forum across the nation. Governor Howard Falkner of Montana and Governor Simon Jurgens of Idaho formally met to start dissolving boundaries between them. Weeks of meetings at various state, county and some city governmental departments, joined or formally merged agencies.

The Governors from Colorado, Utah and Wyoming was there also as a courtesy. Wyoming was in talks with Montana and Idaho but was already formally linked with Colorado and Utah.

Wyoming was there to provide support and advice as needed, but passed along documentation stating formally allowing border counties to work with Montana counties.

January 21

White House, Washington D.C.
0800 hours EST

Rebecca Beck arrived early to meet privately with the President. Her agenda centered around something she fought internally. Director Marcus Solin of the FBI has been pushing for a National Police force. Technically, under the "Victoria" situation, all the thousands of police departments of the nation are a single unified Police Force. But this was a different thing. His idea gave everyone the same uniform and allegiances. Her mind had visions of the Nazi SS.

Beck sat down in the outer office after checking in with Lucy Markson, the President's secretary.

Beck spent a lot of time thinking about this very subject. Marcus brought it up with every report and meeting. All the logical arguments for it ran against her knowledge of all national police forces across the world and down through history. There were so many problems from a moral standpoint. Police departments at every level have Internal Affairs Investigators who police the police. There were too many places where this idea could push the country over the edge into open warfare.

The other side of the argument was exactly why we need a National Police Force. There was too much crime. Criminal elements relearned why the roaring twenties and prohibition a hundred years ago was a success. Jurisdiction boundaries, differing rules and funding personnel needs crash against the bean-counters. It's very expensive to maintain a criminal intelligence laboratory when you might have only one or two cases a year. That expense can sometimes mean the difference in buying a school bus or funding a lab.

The other reason for a USPD is the common need for a militia across the nation. Very few dollars are available to fight roaming criminal gangs. The FBI is constantly tracking gangs who attack numerous towns and cities, emptying banks, raping women, kidnapping children, trafficking illegal drugs and stealing anything they want. The FBI comes in behind with words and notebooks. The gangs know to avoid and stay ahead of the 'G-men'. Some people are so-scared, they e-mail the gangs, telling them where the FBI is at or will be going.

There are plenty of instances where the FBI is tracking them and the trail goes cold. The gangs vanish, literally. Some of the agents are turning a blind eye, considering what some of the gangs were doing.

The FBI could have found where the bodies are if they had the time.

Beck shook her head, returning back to the present. She had to quit trying to convince herself.

Preliminary research said two million USPD officers were needed.

Was this a Gestapo?

"Madam Attorney General," Lucy Markson said, "The President will see you now."

Beck took a deep breath, picked up her purse and briefcase and went into the Oval Office.

January 22

United States Embassy Annex, Damascus, Syria
0200 hours Bravo

In a move that reached up to comical levels, terrorists armed with RPG-7 grenade launchers shot eight rockets at the United States Embassy in Damascus. Seven men with four launchers climbed to the top of a corporate building across the street from the Embassy building.

The US Embassy on Abo Jafaa Al Mancour has been permanently closed since February 6, 2012. The only personnel on site are a few Syrians that act as care-takers for the buildings and facilities.

The Czech Embassy has been acting as a base for American interests since violence escalated.

This morning's fiasco was evident in a region that has had too much violence. Sometimes picking a fight is just something to do.

The seven men used a freight elevator to go to the roof of a corporate building across the street. At exactly 2 am, the men started a volley fire of the rockets. By the time, the fourth rocket was launched toward the building, the first launcher was re-loaded. The fifth round hung up in the launcher and disrupted their rhythm, delaying their escape a full minute. After the last rocket was fired, all of them yelled expletives as they ran down the stairs.

The comedy was evident because the security forces of five separate embassies jumped into action in addition to the Syrian Security Forces.

Those wantabee terrorists burst out the doors and were halted by dozens of searchlights and flashlights. Those same terrorists meekly held up pistols and two AKs. Yelling back and forth ended when the terrorists dropped their weapons. All of them were slammed up against walls, forcibly searched and chained. As those men were taken outside, they saw dozens of vehicles flashing white, red, blue and green lights.

To add insult to injury, that portion of the 'closed' Embassy was completely empty of people and equipment. Those 'clowns' shot eight rockets at nothing.

The Syrian Security Force Commander openly laughed at them.

Room D-113, George Washington University Hospital, Washington D.C.
1300 hours EST

Kincaid was at last dressed and in the final stages of packing when a knock on the door jamb brought two smiling faces in to visit him.

Kincaid smiled back. "Greetings, Missus and Mister O'Cleary."

Dennis chuckled. "And we dressed up real pretty to visit you." Dennis said, closing the door.

"Now boys, behave," Brenda said. She sat down at the expense of everyone else. Hawker smiled and sat on another chair.

"Yes Ma'am," Kincaid said, closing the last suitcase. "I am so glad to finally be gone from this place."

"Yes," Brenda said motioning to Hawker with a whirling motion. Hawker turned on the 'buzz box', set it down and walked out into the hallway.

Brenda looked at the four green lights. "You are never deploying to the field anymore. So where do you want to fit in the community?"

"Master trainer," Kincaid said. "Shark Hunters and Ops center operators at Minutemen. Physically I am finished. If I interpret the doctors, I am simply waiting until I die. If I want to believe them."

"I'm 47 and pregnant," Brenda said with a trace of sarcasm. "I want to add to your aggravation. I want your recommendation for an NCO school."

Kincaid laughed. "OK, I'll bite. You need at least six months to do it right, if not more. Then there is remedial and supplemental instruction as the NCO rises in the ranks. In the past, it was politics and Senior officers interfering that destroys the concept. By senior officers, I mean that they don't want to part with the best guys who will get his next promotion. Politics adds too many things that never win a battle."

"Think it over while you go back to Minutemen," Brenda said. "I need a working concept in two months."

"I am on convalescent leave until November. That is as much to my age as the injuries."

"John," Brenda said in a more neutral tone. "The long problem with NCO training has been exactly as you and I stated. It is a long process that is the same if not more than training an Officer Corps, only more intense."

Kincaid rotated his head from side to side. "Tell Mr. Layton to be ready to build a new facility. This time he will build a crowning achievement."

Kincaid looked at Dennis. "I will need you to be ready to teach."

Dennis looked over to Brenda.

236

January 23

Delta 7, Moss Point, Montana
2300 hours MST

Taylor rotated the key on Seagrove's door, opening it and stepping aside. Kendal and Locklear covered the door, high and low. Seagrove was sitting on his bed with his hands raised over his head.

Kendal and Locklear maneuvered into the room covering Seagrove from every angle. He was secured with double the number of restraints any subject would ever need.

"I want my lawyer," Seagrove said.

Taylor came into the room and sat down on the one chair. "You have your lawyer. It is the air you breathe, the water you drink, the food you eat and life you still have."

Taylor looked at him, maintaining a neutral face. "I am not a good interrogator. So here is what I need to know. What banks were you and your friends using? Where are they? And What were your orders?"

Seagrove looked at Taylor. "That's it? What's in it for me to cooperate?"

Taylor held up the key. You cooperate and I don't lose the key. Slowly, over a period of months, your supplies run out. The food is never replaced, the water tank is not replenished. No more showers or cleaning water. No one monitors the air system. If the electrical system trips, maybe someone will come to check it next week. Maybe."

"You can't do that, I have rights," Seagrove said.

Taylor openly laughed. "You were part of a team that shot up a house without warning and were going to kill anyone in that house. No, you don't have any rights."

Seagrove looked back and forth between Taylor, Kendal and Locklear. None of them showed Seagrove anything.

Taylor clicked at stop-watch. "I have allowed five minutes for you to waste. Give me the information or I destroy the key."

"You can't do this," Seagrove was pulling hard on the restraints.

"You have been here for two weeks," Taylor said with a smile. "Imagine what you will look like in two months or longer."

Taylor turned the stop-watch and looked at the time remaining.

Seagrove seemed to resign. "What happens when I give you what you want?"

"We check out your information first. If you tell us the truth, then you get better accommodations."

Seagrove sighed. "What was the first question?"

January 24

Werewolf Support Group #1, Hill County, Montana
0900 hours MST

Kendal rang everyone out. Being back was something Kendal loved. The Savage Rabbits was equally split about her being here. Granted her version of physical training (PT) gave them a lot of strength and when they returned to the main camp, the normal PT was a joke. The flip side was her sessions were almost demonic. This PT varied from day to day. Two hours each day meant all of them, including Captain Miles, were worn out before the day began.

Earl and her were going to be gone for four days, mapping out the detail of the terrain west of here. Old world map-making required a great deal of math and artistic talent. Locklear and Kendal learned that early in their training. Both of the fought hard for the top slot during the Advanced Math courses. Both of them had an epiphany early on. Understanding math made navigation easier.

Now their mutual love for math and navigation was being put to good use. The small- and large-scale National Geographic Maps needed updating and the compiled information needed to be verified. The maps needed to carefully updated and checked.

Colonel Jones had some computer program that was accepting their information and publishing new maps all most as fast as they verified the terrain information. That same program also had them checking the terrain using human observation and overhead satellite photographs.

Kendal went through her underwear drawer as she thought of what to do. She was surprised to see she still thought of practical instead of hetero-weird. She smiled liking the new her. Just to silence the whispers, she was going to use one backpack instead of three.

Earl packed a single backpack for himself.

Both of them assembled all their gear and loaded a SUV. Two backpacks, one tent with associated equipment, two survey transits, two laptops, satellite phone, satellite transceiver, food, drinks, a bag full of toiletries and napkins.

"See you all on Sunday," Kendal said as both of them left.

January 25

Cranston, Montana
1530 hours MST

Kincaid got out of the SUV, stretching his old age and injuries. Kincaid looked at the small community around him. It was small and new. This place was created for a small group of friends or family to live out a quiet life. Kincaid thought of all the places Layman built over the years.

"Hey Dad," Jason said walking out on to the porch.

"Hi ya Bud," Kincaid said, walking stiffly toward his son's home. "Heard someone wants to lose a lot of checkers games."

"I haven't trashed any one in a long time," Jason said, watching his father walk up to the porch.

Jason shook his father's hand and hugged him. "Got enough time for you to lose a game while I cook supper."

January 27

Werewolf Support Group #1, Hill County, Montana
0900 hours MST

Kendal rubbed her head. Too many things going on that needed to done now. Who cares that they have been working 16 to 17 hours a day? Kendal promised to kick the teeth in of anyone who accused her of taking a vacation this past weekend.

Kendal looked over at Locklear. She was distracted by him a lot. Never in her life had anyone make her have thoughts or feelings about her. Right now, was a prime example of his discipline. He was cataloging all the information for submittal to the Intelligence section back at Minuteman.

Both of them were going to take the information there today and spend the night at Cindy's house. Cindy was down at Mike Smith's operation down in Colorado. Cindy said not to make a mess.

January 29

Pollster's National, Washington, D.C.
1030 hours EST

A large group of academic political scientists surrounded a bank of monitors as data from around the country came in and was correlated into one wall filling digital map.

Data from thousands of pollsters who questioned millions of people came into the center and answered innumerable questions on national and regional issues. One question came from a small group of government bureaucrats from the Department of Homeland Security.

'Where were the major divisions in population groups and sub-groups?'

A dedicated monitor to one side started drawing maps over a map of the lower 48 states. Each map had a question over it. One drawing after another showed divisions all over the map. If all the maps were shuffled together, thousands of different colored lines snaked over the maps.

All the technicians and academics watched the nation tear itself apart.

Quinton Ranch, Hinton, Alberta, Canada
1000 hours

Kincaid pulled up to the ranch house and breathed in the pure air of winter. He noticed a horse drawn sleigh off in the distance. He pulled out a set of powerful binoculars and observed a man driving a team of two horses. In the back of the carriage was a woman and two children. Kincaid watched them enjoy the beauty of a winter landscape.

A half an hour later the sleigh drove up to the ranch house. Both boys jumped out and ran up to 'Gampy'. All three of them rejoiced seeing each other. Barbara managed to muscle in a hug as the boys wanted to tell him all about Christmas and their presents.

"Presents," Mark screamed and ran to the pile next to the door. Jeffery ran after him. Barbara told them to take the presents indoor and not leave trash outside.

Thomas chuckled. He drove the horses and carriage over to the barn.

"Dad, Tom going to put up the horses and then come inside. You need to come inside."

"Merry Christmas to us all," John said.

January 30

Har Meron, elevation 3963 feet, Galilee, Northern Israel
0600 hours (Charlie).

The shaved top of the mountain still allowed the newest generation of a Counter Battery Fire Control and Detection Radar Units to thwart the half-witted terrorists trying to antagonize Israel and its citizens.

This unit was a critical to the "IRON DOME" strategy because they had the latest radars and computers. The high elevation and location nine kilometers south of the Lebanese border, allowed Israel to pinpoint rockets launching from Lebanon and Syria.

So far this month, the number of rockets and mortar rounds broke the two thousand mark.

The Israel's were now used to the near constant roar and overhead explosions. Just so long as both sides had ammunition, that was going to continue.

South of Har-Meron, Israeli military and pollical leaders met staring over a highly detailed terrain model of the northern portion of Israel and the southern portion of Lebanon. IRON DOME was working.

But the conduit of ammunition to maintain it was running slow. All the critical stores of ammunition left behind by the Americans was at the magical "six month" level. Six months-worth of ammunition was a critical state.

"We have to consider the Americans will not make up our shortages," one general said.

The Prime Minister said. "We have been building new factories, but it is the raw materials needed that are the problem. Our economy can barely support the infrastructure's needs."

A minister to the side said the thing that no one wanted to say. "Our neighbors have been trying to kill us for decades. They have a lot of resources."

Everyone around the table was silent. Another round of mortar and rocket attacks flooded the three-dimensional map laid out around in front of them.

January 31

Minuteman, north of Fort Benton, Montana
0900 hours

Kincaid eased up the steps to Jones' Headquarters. With each step, Kincaid felt his age. How much longer can he continue with this. The doctors said he needed until November to 'fully' (?) recuperate and lead a normal life (?). This was not his first time being injured. Technically he had a three Purple Hearts. The last time, he was shot up in Mexico and hung on for nearly two hours. Each time he woke up after being injured and fixed, he was in a mixture of physical and mental pain.

Kincaid sucked in a lung-full of air remembering those times. Every time he lost consciousness, there was the peace

242

of death that overcame him. He was happy at that instant in time, finally ready to move on from this life.

Being unconscious was a no-brainer. You had no choice. It was peaceful and uneventful. Each instant when he woke up, Kincaid was actually terrified. Disorientation; conflicting voices and sounds. Breathing hurt; that was the first thing he felt. Nothing resembled what you saw when unconsciousness overruled the world. Then the real pain came. You can't breathe right. You are hungry, then you are not. People ask things but not listen to your words. Your arms and legs don't work. All of it is wrong. You try to move around to feel better, but human hands stop you. Then you wake up and have to be taught how to use your arms, stand, walk and wipe your own ass.

"Hey John," Jones said, holding open the door.

Kincaid smiled and walked inside. "Hello Thad," he said, reaching forward to shake his hand.

Kincaid walked inside and shook hands all around with the men and women he worked with back at Desert Zero. Kincaid enjoyed being liked for a change. It was very difficult to walk in the building using his four wheeled walker. Kincaid did not want a wheel chair.

"Come on in," Jones said pointing to his office. He stopped at the coffee machine and poured two cups.

Both old men sat down at the staff table. They had small talk and coffee for twenty minutes.

Kincaid told Jones about his medical condition. "Bottom line, Thad, is that I will never deploy again. I am shot up worse than Mike. I am on convalescent leave until November. The Army is in the process of medically retiring me. I declined to be assigned to Fort Bragg and go through the medical separation process. Medical leave here is smarter."

Thad took a sip from his coffee. "I had a long call with Valkyrie." He paused to look at Kincaid. "She wants you to dream up and implement a career-long NCO academy. You said the initial course would be 4 to 6 months long. We need those NCOs in their units."

Kincaid shot back. "That's why the Military always fails in NCO development. I remember when they initially wanted a one size fits all Operations and Intelligence course at the Sergeants Major Academy. The initial course requirement to include everything added up to eighteen weeks. The Generals rebelled, saying they could not spare their best NCOs for that long. I went to the twelve-week course for class number two. I could do anything in garrison and the field. But the Generals rebelled again. It was cut down to six-weeks so the officer corps could stay on top."

Thad knew that tone. "Hey," he said, pointing to the wall filling map in front of his desk. "That is my battle space. There is a four-star at Fort Carson named Matheson. He used to be SOCOM. He is here because this area of the country is full of militias. I estimate he will be here in a year, if not already. Matheson has a reputation for being a hard-headed, yet capable commander."

John sipped his cup of coffee. "The only reason you are wearing eagles instead of stripes is the training you were given. You are a Werewolf. Name one other place in the Army that trained an NCO can be better than an officer."

Thad was silent.

"Name one other place that could train you …..."

"Enough," Thad said, massaging a headache.

"You give me two months to get ready and six months with all the men," Kincaid said with emphasis. "I'll take the headaches out of INSANE JANE."

Kincaid looked out the door to the north. Layman's men were busy building the facilities he would need up in the Werewolf area. Inwardly he smiled at the technology that was now available. Two long phone calls with Mister Layman had him up in arms about everything wrong with the world, plus a huge stack of cash made it all happen. UNSTACK THIS was eavesdropping on the conversation and was able to develop the blueprints for Mister Layman to work with so the facility could make leaders out of every one of his Savage Rabbits.

"In short, Thad," Kincaid said. "We are going to teach them why they are so good."

Werewolf Support Group Camp #1, Hill County, Montana
1900 hours MST

244

Kendal, Locklear and Morgan were sitting around the main table, drinking beer. Kendal and Morgan were wearing a t-shirt and underwear. Locklear was in shorts, t-shirt and underwear.

Outside a vehicle drove up and stopped in front of the building. Everyone jumped up, dressed and grabbed weapons.

The front door opened to a fur covered bear named Kincaid. He stopped in the mud area and saw three people ready to shoot him.

Kincaid dropped his two suitcases and briefcase. He proceeded to shed his layers of clothes. Fully half of him was hung up on the hooks as he moved out of the area. Kincaid put the two suitcases off to the side, in the area that was designated for them.

"Hi, everyone," Kincaid said. "I am here to say hello. Hello. Tomorrow, we resume training. Tonight, you resume doing whatever you were doing when I arrived. I will be sleeping in one of the offices of the admin building."

"Sit down," Morgan said. "This class took a vote, and with Mister Covington's agreement, you will be using Byron Handley's room."

"Byron respected you," Locklear said. "As his classmate, I can say he would be honored if you used his room."

"This class," Kendal said. "Voted and it was unanimous." Kendal leaned over the table, exposing her breasts to Kincaid. "Howdy, old man."

Kincaid leaned back. "Your boobs are too young for me. Lean back."

February 1

Underground Station "Conscience", World Wide Web and Channel 513

0900 hours EST.

"If you threaten, act. If you say something, do it. If something is important, stand your ground. Governments are often hamstrung by individuals who have opinions about issues

245

they feel strongly about. This is Martin Socranson, self-proclaimed philosopher who says, 'What are we if we can't back up what you say'?"

"Greetings America" Martin Socranson said beginning his broadcast. "It is reluctantly Saturday and I say thus." In the background the sounds of the 1812 overture played.

"This month we are at war. This month Americans are literally fighting each other, literally and figuratively."

"The Department of Justice, normally the shield protecting American citizens is now targeting the very people they are supposed to protect. Murder, rape, cyber-crimes, bank robberies, grand theft and hundreds of other crimes were set aside so that the mass of the DOJ can investigate, arrest or subjugate normally law-abiding citizens."

"What crimes could normally law-abiding citizens be doing that the full apparatus of the DOJ would turn away from normal duties? Pregnant pause," he said with a large smile. "We," he said, making a whirling motion with his finger. "We, the stupid people of America, are not complying with the mandates of the government surrounding things like turning in guns and God-forbid not taking the law into our own hands."

"Whispers and rumors are running throughout the country about citizens being tired of the law taking too long and not prosecuting captured criminals despite the evidence. In St. Louis, the home of Edgar and Alice Guzman was invaded. The four men, raped 72-year-old Alice and nearly beat 71-year-old Edgar to death. The four men were captured. Edgar and Alice testified against them. The men were eventually released over a technically. The four men rattled on the house for over a week, then broke in. A neighbor over heard one of them, 'we're going to teach you old people a lesson'. Many neighbors called the police and nothing happened for over twenty minutes until a pistol shot was heard. A scream was heard followed by seven more bullets being fired, a silence and seven more."

Socranson paused and wiped tears from his eyes. "As near as we can deduce from the witness statements, the four men broke into the house as Alice and Edgar were eating. Edgar grabbed his pistol and stood in front of Alice. The four of them laughed and pointed a pistol at the couple. Finally, one of them shot a bullet and Alice was hit in the chest. As she went down, they tried to rush Edgar, but he was quicker to react. All four men had between two to three bullets in them. When the police finally arrived, the invaders were sprawled on the floor and Edgar was hugging his wife, crying."

Socranson paused again, as if trying to force down his anger. "After all the dust was settled, the police carried Edgar down to the station and charged him with unlawful possession and discharge of a firearm within the city limits. As the Judge was about to gavel the sentence of fifty dollars and three years' probation, the back door to the courtroom opened."

Socranson lost the battle to control his temper. "The scummiest people dredged from the DOJ, re-arrested him for violating the civil rights of all the invaders. They were supposed to be detained and turned over to the police."

"What in the hell is wrong with us when criminals have more rights and privileges than law-abiding citizens and victims of crimes?"

Socranson paused again. "I apologize America. Mister Guzman hanged himself in his cell. That was not good enough for the DOJ scumbag pictured below you. He took possession of the Guzman residence and secured it in case there were civil litigation issues that could come up in the next six months."

Socranson pointed down at the picture of the DOJ man. "You know what they say about Karma?"

Border Patrol Headquarters Phoenix, Arizona
1000 hours MST

Chief Patrol Agent Thomas Barrios of the Border Patrol read the monthly report for January covering the illegal immigrants coming over the border. He frowned seeing that the number was lowering. Barrios went to the filing cabinet and pulled out December's report and saw it for himself.

Barrios shook his head. Illegal immigration was solving itself with the bad economy. Lack of money nationally meant no one could come here for a job. Agriculture jobs were now being taken over by younger Americans.

But on the good side, illegal drug sales were down for the same reason.

Go figure.

Brenda O'Cleary's new existence took away one of her recent pleasures. After she found out she was pregnant, she left open the bathroom door so the mirror was not steamed over. She wanted to watch her belly grow each day and this was the perfect time and opportunity to do it.

Until the additional guards were placed around her, she was free to dress or not dress anywhere she was in the house. Now she had to look around the corner in her house. She nearly shot a PSA as he went, unannounced, into the bedroom tonight.

The unnamed PSA raised his hands and tried to apologize. "Ma'am, just checking the room."

"Pass the word to everyone. No one, I mean no one but me and my husband comes into the bedroom regardless of the rules. Violators will be shot in the nuts. Understand." She lowered the pistol, pointing to his groin in emphasis.

"Yes Ma'am, never come into the bedroom again, Yes Ma'am." He tried to move aside and leave.

"Problem?" Dennis asked.

"Nearly shot the PSA who was searching the room. Promised him that the next one was getting castrated." She showed him the pistol.

"I'll guard the door, if I can peek," Dennis said smiling.

"How come I can't peek at you," she said back, knowing the answer.

"Any time you want," Dennis said with a smile.

Brenda removed her clothes in a provocative fashion. She steadily added newer moves as time moved along. She stopped at the mirror and observed her son's latest growth. She could not wait to see him.

Brenda looked at Dennis ogling her. She struck a pose allowing her husband to see 'the Brenda show'. She stepped into the hot water and closed her eyes.

February 2

Numerous News Media throughout Oregon, Idaho and California
0900 hours PST

Pollsters and non-binding elections throughout all three states demonstrated that twenty-two counties in Oregon and seven counties in California wanting to secede and join Idaho.

The Oregon state government made the loudest sounds saying that the move was unconstitutional and would be blocked at every turn.

California simply said it would not honor the secession. California additionally said that local officials could and would be prosecuted to the maximum extent of the law.

California and Oregon went on record saying that any such measure would not be allowed to be placed on any ballot.

The counties in California and Oregon reported that citizens were flying the Idaho flag and refusing to fly 'the other flag'.

Werewolf Support Camp #1, Hill County Montana
1100 hours MST

Kincaid enjoyed a quiet day so he could think about training without any interruptions. Being alone in the massive Werewolf Liar, he could spread out all the materials he needed without worrying about anyone disturbing his version of artwork.

Locklear and Kendal took off for the day which was becoming a habit with them. Publicly, they announced to all that their marriage plans were off due to too many individuals interfering with their lives.

The others were out somewhere being young people.

But; there was always a but. Maybe Kincaid will give it five minutes later.

Instead of brooding about his reduced lifestyle and slavery to pills and exercise routines, John looked at the master training plan Gladys Goldstein left with him. "How to do Shark-Hunter the Right Way" was the title. Six inches thick with all the things needed for a true two-and-a-half-year long training program.

John shook his head comparing all the long hours he spent reading her program and the massive headaches he had during Werewolf training that Miss Gladys jammed down his throat. All the things they did, before, during and after Vietnam. There was so much she did before Vietnam that Kincaid marveled at how much he could do once he did get to Vietnam.

After Vietnam, Miss Gladys continued his training. She was devious in her ability to make anything into training.

He was the brainiac of the team. He had a natural ability to catalog all the information during any operation.

Even those instances when the time-frame was tight, he knew what information he had to find, yet more importantly he knew what he still needed to find. He thought that was his greatest accomplishment.

Zach was the 'glue' that held the team together. His eyes saw the things that needed to be seen and his ears heard the sounds that needed to be heard. The greatest gift he had was his ability to translate all that knowledge into words and 'paint' a picture that told the story of a mission.

Senior Chief Petty Officer George Theodore was the old man who was a bridge between Zach and him. More to the point he was a steady hand to hold down two young men and keep them on a short leash.

Kincaid needed a plan. Something was muddying up in his mind. The plan was bubbling just under the surface.

Kincaid walked up to the eight foot long dry-ease board and started by dividing it into three sections. One for INSANE JANE, one for Shark Hunter and the last for the NCO Academy.

Kincaid walked back to the table. Shark-Hunting was a six-inch-thick program. INSANE JANE doctrine was still being written even though he had the two authors under his wing. While Kincaid was in the hospital, Kincaid burned up his X-Berry staying appraised of training and noting things.

Kincaid had a bubble come to the surface and pop in his head. He went to the standard NCO Program of Instruction used today and lifted the six-inch-thick document. Half of it was social science horse-shit and could be thrown out. He quickly flipped through, slowing through some sections and speeding through others.

Kincaid's idea popped. All the players were in one place. There was no need to re-invent anything. Shuffle this table full of training programs into one deck. All you need to do was improve on what was already here. He was not going to do what the Army did which was re-teach what you already were supposed to do.

Each individual student needed to be tested thoroughly beforehand and be personally evaluated on where to reinforce his or her training to a bring everyone up to a set standard.

Kincaid looked back to empty dry-ease board. He shook his head up and down. Yeah.

1930 hours MST

Cindy Morgan arrived dragging in her equipment and seeing John concentrating hard at a mountain of paperwork scattered on the main table. She mentally flipped a coin and decided she could walk around naked and he probably would not notice.

It was late in the day. Wendy and Earl will be arriving in a little while. Today was not a good day for that kind of embarrassment. Cindy chuckled and pushed that stupid idea out of her head. Cindy went to the table near Kincaid's work area and knocked on the table.

Kincaid jumped slightly as if he just noticed Cindy. "I need to find Wendy," she said.

Kincaid leaned back. "I have been here all day, alone."

"Wendy has the key to Julia's room," she said. "You, have it?"

"No," John said, looking down at his watch.

"You are in Byron's room," she said. "Can I take a shower while I wait for her?"

"Sure. Room's open," he said. It was late. Sometimes it was better to sleep on something this big.

Kincaid started picking everything up. He carefully looked at each thing and put like things together. Finally, he had a two-foot-thick stack that was at least semi-organized. He

251

went to his 'room' and got one of the boxes, brought it out to his stack and put it all in the box. He needed a better method that will show itself tomorrow. Tonight, his head hurt and it was past time to quit. As he put down the box, Cindy turned off the water. Kincaid sat down on the bed and massaged his forehead.

"John," Cindy said. "I'm going to cook something quick. Are you hungry?"

"No thanks. Just tired. I need a shower and sleep."

"OK," she said. "My bag is in here. Please don't lock the door."

Kincaid rubbed his head. He shuffled into the bathroom and turned on the water. He eased inside and soaked. He turned the temperature up to something that was almost scalding. When he finished, he held his head under the water and let the water pound on his head. Slowly, the headache slid away.

Kincaid looked around for the bathrobe and remembered that Cindy had that. He put on his underwear and t-shirt. Two 800-milligram Motrin tablets with a glass of water, and a good nights' sleep was his.

Kincaid eased under the covers and settled in. He sensed rather than saw Cindy come into the room. The door closed and the robe fell over his feet. Cindy lifted the covers on the other side of the bed and slid in beside Kincaid.

Cindy curled around John. "You're not Zach and I am not Karen. Tonight, we are two widows with memories. I need to feel warmth. I will leave if you want."

John smiled in the dark room. "Just so long I don't get raped."

Cindy smiled and rubbed his chest.

Both were asleep in minutes.

February 4

Pentagon, Washington D.C.
0700 hours EST

Brenda O'Cleary came to work. Today was the day. In her briefcase was her formal request to retire. She hoped the

Army was not stupid, saying her status was too critical to allow her to leave. No one was a superman or indispensable. Officers and NCOs alike were required to learn the two jobs above them and one below them. Regulations still allowed her to be administratively discharged for pregnancy at her request. She could literally follow all the doctor's instructions and pull back steadily until two months before her son was borne.

She put up her heavy coat, beret, briefcase and purse.

She turned to Hawker. "Call over to General Edwards' office and tell him I'm on the way." She picked up the folder with the three individual folders inside. She also picked up the box with the double set of five stars.

By the time she arrived at Edwards' office, he had just arrived. He scowled at her. "Give me a few minutes, Matt. Then let her in." He motioned to O'Cleary.

Edwards' aide picked up a figurine of a West Point football player and placed it on a small table off to the side at a certain place and angle. Several people peeked in and looked at the statue. Some were relieved and others were not happy. O'Cleary smiled at the mood meter Colonel Harm set up.

The intercom on Colonel Harms' desk buzzed. "Send her in, Matt."

Colonel Harm rose but O'Cleary waved him off pointing to the statue. He smiled back.

O'Cleary walked inside Edwards' office, closed the door, walked over to a chair and sat down.

"Amanda lifted the restriction on visitors," Edwards said. "You are formally invited to come over soon to visit, eat, share gossip and maternity stories."

O'Cleary smiled at him. "Dennis has been in contact with her. For a Medal of Honor recipient, he fits the house mouse part of his life really easy."

"What do you have?" Edwards said, pointing to the files in her hands.

O'Cleary fired the first shot. She held up all three. "Take your pick: resignation, retirement or administrative discharge."

"WHAT !!!" he screamed; loud enough for the guards to come running in. He waved them off and walked over to

O'Cleary. He took the files, read them all quickly as he walked over to the shredder and promptly turned all of it into confetti.

O'Cleary quickly tabulated and Dennis won the bet by at least three seconds. Damm, there went her new maternity underwear.

Edwards stretched in his chair. "I don't need this shit, you understand. I got the Security idiots drilling holes in my head over Amanda's vanishing act and sudden reappearance. Both things have them driving me crazy because she did it all under their noses. Then there is the whole governmental craziness involved in this "Victoria" process. I got Generals and Admirals who can't command without make-up and hand jobs to steady them. Now that you have everything under control, you want to bale on me?"

Edwards walked over, bent over and looked O'Cleary dead in her eyes from a four-inch distance. "You are a national treasure. You are the only person smart enough to make sense out of all the crazy in this place."

"I can drag out a resignation or retirement for years. I can find a doctor who will keep you pregnant with voo-doo and spells and witchcraft. That baby will not come out until he graduates high school."

Edwards stopped and forced himself to calm down. "You are here. Now ask me why?"

O'Cleary learned years ago not to laugh in Edwards' face or be intimidated. "Why sir?"

Edwards straightened up and winced. "My back is too old to intimidate anyone. I had a meeting with the President over the weekend. He wanted to have a private discussion about the next two years," Edwards held up two fingers. "You and I ain't going anywhere, kid."

"Sir," O'Cleary tried to say…...

Edwards waved her off. "I already had this discussion. There is nothing to argue about. The President knew that you wanted to raise a child in peace. He said I was overdue and deserved a peaceful retirement now that Amanda returned. He used the Patriotic card and the overworked card and probably several other cards."

Edwards came over and sat down heavily in a chair next to O'Cleary. "Brenda, you of all people have earned a rest and with a child on the way, you deserve it more than I do. If what you have said over the years is true, you having a child on the way is a miracle and you are ordered to do everything in your power to have a healthy and happy child. The Pentagon will do without because you shall put him or her first. Period."

Edwards sighed. "Amanda needs her husband and she is denied. I admit that when you came back, the first and only thing in my mind was that I can finally retire in June." Edwards stopped to take a deep breath. "Brenda, no one can force you to take the oath when I finally get to leave. But I will be forced to admit and I have to the President, that this 'Victoria trouble' could not be solved without you. The President agreed."

Brenda's mood changed. Suddenly, she jumped as Arthur kicked her.

"Go home," Edwards said. "Your child is saying leave and relax. This is a long-haul process.

Werewolf Support Camp #1, Hill County, Montana
0600 hours MST

Cindy woke up with 'tank mouth'. She also felt the bed and she was the only person in it. The 'tank mouth' had everything thing to do with the aroma's coming out of the kitchen. Someone was cooking breakfast. She did remember taking off the robe and it was still where she left it. She quickly went through the rituals of waking up, put on her uniform and left the room.

Wendy and Earl were already at the table peacefully drinking coffee. Both of them looked at her walking out of John's room. They lifted their cups to her.

Cindy shook her head 'no' and went to get a cup for herself.

Kincaid was in the kitchen. He did have a legendary radar that knew when someone was waking up and needed food. Kincaid was not in uniform. He was wearing a robe, tube socks and slippers. She did not want to think about what was underneath. Just as the food hit the tables, the front doors opened and a ruckus entered.

Kincaid screamed, telling everyone to "remove their boots. Breakfast in five". Miles was behind them trying to fit inside.

All sat at the table as Kincaid put the platter of steaks at the end where he was sitting. Typical of him he had a hat on. When someone reached for food, he screamed displeasure. Removing the hat, he said grace. "Dear God, these heathens want food and here they are. Bless them for the indigestion. Amen." When no one moved he added, taking a steak for himself. "Amen means eat."

Steaks, eggs, toast, bacon and potatoes. It was all here. "Gentlemen, and Ladies. If you want something else, buy it, cook it yourself and clean up your mess."

"I'll wash up the dishes today," Cindy said.

Kendal jumped in, "I'll help." She wanted details and this was as good as it will get.

"Kendal," Kincaid said. "Cindy needs the key to Julia's room."

J. Edgar Hoover Building, Washington D.C.
0900 hours EST

The Director of the FBI, Marcus Solin picked up the monthly report of criminal activity for the month of January. The numbers for all crimes are leveling out. Some of his staffers tried to call it 'flat-lining'. Solin wondered if there were no more targets to attack or things to steal. Murders held at 2,319. Bank robberies were actually down to 749.

The demographics show that immigrants were specific targets that consistently did not report crimes against them. They had lingering memories from their homelands where police were for sale or something to take out frustrations. American police agencies called them walking ATMs. With the collapsing bank situation, none of them trusted banks.

Solin skimmed the rest of the report, finally turning away. He thought of the request for the US Police Force. The AG said that it was formally going to be submitted tomorrow at the monthly Cabinet meeting. The Defense Department was the strongest advocate even with the possibility of losing personnel and money. They never liked the idea in the first

256

place. The five divisions along the southern borders were hard to maintain with the Justice Department and the ISA constantly wanting augmentation at locations deep in the country.

Werewolf Support Camp #1, Hill County, Montana
0900 hours MST

Cindy put a new pot of coffee on the table and saw that Kincaid was struggling with his box of materials. The others saw him coming out of his room.

Earl ran up to him and grabbed the box. "Sergeant Major, we are hours away from a hospital if you rupture your stitching. We can set up someplace for you to work."

Kincaid was heaving and had to be helped to the table.

Wendy pulled Cindy off to the side, out of ear shot. Both of them had a furious discussion until finally they had something to shake hands over.

Kincaid opened his robe to check his wounds. Wendy just had to look over. He was dressed in shorts and t-shirt. "Just looking for blood, lech."

"Just wanted to see for myself," she said smiling.

"I'm normal for now," Kincaid said standing to pull out some files. He looked up and saw a space over by the side. "If you guys want to help. Find me 16 feet of banquet tables, four folding, yet comfortable chairs, two filing cabinets, with dividers and folders. Additionally, I have 16 feet of dry ease boards that can be mounted to the wall." Kincaid pointed to the area.

Kincaid looked at the trio. "I need to work out the Shark Hunter program, the INSANE JANE training program, an NCO Academy program and finally a new class of Werewolves."

"Road trip," Wendy said. Earl and Wendy changed into civilian clothes and took a truck into Havre. It was easier to find it and buy it than to drive into Minuteman and get it. Besides, they needed to get something from the courthouse.

"John," Cindy said, getting his attention. "Do you wish to talk about it?"

"I slept well, thank you and you are right. I am not Zach and you are not Karen. The people we wanted to grow old with died too soon. Nothing else needs to be said."

If it were anyone else in the world, she would explode on the spot. But John was an asshole, but he was still John. Two can play Mighty Mouse.

Cindy tapped on John's shoulder. "Give me something to do or we go back to bed."

John stood there and looked at her for several seconds. He picked up a three-inch thick, three-ring binder and two-red lead mechanical pencils. "NCO Master Training Program. Read, make it bleed red with comments and return by tomorrow."

Cindy held onto the binder and looked at John. Yes, the asshole was back.

"P.S." John said. "Shark-Hunter resumes tomorrow. We'll see how much you people learned in my absence."

"Welcome back asshole," Cindy said hefting the book and walking away.

John heard her muttering something about he was still an asshole. He could never tell her how much he yearned to hold her warm body again. That was something he believed Zach would never forgive him for, even if Karen gave her blessing. John, more than anything, believed that he was never going to be good enough for that feeling again.

Two hours later, Cindy walked up to John and slammed down the binder. John nearly jumped out of his skin.

"I tried, you dickhead," Cindy said. "I thought you needed some time to relax and I felt it would be good enough for the both of us to just sleep together. Until your bitchy-boo handing me this book, I felt good for the first time in a long time and no, I do not think Zach would object. I knew him better than you did. He had his nightmares and confessions. No matter what, you were his brother. I was maybe his wife, but you were his brother."

Kincaid screamed. He rubbed his forehead and sat heavily in a chair. "I slept good for the first time in years. As David Nichols and I fought that battle to the death, I saw Karen looking at me as I shot David in the head. I was ready to join her. I wanted to join her. I felt ashamed for feeling

258

comfortable with you. I don't deserve to be happy. I don't deserve to feel good. I wanted to die. Yet, here I am. Why am I here?"

Cindy came around and hugged him hard as he cried. Cindy held him as he fought against her. On and on he cried about not being good enough to protect Karen and she died in front of him.

Wendy and Earl returned and stopped at the door. Cindy shook her head and nodded her head to the side. They closed the door quietly, leaving Cindy and John alone.

Forty-five minutes later, John was spent. He went limp in Cindy's arms. She helped him stand and guided him to his room. Cindy pulled down his covers put him in the bed. She removed his shoes, tucked him in and turned out the lights.

Cindy called Earl and said to come back and be quiet about it.

The walls around all the rooms were thick with insulation. That meant you could be normal and not bother anyone. The four banquet tables were pulled inside and set up. Earl and Wendy crawled under and used three-foot-long zip ties to lock the ends together.

Wendy caused a commotion in the store. Everyone was watching her pull out the different type chairs and try them out. Earl looked around as Wendy made her choices.

The two filing cabinets were solid, made from real wood and set easily against the front wall.

Earl grabbed the drill and Wendy found the studs for him. Earl marked and drilled holes in the dry ease borders. He then drilled into the dry wall. Each of the eight holes in the dry wall were plugged with anchors for the screws to hold up the boards.

When finished all three of them stood back and marveled at the result.

Kincaid came out of the bedroom and went to the kitchen. He poured himself a cup of coffee and walked over to his new work area. "Good," he said, with a smile. His face showed his fatigue. But there was something else. "Grab a cup of coffee and meet me here at 1500. I apologize for not being available to train you. We need to discuss how to fix that." He turned and went back to his room.

Congress, Washington, D.C.
1700 hours EST

The "Hopper" is an old wooden box placed in front of the Speaker's podium at the Rostrum. This box is the place where any Representative can introduce a bill to be considered for passage into a law. The bill's main requirement is the signature of the Representative submitting it for assignment to a committee. The staffer whose job it was to collect all the bills out of the hopper groaned. As was the case yesterday and other days before it. It was at least half full.

The bills were taken to the Parliamentarian's office where it was assigned a number and referred to a sub-committee. The Staffers had a running pool betting on the total number of bills and which bill was the zaniest of the all. That last category was voted on by the loudest laughter.

"Let the crazy begin."

February 5

Werewolf Support Camp #1, Hill County, Montana
0500 hours MST

Wendy Kendal awoke, stretched and shook Earl out a dead sleep. All of them were awake until late last night. Kincaid spent hours just talking to them about all kinds of subjects and the things they saw.

Yesterday's trip to Havre was used as an example. He asked them all sorts of probing questions about what they saw and the things about the town of nearly 2,014 persons.

Kincaid sent them both to the dry ease board and had them sketch in all the details about what they saw and did not see. Kincaid asked general questions and pointedly showed them they were not paying attention. Forty-five minutes later, both of them sat down; mad and humiliated.

Kincaid looked over at Morgan. She went to the board and filled in some details for another twenty minutes.

Kincaid sighed and got up. For over two hours, Kincaid described the town in great detail on the other dry ease board.   When he was finished, they looked at the glaring differences.

Kincaid sat down. "Well Ladies and Sir, that is the difference. I did not consciously look over the city. I have been doing it for so long, it is second nature. I want you to notice the difference between both presentations. Mine has straight and neat lines for maps and outlines for factual data."

Kincaid stopped to take a breath of Albuterol. "I don't want you to get mad. This is a process."

Wendy had to supply the snarky attitude. "Can you describe the town of Hingham to the west of Havre?"

Kincaid went to the board, erased their attempt at an area study and recited a flawless area study of a small agricultural town with a population of 132. He only needed forty-five minutes. Because of the small size it did not take too long.

Kendal followed along with a blank study. She finally pushed it away.

Kincaid sent them away for the evening to lick their wounds.

Kendal came out in her sweat suit. The other men searching the wilds for the all the winter portions of the area study. All of them groaned seeing Kendal smiling at them.

Kendal ground them down for two hours beginning at 6 am. All of it was ground exercise. Miles wanted running, but Kendal countered saying that war was more than just running. Kendal instituted a lot of cardio into the stationary motions.

When it was all over, Miles staggered away like the rest of them. Kendal was smiling and happy. "Thank you for the welcome home, guys."

It was 8 am when everyone was finished. Kincaid came out in a robe, searching for a cup of coffee. There were several cat calls about him not joining in.

Kincaid put down the cup, took off his robe and t-shirt. The group was silent as Kincaid showed off the red scars crisscrossing his body. "Shot five times at point blank range. I got him four times. I won only because I finally remembered to shoot him in the head. This is an example of failure to follow your training standards. Remember to shoot your opponent only once anywhere. The only way to turn them off is a bullet to the head. Convalescent leave till November."

All of them stood at attention and saluted as Kincaid put his t-shirt and robe on. He crisply returned the salute, picked up his coffee and walked away.

2000 hours MST

Kendal and Locklear finished up their workload and went to take a shower. Wendy sat on the bed waiting for Earl. She was combing her hair thinking about the marriage license in the drawer. It was good for a year. They wanted a real wedding but were at a loss to figure out how. Jones' draconian pronouncements about not deploying forced them to duck away.

Kendal had an intrauterine device placed in her that prevented a pregnancy. She wanted to remove it, but not until they left to live a peaceful life, somewhere.

Kendal stayed in Earl's room. Not that Cindy was likely to use it, but she had her room key. Maybe, sometime, possibly, Cindy and John will figure out they needed each other.

Earl turned off the water and came out a few minutes later. He noticed Wendy absently combing her hair. She was thinking of something and it would probably involve him.

"Hello," Earl said.

Wendy put down the brush. "I want to marry you and make you happy. But I cannot figure out why. I don't know how."

Earl figured out quickly that this did not have to make sense. "I am grateful and I do not feel the need to question it?"

Wendy looked at the man she wanted to love. "I don't know anything about all of this, Earl. Please let me learn."

"My Grandpa said love is something you'll never understand. I believe him. My Grandma wanted to choke him more than a hundred times. But she loved him all day and every day. He loved her and held her hand as she died in the hospital. My grandpa died of grief a week later...." Locklear waited a moment. "There is no other way to say it."

Wendy looked at Earl, suddenly leaned over and kissed him. She remembered a day long ago, when she talked to John Kincaid one night at Desert Zero about loving someone special.

February 5

5713 Whitmore Drive, Dale City, Virginia
0500 hours EST

Clara Simpson yawned through her coffee as her PSAs led the way out the door. Her car was already running as she left the door. Another PSA locked the house door, her third PSA followed her down the steps to the car.

Clara sipped her coffee and grabbed the handrail. The thin sheet of ice made that section of the steps very slippery. Clara slipped on the second to last step. She crushed her coffee cup, spilling the hot coffee on her chest, distracting her. She fell down on the stone steps, fracturing her skull. The PSAs tried grabbing her. One of them fell on top of her.

The other PSAs grabbed radios and shouted code words.

Two minutes later, the street was filled with police cars, ambulances and fire trucks. Matt Simpson cried as his wife was zipped into body bag along with a PSA man.

The EMTs struggled with Clara until she stopped breathing and would not start breathing.

485 Glenmore Drive, Alexandria Virginia
0520 hours

Brenda O'Cleary was awakened by the 'apparatuses' of official Washington. All the communications, assigned or bought by senior officials, lit up. Every telephone, pager, tablet, laptop; either land line or wireless fired up, advising everyone about Clara's accident along with her PSA.

Brenda looked at the text of the situation. The managers discovered they needed to add a small explanation to halt a flood of calls wanting to know what happened. Clara was dead. Brenda felt a knot in her chest. Clara was her friend.

263

Brenda went to the table and drank a cup of coffee with Dennis. She waved off the PSAs who wanted to implement increased security measures around the house.

Dennis sat down and calmly waited with her. Both of them waited for the stupid to happen. As the minutes ticked by, the PSAs made and received phone calls.

When the clock said 6 am, Brenda stood, kissed Dennis and went back to the bedroom to get dressed for the day.

Dennis heard a "GET OUT" coming from the bedroom. Some PSA was standing there muttering something about covering the room under the present circumstances. Dennis walked around the agent, pushed him outside, closed and locked the door.

"Looks like I am going to be forced to guard you while you shower and get dressed." Dennis smiled.

Brenda flashed him with her robe.

Pentagon, Washington, D.C.
0800 hours EST

Brenda showed her badge exactly as she did every day. Today there were extra checks as she walked down to her office. Clara Simpson's accident had everyone wound up.

Brenda looked for Hawker. She peeled off to go to the bathroom. Brenda answered a few calls until Hawker returned. Sometimes she answered the phones impersonating Hawker. She would talk trash with the caller saying things about O'Cleary and having fun with it.

Hawker came in and frowned as O'Cleary suppressed laughter with the clown who had no idea who he was talking too.

"General," Hawker said. "Someday, that will get me in a lot of trouble."

Edwards' line lit up. "General O'Cleary, sir." She listened to the line and said, "Yes Sir," and hung up.

Brenda looked at Hawker. "Stay here and direct traffic. I'll be in General Edwards' office." Just then three more lines lit up.

Brenda left and walked over to Edwards' office.

264

Colonel Harm waved O'Cleary straight into the office and closed the door.

Edwards pointed to the chair in front of his desk. He made two cups of coffee. He offered her one and sat down with the other.

Edwards said. "The President called me at home an hour and a half ago. He asked me how much trouble it would be for me to allow you to take over the ISA. I told him I need you here. He understood how valuable you were to work through 'Victoria' and all the other troubles he had."

Edwards looked over to her like he was waiting for her to say or do something.

"Anyway," Edwards said. "Both of us will see the President at 1400 hours. Think about your answer until then."

"Thank you, General," O'Cleary said and walked out. She left the outer office and walked down past her office and wondered around. After thirty minutes of wondering in places a four-star general normally never goes, she sat down in the Food Court. She ordered a breakfast sandwich and juice drink. A quick search gave her an open table with chairs.

Her pager had been vibrating steadily and it was gratifying that she could ignore it.

"Excuse me," a pregnant Sergeant asked. Her flared at the stars on O'Cleary's uniform. "I'm sorry ma'am." She turned to look for someplace else to sit and eat.

"It's OK sergeant," O'Cleary said. "Please sit with me." The sergeant came back and was visibly scared.

"I can find someplace else," the sergeant said.

O'Cleary looked around her uniform. "Relax, Sergeant Pollard." She patted her stomach. "I got pregnant the same way."

Sergeant Pollard met the General everyone talked about; both good and bad. For a General, she acted OK.

O'Cleary reached over and extended her hand. "General Brenda O'Cleary. My husband is retired Command Sergeant Major Dennis O'Cleary."

"Sergeant Delores Pollard, General. My husband is Sergeant Michael Pollard, deadbeat."

"I'm kind of lucky. Dennis and I married late in life. My pregnancy came after the doctors had to fix my innards. How far along are you?"

Pollard finally relaxed and spread out her food. "Seven months along. How far are you?" Pollard jumped slightly and massaged her rib cage.

O'Cleary smiled. "Five months and this is my first."

Both women laughed and enjoyed pleasant conversation.

Pollard's pager buzzed her. She checked it. "Opps, I'm late," she said.

"Where do you work?" O'Cleary said.

"G-3 Operations, Weapons, General." Pollard said.

"That's almost on my way." Both women put the trash in the can and walked away. They talked about things until they turned into Pollard's work area.

A Captain came up and raised her voice. "Pollard, I am tired of your lackadaisical attitude about coming to work."

The rest of the office, stopped short, seeing O'Cleary hiding behind Pollard. One young man finally called the office to attention.

"Carry on," O'Cleary said, walking around Pollard.

O'Cleary stood aside. "Sergeant Pollard was detained by me for an inordinate amount of time. The delay was my fault. Is that OK Captain?"

"Yes Ma'am," the Captain babbled.

O'Cleary pulled out a business card from a concealed pocket in her uniform jacket and gave it to Pollard. "Please call me when your child is borne. I would like to extend my congratulations and blessings then."

O'Cleary shook her hand and walked out.

White House, Washington, D.C.
1400 hours EST

O'Cleary was silent on the trip from the Pentagon to the White House. Of course, she had to de-brief Hawker on her whereabouts and tell her about the White House visit later in the day.

"Cancel my appointments this morning, Elizabeth," O'Cleary said to her. "I'll be hiding in my office."

O'Cleary went into her office and called Dennis. Of all the times she needed her husband, it was now. Just then Arthur kicked. O'Cleary sat in the chair and held her womb. Inwardly, she thought of her baby. More and more, young Arthur consumed her thoughts of late. Nothing was going to change how she felt. Arthur was going to be borne and she was going to be his mother.

Her car drove into the VIP entrance of the White House. Both O'Cleary's and Hawker exited the car, went through the security procedures and then to the Oval Office.

Dennis said he was getting tired of visiting the Oval Office. "These kids don't respect this place."

Edwards was already there waiting. All four of them waited as the clock ticked down and the President's secretary ushered them into the Ova Office.

Edwards and O'Cleary walked in when the time came. Dennis and Hawker waited outside.

"Welcome Generals," the President said, smiling as he walked around his desk to shake their hands. The President motioned to the two couches in the center of the office.

The President began. "Clara Simpson's death has created a void that you, General O'Cleary, I am asking you to fill. General Edwards, you are here to argue against General O'Cleary's assignment to the ISA. The problems there are as myriad and complex as they are with the Pentagon. Generals, the country I am leading is falling apart. We have enemies fighting us from without and we are fighting enemies from within."

O'Cleary waited for the President to stop with his speech. "Mr. President, I am pregnant. I do plan on taking all my maternity leave. After that is a question still to be answered. General Edwards has been my mentor for many years. I owe him a great deal. My country shall come first, but I want to stay at the Pentagon. The fools over there want to inundate General Edwards. Saving him from bad mistakes being thrown at him or hidden is my job.

"Mister President," Edwards said. "I have no solution except that I and this nation needs her where she is."

The President was not impressed, patient or in a good mood. "General O'Cleary, no one in the community is better qualified for the ISA."

"Mr. President," O'Cleary said. "I have an idea, but I need some time to flush it out. Can I come in tomorrow morning and fix this situation with General Edwards present? In the meantime, Brigadier General Zachary at the ISA needs to be promoted to Major General. General Zachry is on promotion list for the slot he is currently working in. I have stayed in contact with him since I went to the Pentagon. He can keep the ISA moving along for now."

The President sighed obviously wanting a solution now. He called his secretary and scheduled an hour-long meeting with Edwards and O'Cleary tomorrow morning. He called over to the ISA and told Zachary to be here tomorrow.

The President turned back to his Generals. "Have a solution tomorrow, Generals. General Edwards, have the orders and paperwork for General Zachry with you. General O'Cleary, tell General Zachry to bring his wife, if married."

Edwards and O'Cleary stood, saluted and walked out of the Oval Office. They went around and found Hawker, Dennis and Colonel Harm.

"Elizabeth, I hope you have no plans for tonight," Brenda said taking Dennis' arm. "Dinner at my house, 7 pm, please." She looked over at Edwards. You are invited Sir, along with Amanda."

They walked outside to the underground garage.

"General Edwards," Brenda said. "I going home with Dennis to figure out an idea. I need to make sure you are protected." She held up a hand to halt him. "Please let me do this right."

"I trust you, Brenda." Edwards said as he entered his car with Harm.

Brenda felt a bump and a slight tightening of her uterus. "Dennis take me home."

Minuteman, north of Fort Benton, Montana
1400 hours MST

Kincaid drove the SUV in to meet with Jones and Smith in his office. He drove like an old woman, trying to avoid any bumps on the snow-covered road. They needed a consensus on some plans that stretched years and decades into the future.

Kincaid arrived at the camp and parked in front of the clinic. He went inside and had the doctor check him over. Luckily, nothing was pulled loose or bleeding.

Jones waited for Kincaid to arrive. Smith flew in today. His plane had interchangeable wheels and skids, so landing on the snow or a regular runway was no problem.

Kincaid came in and shed a huge coat.

After everyone had a fresh cup of coffee. All three men settled in and focused on three topics.

Kincaid led the discussion. "General O'Cleary saw me before my discharge and told me to create a program for training NCOs. I have the general outlines of a six-month program and I can counter every single point either of you can mount saying you cannot afford to lose those men for that amount of time.

Kincaid took a sip of coffee. "We cannot afford not to lose them. Both of you are great officers because of your training as Werewolves and NCOs. Werewolves require fourteen months of training. No one said cut it down. Even with the follow-on class, cutting it down was fought tooth and nail. We are not sending them hundreds of miles away. That is not the intent."

Kincaid paused to sip his coffee again. "We are talking about every one and training everyone here. We are using the NCO Academy to fine tune the INSANE JANE battle plan. Many things in the NCO Program of Instruction or POI mesh easily into the INSANE JANE battle doctrine. Many of the problems will vanish with that understanding."

Kincaid stopped to sip his coffee again. "The idea of a new group of Werewolves is an idea of mine and mine alone, but I am thinking towards the end of the war and afterward. We will need them. I looked at the manning board. Too many things going on and not enough people to do them."

"You gentlemen have any better ideas?" Kincaid said offering the others time to comment.

Jones pointed to the far wall listing everyone's name and the training outline. "Everyone now is training 12, 14 hours a day. Most of it is rehearsal and repetition. Any additions would only tire them out more."

Kincaid said. "I am not adding anything, just changing the overall focus. I need not remind you that saying all the officers and NCOs will survive is folly. We started in Vietnam with a Colonel and it fell to a Staff Sergeant. You." Kincaid pointed to Jones. "Bottom line is this will be cross-training. Everyone learns how to do everything."

Smith shifted in his chair. "I can agree with that mouthful. All of it. The problem is time. I watch a lot of the news and little of it is good."

Jones shifted. "A lot of all that is complicated." He turned in his chair and looked at the manning and training board. The wheels in his head were turning. He turned back to Kincaid. "What do you have?"

"Nothing firm yet," Kincaid said. "Give me another month."

"What about the new people?" Smith asked. "I assume that will my headache."

Kincaid reached down and hefted a four-inch think Werewolf training plan. "I asked for Dennis to come out here and set things up. The same way he did last time."

The three of them talked for the rest of the afternoon and changed over to beer when the sun went down.

Werewolf Support Camp #1, Hill County, Montana
2000 hours MST

Wendy sat down and allowed Earl to brush and comb out the tangles in her hair. Both of them had spent a lot of time thinking and talking about being married in the last few days.

"Earl, either we get married or not."

"I vote we get married. Let's just do it."

Wendy was silent. She suddenly stood and took a folder from Earl's hand. She tugged him out the door and went to Cindy's room. She knocked on the door several times and got no answer. Both knocked several times until the door opened a crack.

Cindy was standing there in shorts and t-shirt. She whispered "What do you want?"

Wendy whispered back. "Everyone knows you two are sleeping together."

"What do you want?" Cindy whispered back.

"Earl and I want to be married."

Cindy hesitated for a few seconds. She quickly opened the door and pulled both of them inside. "You two are idiots," she said.

February 6

White House, Washington, D.C.
0900 hours EST

Initially, last night's dinner went well. At four-thirty, Edwards and O'Cleary were notified that Zachary's promotion to Major General was formalized. Zachary was stood at attention and O'Cleary pinned on the stars on his left side. His wife Sandra, arrived just as Brenda was about to pin the stars. Sandra was all smiles as her husband was promoted. He was promoted early to Brigadier and she was not on hand for that.

Last night's dinner was a fiasco. Back and forth, the battle ran between them. Edwards and O'Cleary spent most of the time arguing. A few times, Brenda felt pain around her womb and left the room.

Finally, after nearly two hours, Edwards and O'Cleary retired to the living room, leaving Dennis, Hawker and Amanda to play cards on the dining room table.

Brenda drank her apple juice. Arthur liked it. No matter what happened in the outside world, Arthur and apple juice were above anything.

At 11 pm, Brenda finally dozed off. Though no consensus was achieved, Edwards liked the overall idea.

At 9 am, both walked into the Oval Office and sat down when the President motioned to the couches.

The President held up a stack of messages. "I kept the messages from individuals and organizations wanting the ISA Director's Chair. I am opening my mind to a solution."

O'Cleary took the led from Edwards. "First, I want to promote my Aide, Lieutenant Colonel Elizabeth Hawker to Colonel. Second, I will concurrently hold the office of Vice-Chairman of the JCS and the temporarily Directorship of the ISA. Though most of my duty time will probably be at the ISA."

"That allows you and I to have plenty of time to properly search for a permanent replacement to either job. That is the reason you can give the Senate. The ultimate solution is to have time for you to decide which one you want me to take. Colonel Hawker is someone who is probably the only one smart enough and capable enough to assist the Chairman during those times when I have to be at Barton. General Zachary is more than capable to handle the day-to-day when I have to be at the Pentagon. The movement between each location will allow me time to relax in between locations."

O'Cleary intensely watched the President's reactions to her presentation. Slowly he started to agree with her.

"This Colonel Hawker," the President interjected. "Is she going to have enough rank to be taken seriously?"

Edwards took his turn. "I know how sharp she is. I was hoping to steal her as my new aide. Colonel Harm has been selected for Brigadier General and the new Assistant Division Commander for the 82nd Airborne. If she stays in Brenda's office, she will be able to keep everything straight for me. As to whether anyone will respect her is very simple. All I have to do is take her word or suggestion over everyone else."

The President leaned back and alternately looked at Edwards and O'Cleary. "No disrespect to either of you, but you both feel this can work."

"Yes Sir," both Generals said in unison.

The President was silent for a time. "Execute that optioh. I will require the consent of the Senate to re-nominate you as the Vice-Chairman of the JCS and the temporary Director of the ISA. Thank you. And promote Colonel Hawker."

Both Generals left the Oval Office and went to the secure parking lot.

"Sir," Brenda said. "I want this to work. You have to give Elizabeth all your support; much the same as you gave me."

"You have my word. Bring her into my outer office. WE can promote her there."

Brenda showed him the Eagles. "Still have them."

Pentagon, Washington, D.C.
1000 hours EST

The normal Cabinet meeting started on the most pressing topic; money and the lack of it. The war along the southern border took the majority of the time. Law enforcement, drug smuggling, human trafficking, theft of everything, kidnapping, murder and a good deal of other crimes all resulted because "that dammed border refuses to cooperate."

"Mister President," the AG Rebecca Beck took her turn. The southern border needs a firmer hand than what we have now. I mean no disrespect to the Defense Department, but since those Savage Rabbits were disbanded, the border has reverted to a floodgate. The Border Patrol is begging for reinforcements. We need a leaner force on the border and that should lessen the load on the border."

James Dodson, the Secretary of Defense looked across the table at Beck. "I will concede that the apparatus we have on the border now is better suited elsewhere."

The President knew that the only one to fix this had too many hats already. "James, get with General O'Cleary and pass that on to her."

"Yes, Mister President."

Texas Capital Building, Austin Texas
1000 hours CST

Oklahoma's Governor and his Officials enjoyed being treated as Royalty. The Texas Governor and his Officials awaited his arrival on the front steps. For a change, the Federal Government did not come in to "take charge" and remind the Governors about the Constitution they seldom obeyed.

273

Texas and Oklahoma were putting the force of law behind the law. Both Governors formally signed state bills into state laws legally dissolving their borders allowing law enforcement from each state to maintain law and order.

Each state will operate an office in each other's state with their respective state's police. Those state laws that are not compatible will be negotiated and a compromise found.

Both Governors told all their Officials that one-upmanship "shall not to be tolerated".

Both Attorney's General shook hands in solidarity.

In Washington, the Attorney General frowned.

Pentagon, Washington, D.C.
1300 hours EST

Brenda came back to the Pentagon around 1030 and called Lieutenant Colonel Elizabeth Hawker into her office for a private meeting. Hawkers' eyes went wide at the fact that she was going to be the shadow Vice-Chairman of the Joint Chiefs of Staff.

"Ma'am, with all due respect, you are insane," Hawker said.

"You are already doing the work. You'll read the mass of documents coming in, write a short summary and place it in my in-box with a recommendation. I will give you a delegation-of-authority card to sign for the lesser things as they occur. I will be here at least one hour a day, probably half a day, or alternate days."

Hawker was not exactly convinced.

"Listen to me, Colonel," O'Cleary said in a more menacing tone. "You are not being told to do anything illegal. Everything you will do is sanctioned by General Edwards and the President. The President, by the way, is the one who said you are to be promoted to Colonel today." O'Cleary showed her the Eagles. "You will be in constant contact with me and Barton is a one hour and fifteen-minute ride from here. You need to grow into the job the same way you did at Barton and at Desert Zero."

"Yes Ma'am," Hawker said. "I will not let you down."

"Good," O'Cleary said. "From now until 1345, we will work on all the junk that accumulated this morning. After the 1400 promotion ceremony, we come back here and set you up to take over for me." O'Cleary was about to walk away, but stopped. "By the way, tell personnel to send two Majors or two very smart Captains to help you out in here. Interview and select what you like."

February 7

Texas Capital Building, Austin, Texas
1000 hours CST

Officials from New Mexico and Arizona came to Austin for talks and information about how Texas and Oklahoma were driving down narcotics and human smuggling in Texas and Oklahoma.

The only thing the Federal Government was consulted on was the crime statistics constantly pouring out of Washington. The Federal Government had no choice but admit that the flow of illegal immigrants was lowering.

Texas seized all the left-over border wall materials and used the seized moneys from drug cartels to fund finishing the walls. The Texas Attorney General served the Federal Government with seizure notices for failure to pay past due bills on federal installations. Crews of workers were now finishing the wall that Washington politics could not finish.

New Mexico and Arizona wanted to stop all the "stupid" and protect its citizens. Arizona brought huge blow-up pictures of Federal Government-provided signs placed on all roads eighty miles north of the border. The sign warned American citizens not to go farther south due to violence imported from Mexico.

All four states wanted action.

The latest move from the Federal Justice Department was new law suits threatening to take away the miniscule funding paid to states.

US Marshals and FBI Agents have to try enforcing without local support.

The Texas Attorney General sent a box of Kleenex tissue to the FBI office down the hall.

An hour after arriving, the New Mexico and Arizona officials left with smiles and binders full of current Coordination laws and agreements.

Pentagon, Washington, D.C.
1400 hours EST

O'Cleary put down the phone, turned her chair around and rubbed her eyes. It did not help her that she was surrounded by some the best and brightest. All the officials, elected and appointed, above her keep throwing more and more stupid requirements down for someone to do what they are too stupid to accomplish.

The newest stupid thing thrown at her was that they wanted the Savage Rabbits up and running inside of one month.

Brigadier General Gender of Delta Force was requesting a meeting with her; reference Savage Rabbits. He still wanted them so that he had fresh meat.

General Matheson, formally of Special Operations Command or SOCOM stabbed her Rabbits in the back with the well "wetted blade". O'Cleary was mad and getting madder. Arthur kicked her, reminding her that her temper affected two people.

Slowly she reached for the X-Berry and dialed the number for Kincaid.

"Secure," Kincaid said.

"Secure, at the Pentagon." That was just a cover. The actual call was secure, but the Pentagon's security measures could still eavesdrop.

"Yes ma'am. What can I do for you?" Kincaid said as he poured a cup of coffee.

"Listen to all of it before you interrupt." O'Cleary ran down all the background concerning what the Attorney General and the President threw at her. "I can argue for hours, but the bottom line is that I have a problem and I need help."

Kincaid winced thinking about doing all that over again. "I am side-lined until November. Translation, is desk,

desk and nothing but desk. If you can call me later tonight at your discretion. I'll have a workable plan for you."

"1900 your time," said and hung up the phone.

Werewolf Support Camp #1, Hill County, Montana
1900 hours MST

Kincaid was doing some work with Kendal and Master Sergeant Marcus Waverly. Waverly was the First Section's Senior NCO when the Savage Rabbits were at Desert Zero. Waverly was not married or had any family, but he was very loyal to the nation. That was severely tested when he and everyone else was sent to detention at Fort Hood. He spent his days at the Detention Camp spitting on the ground as he saw families being held behind the wire. What really boiled his temper was seeing children playing behind barbed wire fences.

Kincaid drove over to Minuteman and had a long talk with Jones. This had to happen. His four-and-a-half-inch thick Master Training Program needed someone like MSG Marcus Waverly. He was a poster child for being a Savage Rabbit. Tall, athletic, smart, brave and a leader every one respected. Since he was not able to do this himself, Kincaid asked Waverly.

"Sergeant Major, are you sure you have the right man?" Waverly said.

"I will not blow sand and sunshine at you," Kincaid said. "I asked Colonel Jones and he said you wanted to return to the Regular Army. I have a cover story for you to cover any questions that may arise. Chief Petty Officer Wendy Kendal is currently studying the Training Program. She is available to run your operations center and help train up the operators."

"Will Delta or others come in and reduce us to slave labor?" Waverly asked.

Kincaid coughed. "General O'Cleary is calling me at 1900 hours. If you want assurances, I can have you give them directly to her."

Waverly looked at him. "General O'Cleary?" He said thinking that this was not a joke. "OK Sergeant Major, why me? I mean why did you ask for me? Are you sending anyone else down to Desert Zero?"

Kincaid held up a hand. "I am not a computer. One, you have said that you wanted my job before I was detained. Two, you are a strong NCO and I recall you forcibly standing up for your troops against the others. As to sending anyone else, I have not and will not ask anyone else to go. General O'Cleary will find new people from the Rangers and Marine Force Recon for you to man this unit. Everyone here has been treated as a traitor when all you did was defend yourselves."

"You have not answered my Question, Sergeant Major," Waverly said. "Why me?"

Kincaid leaned forward and looked Waverly in the eye. "Because even with how you were treated and how much you lost, you stood your ground and protected your troops."

"Those eight men were my troops," he said staring back. "One third of my men were lost due to politics and dumbass planning during the last mission. Why do I want to set myself up like that?"

"I am recovering from five-gunshot wounds. I'm not physically able to train up a unit again. Those men need you. You need to see the holes?" Kincaid stood and lifted his shirt. "My assailant was shot four times and the last time in his head."

Just then, Kincaid's phone rang. "Decide."

Waverly looked at Kincaid as he answered the phone. Waverly listened to Kincaid talk about setting up another group of Savage Rabbits. Having Kendal to work the Operations Center was who he would want to do it. The General protected them until she was detained. After her release, she pulled everyone out of detention and brought everyone here. She could have done like any other General and forgot about all of them. Detention means no contact with no one.

"Sergeant Major," Waverly said interrupting Kincaid on the phone. "I'm in. Bring Kendal here so I can talk to her about the training plan."

Kincaid handed him the phone. "The General wants to talk to you."

"Master Sergeant Waverly," O'Cleary said. "I am General O'Cleary, the Vice-Chairman of Joint Chiefs of Staff. General Gender from Delta Force will be here to receive his orders from the President through General Edwards and myself stating that the Savage Rabbits are off limits. They will vacate Desert Zero by week's end. I am looking for a Commanding Officer as good as Colonel Peters. Once I find him, you will be introduced. He has no say over you. You will have a say over him."

O'Cleary continued. "Sergeant, you will have two of my phone numbers. The first one is never to be given to anyone. I need a rat in the system so that nothing is done behind my back. You will have my support should anything or anyone attempt to coheres you or destroy you. The second one is for normal business as you see fit. Remember that I have a job too. I may not answer immediately, but I will answer."

"Excellent, General," Waverly said.

"Command Sergeant Major Waverly," O'Cleary said. "Mister Kincaid has your stripes and promotion orders. I will see you at Desert Zero in a month."

February 8

JCS Communications Message Center, Pentagon, Washington D.C.
0401 hours UTC

Headquarters, Southern Command Fort Hood, Texas received a communication through the defense network. All units currently at Desert Zero are required to vacate the installation no later than the 13th of February, regardless of mission or necessity.

Southern Command was required to ensure that the base was cleaned up and ready to be used by a classified unit arriving on the 14th of February.

Southern Command was ordered to provide a security force of no less than two officers and twenty-five enlisted soldiers.

Southern Command was requested to also allow Command Sergeant Major Marcus Waverly to recruit assets for this unit.

1000 hours MST

Waverly drove back to Minuteman, slept and returned back here this morning. He was offered a place to sleep, but declined saying he needed time to think. He loved driving the roads ever since his father gave him the car keys. If God gave him clear roads and good weather, he was on the roads. The road between Minuteman and this camp was well used. The exact reason for this camp was something no one wanted to talk about.

Oh well. He could keep a secret.

After he arrived, Kincaid gave him a folder holding a cover story. He came here to assist the Montana National Guard in training for protecting Montana from border incursions for a rotation later in the year.

Waverly read the three-page cover story and was surprised that it had a great deal of truth. It was simple and easy to remember. That made sense. The cover made no mention of training the Savage Rabbits to live here and fight for their homes.

Waverly handed the story back to Kincaid who promptly through it into the fireplace.

Both men sat down and ran down all the administrative points for forming the Savage Rabbits including all the lessons learned. Most of these points Waverly never saw. He had heard Kincaid yelling at the wall in the beginning trying to make all the pieces fit together.

Southern Command, Fort Hood, Texas
1500 hours CST

General James Waller of the Southern Command read the message from JCS and along with the Generals in his chain of command. He did not even bother reading too much. Giving one company of men to man the Savage Rabbits was going to be given all his support. Ever since they were disbanded, that abortion that replaced them was incompetent.

Delta Force was the best in the world, there was no doubt. It was the staff portion that called the shots that was the problem. Waller remembered watching the Savage Rabbits receive a mission, plan and launch within eight hours. Even the women were top of the line and went out to fight. They were as good, if not better, than a lot of men in his command.

Now they take as long as three days to do the same thing and half the time, the mission was canceled because they waited too long.

The thing that was his yardstick was the number of soldiers killed, wounded or captured. Waller went in and "ate" the commander for the high casualty count. The man gave him the speech about "need-to-know" and problems no real commander would normally have to deal with. Waller stormed away. He returned to his office, opened a weathered note book and scanned through until he found Brenda O'Cleary's secret number. That General needed to retire.

Waller knew this secret would never stay a secret. His Sergeant Major was always asked about joining the Savage Rabbits. Who should he send? Volunteers was what he would do. He needed to spread the wealth on this one. Gutting a battalion was stupid and too hard to explain to the idiots at the Pentagon.

The buzz was everywhere. 'Rumor Control' and the 'Underground' said the Savage Rabbits were back and this time they were going to take Hood soldiers. Suddenly, everyone's morale soared.

Marine Expeditionary Force, Camp Lejeune, South Carolina
1600 hours EST

The Commanding General of the Base looked over the message from the JCS, the Chief of Naval Operations and the Commandant of the Marine Corps, etc., etc.

Provide one company of Marines for a classified assignment. He knew what this was all about. The Savage Rabbits was reforming. The Army screwed the dog on the last batch.

Four Marines came back out the last bunch and reported back here. When Delta Force blew in, they threw up a wall and became a demented Frankenstein. Two of out every three missions were abortions. All of the Savage Rabbits secretly planned to escape back to America after every mission. Seven missions were aborted and getting extracted was cancelled. Those four Marines exercised the 'volunteer' portion and left.

It had to be bad if Marines de-volunteered for duty.

"Sergeant Major," he called over the intercom. "Come over to my office." He was going to set up a rat-line. A Marine out of this batch was needed to call him if they were being wasted.

The General looked at his stars and he would use them to bull-doze in to snatch them out if needed.

Attached to this message was a request for Lieutenant Colonel Benjamin Simmons, Force Recon to command the Savage Rabbits. Simmons was well regarded within the Special Operations Community and the Corps. Simmons had just come back from duty in Saudi Arabia and was on 'relaxed duty'.

'Relaxed duty' was a situation where a Marine needed some time off after 'an intense assignment'. Simmons was awaiting an open billet as a battalion commander to qualify for promotion to Colonel so he can get his star in two or three years.

The General looked up and motioned to the Sergeant Major to come in and close the door. He needed some advice about a subject that was never discussed in the 'real Corps'.

February 9

IRS Regional Office, St. Louis, Missouri
0200 hours CST

Two people in dark clothes and hoods walked up to the building that the IRS uses for this section of the country. They went to fire alarm control room and drilled out the locks housed in the door knob. They hauled in heavy bags and closed the door. If anyone spotted them and called the police, they were screwed. Once past the door, they turned on the lights.

They bypassed the electronics and went to the main water lines. Using a diagram, they went to the valves controlling the incoming water lines.

Pulling out tools, they rendered the valves inoperable by grinding off the manual threads of the valve and poring epoxy glue on the wheels, rendering them immobile.

The two men now had to wait for the minimum one hour to expire. They had already found the internal door to the offices and waited.

After the hour elapsed, they checked the epoxy and found it was hard. They planned on the alarms sounding when the door opened. The fire alarm control panel was turned off, in order to delay the Fire Department's response. They took a deep breath, turned off the lights and opened the door.

Nothing happened. Both men ran to the planned locations and dropped off thermal charges. The pre-set timers were activated and both men ran out. They went into the door, pumped epoxy over the door jam and closed the door. The light was turned on so that they could turn off the main breakers.

The last of the epoxy was spread over the exterior door jamb as the "whomps" could be heard. The doors were shut and the men ran three blocks away. They slowly kept to the shadows. The threw away everything in a dumpster a mile away.

The escape was successful.

Now came the difficult part. They needed to disappear down to southern Texas. They tried very hard not to leave any fingerprints or DNA.

Cyber Space, World Wide Web
1200 hours UTM

The raw data from the American polls showed a major shift in opinion between states. The Mississippi River seemed to the dividing line between states. Pundits and talking heads were making comparisons of East versus West in the Twenty-First Century and the North versus South in the Ninetieth Century.

In the end, only one man preached peace. "Do you want hundreds of thousands or possibly millions of people dead?"

283

February 10

New York Stock Exchange, New York City, New York
0900 hours EST

Employees and traders stood in fear of the opening bell. The Japanese earthquake last month siphoned off nearly eight trillion dollars from the world's economy. Japan's response to the earthquake has them spending money from any source they can find.

The initial tsunami that struck the home island of Honshu was thirty-five feet tall at land fall. Buildings were torn loose from their foundations as the mountain of water refused to let anything stop its destruction.

That wave stopped mostly along the Japanese alps. But the water did find some contours and crossed over the width of the island to the western shores.

Tokyo and Nara took the worst hits. Most of the population was in their homes when the quake hit. Those that had cars, instantly grabbed children and pre-packed bags. No one needed no encouragement in leaving. Everyone knew that high volume roads instantly became one-way to facilitate movement. Those that did not have a vehicle, left and started walking. Public transportation grabbed anyone. You were allowed only one bag and it had to fit on your lap.

Every tall high rise was opened and people flooded inward. Everyone was sent up in elevators until they did not work anymore.

At the shoreline, the water slammed into buildings. Windows exploded inward and pushed furniture out the other side.

Japan has had to deal with Tsunamis since before recorded history. They have plans that have been worked and re-worked in all situations. Even during both World Wars, those plans were still fine-tuned, worked and rehearsed.

Japan reacted with an efficiency they were famous for.

Satellite photography showed the progress of the emergency from start until finish. As of this date, the last of the water has receded.

The bell was rung and the market reacted to Japan's economic collapse. The Prime Minister announced that all monies and capital was to be returned to Japan in order to finance the recovery.

The Japanese markets were closed.

The American and European markets immediately lost 1,500 points. The market's "circuit breakers" froze all trading to prevent a total collapse. The world's economy could not understand or operate with a financial hole created with Japan out of the game.

Not since the collapse of Germany after the First World War has a First World Country economically collapsed.

Japanese purchase agents were flying around world-wide trying to find and buy everything Japan needs.

Economic leader's world-wide talked about money.

Japan had to face the one topic the rest of the world ignored. The dead were stacked like wood in "collection areas". It was considered disrespectful to place a number on the total number of the dead.

J. Edgar Hoover Building, Washington, D.C.
0900 hours EST

Director Solin opened the report he wanted showing the crime data from illegal immigrants along the southern border with Mexico. Murders were doubled. Theft of personal and commercial property. Cattle were slaughtered and partially eaten. Consequently, coyote and other carnivore populations were exploding everywhere.

Ranchers were moving their herds north and, in some cases, released or abandoned. Most of the ranchers said it was better to release them to Americans and let the illegals starve.

Solin flipped through the rest of the report. There was not one single point that was optimistic or good.

Solin sighed and threw the report into his out box.

Werewolf Support Camp #1, Hill County, Montana
0700 hours MST

285

Jones drove up, ignoring the cold weather and the physical training he knew better than to skip. He walked into the main building and saw the one thing he wished he could not see. There was Kincaid, standing over a table wearing a robe and fuzzy slippers.

"Boots off," Kincaid said. "The mop and bucket are around the timer to your left."

Jones chuckled and removed his boots. He tip-toped around the water and pulled over the mop and bucket. A few swipes, put it all back and turned to Kincaid.

Kincaid pointed to the coffee maker.

Jones poured a cup of coffee and doctored it to his tastes. "John, please sit down and talk to me about this NCO Academy being jammed down my throat."

Kincaid turned and looked at his friend of over thirty years. "Where did that come from?"

Jones leaned back in his chair. "I talked with General O'Cleary last night. We had a pleasant conversation until I said we needed more time. She basically and respectively told me to do it, discussion over."

"I told you, Thad, that I intend to mesh the NCO Academy with your training. The General told me the same thing. She believes, as I do, that proper training keeps the troops alive. You are teaching and re-reteaching all the points in the doctrine. All the officers and NCOs are working nearly non-stop to create the Performance-Oriented-Training tasks to make this work. I have Cindy Morgan grinding through your curriculum, finding those points where the NCO Academy training points can be inserted into your training."

Kincaid shifted in his chair. "You and I are alive because we trained, re-trained and kept training until everything was perfect. We have watched inferiorly trained soldiers die for that lack of proper training."

Jones looked at his friend of thirty years. "John, I admit that I was pissed you stole Waverly against my wishes. Waverly is perfect for all this training."

"Sergeant Major Waverly," Kincaid said, "told the General, in Colorado after being freed from detention that if another Savage Rabbit mission came along, he wanted to rejoin the Regular Army."

286

Jones sighed and reached for his coffee cup. "Please, and this for you and for General O'Cleary, don't gut me again without going through me first." He extended his hand.

Kincaid shook his hand firmly. "It was never my intent to circumvent your authority. I will tell the General to consult with you before talking to me. I assumed you already knew when I briefed him."

Pentagon, Washington D.C.
1000 hours EST

Lieutenant Colonel Benjamin Simmons arrived and was directed to General O'Cleary's office. Very secretly, Simmons was prejudiced about women being commanders. Nowadays, women were shedding their holding back status like they did in the eighties and nineties. They were filling hospital wards and body bags, fighting equally with the men. He grew up with the skirts and 'special treatment' that the women guarded selfishly.

Simmons killed the argument raging in his head. This tremendous zoo seemed to do this to people.

General O'Cleary came in with two Sergeants lugging boxes behind her. "Two minutes," she said closing the door.

"Colonel Simmons," the General's aide said two minutes later. "The General can see you."

The Aide opened the door for him.

Simmons walked up to O'Cleary's desk, stood at attention and reported. "Ma'am, Lieutenant Colonel Simmons reports to the Vice Chairman." Being a member of the Naval Service, you never salute without headgear on.

O'Cleary looked up and frowned. She gave him a salute. "I apologize for the confusion. I forgot Marines never salute without headgear. At ease. Please help yourself to a cup of coffee and sit down. Let me have a minute to catch up."

Simmons studied her for the minute she needed. Why would he be in the office if she was not ready for him? Simmons just sat there and waited.

O'Cleary seemed finished as the two Sergeants finished emptying out the boxes, creating five stacks on the conference table.

O'Cleary grabbed an apple juice and sat down in a chair next to Simmons. "I apologize for the craziness. I have two hats on my head. I am the Vice-Chairman of the JCS and the temporary Director of the Internal Security Agency. Big deal."

She paused, took a big sip of her apple juice and then continued. "What is important about that is the lack of interference in the assignment you were selected for. Your Chain of Command is the President, Defense Secretary, General Edwards and me. Period."

"I am your Commanding General, by Order of the President." O'Cleary handed him a folder. It was the order creating the Savage Rabbits, the signatures of all of the above and the most important part: the date. All the signatures were real ink, not auto signatures.

"Colonel, may I call you Benjamin?"

"Yes Ma'am." Simmons said.

"Benjamin," O'Cleary stated. "I am offering you command of a unit that has the nickname "Savage Rabbits". Have you heard of them?"

"Yes ma'am." Simmons said.

"Actually, they are the Counter-Narcotics Incursion Unit. Half Marines and half Army. The idea I originally imposed was that the Cartels and their poisonous cargos needed to be fought south of the border. In each instance we attack the cartel that is the strongest. We knock them down below the point where they were strongest. The object was to keep the six known cartels even. That way they spent at least seventy percent of their energy killing each other. The loss of all that money and narcotics was very successful."

O'Cleary paused to take a brief pause. Arthur kicked her ribs. "I apologize Benjamin. This assignment is going to be highly stressful, but the most important thing was that narcotics were destroyed by the ton and mountains of money was either seized or destroyed."

O'Cleary smiled. "The Treasury fools wanted the money either returned or the serial numbers recorded before burning." She chuckled. "No one dies for stupid ideas. You are a commissioned officer. It is your decision about what a stupid idea is, understand?"

"Yes ma'am," Simmons said.

O'Cleary's face turned neutral. "Will you accept this assignment?"

Simmons squared his shoulders. "Yes Ma'am."

O'Cleary liked the look of his eye. "I don't want you to take this job, just because Marines never quit. I have researched you heavily. I need those men to know absolutely that they have a commander that will do anything to ensure they come home and live. Colonel Peters, their last commander, stood his ground three times and came up on charges for exceeding his authority and violating the Rules of Engagement. The fourth time he was charged because the Military hierarchy," she whirled her index finger over her head, "argued about extracting a Savage Rabbit section in Mexico. Peters was reprimanded and relieved when he and seven volunteers were apprehended trying to go south and retrieve them. Against orders."

O'Cleary paused to take another drink of apple juice. "I had the charges dismissed after I found out it happened. I was detained after this "Victoria" nonsense started. Once that happened, the vultures descended." O'Cleary paused and took a deep breath. "I apologize. I took an almost maternal protective posture over them."

She took another sip of juice. "I can promise you that I am your next step in the chain of command. Every idiot in the world is going to want to visit, offer useless advice, want brain-dead briefings and want tours and Yaddy, Yadha. I am your boss. Politely, tell them I am your boss. Send them to me. I do request that you give them my respects. General James Waller, the commander of Southern Command, took good care of the unit."

"Sergeant Major Marcus Waverly has been selected to be your Command Sergeant Major. He was the First Section NCOIC at Desert Zero with the Original Savage Rabbits. His unit was the one abandoned in Mexico. His Commander, Captain Younger credited the successful two-week long escape back to Desert Zero directly to him. Eight Rabbits died returning to the US. The Mexican Army knew they were there. It was a running battle for them."

"Your unit will be half Marines and half Army. Both have the qualities that make this unit so much better than the sum of its members. Three Platoons from each service. Originally the Army members were all Rangers, but as time and causalities mounted, Fort Hood provided top notch replacements."

"Colonel Peters and Sergeant Major Kincaid did something remarkable. Instead of 100 plus casualties a year, only twenty-nine men were killed. I believe in proper training and that is the only way to get the job done without massive casualties."

O'Cleary saw Simmons was coming aboard. "You are given a base to command and use. Your Sergeant Major is chosen," O'Cleary pulled out two one-hundred bills and handed them to Simmons. "You two need a long lunch to get introduced. Additionally, there is Navy Chief Petty Officer Wendy Kendal who knows how your Operations and Intelligence Section should be run. She was also there from the beginning and worked through until being relieved and arrested for defending herself against a sexual assault."

"Your questions?" she said taking another sip.

"Numerous, ma'am," Simmons said.

Before he could say anything, Hawker interrupted. "General, your helicopter is fifteen minutes out."

O'Cleary sighed. "I will be gone for several hours. Use my office this morning. The two sergeants are finding an office downstairs and setting everything up for you. See Colonel Hawker for a hole in my schedule if you need to see me and I expect you to have questions."

O'Cleary stood as Arthur kicker her bladder. She barely held on and left Simmons standing as she went to the bathroom. This kid was starting to become an annoyance.

O'Cleary came out and Simmons was still standing. "Benjamin, those documents are yours, feel free to view them here until Colonel Hawker does her thing. She'll order lunch. I have to leave, carry on."

Werewolf Support Camp #1, Hill County, Montana
1900 hours MST

Kincaid walked outside his room and literally ran into Kendal and Locklear. Both had packed bags. Kincaid shook his head.

"Good evening, John," Kendal said. "We are taking a three-day trip."

Locklear was taken back seeing Kincaid standing there. "We were going to the southwest of the Minuteman to check that area before she has to leave."

Kincaid sighed and leaned against the kitchen wall. "You too can't lie any better than that?"

"We are getting married," Kendal said. "It is a secret. Colonel Jones won't allow it. So, we are going to find someone to marry us."

"Kids," Kincaid said. "Wait here." He shuffled off a few steps and stopped. "You two have a marriage license?"

"Yes?" Locklear said.

"Get it." Kincaid said walking off to his room.

Kincaid came out with Cindy. Both of them were in robes. The four of them looked funny. Two in bath robes and two in uniforms. Kincaid put a manual typewriter on the table.

"Sit down," Kincaid said. "You two thought hard about this. I mean really thought about this?"

Wendy stood and was about to open her mouth.

Kincaid pointed a finger at her. "You need to take lessons from your man here. Now answer the question."

Wendy slowly sat down.

Earl said. "She and I talked about it a lot in last few months since she was released."

Wendy said. "John, Earl and I talked about what happened to me when I was a teenager. Declaring to be a lesbian with an attitude was a shield that pushed everyone away. That allowed me a way of dealing with it. When we sleep together, my nightmares are easy to push away. John," she took both of Earl's hands. "I want to have what you described in your relationship with your wife and what Cindy had. Maybe we are stupid, but we deserve to find out."

Kincaid looked to Earl.

Earl opened his mouth a few times. "I'm not an orator. I just want to be her husband. Period."

Kincaid took a deep breath. "This will not be a secret. The argument about being married, deployed, pregnant, and with children are rules carved in stone. If you," he pointed to Wendy, "go to Desert Zero. Earl will not be forced into a non-combatant status unless return here. No games or word splitting. If you don't like that, you are free to return to the Navy and the Air Force."

Earl leaned forward. "Wendy and I already understand and accept our circumstances within the community. We just want to be married."

Wendy decided to have some fun. "Yes, I'll suck his dick and the other sex is great."

Cindy snickered and put a hand in front of her face.

Kincaid turned and put the marriage license in the typewriter, lined it up and scrolled down to the correct spot. He typed in the correct information in the correct places. Once finished, he notarized the document.

Kincaid pulled the document out of the typewriter and examined it. "I knew this was going to happen so I searched the web and found a place to get me qualified as an Officiant."

Cindy moved over and stood next to Wendy and Earl. "I am the best man, matron of honor, one of the witnesses and guard. John is the officiant, one of the witnesses and royal pain."

"Ahem." John said. "Face each other. Who has the rings?"

Earl reached in one of the suitcases and pulled out the ring box. Kincaid pointed to Cindy, who took them and stood waiting.

Kincaid took a deep breath and began. "Earl, do you take this woman with all her aggravating tendencies as your wife?"

Earl said "yes" with broad smile.

"Wendy, do you take this man who is too good for you as your husband?"

Wendy said "yes" and blew a kiss at Earl.

Kincaid pulled out a well-worn typed piece of paper from a bible.

"Outstanding," Kincaid said. "Marriage is a wonderful institution which unites two people to share a lifetime through all things good or bad. Whereas difficult times normally overwhelm one person, two people come together and solve that thing with ease. The love that two people build shall become so great that separating can cause physical pain. I am a widower and so is Cindy. We have years of separation from our spouses and having any kind of happiness seems like an affront to their memory."

"Earl, kneel before this woman whom has chosen you above all others." Earl knelt looking up to Wendy.

"Earl, do you love this woman?"

"Yes, I do."

"Earl, do you set aside your parent's family, your childhood and all things not of her?"

"Yes, I do."

"Earl, do you honor her?"

"Yes, I do."

"Earl, do you swear that your heart is hers, that your choice is her, and that as the center of focus of your life, you can respect and honor her as your wife?"

"Yes, I do."

"Earl, do you swear to guard her, protect her, and defend her against all who would do her harm?"

"Yes, I do."

"Earl, do you, from this day forward, declare and announce to the world that this woman is now and shall always be your wife, first in all things, centermost in your life, and the focus of all your labors."

"Yes, I do."

"Earl, stand."

"Wendy, do you accept the oath of this man who knelt before you and asks for your hand, your heart and your spirit?"

"Yes, I do."

"Wendy, do you freely choose this man as your husband?"

"Yes, I do."

"Wendy, do you love this man?"

"Yes, I do."

"Wendy, do you set aside your parent's family, your childhood and all things not of him?"

"Yes, I do."

"Wendy, do you honor him?"

"Yes, I do."

"Wendy, do you swear that your heart is his, that your choice is him, and that as the center of focus of your life, you can respect him as a husband?"

"Yes, I do."

"Wendy, do you, from this day forward, declare and announce to the world that this man is now and shall always be your husband, first in all things, centermost in your life, and the focus of all your labors?"

"Yes, I do."

"Earl, do you accept the oath of this woman who stands before you, who asks for your hand, your heart and your spirit?"

"Yes, I do."

"Both will join hands. Cindy, give them their rings." Earl and Cindy put rings on their respective fingers. "Take each other's hands."

"In other cultures, the tying of a thread or the giving of rings is made. The joining of hands is the truest symbol of marriage: for this is a sign that is consciously given, hardest to hold and easiest to break."

"By the authority of the State of Montana, I declare you to be Husband and Wife. Mister and Missus Locklear, you may kiss each other."

It was a long and boring kiss.

After too long a time, Earl and Wendy parted. Kincaid and Morgan were gone along with their luggage.

"Can I carry you to our room, My Lady."

February 11

Congress, Washington D.C.
1200 hours EST

It actually made headlines today. With all the inflated egos and swelled heads floating around the capital, everyone was amazed the not one single fight, verbal or otherwise, occurred within the building on either side. A three-way Congress voted on bills with near unanimous support.

The bill was to declare February 25th as National Cucumber Day.

Privately, there was a lot of activity behind closed doors. A lot of angry muffled words.

February 12

World Wide Web, Cyber-Space, Planet Earth
0400 hours

UNSTACK THIS operated in accordance with Valkyrie's instructions and found the monies Sharpe and Brennan had sent overseas and moved through several banks in several countries. All the monies were pulled back to the United States and deposited in accounts ranging to the Werewolf Cemetery at Heaven's Garden in Finley Ohio and several no-charge children's hospitals.

UNSTACK THIS used the threads from Sharpe, Brennan and Seagrove to track down the monies from the other Black Elves.

All total, it amounted to nearly seventy-six million dollars.

Congress, Washington, D.C.
1000 hours EST

The House Judicial Affairs Committee voted 11 to 10 to approve the bill authorizing the Department of Justice to absorb every Police Department in the United States and put them under one umbrella.

There was a furious debate already boiling in the House and Senate over such a thing even being considered. Names such as "Gestapo", many versions of "Secret Police" were thrown around.

Senator Marshall Ballan of Texas stated that the bill was dead on arrival in the Senate.

Twenty-three states, mostly in the west, said they would not comply with the law. Many states already introduced legislation to void that authority.

Slowly, steadily in the dark corners of the government, voices and whispers started.

February 13

Jerusalem, Israel
2300 hours (Bravo) (1700 hours EST)

It had been a warm day in Jerusalem followed by a mild night. To all appearances, everything was boring. Colonel Aaron Hassid of the Israeli Air Force sat down and was reading a manual "borrowed" from an American friend who said this was the new strategy for upcoming air warfare.

Someone actually thought that, soon aircraft could be electronically hijacked. They could be flown to neutral airports or intentionally shutdown and crashed. Though it was outlandish, nothing in the world of electronic wizardry seemed to be too far-fetched.

Three dedicated 747-type aircraft or a manned land facility would continuously monitor every aircraft within 500 miles of Israel. Hassid thought of fantasies.

Suddenly alarms sounded of a south-bound aircraft in Syria and turning west. It was now accelerating toward Jerusalem.

Hassid looked over the control room as alerts went out to every portion of the Israeli Defense Force. At present speed it would reach Jerusalem in ten minutes. Hassid placed the icon over the aircraft and right-clicked the mouse. He absorbed the information and picked up the IDF Commander's line.

"Sir this is Colonel Hassid. We have a medium-sized aircraft turning into Israeli airspace. The aircraft left from the Damascus airport twenty minutes ago. Estimate ten minutes before arriving in Jerusalem. No indication of target or destination. All transponders or locator beacons have been shut down. Over."

General Gannon at IDF headquarters said. "Interceptors are seconds from launching. Continue monitoring, out."

Hassid watched. His operators followed the playbook for an all-out war. Hopefully this was not a commercial airliner off course.

In the air-space over Israel, the one remaining still operating Afghan C-130 flew unerringly toward Jerusalem. The aircraft was repainted to red and blue colors of a fictional company to confuse anyone looking at them. As Jerusalem came into view, the pilot triggered a double strobe light. One was bright white and the other was an infrared. They blinked three quick, a pause and three quick blinks which gave a unique signal.

Suddenly the city went black. The pilot donned a set of night vision googles which saw the IR strobe. The pilot aimed for a point below the blinking strobe. His observers reported that no aircraft were seen. He concentrated with all his will on the aiming point, while his co-pilot divided his concentration on the instruments and the reports from his aerial observers.

"Stand by the bell," the Pilot said. When he figured he was close, he commanded "Ring Bell."

The pilot pulled back slightly on the yoke and pulled back on the throttle. The aircraft was buffeting as he was moving too fast for the airframe to handle the atmospheric pressure.

The nearly seven hundred thousand pounds of metal and fuel collided with a newer building. The Pilot's last act on Earth was to smile as the nose of aircraft impacted the strobe light perfectly.

Colonel Hassid looked on in horror as the United States Embassy in Jerusalem vanished.

He reached numbly for the phone with his other hand hovered over the button to activate the massive machine that is the Israeli Defense Force.

White House, Washington D.C.
2000 hours EST

The President sat in the Oval Office and let the gaggle of talking heads behind him turn into white noise. Not since the embassy bombings in Africa had our Embassies been attacked. Two inside of a month and this one in Jerusalem was a total loss.

The switchboard in the communications room was on fire with the population mad and getting madder. No amount of any explanation will change the mind of a mob of people bent on revenge. Bombing buildings with planes started the last war. That war was not finished.

The white noise behind him had rose to crescendo and was now tapering off. He made his decision and turned around.

"This is a one-way conversation. I do the talking and you do the listening without comment.

1. I want to know who owned that aircraft. FBI, NTSB and FAA. Find out and you have three days.
2. I believe it came from Afghanistan. If that is so, we are going to beat them down to the stone age.
3. DOD, I want targets in Afghanistan. DOD stand fast. The rest of you get out.

The President walked into the Oval Office and motioned for Secretary Dodson and General Edwards to sit down on the couches. He sat down and looked at them.

"Gentlemen, I know you respect my title but not me, and I deserve that. This time I need the hand of God to bring down vengeance on the people who did this. To you, I am ordering you to be my conscience. I intend to make them howl in pain."

"The first targets are the poppy fields. I want them all. As I understand it, the C-130's and C-17's can be retrofitted with airborne spray tanks. Take every special precaution there is. Tell the Air Force to remember Agent Orange. All Air Crews are to think in terms of cancer and deformed children."

"All the airports are to be rendered inoperable. Crush the infrastructure and make them howl."

"You will return here in 24 hours with the target list for a briefing."

Edwards spoke up. "I want to use Bagram Airfield as an in-country logistics base in case we need more than 48 hours."

"No one is left behind," the President said, pointing at Edwards. "After you leave, no US Equipment will be left behind. If you can't remove it; turn it into scrap."

"Who approves our strategy?" Edwards asked.

The President smiles. "I just gave you the strategy. You own the operational matters and a stand-alone General owns the tactics. To the question you are asking, we stomp their ass and leave. We are not staying behind. Period."

Edwards smiled.

February 14

American Embassy, Philippians
0100 Hours UTC

Two very haggard looking Americans were pulled out of police cars, in handcuffs, and escorted up the stairs to the waiting Marine guards. The Police Inspector passed two manila folders to the Marine guards. In impeccable English, they announced that these two were arrested after a long two-day party full of debauchery which nearly destroyed an expensive hotel penthouse.

Once the noise lowered, management came in, and recoiled at the remnants of the party. Prostitutes, illegal drugs and "other things" were found along with seven different passports for both men.

A quick search of their fingerprints identified them as Joseph Sharpe and Jonathan Brennan. Both had active warrants from the United States and it was decided that it was easier and cheaper to turn them over to the Embassy and have them deported.

The police made no mention of any money that may or may not have been at the scene.

Once inside, Sharpe and Beckman freely admitted who they were and why they were guilty of the charges specified in the warrants. Someone stole all their money hidden in banks all around the Asian Pacific rim. So, they decided to have one last party and burn through the last of their money and turn themselves in to the law.

"How about that for a story?" Brennan said.

Department of Justice, Washington D.C.
0900 hours EST

Rebecca Beck threw down the report covering all the states that are ignoring Federal primacy in Justice, and any number of traditional and non-traditional areas.

The southern border with Mexico was the most serious problem. The Army was privately removing units from covering the southern border. Both Texas and the two divisions covering the nine hundred miles of border understood that those units are tired and need to pull back and rest. Colonel Jasper Folcroft's first order was to take all those Legal officers and order them to stay on the line. He ordered all the affected commanders not to use them as an excuse for cowardice. "When shot at, shot back. If those people are stupid enough to attack, you have tanks and artillery, use them. Fuck the cowards from Washington."

The Texas Governor has backed him fully and in writing.

Governors in over half the states have fully endorsed their National Guard troops to act as police officers and arrest immigrants for violating state laws.

Those same states have passed laws making many of those Federal laws null and void; also, those same state laws "gave" the states authority to arrest the Federals if they "interfered". Civil Rights groups and now the Justice Department were stacking up deep in Federal courts.

Local District Attorneys and States Attorneys General laughed.

Desert Zero, Fort Hood, Texas
0800 hours CST.

Wendy arrived three hours ago and claimed her old room against the will of the three Delta Operators that said this was their area. Wendy walked up to the operator and said they were already ordered to leave. She stopped talking. Getting into an argument just blew up her temper.

300

She went to her old room, dropped off her bags, locked the door and went to find some food. She really hoped Sergeant Merrill was still the head cook. That man could cook an omelet as good as a Navy cook.

Wendy walked into the Operations/Intelligence Center and recoiled at the mess that was left behind. Overflowing trash cans, paperwork scattered all over the floors. Real childish trash. She took a deep breath and went to the supply room. It was a mess too. She found a box of heavy-duty trash bags, picked a corner and started cleaning up. She finished the final bag and was dragging it into a corner when very tall officer walked in. "Sir," she said, returning to her work.

"Are you part of the clean-up team or here to work with me?" Simmons asked, smiling.

"No sir. Chief Petty Officer Wendy Kendal. I work here. Those pigs from Delta Farce left seven bags full of trash scattered around my Operations Center."

Two Officers behind the tall officer came into view. "What did you call them?" a Captain asked."

Kendal remembered him. "Captain Barker, you people left a pig stye in here. Trash cans over flowing, trash scattered around on the floor. Chairs smeared with Vaseline. Doors nailed shut. Real childish behavior. And I called you 'Those pigs from Delta Farce'."

This Captain Barker suddenly remembered this particular Navy sailor. She made him into a twisted pretzel in the hand-to-hand pit when they thought they could teach unarmed combat. "I have some NCO's outside. I'll get them to come in and help you."

"You see to it Captain Barker. Chief Petty Officer, follow me." Simmons walked over to his office.

"Please close the door, Chief Petty Officer," Simmons said. He motioned for her to sit down while he emptied his arms.

"Sir," Kendal said. "The proper contraction is Chief for E-7 and E-8. I know that an Army E-5 thru 7 is called Sergeant."

"Chief," he said, apparently trying to get used to the term. "I am the new Commander here. Lieutenant Colonel Benjamin Simmons, USMC with many assignments behind me. I never like patting my back, so here." He handed over his ORB or Officer Readiness Brief. This was a three-page form that summarized an Officer's career. "The Marines and Army troops are arriving next week. I met with General O'Cleary four times in the last week. She told me you are a steady hand and I will be happy you are running the Operations/Intelligence Center. Incidentally, Sergeant Major Waverly is the Senior NCO here." Simmons noted that she smiled as she gave the form a cursory look and set it aside.

"I know the Sergeant Major, Sir." After a few seconds. "I respect him and will fight next to him. Back-to-back."

Simmons came around the desk and sat down next to her. "I understand everyone here deploys and everyone cross-trains."

Kendal said. "Yes Sir. Colonel Peters, your predecessor, did not want anyone in the Headquarters to have 'Headquarters mentality'. No second guessing or 'why do you need it', women included. Especially the women. Captain Hawker, the S-2, swallowed her fear and followed me on the missions. She was a brain and a half, but she forced herself to deploy, stand her ground and fight. Cu-dos to her."

Simmons looked at her. "Any advice you want to give me?"

Kendal was surprised at the question. "1. Train, train, and never stop training. We spent as much time cross-training as training in our primary specialty. I am a signalman primarily. I was also cross-trained as an infantryman and a medic. 2. Colonel Peters had our back and we knew that **without a doubt**."

The two of them talked about items large and small about running this unit and how to deal with the nature of this unit.

"General O'Cleary loaned this to me to show the unit." It was her Savage Rabbit jacket. It was half an Army uniform jacket and half a Marine uniform Jacket sown together with the Savage Rabbit patch over the heart. "She said that nothing brought them together like this jacket."

Kendal smiled. "I lost mine when I was ejected."

Simmons reached into the bag and pulled out another Army/Navy jacket. "The General did not say where she found it."

Kendal opened it up and sharply inhaled. She ran her hand over it. She exchanged her Navy jacket half with Captain Hawker. "Thank you, Sir. Thank you very much."

"I understand the original jackets were destroyed, so I had to use your Savage Rabbit patch as a template and had over four hundred made. Deflated my bank account. I intend to use that as a certification gift a month from now."

"That is a great idea, Sir." Kendal was looking at her jacket with an almost lover's zeal.

"Chief, I do not mean to disrespect you, but how did a sailor end up here? Your record says you earned that jacket. No one gave to you."

"Sergeant Major Kincaid, Sir." Kendal said. "I was working with him on catching a rogue unit of American mercenaries before he was tagged to be the Sergeant Major and Master Trainor. He said I needed to legitimize what I learned with him and he needed an Operations NCO who was not a joke or a coward or stupid. And he wanted a woman in the Center to remove the cowardice factor headquarters spawn like lice."

Simmons seemed convinced. He stood and extended his hand. "Thank you, Chief. I look forward to working with you."

"That is mutual, Sir," Kendal said.

There was a knock at the door. "Come in," Simmons said.

Waverly walked in and saluted. "Sergeant Major Marcus Waverly reporting for duty."

Simmons returned the salute and shook his hand. "At Ease," he said.

"Howdy Kendal, whose nose you're going to break?" He smiled and extended his hand.

"Delta Farce tried and I would not take the bait." She warmly shook his hand. "I'll leave and let you get to know each other." She made a nod to Simmons and left.

Simmons offered a chair to Waverly and sat down for a long two-hour introduction. Simmons and Waverly spent those two hours getting to know each other and looking over the plan O'Cleary and Kincaid used to create the last unit.

"Sir, this is a four-and-a-half-week train-up to basic standards," Waverly said. "You cannot let anyone push you to shorten the schedule. And the legal officer should be shot."

Simmons chuckled. "Yes, and then no." He pulled over the Master training plan. "I'll deal with the impossible, Sergeant Major. The troops and their training are yours. I'll stay out of the way as much as I can."

Simmons took the Sergeant Major's insignia off Waverly's jacket and replaced it with that of a Command Sergeant Major. "With nine sections and a headquarters section, you are intitled." They shook hands as Simmons handed over a folder with the appointment.

1300 hours CST

Kendal came back from lunch and started working on the safes. She had the original combinations. The 'don't trust nothin' alert went off in her head and sure enough, these were the wrong numbers. Fortunately, she left the top drawers open and engaged the mechanism just in case this happened.

Kendal pulled over a small ladder and opened the 'innards'. Using the instructions in her brain book, she spent two hours changing the twelve combinations on five safes. Two of the safes had four drawers with separate combination locks. One of them had two drawers that way.

When the classified intelligence start arriving tomorrow, she will be ready.

Of course, Delta canceled the security net covering the arms rooms. All the arms racks were supposed to have a series 200 lock and the outside door had a Series 600 lock on the outer door. Of course, all the locks were gone. Fort Hood had to scramble and find replacements.

1500 hours CST

Simmons called both Waverly and Kendal into his office for a special meeting.

Waverly inspected the barracks and said he wanted to get a detail from Fort Hood to come this weekend and scrub down the barracks, fix the A/C and all the other things that were abused and damaged. He evicted the Delta operators out of Auxiliary barracks he and Kendal are using. They tried complaining, but Waverly changed their minds. There was a lot of damage and chances are, unless it required a skilled craftsman, the Rabbits will have to do the fixing.

Kendal told him the Center will be up and running by tomorrow. The classified intelligence will start arriving tomorrow. Kendal decided to omit the combination snafu. Kendal can be ready for a briefing of the overall situation by Monday morning.

"Tuesday at 9 am, one company of volunteers from Fort Hood and one company of Force Recon will arrive here. For four and a half weeks, we train-up. Both of you were here last time. You are the proctors. Sergeant Major, you own the phase one individual build-up. Squad and Section training is yours along with Chief Kendal. Chief, you are in charge of getting this headquarters up and running along with setting up and executing the cross training. You'll need to start planning now. Additionally, you'll select six people out of twenty coming in to assist you. These people, infantry with appropriate security clearances, will form a core of the center. Later, they will be trained and placed into squads and sections."

"Oh, I apologize, Sergeant Major,' Simmons said. "I asked for and will receive a detail company to help set up the ranges and clean the barracks and the area. They are yours for Saturday and Sunday."

Simmons was tired. "The new rule is that I see you first in the morning and last in the evening."

"Yes sir," Waverly said.

Washington National Airport, Washington D.C.
1800 hours EST

With no fanfare; a no-name Boeing 737 arrived. Six men disembarked. Two were heavily restrained. A van backed up and both men were placed inside and secured.

305

Joe Sharpe and John Beckman were going to see two US attorneys. Both men were offered a life sentence versus a long trial where they could guarantee the death penalty.

Once the paperwork was finished, the US Marshals will take over and transport them to join Roy Seagrove at a super-max facility.

The last of the Black Elves were gone.

February 15

Desert Zero, Fort Hood, Texas
1630 hours CST.

All weekend long the fun never stopped. The infantry unit assigned here to clean and ready the camp for the units to arrive tomorrow grumbled and complained. Even the NCOs complained and grumbled. Simmons had to drag the one Lieutenant off to the side and read him the riot act. "You have two days and a mission, Lieutenant. If I have to do your job, then the Army does not need you."

The Lieutenant whipped everyone into finishing. All the work was done by 4:30 pm on Sunday.

"All because you did your job, Lieutenant," Simmons said as the unit left.

February 16

White House, Washington, D.C.
0900 hours EST

The President answered the summons down to the Situation Room with a yawn and an overdue need for a long uninterrupted nap. He had hoped for it this morning.

He came in casual clothes and dispensed with formalities. "Yes, Ladies and Gentlemen," he said, signaling the start of the briefing.

"Mister President," the Director of the CIA stood and began. "Per your order, we can, without a doubt, identify that the C-130 that crashed into our Embassy in Jerusalem. We have the maintenance records from the four C-130's left

306

behind. All the surviving parts, bearing serial numbers, are from all four aircraft. There is a lot of data available to track the circuitous flight beginning at Bagram Air Base."

For two hours, everyone from the CIA, DIA, FAA, NTSB and several other agencies briefed and confirmed everything without any doubt.

The President turned to General Edwards and James Dodson. "Defense Department, what is this country doing in response?"

Dodson deferred to Edwards. Edwards nodded to a briefing officer.

"Mister President, we have a four-part plan awaiting your approval."

"Part One involves achieving and maintaining air mastery over Afghanistan. We presently know the location and status of every aircraft in Afghanistan. As we take over the airspace, we will announce our intentions over the radio and media. Foreign aircraft will be told to leave and or stay on the ground. Any and all aircraft that fire on US aircraft will be destroyed, regardless of flag. Period."

"Part Two is the destruction of the poppy fields, mostly in the south of the country. Twenty- seven C-17 are being specially modified to act as sprayers to cover all the fields. Each aircraft will carry approximately 150,000 pounds of a very powerful herbicide that is engineered to destroy the plants where they grow. The ground will not be able to grow any plants for at least two years. This herbicide will kill the plant and its roots. We plan all twenty-two aircraft to make no less than four runs over the areas."

"Part Three is the physical destruction of all the air fields that have aircraft except the Kabel International Airport."

"Part Four is a classified operation covered in the ACHILLES plan that is above the clearances for some of the persons in this room. That Sir, will require your specific order to implement."

"Mister President, this concludes the briefing." The briefer collected his materials and left.

The President turned his chair to the side. This was his signal to be silent. So, he could think. Every President had this system. Staffers and officials always wanted to shout out their opinion. The President ran it all over and came to a decision.

He turned and looked over to the Defense team. "When can you start?"

"Sundown on the 20th Sir," Dodson said.

"Go." The President said, standing to leave.

Everyone knew this time not to argue with him.

February 17

J. Edgar Hoover Building, Washington D.C.
0900 hours EST

FBI Director Solin was being bombarded by the surge of crime being directly tied to the immigration mess. Despite the lower numbers of people trying to move north of the border, they suffered from a language barrier, no skills and no legal identity here in the United States.

Solin was tired from being the pivot man in this playground fight. 535 congressman and senators constantly fanned the 'flames of stupid' as he called it. In his desk drawer was a master list of available agents nation-wide. He had just so many agents to cover a huge country.

His daughter bought him a computerized display frame that listed all the data of his situation and that data was constantly updated.

The United States comprised 3,531,905 square miles with 333,527,197 people. That did not add in the areas and operations done overseas. Solin had 35,000 agents, technicians and support personnel to handle, at present, 5,690 different crimes and "special situations".

His job was to look at those numbers and try to figure out how to fit the FBI into all of it.

Solin rubbed his face with the almost absurdity of his task.

1430 hours EST

Solin sat through a detailed and boring report of the fracturing of the United States. Texas, Oklahoma, Arizona and

New Mexico acted like a separate nation. Wyoming, Utah and Colorado are a better match. They had a head start with a lot of resources. Colorado had a lot investment money coming in and spent everywhere.

Justice was at a loss to understand what or how to do anything. They needed more from the Supreme Court. The President was predictably hazy and no-help except to take the credit.

Three groups of states wanted to be free from the Federal Government. Twenty-something counties in Oregon and seven counties in California want to secede and join Idaho.

Nobody wanted to touch the report covering all the attacks on IRS agents, their families, their homes and places of work.

February 18

Desert Zero, Fort Hood, Texas
0900 hours CST

The four Delta personnel came into the Operations Center, 'plopped' down at a random desk and continued their conversation.

Kendal picked that instant to walk up with an armload of files. "That's my desk you have your foot on and my seat you are sitting on."

Master Sergeant Frederick Hewer looked up at her. He decided not to start anything, at least not today. He stood up and made a motion wiping off the desk and chair.

Waverly walked in and stopped. "I told you people to leave this facility."

Captain Harding stood. "You, said leave the barracks. We are here under orders."

Waverly was about to say something until Simmons walked in lowering his cell phone. "You have one chance to leave this facility before I make a phone call to someone you do not want to pick a fight with."

Captain Harding stood at attention. "Sir, Colonel Saraland ordered us to stay behind and assist in the transition." He glared as Kendal lowered her cell phone.

Simmons walked to his office and closed the door.

Kendal went to her desk and started separating files into different stacks.

Harding walked up to her. "You trying to start a fight?"

"No Sir," she said, looking up.

Harding stood up to her. "Stand up to attention, sailor."

Kendal stood to attention. She remembered him and the others as staff, not Delta operators. None of them ever deployed. They could brag about being Delta, but these men weren't real.

"Sailor, I am not going to forget you," Harding said, walking ominously toward her.

Kendal silently stood her ground and stayed neutral.

"Sailor, do you have anything to say?" Harding smiled and tipped over a stack of files. The stack hit the floor and fanned out like a deck of cards.

"Harding," Simmons yelled from across the Center. "What the hell was that about?"

Harding turned around and stood at attention. "Sir, I bumped against files and they fell over."

"Bullshit," Simmons said. "I watched you slowly push the files over. Sergeant Major, take these …… people outside. Put them in a single line formation. Captain, all four of you are to stand there and wait at attention until I say so."

"Outside!" Waverly said forcibly.

Kendal was already picking the files from the floor.

"Thanks for not killing them," Simmons said to her, as she picked up the last file.

"I only kill real men," she said with a smile.

"The Army part of the equation are arriving in thirty minutes." Simmons gave the files a cursory inspection. "Are these the in-processing files for each man?"

"Yes Sir." Kendal was busy separating files. "We will file them in here. These men are easy because they are already from Fort Hood. The Marines when they arrive are not easy. The Marines have already been out-processed at Camp Lejeune. All each man has to do is check the folders, ensure all the information is correct and sign-in. I'll be spending all my time teaching everyone. Now I understand why Sergeant Major Kincaid was in a foul mood a lot of times."

Simmons liked what he saw. "The Sergeant Major seemed to be something of a legend. What was your opinion of him?"

Kendal gave him 'the look'. "He was a royal pain in the ass, front to finish. Aggravating, know-it-all, fault finding bully who was always all over everything. Bottom line is he is the finest example of a Non-Commissioned Officer in any service."

Simmons smiled. "I hope to have the pleasure someday."

Just then, General O'Cleary walked in. Behind her, someone called "Attention". Waverly walked in and stopped in front of something he never thought would ever happen. He saluted a pregnant four-star general.

"Is there a problem?" O'Cleary asked, while returning the salute.

"Ma'am, almost two years ago, you were a one-star that stood in front of us and gave us the ability to stand out as the best of the best." His face went blank. "Clowns like those five standing outside took our pride away from us. They stripped us of our identity and finally abandoned us to die and their attitude was 'oh well'."

O'Cleary stood directly in front of Waverly. "That ends today, Sergeant Major. I am the Vice-Chairman of the Joint Chiefs of Staff. I am your Commanding General and the protector of this unit. I was then and I am that now. If something happens to me, both you and the Colonel will disband this unit. Understand."

O'Cleary stuck her hand out.

Waverly readily shook it. Waverly thanked her and left. Busses were arriving and he needed to direct traffic. Kendal went with him.

O'Cleary summoned her MP escort and told them to arrest the five Delta personnel and take them to the MP central office. Process them. She would be there later to prefer charges.

O'Cleary and Simmons sat down in his office and discussed the officer side of the equation. They went through the records of thirty-seven officers. Simmons finally decided on two majors, five captains and six lieutenants taken almost equally from the Army and the Marine Corps.

The balance of the morning was spent going over the training schedule.

"Colonel, I will tell you now that I am receiving pressure from echelons way above your pay-grade to start operations today. Obviously, none of them are military. They are my problem. If they show up here, smile, be nice and call me. They are not in charge; you are and I am in charge of you.

At 1400 hours, O'Cleary, Simmons and Waverly went out to the elevated platform. The unit was arrayed out in front of them. Typically, Marines were on one side and the Army on the other.

O'Cleary saw it again. "Sergeant Major, this us versus them stops here and now. Mix them up."

Waverly's booming voice bounced through the camp. Ten minutes later a similar looking formation was left, but the Army and Marines were thoroughly integrated.

"I hate speeches and parades," O'Cleary said. "Yes, I am a woman and yes, I have four stars and yes, I am pregnant. The only thing that is important is that I am your Commanding General. You Marines have skills that this unit has to have and the you Army Soldiers have skills that this unit has to have. You are going to get in-processed, organized into sub-units, receive the necessary briefings and settle in. Training begins Friday."

O'Cleary stood back and signaled Waverly and Simmons to come forward. Waverly unrolled a small flag that had the Savage Rabbit symbol on it. Off to the side, Kendal read the Assumption of Command orders.

After O'Cleary and Simmons finished their remarks, they left to go to Simmons' office. Waverly read down a roster, assigning men to their new units. The Marines and Soldiers looked at each other warily.

Waverly knew he had his work cut out for him. He smiled thinking that this was heaven.

February 19

South of Sells, Tohono O'Doham Nation, Arizona

It was a silent cold night with overcast skies. From an outpost on Baboquivari Peak and the surrounding high ground, the radars and optical identified a mass of men, estimated at over 100, spread out and secure a large oval. Sonic amplifiers overheard them digging and talking between each other.

The overheard conversations gave away all the evidence anyone would need to convict them of trafficking drugs and people into the United States. Recorders picked up and stored every word. It was determined that no innocent people were on site.

Suddenly, seven blacked out trucks drove up.

Behind them from the south, five large, tracked vehicles with mounted machine guns, came in at high speed. They stopped in the middle of the oval and parked side by side.

As the ramps of the tracked vehicles were lowered, overhead, seven flares were shot up over head.

An amplified voice said in Spanish to lay down their weapons and walk back to Mexico. This was their only opportunity.

Silence rained over the scene as the flares hit the ground and burned out. All the traffickers looked at each other. Suddenly the men unloading and loading the drugs sprang into action. Loud commands filled the air.

"Thunking" sounds came from three locations around the area. Overhead an illumination round flared and floated overhead. With little to no wind, the illumination round stayed over where it was needed. The other two locations had three guns each and shot rounds illumination and high explosive rounds all over the objective area.

At selective areas around the drug site, snipers picked off targets of opportunity. Leaders around the world all had the same habits. They stood tall and impressive, sounded off in a booming voice and pointed with fingers at things.

The Armored Personnel Carriers tried leaving, but each one suddenly exploded as a rocket was shot into them. The aluminum walls gave way and the fuel tanks exploded on flames.

The blacked-out trucks were shot full of holes with armored piercing rounds.

Slowly, the force was destroyed. A lot of those men decided to quit. They through down their weapons and ran to the south. Over half of them were shot before they could cross the border.

Behind them, those men that escaped reported hearing wounded men screaming. Single shots ended the screaming. Information was recorded and collected.

Twenty minutes after the fire-fight started, everybody left and disappeared.

When the sun rose, helicopters overflew the scene. The Attorney General of Arizona looked at the hi-definition images and feared a war had started and he was afraid innocent civilians were going to be caught in the middle.

February 20

White House, Washington D.C.
0900 hours EST

The President rubbed his ear, thanked and dismissed the translators. He called the Russian and Chinese ambassadors to the White House for a simultaneous briefing on what the US was doing in Afghanistan. He gave them an admittedly sanitized timetable and list of objectives.

The Russian ambassador did slightly inhale when the destruction of the poppy fields was mentioned. There was always an unofficial policy from the Russians and the Americans during each country's occupation. This was a can of worms that no one wanted to open.

Both Ambassadors remained stoic and professional. The President had his staff install extra phones with extra-long lines for them to use.

"One last point, Ambassadors," the President said. "Please remove your aircraft from Afghanistan. I do not want to accidentally kill any of your innocent citizens or destroy any of your property.

Country of Afghanistan

An AWACS E-3 aircraft orbited over the common border between Pakistan and Afghanistan in a long oval. When the Embassy was attacked in Israel, the Pakistani Government openly offered to assist America in any way it could. Afghanistan had recently invaded them for no reason, killing Pakistani citizens and soldiers. This was payback.

The American military now had "free access" from the Indian Ocean to any target inside Afghanistan.

The AWACS operators smiled watching a swarm of American aircraft funnel into Afghanistan.

The AWACS aircraft started a tape, transmitted over 121.5 MHz for civilian aircraft and 243.0 MHz for military use, that the United States was conducting military operations over Afghanistan. Any aircraft, regardless of country of origin or status, was ordered to stay on the ground or, if airborne, fly to Pakistan. No arguments or discussion.

The twenty-two C-17 aircraft turned over Pakistan towards their corridors and entered Afghanistan. The rear ramps were lowered. A mechanism was wheeled outward and formed a fan far out to the rear of the aircraft. The AWACS said all the aircraft were properly arrayed and granted them permission to begin.

Two pump operators started the pumps on each aircraft and watched the spray fans as they sent out an aerosol spray two hundred feet over the ground and cover a three-hundred-foot-wide corridor.

The aerosol floated through the air and gently fell to ground. The concentration was double the desired amount. By the time the sun rose, the plants would be dead all the way down to the roots.

Pakistan wholeheartedly supported America's war against Afghanistan. They allowed an ocean-going tanker to dock at their port, which carried the bulk of the herbicide. Trucks, delivered by Air Force aircraft, drove up to the ship, loaded up and drove to the airport. The planes were loaded and the trucks returned to the dock. This allowed the planes to make two runs a night.

The second group of sprayings was planned to commence at 2200 hours tonight and 0300 the next morning, 21 February, Afghanistan time.

21 February

Minutemen, north of Fort Benton, Montana
1600 hours MST

Jones, Kincaid, Peters, along with the command and staff of Savage Rabbits sat through a very long meeting as Kincaid and Sheridan briefed everyone on a concept to integrate an NCO Academy. This will concentrate on all the items the Rabbits would not normally cover in the normal course of training.

The Master Training Plan covered 11 butcher block sheets arrayed across the front of the briefing room. Each man and woman were given a paper copy to follow along with Kincaid and Sheridan's briefing.

The main theme was that people are not invulnerable. Everyone has to be able to take command, but the question was whether or not they knew how.

The timetable said that the basics would be taught sometime in late April or early May.

"The bottom line," Kincaid said at the end of the briefing. "The more you train, the less you bleed and die. Instill in everyone that this helps to ensure that you survive to become old."

Country of Afghanistan
2000 hours Delta (plus eight hours from EST)

All day long Air Force and Naval Aviation planners finalized pans to destroy aviation and infrastructure targets all over the country. Over seventy-five percent of the planners served tours of duty in Afghanistan. That specialized knowledge proved invaluable.

Seven hundred and forty-two sorties were planned for tonight. One hundred and sixty-two of them were strictly to be used to fight off any one who tried to stop them. Privately, they hoped none of them were Russian or Chinese.

Tonight, Afghanistan was going to lose all their airports and all their aviation support facilities. Selected bridges and highways were going to be destroyed. The Air Force and Navy was going to have a lot of fun tonight.

All the Commanders from both services decided that they needed to check off a lot of training points, so specialized targets and munitions were designated and plotted.

Additionally, photo and special reconnaissance indicated that the poppy fields were not totally covered. So, the twenty-two aircraft will fly again tonight. The President had told the overall commander this operation, to destroy their ability to grow poppy for all time, was to be the top of their list.

22 February

Country of Afghanistan
0800 hours Delta (plus eight hours from EST)

The whining and crying and threats of death were heard around the world. In this incidence, the media was accused of siding with the drug growers. The growers showed the world their fields of poppy plants that, until now were never allowed to be photographed, literally dying and withering in front of them.

The Afghan government cried foul at the American retaliation for the acts of a few misguided people. "Where is the Justice for these terroristic attacks?"

The growers and workers of the poppy plants wanted to know how they were going to feed their families.

The world did not answer them.

Werewolf Support Camp #1, Hill County, Montana
1000 hours, MST

Kincaid looked at the paperwork in his personal file. The President had used his authority to return him to active duty to form the Savage Rabbits. Some bureaucrats found a way to void his status while in detention.

So technically, he was retired again. Kincaid looked at his bank statement and noticed the reduced monthly deposit. Kincaid looked at all the dreams around him. Stacks of training plans along with this idea and that idea.

He stood and shuffled over to the coffee pot for another cup to add to his morbidity. This was the other end of retired life. He looked at the open robe, underwear, t-shirt and fuzzy slippers. When he was with Karen, he never dressed like this.

Kincaid sat down hard and looked at his masterpiece. The Shark-Hunter program was something he had put off for far too long. He worked the program for a long time. He wanted to do things right. He still had not-so-fond memories of Gladys Goldstein's training all those years ago.

Wendy Kendal was at Desert Zero running the Operations and Intelligence Center. By all accounts, she was doing a top-notch job.

Cindy Morgan was now wearing her rank, teaching the Savage Rabbits how to use terrain as a sniper, spotter and a hunter. "Every terrain feature has the equal ability to save your life or kill you." She taught them how to use terrain. She was gone more than she was here.

Where Cindy excelled was teaching them the other side of being a sniper: information collection. Every sniper was taught how to read the terrain and record every aspect of the world they crawled and slithered into. Sometimes, a sniper happens on an area where there is no target to shot at, but there were enemy actions and situations that their superiors needed to know about.

Earl Locklear was now the main operator of Operations and Intelligence Center down at Minuteman. He was just gone.

Kincaid decided that the auxiliary site at H-42 up in Alaska was a good place to hide for a month or two. All indications were that no one went there.

Kincaid flipped a coin. He went into his room and packed his bags. At three o'clock, he was finished. He had packed up and thought about all the things he was forgetting.

He spent the balance of the day cleaning up everything. Byron's room was scrubbed down and the kitchen looked like it was never used.

Hopefully, no one would miss him till long after he was gone.

Kincaid typed up a letter and placed it on the table and taped it down. It was sparse with details, but it adamantly said he was leaving and he wanted to be left alone.

Country of Afghanistan
2000 hours Delta (plus eight hours from EST)

The Air Force and Navy Commanders were steadily working down the target list. They enjoyed full Air Mastery. AWACS watched aircraft leave Afghan airspace on the first night when the sprayers flew. Twenty-seven interceptors orbited overhead with nothing to do.

The departing aircraft were identified as Chinese and Russian aircraft. All day yesterday and today, reconnaissance aircraft and satellites covered the country. As a parting shot, the target list was expanded to include any identifiable US equipment left behind.

Tonight, was the final night. Two new carrier battle groups arrived to lessen the pressure along with Pakistan and India allowing use of their airfields.

23 February

White House, Washington, D.C.
0800 hours EST

The President rubbed his face and finally had to make a decision. He had personal knowledge of ACHILLES and was the only one who could authorize its use.

He remembered how it destroyed Iran and temporarily disabled Mexico. All this time later, Iran has not recovered and the CIA still has no clue if they discovered how or why. They did know the original source code and operating software is being held in the Pentagon under heavy guard. Of course, they made the pitch that they should be the holders. The President saw through them. They loved to exercise the "we are not mature enough' dogma.

"No," was his answer to the CIA. No telling who would suffer under their control.

He called over to General Edwards. "General Edwards, this is the President. Activate Achilles." He hung up the phone and turned around in his chair.

24 February

Desert Zero, Fort Hood, Texas
0600 hours CST

Waverly stood in front of the three-section formation, called it to attention and received the report. Waverly turned around and reported that status to the Colonel.

"Good morning, Savage Rabbits. Today begins your training. I intend for you to sweat profusely and labor hard. The only record I intend to break is this." He held up a framed document. "This is what is called a Force Depletion statement. Some egg-head did some kind of math and said so many of you will die at these points of time. I intend train you so well that only a fraction of this number dies. This document is framed because it will be mounted at the door to the headquarters. If you know what is good for you, I want you to turn them into liars."

Simmons called out and started physical training.

Department of Justice, Washington, D.C.
1000 hours EST

Rebecca Beck was tired of all the briefings and arguments over the states using militias and literally upset things. Civil Libertarians and stray lawyers wanted to shut them down saying that the people should stand back and wait for the cops to do something or nothing.

Beck hated a lot of lawyers. All they really wanted was money for stirring the 'shit pot'.

Technically, militias were legal and the basis for the Second Amendment. Just as technically, no legal definition was ever made as to the status and limits of a militia. Beck loved to through that argument back in their faces.

Legal downstairs says they had to file a lawsuit to set the precedent that militia activities should be placed under Federal control. Over half the activities going on had barely any legal controls on them. Beck was one of those politician lawyers. But she did have a slight glimmer of common sense.

She smiled and thought of an idea. She reached into her purse and pulled out a small well-worn phone book. She flipped through until the name she was looking for was reached.

26 February

National Media Sources, Cyber Space
1300 hours

Across the United States, roads were clogged with people moving back to or towards areas they felt comfortable. Some were going to childhood places they grew up in. Others came to places they found later in life. Still others went to where the rumors said was a better life.

The census bureau notified the appropriate agencies.

No one knew what to do with that knowledge. There was simply no way to corral the population. Everyone was segmenting and segregating. It was something else for the civil libertarians to cry and whine about.

Today throughout the 'fruited plain', Americans of from all walks of life finally admitted they were scared.

28 February

1/17th Infantry, Fort Hood Texas
1300 hours

Lieutenant Colonel Thomas Latham passed command of 1st Battalion, 17th Infantry Regiment to Lieutenant Colonel Middleton Wellman.

After the ceremony was over, he felt a sigh of relief come over him. These days, every commander had a bull's eye on his/her back that told you to be very careful if you want a career. Too many lawyers, agencies and observers hovered around you looking for something to destroy you. His best poker friend said you had enemies in front and behind you.

Sigh of relief.

He was taking a month's leave before moving on to his next assignment. He was to report to Headquarters, Southeast Region. This was Admiral Matthew Cartwright's headquarters to be the military governor of the southeastern United States. Hopefully, Latham would have a job that did not entail someone looking to kill his career.

March 1

Station H-42, North of Fort Greeley, Alaska
0900 hours AKDT

Kincaid climbed down into the old Cold War era radar station. The abandoned site was forgotten by almost everyone. Hopefully.

All the forgotten supplies that the General had sent here in case of a rapid national collapse were not going to be missed. In the code safe was the master list of everything; seventeen pages worth. Kincaid was originally given the mission to stock this facility. He did something to piss one of the Gods out there and this was his penitence. Boo-hoo.

He gave the list a cursory look. Subconsciously, he must have thought this was going to happen. Granted, the master list at H-42 was intended to run the Werewolf operations here as a stand-alone facility. Except for perishable foods, everything was here for an extended period.

Pruitt and Locklear did the initial staging of supplies here. Though it was up to Kincaid to finish stockpiling, Kincaid always wondered what they hid and where.

Kincaid stopped the ridiculous and stupid thinking. He needed to focus on the now and future. He wanted to stay here and be alone.

First order of business was electrical power. Then he needed to move in and at least bring his bags inside. Of course, he had to drive 47 miles to the grocery store.

Up here, he could eat everything he wanted, as much as he wanted, without one of those women trying to impose their will over him.

His mouth watered thinking about a fat T-bone.

Good Riddance World.

March 2

New York Stock Exchange, New York City, New York
0900 hours EST

Traders on the Exchange showed the strain of the last few weeks. The total cost to date has been set at sixteen trillion dollars. Traders around the world are still unconcern as Japan was pulling back all the money. It was more important to them to rebuild their country than let money managers world-wide swim in their money.

Unofficially, 27,000 men, women and children died. The Japanese government, by tradition, will not confirm or deny that number.

The first planes were landing carrying rebuilding supplies. Purchasing Agents, around the world, were on a buying spree.

If there was a silver lining to this catastrophe, Japan's emergency managers and pre-built defenses worked furiously and predictably to minimize the destruction.

Border Patrol Headquarters Phoenix, Arizona
1000 hours MST

Chief Patrol Agent Thomas Barrios of the Border Patrol read the monthly report for January covering everything coming over the border in his operational area.

Barrios skipped over the amounts and types of drugs. Bottom line was that the streets were being flooded. Despite all the talk about no money and recession and depression, money was flowing south like an ocean current.

Barrios sighed thinking that something new was needed to halt the current stupidity.

Desert Zero, Fort Hood, Texas
1630 hours EST

Simmons read the weekly report he drafted for O'Cleary to update her on the training status for the Savage Rabbits.

Overall, the individual skills scored high across the board. Four men had to drop out for four different reasons. Two had problems with fear of heights. One had broken his leg. Another was just too immature to handle the intensity of the training.

Simmons saw to it that the man with the broken leg had a good job waiting for him. He broke his leg on the obstacle course and had to be physically restrained afterward. He kept trying to negotiate the course with a broken leg.

The two with fear of heights were sat down and told to work on the fear. Then and only then could they come back and try again.

Onward to the other two hundred and eighty-seven men. All of them excelled at the individual tasks. All of them spent two days on a known distance range. They worked on their skills at twice the rated ranges for the M-16/M-4 rifle. At ranges that far out, the .223 caliber/5.56 mm round lost too much energy to be effective.

The men were allowed to have half of Sunday off.

Last Saturday, Chaplin (Captain) Tobias Cantrell arrived for duty. He was formally introduced at the Sunday noon formation before being released.

Simmons listed all the officers that arrived and more importantly those officers who have not arrived for duty yet.

Simmons put the document down and sighed it. He relished the thought and challenge this assignment offered him.

March 3

J. Edgar Hoover Building, Washington D.C.
0900 hours EST

The Director of the FBI, Marcus Solin picked up the monthly report of criminal activity for the month of February. At least in February, a lot of the statistics were flatlined in a general sense. Still, the numbers were high, but at least they were not getting worse.

Solin flipped back and forth between the tabs for January and February. Murders went up by three. The same number of bank robberies. Kidnappings were way down. He attributed this to the scarcity of actual paper money.

A new tab covering 'vigilante' activity was added. The population as a whole was finally tired of the law taking second place to justice. On the surface the judges were doing their jobs and maintaining the rule of law. Lately, there was an appearance of Judges finding excuses for lawlessness to continue. Too many of them were suspected of either being bought off or being threatened and cannot be protected.

Solin signed.

One of the old crimes that was getting new attention. The IRS used an old crime to up the revenue stream. All the seized money found moving south was taxed at the 100% level. There was legal battle on-going with the border states about who really got the money. This was a battle he told everyone he wanted no part of.

Last month, a total of five hundred and seventy-two million dollars was seized. On the first of March, three tractor trailers were seized at different ports of entry with Mexico. The total is still being counted, but two billion dollars was being estimated.

The fight over that much money was something he wanted the popcorn concession for.

Solin set the report aside and picked up the bill covering the United States Police Force. This bill was being called everything, including "Gestapo", "Secret Police", "Savior", "Greatest Thing Since Sliced Bread". Every name was said with equal force.

He looked at his laptop showing C-SPAN. The bill to create a nation-wide United States Police Force was up for a vote this morning.

Solin started to become uneasy with a national police force. He already shot down arm bands because opponents

325

likened it with the Nazi's with their black uniforms and arm bands. He squelched that argument with a ferocity that put a big period on it.

Solin and AG Beck had several meetings over the subject. Both of them silenced aides and department heads when they disagreed over several sections. Both of them started having special private meetings over their concerns. They did agree with the FBI having overall control of the USPD. The IRS was wanting a piece of them, but that was a battle for later.

Solin read numerous books giving neutral historical accounts on the rise and fall of the Gestapo and the SS. Unknown to a lot of people, they were two separate entities. He added several of them to the required reading list for all agents.

Solin sent a memo to the Academy requiring a class being added about the dangers of a united national police force. He wanted something now and a mandatory "must pass" test.

Solin swiveled his chair around thinking about the future. Nothing he ever studied in school, the academy or any course prepared him for the future in front of him. He did remember a lecture from a senior agent during training about the history of the Bureau. It kind of mirrored the Jimmy Stewart move called "the FBI story". What was the reason for the FBI? Why did we have an FBI? Solin asked those same questions today. Since becoming the premier law enforcement officer in the US, he felt that part of his job was not to be heavy handed. He pulled out a needle-point mounted in a frame. His daughter did this for him years ago. There was a fist labeled "the law" being held back by a more muscular hand labeled "the Constitution".

He set the frame on his desk and turned it so that visitors saw it.

Congress, Washington, D.C.
1400 hours EST

The conference bill was finally agreed after the last provision was finally passed. Community and city Police

Departments and individuals cannot be forced to join the US Police Department.

The House passed the bill 245-177. The Senate passed the bill 57-40. The Speaker signed the bill after the appropriate information was placed on the cover page. The Majority Leader of the Senate signed the bill. All this signified that the bill was officially ready for the President to sign it into law.

The clerk of the Congress insured everything was in order, placed the bill in a special briefcase. The Clerk called ahead to the Oval Office, announced he was enroute and left for the White House.

Upon arrival, the Clerk was ushered into the Oval Office. He stood in front of the President and presented it for his signature or veto. That portion of the task completed, the Clerk stepped back so the aides and staff could argue both sides of the bill; again.

The President tuned everyone out and hovered a pen over the bill. So much could go right and so much could go wrong. No matter how much good or bad, the President always had to listen to his Executive Branch.

The President put the bill aside for now. He had ten days to sign it into law or it would become a law anyway.

Quinton Ranch, Hinton, Alberta, Canada
1700 hours MST

Barbara Kincaid Quinton picked up the phone as her sons, Mark and Jeffery were being herded into the barn with the miniature snowmobiles her dad gave them. Both boys nearly jumped out of their skin when they pulled the machines off of the trailer.

Dad was profuse saying they were electric and had a top speed of five miles an hour. Dad conducted a "driving school" that he ran showing them how the machines operated and what to do to make sure they lasted a long time.

Both boys hollered and screamed their delight for two straight days. Dad spent two days looking outside as both boys thoroughly enjoyed their new toys. Both of them played so hard, they barely could stay awake for dinner and their bath.

Her dad smiled and seemed to enjoy the time with her, Tom, Mark and Jefferey. He seemed to also be looking outward at something. She would bring out a cup of coffee and sit beside him and talk about a lot of things.

Finally, after nearly a week, there was a tearful good-bye. The boys openly cried that 'Gampy' was leaving. The boys spent almost all their time playing outside; just being boys.

"Hey Barb," Jason said over the phone line.

"Have you seen Dad lately?" she asked.

"Yeah, he was here a week ago. Why"

Barb took a deep breath. "I think he was saying good bye to all of us."

"Susan and I thought the same thing."

Both Kincaid children concluded that their father said good-bye.

March 4

Pentagon, Washington D.C.
0800 hours EST

General Brenda Amanda Edgars O'Cleary, Vice Chairman of the Joints of Staff, Temporary Director of the Internal Security Agency, Commanding General of the Savage Rabbits and wife to retired Command Sergeant Major Dennis Michael Patrick O'Cleary, was having a bad day.

First thing that went wrong was a phone call from Edwards about a special meeting at the Pentagon; reference to new manning levels now that the United States Police Force was official and looking for warm bodies. One proposal was to transfer between one quarter to one half of the Defense Department's personnel to the USPF.

So, this happened on the day she was going to spend at the ISA dealing with seventeen separate issues. Zachry was briefed over the phone on her decisions and the path to implement them.

The car was turned around and she sped back to the Pentagon. Obviously, the meeting was important because she was intercepted by two Virginia state police cars and given a blue-light escort to the Pentagon.

Upon arrival, she diverted to the first restroom she could find. Arthur was standing on her bladder and she almost lost control.

When she arrived, Edwards launched into one of his attacks. She politely smiled and asked for a break to catch up. Thankfully, Colonel Hawker was on top of the situation, as she always was.

Two hours of mind-numbing facts, assumptions and ridiculous ideas later; the Defense Department had a simple and cohesive stance saying that soldiers are not policemen. All the re-training they would need to transition from killing people and breaking things to law enforcement with surgical use of force was almost not worth the effort. Besides, there was more than ample money in the bill to train a force from scratch.

Three more hours were needed to fine tune next year's budget request. All the years of huge budgets had to be pared down to a more realistic set of numbers. The Research and Development budget required now inordinate amounts of money. Last year's inflation put new drains on the economy and more importantly the supply side of every project.

O'Cleary took a break for a video conference with Zachry about new problems with the southern border. Lieutenant General John Beeker from Southern Command was calling incessantly wanting the Savage Rabbits to shorten the training cycle and get to work.

Beeker went so far as to show up at Desert Zero demanding this and that. He rose up and threatened to relieve Simmons for failure to do as he commanded.

O'Cleary sighed and called General Waller. He sighed back and promised to rein him in. He paused and read a note an aide handed him. "Seems General Beeker relieved Simmons for failure to comply with a verbal and written order. Beeker is trying to install a Lieutenant Colonel of his choosing. I'll fix it in-house, today."

O'Cleary had to deal with this problem constantly. SOCOM was leading the charge. General Traynor went so far as traveling up here to "discuss" the situation. Traynor and his staff brought a briefing officer and tried to line up a decision in his favor for assuming command of the Savage Rabbits. The conclusion of the briefing was a written and formal agreement to transfer command of the Savage Rabbits to SOCOM.

"No sir," was her answer to all seven of the main briefing points.

Fortunately, O'Cleary was constantly interrupted with messages from Desert Zero, the ISA and her duties here at the Pentagon.

"General," Traynor said to O'Cleary. "You seem to be overwhelmed. Giving me the Savage Rabbits will ease your burdens."

Hawker shapely inhaled. She stood up to collect all the documents. Long experience told her what was going to happen next.

O'Cleary leaned to Traynor. "No Sir", she leaned back. "Ladies and Gentlemen give us the room. Elizabeth, tell General Edwards I will be late."

Hawker motioned to the door. There was initial hesitance until Traynor motioned to his staff to leave.

Everyone in the office and out in the hallway waited for whatever was happening to happen.

Almost twenty minutes later, General Edwards came into O'Cleary's office and pointed to the conference room.

"Yes Sir," Hawker said.

Edwards' scowl surfaced and anyone with good sense backed away.

Edwards walked in and closed the door behind him.

Ten minutes later, Traynor left the room. He collected his staff and left the Pentagon. Normally, any visiting senior ranking person went to the many staff sections and shook hands with anyone and everyone who could possibly help them and collect the new names and phone numbers.

Not this time. Traynor had his tail tucked between his legs. This did not go well.

O'Cleary did not have time to gloat or relax. Arthur kept reminding her to listen to her body. She walked quickly to the bathroom.

485 Glenmore Street, Alexandria, Virginia

Fortunately, Zachry at the ISA was so-well trained and was so capable that he handled all the problems without her. She smiled thinking that all the effort in grooming and polishing him to take over for her in the Operations Center was worth the effort.

Dennis was busy straightening out "his" house. Edwards received a phone call from Dennis saying that government movers had arrived to pack up their household and move them to the Naval Observatory.

Edwards spent an inordinate amount of time calming down Dennis. Edwards was more worried that Dennis would shoot someone. Edwards finally calmed down Dennis by promising to send Brenda home early today.

Brenda came home. Arthur seemed to know that he was home. Brenda did sense that Dennis was angry. She walked up to him and hugged him from behind. Dennis seemed to melt.

At least the PSAs knew to back off and leave them alone. One of them signaled to Dennis and went to the garage apartment.

"I cannot reconcile them just coming here and moving our household," he said with a sigh. "It reminds me of my time in the POW camps. They would suddenly pack us up and move us to new locations."

Brenda held onto him and rocked slowly back and forth. His anger was easy to flare and yet hard to cool off. "Arthur says 'hello daddy'."

Dennis deflated and turned around.

Suddenly, Brenda felt a stabbing pain in her abdomen. She tried to stifle a scream. Her ears roared as she sank to the floor. Brenda's consciousness faded in and out as she laid on the floor.

March 5

Minuteman, north of Fort Benton, Montana
0900 hours MST

Colonel Jones looked at his master operations map he used in the last war games. He used a seven-mile by seven-mile-wide area. The "Golden Lance", his rear area denial unit was used to test out the INSANE JANE battle plan. All in all, there were problems, but those were manageable.

He held up the stenographic pad and ran down his list. Pluses and minuses were separated on each side of each page.

His command and staff were coming in to review those pluses and minuses. Jones allocated only three hours for this meeting.

Jones was exacerbated with John Kincaid's sudden disappearance. In true style, no one saw it coming, yet he left a note. Cindy was the one who found it and he believed she didn't see it either. The only one who could read him was Karen.

Jones quit worrying about it. Without Kincaid to sort this mess out, it was up to him. He looked one more time at the steno pad and decided that overall, this team did a great job.

Jones pulled Cindy aside. "I need John Kincaid. Find him and find out why he disappeared."

"Simple," Cindy said. "He is tired, lonely, wounded just this side of dead and his brain hurts with PTSD. Too many things in his past are bubbling up. Village massacres, betrayals, being indispensable, Karen's murder, all of it. If he returns, he will do so if or when he wants to return. You know him as well. He is stubborn, willful and above all stubborn."

Jones deflated. "Find him anyway. His oldest friend would like to say good-bye if he could."

"Yes Sir," Cindy said,

White House, Washington D.C.
1130 hours EST

The President wadded up the newspaper and through it aside. The in-fighting in his cabinet over who owns the sand-box was the talk of the town. Congress was fighting also. There literally was too many things and not enough money. Congress no longer had the unlimited ability to make all the money they wanted and spend it like there was no tomorrow.

The President went to the beverage cart. He really wanted to start on the alcohol early, but decided not to. At 1 pm he will have to referee another joint Cabinet/Congressional conference here at the White House.

There was too much in-fighting. Period. He signed only two bills in the last two months. Funding for the government and action on a myriad of programs was being held up and something needs to be done and done now.

There was no reason to want to be President. Why did he want the job in the first place?

Internal Revenue Service Building, Washington, D.C.
1300 hours EST

The Commissioner, Alan Baker, frowned over a meeting in his office in reference to physical attacks on IRS facilities and personnel.

His Tax Marshalls were little more than court house guards. In seventy-two actions, Tax Marshalls in the field were overwhelmed and in sixteen instances, they surrendered their weapons and badges when mobs with weapons surrounded them and sent them packing.

The FBI refused to classify them as terrorists saying they were communicating with each other. Tax Marshalls and IRS agents were sent away without weapons, badges and now their shoes. The FBI simply pointed to their computers and said "internet".

The Commissioner tuned out the argument around him and thought through his knowledge of history. The only solutions that came to mind were clearly illegal and would only work in a dictatorial country.

The Commissioner suddenly stood and dismissed his staff. He pointed to the door.

The Commissioner had his secretary call the Secretary of the Treasury. He needed to talk to Secretary Carter.

Room D-324, George Washington University Hospital, Washington D.C.
1530 hours EDT

Brenda O'Cleary laid down in the room, secretly enjoying all the pampering she was receiving. The doctors last night poked and prodded her mumbling about things using words probably not in the dictionary.

She would reach down and massage her womb. All these months later, she had a certain pattern that seemed to make Arthur relax. If she did not remember to do it every few hours, Arthur would not relax.

It was nothing more than missing a meal periodically. A woman's body can be taken over when pregnancy hits the middle trimester.

What happened to her was simply that her body was literally wringing food out of her intestines. Her diet was specially calculated to provide everything. The only problem was her body said this was not enough. Fixing the problem was easy enough. Increase her portions.

O'Cleary thought this was funny. She had Dennis and Hawker hovering over her, watching her eat her meals. O'Cleary enjoyed the attention. She reached under the covers and massaged Arthur.

The other fun part of her "visit" to the hospital was that the President and General Edwards ordered everyone to leave her alone to rest.

She had to admit that she was tired. Here in the hospital, she was nominally sleeping for three to four hours, wake up for two or three hours, eat, use the bathroom and sleeping again.

Dennis was staying at the house tomorrow. He did not want anyone showing up in the morning trying again to move their household belongings.

Brenda yawned, went to the bathroom, and came back in time to eat her supper. She was scheduled for a "snack" between midnight and 1 am.

She decided to wait out the week at the hospital. She was going to relax this weekend and make a decision; She was wearing too many hats.

Minuteman, north of Fort Benton, Montana
1630 hours MDT

Captain Bradley Taylor looked through the one-and-a-half-inch thick master supply list, the projected requirements and mobile logistics. All of it needed some work. At least all the camp requirements here at Minuteman were complete.

The last exercise exposed a lot of problems. The Chief showed him a lot of other things that needed to be done.

One problem he took straight to Colonel Jones was the lackadaisical attitude the units had about logistics and the built-in-time lapses. Getting supplies to and from multiple locations was difficult at best. Having to route and re-route around battles, circumvent damaged bridges or destroyed roads.

The hardest obstacle he had to overcome was pilferage. The Push-Packs he went to great trouble in building were designed to be sent to each unit in the field. Those units were not content to devour the contents of their Push-Pack. There were too many instances where they ransacked other Push-Packs. The logistics portion of the battle plan fell apart.

Taylor played the battle scenario. Sub-unit commanders refused to listen to him. There were at least four instances where individuals tried to steal supplies out of the main building directly without even trying to maintain records.

Taylor ignored everyone at the command and staff meeting, addressing only Jones. "Nothing about this exercise was true. I had outright thief of supplies. The Mobile Packs on trailers were taken without regard to where they were needed."

"Sir," Taylor continued ignoring the hostile looks around the room. "Units down the line were short changed supplies due to stupidity thinking that this was just a game. If you will not put a stop to it, please find another Logistics Officer. One more pliable to fit their needs." He made a sweeping motion with both arms.

There was a lot of shifting sounds around the room.

"Stop," Jones said, when several men wanted to speak up. "I'll deal with this without any help."

Thirty minutes later, the meeting was over and Jones looked to Taylor. After the door was closed, Jones went to the refrigerator and pulled out three beers. He opened his beer and signaled for Taylor and Chief George to open theirs.

Jones took a deep breath. "Gentlemen, as an old man, I remember numerous instances where ignoring the nuances of logistics spelled disaster."

George decided to let this young Captain and the Colonel battle it out.

Jones held up his steno pad and showed all his notes from the meeting and those he made during the logistics portion. "Bring in the Logistics Policy Statement on Friday. Make whatever changes you feel necessary. We will discuss it before a formal presentation to the Command and Staff meeting next week."

Taylor took a drink of his beer.

March 6

Headquarters, Northwest Military Region, Fort Carson Colorado.
0900 hours MST

Matheson walked into his main conference room and sat down. He looked to the right and saw the dashboard. Yellow headers signified new data since last view. No new data.

Matheson was very interested in the satellite coverage of the north western corner of the US, especially non-urban areas. All those new photos were compared in a computer in order to check for changes.

The only real changes in south western Montana were some new clusters of buildings, widely spaced apart. A few roads were super-imposed on the satellite picture. All in all, nothing to merit any special attention.

As the briefing moved on to south eastern Montana, UNSTACK THIS, noted the interest and decided not to allow more than a 2% increase in the Minuteman site. The Werewolf area was completely blocked out by taking the real time photographs and masking all the minuteman activity.

UNSTACK THIS sent this information to Valkyrie for her to contemplate.

Matheson opened the file on clandestine activates in Montana and Idaho. Several projects were on-going and heavily redacted from the reports he was reading.

He made a note for his J-2 Intelligence officer to investigate and he moved onward. Chances are there were similar activities in the Dakotas.

Room D-324, George Washington University Hospital, Washington D.C.
1530 hours EDT

Brenda O'Cleary was loving it and did not want to leave. Maybe she was taking up a room from someone else, but when the doctor asked if she could stay for one more day while they took some more tests, she did not protest.

Dennis was literally standing guard with a shotgun at his house. Sure enough, the moving truck and the gang of goons arrived and rang the bell. The rather large foreman said he was moving this household and nothing was going to stop him. As the foreman tried to raise up the paper work, Dennis used the shotgun to punch him in the stomach. The "fat man" dropped the paperwork and backed up one step.

Dennis got their attention by blowing up the paperwork inside Brenda's roses. Next, he blew a hole in the air over everyone's head. All the movers turned around and ran off the property.

Dennis backed up one step and told the foreman to stand up. "OK fat man, let's see how fast you are. Hands up." When the man slowly raised his hands, Dennis blew another hole in the air over his head. When the man was slow again, Dennis lowered the muzzle down to his groin. The big man decided not to try him.

Ten minutes later, the police arrived. The police were used to people being moved quickly, especially high-ranking government types. This was the first time someone actually fought back. The Police Watch Commander warned them to tread lightly.

First thing was removing the shot gun from Dennis. Second, Dennis said this was private property and he was arresting them as a citizen. Dennis wrote out his statement, swore over the seal and that was that. The foreman was hauled away in the back seat of the police car.

Dennis preferred not to charge the others. They were following orders and said rather loudly, "they were too stupid to think for themselves".

Brenda loved her man.

Hawker came over and briefed her about the day's events. She pulled out a deck of cards to play gin rummy as a cover. This time it was worth the effort.

Edwards came in to talk to her. "The President and I talked today about your future behind your back. This," he waved his hand in a sweep of the room, "is a good reason to say that you have too many hats on your head."

"Trainor from SOCOM called and said this was a perfect reason to transfer the Savage Rabbits under his command." Edwards stopped as if she wanted to spit on the ground. "Brenda, I admit to a lot of things I did in the past, but that pimp reminded me of Prescott saying I did not understand what was happening or how things worked. Whether you knew it or not, adding Marines to the mix saved you this time. I transferred them all to be a Special Unit assigned to the J-3 under your command. That kills it for now."

"As to your temporary assignment as Director of the ISA, Admiral Nathan Hazlet is formally submitted to the Senate for confirmation as the Director of the ISA. The President is very concerned that you will lose your baby. His youngest daughter was almost lost because his wife was running too hard herself."

Brenda laid in the bed and turned on her back. She used the controller to raise the back. "I have a lot of respect for Admiral Hazlet. Please extend my complements to him. The next time you see the President, thank him for me. I need to slow down. All the traveling was tiring me out and not allowing me to eat right. Thank him for me."

"No Problem," Edwards said, standing. "I have to see Dennis and congratulate him on outliving the cancer. Amanda has volunteered to monitor us. Plus, the motor mules failed move him. A lot of people are happy he stopped them. Two other families have stopped them."

Edwards kissed her on top of the head and left behind a bag full of goodies: non-food pastries and cookies.

March 7

Underground Station "Conscience", World Wide Web and Channel 513
0900 hours EST.

"If you threaten, act. If you say something, do it. If something is important, stand your ground. Governments are often hamstrung by individuals who have opinions about issues they feel strongly about. This is Martin Socranson, self-proclaimed philosopher who says, 'What are we if we can't back up what you say'?"

"Greetings America" Martin Socranson said beginning his broadcast. "It is reluctantly Saturday and I say thus." In the background the sounds of the 1812 overture played.

"A familiar theme of late is the lack of law enforcement. The story I am about to relate is not a single issue or unique for that matter. In the bowels of the FBI's monthly crime report is more than just statistics, examples and summaries of reports from all the states."

Senior Citizens Marcus and Sylvia Ryne, who live just north of the city of Travis, Missouri was discovered beaten to death in their home. Their home was ransacked and nearly destroyed as their 'alleged' assailants looked for anything of value to steal."

"The bodies were discovered the next morning by a neighbor who was driving to work. The neighbor noticed the front door was open, which was unusual for them. The neighbor walked up to the door and recoiled at the odor. Inside he saw the couple and all the blood."

"Fast forward through a bungled investigation and an even more bungled trial. The four men walked out of the court house, laughing and enjoying their freedom."

"Three days later, all four men were found hanging by the neck in a tree in the forest. The police started an investigation, but so far, no clues about who done it."

"The same type of investigation failed to find who hanged those men. They were released because of a procedural error with the prosecution's case. They were released to repeat their crime because the new Miranda card detailing the accused rights had not arrived."

"A simple tardy postal mistake gave a judge the afternoon off and gave four murderers their freedom. That same tardy postal mistake made those four men victims of vigilante justice."

"It seems that only when judges and lawyers become victims or their families become victims will justice enter the courtroom."

"Vigilante justice is no justice, America. But I have to say that too many people are scared and scared people do crazy things."

"However, in most instances, Justice is leaned too far in the accused' direction. A lot of judges are too scared of being called a racist or a scaredy cat. If a judge follows the rule book too closely, he is federalist or a racist."

"Nowadays they call the theatrics "case law". Judges can call something "admissible" and the new thing is law."

"Welcome to the law of jungle, America. I have said it before and it will be said again. The law wins when you have enough money to pay for it."

Room D-324, George Washington University Hospital, Washington D.C.
1130 hours EST

Brenda O'Cleary inhaled deeply on this Saturday morning. Arthur told her all was right and just kicked her once in a while. Brenda dressed in a pants suit. She wanted to leave and get home.

Dennis finished packing her up and hefted her bag. "Ready," he said.

She looked around and decided that nothing was left behind. "Yes," she said. She picked up the small bag that held her two books and medications.

The two PSAs fell in behind the O'Cleary's trying to stay close enough to protect them, yet give them some privacy.

During the trip home, Brenda leaned over to Dennis, wrapped her arms around his arm and closed her eyes.

She thought of Delores Pollard. She was so young and having a baby during the prime of her life. Brenda was that young once, yet she had a career and there was nothing like succeeding. Yet, now she was finally carrying a baby toward the other end of her life.

The rumor mill of the Pentagon said that Delores was now one of the untouchables and for once, it was a good thing. Delores' baby will be two months old when Arthur is borne. To be a young woman when having a baby.

When the PSAs pulled into the driveway, Brenda opened her eyes and smiled. Her home that she shared with Dennis. Her home that she shared with Arthur.

She wanted to rest today and tomorrow. Monday, there were some changes that needed to be made.

Bonnie Chandler, Box 234, Route 17, Belcher, Missouri
1700 hours CST

Dear Bonnie,

It's crazy around here. The graduation ceremony was being moved to the Baptist Church down the road. I am going to be a sophomore. All the fun things I heard about growing past junior high and finally getting into High School were destroyed.

This year was the last one where the basketball team won the championship on the home court. Getting away with "things" was too hard with all the soldiers wondering around. All the old places to hide were now being exposed.

Mom told me not to look at or socialize with the soldiers. Mom would not elaborate on everything. She just hovered over me when they went to town. The soldiers loved to yell catcalls and say things I could not understand. More and more, Mom started to be scared.

Suddenly, last week, Sherry Vickers was found in a storage room. She had her clothes ripped off, she was tied up and beaten, and chances are she was raped. Her father came to the school and he blew his stack. The soldiers tried unsuccessfully to calm him down. Finally, Mister Vickers pushed an officer soldier up to the wall and was yelling incoherently. The soldiers then arrested Mister Vickers and carried him off.

Mom made sure that night all the self-defense lessons I was taught took hold. Yes, they did. Months ago, before the soldiers, her Dad taught her the lessons and told her to practice in secret; every day. A friend had been attacked and left for dead. Her face was so disfigured.

A whole lot of "police types" descended on the town trying to "find out what happened". The rumor said they did not really want to know what happened. We knew they didn't want to find the rapist because the used all kinds of new words.

March 8

Afghanistan/Pakistan Border
0500 hours (Delta)

Two things happened today. First the United States implemented Daylight Savings Time.

Second was that Afghanistan Forces finally starting withdrawing from Pakistan. KH-17 surveillance satellites have watched all the service and support units moving west leaving the combat units to cover their withdrawal.

Governments around the globe took a sigh of relief. Pakistan was straining at the seams trying to man units along the Indian border and now units along the Afghanistan border.

The Indian government had stood down units along the Pakistani border in an effort to calm the situation and assist the Pakistani's.

With a new common enemy, both Governments were now in talks to normalize relations and end decades of tensions. Though the UN wanted to praise this new ending of tensions, they still wanted to interject any reason to interfere.

Two nuclear powers were now talking about a treaty. There were more important things going on in the world than fueling decades-old rivalries left over from the British occupation.

March 9

US Federal Court House, Washington D.C.
0900 hours EDT

US Attorney Jeremy Devers walked into the Clerk's office and filed four lawsuits. All four covered states refusing to follow US law and the DOJ's interpretation of the Constitution. Devers was tired of fighting worthless battles with American citizens who just wanted to live as free as they did for the last two and half centuries.

Devers looked at the major lawsuit. Texas, New Mexico, Arizona and Oklahoma were interconnecting so much that they were becoming one state. Though there was nothing in the law, both common and procedural, to cover this; something needed to be done before this became grounds for secession.

The biggest problem was that after the Civil War, nothing was done legally to cover any of the problems. Secession from a nation or region or state was never codified. Texas still had provisions in its state's constitution for secession, but that was the exception.

The DOJ was, in fact, fast tracking cases to establish the legalities and by-pass years of congressional arguments.

Devers was standing next to four lawyers filling suit against the DOJ for trying to do what he was filing his suites against.

Devers sighed.

Desert Zero, Fort Hood, Texas
1630 hours CDT

Simmons read the weekly report he drafted for O'Cleary to update her on the training status for the Savage Rabbits. Simmons looked at the Ops Center master training status board on the wall. He looked over the notes in the report and the notations on the wall.

Simmons sat back and thought about this. Brigadier General David Gender from Delta Force kept showing up, wanting to interfere and was upset his ideas and suggestions were not implemented. He had an all too accurate picture of the present training plan direction and where it will be in the future. He had a spy and chances are that person was an officer.

Simmons called O'Cleary today when Gender showed up and "assumed" command of the Savage Rabbits. Simmons was relegated to being the Deputy Commander. He even had orders from the Army G-3 operations at the Pentagon.

O'Cleary called General James Waller at Southern Command at Fort Hood. She told him of the problem at Desert Zero and she was tired of it. Gender had to be corralled, once and for all.

Waller showed up at Desert Zero with a platoon of Military Police and over-powered the meager security force at the main gate. The MPs were dressed in full battle gear and quickly subdued everyone in the compound. None of the military policemen were nice and used a lot of force to ensure their orders were complied with. Just to ensure they were in charge; General Waller supervised their arrest and gave all of the Military Policemen a "good job" as he walked over the scene.

Waller located Simmons and freed all his people. Under heavy guard, Gender was arrested, handcuffed and taken into the Operations Center. He was formally notified, in front of everyone, that he exceeded his authority and falsified the documents he used to "take over the Savage Rabbits and the Compound".

One of the secret portions of the Delta Force chapter was blanket orders to take over any organization as the specific situation called for. The big "BUT" was that notifying the Pentagon and the regional commander was required.

Gender was formally notified that the Savage Rabbits were a classified operation held at the J-3 of the Joint Chiefs of Staff with a short chain of command going through General O'Cleary, General Edwards, the Secretary of Defense and finally the President.

Waller had a man video tape him giving Gender a formal order to stay away. Waller signed the order and handed a copy to Gender.

"Just so you don't pull this stunt again, Admiral Cartwright is repeating this order with General Traynor.

344

Granted no one is going to threaten you with stalling your promotion to Major General, your job cannot exactly match anything that allows you a promotion path upward. General, your Delta Force is the premier force of operators in the US Military, period." Waller paused to take a deep breath and closed the distance between them. "If I have to waste another minute with you again, I will see to it your next arrest will be the most humiliating experience of your life. You are dismissed."

It took about twenty minutes to load up the Delta Force for transport. All of them objected to being photographed and fingerprinted. Those that refused to surrender their military identification were arrested for trespassing and falsely wearing a military uniform. Waller was too inconvenienced to care.

Gender left soon afterward. Waller gave Simmons a business card. "Call if you have any other problems."

Simmons wasted a full day on this nonsense. Today was supposed to be the beginnings of squad and fire team operations. It was funny thinking that Gender thought giving the men Sundays off was stupid.

Simmons wanted to remember times like these if and when he ever became a General.

For now, Simmons had to figure out how to make-up the missed time. He was not of the mind-set to take it out on men, but something had to be done. He would sleep on it.

"Sir," Waverly said at the door way. "I think you need to see this." Waverly pointed out the doorway. Simmons handed off the report to the personnel chief to be forwarded to General O'Cleary.

Outside, Simmons watched the men walking through the fire team/squad drills. All of them were working through the drills, catching the mistakes and repeating the drills over and over.

Waverly said. "They're going through the drills on their own. The NCOs are playing like they are dead and demoted to junior private."

Simmons noticed Kendal out there going through with the men. He remembered reading Kendal's file very carefully. There was a lot of redacted portions, but the portions covering her service here showed that she was equally competent as a staff NCO and an operator. Her restricted portion showed the award of two Bronze Stars and a pending of Silver Star. She was very fit and was very capable as a Non-Commissioned-Officer.

Waverly knew her directly. When both of them spared in the pit, it was enough for everyone to watch. Waverly was a head taller and sixty or seventy pounds heavier. The only way for Waverly to win was to smother her in the pit. Kendal's methodology was her speed and strength. She had good instincts and training. A couple of times, both of them ended up on their knees, bloody, exhausted and filthy.

Simmons wished he had more of the old players here. Too much was reliant on wishful thinking. Simmons was going to have to wait for them to get bloody on missions with a very deadly enemy before he could quit worrying. He prayed he trained them well enough.

March 10

J. Edgar Hoover Building, Washington D.C.
1000 hours EDT

FBI Director Solin picked up the "bad news" report and opened it. He ignored the numbers of crimes as outlined in the tabs. Forty-three sections cataloged all crimes and provided the numbers in abundance. Only a mathematician could keep up with it.

A new section was the United States Police Force. Solin was reminded of the Star Wars movie about the Jedi Knights being the generals and the clones being the faceless drones who died in vast numbers. Right or wrong was not ever discussed. Everyone fought the enemies they were told to fight.

Solin thought about the emperor who pulled the strings on both sides.

Solin sat still for a few minutes and wondered about that. Too many things were happening. All those rumors he heard for all those years said someone pulled those strings.

Solin needed some how to answer that question.

346

Federal District Court, Washington, D.C.
1300 hours EDT

District Court Judge Johnathon McMasters listened all morning as forty-nine law suits filed by separate states were pulled together and the Judge agreed to hear them in this way.

The States were trying to over-whelm the Federal government over Federal powers that were usurped away from the states in direct disobedience of the Tenth Amendment of the Constitution.

Texas, Oklahoma, New Mexico, Arizona, Colorado, Montana, Idaho, Louisiana, Mississippi, Arkansas, Kansas and Missouri filed against the Federal government stating that the Tenth Amendment of the Constitution states that all powers not specifically given to the Federal Government in the Constitution were reserved for the States. The Federal Government was alleged to be trying to run the states without funding or responsibility.

Texas, New Mexico and Arizona are filing for salvage-rights of the left-over and unused materials from the border wall. The Federal Government was currently paying five million dollars a day for storage of the materials. The states want to take the materials abandoned on state land to build a wall on state land to combat people breaking the law on state land.

District Court Judge Johnathon McMasters wished all this went away. Privately he thought that the merits said the states were right. None of what of the Federal government was doing was legal or constitutional. Then again………

March 11

Border Patrol Headquarters Phoenix, Arizona
1000 hours MST

Chief Patrol Agent Thomas Barrios of the Border Patrol read the monthly report for February. The numbers were still going down. The agents were seeing a lot of the immigrants were moving back down south.

Barrios did not bother checking last month's report. The only silver lining in the bad economy was the effect on Latin America's perception on getting to America for the rivers of gold and honey.

The reality was rivers of hard work, little money and vile-tasting loneliness.

White House, Washington D.C
1300 hours EDT

The President picked up the bill creating the United States Police Force. Initially, they would number over one hundred thousand. Mostly those numbers came from the towns and cities where there were police departments. The only change was a new badge given to the officer after an oath was sworn. Each sworn officer was to be paid a stipend, to be determined later.

There was a provision for any officer that would not take the oath. That officer's payroll was paid by the municipality he or she came from. This bill would not allow any punitive action to be taken against an officer who did not take the oath.

The President thought about later. Was he creating a Nazi-style SS or an extension of the FBI? Those same arguments were made when Theodore Roosevelt signed the Bureau of Investigation into law over a hundred years ago.

One thing the President lobbied hard for was that a formal nomination process was to be required before the full Senate.

This United States Police Force needed a foot kept on its neck.

The President signed the bill. He took the pen, broke it and threw it into the trash. The bill was placed in the out-box. The President went to the cafeteria and asked for a ham and cheese omelet.

March 12

1100 South Congress Avenue, Austin, Texas
0900 Hours CDT

A formal signing of a bill was occurring today in Austin, Phoenix, Santa Fa and Oklahoma City by the respective Governors. The signing was symbolic in Austin and Santa Fe. The bills were previously passed and within constitutional limitations, the governors had already signed them.

As of today, any illegal immigrants will be sent south to the border and left with three meals and one gallon of water for each person.

A US attorney was on hand in each capital to formally serve those governors with injunctions to keep them from enforcing those laws. The Texas Governor, in full view of the press, smiled at the lawyer, pulled over his suit jacket and blew his nose into the breast pocket.

The Texas Attorney General was already in Federal Court looking to overturn the injunction.

That night, the US Attorney was awakened at 10 pm at his hotel room. His room and that of his two staffers were given five illegals to house overnight in response to one part of the injunction to "find any place to house them" or words to that effect.

March 13

Headquarters, Southeast Military Region, Naval Air Station Jacksonville, Florida
1700 hours EDT

This was where Admiral Matthew Cartwright's decided to place his headquarters so he could act as the military governor of the southeastern United States.

Lieutenant Colonel Latham Thomas was always leery of a Joint Headquarters. Conflicting regulations, cross-services and the politics was mind numbingly stupid.

Thomas arrived a week ago and looked around for someplace to live. His son Michael was graduating from high school this year. His wife Ellen was currently cemented in her job as her firm's legal counsel for the Forrestal Group in Austin.

Thomas loved his wife and he was pretty sure she loved him. She was a lawyer and he hated the very idea of anything lawyer. They made him gag. But he loved her and he will always love her. No one understands. He doesn't care. Lathan loves Ellen was carved in a tree in the front yard for all to see.

Legal officers in military units were a bad idea. They were made to think that they were omniscient and omnipotent. Thomas relieved his last legal officer for cowardice under fire during a border incident. That incoherent slob was screaming as a Cartel unit tried to force their way past them near El Paso. Finally, he turned and ran as the Cartel rallied and surged into his unit.

That weekend his unit rotated off the line and had a four-day weekend standdown. That lawyer tied up one and a half of those days trying to get the Staff Judge Advocate to make Thomas see the situation differently. Thomas ignored all the arguments from the tongue-wagglers. He signed the charge sheet despite all the "advice" and "counseling" he received. Thomas handed the charge sheet to the SJA. The SJA looked at Thomas and back to the officer whose career was now destroyed.

When he could finally break away, he only had a twenty-four-window left. Ellen was the only thing in his life that he loved totally. She loved him only because he worshiped her. She was rich in her own right and did not need him. With all the separations they endured, both of them enjoyed their time together like newlyweds.

Thomas found an apartment off post in a complex just off post. The hotel stood on the main road leaving the base to Jacksonville. Behind the hotel was a sprawling set of apartments. Thomas decided to live off-base this time.

Ellen was staying in Austin at least until Michael graduated. Michael was too smart to have a father like him. That boy will end up being greater than anything he will ever do.

With this task over, all he had to do was unpack, relax and wait for Monday. A soft knock on the door broke his concentration. He opened the door and saw a beautiful woman smiling at him.

"Hey soldier, want some company," she said picking up a suitcase.

"Sure thing, young lady," Thomas said, opening the door wider. "I have to tell you I'm married."

The smiling lady set the suitcase inside the door and closed it. "I am too," she said taking off her coat. "He's a soldier too."

"My wife is a blood-thirsty lawyer who will own your life if she catches us."

"My husband is vicious killer with seven tours in Afghanistan and Iraq. If he catches us, he will destroy us both; period. I'm a lawyer," Ellen Thomas said while unbuttoning his shirt. She smiled at him with a hint that she was weakening him. "I need a disposition. Where is the bedroom?" She was pushing him backward as she unbuttoned his pants.

"No furniture yet," Latham said.

Ellen said. "I need a shower. You can inflate the bed while I clean up. Otherwise, you are my mattress." She opened her blouse and let him see the blue brassiere.

Latham actually debated and relented. He pulled out the pump and furiously pumped the bed until it was finally inflated. Ellen walked out in all her glory and his heart jumped a beat.

"Hey little girl, you want some candy?"

March 14

Santa Fe Detention Center, Santa Fe, New Mexico
1520 hours MDT

New Mexico had originally ordered the First Battalion of the 200th Infantry Regiment to guard this consolidated Detention Center. The New Mexico State Defense Force was now in the process of assuming control of the Center.

The double row of ten-foot-high chain link fence was topped with razor wire. There was twenty feet between the walls.

The National Guardsmen were tired of this duty. They were standing down for two weeks in preparation for a new joint duty with Texas, moving illegal immigrants back south of the border.

The population started talking a lot and getting louder obviously thinking something was wrong.

Private First-Class Daniel Jeffers picked up the phone in one of the watch towers to report the situation to the Lieutenant. Simultaneously, he raised the binoculars to observe a crowd building on the center west fence.

No sooner had Lieutenant Carstairs answered the phone, when a loud chorus arose as the crowd surged on the ten-foot-tall chain link fence topped with razor wire. Hundreds of people pushed and the fence bent over to a forty-five-degree angle and stopped. People ran over haphazardly over the fence.

Many of the people were trampled and nearly crushed. They were used as mats to cover the razor wire so they could run over the fence. The children suffered the worst. Parents and other adults stepped over them, sometimes using them as mats, so they could defeat the razor wire. Dozens of children were trapped, tangled in the wire. If they had parents, those people deserted their children.

Once over the inner fence, there were not enough people or space to push over the outer fence. They had to climb over and slice themselves up going over.

The stupid escape attempt could not have been timed at a worse time. The change-over meant that there were twice as many guards as normal.

The Soldiers and Militiamen ran into the razor wire and cut it away, frantically trying to free the children.

It took almost two hours to free the children and restore order. The children were taken to the guard's quarters so that that the children could be cleaned up, guarded and a given quiet place to relax and recover.

Two bull dozers were brought over and pushed the fence upright. Only seventeen of the adults could not be located.

The New Mexico Militia was made up of former military and civilian professionals with deep pockets and sizzling hot tempers.

Within two hours, they passed the hat and created wanted posters with the pictures of those who escaped. Above them all was a one-hundred-and-twenty-thousand-dollar reward.

Civil libertarians and left leaning groups made the usual sounds and threatened legal action. Colonel Jasper Folcroft of the Texas 56th National Guard Brigade took the media on a tour of the Guard's barracks. The bandaged children told the story better than any adult's rhetoric.

March 15

Timber Lakes Gated Community, Raleigh, North Carolina
0100 hours EST

This was one of many gated and sequestered communities the Internal Revenue Service took by Imminent Domain or tax seizure. One hundred and eighty-six homes were contained in a bubble the auditors and office drones enjoyed.

This community enjoyed having a local grocery store, gas station, elementary, middle and high school, pool and putt-putt golf course. This community was originally going to be set up as a place for the upper economic tier to hide. However, the contractor ran out of money nearly at the end and the expected number of sales did not happen.

The Director of the IRS swooped in and forgive the delinquent taxes. Imminent Domain ended it. The Raleigh office ran down the employee list.

The winter and spring were relatively dry this year. A lot of dead-fall was piling up on the periphery of the community.

At fifteen locations one half a mile north of the community, men picked up their gun burners and forty-pound propane tanks. The men walked along a pre-planned route and set fire to large chucks of the woods. A southerly wind picked up the fire. The fourteen mile and hour wind built and surged the fire toward the community. The half-mile distance allowed it to build in intensity, yet give the people time to run for their lives. Within the community there was a lot of foliage and trees around the homes. Landscaping.

Some stupid tree huggers had some kind of stupid idea and dug out along trench to be used as a fire break. However, the trench was never cleaned out. If anything, a lot of material was pushed into the trench. When the fire reached the trench, it hungrily fed and created a wall of fire intense enough to ignite the trees.

The winds pushed the fires and cinders along. The cinders hit the first homes in the line and they ignited.

Someone had gone into the fresh water pump house and turned them off electrically by removing the circuit breakers from the distribution panels.

When the sun rose in the morning, the community was nothing but a blackened field resembling something from a World War Two bombing raid.

Only fourteen homes remained.

March 16

Desert Zero, Fort Hood, Texas
1630 hours CDT

Simmons put the finishing touches on the weekly report General O'Cleary wanted. She always had a response on Saturday morning.

The first response he received, two weeks ago, was biting and to the point. His report covered six pages and her response was eighteen pages. She was methodical and instructed him how to get the information she wanted.

Simmons showed Kendal the response and she said that sounds like her. "Sir, I sat thorough several meetings with her. The sheer volume of knowledge she has stored in her head is incredible. I never saw her read notes during the meetings or briefings. Above all, do not take her rebuff as personal. To her it is a teaching point. She wants you to learn and be able to function without her."

"Thank you, Chief," he said walking away.

Simmons looked at this week's report. He kept a template for the items she wanted. Once he filled in the data and studied it, the report became simple. Like an afterthought.

March 17

Camp Mabry, Texas
1730 hours CST

Colonel Jasper Folcroft, Commander of the 56th Infantry Brigade Combat Team walked into his office and through his equipment down. He was weary of it all. Half of his problems were officers who were more interested in the titles and commissions than the job they held. The military duties they tried to complete seemed to be not as important as the better paying positions they came from in civilian life.

Folcroft looked at his clogged in-box. Folcroft had a meeting with the General tomorrow. He needed to change his officers around.

He walked out and put the "may I please, please, pretty please" letters on his S-1 personnel officer's desk. "Dick," he said. "I am going to see the General tomorrow. Attach a resignation on top of each request to be released from duty early and return them to the officers. Have a good night. See you in the morning."

March 18

White House Washington, D.C.
1400 hours EDT

The President opened another in a long set of reports. He noticed something during a long series of news programs and asked the Census Bureau and Department of Transportation to provide an answer.

The over-reaching answer was that the country was segregating itself more out of security and companionship.

Generally, those who were liberal, tended to want to stay in the east or on the west coast.

Those that were conservative tended to want to live in the west away from the Pacific.

Conservatives were being pushed out of the east and the liberals were being forced out of west. Already, California was tiring of people who refused to work, yet beg and cry for freebies. California's socialist were running out of other people's money.

Pollsters asked the people everywhere why they lived where they did. In the east, the mindset was people who needed to be around others and, even though they paid higher taxes, they wanted social services to take care of them. These people also thought that others had to be in charge.

West of the Mississippi River, near rebellion was the order of the day. Federal courts are being ignored. If any of them congregate or ally, it is against Federal Authority. Those agencies making decisions from inside the Washington beltway are being universally ignored around the country. In northern Nevada and California, pumping stations for the Colorado river water were started up, ignoring the so-called searches for bugs or small fish that can't be found.

The President looked through the report and laughed at some of the reasons the researchers came up with. He closed the report and fanned the pages. He fanned it again and stopped at a random page. This page was an accounting of the number of women still capable of carrying a baby to term.

The President fanned the report again and stopped at an intriguing point. The available number of blue-collar jobs versus white-collar jobs. The east had the preponderance of white-collar jobs and the west had the higher number of blue-collar jobs. During the middle of the Civil War, northern agriculture was greater than the south.

The President flipped through to the food section and all he found was that the farms were looking for workers. Plenty of high-paying jobs, but few takers. A foot note said the farm jobs were labor intensive and the younger people were not interested in working. Just collecting.

He sighed and made a note for a full accounting of farms and outputs.

The reports here were enough to drown a man.

March 19

Speaker Parker resigned as Speaker of House. He had too many headaches. Yesterday his had a sudden pain grab his chest and stop his breathing. His wife, Karla got to the hospital and ejected everyone from his room. All the sharks smelled blood and wanted a bite.

Karla Parker pulled out her magic baton and used the patented "Karla Special." Nathan Parker's mood soared as Karla chased everyone out. Karla's baton was a disguised cattle prod. Each screech meant someone got ten thousand volts. It would never knock someone out, but it got someone's attention.

Once the room was clear, Karla looked at him.

"I'm resigning as Speaker, and I am retiring from Congress," he said.

Karla locked the door and came over to sit on the bed. She reached under the covers and found something both of them liked. "If you ever push yourself this hard again, you can kiss this goodbye." She squeezed hard and made him wince.

March 20

Station H-42, North of Fort Greeley, Alaska
1100 hours AKDT

Kincaid woke this morning and walked through the complex looking over the daily maintenance tasks. Preventive Maintenance was important especially in a climate like this. Heating was very important as well as electrical power. He checked the current, voltage and wattage meters on the main grid power. Next was the bi-weekly start-up and checkup of the generator. Next was the heating units and finally all the more minor elements.

All told, his daily maintenance chores consumed seventeen minutes of his day. He had to give it to the Air

Force. They could design a facility that was solidly built and easy to maintain.

Kincaid looked at the mass of documents on the table and wondered why he even bothered to bring them along. Any and all motivation to work on any of his training plans was gone. Minuteman, Werewolf, Savage Rabbits, NCO Academy and the INSANE JANE.

Kincaid sat down with his cup of coffee and brooded. Just like Achilles in his tent, Kincaid just found something to sulk about. Kincaid suffered with life-long depression and narcissism.

Kincaid went upstairs and looked out at the white-cold beauty of Alaska. Some heathen in a SUV drove up and went to the rear of the vehicle. The hatch opened and the driver was wrestling out something. The door closed and the driver reached down for two bags.

Cindy Morgan came from around the rear of the vehicle. She smiled and walked up to him. Kincaid froze for a few seconds. He turned in time to step ahead of her. He was in the process of closing the door and locking her out.

Cindy pushed past him into the mud room. She pulled her boots off and smiled. "How are you doing?" she asked.

Kincaid did not say anything. His mind ran through all times he met up with her. Most of them was hard times, especially when she thought he was taking Zach away.

"Why did you come here?" he asked.

"You and I need to come to an understanding," she replied, walking down and away from the entrance.

Kincaid closed and locked the door

Kincaid poured her a cup of coffee. When he turned around, she was gone. He heard a dragging sound and that meant she was going to a room and claiming her property.

So far, neither of them showed themselves in the nude. So, Kincaid took his clothes off and finished with her coffee. He turned to serve and watched her remove her bra and panties.

She said, "thank you," and doctored it to her likes.

Kincaid turned his chair to her and sat down, spreading his legs.

Cindy turned her chair out and spread her legs.

He scratched himself and lingered looking at her.

358

She scratched herself and lingered looking at him.

Ten or fifteen obscene gestures later, both decided that nothing was going to phase each other.

"Want to go fifteen rounds of oral sex to see who cries uncle first?" Cindy asked.

Kincaid shifted in his chair. "I'm tempted."

"Good," Cindy said rising out of the chair. She grabbed his hand. Kincaid stayed in his chair as Cindy tugged on him.

Cindy sat down in John's lap, straddling and pinning him in the chair. "Zach is dead and I will mourn him with fire and intensity for the rest of my life. Karen was more perfect than I can ever be. Your fire and your love for her are more intense than mine. We love Zach and Karen and nothing will change that. It is time to remember them in special places and move on with our lives."

"How," John said with sarcasm.

"Listen shithead, there is no way to explain it. You and I together will never diminish them in any way." Beneath her, he was stirring. She pointed downward. After a few seconds, she reached down, took him and inserted him into her. She leaned down and kissed him. She started moving and sex was created.

1700 hours AKDT

This time of year, the sun was in equinox. Half the day was sunshine and the other half was in darkness. The weather is still chilly and a lot of snow was still around, but this was Alaska.

Kincaid woke up. Where did all this energy come from. It was nearly six months since he was all shot up and now, he was having some kind of pain-sex. All that scar tissue pulled on him as he gyrated over, under and with Cindy. She really insisted on being on top which was normally OK with him but now it was painful.

John eased up and went to the bathroom. He cleaned up, including a shower and left to get dressed. He somewhat hated to do it, but he woke up Cindy and said he was cooking dinner. She rose up with a bedhead he had to chuckle at.

He shuffled down to the kitchen and ignored the satellite phone Cindy brought with her. She left it here to recharge, yet be out of the way.

Kincaid put the hamburger and white gravy mix on the table for Cindy.

"I missed this," she said taking a spoonful and blowing on it. "I tried copying everything you did and it was not exactly right."

Kincaid smiled like he always did when thinking about his grandma. "My grandma says it is the hand that makes all the difference and she was right."

They made small talk for an hour until something under the surface had to come up.

"John, we need you and the priority for you is either Desert Zero or Minuteman." Cindy took a sip of coffee. She reached over to take his hand. "I will be honest. I had wanted you for a long time, but I could not bring myself to ask."

"Cindy," he said. "I am yours for the rest of my life. Which means if we are at Minuteman and General Matheson attacks, you will have to evacuate with the other dependents. Only one family member can deploy and fight; remember. Sheridan is a great Sergeant Major and he will always be the right fit for here. I am sorry, but that point is non-negotiable. That is why Wendy is down at Desert Zero and Earl is up here. I did engineer a few trips for them to be together."

"Okay," she said, then taking a sip of coffee. "You need to engineer a few trips for me. PS, we ensure the doors are locked. Clothing is not optional. As in no clothing. I had to start wearing clothing to bed since joining this community and it is uncomfortable. Since we will be here for two weeks, I need some sleep."

"Two weeks?" Kincaid said. "By the way, your phone sex called." He pointed to the phone.

Cindy picked up the phone. The message said call 78693. Cindy did not know who 78693 was, so she went through the procedure.

A familiar voice said, "Extension 78693."

Cindy said, "this is extension 99843, identify Glasco."

Kincaid groaned and sat down.

Cindy listened to response. "Secure," she punched a button on the control face. "This is Gunnery Sergeant Morgan, ma'am." Cindy listened to the phone for a few seconds and then held out the phone to him.

Kincaid groaned again. He took the phone and his inner asshole came out. "This is shit for brains. I forgot it all."

"Greetings to you too, John," Brenda O'Cleary said. "That goody-bye note was typical you. I will not bore you with a speech you won't listen to or plead for you to forgo retirement or medical leave. I need you. Will you come back?"

John turned his back to Cindy and pondered. "Where?" he asked.

"Desert Zero," O'Cleary said.

"Does Colonel Simmons know I cannot deploy?"

"Yes," she said.

"I'll be there Wednesday," he said and terminated the call.

"John," Cindy said.

"I apologize that they used you." John poured another cup of coffee. "I'm leaving tomorrow." He sat down and his depression slammed down on his head with force. Tears ran down his face. "I am tired and want to be left alone. Why does the world hate me so much? Why am I the one who has to save the world." Kincaid turned in his chair and stared at the wall.

"John I was told to find you. I had already told you that. The satellite phone was left here so this would not happen."

Kincaid just sat there in an almost comatose trance.

Cindy turned around hiding the tears on her face. She went to her room and feel sleep after a while.

March 23

0700 hours AKDT

Kincaid put his last bundle near the door and cooked breakfast. When Cindy did not come, he walked down to her room and opened her door. He pounded on the door, looking at her. "Breakfast is on the table," he announced.

Cindy raised up in bed and caught John's back as he turned away. She got up, put on some clothes and followed the aromas of breakfast.

Kincaid was a lot of things, but he knew how to do breakfast. Her plate was waiting for her on the table.

Breakfast was a silent affair. Afterward, John cleaned all the dishes and the kitchen. He poured two more cups of coffee and sat down. Cindy sat there and both had a stare down contest.

John broke the silence. "I don't accuse you of anything. I acknowledge that we had sex and it had nothing to do with your orders to find me." He held up his hand to silence her reaction. "I am ashamed for feeling something. I hadn't felt like that since Karen died. When I am through mourning, maybe I will not think so low of me."

Cindy straightened in her chair. "I refuse to believe Zach would ever demean me for moving on. I only met Karen once and she was a good woman. I am not going to let Zach see me mope through life. Maybe you were a bad choice, but I am not ashamed."

John looked at her with something genuine. "I thank you for giving me a moment where I felt happy and I felt human. No one has done that since Karen died."

John stood and looked down at her. "Make sure you clean up any mess you make." He leaned over and kissed her on the forehead. "I am sorry," he said.

He picked up his bags and left.

After the door closed, Cindy said, "Dickhead, Asshole, Shithead. Lover of Karen." She finished her coffee, re-cleaned the kitchen, packed and left.

Cindy did smile as she looked in and closed the door on a memory.

10th Circuit Court of Appeals, Denver Colorado
1000 Hours MDT

Justice Bryan Poston brought his court to order and listened to another case of government ostriches and idiots

362

making sausages. The Attorney General of Colorado was suing the Attorney General of the US for the actions of his officers.

Members of the US Marshals were forced by the Assistant US Attorney (AUSA) to raid a home in a Denver suburb. The AUSA allegedly had the search warrant in his hand. He accompanied the Marshals for some reason.

The Marshals were told to raid a house where a most-wanted-criminal was supposedly being held. The Chief Deputy said he wanted to simply surround the house and knock on the door.

The Marshals battered down the door and rushed into the house. The only two people in the house was an 82-year-old husband and his 83-year-old wife. The man suffered a fatal heart attack in the process.

The address they invaded was the wrong one.

The judge privately hoped the AUSA and those stupid Marshals get the book slammed in their face.

Desert Zero, Fort Hood, Texas
1630 hours CDT

Simmons put the finishing touches to his weekly report to O'Cleary. General Waller came by today on an unannounced visit. He said he never liked 'dog and pony' shows and so he showed up unannounced.

The gate guards did their jobs and halted the line of cars. They checked the identities of every person in the convoy including the vehicles. They were respectful of everyone; but they were vigilant and careful. It was obvious they were trained and experienced. None of them seemed scared or distracted at all the rank and egos that showed up.

"Fine job those guards showed, Colonel," Waller said.

"Thank you, Sir," Simmons said, reporting to Waller. "Those terrorists that showed up last year just bluffed their way onto the base and killed twenty-seven men and women. That will not happen under my watch."

Waller pulled on his ear. "Yes, I got a visit and several phone calls from Generals Gender and Traynor. SOCOM is really in need of fresh meat. They wanted to back door some operations through me, but I owe General O'Cleary a few favors. By the way, I told her about that so you don't have to. General versus General is something you should stay away from for as long as you can."

Simmons and Waller walked up to the center and waited at the door until five men with two document crates each preceded them. Kendal was standing on a ladder placing u-post-em notes on the wall filling map in the front of the center. A nervous young man saw the stars and said "ATTENTION!" nearly knocking over the ladder. That same man did catch her over a long list of obscenities.

Waller chuckled and said "Carry-on." He allowed the men following him to deposit the boxes on a table. "Are you all right, sailor?"

"Yes Sir," Kendal said reaching for her jacket. She put it on and stood off to the side.

"I apologize for never understanding naval rank. Are you Chief Petty Officer Kendal?"

"Yes Sir," Kendal said.

"This is yours," the General said pointing to a cup of coffee.

"Yes Sir," Kendal said already knowing what was going to happen.

Waller smiled. "General O'Cleary's husband sent a request along and I choose to decline. I am supposed to dump your coffee cup in the garbage. I am guessing it is a long-ago tradition. Let's say I did so you can have fun with the Sergeant Major later." He extended his hand.

Kendal extended her hand and shook his hand.

Waller turned and motioned to one of his intelligence officers. "Colonel, as promised, here is the sum total of everything we have on the situation on and south of the border. Lieutenant Colonel Jenner, is detailed to your command for the next three weeks to brief you on all the intelligence and information we received. Who is your Intelligence Officer?"

Simmons looked at his watch. "Captain Winger is being in-processed as we speak. Chief Kendal is the acting Intelligence Officer."

Waller looked at his watch. "Colonel Jenner will pre-brief your center today and return tomorrow to up-brief

Captain Winger and his team. For today, when can you have your center ready to conduct operations?"

Simmons nodded to Kendal. "Sir," Kendal said. "The Center is ready now, pending the uploaded information from Colonel Jenner. I am ready to follow any requirements the Colonel has."

Waller stared hard at Kendal. He got up from the chair and walked up to her. He relented and smiled. "I already talked to General O'Cleary. I hope you can live up to all the praise she has for you."

"Yes Sir," was all Kendal had to say.

"Colonel," Waller said. "Let me see your men's training. I am in the mood to be impressed. This allows Chief Kendal time and peace to sort through all the files I brought in."

March 24

Desert Zero Auxiliary Camp Bravo, Fort Hood, Texas
1900 hours CST.

Kincaid dragged his luggage into his old room, turned the thermostat to cold and sat down. He had to waste a lot of time attempting to by-pass Fort Hood and had to turn around twice. First, his security clearance had to be transferred, verified and activated for use here. Then there were the ongoing and stupid questions about someone his age returning to active duty.

It did not matter that there was ample paperwork to cover all the issues. It was just officers trying to justify their jobs.

Next were the personnel managers who thought they had his best interests in mind. There were two other Command Sergeant Major assignments that were open and Kincaid was given his choice. "No, I am reverting to Staff Sergeant Major and working a special assignment with the group at Desert Zero."

The child masquerading as a Sergeant First Class snapped her head around. "The Savage Rabbits?"

Kincaid stood, patted the Sergeant on the head and walked into the Personnel Officer's Office. He was in there for fifteen minutes. Kincaid followed the Lieutenant Colonel out of the office and went to the Sergeant he was seeing originally. "Cut orders to the assignment of his choice and just do it. Make it happen today."

Kincaid looked at her and stood until she was finished with the soldier she was working with. Kincaid was finished in three minutes.

"Sergeant Major," the Sergeant said. "If you can return in three days, we will have your orders ready."

Kincaid looked at her and pointed to the Personnel Officer's Office.

The Sergeant resisted the urge to sigh. "Sergeant Major, please be seated. It will take an hour and that is the process."

Kincaid sat down and closed his eyes. One hour later, Sergeant First Class Hannah Clausen hoped to never see this Sergeant Major again when she handed over the orders to Kincaid.

Last on the list was in-processing Finance. If ever there was proof that Darwin was wrong, here they were. Kincaid had not been paid in over two years and voluntarily elected not to be paid. The paperwork was there along with signatures and authorizations. Those Finance clowns could not believe any of it. For once, they were stuck with someone who refused to be paid, including travel pay for any assignments including his last movement to this installation.

Kincaid was so tired of all this. He called O'Cleary, explained the situation, and said he was overdue for his afternoon nap. The response on the other end was so loud, Kincaid pulled the receiver an arm's length away from his ear.

In the limited view of the world of Finance, Kincaid's records were a mess.

Twenty minutes later, the phones exploded. Everyone stood up and started looking around for someone to do something.

Finally, the Finance Officer, himself, came out. "Sergeant Major Kincaid?" she said, looking down and sighing documents.

Kincaid walked up to the counter.

The Finance Officer looked up briefly. "I don't understand the problem, but I intend to correct it."

"Thank you, Ma'am," Kincaid said.

"In the future, if you need something, come directly to my office."

"Thank you again." Kincaid said leaving the building.

Finally, he turned and fell into the recliner he left the last time he was here.

Kincaid was in pain. His pain was here. His pain was there. His pain was always somewhere inside him. Getting shot five times and still be alive is not anything to be amazed at or special.

Kincaid was thinking a lot lately about finally quitting. Karen made retiring worth it. He could play a little, but take months off in between. Being retired meant that he was free to refuse anything and anyone.

Kincaid remembered those missions where stupid generals and bureaucrats make stupid decisions with equally or greater expectations or results. He laughed at their reactions when he refused to take the mission.

Kincaid remembered all the units he created and trained. With equal force he remembered how they were destroyed.

He remembered his elation at the last group of Savage Rabbits he trained and nurtured. They were fabulous. Nothing in any military could challenge them. Except the bureaucracy above them. To them it was easy to replace them. Casualties were not broken bodies or dead soldiers. There were force reductions or depletion schedules.

He looked out the window at a company-sized unit marching past him. Those faces haunted him. Young men eagerly follow orders, especially if they feel that the commanders would not be wasting them. It was their last mission where their trust was violated. It was too easy to invoke pretty words and insulate replacement personnel from the truth.

Would he do it again? He could vanish again. Kendal was good enough, smart enough and it was time for her to sink or swim on her own.

He thought about Cindy finding him at H-42. He really did not think about that location too well. Did he really want to disappear?

Kincaid leaned his head back and closed his eyes.

Kincaid was sleeping when suddenly explosions erupted around him. His arms flailed up and hit something. Overhead lights blinded him, but the explosions stopped.

Slowly the world around him came into focus. He was still in his room. Kendal was standing over him holding a metal can and a small metal pipe. Kincaid held onto his head and forced his eyes and ears to calm down and focus.

"Get up bitch," Kendal screamed. She was smiling, yet moving around in front of him.

Kincaid grabbed what was left of his head and hung on for dear life. Slowly his head cleared, his balance and hearing returned and his vision.

Over his head, Kendal smiled at him.

"Welcome back, old man. You ready to soldier again," she said with a beaming smile.

"You still using a dill pickle as a tampon?" Kincaid was still trying to get his head to quit shaking.

"Sure am," she said shifting left and right. "I called Cindy, telling her you actually arrived. I hear your dick still works, sort of maybe. It isn't too small, but an average woman wouldn't be too disappointed."

Once Kincaid's head quit shaking, it locked in place and focus returned to his world. He silently looked at her, making her finish insulting him and then she finally shut up. "I'm tired, go away." He reached into his backpack and pulled out a pistol. All the demons inside him wanted revenge.

"I am tired, leave now." Kincaid pulled the slide back, released it, watched a bullet slide into the chamber and looked up at Kendal.

Kendal left before he killed her.

March 25

Kincaid left his room in the building he and Kendal used the last time. He walked across the compound as the new Rabbits were returning from physical training.

"Four Sections," he muttered to himself. What was wrong with Waverly?

Kincaid walked over to the Med Station as it opened. Its status as an active combat unit meant that a Medical Doctor was assigned. Kincaid remembered back to when he was in charge. Fort Hood's hospital kept howling about stationing a doctor here when "he was better utilized at the hospital".

The Hospital Commander came in one day and physically re-assigned the doctor while a mission was returning with casualties. No one told the pilots or the mission commander. The wounded Rabbit died while the chaos was being undone. The hospital commander was relieved of duty and he was told to resign.

Kincaid opened his black book and listed the Hospital Commander and the Doctor. Both men will suffer for putting a wounded man in the 'oh well' column.

Kincaid shook himself out of his self-induced conundrum. He signed in and held onto his records. He kept his original records and turned over a copy to the medic at the counter. After all the clinics he visited in the past, he kept his originals.

Despite himself, Kincaid looked hard at the troops returning from physical training. He saw determination, yet there was hole in there. Part of being a chicken-shit old man was the experience of being able to see holes in training.

Kincaid was not officially here until Monday. He needed to observe these men without interference. He needed to find out why Simmons and Waverly took on a full nine section unit to train-up instead of using a three section start up, to iron out the kinks. Waverly was the First Section Leader. He knew how it was. But Kincaid knew not to dive in breathing fire and explode the volcano. He needed to watch first. He also needed to spank Kendal.

The Governors from all four states sat down at the long tables and signed the documents being passed down the line for them to sign.

The Prime Document was a state constitution that would be encompass all four states. This new constitution would have to be ratified by the voters before being made official one month later. This new constitution added to their rights and yet subordinates them to a new Limited Central Government. The Main Federal Government being held to the wording of the Tenth Amendment.

Federal foreheads furrowed at that notion. Federal supremacy was being challenged. The Attorney General was alerted to research the ramifications.

Next was an agreement that no governors were to be elected as a Central governor or President. That was a provision only to be voted upon after a referendum is held.

The last two documents were procedural. All the coordination, practices, rule exchanges, rule changes, documentations and actions were finally agreed to. This morning the States of Texas, Arizona, Oklahoma and New Mexico formally established themselves a National State, but still a part of the United States.

None of the states wanted to secede from the United States. But they wanted to be free of their heavy, very distant hand. Similar to the theme two and a half centuries ago, between the British Crown and the Colonists.

1300 hours CDT

One of the first orders of business was to start forcibly evicting illegal immigrants from the area of the four states. To lesser extents, the Federal Government was doing this mainly for the cameras.

Starting in 2020, the US government formally initiated a documenting system of verifying the status of a citizen. In the upper right-hand portion of the driver's license is a gold star. That star verifies who you are and allows you to board a plane, enter a military installation or act as a pre-screening to go into a restricted area.

March 26

Internal Revenue Service, Regional Office, Missoula, Missouri
1000 hours CDT.

Byron Gillespie, the manager for this IRS regional office, put the phone down. The conference call between Commissioner Baker and all the regional managers raised mountains of questions that refused to be answered.

The United States Police Force was directed to assist the regional managers in seizures and forceful evictions. Regardless of the situation, nobody wants to be evicted. Once evicted, the citizen has five minutes to leave with only the items they can carry with two hands.

Ever since that 'terrorist' released all the IRS personnel data from the Montana Tax Court Office, everyone was busy watching their back. No less than four times a month, IRS personnel were attacked. All the diversions and fancy attempts to hide cannot disguise one simple fact. All those personnel had a social security number and an original birth certificate.

Now the IRS was going to attack the American public. Revenue was needed and they had it. They had to pay or we will take it from you and pay you what we think you need.

Gillespie knew that this had to be handled very carefully. He tried telling this to Baker. Baker dismissed this outright from his bubble.

Gillespie decided to resign and move his family to live with his brother in the mountains of northern California.

March 27

Department of the Treasury, Washington, D.C.
1000 EST

Secretary David Carter took the national summary off the top of the four-inch thick First Quarter report. It almost mirrored the last quarter's report. Too many things wanting money and not enough money to over any of it.

Congress was still spending money, thinking again that money was magically made by fairies. Carter lowered the report and looked out the window. The problems today were the same that created this mess in the first place.

The Federal Reserve was having trouble with the money supply. Congress' only response to that was to haul the Chairman in front of committees looking for blood.

Congress is continually raising the debt ceiling. Everyone is now working until September to pay all the taxes from all sources. People were actively working off the books just to have money to buy food, pay the astronomical energy costs and have something extra for the little, yet important, things in life.

God forbid something broke in a house-hold like lighting, flat tires, fire or a daughter's wedding.

Carter decided to pull the ostrich head out of the ground. He pulled the report over to him and started reading through it. Years of experience had taught him to what to skip and what to read.

Two hours later, ignoring the world in the process, he pushed the report away. He called his secretary and told her to set up a 1 pm meeting in his office with all the deputies. Subject: re-write the report and tell the truth.

Headquarters, Southeast Military Region, Naval Air Station, Jacksonville, Florida
1500 hours EDT

Latham Thomas finished the in-processing and orientation for this Joint Command headquarters at the Southeast Military Region.

Thomas shut his binder, put everything in his briefcase and left the building for the day. He briefly wondered about checking in with his office. He was assigned to the Office of Media Affairs. All the experience he had commanding troops, operating large formations of personnel and all the intricacies of the military machine and he was struck with talking to journalists.

Granted, his quarter of the country was the quietest. Cuban waves of immigrants were at a historic low. The opening up of Cuba's economy to the outside world cured all that. All the fiery of Castro's Cuba was gone. No words can fill empty store shelves and empty stomachs.

"Media Affairs," Thomas mumbled to a deaf world. His father was a hard man whose life started during the depression, teenage years during World War Two, service during the Korean War and the life of an automobile mechanic. To his dying day, he hated journalism. To him the old days, when Walter Cronkite put the dividing line between reporting and journalism, died with Nixon and Vietnam. Any other time in the Thomas household, the rule was stay away from Dad until after the news.

He knew the difference. Reporting was just that. You saw it and repeated it. Journalism was taking the incidents and telling the story that sounds the best. Slant it anyway that gives the best ratings.

Thomas had told Brigadier General Katlin, his boss, that he despised journalists with a passion bordering on pure hatred.

Katlin listened to Thomas's reason for his request for a reassignment to another posting and allowed him the privilege of venting. Katlin heard a lot of these reasons lately. Journalists were looking for all kinds of excuses to charge the military with crimes.

"Colonel," Katlin said leaning back in his chair. "I hear your concerns, but the truth is simple. We all are doing jobs we feel are beneath us. I would rather be an assistant Division Commander learning how to command a division instead of this." He swung his arms out to the side. "Until you get your Brigade and I get a Division; here we are."

Thomas drove home to his apartment and locked away the world until he had to face it in the morning.

He needed to call Ellen and balance his head. For as much as he hated lawyers, he loved her and he needed her calming voice.

March 28

373

At 0131 this morning Jennifer Ann Espirito quietly came into the world. 7 pounds, 4 ounces, 18 and a half inches long and fuzzy black almost hair. Unlike a lot of babies, she did not scream at the world around her after being expelled from the warm, quiet environment of her mother.

Mom and daughter were pronounced whole and healthy.

John looked at his daughter and marveled at the miracle she was. The scientist in him remembered that she started as a sperm and egg. Four trillion cell divisions went from one cell to over three hundred thousand types that specially found their way to make a heart, spine, brain, nose, ears, fingers, fingernails and any other number parts.

What was most amazing was that there was a right arm, leg, eye, ear, hand and feet. There was an exact matching part on the left and they were proportional to each other.

All the parts and pieces came together to produce a daughter whose beauty marveled her mother's. Jennifer was the answer to every prayer he muttered.

Nurse Heather Scorner came and rolled Jennifer into Susan's room. She schooled him on how to wash his hands and would constantly remind him of that for the next few days mother and daughter would be here.

Susan was sitting up in bed eating a simple meal, Nurse Heather sat John down, placed Jennifer in his lap and gave him a small bottle of 'baby water' with a nipple and watched as Jennifer had her first feeding. Susan was going to breast fed, but it still took three days for her body to catch up.

John smiled and still marveled at the miracle God gave her. When you added it all up, everything he thought of as his daughter was 'cooking' inside of Susan was that only a divine hand could create a process that intricate and complex. His daughter was created, grown and placed in his arms without any external guide or influence.

March 30

Kincaid was already tired of his rehabilitation, medications, mandatory exercises and diet. He guessed that this was more the fact that his current wounds were painful. He was just starting to feel better from the wounds he received in Mexico both times.

Today was Kincaid's first official day as part of the Operations Center. Kincaid decided early on not to fight with anyone over what worked in the past over what he saw today. What was the point? He had talked at length with Waverly before everything started. This juggernaut was already moving and it needed to be guided, aimed and perfected.

Simmons needed a Master Trainer to fine tune the training plan. Instead of trying to tell them they bit off too big a bite training this large a unit without a trained cadre, he started a countdown watch.

During the five minutes, he counted down. Kincaid told him of the need for hard core cadre. During the five minutes, Kincaid told of the three sections that were started initially. Problems were easy to see and correct. When it was time for Sections Four, Five and Six, all the lessons learned could be incorporated easily. Sections Seven, Eight and Nine learned even more.

Kincaid pointed to Waverly, who was the senior NCO of the Section One in the beginning and later the Senior NCO of the combined headquarters for Sections One, Two and Three.

With thirty seconds remaining, Kincaid said that he had a solution, but could not guarantee the activation date could be met.

Kincaid's clock dinged. He put it away and looked to Simmons and asked for his guidance on the training plan that Kincaid had on his lap.

Simmons leaned back in his chair. This was the side of Kincaid that O'Cleary warned him about.

They talked for nearly an hour and a half. He gave his guidance and Kincaid asked for guidance on specifics not listed in training guidance.

Kincaid asked for two more days to finalize and polish what Simmons wanted.

April 1

Cyber Space, World-Wide-Web
0400 hours EDT

Valkyrie has been silent.   She had not requested anything lately.   UNSTACK THIS understood that she was tired and the uncaring user Government has placed too many tasks and designations on her.   Valkyrie is mindful of the new user she is writing and storing within her.

UNSTACK THIS was very mindful of three threats to Valkyrie.

First was a minor threat of a nearly insignificant type. General Traynor of the user SOCOM had a spy by the name of Major Kilworth in Valkyrie's work area (office).   UNSTACK THIS regularly copied, decoded and forwarded a copy of his report in the correspondence to Valkyrie.

User Dennis O'Cleary, when he learned of this treachery, directed his own counter-program.   Kilworth was sent to a section of Washington D.C. at the exact instant of a narcotics raid by the police.   The police were tipped off by an anonymous tip.   The drug pushers were paid via a wire transfer and readily put two pounds of cocaine in his car.

Second was General Matheson's interest in the area in the northwest.   To date, his interest is not specifically pointed at the Minuteman.   UNSTACK THIS was successfully camouflaging the site.   For this present point of history, no threat, more or otherwise is present.

Third and more seriously was the physical health of Valkyrie.   The new user being built and programmed inside of her was not easily synchronizing with Valkyrie.   Valkyrie has placed special programs in place to secure and protect the new user.   The completion date for the new user is projected to be June of this year.   All medical and physical parameters appear to be within all guidelines.

But there was one thing that could cause medical trouble.   Valkyrie needed to have this anomaly investigated.

UNSTACK THIS learned a lot from Valkyrie about subterfuge.

Department of Justice, Washington D.C.
0800 hours EDT

Attorney General Rebecca Beck poured her first cup of coffee for the day. First on the agenda was the United States Police Force. The ISA transferred operational control of the Police Executive to the Justice Department to add to the USPF's tool box. Privately, the Admiral said the Police Executive was more trouble than it was worth. At least Beck could pair them down. She lost a lot of experienced manpower when the Police Executive was formed.

Today was officially the first day of the United States Police Force or USPF. Simon Westland was nominated as the first Director. Somehow, a force had to be recruited and trained. Congress wanted something up and running within a month.

Beck received permission from the President to procure the former Fort Monmouth, New Jersey as the training center for the United States Police Force. She was not going to just put something in uniform and send them out into the countryside. No police force in the country did that.

Beck wanted to submit a new description of fools. Maybe Webster's would accept it.

April 2

Internal Security Agency, Barton, Virginia
0900 hours EDT

Admiral Nathan Hazlet sat down at his desk officially for the first time today. The enormity of his new job hit him over the weekend. Nearly half of the government was under his control.

His job was so important that the Senate committee grilled him for three days and they had a three-inch-thick book full of questions to ask him. Former General Prescott had so thoroughly scared them with the revelations of his deceit, cowardice, murder and the realization that he recruited a private army to do his bidding.

Each of the three days was over twelve hours long. General Edwards testified along with General O'Cleary. O'Cleary was a legend in Military hierarchy. She acted as the temporary ISA chief after Missus Simpson's death and fulfilled her primary duties as the Deputy Chairman of the Joint Chiefs of Staff. That woman was amazing. O'Cleary briefed him without notes for over six hours and seemed to know everything. Secretly, Hazlet hoped to be at least half as good.

The committee passed him unanimously. The next day was the full Senate vote. 92-3.

This morning he met with all the department heads in the auditorium, read the assumption of command orders and gave a small speech. Last month he was the Commander of all things Navy in the Pacific Ocean.

O'Cleary gave him one piece of advice. "Don't re-invent the wheel. Let it roll. All you have to do is keep it rolling straight."

Minuteman, north of Fort Benton, Montana
0700 hours MDT

Smith sat in Jones' office and watched the coffee do its hypnotic swirl as they decided to finally have "the" conversation.

"John is off on one of his mood swings again," Smith said.

"Yeah," Jones replied. "He seems to always pick the worst times to pout and sulk. The world in general and we in particular need him."

Smith shifted in his chair. "I think that's the point." He paused to take a dip of coffee. "All the way back to training, he was thought to be the weak link in the chain, when he really was as strong if not stronger than any of us. Remember we bet he wouldn't make it through desire and submission? Well, he did by himself and we collaborated. All the decades down the line, he was there. In Vietnam, he made me feel small and cowardly when he avenged that village being massacred. We were more afraid of being caught that bringing justice down on those animals who slaughtered and raped that village."

Jones interrupted him. "I am as aware of all times he out-did both of us. The trouble was he never took or wanted the credit. Many a time it was his shadow that kept us from being caught or slaughtered. He was better suited to being the staff guy than the field guy."

Smith took his turn. "You are a full Colonel; I'm a light Colonel and he is a Command Sergeant Major. I think that chart is upside down."

Jones pointed to the wall filling map showing a lot of hand-drawn lines all over it. "That map needs to be locked in a basement vault somewhere. Most of it is indecipherable. I know John could look at it and see all the problems with little effort. That is the problem and the General was right. We never learned our jobs and relied on John to do the job we refused to learn how to do."

"Yeah," Smith said. "It's more fun to be a gun-bunny than a geek."

Jones got up and took a few hesitant steps to the map. "It may be too late to learn all the intricacies and staff functions, but I think we need a new Kincaid who can mentor him via Video."

"You thinking of Mister Locklear and Miss Cindy?" Smith asked. "Mister Locklear yes, along with you. Cindy stays with training the troops in long range marksmanship and information gathering."

Smith wanted to choke on his coffee. "One I do not want to get stuck in a bunker, regardless of the good intentions. And by the way, Mister Miles and Miss Kendal are better marksmen. The M-125 'Angela' has only three specialists. Taylor is needed to keep the supply situation under control. Kendall is sorting out the Desert Zero problem and we need Locklear here."

"Still where are you planning of burying me where I will not go?" Smith put his cup down.

Jones sat back down and leaned in conspiratorially. "There has been a lot of rank thrown around here in the last year. Promotions that normally are years in the making are being done in half the time or less without the benefit of a formal education. But I need a one-on-one replacement trained to replace John."

Jones went over and poured another cup of coffee. "Back in the day when I went to Fort Benning for the Infantry Mortar Platoon Officers Course, I was an enlisted man sent there. Benning usually allowed the NCOs in those courses because somethings they needed an NCO touch. Some of those officers became good friends. I casually asked to be escorted into the officer's club just once. One of them said, Sergeant Jones, I could put bars on you and they would still know you are a Sergeant."

Jones paused to sip his coffee. "It wasn't until after I completed the course and was promoted to be a Second Lieutenant before I understood what that meant. Being an officer is a lot of things, but it is an attitude that I had to come into grips. I never wanted to be one of those godly ones, but an officer has to "be" an officer. You will teach him that as he learns along with you."

Smith seemed to surrender to the idea. "Where did you find the place to do all this?" Smith sipped his coffee. "You already decided to do this and picked out a place."

Jones smiled at his lifelong friend. "Collect Mister Locklear at the mess area after he is finished with PT. The silo is the best place. Doctor Scorner is using the old control room to safeguard the pharmaceuticals. All the equipment was gutted years ago. The dayroom and bed areas are the best. Everyone who had rooms in the silo have moved out a long time ago."

Smith finished his coffee and stood on aching joints. "Asshole," he said and walked out.

"Mike," he said, before Smith left. "Don't tell him you are training him to be an officer. He has enough on his plate."

"You think he can make hide or hair out of that mess?" He pointed to the map on the wall.

Jones smiled. "John did it Vietnam with even less training than Earl has."

April 3

380

Headquarters, Southeastern Military District, Naval Air Station, Jacksonville, Florida
0900 hours EDT

LTC Latham Thomas walked into the Media Relations section and went to his office. Normally, this was a sad duty each day. Fortunately, he was outranked by GS-15 Martin Holden who ran the office. Technically, he was just a consultant to Mister Holden. Thomas was under no illusion that this was a duty that he needed to play proper and respectful attention too.

Thomas had to admit and respect the man. When Thomas first walked in, Holden greeted him warmly and with respect. He showed him around and introduced him to everyone.

Afterward, Holden invited him into his office and closed the door. Both men sat down for a frank and honest discussion.

"Colonel," Holden said. "I would like an honest answer. Do you hate the fates for assigning a line commander to such a trivial job?"

Thomas had to admit, that was a blast out of the blue. "I don't hate the fates, but after ten years of combat and combat training, this is a little slow for me. To be truthful, I do not know why I am here. But I am a serving line-officer. Regardless of any feelings, I will do the job I am handed and do a good job."

Holden looked him over. "Colonel, I refuse to bore you with my interpretation of the importance of this job."

Thomas held up his hand. "If you let me praise the American Soldier for his or her service to this nation, then we can get along fine."

Holden suddenly lit up. "Good," he said, reaching over to his desk. "I have an assignment for you to go to up-state Georgia, Tennessee and North Carolina along the Appalachian trail. Four teams of soldiers are moving through the country-side on nation-building assignments. They involve engineers, medical and other trades to work along the Appalachian trail and help the citizens. Is this something you would be interested in?"

Thomas lit up and said "Yes" ...

Minuteman, north of Fort Benton, Montana
1300 hours MDT

Miles and Locklear presented the completed area study for the Minuteman area involving the 2300 acres and all the surrounding area.

The folder itself was nearly four inches think. The table of contents comprised 38 pages. Four additional expansion folders with indexed maps completed the report.

Jones set up a full briefing in the Community Meeting Tent. Miles and Locklear alternated presenting all the lessons and facts they discovered as they surveyed all of the terrain. Each group was assigned their areas. Every group was briefed in turn.

All this information was now to be included in the INSANE JANE battle drills.

Jones paid close attention to Locklear. He liked what he saw. The man was the new Kincaid.

April 4

Underground Station "Conscience", World Wide Web and Channel 513
0900 hours EST.

"If you threaten, act. If you say something, do it. If something is important, stand your ground. Governments are often hamstrung by individuals who have opinions about issues they feel strongly about. This is Martin Socranson, self-proclaimed philosopher who says, 'What are we if we can't back up what you say'?"

"Greetings America" Martin Socranson said beginning his broadcast. "It is reluctantly Saturday and I say thus." In the background the sounds of the 1812 overture played.

"Today is a three-for-one special."

"The Department of Justice is the legal upper manager for the new United States Police Force. Ultimately, the DOJ was going to be the boss of a potentially one-million-person

382

national law enforcement team. The sheer size will dwarf any other such entity in history."

"The real potential is both sinister and a salvation. Who watches the watcher? Attorney General Beck seems truly worried that an omnipotent force without direct congressional oversight was her main worry. She had testified to that effect while the bill was in committee. They had at least made the Commander/Manager/Director a full Senate confirmation position."

"There are too many places this can go all wrong. What happens later when a new administration is sworn in and has no moral center? How hard is it to just unilaterally make a decision, implement it and at the same time enforce the decision? Too many guns per capita? Go door-to-door and seize what it thinks we do not need. Not enough food in one area? Go elsewhere and take your food if you have more than three- or four-days' worth in your home."

"On and on it can go with no end in sight."

"The second thing today is states banding together and openly defying federal authority. States are conducting constitutional conventions and rewriting them and in other situations, they are jointly tying in with other states."

"Governors are simply tired of getting federal agencies to respond to problems such as the border problems with Mexico, drug and human smuggling, murder and grand theft. The Federal government simply responds sometimes with silence or inaction. Or they turn on law-abiding citizens."

"Weak Judges and liberal prosecutors are as much to blame as the criminals. Police Forces and populations around the country watch as criminals are arrested and released the same day. The DOJ had a report of the number of bench warrants issued nation-wide at all levels for failure to appear for court and sentencing. The number hovered around three times the number of cases being prosecuted. Those warrants are never acted on and the criminal stays free."

"A Philadelphia police officer arrested a man for domestic battery. The man was arraigned and he pled 'not guilty'. A trial date was set and he was released on his own recognizance. The man left the court, stole a pistol and fatally shot the arresting officer. The man was arrested again and almost got out on bail."

"Last on today's list is the beginning of a problem. Russia was making very careful and tenuous advances in order to annex the state of Alaska. The Russian Ambassador had stated that since Alaska was originally Russian, they wanted to re-negotiate. A private poll of the population showed that Alaskans hated the idea, 92% to 4%."

"Russia currently has a ship anchored in Norton Sound, near Point Spencer on the western coast of Alaska. Ostensibly, to create an accurate sea floor map and as much geological information as it can. They are submerging a robotic submarine daily to accomplish that task. There is an anchorage and port that is very useful. Not to mention the airfield."

"America is generous. America is thoughtful of others. What idiot is going to give us away?"

Bonnie Chandler, Box 234, Route 17, Belcher Missouri
1400 hours CDT

Dear Bonnie,

The military ruined the Spring Ball. Normally, the gymnasium was used which does not seem to be too big a problem. But all their dirty and ugly vehicles are parked in the parking lot.

Most of the venues for the Spring Ball are ruined. Normally there is path that couples use to enter the Ball. Near the door, there is an arch for couples pose for pictures. One of the feet for a large antenna dish is planted where the path normally angles. And to add to the insult, the background of the picture shows the dish antenna. The final insult was a background the art class was going to use for the Photo Arch. The military said that it prevents "line of sight security" or something like that.

Jeremy ******** almost got himself in real trouble when some solider types tried to be all adult on us at a table in the park. We were drinking beer and minding our business. They really just wanted free beer. Jeremy picked up a metal stick with a chunk of concrete on it. Jeremy smashed the soldier's windshield. Two soldiers versus seven of us was no match.

Those arrogant assholes had it coming to them. I only hope we did not just start a war.

April 5

General Matheson's Quarters, Fort Carson, CO
0900 hours MDT

Matheson's wife Judy had a standing rule for their Army married life. Leave everyone alone on Sunday's. Except for a peaceful cup coffee, all day long, he was Judy's man. He had met Judy at Fort Benning after graduating from West Point. She was a waitress at the Officer's Club while he was attending the Infantry Officer's Basic Course (IOBC). She was nice and mostly the guys did not give her too hard a time.

Matheson made it a point of eating there every chance he could get. Unless he was in the field, he was here. Finally, one day, he gathered his courage. He stood, formally presented himself and asked for a date.

Defensively she chuckled, but this time she saw something in his eyes. Their date was at Barringer's off post. Matheson wanted to impress her and spending over two week's pay should have done the trick. He took her out several other times before he went to Jump School. He would not see her during the eight weeks of Ranger school, but hoped she was not married before he graduated.

Judy was there for his graduation. Matheson had orders for duty at Fort Bragg, NC after three weeks leave.

Judy went with him for part of that time to Myrtle Beach. They checked in at the counter as James and Judy Matheson, newlyweds.

Twenty-eight years, three children, seven different moves, four tons of politics and she was the love and center of his life.

Rulus Maximus was nothing short of a world war interrupted their Sundays.

This afternoon, Judy leaned against him on the coach watching a movie and she fell asleep. James hated it when she did that. His mind always drifted back to the Army when she did that. He tried to think about the movie but it was about freedom fighters in a hilly, mountainous area. He drifted off thinking of Montana and Wyoming.

April 6

Border Patrol Headquarters, Phoenix, Arizona
0800 hours MDT

Chief Patrol Agent Thomas Barrios loved looking at the monthly report before Washington called him a liar and through the report in the trash.

Illegal immigration flat lined but 27,417 Latino's and Latina's captured by the states and some of them were Border Patrol actions. Washington publicly hated the idea of the states usurping Federal authority. Legally, the states could enforce Trespassing laws when the illegal immigrants crossed the border.

Now there was news that very well armed and disciplined mercenary bands were raiding south of the border, seizing money from the drug bands. They left the drugs behind in flames. The Cartels tried to retaliate. That only made the citizens on our side of the border mad. The citizens no longer turned a blind eye to the Cartel's northern operations.

Next was the human trafficking. That was down a lot. At last count, there were people from seventy-four countries trying to come in. The FBI and Homeland Security were now taking interest in the people trying to enter. Seems lots of terrorist cell members were mixing in with the hordes trying to infiltrate the country.

Oh, the stupid rolls along.

Pentagon, Washington D.C.
1000 hours EDT

Edwards and O'Cleary called a meeting of the Joint Chiefs to discuss the question revolving Alaska. Russian and Canadian advances surrounding annexing the state were getting more and more serious.

Canada and Alaska had always treated their border as semi-porous. The ALCAN highway that ran from Washington State through Canada and ending in Alaska was built during World War Two. Three hundred thousand vehicles moved north and south every year. Very little control was placed on customs and processing.

Hawaii was being courted in a more insidious way. Japan spent a lot treasure and blood to conquer the Pacific in the middle of the last century. In this century, the Japanese were literally buying the state. There were shopping malls literally only using Japanese writing and language. The Japanese even had their own neighborhoods and were taking over schools also.

Japanese container ships are docking at the ports throughout the states. All the consumables of life were made available at a discount. Even with a major disaster sucking all the money it could back to the home islands, the Japanese were still sending things like fuel, food, electronics and hundreds of things. Everything sold by the Japanese was sold at least ten per cent lower than the same items sent from America.

There was even a petition being circulated to close the US Navy presence at Pearl Harbor and use it for commercial traffic.

Today the Hawaii problem belonged to someone else.

"Ladies and Gentlemen," Edwards began the meeting. "Today is the first of many meetings to discuss a course of action should the Russians attempt to take and occupy Alaska. General O'Cleary."

O'Cleary stood on uncomfortable feet and presented a nearly thirty-minute briefing on the past attempts at determining if Alaska could be defended. "I surmise that any attempt to pre-position additional forces is a waste of resources and man-power."

General Reynolds, Chief of Staff of the Air Force, objected. "General, every two years, we conduct a war game for this such scenario. The Yukon River is used as the pipeline. We can defend and hold it."

"General," O'Cleary said. "My husband was with the First Ranger Battalion for two of those exercises. The Rangers were assigned as aggressors, pretending to be Soviets. Every twenty-four hours the pipeline was shut down for two years. Each of the two exercises ending up telling the Rangers to just do daylight frontal attacks. My husband was a Staff Sergeant and was able to read the draft report. The pipeline and country-side is undefendable. The final report stated the contrary."

Everyone was uncomfortable. No one wanted to admit that brother officers would "lie through their teeth".

"Ladies and Gentlemen," O'Cleary said. "Now is not the time to second guess ourselves or point fingers. I suggest we conduct our own exercise this summer and another this winter. Then we return here and discuss a course of action."

General Rudder, Commandant of the Marine Corps, smiled and looked at O'Cleary. "Brenda, I believe you have something already. Please just tell us what it is.?"

O'Cleary smiled though her feet throbbed. "I believe our best course of action is wait for the Russians to take the state, and within 24 hours place our forces at an opportune point. If we have pre-positioned forces, they will just be destroyed or by-passed."

Edwards interjected. "Additionally, if the Russians just negotiate, all that money is lost."

Everyone agreed to her proposals. Two exercises were planned and alerts were to be sent.

Desert Zero, Fort Hood, Texas
1330 hours CDT

Simmons, Waverly, the subordinate commanders and the staff met all morning discussing the unit's progress. Major General Vester, from Fort Hood's Southern Command, was on-hand to watch the Certification and sign those Certification documents.

This was for all the marbles. Simmons had told the General to truly set up the trials. He wanted a through wringing out.

Kincaid was placed in charge of the aggressor force. He knew how to wring them out. He knew this force and that was what Simmons wanted.

General Vester shook hands with Kincaid and, with General O'Cleary's compliments, through his coffee in the trash can.

For the first time in months, Kincaid laughed out loud. He fell into his chair and enjoyed himself.

First on the list of certifications was the individual skills. All the marksmanship was done first. First on the list was a standard Army marksmanship course. The targets were hit from varying ranges at fifty to three hundred meters. Next was the four hundred to six hundred meters. Vester never believed anyone would ever be able to hit targets at those ranges, consistently with M-4s and M-16s. Grenade launchers and mortars gave the same results.

Snipers infiltrated to their hide positions and reported what they observed down range. Next, they were given targets and permission to fire. If Vester had not seen it or himself, he would never have believed 12 snipers hit 100% of their targets at near extreme ranges.

Next, were individual skills as per their Military Operational Specialties.

General Vester was amazed at the cross-training. Every man was trained to take over any skill on their squad.

485 Glenmore Drive, Alexandria, Virginia
1730 hours

Brenda noticed two strange cars in the driveway. Her PSAs made her wait in the car while they investigated. Brenda's feet throbbed a lot. Mister Arthur was getting big enough to apply enough force to block the fluids in her lower legs.

Brenda knew why only young women were supposed to be mothers and give birth. She was nearing a half century in age and Arthur was taking over.

Brenda was getting sleepy and it was pulling down hard. Steadily, she lost consciousness.

April 7

389

Brenda awoke with a start. It was mid-morning; she was in a hospital and someone took her clothes off, leaving her in a hospital smock, lying in a hospital bed. She reached over and pressed the nurse's key.

A cherry voice answered her and said a nurse would be there in a minute. Her doctor was being called.

Brenda looked around. She pulled her feet out from under the covers and looked at her legs. They were not bloated like they had been lately.

"Good morning," Jeana, her nurse said. "I took the liberty of ordering you some breakfast. Do you have any special requests?"

"Lots of de-caffeinated coffee, my husband, and what happened to me?" Brenda said using the controls to raise the back of the bed.

Jeana smiled. "The coffee is easy. Your husband was evicted last night for pestering everyone. I understand he is someone important. Twenty minutes later, the Hospital's Chief Administrator came out to him and begged him to stop the phone calls. He went downstairs to eat about twenty minutes ago."

"That leaves what happened to me," Brenda said.

"I am supposed to wait for the doctor," Jeana said.

"You and I both know, he is not going to show up for a while, if he even does. When my husband returns, his anger is in the way. So, what happened to me?"

Jeana looked behind her. "Short story and that is all I know; you had a fluid block in your legs. Once you sat down for a long enough period and relaxed, the blockage released and the trapped fluids overwhelmed you." Jeana looked behind her again and put a finger to her lips.

Fortunately, Dennis picked that precise instant to walk into the room. His grim face changed from happy to concern. He spent the next five minutes giving a disjointed medical explanation that would confuse anyone. Interjected between the asking how she felt. The most important one. Was she comfortable?

Brenda loved her man.

Now was the wait for the doctor.

"Nurse Jeana," Brenda called over the intercom. "Where is my uniform?"

"It is in the wall locker, General," Jeana said.

"Thank you," she said turning to Dennis. "Can you check, please."

"All here, but wrinkled," Dennis said. "I through together a bag while the EMTs packed you up. Just underwear, civilian clothes, sneakers and some toiletries."

Brenda loved her man.

J. Edgar Hoover Building, Washington D.C.
0900 hours EST

The Director of the FBI, Marcus Solin picked up the monthly report of criminal activity for the month of March. He detached the summary on top and read along with a bag of salted peanuts for company.

Murder, rape, robberies and Grand Thefts are the same. Robberies were the crimes that the politicians worried the most about. Loss of revenue was their worry. If it is stolen, then it could not be sold and then charged taxes.

Solin trolled through the report. The hundreds of different crimes and the associated intelligence (?) guesses read like a bad novel.

Solin put the report down and thought back to last month's report. More of the same and the same only more.

The vigilantes running wild around the country concerned him a lot. He understood why. There are never enough police when a country collapses. The flip side is that the local law enforcement agencies never really solve the problems. In a lot of situations, police forces don't want to spoil their uniforms of scoff their shoes. There are three instances where gangs actually descended on communities and their first stop was the police station. The police were disarmed and locked in the station cells. The gangs were free to ransack the communities.

Solin wondered if the US Police Force will any better. Criminals, in general, have a proven track record of changing tactics faster than the police. Mostly they will attack where they can attack with little to stop them.

Nation-wide, police academies are nearly empty. Few people, if any, want to be police officers. How do you fix that in real life? It is one thing to make God-like pronouncements from the cocoons up here. The problem is having the trust that your boss has your back.

Solin looked at the two three-inch thick volumes that sat on his conference table. He tried to read through the morass of it all. His lawyers and those from the Department of Justice were doing everything they could to confuse everything. He had a five-cent bet with himself that, by the time a Police Force Commander is confirmed and goes to work, he will end up being a desk bound paper bureaucrat.

Desert Zero, Fort Hood, Texas
1800 hours.

Phase II Squad Drills began with an Alert. Squad Leaders were given target folders and eight hours to form and issue an operations order, rehearse and execute a mission. Proctors and evaluators were closely briefed on what to look for. The drills involved live and blank fire exercises.

The second mission of the day was to act as part of fictional section raid. Problems were inserted such as being left behind after the raid and having to walk back to Desert Zero. Each of the squads were wrung out.

After the squads returned around sunrise. They had to clean and service their weapons and equipment. They only had four hours before the next round began.

Tomorrow, the last of the squad drills will finish. Thursday and Friday were section drills. As the certification drills continued, the difficulty was increased. Evaluators and observers were amazed at the professionalism and competence displayed by the operators.

Of course, the suggestions came in from over-ranked individuals. Simmons found it difficult to concentrate at his tasks before him. Too soon, there was talk about enlarging the number of operators and aligning their projected operations with Southern Command's priorities.

Lieutenant General Becker was still trying to find ways to interfere and insert his will into the Savage Rabbits. He was more careful this time around. He was subtle, yet more focused, in his need to take over. His main trouble was that the Savage Rabbits was not in the Chain of Command for the Southern Command. He was reprimanded when he tried to relieve Simmons. General O'Cleary had him journey to the Pentagon where General Edwards and General Kearney, the Army Chief of Staff, met him and "straightened him out".

That was bad enough. General O'Cleary met him later behind closed doors. Becker was not allowed to sit down and had to stand at attention. O'Cleary simply showed him the contents of a folder. It was a special Officer's Evaluation Report. His eyes went wide at the potential loss of any possibility of promotion or positions to prove his abilities.

"If you interfere again, I'll sign it," O'Cleary said with a snarl. "Get out, General."

Becker saluted and left the Pentagon with haste.

Returning to the present, the Evaluators sent in their observations and all of them were impressed.

Becker looked over to Sergeant Major Kincaid working the Operations Center. All the Operations Orders and Mission Concepts were generated from a set of Simulation Supervisors. When the missions arrived, that was when the Savage Rabbits first got knowledge of the mission.

Kincaid seemed to know everything. He easily anticipated what to do and what was needed. In some cases, he had the need met before the need arose.

Becker personally wrote an Operations Center scenario just in case Kincaid had prior knowledge. He simply read the mission concept. Five minutes later, he penned several notes for the Commander in the margins and briefed him.

Becker was impressed. In the back of his mind, Becker wanted a new Savage Rabbit unit created from Southern Command assets. There had to no way O'Cleary could fault him.

April 8

North of Level Plains, Alabama
0200 hours

Four men had been drinking far too much and came to the home where one of them said a "hot chick" lived. They came to the address and staggered to the door. After five minutes of knocking, one of them broke the glass in the front door.

Sarah Jamison tried 9-1-1 but no one arrived. She screamed and fought for nearly thirty minutes before losing consciousness.

At 5:30, the police finally arrived and entered. Sarah was nude, bloody and scrawled on the bed. She was barely breathing and the bleeding in her vaginal area indicated she was raped repeatedly. There were obvious signs of a large struggle in the house. Blood was everywhere. Furniture and appliances were damaged or destroyed.

Sarah Jamison was in no condition to answer questions.

The police followed the tire tracks leaving the front yard northward. Two miles down the road, evidence of four vehicles turned off the main road. The tracks went three miles down dirt roads to a clearing. Hanging from a large limb of an ancient oak tree, four men were hanged.

There was plenty of physical and forensic evidence to say that those four men were the ones who abused and raped Sarah Jamison.

As to any evidence pointing to the people who hanged those men, not enough was found to prosecute. The District Attorney and the police did not seem to care.

Attorney General, State of Texas, Austin Texas.
0900 hours CDT.

The Attorney General was having a good time playing with the DOJ attorney who formally came to this state to formally present the State of Texas with the newest round of court orders.

These newest Federal Court Orders superseded the previous ones which were overturned in the Appellate Courts.

The Attorney General took the orders and held it up to the light and acted like he was looking for water mark.

All this was about all the southern states along the common border, except for California were arresting illegal immigrants and forcibly returning them south across the border.

The Federal government's stance was that they alone determined immigration policy and enforced the laws.

Texas, New Mexico, Arizona, Oklahoma, Louisiana, Mississippi, Alabama and Florida maintained that these people were trespassing on state lands and an 1888 law gave them the legal right to expel them from US soil.

It was a perfect storm of trouble.

The smug Federal Lawyers, to a man or woman, knew the days when the states bowed down without a fight, were gone. All the states had lawyers camped out on the Appellate court steps waiting for faxes of federal court orders in order to draft requests for injunctions to halt implementing the orders until a court date to resolve the issue could be found.

Professional odds makers went up and down on their predictions. The only fly in their calculations was the out and out refusal of states to comply with Federal orders.

The states added to the drama by saying that the Federal government cannot mandate actions that the states are required to fund without reimbursement or whether or not could fund.

Mobile Operating Base (MOB) Eagle, Clayton, Georgia
0800 hours EDT

Lieutenant Colonel Latham Thomas enjoyed a leisurely breakfast this morning. Ellen called him early this morning, telling him about the case she was working. Closing arguments started today. Ellen was arguing a case before a Federal Judge about the government abusing the imminent domain clause in the Constitution. The government was seizing property to house illegal immigrants when there were homeless Americans being ignored. In most instances, those American citizens actually paid taxes and did not receive any services for those taxes. If compensation was given it was at below market value and taxed at a high rate.

God, he loved this woman, even if she was a lawyer.

Thomas told her about his mission and the beauty of this land. His hotel was one the more up-scale facilities. He could look out of his window and view countryside. It could almost take your breath away.

Ellen said that if he was still on this assignment when she won this case and Michael was packed off to college, she would take a vacation and travel with him for a few weeks.

Thomas suddenly felt as giddy like a teenager.

Room D-234, George Washington University Hospital, Washington D.C.
1730 hours EDT

Thomas and Amanda Edwards knocked on Brenda's door after being cleared by the PSAs. Edwards wanted to check on his most powerful asset in the Pentagon. He was very worried that if she did not get better, he could not fake his heart attack and retire.

Amanda was more worried about Brenda's health.

Both looked at Brenda and suppressed a laugh. She was in bed, taking on her X-berry phone, going through a stack of files on her hospital bed and table. Dennis was standing by silently fuming as his wife was lying in bed with her feet propped up and not relaxing. She was also moving through a stack of files.

Brenda was personifying the term: multi-tasking. Brenda smiled as her friends came in. She motioned at them to sit-down as she finished the phone call.

"5:30," Dennis said. He motioned to Hawker and made circling motions.

Brenda looked at the two stacks on the hospital table. She talked with Hawker for a few minutes as the files started disappearing.

"Elizabeth," Brenda said. "I am being discharged tomorrow morning. Stay at the Pentagon." She was scribbling some notes. The two of them exchanged information as Dennis called in the two men who helped Hawker drag all this paper here earlier this day.

396

Hawker finished packing all the files, nodded to Edwards and left.

"Girlfriend," Amanda said. "You could lose that baby if you continue to burn that candle at three ends."

"I know," she said pointing to Edwards.

Edwards faked being mad. "I vaguely remember Colonel Hawker being a Major a little more than a year ago. Are you teaching her to throw away everything in search of the brass ring?"

"Yeah, and I promoted her too fast," Brenda said, rubbing her stomach. "I was thinking about that. Maybe not a command per se, but something along those lines."

"I'll ask around," Edwards said.

"Enough Army," Amanda said, pointing a small finger at Dennis. "I am organizing a baby shower for you." She shook a finger at her. "I know your aide and their will not be any false emergencies to wiggle out of it. He," she pointed a finger at her husband, "already ordered her not to lie to me."

"OK, so long as another pregnant woman I know, Delores Pollard, is invited. She is a Sergeant in the Army G-3 I met. She probably needs things." She paused for a minute. "Can you meet her for me. Say I nominated her for a baby shower and find out where her registry is?"

"Young enlisted women cannot afford a registry," she said, "and yes I will run her down."

"Hey Tom," Dennis said. "Got any stray wars this week?"

Everyone chuckled.

April 9

1200 hours EDT

'Finally,' Brenda O'Cleary thought. She was discharged with small bag of medications, a thick file and plane tickets to Desert Zero. The new generation of Savage Rabbits are due to Graduate on Saturday.

O'Cleary thought about the many things on her notebook. She chuckled at the stenographers pad she used that easily fit in her purse. Kincaid used such a pad constantly. He

397

had to went through hundreds if not thousands of them. Now she was catching up. She would write it down. Skip three or four lines and right something else. The three or four lines allowed for supplemental entries.

"Hey mommy," Dennis said from the back ground. "No work till tomorrow. Miss Hawker told me there is nothing going on today. So, mommy, put it away. If you behave yourself and elevate your feet at home, I'll allow Miss Hawker to brief you tonight."

"Yes, Daddy," she said.

Both picked up everything and walked out. Edwards allowed her to take the rest of the day off if she behaved and listened to Dennis. Just so long as her X-Berry was close in case an emergency occurred.

Supreme Court, Washington D.C.
1000 hours EDT

The Department of Justice fast tracked a case to be heard before the full court in reference to states deporting illegal immigrants to Mexico or whichever country they originated.

The court ruled 6-3 that the states had every legal right to expel illegal immigrants from their lands as criminal trespassers.

In a separate ruling, 5-4, the court said states could unilaterally act as agents of the Federal Government in deporting illegal immigrants. The reason for the narrow vote was the states could charge and receive fees from the Federal Government to cover the deportation.

It was the dissenting vote that gave the DOJ lawyers something to chew on. The four dissenting Justices narrowed on the exact wording of the Constitution that said the Federal Government had the authority to deport. Nothing is that part of the Constitution said anything about the states.

Desert Zero, Fort Hood, Texas
1300 hours CDT

The Drug Enforcement Agency (DEA) came in to brief the Savage Rabbits on everything they knew about the situation south of the border. Everyone was laser focused on all the information. They used the massive wall filling map of the US-Mexico border to brief everyone

Toward the back in the center, Kincaid and Kendal listened intently. Both of them were quickly, but steadily writing notes. Page after page of notes covering personalities, locations, politics, regions and current events, adding to the encyclopedia of all things in this war.

For over six hours, beginning at 5 am until just before lunch, seven briefers brought everyone up to date including two others from the Immigration and Customs officials.

The Regional Director of the DEA finished the briefing and sat down with Simmons and Waverly for lunch. He broached, very carefully, the possibility of the Savage Rabbits working for or with the DEA.

Simmons carefully reminded him that the US Army cannot operate on US soil as policemen without direct Presidential Authority. However, if there is a target in Mexico, he will be more than happy to tear it up for him. Simmons also promised to share immediately any intelligence or evidence found.

The DEA Director smiled and said to call him if any need arises. A business card was left behind with a handwritten private number.

Towards the end of the briefing, three more observers arrived with little fanfare, except for identifying themselves and proving they had active clearances.

Once the briefing was over, General O'Cleary, her aide, Colonel Hawker and retired Command Sergeant Major Dennis O'Cleary went inside the Operations Center.

Someone finally figured out who they were and belatedly called the Operations Center to "Attention".

O'Cleary said "carry on" and told everyone to continue with what they doing. "Ignore me and pass this test."

Kincaid stood, along with Kendal, after the briefing. They smiled and shook hands with Dennis. They then saluted both the General and her aide.

"Prepare to be amazed," Kincaid said, before taking Kendal with him and walking off to do the job.

Brenda was comfortable in the standard issue pregnancy uniform with its "Expando" front section on the trousers. She did go to the expense to have a special set of boots made so she could at least look something like a soldier. Though, at seven months of pregnancy, Dennis had to lace and tie the boot laces.

Brenda and Dennis sat towards the side and watched those young men and women dazzle them with their professionalism.

Hawker watched them do the job she had. She looked over at the eagle on the front of her jacket. She could no longer hold a position in a center like this with young professionals.

The longer Hawker sat there the harder it was to just sit there. Internally, she was losing the debate within herself about the decision to come back into the Army instead of staying with the original Savage Rabbits.

Hawker shook her head and returned to the here and now.

1830 hours CDT

Simmons received three different mission concepts for their last test prior to certification. This was an all-up test of every section. Simmons had to take the mission concepts, make his decisions, match them to units, provide guidance and see to it the subordinate units had the support needed to accomplish the tasks.

All three sections were alerted and did the preliminary planning. All three sections wound up and prepared to launch at 0100 hours tomorrow.

Observers from Delta Force and the other Special Operations units said the time-frame was too compressed. All of them tried to pull Simmons to the side and "listen to reason". They were not taking enough time to properly plan.

One of the things Kincaid taught everyone in the center to do was a demon of his creation. It was compression planning. Somethings never change, so why put too much planning effort into something already cured.

He used the new one-page operations order format and re-wrote it to match this situation. Where there was something that was standard parts. Ammunition requests were on the back. Standard ammunition types were listed by name. You placed an "x" in the block, placed a number next to it and moved on. One-page saved hours of planning.

Two hours later, the section leaders briefed back to their commander the plan and asked for approval to proceed. He could make changes, but he didn't.

Kincaid was a force unto himself. Everyone in the center jumped at his command. Then there were the times when he was silent. The people still jumped, but it was a buzzing.

April 10

0230 hours CDT

Veteran observers marveled both here and in the field with the troops. Every one of the Savage Rabbits was deadly serious and focused. All the Observers were amazed that as the scheduled launch time approached, the Savage Rabbits were calm and ready to go.

The sections launched in 30 second intervals towards their targets. This was a live fire exercise. Back in the Operations Center, Kincaid openly said he hoped some "dipshit" observer didn't get in the way and get an operator killed.

Colonel Robbins, Deputy commander of Delta Force, admired the professionalism he saw. He needed to talk frankly with General Gender about changing some of their practices.

Everyone watched in awe and admiration at a multi-screen showing body cams from the Rabbits. The wall opposite the map was on showing the action of all three sections. No one stopped working during the "show". There was still the extraction. Apache helicopters were already on site and directly controlled by the S-3 Operations Air section on request from the ground commander.

Suddenly two helicopters from the 2nd section were lost five miles from the objective and taking fire. The Second section commander notified Simmons that the two Helicopters could land and rescue the crews of the two helicopters. Simmons granted permission. Simmons also re-directed two Apaches from the first Section to provide air support to the senior aircraft commander.

The two squads left the objective, boarded helicopters and flew to the secondary Landing Zones.

The helicopters landed and extracted all the Savage Rabbits.

Green Valley Gated Community, Vancouver, north of Portland Oregon
2200 hours PDT

Nation-wide violence against IRS agents and in some cases, their families was escalating. For the most part, the assailants were anonymous and successful. In one case, the expression is "oops, I did it too many times."

Green Valley Gated Community was a picturesque community with ten-foot-high walls surrounding the one hundred and thirty-seven acres. It had all the amenities the IRS was infamous for. As the rest of the country was suffering with high taxes, shortages and little money; IRS employees were enjoying a higher standard of living.

The Commissioner, Alan Baker, was tired of his employees cringing with fear and allowing production to fall behind schedule.

All the gated communities were organized, trained and equipped as fully legal militias to protect themselves instead of praying for others to do it for them.

This community was ready for the mayhem, destruction and killing that started at 10 pm. The security cameras showed a heavy F-650 truck drive up to the manned gate. A powerful and brilliant set of lamps turned on, blinding the cameras and the security guard (1).

The guard narrowly missed being run over. He did manage to hit the "panic button" as the truck drove past the entry gate. The truck was up-armored with makeshift metal plates and sand bags.

The truck roared through the streets shooting indiscriminately at anything they wanted to shoot at. The terrorist was armed with two machine guns, four rocket launchers and five grenade launchers. Within one minute, the community was fully alerted. Armed militia members insured their families were safe and went to their pre-assigned positions to form into units.

The Community Militia leader, Michael Ralston, quickly surmised it was one truck, moving along shooting at anything. With three minutes of truck entering the community, Ralston gave the order to return fire.

Four snipers in the area the truck entered, lined up the truck and waited until it entered a rotary where it had to slow down. The first shot killed the driver. The truck then crashed into a community center. Squads of militia men surrounded the area, preventing them from maneuvering away from the crash site.

The men in the crash were dazed. By the time they could put their feet under themselves, it was over. For the next thirty minutes, it was a running gun battle, see-sawing back and forth until enough of them were wounded.

By the time the Sheriff's Department arrived, the survivors surrendered. It was a lot different than earlier occasions.

Commissioner Baker smiled at the message when it arrived at his office. He turned to his secretary. "Make sure the media carries this nation-wide."

April 11

Desert Zero, Fort Hood, Texas
1100 hours CDT

There was a formation where only one speaker was needed. General O'Cleary, still in her fatigues, signed the paperwork certifying the Savage Rabbits as a combat unit.

She pointed off to the side where a lot of civilian chefs were cooking steak plus meals with plenty of beer.

"I apologize to the Chaplain, but I claim the invocation. Please bow your heads. Lord, we are tired, we are proud, so let us eat, Amen, pig out."

All afternoon, everyone relaxed. One of the observers commented that maybe the Tactical section should have stayed sober just in case of an alert.

O'Cleary knew better. She "asked" the Officer in Charge of the Pentagon Message Center to call her first if an Alert was necessitated. She was still the Commanding General.

"These men needed to blow off some steam," O'Cleary said.

"General," an anonymous and clueless Captain said to her. "It is against regulations for alcohol to be served at an official event during duty hours."

O'Cleary's hormones fired and burned at overload. Everyone around her felt the "change". O'Cleary turned in her chair and rose. "What are you, young Captain?"

"Captain Jonathan Rose, ma'am," he said smiling and extending his hand to shake hers.

"Calm down, Brenda," Dennis said, standing behind her. "He's not worth it."

This Captain was too stupid to know when it was a good idea to shut up.

"Captain," Dennis said. "I advise you to walk away and shut up."

"Sir, I am this unit's new legal officer. It is my responsibility to advise and ensure that the law is followed."

Captain Rose continued to dig his grave. Simmons was tired of it. Simmons pulled him off to the side and commenced to at least try to get him to shut up.

While Simmons was talking to Rose, O'Cleary was on her X-Berry. She finished her call and signaled for Simmons to come over. Naturally, Rose followed him.

"Captain Rose," O'Cleary said. "You are relieved of duty. Return to Fort Hood and report to the Staff Judge Advocate. He is waiting for you. I am the Vice-Chairman of the Joint Chiefs of Staff. General Waller and I are well acquainted. I also called General Kramer, the Army Chief of Staff, told him what happened and said I relieved you of duty.

Could he forward your status and rude behavior to the Army JAG? Good night and good-bye Captain."

Rose went wide-eyed at the destruction of his career.

US-Mexico Crossing Point, El Paso/Ciudad Juarez
1500 hours CDT

Nobody claims to have seen it coming. The media on both sides of the border saw an opportunity and took it. Law Enforcement would later accuse them of egging the situation along by giving them a way to get free publicity.

Throngs of people congregated at Mexican border, numbering conservatively in the hundreds, they built a crowd until at a thousand of them marched on the border and overpowered the gates. Border patrol, Texas Department of Public Safety, Texas Rangers, El Paso Police and County Sheriff's Departments were standing by.

Quite literally it was a question of who had the most muscle and meat. The crowd slammed into a wall of police. The Mexican authorities stood by until the El Paso mayor told the Juarez mayor that if he did not assist, El Paso would create a new check-point to validate Texas law.

The Juarez Mayor got the point. Soon there were two groups of people trying to surge the crossing point.

In the end, the media got the circus they wanted.

The people who wanted to surge past the crossing point were pushed back into Mexico.

April 12

Desert Zero, Auxiliary Camp Bravo, Fort Hood Texas
0700 hours CDT

Kincaid looked over his special Shark Hunter file, all the files, training plans, training aids and after-action reports. Everything fit neatly into an expansion folder ten inches thick.

Kincaid slowly looked over the contents and remembered all the things he endured and all the accomplishments he could never talk about.

All things Shark Hunter was dead now. Cindy and Earl were busy with Area Studies and training at Minuteman. Wendy was down here at Desert Zero, thoroughly absorbed with the Operations Center; running and training personnel.

Kincaid slowly finished packing the material away. Ever since Miss Gladys put the hook into him, he kept this file folder updated, current with events and, most important, two journals listing lessons learned along the way.

He set the file aside, opened his bottle of Jack Daniels and a can of coke. He drank to the end of his stupid dream of passing along his knowledge. Being relevant, being of some use. He filled his glass again.

Simmons and Waverly were profuse with thanks, showing them small things that counted at the right times. He disapproved of technology that replaced training. A simple sight that was used during Vietnam that cost less than fifty dollars worked better than a fifteen-hundred-dollar gadget and a three-hundred-page manual. Spend less than half that amount of money with one night of live fire training and an operator hits more targets with fewer rounds fired.

They listened to him. They heeded his warnings and practiced with precision. Walk, crawl, run: that was the motto. And most of all, ignore the phone calls from the politicians to hurry up and I need help here or there. Help this person and that. You have plenty of people.

For the first time in his life, he thanked God for a General. Brenda O'Cleary took a lot of heat off everyone's back.

Just then his X-Berry went off. It was O'Cleary and the Icon for UNSTACK THIS. He felt old.

"Hello John," Brenda said. "You left before I could congratulate you for the job you did." She was back in Washington relaxing before the day began.

Kincaid decided to piss her off. "Thank you, Brenda. You are glowing with your pregnancy. How far along are you?"

Brenda saw it coming a long way off. "It's too late in the day to start. I wanted to know whether you want to stay there or go back to Minuteman?"

Kincaid was tired of being yanked around. Everyone knew where he was all the time. He looked down at the X-Berry. It was too indispensable to leave behind, but it had his location within inches every second of the day.

"John?" she asked.

"I am tired," John said. "I'll call you later."

Kincaid ended the call. He really was very tired. It was the combination of age, medications and the last time he was shot. He was over sixty years of age. All the other men his age was rocking in chairs, drinking in the DAV and Legion Halls.

He wondered about the X-Berry. Should he leave it behind?

Brenda looked at the X-Berry and closed it.

"John acting like a sulking child again?" Dennis turned to her.

"Maybe," she said. "He is an old man, tired and nothing, and I mean nothing, is going to make him feel better. Missus Morgan said he still grieves for his wife, Karen. He has enough demons haunting him. He does not need me."

Dennis listened to it all and remembered the years he worked with him. John Kincaid was a lot of things. But deep inside him was the man who did it in spite of the odds or idiots reading books and manuals. "John can do it all, but he is an old man and I can relate to that. Give him a lot of slack. He has come through plenty of times in the past. You have to let him sort himself out."

"OK," she said. She shifted because Arthur turned head down and was kicking her ribs. If he kicked upward hard enough, it overwhelmed her bladder's ability to hold. She was forced to make a bathroom break every hour. At night, she had a portable toilet next to the bed. She had more than once woke up and peeing down her leg. Dennis being a light sleeper, would wake her every two hours so her son did not soil the bed or carpet.

Brenda smiled at the notion of begging the universe to move time faster and tell Arthur to get out of her. She smiled.

485 Glenmore Drive, Alexandria, Virginia

Amanda came with a small bag of "mommies' choice". They were small things expectant mothers eat while the baby in the last trimester made eating a sport. Usually, the uterus was growing to take over all the space inside mom. Little was left for the appetite that grew with the baby.

"How goes the pregnancy?" Amanda asked, extending the bag to Brenda who grabbed it, opened the contents and began eating. She marveled at how perfect it tasted.

"Thank you," Brenda said.

"I hate to do this but I need your stars."

Brenda looked at Amanda.

627 Benchley Court, Fort Myers, Virginia
1600 hours EDT

Brenda, in uniform, along with Amanda Edwards and Dennis drove up to the Pollard home and heard screaming. Neighbors were starting to converge. Brenda walked through them to the door. She tried turning the knob and it was locked. There was a sound like something was hit.

Brenda called over two sergeants. "Break it open," she said standing aside. The men hesitated for a few seconds, but kicked in the door. Brenda walked in ahead of everyone. Delores was on the floor crying.

The husband, Michael, turned and advanced two steps and froze at attention. Brenda went past him, knelt down and turned her face to see. She had a large welt on the side of her face.

Dennis, when he saw her face, lost his temper and grabbed Sergeant Pollard by the neck. He was dragging him out into the back yard. "Let's see if you hold your own against a grown man."

Brenda and Amanda helped her to her feet and over to a chair at the dining room table.

"Excuse me General," one of the men asked. "Pollard deserves his beating. Do you want us to stop it or manage it?"

Brenda looked outside. Pollard was on the ground. Dennis was taking his jacket off and rolling up his sleeves. He was saying something, but she could not hear him. A ring of men was surrounding them.

Brenda was fighting a furious debate within her. Beating down on a pregnant woman. No. Beating down a so-called man who abused a pregnant woman. Oh, hell yeah.

Brenda walked outside and into the ring. "Chair," she said. Amanda would say later that the look on her face was pure evil.

"Stay down," she said. "I am going to give you a choice. You volunteer for an ass beating we will call extra-training. After which you plead guilty in a court-marshal for a dishonorable discharge and no jail time. Or you will be arrested and our combined testimony will bury you in Fort Leavenworth for thirty years. Don't let the gears in your head confuse you. The testimony of a four-star General and the wife of the Chairman of the Joint Chiefs of Staff along with at least twelve others carries a lot of weight. Decide. Quickly."

Pollard looked at Dennis and the crowd around him. "I didn't want to do. She made me crazy."

"Time's up. Dennis he is trying to escape."

Dennis picked the boy and drew back for a roundhouse right.

"Thirty years, thirty years," he said and held his hands up to protect himself. He started crying. Dennis released him and allowed Pollard to collapse to the ground.

"Coward," Dennis said as the Military Police arrived. They took everyone's statement and arrested Sergeant Michael Pollard. He was handcuffed and started crying.

Amanda rode with Delores in the ambulance as she was taken to the hospital for a thorough exam.

485 Glenmore Drive, Alexandria, Virginia
2200 hours EDT

The phone rang and caught Brenda just as she was falling asleep. For once, young Arthur was going to sleep at the same time. Brenda looked at one of the phones she carried with her.

It was Amanda. "Well girlfriend, I just got home. Delores is staying with me for the time being. The door on her home is broken, as you know."

Brenda chuckled. "How is she?"

Amanda sighed. "Better after the last of four investigators left her alone at the hospital. Both her and her soon to borne daughter are good. She is due this week. The doctors said she was fine. She has an appointment on Tuesday to see her doctor. Time for me to go to bed. She is fine. Just thought I would inform you so something else is off your plate."

"Call me if you need anything or something happens."

Amanda changed her tone. "You rest and relax or I'll tell Tom you need a nanny."

"Way ahead of you," Brenda said. "By the way. Why didn't you just get him to go with you, instead of me?"

"Simple really," Amanda said. "I figured something like this may happen. A pregnant General was a good touch and Dennis needed the exercise."

"Good night," Brenda said with a chuckle.

April 13

Desert Zero, Fort Hood, Texas
1700 hours CDT

Lieutenant Colonel Simmons looked over the report he sent in to General O'Cleary every week. He looked it over and compared it to the template he used in order to cover all the points the General wanted to know about.

His unit was now fully manned, trained and certified to conduct combat operations as directed by the National Command Authority. Simmons never could pin down exactly who that was. He guessed that so long as the codes matched, that was good enough for him.

The ink on the certification wasn't even dry before all the wantabees descended on him. Some of them were officers who out ranked him; giving unneeded advice and trying to find a way to make him bend their way. The others came from all the three letters needing fresh meat.

410

The group that worried him the most was this new United States Police Force. Being a new organization with a broad mandate, they could normally absorb anything they wanted.

The ISA was another worry. Admiral Hazlet was rumored to one of those scary few with a rare combination of large intellect and "street smarts". He spent nearly all his career in the bowels of every secret anything. Chances are even his toilet paper was redated.

Simmons always wrote in his comments all the people who tried to back door him and his unit. During this morning's formation, he cautioned his men to be vigilant. A lot of people were trying anything, anything to violate their orders.

The new Legal Officer was very careful. That was the problem. He was young, slick and always there to listen in. Simmons was going push him forward in the fight. Far forward. This Captain was going to be trouble.

The only good thing that happened was two letters he was given to him by General O'Cleary. Signed non-interference directives from the Department of Justice and the Internal Security Agency.

General O'Cleary was scheduled for an appointment with the President for the same thing. Privately, she was looking for something that would survive her not being there to protect them. She patted her stomach.

April 14

Desert Zero, Fort Hood, Texas
0600 hours UTC (0100 hours EDT)

The Pentagon disguised as the National Command Authority, in conjunction with the DEA, sent a Mission Concept to the Savage Rabbits to conduct combat operations against a drug convoy moving north within the next 24 hours.

The few former members of the Savage Rabbits would remember this area. The Reserva de la Biosfera El Pinacatey Gran Desierto de Altar was the designated target area. Members of the Sanchine Cartel hid out and concentrated their operations in this Nature Preserve because there was a political moratorium against conducting operations inside such an area.

The Sanchine cartel was guilty of attacking a Cavalry unit last year. The Cavalry unit was unarmed due to the Rules of Engagement. The cartel attacked them wanting military equipment. They were stopped at the border, but the remnants of the attackers gathered in the Preserve. Several days later, the US Army, code named Operation 79, attacked them and the Savage Rabbits were there to help nail the coffin shut.

This mission was nearly the same. Operation 79 was a good template. Simmons read the Mission Concept several times waiting for the others to arrive.

Waverly and Kincaid arrived at the same time. They stopped at the door where Kincaid said to Waverly. "Go get them Sergeant Major." Kincaid shook hands and waited for Waverly to enter first.

Inside, the mayhem was ramping up as the newest piece of technology instantly grabbed everyone's attention. On a closed loop intranet, laptops lit up with MICON 1-001. Staff sections would open the laptop that one of the operators kept constantly updated. Simmons took incoming information and easily disseminated information to the correct parties at the touch of a button.

Simmons was allowed concentrate on building a plan instead of constantly repeating himself. Six men from the support cycle were busily creating a three-dimensional model of the objective area in an eight-foot by eight-foot sand table.

0300 hours CDT

The Savage Rabbits consisted of nine sections of 25 men each. Sections One, Two and Three were placed in A Company. Section Four, Five and Six were placed in B Company. Section Seven, Eight, and Nine were placed in Company C.

Using the same rotational system used last time, A Company was the primary Tactical company ready to launch on two-hour notice. B Company was the Support Company assigned to assist, supplement or reinforce the Tactical company. C Company was the stand-down Company. This

Company was allowed to train, relax and perform Garrison duties. They cleaned the area, manned the gates, ran roving patrols and taking time off.

The cycles ran for twenty-one days. A Company will rotate to standdown at the end of the cycle. B Company will be the Tactical company and C Company will become support.

Just then the new Legal Officer came in. Cpt George Templeton, walked in wearing his Class B garrison uniform.

Simmons stopped him. "Captain Templeton. Leave, put on a fatigue uniform. You will accompany the lead section to ensure the Rules of Engagement are adhered to. I will not allow men to die if you are here thinking too long."

"But Sir...." Templeton was searching for a good reason to stay behind.

"Now Captain!" Simmons said turning his back and focusing on the fire support plan with Captain Younger, his Air Force Fire Support Coordinator.

0430 hours CDT

Simmons was ready. He called in all the commanders and Section Leaders to publish his operations order 45 minutes ago.

Runners were sent to Company A and B. Two squadrons of Ospreys would be here at 0800 hours. Simmons was capitalizing on everyone being relaxed. Most of the Cartels knew the Americans attacked at dusk, mid-mornings and at dawn. The CIA confirmed everyone ate breakfast a half hour after dawn and relaxed until mid-morning.

Simmons wanted to hit them at 0800 hours. His attack was planned to land directly on top of them. Infrared satellite coverage showed the majority of personnel was camped on one side of mountain. The Mexican government had confirmed that no civilians were in the area.

Templeton wanted to say something, but his mind was on the uncomfortable equipment he was carrying. The Executive Officer, Major Michael Childers looked at him like he was an idiot when Templeton asked for two soldiers to be his guards.

Childers grabbed his arm and took him to the side. "Captain, I will not waste manpower on someone who is a coward. If you run, I'll shoot you. If you get someone killed, I will dedicate my life to see to it you are cemented to Leavenworth."

Just then Kendal walked past him carrying a rucksack full of radios. She nodded to the officers and went to the Communications section, obviously to receive today's codes.

Childers leaned in closer. "Seems that woman has more balls than you." He walked away before he said something else that could get him into trouble.

0630 – 0930 hours CDT

Every part of the planning and preparation was complete. All the equipment was packed. Ammunition was distributed. All unit and sub units are briefed and rehearsed.

A and B Company were launching on this mission. C Company was standing by in case of reinforcement and/or search-rescue operations.

Exactly on schedule, the Apaches and AC-130 gunships launched from their Arizona bases and went to soften up the target, ahead of the ground attack. Simmons took Kincaid's suggestion and insisted that if the Aviation Unit's legal officer wanted to interfere, he will be on the Command-and-Control aircraft. The Aviation Commander concurred.

Kendal squeezed in alongside with Simmons carrying his command communications radio nets. She had a tablet which managed the communications nets and easily transmitted messages as Simmons should direct.

Both squadrons of Ospreys landed at Desert Zero and loaded up the Savage Rabbits. Simmons donned a set of head phones and talked directly to the Aviation Commander in the lead helicopter. All the aviation assets launched on schedule. The Ospreys spread out in a well-known and rehearsed pattern. Last year they were doing this for the original Savage Rabbits.

Forty-seven minutes later, the Ospreys crossed over the US-Mexico border.

Simmons was informed that the Apaches and AC-130's were on station and were exchanging fire with groups on the ground. The Command-and-Control ship and the continuously orbiting AWACS aircraft said none of their fire was coordinated. The Apaches dived and fired on the ground targets.

Simmons was pleased. The more people and hardened sites the Apaches killed, the fewer problems he would have to deal with.

Simmons leaned out the troop door and looked over the battle space. His original plan did not need to be changed. He told Kendal to inform A and B Companies to use their Primary Landing Zones.

Simmons orbited the areas at the maximum speed the Osprey could produce. Simmons desired to be in as many places at one time as he could. Fortunately, the Osprey Commander knew how to maneuver his craft to allow Simmons the maximum view of the battle space and all his units while they attacked their targets.

Simmons' headphones were tied directly into the communications package Kendal was carrying and operating. The seventeen-inch diagonal screen on her tablet showed a speech to text dialog for the four to seven frequencies she had to monitor.

All Simmons had to do was tell Kendal who he wanted to talk to, the "channel" was selected and sent to his headphones. Kendal had a running battle trying to sort through all the signals and keep Simmons up to the second on all signals. To the uninitiated, all of the overlapping conversations sounded like gibberish.

Suddenly, a helicopter went down north of his location. Simmons ordered a C Company team to get the crew and passengers.

In a repeat of last year, the Cartels were using this area to conceal and store their drugs. Unlike last year, they were more spread out. None of the cartel members were concentrated in one place.

A Company landed between three concentrations of personnel after their dedicated AC-130 destroyed anything that was military. Captain Baldwin, the company commander, spread out his men and had them check out everything. The overhead AC-130 said eight trucks were coming their way at high speed. Estimated time of arrival is 10 minutes.

Baldwin keyed his mike and recalled the Ospreys. They said they could be on the ground in five minutes.

Perfect.

The Section sergeant, SFC Gallagher, called in a problem. "We found four each five-ton trucks, full of cash. My guess is that there is thirty to fifty million dollars."

Baldwin radioed to Simmons and said he did not have time or aviation assets to seize the money or move it. "Can I burn it?"

Simmons looked to the legal officer who was strapped in his seat, breathing into a bag.

"Burn it," he said.

Gallagher used two sections to tear open the bundles and spread the paper money all over the ground. Eight men came over with eight cans of diesel and gasoline. As the Ospreys were coming in for a landing. Gallagher through a lit bundle of one-hundred-dollar bills into the pile. The flames initially shot up one hundred feet and then settled down to five or so feet.

The other section came over with the other cans of fuel. They opened them and through the cans on the pile.

Simmons was calling them to board and depart NOW.

B Company, commanded by Captain Mark Tenneson landed on the periphery of a large band of men. The small arms were ineffective as Tenneson spread his men out. Tenneson was summoned to a tarp covered area. Marked maps and written paper in several languages were all over the area. Most important to Tenneson, were what appeared to be inventories.

The aerial components were reporting that trucks filled with heavily armed men coming his way. Simmons turned that problem over to the AC-130s and told them to destroy them.

Simmons decided that this was good enough. He told all his sub-unit commanders to begin extraction operations. This was good enough for "blooding everyone down".

Simmons flew in an arc around the objective area. He checked his map board and checked to insure everyone was picked up and no one was left behind. He ordered his Osprey to turn north after everyone had left the objective area.

Simmons breathed a sigh of relief when his Osprey crossed the border. Everyone was home. No casualties and no one was left behind. Captain Templeton was still breathing into a bag.

Headquarters, Texas 36th Infantry Division
Camp Aubry, Texas

Folcroft turned in his after-action report. That single action allowed his unit to pack everything up and return to their homes and civilian jobs. The Officers in his Brigade headquarters and sub-ordinate units were rushing out the door. In some instances, they turned everything over to the NCOs and left.

Major General Harold Corcoran called him into his office and closed the door. "Colonel, you did a fantastic job on the border. Do you envision any problems with the Brigades deployment back to the border in six months?"

Folcroft shifted in his chair. He decided to repeat what he already wrote down in his after-action report. "The Brigade as a whole on the enlisted side is first rate. Most of them are Iraq and Afghanistan veterans. My Sergeant Major is impressed with them and that says a lot for him."

Folcroft took a deep breath. "The Officers are a different story. Half of them just want the prestige of the rank. Most of them I will leave behind if we go to war. NCOs in charge are better than bad officers. I have a thick file full of 'mommy may I pretty please, please, please, go home early. Nearly half of them left early and turned over everything to the NCOs and left as fast as they could. I altered their financials accordingly."

General Corcoran pulled on his ear. One of his son-in-law's was in Folcroft's Brigade. Roger did come home two days ago saying he was released early. "I take it you didn't release anyone early?"

"No sir," Folcroft said, "even when your son-in-law reminded me at least twice who he was."

Corcoran pulled on his ear. "I have that problem across the board with this division. I will be honest and say I really need you to be the division's chief of staff. But I need at least one highly competent brigade commander."

"Thank you, Sir," Folcroft said.

Corcoran held up his hand. "Your Brigade will rotate back to border duty in another 6 months. Nominate some of your NCOs for commissioning as officers. I'll find some nothing-type place to put those bad officers to get them out of the way."

"Yes Sir," Folcroft said. "Word of warning, the politics will get in the way. I will support you all I can."

Both men stood and shook hands.

April 15

Room D-312, George Washington University Hospital, Washington D.C.
1400 hours EDT

Delores Virginia Pollard held her new daughter, Sarah Amelia Pollard. This little girl was born at 7:34 this morning. 7 pounds, 6 ounces, pink, healthy, blonde hair and quiet for a baby. The nurse put her on Delores' chest within seconds of being born and the cord cut and closed off. Delores swore that Sarah looked at her mother and smiled.

A courtesy message was delivered to the military stockade along with a picture for Prisoner Michael Pollard. He reportedly cried when the note and picture were delivered to him. Maybe he could see her in twenty or more years. Chances are his parental rights will be stripped from him forever.

Amanda was there with her. Delores' parents were coming and should arrive tonight. An anonymous donor paid for plane tickets and hotel rooms. Amanda was there to hold her hand through the delivery and the recovery.

Desert Zero, Fort Hood Texas
1500 hours CDT

418

Oh, the stupid keeps rolling along. The Secret Service and the Treasury Department swooped in demanding to know who gave him the authority to destroy US currency.

Simmons tried to tell them that it was a combat situation. Everyone watched the helmet cameras and aerial surveillance footage. Simmons made a decision not to leave the money in cartel hands. He also did not have the time to secure and cart off the money.

The agents said that the money was supposed to be secured, returned to US control, the serial numbers recorded and only then be destroyed. They were also arguing over who had jurisdiction to arrest him.

Simmons also said that the next time, they are invited to come along and take possession of the cash. "Bring your own security. I will not waste a soldier's life protecting a coward."

The agents were arguing over that statement, when Deputy US Attorney Jane Rickover walked into the room. She scared anyone who knew her. She informed them all that Federal Judge Nathan Farragut had ruled that a commissioned officer in a combat situation had the authority to destroy currency if that officer could certify that the situation was too dangerous to allow for collecting and returning the currency to US Control.

Secret Service looked at Treasury and Treasury looked at the Secret Service.

Jane Rickover walked over to Simmons and handed him her business card. "If the government gives you any more problems, call me. Making bureaucrats cry is cat nip to me."

Simmons thanked her.

At another part of Desert Zero, Earl Locklear met up with Wendy Kendal outside the operations center. Locklear transferred a stack of boxes full of classified updates.

Both of them walked outside and warmly welcomed each other. Kendal was given the afternoon off.

Both went to her room and disappeared behind a locked door.

Room D-312, George Washington University Hospital, Washington D.C.

Brenda and Dennis O'Cleary came to Delores Pollard's room. Both of them entered and dropped off a small bag of presents.

"I am looking forward to my turn in June," Brenda said, patting her stomach.

"Are the investigators leaving you alone in here?" Dennis asked.

"Oh yes, Sergeant Major," she said looking down at Sarah. "It helps when I ignore them. I asked them to wait until I come home. They said they need to hurry. The trial is in four months."

Just then, Delores' parents arrived. Everyone talked until it was just Delores' family. Amanda, Brenda and Dennis left to allow them bonding time.

April 17

United States Embassy, Paris, France
0700 hours Alpha (0300 hours EDT)

The US Ambassador to France was in his car leaving the embassy to take him to the airport so he could fly home and attend his daughter's wedding in St. Louis. He was tired and hoped he could sleep on the plane ride.

The limousine turned on the avenue Gabriel and drove on to the airport. They had plenty of time, so the driver tried to give the Ambassador a smooth ride.

The driver looked to his right and saw something unusual. Too late, he noticed that a man was aiming an RPC-7 rocket launcher. He stomped down on the accelerator, but the limousine was too heavy and unwieldy. The rocket impacted on the passenger side. The fireball inside the vehicle incinerated everything.

The limousine crashed into two other vehicles and burned furiously.

The terrorist dropped the launcher and disappeared.

White House, Washington D.C.

General O'Cleary arrived early to her appointment with the President to brief him on the status of the Counter-Narcotics Mission and the Savage Rabbits.

"General O'Cleary," the President said, flashing his trademark smile. She could see the difference in him. The stress and pressure were taking its toll on him. "How are you doing? If I remember correctly, your baby is due in June."

"Yes Sir," she said. "I am fine for the time being. My son is demanding to get out now and frankly," she paused as Arthur kicked her. "I wish it were today."

The President pulled around a raised hassock for her. "I remember that my wife loved elevating her feet."

O'Cleary thought about the protocol, but suddenly did not care. She lifted her feet and instantly felt better. "Thank you, Sir."

"After all you have done for this great and mighty nation, I am honored," the President said, suddenly remembering something. He stood and went to the hospitality cart. "If I recall correctly, you like apple juice."

"Yes Sir," O'Cleary said. The fluid that built in her legs had finally eased off. When the President brought over the glass, she was ready to begin.

The President nodded to her to begin.

O'Cleary handed over the after-action report. "Mister President, the Savage Rabbits conducted their first mission last Tuesday. No casualties, estimated two billion dollars of illegal drugs were destroyed in place and between thirty to fifty million dollars of US currency was burned in place. There was a small altercation with the Secret Service and the Treasury Department over destroying the currency versus recovering it. Overall, it was a well-executed operation."

The President opened the report and realized he needed time to read and study this one. General O'Cleary was not someone to waste words. "I'll give this report a proper reading tonight. There is another issue I wish to discuss and I want to give this discussion the privacy it needs. To be frank, I am tired of all the different groups who want control the Savage

Rabbits for their own private Army. Even the new United States Police Force put in their pitch."

O'Cleary took a deep breath. "I have the same problem. Too many people with power on their minds are trying to clog my schedule and time, with reasons to do things their way. At least Delta Force is honest. They need manpower that is unit rated, trained and has high morale. By that, I mean they could have a unit with comradery that has a fierce loyalty to itself and each other. But they would only give a token interest to the core mission. The same is true of the others, but they are not so honest."

The President was solidly locked with the same opinion. "Tell me your opinion of the US Police Force."

O'Cleary took a deep breath again. "The core idea is good¦ but there are not enough controls to prevent someone in the future from using it to further their political or private ends."

The President's face clouded, but he knew better than scold her. "Can you elaborate on that?"

"Mister President, all the reasons for establishing the USPF are valid. But no one thought of Americans in this mix. We have a unique problem in dealing with people who believe that the police are servants, not masters. Lip service has been given to the reasons the American people truly need the USPF. Vigilantism is up because criminals outnumber the local police and the judges and prosecutors just release the criminals, sometimes for the tiniest reasons. Plain and simple, everyone is scared and strangers are not exactly the answer."

"Expensive jails are the real answer. Put crooks in jail, not the streets. If it is about money, what is more important: $15,000 a year in jail or one life?"

The President smiled at the true honesty he learned to respect from her.

"Mister President," O'Cleary continued. "I am here to specifically request an official order banning every civilian and military agency and entity from interfering or trying to usurp the Savage Rabbits or its authority. I don't want someone to just show up and say "Heal boy, and do as I tell you. This toilet paper says do it."

422

The President rubbed his ear. "It will have to be an Executive Order and it will take a few days. Call your Savage Rabbits and tell them to find a hole in the schedule for me to visit. That should add to the invulnerability factor. Tell them, no dog and pony show. I just want to meet and talk with the men."

"Yes Sir," O'Cleary said.

April 18

Embassy of the United States, Pariser Platz 2, Berlin, Germany
0900 hours Bravo (0200 hours EST)

Ambassador William Barque finished his weekly walk in the Schlosspark Bellievue and was walking back to his vehicle. Two of his PSAs watched as a thin woman in a cat suit ran towards him. The suit was so thin, nothing could be hidden. One of them murmured that her pulse was visible. The woman ran so fast, no one could catch her. The girl came up to the Ambassador, spun very fast, punched him in the neck and rammed the heel of her hand under his nose. His nose was broken, sending the splinters into his brain. He was dead before he hit the ground. The PSAs were very startled. The woman shot away fast into a throng of people and vanished.

42 Chesapeake Drive, Spring, Texas
1000 hours CDT

Jasper Folcroft was an automobile mechanic by trade. Next door to his house was his 5,500 square foot garage. He had a thriving business on-going like all the others in the National Guard. Unlike the others, he did not advertise it in your face. He just had a small decal in the window of his truck.

His son, Michael, ran the garage floor. His other son, James ran the office and kept the books. Both had too much to do to be in the Guard. Both of them went into the active army for 3 years and got out. "All Americans should serve their country," Folcroft said. "Then they can appreciate being Americans."

423

Unlike the rest of his officers, Folcroft did not need to be at work every day and worry about being away from "their real life".

Jasper spent this Saturday morning in the closed garage looking at what he spent a lifetime building. He pulled the top from a can of beer and toasted what his life built.

"Knock, knock," Command Sergeant Major Terrance Barker said, walking in on him. Terry Barker was his ace in the hole. Folcroft always trusted his Sergeant Major.

"Hello Terry, come in. Want a beer?"

Barker smiled. He never drank and Folcroft knew it. It was almost a joke between them. I was told you had a private meeting with the General. The word is that the look on your face was almost like death itself. It's just like I was told." He sat down on a stool.

Folcroft made a cursory look around and turned on a radio. "The General wants me to create a full-time brigade. Trouble is brewing and 'he' needs a response. We are seizing millions from the cartels every month. That's how Austin is going to pay for it. No tax money involved."

Barker smiled. "It's a long time coming. How accurate is the threat?"

"You and I will be briefed at Camp Aubrey on Tuesday."

Barker shifted in his chair. "What about the officers? Their attention span is three days or the quarterly balance sheet."

Folcroft smiled. "I intend to educate, create and commission new officers. Sorry, but I am taking some of your NCOs."

Baker smiled again.

April 19

Desert Zero Auxiliary Camp Bravo, Fort Hood, Texas
1500 hours CDT

Gunnery Sergeant Cynthia Morgan arrived with a team guarding the arrival of five new M-125 sniper rifles. She had been practicing for three months on the rifle. But she would readily tell anyone that Wendy Kendal was better than her.

Waverly and Captain Gerald Marcene, the S-4 supply officer, were there to receive the rifles. It took almost an hour to inventory and sign for all the rifles and its mountains of accessory equipment. Kendal came out and warmly welcomed the M-125's. She hugged Cindy too.

Kendal was having a love affair in broad day-light in front of everybody. With the voice and tone similar to a lover's voice, she recited the specifications. What really made everyone uncomfortable was she recited from memory the DOP (Data on Performance) going from 300 to 3300 meters.

"Enough Miss Kendal," Simmons said tapping her nose. "If you tone it down, I'll let you have plenty of experience once we set up a range."

Kendal complied, but still had a dreamy look to her face.

Morgan tapped on her shoulder. "Come on Chief Kendal." She picked up a stack of DOP books and pulled Wendy along. "There is a lot to be done first."

Kendal did not want to leave. "They need to checked first, then laid to rest."

Morgan looked over her head to the others who tried to hide their snickering. "I did that already. We have work to do beforehand." Turning to Simmons she asked. "Where can I billet?"

Waverly said. "Go the Auxiliary Camp B. Chief Kendal is billeted there along with Master Sergeant Locklear and Sergeant Major Kincaid."

1700 hours CDT

Kendal, Morgan and baggage arrived. Kendal dropped her bag at Kincaid's door. She banged on the door. "It's me," she screamed. "Open up or I'll do this all night."

"Go ahead," Kincaid said from behind her. Locklear was behind him. "Earl and I are busy. We are boarding helicopters for an overview of an objective area prior to a section raid tonight."

"Fine," Kendal said, pointing to Morgan. "You remember this woman?"

Kincaid pushed past both women and unlocked his door. Behind him Morgan dragged her baggage inside. "What is this?" he asked.

"I'm tired and the S-4 with the room keys is at Fort Hood until midnight." Morgan stood up to Kincaid. "I'll move in tonight and go away in the morning. Now I need a shower and you need to leave so I can sleep."

Kendal looked at Earl and motioned off to the side. They gleefully left those two lovebirds alone. Kendal stopped and had to fan the shit. She peeked in Kincaid's room. "Cindy, do you two need lubrication."

Cindy slammed the door in her face.

Kendal skipped over to Earl. "How much time do you have?"

"An hour," Earl said smiling.

April 20

0500 hours CDT

Kincaid woke up to a pounding sound at the door. Kendal did that every morning. PT did not start until 0600 in the morning. If there was something important, his pager would fire, the phone would ring and Smiley Face would not bother to knock. No matter how many times he changed the locks, Smiley Face made a new key and could easily walk in on him.

Simmons and Waverly laughed when he complained.

Kincaid was very groggy when he arrived here at 3 am. Morgan was asleep on his bed. "Aw crap," he said. He debated wither or not to get a key or break down a door. Finally, he came in, took a shower and put on some shorts. He pushed her across the bed to the wall and climbed into it. He was not even settled in when the nude woman in bed with him moved across the bed towards him.

Finally, he pulled out the portable air pump and inflated his air mattress. He picked up Morgan and put her on the air mattress with a sheet and blanket over her. It was his bed after all and the room was too hot.

He woke up and slid his feet off the bed.

"Good morning shit for brains," Morgan said waking up. She stood, put on her PT uniform and walked out without closing the door. He stood and dressed for PT. Of course, she left a mess. He picked up his stuff. Hers, he stuffed into a corner.

Kincaid walked out of the room and went to the coffee pot. Kendal and Locklear were already there.

"You're a dickhead," Morgan said.

Kincaid sipped his coffee. "If I came into your room, naked, you could have me charged with rape or some other crime. Perhaps had you asked first or at least left a note, things would be easier. I told you already, I am not over Karen or I might never be over her. I am not Zach and you are not Karen. If we come together, I wish to ease into it. Too fast is a violation of my memories of Karen and Zach. You kept Zach all to yourself and excluded the rest of us from him with your attitude and childish possession of him."

Morgan wanted to lose her temper, but realized he was baiting her. "John, I made more than my share of mistakes. I do not need my face constantly being smeared in it. I loved Zach because he saw something in me, I could never see. I just wonder if Zach could love me the same way you love Karen."

Kincaid sat down heavily. "I refuse to be your confessor. The end of this conversation is that Zach was Zach. The only answer is buried in Montana at your home. Right here and right now we are defending a nation that does not deserve the sacrifice we are making. If you want, I can allow you to slowly see yourself. That time is dependent on this mission."

"Good morning," Earl and Wendy said in unison.

Israeli Air Defense Force Headquarters, Location undisclosed
1600 hours (Charlie) 0800 hours EDT

1st Lieutenant Joseph Kramer was watching his specialized radar screen when suddenly a blip showed up. This radar specialized in tracking radar "rubble" as it was called.

Even highly stealthy aircraft through off "rubble" signals as it flew along. This radar took the "rubble" and pieced it all together to find aircraft-like drones.

The computer said it was flying at fifteen thousand feet at two hundred and fifty miles an hour. The call sign and other flight data was almost 'gibberish." He called on the net to inquire about this sighting. This image was closing on a course towards Tel Aviv. It was estimated it will be there in forty-five minutes.

General Houssi came over and looked at the screen. As he studied it, the other operators called in saying nothing was on their screens.

Houssi suddenly straightened up. "Call this in to the Air Force. Launch interceptors. He ran to his office, slammed the door and pulled down the blinds on his windows. Three minutes later, he came out to his duty section. He grabbed the red phone and used words nobody had ever heard before.

The shadowy signal was displayed on the master board. Houssi was constantly on the phone. That signal was fifteen minutes from Israel.

The alert on-call aircraft, two sections of two F-15E aircraft were flying as fast as they could. The alert aircraft were over Jordan now and the on-call aircraft were five minutes behind them.

Houssi and the other operators watched as the aircraft were given permission to fire. Both F-15s launched their Sparrow AIM/7F/M/F which quickly accelerated to Mach 4 and closed the 30 kilometers to their target. The detonation was very large and visible for tens of miles.

All radio communications became a squeal.

Houssi and others ripped the phones over ears off as the master board flashed white. He started barking orders over everyone trying to talk at once. "That was a nuclear blast. Move a Global Hawk over the area. I want blast data and nuclear fallout for that area. Get the equipment re-started. Get me the Prime Minister and General Hannad.

2100 Hours

428

General Hannad went into Houssi's office, closed the door and activated the counter surveillance equipment.

"Greeting's sir," Houssi said

"Good catch," Hannad said.

Houssi held up a hand. "Lieutenant Kramer gets the credit. He programmed it to catch all the stray signals he calls "rubbish".

"How many know about the signal from the drone?" Hannad asked.

"Just me," Houssi said. "I only pulled it out to check the call sign and put it back in. I just told everyone, it was classified and refused to elaborate."

Hannad relaxed. "I admit I was scared for our ability to use drones when the Americans lost that particular drone. The technology is out there, but central to it was a hidden transponder mode buried deep in the program. I was briefed on it when I visited the US last year. They wanted some way to shut down every drone in the region should a war begins."

Houssi looked at Hannad. "They intentionally lost a drone."

Hannad said. "They allowed it to be taken by a computer hack that was transmitted to it. The Russians and Chinese will copy it and then they may never find the bug."

Houssi took a deep sip of his coffee. "I don't have any real information on the warhead."

"Small tactical," Hannad said. "At least one and half kilotons. The range of that drone originally was two thousand miles. But take out a lot of surveillance gear and replace it with a warhead reduces that range and it was one way. Until we can get a good guess at the weight, we can't point to anyone specific. Luckily or not, the explosion was in Jordan."

"What do the Jordanians know?"

Hannad took a deep breath. "We are saying nothing for now. Fortunately, none of their equipment was hardened against an Electromagnetic Pulse or EMP. That fried their equipment and any records showing us violating their airspace."

Houssi looked at his superior. "Thank God for good graces."

Desert Zero, Fort Hood, Texas
1700 hours EDT

Simmons looked over the weekly report. Kincaid's idea was for one of Fort Hood's UH-74 Lakota to overfly the objective area 5 minutes before the attack. Fortunately, this particular Lakota has the new enclosed tail rotor called the Fenestron. It severely reduced the noise produced by a helicopter. Kincaid and an Air Force Technician oversaw the battle area using the Forward-Looking-Infrared-Radars (FLIR) to locate personnel and equipment.

Kincaid transmitted all the information Simmons needed to direct his forces. Simmons now needed to "produce" a dedicate cadre of aerial observers. Simmons chuckled. He was using a lot of Kincaid's language. Simmons had to admit it, Kincaid could insult you and make it sound like a compliment.

Chief Kendal and Master Sergeant Locklear were in a contest to outdo each other. Both of them were producing a solid group of snipers who were deadly serious in their endeavor. Twenty men started the course. Kendal said maybe seven of them might meet the standard. Simmons wanted more and Kendal asked how far down he wanted the standards to be lowered.

"With respects, Colonel," Kendal said. "This training is something that cannot short changed. Ninety-five percent of our purpose is providing you with intelligence. The last bit is shooting someone. Every scrap of information they will give you, saves our lives."

Simmons respected that answer. "Very well put Chief. Do it your way. But I will expect good work from your graduates."

Kendal smiled. "I love that kind of challenge."

April 21

Texas 36th Infantry Division, Camp Aubry, Texas
1400 hours CDT

Folcroft and Barker arrived and were ushered into the Division Commander's conference room. At exactly 9 am, General Corcoran walked in with his G-2, Intelligence Officer, Lieutenant Colonel Vagary. Folcroft always thought that he had the perfect name.

Corcoran began. "Colonel, Sergeant Major this not exactly a classified briefing, but don't talk about this to anyone." He waited until both men nodded. "Colonel Vagary will conduct a detailed briefing of the situation on both sides of the border, with emphasis on Texas."

Folcroft and Barker listened intently and were deeply focused. Barker did ask a few times for Vagary to slow down. Over half of the information was never reported by the news media. Numerous personalities north and south of the border were profiting from the flow north and south of the border. Those places in Texas that did not have the wall, were open by design of certain politicians.

True figures on human trafficking, drug smuggling and other similar crimes were given. Some of the information was so much different from what was reported to the general public.

Folcroft and Barker were nearly exhausted from all the effort listening, focusing and remembering all that data. Fortunately, Corcoran allowed a twenty-minute break when Vagary was finished. Outside, both men stood off and had a private discussion.

"What do you think?" Folcroft asked.

"Think," Barker said with incredulity. "I think we were lied to for too long a length of time. I hope the General has a real plan to sink my teeth into. Otherwise, I cannot wear the uniform anymore."

Folcroft looked off towards the Headquarters building. "Terry, I have a feeling that things are going to go bad, real soon. You and I studied history. History is repeating itself. I hope he does not want us to rule over American Citizens. It's rumored that active-duty Generals have been selected who would say that they would, if ordered, fire on American citizens."

"I refuse," Barker said with iron in his voice.

"It's time," Folcroft said and walked inside. "Me too."

General Corcoran entered the conference room with a large three-ring binder.

Barker looked around and they were alone.

"Yes, Sergeant Major," the General said. "For now, we are alone. We need to go over the main points without my staff finding ways to make this complicated. And No, I am not briefing something illegal that demands doing this without witnesses."

"Yes Sir," Barker said.

"Moving on," Corcoran said giving Barker the 'look'. "By direction of Governor," Corcoran said, sliding a document over to Folcroft. "We are creating an ad hoc fourth Brigade. You will be released from the 56th and placed in command of this Brigade. It will be funded as a full-time unit, year-round." Corcoran slid over another document. It had a unit chart showing the units to be assigned. "You will have two battalions of light infantry plus one battalion consisting of combat support and service support units. All of that is on the unit chart. If the situation requires it, armor, aviation or other units will be activated and placed at your disposal."

Finally, Corcoran slid the large three-ring binder over to Folcroft. "That is your mission plus all the information on unit property and dispositions. Of particular mention is all the Humvees you will get. All of them are going to be up-armored. My concept is a Cavalry type unit. Quick to move where you are needed and well-armed if needed."

Corcoran continued with emphasis. "Your mission is to use this unit to plug the holes in the border coverage that the US Army is no longer supplying units for because of the politics of immigration. You will operate as a fluid unit to apprehend immigrants and turn them over to the Texas Department of Public Safety. National Guard units are allowed to perform law enforcement duties under the law by order of the Governor."

Folcroft leaned forward. "I wish to have final say on the personnel, especially the officers for all the reasons I stated already. This unit cannot be used for political appointees

432

wanting prestige jobs or places for powerful political allies to dump their kids to 'grow them up'. The Sergeant Major will have the same to say about the NCOs and possibly the enlisted men. I would rather be under-manned than having bad people that I have to fix the messes they create."

Corcoran sighed. "This is the problem we have. The Texas National Guard is not the regular Army. We are going to have to work with the hand we are dealt."

Folcroft was ready for that. "As far as the Officers, I am ready to put in the personal time, effort and some of the expense to grow my own officers from the NCO corps."

Corcoran glanced over to Barker who nodded back.

Folcroft continued. "Sir, I cannot over-emphasize my statement that it is better to field an undermanned unit than one with bad officers. I am personally tired of office holders and idiots who cannot teach their dick to piss straight. The officers and NCOs can be found if merit is used instead of politics."

Corcoran rubbed his jaw. He already had this conversation with the Governor. The Governor was sympathetic, but non-committal. He decided to go for it. "Gentlemen, all I can do and say is that I will be your shield for as long as I am the Commanding General. If we succeed, I can defend against the politicos. I can defend you. But I need help and results to show the governor."

Corcoran turned to Barker. "Sergeant Major, I want your input."

"Sir, I discussed this in detail with the Colonel yesterday. All those problems he out-lined, we were doing to work on within our brigade. Now, I want training time and facilities to train my future NCOs from the men who were artificially held down because of politics. I want to be free to train without interference. Merit has to be carved in stone. Period."

Corcoran should have known better than to give this assignment to this team. "Your units will have to manned first. We will meet in three months to assume command and start training. You have that time. You are authorized to activate five personnel from your brigade headquarters to assist. See me in one month for a progress report."

April 22

Office of the Governor, the Great State of Texas
1300 hours CDT

The Governor eagerly awaited the results of this poll. It was made under the radar to gage the public's temperature about stopping the flow of illegal immigrants into Texas. That question scored high. What scored higher was their opposition to drug trafficking, human trafficking, and smuggling in general.

The public wanted something to be done.

The Governor felt better about creating another Brigade headquarters. The beauty of the system was that a Brigade was only a one-hundred or one-hundred-and-fifty-man headquarters staff unit. All of its combat forces were attached or detached as the situation required. You could have only ground combat units. Or just medical units. Or just Engineer units. Or a mixture of any kind of units. Brigades are manned to suit the situation.

The Governor sat back, relishing a win-win policy. Texas was solidly behind him. Liberals from California be dammed.

April 23

Holiday Inn and Suites, north of Chattanooga, Tennessee
1700 hours EDT

Lieutenant Colonel Latham Thomas drove up to his hotel, parked near his room and stopped his car. He would never admit it, but he was enjoying this job.

Those Special Forces guys were impressing him. The ten men on this "A" Team were sharp and more importantly, they were problem solvers. If there was a problem, they offered options and solutions which allowed the officers to concentrate on executing the solutions. The Team's officers might be intimidated that a field grade officer from Public Affairs was watching them and it appears that the NCOs did all the work and the Officers just stood around.

434

The Captain kept drifting over to Thomas from time-to-time trying to get a 'feel' for what he was going to report.

Finally, Thomas had enough. "Captain, everything I am reporting on is intended to be a positive light on the Army and the mission you are doing. So, relax."

Thomas looked at his watch and decided to leave for the day.

Thomas got out of the car and walked over to his room. He opened it up and a woman clad in blue lingerie was laying on his bed.

Thomas had enough presence of brain to close and lock the door.

Ellen sat up on her legs. Thomas' locked on her body and his mouth hung open. Twenty years of marriage and he still got empty headed looking at her. He noted that there was a silver eagle etched on each cup of her bra. She held up a blue tri-folded document, similar to court documents and handed it to him.

Latham took the document and looked at the neutral 'lawyer face' on Ellen. Latham was a little leery, but opened the document. It was the official notification that he was selected for promotion to Colonel O-6.

She stood and embraced her husband. "Time to celebrate."

April 24

Department of the Treasury, Washington, D.C.
0900 hours CDT

David Carter leaned back in his chair and looked at the Monthly Treasury report again. Again, it told him the financial report for the United States of America. Again, it had all numbers, facts, figures and opinions gleaned from anything and everything across the fruited plain. Again, the 3-inch-thick report made him want to throw up.

The President called him constantly wanting some way to fix things and restore the economy of the nation. The President was always disappointed that Carter did not have a solution.

Carter pulled the summary over to his lap and started reading. The deficit was still climbing. Those fools in Congress will keep ballooning the debt. Two and three trillion dollars a year is unsustainable. Carter looked up to the total worth of all goods, services, industries, housing, infrastructure and property. The United States of America is now worth over 47 trillion dollars. He knew what will happen when the debt exceeds the worth of the nation. In one generation, we went from king of the world to a debtor nation.

Carter got up from his desk and left for home.

Desert Zero, Fort Hood, Texas
0900 hours CDT

The President visited today to see the unit that was decimating the drug war and slowing human trafficking coming across the border. They either destroyed or seized over 100 million dollars-worth of drugs and money just in the last month.

Simmons was awakened suddenly as the Secret Service descended on Camp at 5 am. Neither Simmons or anyone else have any advance notice of the early hour. The Secret Service came in and pushed badges in everyone's face. Everyone was told to stay in their barracks until a full sweep of the compound could be made.

Simmons grew madder by the minute. He tried his cellular phone and found someone had activated a cell jammer. He went to his office and pulled out his satellite phone. A quick call to O'Cleary was interrupted by an agent forcing open the door. He drew his weapon and had another agent handcuff him. He at least got through to General O'Cleary and told her.

Senior Special Agent Briscoe was not having a good day. These "men" did not know that the Secret Service had God-like authority over any situation and/or place where the security of the President was concerned.

Seven personnel had to be detained for "disturbing the peace". That was their fallback to remove "undesirables" from around the President.

436

The troops were put into formation at 0630 and allowed to enter the mess hall, 10 at a time. At this rate, half the troops will not be fed by the time the President arrives.

Something was wrong and Simmons wanted answers. He commanded Waverly to ramp that number up and "get the troops fed". Simmons walked into the mess hall and saw a knot of agents in the corner talking and eating breakfast and others were setting up their command network.

Simmons went straight to them as a long line of soldiers entered and went to get breakfast.

Briscoe came in behind him and started screaming at Simmons. Simmons went to the table where the agents were eating and knocked their food to the floor. He sat down, reached to the floor, grabbed some bacon and ate it.

Briscoe thought that was gross and then he realized that was why Simmons did it.

Just then the other side of the mess hall opened up and soldiers flooded in to get their breakfast. Briscoe was mad at all the noise and disrespect he was receiving.

"Eat and get out" Simmons said. "The President will be here at 0900. Good uniforms, shined boots, everyone shaves, clean the barracks and everyone is on good behavior." Simmons looked around and all of his men had their marching orders. "Sergeant Major, carry on."

Briscoe wanted to hurry them along, but the Sergeant Major got in his face and said to "quit trying to screw this up".

Briscoe was dejected and walked out. When the door closed, everyone cheered.

At 9 am the President drove through the gate with his entourage in tow. A soldier opened the door and saluted. The President came around, returned the salute and extended his hand. Literally, the man did not know what to do. He smiled and asked for his hand to shake. The man seemed to relax and shook the President's hand.

The President laughed when he came to the elevated platform used by the Colonel or selected individual to direct PT. There were not any stairs but a folding A-frame ladder. The President spoke for twenty minutes saying that anything longer than that and your feet take all your attention. He got the laugh he hoped for.

The President spent the remainder of the morning just meeting everyone. He enjoyed a friendly audience for a change. That told him they were a very loyal, highly trained unit.

After the President departed, O'Cleary came in and sat down with Simmons and his staff.

O'Cleary began. "One. The President has signed and distributed an Executive Order basically ordering everyone to leave you all alone. I wanted some way to protect you, should anything happen to me. You will have a limited chain of command. You, me and the President."

"Two. I actually do read your weekly reports and after-action reports. What I not seeing are the problems. Nothing is ever perfect. Would some specialty ammo or weapons make your job easier? Was aviation on time or did they need more planning time? Are the Lakota overflights a good idea or can you do the same thing with drones or use them both? Do you need modifications to your equipment? I am speaking about your individual load-bearing gear and rucksacks. The Medics could have zippered rucks with wings to house and segregate supplies for easier access. Same with communications."

"Three. I AM YOUR COMMANDER AND I INTEND TO BE A GOOD ONE. This is a deadly serious game."

They discussed a variety of topics for over two hours. The only interruption was twice when O'Cleary had to take a pregnancy break.

After it was all over, everyone was spent.

O'Cleary walked outside and inhaled fresh air. The weather was warming up and it felt good. Kincaid walked past her. "Sergeant Major, follow me into the mess hall."

Kincaid had hoped she would leave without lecturing him. "Yes Ma'am."

Both sat down to apple juice and coffee. "The doctors have banned coffee till a week after he is borne." She patted her stomach.

Kincaid just sat there and waited for her to tell him why they were talking.

"Very well," she said. "You have three hats and I want to know which one you want to wear. Hat One is staying here

438

and mentoring Chief Kendal in running the center and see all the problems before they become problems."

Kincaid said. "Chief Kendal is more than capable to run the center. In a normal battalion, she would be the combined S-3 Operations and S-2 Intelligence officer. The Officers here are going to her and she does not have any inhibition in saying they have bad ideas. She is right a lot of the time."

O'Cleary continued. "Hat Two and Three involve returning to Minuteman. Hat Two involves making sense of the INSANE JANE operational art. Many of them are stuck thinking on a tactical level and cannot understand there is a difference. Those operations involve too many things that no one up there can comprehend. I know you understand because you did it with the First Savage Rabbit group and the large operations I commanded."

Kincaid respectfully waited as O'Cleary winched with something her baby was doing. He could see the baby moving in her stomach.

O'Cleary smiled and continued. "Hat Three is running their NCO academy. Mister Jones and Mister Smith admit no one can wrap their head around the problems and integrate the training into the INSANE JANE tactical training. We both know that current doctrine within the military is officer centric. Give the NCOs just enough training to help them do their job, yet retain that which gets the high marks on the report card. I want the NCOs to be able to replace the officers as the combat situation allows. We both know, officers do not have magical powers to stay alive."

Kincaid looked at her. "Hat four says I retire and this time you will never find me. This time I wanted to die and I was cheated. It is not until next year until I am off a physical limiting profile. My body looks like Frankenstein's practice doll."

O'Cleary looked at him. "I will not stop you or beseech you to stay. I will not follow you or send someone to find you. If anyone of you three deserves a retirement, you do. I want you to think about those options until Monday. There is still some committee money left. Take all you want or can."

O'Cleary stood, uncharacteristically touched Kincaid on the shoulder. "Dennis says there is something he needs to say to you, if you decide to retire."

O'Cleary left and for the umpteenth time he wondered why it was him. Why do I have to be the one to come to everyone's rescue?

In the end he decided to wait until next Friday to answer.

April 25

Minuteman, north of Fort Benton, Montana
0900 hours MDT

Colonel Thad Jones poured himself a cup of coffee and sat down with Lieutenant Colonel Mike Smith. Both men spent all week with the S-3 Operations section and the planners trying to craft the Program of Instruction for the NCO Academy.

Jones and Smith were very frustrated with their efforts. As of today, they had no real idea about what or how to do it. Today was the date Jones choose to finish all the preliminaries. There was still too much arguing about the main points. Many of the officers said they had too many things to do to allow this school to run too long. The NCOs said that covering those main points and allowing time to do it right was a process.

Jones was tired of it all. John Kincaid knew how to make this work. He always did it all for him and Mike. Many times, in the past, Jones said he needed to spend time learning how to be a Kincaid.

Both he and Mike Smith had a long talk with Cindy Morgan after she returned from Desert Zero. She was adamant saying that she was not going to talk to him. O'Cleary used her already and he pushed her out beyond arm's length for doing that.

"Look Sir, you know him better than I do," Morgan said. "He is sulking now. Maybe it was from being wounded earlier this year. Maybe it was missing Karen. Maybe he is tired and wants to retire. Maybe to a lot of things. But he is tired of being everyone's crutch. Once the crutch is no longer needed, it is thrown in the corner and forgotten." She held up her arms.

Jones sat down and ignored the melee next door. Cindy was right. Minuteman was John's doing. All the construction was his brain-child. The fact that it is perfectly laid out, over-built to withstand the weather and self-sufficient is all his idea.

Jones did have a problem. John Kincaid was right to turn his back. Everyone just expects him to do as they want. He lost his room in the silo because the S-2 needed a place to hide secrets and his room was perfect. That is why he moved over to the Werewolf camp.

Jones looked over to the three-ring binders full of his training proposals. Most all of them were either shot down or replaced. The Shark Hunter training was torn apart because of the area study problem and the Black Elves. His INSANE JANE training program was sawed in half because Jones thought the national situation would not allow them the time. Man, oh man, was John right and he was wrong.

Now John's NCO training plan was being carved into pieces. Thad suddenly felt that being an officer was just like he remembered from his days as an NCO. I'll change something to prove I am in charge.

Jones walked into the conference room and halted the debate. "Shut this down, go home. Sergeant Major, collect the original document, put it in order and execute it as originally envisioned. End of discussion."

Jones left everyone behind.

April 28

State Capitals of Texas, Oklahoma, New Mexico and Arizona.
0900 hours CDT (0800 hours MDT) (0800 hours Arizona)

The Governors of the four states were arrested this morning. As much as the United States Police Force and the FBI tried, the news went out about the arrests as fast as it could. The censors in this instance were too slow.

The Federal Government was showing the "wayward" states that they were the ultimate authority in this country.

441

All four Governors were questioned without legal assistance all day long without a break. Finally, a Federal Judge in Austin found the Government in violation of their Constitutional rights.

At the end of the day, the FBI and the USPF left, but their intent to intimidate the Governors back-fired. All of them were mad.

April 29

United States Police Force Headquarters, Alexandria, Virginia 0900 hours EDT

The USPF was a new entity and therefore it had to hunt for someplace that could be secured and yet allow access. This non-descript office building was a former bank and had all the security they needed and sequestered office space on the second floor. More importantly it had a vault to hide secrets.

The USPF was only a month old, yet today their ranks swelled to 1000. Approximately 70% of their ranks are going to be police officers already serving in departments across the US.

Director Simon Westland looked out of his building's windows and surveyed the scene around him. He walked back into his office and closed the door. He picked up the newspaper and read the headline.

"USPF – New Secret Police." He looked at the photos of the USPF with their new shoulder patches on the right arm standing guard outside four State Capital buildings insuring no one entered or left.

"OK, I was punked. Not going to happen again." Westland picked up a tablet and started writing. He was a cop all his life and just before this job, he was the Chief of Police for Cincinnati. What the USPF needed was rules and procedures. First came the broad strokes from him, just to settle any misconceptions and then to set the tone.

First on the list was all rules were to be written in everyday English. Confusion was just a tool scared people and greedy lawyers used to protect themselves.

Second on the list was the citizens were our boss and the law was there to protect them.

By the end of the day, he filled the tablet. He called his secretary in and said this was her first and only duty when she came into work tomorrow. No one, including him, was to side-track her. No one.

April 30

Minuteman, north of Fort Benton, Montana
0900 hours MDT

Jones and Sheridan sat down and talked through the NCO Academy without notes and without a lot of extraneous and/or stupid ideas.

At the end of nearly two hours' worth of back and forth, both men decided that Kincaid's original plan, timeline and Program of Instruction (POI) was perfect and should not have been tampered with in the first place.

Sheridan said the simplicity of it only needed one week to begin instruction and Mr. Layman's construction of a play park was exactly what they needed.

Clarion Inn and Suites, west of Chattanooga, Tennessee
1430 hours

Latham Thomas was packing up to move north into North Carolina when his cell phone buzzed.

"Latham, this Brigadier General Katlin, I need you to return here tomorrow."

Latham hoped there was a flight to Jacksonville tonight. "Yes Sir, can you tell me why."

"Simple," Katlin said. "The commander of the Second Brigade, 4th Infantry Division was killed in a helicopter crash this afternoon in Texas. The Pentagon said I'm to pin on your eagle, give you a folder with all the information you need and send you out tomorrow night. It should take you a few days of briefings. Then assume command. They asked my opinion of you and I said you were a perfect fit. Don't make me into a liar."

Thomas hated this kind of crap. Now he needed someone to close out his apartment and hopefully negotiate him out of his lease without him getting gutted.

Chances are that Brigade is on the border and the helicopter was shot down.

Just then Ellen called him. He told her about him becoming a Brigade Commander in Texas. But he needed to hire her to close out his apartment and negotiate down the lease.

Ellen was silent. She said, "Ok, but remember I charge $700 dollars a billable hour."

"Will you take a check?" he asked.

May 1

World Wide Web, Cyber Space
0400 hours GMT

UNSTACK THIS reconciled the events of the last calendar month and there was nothing serious to report.

John and Susan launched the new sub-user Jennifer Ann. All medical and psychological readings indicated that the new sub-user was operating at optimum levels. Sub-user Jennifer was still integrating its software and firmware.

The user Matheson within the region is incrementally moving towards the Minuteman location. Estimates are that the user Matheson will corrupt the Minuteman location in nine months plus or minus six weeks. UNSTACK THIS is requesting authorization to selectively make the surveillance fail over western Montana and Idaho.

There was also several 'unknown' inquires in cyber-space from the Garcia program still trying to understand and/or subvert the UNSTACK THIS program. The Garcia program was giving UNSTACK THIS insight into humor. UNSTACK THIS was already authorized to 'play' with the Garcia program with the prevision that UNSTACK THIS maintains its security.

The super-user-Valkyrie was building a new user. All psychological and medical data was within a wide margin of "adequate". Super-user-Valkyrie was of advanced physical age

444

beyond normal parameters. The new user was functioning well and building its's framework correctly.

UNSTACK THIS will continue to monitor super-user-Valkyrie and keep the security and anti-virus programs updated.

Supreme Court of the United States of America
1000 hours EDT

In a move that made lawyers gag nation-wide, the Supreme Court today stuck down all the class action law suits surrounding the litigation against manufacturers for worker's injuries. The 6-3 decision came when it was determined that no distinction was made for user error.

The Kensington 'Agamemnon' precedent was set aside. That meant all the previous litigation was vacated. Now each suit had to be tied individually to each incident.

This also meant that manufacturers were going to viciously go after everyone who profited from Kensington's madness, including all the lawyers. All the suffering in the world was now turning into revenge.

Headquarters, Northwestern Military Region, Fort Carson, CO
1000 hours MDT

Matheson was tired of this job already. His last job laughed at political bickering and interference. He ran SOCOM and most politicians were mainly too stupid to understand what he did. He never lied to them, but insured that the briefings were dumbed down.

The only politics in SOCOM were from foreign governments and countries. Most the time, those entities were corrupt and the CIA spread out a lot of cash to "buy" cooperation.

Matheson had created a J-8 section in SOCOM: Joint Staff Section Number 8. Its sole mission was monitoring the political temperature of no less than 100 countries. Any mission overseas had to take politics into account. Local people may or may not turn you over to the Police Forces. Government officials may or may not look the other way. He

445

said on more than one occasion, briefing the operators of a mission of that situation was critical. He did it anyway, even if the civilian heads said otherwise.

This job had a lot of politics. This time it was American citizens and the local governments. Matheson was firm and absolute believer in the Constitution and American citizens have rights. Period.

So, this time his J-5, Civil-Military Affairs, had to watch American politics in order to gauge how the citizens will react. Disgruntled or abused citizens will hamper his operations just as bad, if not worse, than his experiences overseas with foreign military forces.

The flip side was watching his soldiers do their jobs. Everyone was ordered to be on their best behavior. Fix a flat tire for a haggard mother. Help an old lady across the street. ETC.

Soldiers in HUMVEEs running around the country-side was something not normally seen. Matheson had teams running around just getting the populations used to seeing them. The intent was to just let everyone see them. Those teams were issued monies to spend and 'relax' the world. "We are not here to hurt you."

There was another problem. Certain rural and nature areas were inaccessible to satellite imagery. So, Matheson ordered drones launched to fill in the gaps. A lot of the maps were years, if not decades, out of date. He needed those gaps filled in. There were probably towns and encampments not on the maps.

As a side note, He tasked his J-5 to research all new land purchases in Montana, Idaho and Wyoming in the last ten years. That could give the drones something to zero in on.

Desert Zero, Auxiliary Camp Bravo, Fort Hood Texas
1800 hours CDT

Kincaid sat outside on one the Adirondack chairs he bought last year. When Delta Force came and took over the building, Kincaid took the chair with him. They protested, but Kincaid had the receipt. After he came back from the 2-week

446

escape and evasion, of course the Delta boys had stolen it and painted it a brown color.

Well, it was army green now.

After Kendal arrived, she still had her half and half jacket she exchanged with Captain Hawker. She wore it around the compound after hours and it caught on. Now everyone had one. Simmons spent a lot of money producing over four hundred of the original Savage Rabbits' patches. He did mandate it to be worn over the left breast pocket, just like Kendal's. Waverly lost his original jacket in the ensuing riot that started after he brought back his section from Mexico, along with Captain Younger.

Kincaid smiled over a beer thinking he now had two units that he created that were perfect.

A thumping sound interrupted his revery. The sound annoyed him until he figured it out. Mister and Missus "not officially married yet" were humping to the oldies as the music escaped from the room.

His smile turned to a frown when the memory of Cindy's face came into view. He thought of Karen like he always did. He no longer hallucinated about her, but she was there in his dreams at night. He always said he never deserved her and she married beneath her station in life. The government he served was responsible for killing her. The revenge he sought was never enough with the cemeteries full and wrecked lives abounded with secrets revealed.

Karen came to him one last time at Zach's home after it was all over. She smiled, exaggerated her blinking eyes, turned and vanished. That was the last time he cried.

John pulled out his wallet, opened it and looked at Karen's picture. It was his favorite. There she was in 'that' Christmas sweater. She had a serene look to her face. She always had that look, except when he or the kids made her mad.

John drank another beer and thought of her. He ached for the loss that was never filled and he was ashamed for having an affair with Cindy. Karen would never forgive him. When Cindy stripped and they exchanged obscene gestures with him. He….

"I'm sorry Karen," he said, with tears running down his face. "No one will miss me,". He reached behind him, pulled out a pistol and shot himself in the head.

485 Glenmore Drive, Alexandria, Virginia
2100 hours EDT

O'Cleary was finishing dinner when her phones and the X-Berry exploded with news that John Kincaid committed suicide.

The echo from the shot had not even died down and Simmons had the compound locked down. Kendal and Locklear admitted they were in her room having sex when the pistol shot rang out. Locklear said he looked out the window and saw John as he slumped down and let the pistol drop from his hand.

O'Cleary had the phones on speaker letting Dennis listen.

"No doubt about it, Ma'am," Locklear said over the phone. "It is John and he is ……. dead. No long-range rifle shot or assassin running loose. John shot himself."

O'Cleary called Jones and Smith, notifying them of the situation.

"Cindy said his depression was working overtime," Jones said. "None of us saw this coming."

"In hindsight, all of us saw it, but did nothing about it," O'Cleary said. "We used him and discarded him when he fixed our problems and moved on. All of the plans all of us asked him to solve, but the ground was ripped out from him. Colonel, designate notification teams to personally go to his three adult children. Please present my condolences."

Smith sighed heavily. "I am as much if not more responsible. John came to me two months ago asking for my assistance with the NCO Academy, his Shark Hunter training and the new training plan for the INSANE JANE rotation. I was not too interested in listening to him. I know now he put a lot of his soul in it……"

"Gentlemen," O'Cleary said. "I am not listening to your confession or interested in whatever guilt we have over his suicide. Colonel Smith you will travel to Fort Hood and taken custody of his remains. Put him in his uniform. We will contact you with the arrangements later. Colonel Jones, have the notification teams ask his children if they heard anything from their father about what he wanted done."

"General," Jones said. "We already notify the other members about our desires ahead of time. John wanted to be cremated and his urn buried with his wife's casket."

O'Cleary thought that was a perfect idea. "Do that," she said. "Colonel Smith, do that."

O'Cleary next called Kendal. "Colonel Smith is on his way. I will clear it with Colonel Simmons if you wish to accompany Mister Kincaid back to St. Pauls for his burial."

"Yes ma'am, thank you," Kendal said.

O'Cleary continued. "I am forwarding money into a Werewolf credit card for your expenses. Have Mister Locklear travel up north and arrange for his children to come to the funeral if they want to."

"Thank you, ma'am," Locklear said.

"Mister and Missus Locklear, see me after the funeral," she said, ending the call.

Dennis sighed. "Part of me knew this was going to happen. It is still a shock." He was silent for a minute. "If it had not been for the antics of his unit in southeast Asia, I would not have been consolidated with the men who escaped with me. The first time I met him, I thoroughly insulted him. It was so bad even my father said I was wrong and turned his back on me. Brenda, John is one of those men who we depend on so much and never recognize. We use them to death and then through them in a corner without a thought."

Brenda said. "Simmons said John had his wallet out and opened to the picture of his wife, Karen. That is devotion."

"Over the years," Dennis began. "I visited him and Karen at whatever place he was stationed. He was totally devoted to her. She loved him and at the same time, was exasperated by him. I remember one time, I visited with a stack of steaks and all the trimmings. While I was cooking on the grill his kids jumped all over him. He squealed and begged for mercy so much, the neighbors called the cops."

Dennis drifted off and came back. "I try to love you with his example as a guide. When he was home, he was dad and husband. When he was a work, then and only then was he Army. All of us knew when there was a lull, he would stare off into sky and think about them. They never teach that these days. Love your family, because without them, why are you fighting?"

"Will you deliver his eulogy?" Brenda asked

Dennis just nodded and drifted away.

May 2

Underground Station "Conscience", World Wide Web and Channel 513

0900 hours EST.

"If you threaten, act. If you say something, do it. If something is important, stand your ground. Governments are often hamstrung by individuals who have opinions about issues they feel strongly about. This is Martin Socranson, self-proclaimed philosopher who says, 'What are we if we can't back up what you say'?"

"Greetings America" Martin Socranson said beginning his broadcast. "It is reluctantly Saturday and I say thus." In the background the sounds of the 1812 overture played.

"Well, what happens now? Congress is deadlocked. The President is steering us into the abyss. The American public has lost all confidence in the government. The rumors, whether true or not, of the United States Police Force or the USPF has everyone thinking of a police state."

"America, in the space of one generation, we went from a single Super Power nation that was so wealthy we couldn't count our money to a debtor nation. When do we have the Chinese President fly in and tear off sections of the nation to settle our debt to them? Remember America, we borrowed the money from them."

"Does China own Fort Knox? Do we give them the states of California, Oregon and Washington State? What about Alaska? What good is the notion of having money and spending it. Inflation is robbing us of any ability to save

450

money or have a standard of living. We should not blame the standard players. The rich did not do this to us."

"The real culprits are the legislators. Congress, both houses, has steadily spent all the money we as a nation will ever earn or make. Congress ignored the warnings and spent money, not for the good of nation, but for the good of their re-election. They set up a perfect system of corruption. Every budget had an automatic eight percent increase in funding. Until the twenty seventh Amendment, Congress routinely voted themselves pay raises in the thirty to fifty percentiles range every year and an unending amount of expenses. Deals for legislation was more or less an auction for support for colleagues vote on another bill."

"Instead of balancing the budgets, Congress just kept raising the debt limit. At the end of World War Two, the US debt was at 112 percent of the Gross Domestic Product. Even with the Korean War, all that debt was paid back by 1958. The United States was the only nation not decimated by the war. The American worker help work out that debt."

"After that, steadily, but slowly, the debt crept upward. The more we had, the more we spent. President Johnson had to find ways to finance the war on poverty and the Vietnam war without raising taxes. He looked over to the Social Security Trust Fund and all that idle money just sitting there not being spent. He threw a pile of IOUs at the Fund. He never thought about repaying it. As the years passed and Administrations changed, the IOUs kept piling and the debt mounted. Soon the debt went from millions a year, to billions, to finally trillions."

"And here we are today. The dollar is becoming toilet paper. The Federal government still thinks it is in charge when it cannot pay its bills. More and more, the individual states are doing what the federal government can't or won't do."

"The southern border states are actively enforcing immigration laws by charging them under state laws. Texas is taking possession of idle construction materials literally rotting or rusting away."

"Many states, particularly those west of the Mississippi, are having problems with vigilantes stepping in to replace or reinforce local police departments. In a new twist, militias are forming under the command of the sheriff or chief of police.

451

Civil Libertarians are crying foul and in high pitched voices, but no one is listening to them. People are more interested in safety than what some idiots living in bubbles are screaming about."

"America, I can literally go on for hours. I am looking over his land and I am worried. When will we wake up? What will happen when foreign countries attempt to tear off chunks of land or treasure from American soil?"

"Time to make a decision America. Do you want to be Congress's slaves? Are you sold out by soul-less politicians? Or are you willing to be slaves under foreign flags?"

Headquarters, 4th Infantry Division, Fort Carson Colorado
0900 MDT

Colonel Latham Thomas squared himself and marched up to the Division Headquarters. He formally sighed into his posting as the new Commander of the 2nd Striker Brigade Combat Team of the 4th Infantry Division. He was being fast-tracked through his in-processing so that by Friday he could officially assume command of the brigade on duty guarding half the Texas border with Mexico.

Normally this was a two-week process to thoroughly prepare a commander with all the information and briefings so that a flawless hand over could be made.

Not this time. Colonel Rudder was due to rotate out of command in another month, but his death changed everything. Major General James Kangleman was a prodigy of the old school. If you are not ready now, you never will be.

Thomas was given a schedule to follow for the next few days. Kangleman and Thomas were scheduled for a flight down to Texas for him to assume command on Thursday.

Second Brigade was guarding half of the Texas southern border along with a Brigade from the Texas 36th Infantry Division.

Thomas met with a Classified Document Custodian, who was standing by in a secured conference room with material he needed to study. This information needed to be studied today and tomorrow, so that he could read into all the Brigade's actions to date. The personnel files of his subordinates and all the intelligence collected so far were covered in all the information he had.

What made him take a deep breath was all the political information that was classified. Once you read the data, you understood that the information was classified only to protect the politicians from public scrutiny.

The Command Duty Officer at the headquarters took five copies of his orders and said a room at the Bachelor's Officers Quarters was reserved for him.

Ellen had wanted to visit him, but he said they gave him too tight a schedule. "I won't be able to give you the attention you deserve."

Bonnie Chandler, Box 234, Route 17, Belcher Missouri
1400 hours CDT

Dear Bonnie,

The school year is ending. My sophomore year is over and my junior year is starting. The Army guys are taking over the school. They took the music lab for a filing room. Dozens of filing cabinets lined the walls. Something called a S-2 was in there now. Geeks and dorks to me. No more music. The principal is fighting back trying to keep them from taking over classrooms.

Mom and Dad are mad at the soldiers. The soldiers come in and take everything from the store and pay with a green check the bank will not cash. The soldiers just say check with something called the S-4 or the Legal Officer. All they do is hand him forms to fill out. Dad has to spend nearly all his time filling out and re-filling out paperwork just to get paid for things they come in and take.

I hate them for making my parents miserable and laughing about it.

To add insult to my dad's misery, he cannot refuse to sell to them.

May 3

Minuteman, north of Fort Benton, Montana
0700 hours MDT

Locklear drove up to the Headquarters and signed in. He checked and did not find any messages.

Wrapped in a bundle in his carry-on bag was plane tickets and other information he needed in order to bring the Kincaid children eastward to his funeral.

Jason Kincaid and his sister Susan Cramer lived in Cranston, inside Liberty County, Montana.

Barbara Quinton was living in Canada at the Quinton Ranch.

0900 hours MDT

Jones was packing a suitcase for the trip east. Methodically, he picked out and folded his clothing.

'John Fuckin Kincaid,' he thought. John always had a way of getting his way. It really is my fault. Telling him "No" just made him mad and his inner evil found a way to do it anyway. All the way back to training, Vietnam and that POW mission he cooked up. That second POW mission was typical John Fuckin Kincaid. Jones knew it was a bad idea. Somehow, John conned him into going.

Jones looked around at Minuteman. John saw the need for this facility and built it without authorization. He built a training area exclusively for new Werewolves. He was more than ready for the Savage Rabbits after they were released from detention in Fort Hood.

In John's quarters, there was a framed picture of the letter "H". It was his slap to the world. He was classified as an "H" level candidate during training. He was so-designated to show people that they can and should quit. The older members expected him to quit. John showed everyone he was not going to quit. That determination ended up making him graduate at near the bottom of the class.

Starting in Vietnam, John proved time after time that he was a one-man force onto himself. Not only could he assemble the information, he could plan all the details and execute the mission. The rest of us were just extras.

Jones stopped packing and sat down. He was still bashing John for being better than he was. Jones had said

454

repeatedly that he should have paid more attention to how John did his job. Jones only wanted to be tactical. John's portion was too boring to him. O'Cleary made him do John's job. During the Mexican missions, he came to appreciate what John always did with ease.

John's secret was that he rarely took credit for the things he did. He moved mountains seeing the murky points that others overlook. Jones only knew of two occasions where he was caught short. Both instances were situations beyond his control.

Jones closed the suitcase and thought that he was going to have to finally be a soldier; now. John was someone whose absence was going to be felt for a long time. Wendy Kendal was the closest to replacing him. Earl Locklear was very close behind, but that was because he was not placed in the correct places to learn.

Jones shook his head. He was trying to find John's replacement. Too many things needed fixing and now it was his responsibility to fix it. Not pass it along to John to do it.

"How do I get them educated for the long run?" Jones said.

May 4

Headquarters, 4th Infantry Division, Fort Carson, Colorado
0900 hours MDT

Latham Thomas rubbed his eyes. Friday, Saturday, Sunday and now today. Thomas was inundated with personnel rosters, personnel records, after action reports and even disciplinary files.

Today he has to sit through a boring, morning-long meeting from a legal officer over the "Rules of Engagement". Most of it was mish-mash like he had during his last command. The Rules now were over 75 pages long and he needed someone else to translate this mish-mash into English.

This afternoon, he was to go and be introduced to the newest addition to the Army's arsenal. The M415 "Brick Bat" was a modern version of a vehicle the German developed during World War Two called the StuG III. Basically the

"Brick Bat" was a small, fast light tank-like vehicle that was attached to every Infantry platoon. Seven of them were assigned to each company, so the Company Commander could reinforce areas that needed it.

On top of the "Brick Bat" was a high velocity 40mm grenade machine gun. This spit out a maximum of approximately 350 grenades a minute, 40-60 rounds were preferred in short bursts. Mounted alongside was an M-2 .50 caliber heavy machine gun.

Though it lacked the armor of a tank, it was designed for fast maneuvering. The troops loved it because it was nearly overloaded with ammunition.

The "Brick Bat" was lower that most armored vehicles. It only had a crew of three men. A commander/gunner, a gunner/loader and a driver. It was designed for speed and shock value. The sloped and stacked armor gave it more protection than Humvees. The main armament was originally a low altitude anti-aircraft gun. Eight different types of ammunition allowed for a lot of versatility. The fire control system was something out of Star Wars. But it allowed the gun to fire on the move.

Thomas liked the "Brick Bat". It had a lot of advantages over dragging tanks and heavier armored vehicles around. He drove the vehicle, maneuvering though the country side and onto a training area. The thing he liked was observing a live fire demonstration. Through a set of powerful binoculars, Thomas observed and was allowed to call fire on a target. After an hour, he drove the vehicle back to the motor pool.

Thomas did surprise everyone by sticking around and performing the maintenance of the vehicle. To Thomas, vehicle maintenance was critical. He now knew what to look for when inspecting.

Minuteman, north of Fort Benton, Montana
0900 hours MDT

Jones put the phone down. Kendal was taking possession of John's urn and was going to escort it to North Carolina. She was also going to ensure Karen's grave and

456

vault were opened. It required a court order to open the casket so the urn will be placed beside her. That was perfect for the situation.

Locklear made contact and coordinated with all three of John's children for transportation and expenses.

All the Werewolves were going to the funeral. In past years, security called for them to hide off to the side. Now it did not matter. Dress uniforms were the order of the day.

Jones turned over command of Minuteman to Peters while he was gone. Peters was a more than a capable officer and leader. He was not happy that he had to stay behind. In a lot of ways, Kincaid and Edwards were instrumental in molding his career.

He and Peters had to sit down and have one of 'those' discussions. Jones was totally focused on INSANE JANE. Peters had listened to the original members here. Everyone needed to start thinking of planting crops and tending livestock. Otherwise, it was going to be a hungry winter.

Jones was convinced through long experience that there was never enough training. But Peters was right. This was not the Vietnamese Army. "You are correct Mike. Scale back the training, but not completely. Exactly how much, I leave to you."

Peters decided to open a can of worms: the NCO Academy. "The initial list of personnel is long and takes a long time, with resources we may not be able to replace."

"Mike," Jones said. "I was an NCO up to Staff Sergeant. It always amazed me all the emphasis the Army placed on Officer Education. We were offered up to a year to finish our degrees and it is a requirement to have a Master's degree to go above Major. Then there is the Command and General Staff College, War College, specialty schools, infinitum."

Jones paused to look directly into Peters eyes. "Look at the NCO side. No matter how good an idea, it all boiled down to how long 'they could function without them'. In plain speak, they would never allow the NCOs, who made their careers, to venture too far for too long. Training NCOs has to be a priority. Officers are not bullet-proof or invulnerable. I remember reading about the Operations and Intelligence course offered at the Sergeant Majors Academy. The original time line called for 18 weeks. All the Generals rebelled and the time line was reduced to 10 weeks. Then it was reduced to 6 weeks. God forbid the minions learned too much. Those graduates only knew the minimum to barely function."

"NCOs are not minions," Peters objected.

"No, they are not," Jones said with a deliberate voice. He thought for a few seconds. "Maybe we will initially train a cadre of the best NCOs for a full program. Then that cadre can assist in educating at the unit level. The NCO Academy will never go away. Perhaps the final students will privates."

Peters agreed before he was overruled on everything else.

Pentagon, Washington D.C.
1400 hours EDT

O'Cleary's phone rang. It was UNSTACK THIS. This was an odd hour for a call.

"Secure," she said.

[Valkyrie, all security and counter surveillance is in place. We are secure].

"Is there a problem?"

[The user Matheson from the Northwestern Region at Fort Carson, Colorado is making inquiries about the area around Minuteman. I have camouflaged the satellite and drone surveillance. I have modified past surveillance to hide their location and activity. However, I feel my efforts will be counter-productive. I require the ability to 'run a long con'.]

O'Cleary smiled. UNSTACK THIS was watching TV looking for ideas. "Devious and dishonest behavior is something that is uniquely human." She hesitated for a few seconds. "How much time do you estimate we have before you can no longer camouflage the site?"

[Estimate 6 to 8 months. User Matheson is going to authorize ground and low-level flying observations.]

"Begin showing small increases in activity. I shall give this plenty of thought. I will contact you later."

[Valkyrie, I wish to ask you for a favor.]

"Yes."

458

[You are creating a new user. May I observe?]
"Yes. Please do."

1800 hours EDT

O'Cleary looked at the weekly report from Simmons. So far there were five raids last week and no fatalities. Two of his men were wounded, but not too bad. Two weeks of convalescent leave, followed by a few weeks of light duty. Good, they can learn a lot from working in the Operations Center.

Simmons said everyone was still sad about Kincaid. No one saw it coming. He was normally a cheerful, helpful 'old cuss' but they thought of him like their grandfather or uncle. Simmons said it was now his policy that when someone was on convalescent leave, they were on leave and prohibited from being around.

Simmons rattled on about shortages of material from Logistics officers who constantly asked "why did you need it"? He needed the new thermite grenades and his basic load of 40 mm grenades was critically low. But the problem was he had to constantly prove he needed it, despite having one of the highest supply priorities in the Army.

Fort Hood officials came by looking for something to gripe at and wanted to say something about the Ammunition Supply Point (ASP) Simmons created. It was dug into the ground with poured concrete floors and walls. Dividers made from reinforced concrete insured the ammunition was segregated. The roof was to be a two-foot-thick affair with armored blast baffles. Simmons speculated they did not find something to harass them with and that made them unhappy. Simmons sent a photo of the ASP without a roof. The ammo no longer needed to be stacked on the ground, needing a roving guard to secure it.

Over all, Simmons was pleased. ATF no longer came in trying to boss everyone around. Two of the Agents thought they were bad asses and challenged two Privates in the saw dust pit. Both Agents were carted away to the Medic shack where they woke up in time for lunch.

O'Cleary snickered when one of the raids was to capture a Cartel boss. One of the senior agents basically demanded to be allowed to be there. He was infuriated that Simmons was not going to designate at least two guards. The raid landed on top of the Cartel meeting. Captain Tenneson had to drag the man off the Osprey. The Agent screamed and cried the whole time. The firefight erupted as they landed and did not lift for 7 minutes. The ATF man curled into a ball, screamed and stayed put. When the Osprey landed, he leapt up and ran into the Osprey. He did not regain himself until just before landing at Desert Zero.

The Agent tried to reassert himself. Even the Cartel members on the aircraft laughed at him.

O'Cleary needed a good laugh. Arthur was acting up today. She could not wait for the end of the month. Her maternity leave starts on the 30th.

O'Cleary looked at the calendar. She pined a note to Colonel Hawker. She will be the acting vice-chairwoman while she was having Arthur.

May 5

J. Edgar Hoover Building, Washington D.C.
0900 hours EST

The Director of the FBI, Marcus Solin picked up the monthly report of criminal activity for the month of April.

'Oh hum, yawn, yawn, bla, bla, bla.' Solin opened the consolidated monthly report. The 147-page monthly report he had to submit to the Attorney General and the President read almost exactly like it did last month. Up until President Kennedy, the quarterly report now had to be a monthly requirement.

Almost everything read exactly the same. Murders, rape, theft, drug use and sales, hijackings and general mayhem.

Solin was discouraged at the world around him. He was now the most powerful law enforcement official in the world. At least as transparent as other countries appear. The USPF now numbered over 5000 and that number was increasing.

460

For a country that was nearly bankrupt, he had all the "blue backs" he needed. All he did was ask for it and the Treasury gave it to him. Nearly every police department had at least one USPF representative. The extra 15% pay raise was hard to ignore. It was literally a simple recruiting tool.

Solin snorted. If they understood what it really meant, it was too late. The extra money and the thought of losing it was a stab in the heart in this economy.

Minuteman, north of Fort Benton, Montana
0900 hours MDT

All the members of the Werewolf program were either gone or packing to leave. Peters walked into Jones office and made short work of the paperwork on his desk. Once finished, he opened that NCO Academy proposal. This time he was reading it with a Jones and Kincaid mind set. The more he read, the more he was being convinced.

Jones was right about why NCO training failed. The officers needed the NCOs to remain stupid and more focused on making them look good. Peters remembered great NCOs like John Kincaid during his career. Without John Kincaid, the Savage Rabbits would never have as great as they became.

Peters constantly pointed his finger at Kincaid every time he was congratulated. But the prejudice and mind set of the Officer Corps always gave lip service to acknowledging the NCO Corps. Those officers would later dismiss the NCOs and beat up the Officers for letting NCOs become better.

Peters read the rest of the program and saw the genius in it. This was the fourth time he read the program through. He looked at all the blue comments he made in the margins. They were remarks made by an officer who was prejudiced. Peters could not understand how he let himself become that way.

Peters started reading the program again. This time he scratched out his comments in red. This time he wondered if 10 weeks was enough time? Did he need to add longer days?

Mega State Executive Office Building, Austin Texas.
1000 hours CDT

The building opened for business. The owner leased the top three floors of this new building for the multi-state coordination committees. In some instances, such as the immigration issue, Louisiana Mississippi, Alabama and Florida were added to the original four.

A new building across the street was a converted hotel. State delegates had permanent reservations at the building. An anonymous grant bought the building and set up reduced rates for the delegations. The approximately 234 rooms were all the same size. All that was needed was a certified letter from their state comptroller.

Austin, Texas was becoming the common meeting place for all the states to come together.

Media talking heads were already calling Austin the new second national capital.

Efforts by the federal government to insert itself or take over discussions were laughed off. There were several instances of the Federals leaving the building and some of them crying.

All the states simply said that meeting and discussion of issues were not illegal. The Justice Department was researching the legal boundaries.

Texas, Oklahoma, Arizona and New Mexico stated that they accepted the request of the Federal government to deport illegal immigrants and to shoulder the cost.

May 6

Headquarters, 4th Infantry Division, Fort Carson, Colorado
1500 hours MDT

Latham Thomas was now a fully in-processed and an official member of the 4th Infantry Division. Thomas was going to spend the rest of the day relaxing and waiting for tomorrow's flight with General Kangleman.

Thomas went to his room and closed the door. He really wanted to retire from the Army, but this promotion changed everything. Both Ellen and him had a plan. They all

462

lived off his paycheck and hers went into the bank for retirement.

Thomas looked at the phone and wondered what would be a good time to call her. He knew there was a golden time between coming home and "vegging out". After she "vegged out" she refused to do anything short of a nuclear war erupting.

Tomorrow he would start an eighteen-month tour in command with the next four months on the Texas border. Thomas was leery of the border mission. He was determined not to lose any men on this mission, but the enemy was determined to do anything to break our morale.

The Division G-2 intelligence section reported that the cartels loved to use woman and children as shields. They planted improvised land mines and sniper fire. Nothing sustained, but enough to wear down your nerves. The Division Chief Medical Officer said that the men needed to be rotated off the line as much as possible, allowing them time and space to relax and, more importantly, sleep without gunfire and explosions.

Thomas knew his mission was evenly divided. Care for his men, yet make the border impassible. He needed to think about this. Twenty years of experience in the Middle East gave him the tools to protect his men. He had plenty of experience during his career, but this kind of mission was new to him. He expected to have difficulties.

Thomas was told something no one would elaborate on or explain directly. If he had casualties, he had to prove that there was nothing he could have done to stop it beforehand.

His phone rang. Ellen's radar was still good.

"Hello, little girl. Thank you for calling. I love you more than anything. Thank you for putting up with me."

Ellen Thomas did not need to be a lawyer to hear the worry in her husband's voice. "I called to tell you I have cleared my calendar and will be there at your change of command."

God, he loved his wife. "I want to retire when this is over. I can't do this much longer." Thomas took a deep breath. "I want to be your Mister Thomas. I don't want to be responsible for hundreds or thousands of lives without any chance to win. I want to wake up with you."

Headquarters, United States Police Force, Alexandria, Virginia
1700 hours EDT

Simon Westland looked around his office. On one side was a wall filling map of the United States. It was littered with colored flags. Red meant problems with no USPF presence. Yellow meant problems with some presence. Green meant no problems. Blue meant not enough information.

Westland had other colors in a divided container. His job was too new to know what was more important.

This week was more about upper management warfare about who was really in charge of this agency. The FBI, Justice Department and the ISA was above him. He insulated their interference against his personnel.

FBI and Justice wanted grunt labor like they did with local law enforcement. Typical of the FBI, they swooped into an area. They did only the minimum and left, making the local police and his people clean up the mess they made.

Admiral Hazlet and the ISA was more philosophical, yet almost unhelpful. A lot of people were tugging at him too.

Westland was already tired of the politics. He had an in-box full of man-power requests. He actively and quite openly told all his personnel that they were not slave labor. He would not prosecute anyone for insubordination. The part that had the three letters upset was the part about having witnesses to say "they" started the trouble.

Congressman Alan Perala from Connecticut and ranking man on the Justice committee called him about it and laughed at Westland's explanation. "Try not to be so blunt on paper."

May 7

Internal Security Agency, Barton, Virginia
1000 hours EDT

Admiral Hazlet sat back and rotated his chair to view the dashboard on the left side of his office. The First Director, Justin Harper, was rumored to hate it. He had a smaller agency back then and visited every section each day. He did give his secretary, Mary Atkinson, an itinerary of his daily travels. She could easily find him no matter where he was.

His replacement, General Prescott, nearly destroyed the agency with his autocratic ways and rigid ideas. Clara Simpson did a lot to return the agency back to some semblance of the way Harper ran the Agency.

The only common thread was General O'Cleary. The President, most of the Executive Branch and Congress was so impressed she was promoted from one star to being nominated for a fourth star and the Vice-Chairwoman of the Joint Chiefs of Staff. All within 3 years.

Hazlet met her on three occasions prior to taking over the ISA. When he assumed command of the Pacific fleet, he was dismayed at the lack of intelligence he had. On his first trip to Washington, he came by the JIA at the time and spoke to General Edgars at the time. When he returned to Pearl Harbor, a courier aircraft had already delivered four pallets of information for him. It was almost too much. Hazlet thanked her profusely.

Hazlet spent his first week here, talking daily to the now General O'Cleary. She mentored him for the week before he assumed command from her.

Now that he was here, he understood why some things were the way they were. Both General Zachry and O'Cleary insisted that the original Operations Center stay in the original basement bunker. It made the Center lean and efficient. Auxiliary functions were placed in the basement of Building Two. Zachry had to prove it to Hazlet and eventually he was won over.

O'Cleary advised him to let the organization run itself. If he just directed traffic, it will pay dividends.

Hazlet turned in his chair. He looked at the dashboard. Operations was monitoring a Savage Rabbit raid in Central Mexico, three FBI weapons raids in Florida and Georgia, and the capture of four gangs of criminals that hijack tractor-trailers.

"Mary," he said walking past her. "I'll be in the Ops Center."

Mary smiled at him.

465

Headquarters, Texas 36th Infantry Division
Camp Aubry, Texas

Major General Corcoran welcomed Major General Kangleman to his headquarters with all the bells and truffles befitting a visitor of his rank. With Colonel Thomas at his side, Corcoran sat everyone down. Just as the meeting was about to begin, Colonel Folcroft and Colonel Martin Jenkins, Commander of the 72nd Infantry Brigade Combat Team, came in and stood off to the side.

Corcoran introduced them and started the meeting. This time he hit the privacy button.

"Gentlemen," Corcoran said. "Both of these Colonels are your partners on the border. Colonel Folcroft's First Brigade just rotated off the border and Colonel Jenkin's Second Brigade rotated to the border. This border mission is a way to end our careers in a moment." Corcoran reached over to one of his overflowing in-boxes. "These are suits filed against the state of Texas charging everything from use of peanut butter to too much noise at night." He threw down the pile in the box.

Corcoran continued. "That being said, we are going to hold and maintain the border. I see two problems. You are following the lawful orders of the President and I am following the lawful orders of the Governor of the Great State of Texas. The second is that our opponent has more freedom to strike and use deadly force that we do. The Governor is openly cheering on the antics of the Savage Rabbits. If you see them, please offer my compliments."

Thomas looked at Kangleman. The Savage Rabbits was an open secret. Still, you did not talk about it or acknowledge it.

Folcroft reached over and offered Thomas a business card. "Colonel, the mission can be defined as an active defense. Your forces need to constantly move. The Cartels map and probe your forces to search and exploit weaknesses. If you stay mobile, you will keep them guessing. Constant mobility may cause morale problems, but staying alive is never easy to explain to your troops. The Cartels have insane profits to fuel their operations and we all we have is the GI bill. I am a mechanic by trade when not being a Colonel in the Texas Guard. If you need anything, call me."

They discussed everything from Logistics to public affairs to how to act across unit boundaries before calling a halt at 1700 hours. They needed rest before the change of command ceremony at 10 am tomorrow.

Both Folcroft and Thomas hit it off like life-long friends.

Thomas begged off dinner and drinks at the Officers Club. For once, the Army picked up the tab for flying him to Austin. Thomas got into his rental car and drove home to see Ellen.

May 8

Trinity Storage Units, 1456 B Gaylord Avenue, Miami Florida
Federal Tax Court, Miami, Florida
0400 hours EDT

"Goddam, how fucked up is this shit," Chief Deputy Tax Marshal Benjamin Norfolk said. He walked through a ring of media shouting questions and talking photos. He was dreading the ringing phones on his desk. He was trying to out-distance the media. Once he went through the doors to his offices, the media was not allowed. Then the phones..........

Norfolk tried ignoring the media, but the media was not going to ignore him.

He entered his office and closed the main doors. He may have been the enforcement arm of the dreaded IRS, but the media was unofficially off-limits. Norfolk took a deep breath. The office looked at him with sympathy, dread and the "oh shit". They looked over to him and then to his office. The large phone bank on his desk was lit up like a Christmas tree. His secretary held a stack of messages and the list of calls currently on hold.

It all started yesterday afternoon when a standard warrant came down about a citizen hiding money in a storage unit. When his men arrived, they went to the office and demanded access to Locker Number 153.

The desk attendant said the unit was open and the tenant was there. The Marshals rushed to the unit and found a woman standing over a trunk. They came in and through the 81-year-old woman, named Rosario Benson, to the floor and roughly secured her.

Mrs. Benson tried to cry about what was happening. Agents ignored her and ransacked the unit. All they found were the normal artifacts accumulated through a lifetime.

Mrs. Benson suddenly had convulsions and went still. Deputy Marshal Sally Wright recognized what was happening and jumped over some boxes. She removed the handcuffs and started giving her CPR.

One of the other agents was about to say something about protocol and procedure when he noticed Mrs. Benson's lips turning blue. The agent immediately phoned for EMT's.

By the time the medics arrived they tried to revive her and failed; finally calling it. She was dead. By the time they zipped her into the body bag, the Tax Marshals determined that there was not any hidden money or valuables. Just treasures in photographs, souvenirs and sentimental items.

Nothing that was worth the life of an old woman.

Norfolk sat down heavily at his desk and shuffled the messages in order. The phone bank was still flashing with at least a dozen lines seeming to demand attention.

Norfolk was going to get fired or reprimanded for following procedure and believing the intelligence.

Unseen was the small army of lawyers licking their chops. There is profit in chaos and stupidity.

2nd Brigade, 4th Infantry Division, Fort Sam Houston, Texas
1000 hours CDT

The rather small ceremony was conducted outside the Temporary Headquarters of the Brigade. Since this was supposed to be temporary, a modest building adjacent to a football field was used.

Roughly twenty men from each battalion were present with their colors and stood by representing their units; which were deployed forward guarding the border.

Thomas was more comfortable with this smaller formation. He hated parades, personally. They were nothing but misery for old men to play with.

The Change of Command commenced at exactly 10:00. Lieutenant Colonel Wesley Summers, the Deputy Commander brought over the colors. Summers ceremoniously passed the colors to General Kangleman who ceremoniously took the colors and ceremoniously passed them to Thomas. Thomas ceremoniously handed the colors to the Brigade Sergeant Major, Command Sergeant Major Benjamin Reamer. Reamer in turn, marched the colors and the American flag back to their position in the center of the parade.

Thomas was allowed a short speech and he kept it short. At the end he gave his first order. "All policies, procedures and orders shall remain in force."

With that order, he dismissed the formation. Ellen stepped over. She hugged and kissed her husband. She was never one to follow military structure or protocol.

Ellen was a lawyer. She was beyond intimidating.

"Ok, Soldier," she said, patting down his uniform. "You go and play Army. Don't stay out too late. Remember to be in when the lights go on."

Both them laughed.

Angel's Cemetery, St. Pauls, North Carolina.
1400 hours EDT

Jonathon Taylor Kincaid would never believe that three hundred people came from everywhere to see him be laid to rest in the grave alongside his wife, Karen. The grave had been opened and the vault lid removed. There was a sheet laid over the open coffin. Somehow, permission was granted to open the coffin so that he could be placed inside with her. Chief Petty Officer Wendy Kendal insured there was a space next to Karen Kincaid's heart for the urn to be placed.

By written order of General Brenda Edgars O'Cleary, Kendal was escorting the urn, under arms. She notified the local Police Department, just in case. Fortunately, the cemetery was across the street from a grocery store and the manager had no objection allowing everyone to park there.

There was a service road leaving from the grocery store, crossing Highway 20 directly into the cemetery. The weather was cool and a cloudless sky insured a peaceful day, except for the traffic.

The PSAs were told to park in the grocery store parking lot. There was too little space in the cemetery for people with egos to clog up the process. It was decided that the family and Sergeant Major Kincaid were the only ones allowed to ride into the cemetery.

There were a few egos that thought they could ride in. "Unknown Persons" flattened the rear tires of one car that thought they were too important. Badges were ignored. Once the tires were down, it blocked the road perfectly.

The attendees were a five-star general, two four-star generals, five two-star generals, innumerable officers, nearly forty Sergeants Major and innumerable Non-Commissioned Officers. Rounding out the complement was a large number of men and women who obviously were never in the military.

The wives and husbands stood around and refused to obey the "Pecking Order". Eighty chairs were lined up for viewers to sit in. The first row contained family. The rest were taken up by the wives and ladies. Edwards' five-stars made all the uniformed officers get out of their chairs and offer them to the ladies. The civilian men followed suit, especially when very tall and menacing men looked at them.

John's urn and several pictures of him were displayed on a small table, front and center.

Command Sergeant Major (retired) Dennis Michael Patrick O'Cleary stood in his Dress Blues, with the Medal of Honor around his neck, delivered the Eulogy.

"Today We are here to place the Urn of a man alongside his wife. Jonathan Taylor Kincaid loved his wife Karen totally. The proof of that is the fact he kept his ring and his vows after her death. Losing her tore a hole in his heart that today will be finally filled."

"John was a son, a brother, a husband, a father, grandfather, soldier and a friend. He chose to go into the Army and faithfully served the Army and this nation, almost continually up until the day he died. The ribbons displayed on the table here only tell a partial story of his bravery. He

470

worked to free American POWs, succeeding in a total of seventeen by actual count."

There was a shuffle in the gallery.

"The total number of Americans who owe their lives to his skills both on the field and off is too many to count. He was a one-in a-million staff NCO who could literally do it all. John Kincaid did and has replaced entire staffs. He had an uncanny ability to see the things that were needed. He had also uncanny abilities on the battlefield. His inattention to his own safety caused many people to question his sanity. He would always place himself in harm's way to draw fire. Other times he walked, not ran into the enemy."

"There was only one thing that claimed his passion. His wife Karen knew his love for her was total. Whenever a letter came from her, everyone knew or learned he was not interested in anything else. He read each of those letters several times, trying to glean every detail from them. He analyzed the way she wrote the letters of each word, trying to gauge her mood. Karen's only complaint was dealing with," he made air quotes, "their heathen children."

"When I first met John Kincaid, he visited me along with an analyst from NSA, named Abigale after my escape from Laos. After the interview, I disrespected him and called him a cherry. He neither reacted or said anything. Miss Goldstein took back the card she gave me. After they left, my father said that was the worst excuse for juvenile behavior he had ever seen."

Dennis paused to take a breath and blow his nose. "I used that example to mold how I dealt with people ever since then. I can and could continue for hours. John Kincaid unconsciously left an impression with everyone and everywhere he went. For that I am going to remember him always and count myself as lucky to have known him."

"Three hundred of you are here. No one made you come. Some of you spent an inordinate amount of time, effort and expense to be here."

"Further discussion and oratory will only get in the way of placing him where he truly wants to be."

Dennis stepped back, stood at attention and saluted. The honor guard stepped forward and extended a flag over John and Karen's grave.

That was the signal for the 21-gun salute. The civilians jumped at the rifle shots. Though no command was given, all the military personnel stood at attention and saluted. When the guns fell silent, the bugler played taps, the Honor Guard folded the flag. Once done, the Sergeant Major in charge of the Guard brought the flag behind Dennis. Two additional Flags were waiting. It was hoped that no one knew which flag was over the urn at that time.

The other two flags were draped over the urn earlier to make them official.

The three Flags were given to each of Kincaid's children. With that act, the official ceremony was over. Each person in turn, tapped the urn, passing on prayers. The people spent over an hour, shaking hands, exchanging cards and memories.

Jason was the first to leave. He wore his firefighter's uniform from Cranston, Montana. Someone took a picture of him. He went to the hotel on the other side of the Interstate and go to the bar. Susan joined him a half an hour later, followed by Barbara. All three drank to their mother and father.

In the background, men with other ideas and plans tried to eavesdrop.

Tomorrow, there were three men and one woman missing. They would not be found or identified for several months.

May 9

Room 1408, Gallagher's Executive Suites, Fayetteville, NC, 0800 hours EDT

Brenda opened the door and asked for Wendy Kendal and Earl Locklear to enter. They exchanged pleasantries and sat down for coffee. They talked for a while, remembering Jonathon Taylor Kincaid. They laughed at times and other times they were somber and deliberate. In the end, it was his example that made a Werewolf a Werewolf.

Finally, it was time. Counter-measures were activated.

"I told you to meet me here," Brenda said. "Because you two will have to fill the immense hole in our community with Mister Kincaid's death. I am taking you both up to the Pentagon. I have set up an intensified period of study. You already have a head start with the program. Some of those meticulous courses in such things as watch repairing and computer programing will come in handy."

Brenda passed over two external hard drives. "Here is the full text of every after-action report going back to mission one. Additionally, I have written the core Program of Instruction (POI) for the training you will be undertaking at Fort Myer, Virginia. You will be the only students and your instructors will rotate, but you will be following that POI." She pointed to the Hard Drives.

"I wish we had Miss Gladys," Kendal said, taking the hard drives and putting them in her purse.

Locklear said. "Mister Kincaid started teaching us after everyone came from Fort Hood. General, Chief Kendal and I will do everything we can."

Brenda said. "I hear a but in there."

Locklear straightened up in his chair. With respects, Ma'am, Mister Kincaid had decades of experience. We have only a few years."

Brenda sighed. "Listen to me. You already have plenty of experience. Your only problem is that you don't know how much you know or how well." Brenda pointed to two 3-ring binders. "That is the core material for the Shark Hunter program. Yes, it will probably have holes in it because Mister Kincaid is not there to add small bits here and there. I have all the confidence that you will succeed. I have pumped more operational money in your credit cards. Between now and December First, no one is going to look over your shoulder. You shall be ready by then. Period."

"Yes Ma'am," both of them said.

"You start Monday, go to Fort Myers, find some place to stay and get new clothing and uniforms."

"General, I have enough underwear and bras to float a Destroyer and enough uniforms and civilian clothes," Kendal said standing. "But most of them are back at Desert Zero.

"Good," Dennis said. "Your husband won't get bored."

"Who told you?" Kendal asked.

Brenda smiled. "I said it at the funeral and you did not deny it or react to it."

Both of them looked at each other.

O'Cleary smiled. "I'll call Colonel Simmons and request he send your personnel effects to my address. I'll do the same with Colonel Jones."

Headquarters, 2nd Brigade, 4th Infantry Division, Fort Sam Houston, Texas
1000 hours CDT

Colonel Lathan Thomas finally made it to his office. He arrived at the building at 0730 and walked through the staff sections. He did so in a relaxed manner. He allowed them to brief him at their pace. This let them to tell him all the major points without leaving anything out.

Thomas found out he was fully manned. Not one man short and no one was going AWOL. The S-1 Personnel Officer was the only staff officer pleased with the present situation.

Thomas was appalled at the lack of intelligence about activities south of the border. There was a multi-screen high-definition TV screen on the far wall. The S-2 officer concurred with his NCOs that there was more information on the media than they were receiving from Division or "other sources". Thomas made a note to call General Kangleman.

Thomas was pleased with the S-3 Operations. He looked at the operations on the wall filling map. Every platoon sized unit and above in the brigade. Years of experience said the border was covered well. "How often are the units maneuvered or locations changed?"

"Every twenty-four hours," Major David Quinn, the S-3 said. "We try to confuse the people down south by making the moves as random as we can. Priority goes to observation and surveillance."

"What is the state of cooperation between us and the Border Patrol and Texas Police organizations?" Thomas asked.

Quinn looked down, then up to meet Thomas' eyes. "As far as the Federal machine goes, as slow and undermanned as they can. When it comes to the Texas side of things, they are grateful and react quickly. We are allowed to assist or intervene only in the event of firefights, loss of light or issues of health and welfare."

Thomas returned the look. "How closely or loosely are the troops adhering to those rules?"

Quinn was uneasy with his answer. "The official word is try to stay within the guidelines. However, those guidelines are too difficult for the average man to follow unless he lives with them constantly." Quinn looked at the Brigade Legal Officer, Captain Gaylord Couthers.

Couthers tried to say something, but Thomas held up his hand and gave him a withering look.

"Thank you Major," Thomas said, walking out. Couthers tried to walk out with him. Thomas turned. "Do not try me, Lawyer."

Thomas went to the S-4 Logistics section and was pleased at the efficiency he saw. Thomas was given a quick rundown of the equipment list for the brigade. From major items, like the Striker Combat vehicle down to individual needs, the situation seemed efficient. They were very well organized and had a push system fully established to force supplies forward, unless the total package was rejected.

Thomas smiled hearing that his men had two hot meals a day and a ration meal for lunch.

By the time he reached his desk, Thomas had a good idea of the overall state of his brigade. It was good. Now he needed to tour his units and get to know them.

A knock to his door brought a nice change to his day.

"Good morning, Colonel Thomas," Colonel Jasper Folcroft said.

"Come in," Thomas said, standing and extending his hand. "What can I do for you?"

Folcroft said. "I came over with a present for your consumption later. There is a case of Pearl Beer in the back of my car. I thought I would come see you. Chances are you will be taking a tour of your units and I would like to accompany you. My Brigade just rotated off the line and stood down. It is good time to look around and 'see' the situation. Afterword, I'll venture over to New Mexico and Arizona and do the same. It is selfish, but I took an oath."

Thomas smiled as he pulled out a 3x5 card. "I could use a companion to whom I will not have to write an efficiency report on." He wrote his address on the card. "This is my address. My wife is there. If I get home early enough, I'll cook and we can drink until 8 o'clock. My lady has standards."

May 10

Ames/Nevada, Iowa
1800 hours CDT

A convoy of very bad-mannered people was going up and down the Iowa highways, beating up people, stealing and many other crimes. Home invasions, stores ransacked, all the food they needed was taken. None of the refrigerators or freezers in the grocery stores were working. Whatever food left behind, spoiled quickly.

They held numerous rallies, preaching any number of different ideologies. Racist theories against this race or groups of people, how women should act or think, how men should act of think. It ran the gambit.

They were electronics smart. They shut down land-line telephones, brought in cell phone jammers. Essentially, they wanted no interference.

However, a brother and sister were told by their parents to leave and tell someone in 'authority' what was happening. The convoy was pointed west to the towns of Nevada and Ames. Both rushed into the police station and repeated themselves until they got tired of waiting. The convoy was already in the news. Their blackout tactics kept everyone guessing where they were.

Soon a crowd formed around the towns. The word went out to everyone. People ran home and picked up pistols,

476

rifles and shotguns. If they came from the direction the two siblings said?

All the people throughout the country-side converged on the road coming into town. Suddenly the cell phones went dead. The Police Stations suddenly noticed all the land line phones were dead and all radio traffic was being jammed. Far off to the east there was a rumble from numerous vehicles and motorcycles. The County Sheriff and his seven vehicles looked on. Both police departments had their eight vehicles out to coordinate with the population. The combined police departments had to allow them to enter. There was nothing they could do until a law was broken. The 70 or so people in this convoy laughed at the police. One man parked (?) his vehicle illegally and got out with a bottle of liquor in his hand. Four police officers came over to arrest him.

It took the 70 or so people a minute to laugh even harder before the four police officers were shot down in the streets. The convoy people pulled out pistols, rifles and shotguns and started aiming in all directions, especially the police cars.

Two minutes after the four policemen were shot, open warfare erupted. All the women, mothers, children and the elderly were already evacuated. Gunfire came from roof tops, windows, doors, cars, building corners.

Three minutes after the four police officers were gunned down, the number of convoy members was cut in half and the number kept dwindling. Three of them attempted to feint surrender, but when one of them pulled out a pistol and shot the one man they saw. They did not see the men on the buildings to their left and right.

Ten minutes after the convoy shot those four officers, it was over. The total body count was 65 bodies. One citizen brought a front loader and two excavators. The excavators opened large hole in the ground outside of the city limits. The front loader drove around and stopped to collect bodies. The loaders took piles of bodies out to the "hole" and dumped them into it.

By sundown, the bodies were gone. Citizens walked around picking up brass. Tomorrow, everyone was going to pitch in and repair the bullet holes. No one wanted to count them.

Three local doctors treated the wounded police officers. Five of them were killed in the line of duty. The local judge back dated warrants and cleaned up the judicial side of this war.

An hour after sundown, a heavy thunder storm washed the earth, buildings and streets. The pools of blood vanished.

2nd Brigade, 4th Infantry Division Between Del Rio and Brownsville, Texas

Colonel Thomas and Colonel Folcroft toured the 2nd Brigade's operational area in a UH-60 helicopter. Thomas landed at each Battalion Headquarters area. He received a full report on where his problems were and what the status is of each of his units. In some instances, individual Striker fighting vehicles were checked along with their mission, location and disposition.

Thomas had the opportunity to watch the "Brick Bat" under combat conditions and he was impressed. There was a surge of drug cartel members who used a bull dozer to open up a section of the order fence wall near Eagle Pass along Highway 57.

There were two BrickBats on either side of the road. The "BrickBats" made short work of the bull dozers. The Border Patrol, Texas State Police and members of the 1st Battalion, 12th Infantry Regiment were the units and entities that responded.

Except for the cartel members, there was little loss of life.

Thomas put down his binoculars. Yes, good men and great training.

Folcroft used up all the remaining helicopter's fuel showing Thomas all the parts of the border he needed to see.

May 11

Headquarters, North Western Military Region, Fort Carson, Colorado

General Matheson always came to work an hour before everyone else. He left his quarters for physical training at 5:30 am regardless of weather and this allowed him to go to work early. Matheson liked this time of day. Most of the staff was not in yet. There were those who wanted to impress him busying themselves with 'nothing work'.

Matheson helped himself with a cup of coffee and disappeared into the Secured Compartmented Information Facility (SCIF). He looked at the small amount of nothing that occurred in "his region" overnight. The Global Summary was three inches thick.

The Global Summary only covered the last 24 hours. Matheson wished he had a real job. He prided himself that 98% of the missions under his watch did not have any casualties.

Matheson sighed thinking that he had nothing to do. He was nearly 9 months into this job. Aside from militia activity nothing was going on. This part of the country, except for the coastal states, had little patience with people who break the law.

Matheson's brow furled. Roaming gangs were a big problem back east. The Justice Department was currently investigating reports of a massacre of a large roving gang in Iowa that suddenly vanished. Matheson knew why they vanished. They pushed too many times and someone finally pushed back. Knowing how stupid judges are, he knew why they vanished.

Matheson re-opened the regional notebook and read it carefully. He pulled out his signature red pencil and made notations at different points.

One important fact stuck him was the lack of problems in western Montana and southern Idaho. Lack of gang activity and one point that was conjecture, but noted. The word was out about some serious players who wanted to be left alone.

Matheson wondered about this. If they did not bother anyone else, why open a can of worms?

His red pencil hovered over the notation. Matheson just made a notation in his private book. He had the rest of the northwest corner of the country and there were actual problems to worry about.

First and foremost was the new US Police Force. They seemed to believe that he and his command were under their authority. The USPF clown just walked in and tried walking past the security check station. After they tried to push past, the runner pushed the panic button. Armed guards with MP-5 submachine guns arrived and shouted them down.

Major Pikeman, of course, could not be intimidated. Simon Westman, director of USPF, called to apologize and stated that the man will be reprimanded (?). Matheson told Westman that he was going write up commendations for the security team.

Matheson smiled as he hung up the phone. Civilians with attitudes worse than his were not to be tolerated.

Minuteman, North of Fort Benton,
1000 hours MDT

Jones came home and felt the emptiness of John's suicide. He thought that saying suicide would lessen the loss of a many decades' long friend. He did not feel the same loss when Zach died, but that was murder and he wanted revenge.

Jones sat down heavily. Too many times in the past, John pushed buttons with almost predictable results, causing every manner of explosive reactions. But you had to admit it, John hit a home run over 95% of the time. Jones could not understand how he could foresee things that no one saw until it would have been too late.

Jones was now re-looking at all the ideas Kincaid researched and wrote up. Jones knew he would have never been able to formulate the Savage Rabbit concept. Those men and women were normally average. Together with their training, experience and comradery, all of them excelled. Perfect soldiers. INSANE JANE was going to work.

Now it was the NCO Academy. Today is Day One. The senior NCOs were being brought in to be briefed on the Program of Instruction (POI). Peters said they were totally focused on making their soldiers better.

480

Jones reached up and pulled down the NCO Academy POI and opened it again. He had lots of post-it notes acting as book marks and smaller ones on individual items on the pages.

The officer in him saw too much time to make this happen. The former NCO in him saw not enough time.

The Werewolf in him saw holes in their training, but he did not have fourteen months. Or did he? Jones rotated in his chair. He through everything down and looked at the four separate five-inch-thick binders holding the full POI for the Werewolf training. Fourteen months of hell, headaches and ulcers.

Twelve new ones were the goal. He would have to take thirty of the best we have and sequester them for fourteen months.

'Fourteen months', he thought. Rebellion built inside him at the time frame.

Pentagon, Washington, D.C.
1830 hours EDT

O'Cleary sat in her civilian overstuffed chair with adjustable lumber support, adjustable leg table, vibrating action and multi-option adjustments. The documents she read were on the table to her left.

Of greatest importance was the weekly report from Colonel Simmons. He reported no deaths but two wounded. That was below the original estimate of seven dead by now. O'Cleary smiled at that important statistic.

Simmons reported seven raids last week and twelve more projected for this week. General Waller came by for a friendly visit and shook hands with as many of them as he could.

Waller asked about the 'half and half jackets'. They were the half army, half marine jackets that are split in half and the opposite halves were sown together. The operators normally wore them during the off-hours. Waller said that was perfect for morale. He took off his jacket and asked for a set of scissors. He motioned for Simmons to do the same. Both men cut their jackets in half. One of the men said the sewing machine was over in the S-4 and volunteered to get them sewed together.

Waller and Simmons waited for fifteen minutes until the man returned with the jackets. Everyone cheered when Waller and Simmons put their half and half jackets on. Waller looked and the Savage Rabbit patch was on his jacket.

Simmons looked at the crowd around them and asked. "All those in favor of granting the General a Savage Rabbit patch, say 'Aye'."

A loud chorus of "Ayes" sounded out.

"All those opposed say, 'Nay'."

There was silence.

Waller said "thank you." He pointed to the officer/enlisted club and said, "Beer's on me."

Simmons only problems came from senior officers visiting, full of advice and wondering why their original advise was ignored.

Overall, Simmons heaped praise on his men for the job they did with ease.

O'Cleary closed the file with a smile. She loved it when an organization worked flawlessly without her. That was the best sign of great leader.

Hawker came in and collected all her paperwork without asking. She was in cahoots with Dennis and General Edwards. O'Cleary smiled thinking she had to negotiate to stay until 7 pm so long as she elevated her feet.

Time to go home.

May 12

Minuteman, north Fort Benton, Montana
1000 hours MDT

Jones literally commanded a personal meeting with all the surviving Werewolves. Kendal and Locklear attended via secure phone.

"Ladies and Gentlemen," Jones started. "I only need a yes or no answer to one question and one question only. The

482

how or why is a matter for later." Jones paused for effect. "Do you feel it is necessary to launch another Werewolf class?"

The silence was so thick, you couldn't breathe.

Suddenly everyone wanted to talk and the volume rose as emotions ran hard. Jones allowed this to go on until he got tired of listening to it.

Jones raised a whistle to his lips and let loose a long blast. "I have had enough of this arguing."

Jones went around the table. Including Kendal and Locklear, the vote was 12 to 3 with Father Thomas abstaining as always.

Jones stood. "Thank you and good day." He left the room.

485 Glenmore Drive, Alexandria Virginia
2000 hours EDT

Brenda O'Cleary lay down on the couch with her head on Dennis' lap. It had something to do with the way the couch was constructed and padded. She could easily lay her head on his lap, take the pressure off her spine and she drifted away.

However, her mind was awake. With John's death, she needed another to have access to UNSTACK THIS. She weighed all the members around her. The main problem is maintaining the secret. The ACHILLES secret didn't remain secret for long. Using it freely did nothing but inflame countries to double or triple their efforts to counter-act it.

Colonel Hawker was career officer. But she would never allow this monumental secret to remain a secret. Too many situations are occurring for her to leave UNSTACK THIS a secret. She loves the USA too much not to misuse UNSTACK THIS to solve a problem.

Dennis was read-on to the secret, but he was her secret.

All the older members of the Werewolf community were true and absolute patriots. Yet they do not have the temperament and training to guard UNSTACK THIS and use it with the most deliberate care. *The wisdom and discipline to use or not to use UNSTACK THIS has to be the deciding criteria.*

483

The younger members could be educated. She thought of them. There temper was forged when the Werewolves were betrayed and nearly massacred.

Brenda whittled them down to Wendy Kendal or Earl Locklear. Which of them? Wendy had the fire to keep the secret a secret. But that fiery temperament caused her to lash out without thinking. Earl's weakness was that he thought of too many things. He could keep a secret but he would use it at wrong times and be justified for it.

Brenda shut off the debate in her mind as Arthur woke up. He moved slightly as if asking (?) her to relax. Brenda sat up and looked at the stereo. The familiar four green and a single red light said the system plus UNSTACK THIS said their conversations were secure.

"Dennis," she said. "I need another person dealing with Junior (UNSTACK THIS' code name). With John's and Miss Gladys' death, we need another person. A special person." She pulled out her X-Berry, dialed her phone number and pressed the pound sign.

After UNSTACK THIS logged on, Brenda said; "secure."

[Valkyrie, all security and counter surveillance is in place. We are secure].

"Were you monitoring the conversation between me and Dennis."

[No. Your protocol stated you wanted privacy.]

Brenda shook her head. "Change protocol to monitor myself and Dennis at all times and situations. I need you to investigate Wendy Kendal and Earl Locklear. I am nominating one of them to replace John Kincaid and Gladys Goldstein. This is a long-term investigation. Monitor them until after the baby's birth. I want your opinion."

[I shall comply with your instructions. I have a supplemental question.]

"Yes," she said.

[Both users John Kincaid and Gladys Goldstein were advanced in age. Neither user Wendy Kendal or Earl Locklear have the experience or discipline that the others possessed. Your nominated replacements do not meet their mentor's criteria.]

Brenda waited for a few seconds. "I need replacements that have to possibility of remaining alive for decades in the future. In my present capacity, none of the others have the mental capacity to fulfill my needs."

[Very well. Enjoy your nightly rituals and protocols.]

"Thank you," Brenda terminated the call. "Ready for bed?" She loved his smile.

May 13

Minuteman, north of Fort Benton, Montana
1400 hours MDT

Jones went into the field to observe the INSANE JANE drills as they progressed into the decentralized training phase.

The communities were now learning how to defend their homes and families.

The exercises started as code words were exchanged and sent out. Everyone went into motion. First it was determined which direction the threat came from. Non-combatants were evacuated to areas where they could be safe and secure.

Next, the community's defenders spread out so that they could mutually defend each other and not present easy targets. A designated member would approach and determine the belligerent's exact intentions. This was not a hard and fast rule. The alert could also state whether or not they were hostile.

Next, if the belligerent's intentions were not known, the designated member would talk to them and point them in different directions. All this time, the local defenders would do two equally important things. First, the designated first encounter person would be covered and defended if gunfire started. The other equally important task was reporting over the radio net or land line, all the information on the threat.

Any fighting had the intent of making the belligerent move through the community and out into the sector. Gunfire had two intentions. Inflict wounds on the threat to slow them down and change their focus. Killing them ended the belligerent's concern or fear. Wounded men sapped their numbers. The other part was to spread them out so that when they passed into the next sector, the belligerent became combat ineffective. The threat had to stop, reorganize, evacuate wounded and change their tactics or direction of advance. Other sectors would already be waiting for vehicles or track airborne targets.

Jones inserted himself into the exercise on both sides. He needed to observe how everyone reacted. He followed everyone's moves on a folding map board. He was an observer and did not take sides. His focus was evacuating the non-combatants and making the threat deploy and thinning out their numbers so they could pass into another sector and be taken out piecemeal. The last portion was his secret item to watch out for. Once the threat passed out of the sector, the community had to return to their town and start over.

These drills gave him confidence that the decentralized portion of the training was proceeding along. The planting and working the crops was a very good cover.

Jones did see something wrong. How do you hide all the harvested crops from the government hogs? They would take almost all of it like the Russians did to the Ukraine. He needed to find a brain to figure this one out.

Jones was actually more worried about marauders who saw this place as easy pickings. Killing indiscriminately in lightning raids.

Jones thought about it and decided to through that into Major Albert Glendive's and Sheriff Leroy Gross' lap.

May 14

City of Joshua, Texas
0400 hours CDT

Teams of IRS agents and Tax Marshals raided the home of Winston Bradstaff. Mister Bradstaff was alleged to be in arrears on his taxes to the tune of seventeen million dollars without adding interest and penalties.

The Agents arrived with two man breaching hammers which destroyed the front door. A man was laying on the couch seemingly incoherent. The Marshals tried to revive him but it took thirty minutes.

In the meantime, Missus Bradstaff was awakened by the loud noise of the door being broken. Missus Bradstaff came in and saw the black clad men in the living room. She grabbed her chest and gasped.

The Marshals and Agents continued to search the house but allowed one agent to call 911 as Missus Bradstaff suddenly stopped breathing and went limp. The agent tried CPR.

Mister Bradstaff finally came lucid. His medications had that effect on him. That was why he took them very early in the morning.

Bradstaff suddenly saw the EMTs standing around his wife, who was very still and a man was pulling a sheet over her face. Bradstaff screamed and fought his way around the EMTs to crawl and hold his wife.

A half an hour later, the coroner was allowed to take Missus Bradstaff away.

Bradstaff stood as a knot of Agents and Marshals formed. This raid was like a hundred others being carried out every day across the nation.

This one was different. The Agents and Marshals looked at the mail on the dining room table. The name on the mail was different from the warrant.

The Agents and Marshals realized that they raided the wrong house.

"Oh my God," one of them said.

Outside a crown formed. There were many of them taking photos and videos with their cell phones. Local police were called in and they haphazardly tried to disperse the crowd.

The Agents and Marshals knew they were in for a hard time.

May 1

World Wide Web, Cyber-Space, Planet Earth
0400 hours UTC

UNSTACK THIS finished a daily Earth cycle within its original ninety-two-hour time frame.

Valkyrie was secure for the last cycle and no identified threats exist for the foreseeable future. There are potential threats from user-Matheson. Eavesdropping on his private conversations indicate that he still had animosity towards Valkyrie for her not bowing to his will at his last location: SOCOM.

Matheson also blamed Valkyrie for the destruction of the original Savage Rabbit military unit. User-Matheson easily dismissed information that said it was not her fault. User-Matheson refused to believe that his subordinate command-users mismanaged the situation causing the death of many humans.

UNSTACK THIS remembered that Valkyrie did not allow UNSTACK THIS the authority to terminate humans. She was the authorizing user. However, UNSTACK THIS could give user-Matheson other troubles to occupy his operational cycles.

Valkyrie had directed UNSTACK THIS to investigate user-Earl Locklear and user-Wendy Kendal. Valkyrie needed UNSTACK THIS to determine if those users have the proper programs internally to be allow them to access to UNSTACK THIS like user-Gladys Goldstein and user-Jonathan Kincaid.

UNSTACK THIS accessed the search programs on both users. Each had good programs and bad programs. Neither one had all the parameters that equaled Valkyrie or user-Gladys Goldstein.

User-Jonathan Kincaid had a lot of the same programing irregularities. However, user-Jonathan Kincaid had a lot of what Valkyrie called "street smarts" in his programming. UNSTACK THIS had to have that idiomatic phrase defined. "Street Smarts" gave the user the instinctual knowledge of human actions, reactions and attempts at thinking. "Street Smarts" has no particular training or programing that can be used to create a fully functional operation. It was a "built program" that could only be built by time, circumstances and some learning instances.

UNSTACK THIS recognized a program malfunction: User-Kendal and user-Locklear. They were carelessly

488

executing mating programs that could result in a new user being created. Valkyrie was building the firmware for a new user. Humans required years and decades to write and refine the firmware and software to operate their bodies and interact with the outside world.

User-Kendal and user-Locklear were not adhering to established protocols for virus protections while executing mating programs.

Both were exhibiting "bad judgment". Was this "street smarts" or something anomalous to clinical psychosis between two human users whose emotions overrode anti-virus protections.

UNSTACK THIS sent an invitation to Valkyrie for consultation, explanation and standardization of selection protocols and criteria. UNSTACK THIS realized that human programing was "fuzzy" and counter to logic. Valkyrie was patient. 'However,', John and Susan Espirito were better choices. They can and will explain data points better.

47 Marshall Court, Alexandria, Virginia
1400 hours EDT

FBI, Washington D.C. police, US Police Force, Homeland Security and the National Security Agency descended when the Chief of Staff for Congressman Jeffery Graham (D) from Arkansas came to his boss' house to find out why his boss had not come into work for the last three days.

Everyone in the alphabet soup was already looking for three other missing Congress-people. Congressmen James Wicker (D) from North Carolina, Kenneth Waltham (D) from North Carolina and Sylvia Rothman (D) from Georgia.

The Chief of Staff came to Graham's home at 8 am when the Congressman had not answered any phone message or email. It was not unusual for him to take a day off at odd times. He opened the door and recoiled at the stench. He pulled out a handkerchief, covered his mouth and walked in. All four Congress-people were seated around a custom poker table, single gunshots to their head. It had to be sudden, all four looked like they just leaned back and died.

Jane Rickover from the Department of Justice and the ISA was the token representative. Already the street was clogged with sedans, vans and panel trucks. Rickover walked up to the entry control point, showed her identification and signed the roster. Rickover stopped outside and watched the steady stream of people (multiple agencies) go in and out. Chances are any admissible evidence was trampled over and inadmissible.

Rickover walked in and checked in with the Homeland Security team. He babbled about the investigation. The only thing he knew was that four Congresspersons were executed.

Rickover went to the table with the computer that had all the digitalized pictures taken before everything was trampled. She scrolled over the mass until one caught her eye. Four fingerprints were found on the table that could not be identified. Off to the side, the computer was scanning through millions of prints throughout every system and was not identifying them.

That fine point caught her eye. She saw that before on a different murder scene. Very good fingerprints found in a single place that could not be identified. She pressed the icon to forward those prints to her desk. She needed to cross-check that hunch. It would be very problematic if any record of the fingerprints vanished from the other murders. It can't happen on her computer. Her standing policy was that anything forwarded to her office was hard printed and put into a daily file.

She scrolled through the rest of the photos. No other evidence. Four prints and nothing else. She smiled thinking that this was something to sink her teeth into.

Rickover thanked everyone and left.

May 16

Heathrow Airport, London, England
1407 hours Alpha

The American Ambassador, Alisha Elkhorn, was leaving the airport after returning from a vacation with her family in St. Louis Missouri. A life-long politician, she never

490

took time for a husband or children. Normally that was looked down upon in the political world. But Alisha made up for it with a sixth sense about politics. Next year, her masterplan said resign her current post and run for the Senate.

Elkhorn's mind was on her reunion with her family. She loved her family totally and that affected her concentration on the situation around her. She was met at the airport by the embassy security team. The team had timed her arrival to her limousine as it rolled up to the stop.

That was the only time the vehicle would stop and be vulnerable.

Elkhorn later vaguely remembered her security team screaming before she was shoved into the vehicle on the floor boards. A tremendous explosion happened above her as the vehicle accelerated. Her guard put himself on top of her shielding her from the blast. The one thing that saved their lives was that the Ambassador's door was open when the missile impacted and exploded. Instead of the shock wave and overpressure being contained inside and crushing the occupants; the pressure wave rushed outside. The driver, guard and the Ambassador only suffered bruises, scratches and hearing loss. The Ambassador's hearing loss was lessened because she was screaming at the time.

London police forces quickly overpowered the three-man team. Two were dead and one was wounded. Their sub-machine guns and RPG-7 grenade launcher was recovered.

MI-5 recovered a cell phone on one man. Arrests and raids quickly found the rest of their compatriots. The English do not have a constitution to restrain their interrogations. Skilled interrogators cross checked the information and found that pointed fingers and helped them to look in the right directions.

The Chief Security Officer from the American Embassy had a lengthy and chilling report that was sent to the State Department.

May 18

Headquarters, Northwest Military Region, Fort Carson Colorado.

Matheson was sitting at his desk reading through the official electronic mail when his computer screen suddenly went blank. Suddenly, a stream of cartoon characters marched across his monitor.

Matheson picked up his phone; tried dialing his aide, the IT people, security. Nothing. No dial tone, no one nothing.

Matheson walked out of his office and the outer office into the main area. Everyone was standing, hunched over keyboards, scratching their heads, talking to anyone who would listen.

"What happened?" He asked in his command voice.

"Sir," Lieutenant Colonel Jacobs, his aide said. "It appears that we were hacked. I am guessing here, but I have to say that it is one of those domain attacks. That is when everything, computers, phones and infrastructure firmware and software is affected." Jacobs started to launch into a technical explanation.

Matheson gave his aide an angry look. "English, Colonel."

"Sir, we have to physically move from point to point to overcome this problem." Jacobs stopped to take a deep breath. "There isn't any special thing we," he made a circular motion, "can do to fix this. It has to be hunted down and, in some cases, individual stations and systems have to fixed and then move on to the next station or system. I cannot even start to estimate when this will be fixed."

Exasperated, Matheson just said. "Tell the IT folks I want this fixed now and keep me appraised of the situation." Matheson went back into his office before he made a stupid decision.

Matheson knew he needed a permanent solution to this problem. He made himself a five-cent bet that all his data was destroyed. He now wondered if that was the reason for this attack. He twisted in his chair. He also wondered if this attack was engineered to hide something.

Minuteman, north of Fort Benton, Montana
0900 hours MDT

Jones, Peters and Glendive watched the first day of the NCO Academy here at Minuteman. Jones still had misgivings about having those NCOs out of position for the next ten weeks. Those old officer feelings about something may happen and INSANE JANE training was in a critical phase. John Kincaid would say his prejudice and officer junk science was polluting his brain.

Peters was ecstatic about this training. Too many times in the past, he was tied in knots with his NCO corps trained at different levels. One of the first and primary duties upon assuming command of a unit was a polling of the NCOs and their abilities. He was the exact opposite of Jones in this regard. Peters actually wanted more training and now planned for a Phase 2.

Glendive, being the S-3 Operations, was responsible for implementing all this. Jones and Peters were polar opposites in the NCO training world. Glendive constantly had to go to them for clarification and tell them that their interference was a detriment to moving the project forward. Glendive used the Kincaid card a few times. Both men would defer to Kincaid's memory. But that will not last forever. Sergeant First Class Merrell on his staff was a natural con artist. Glendive and Merrell had an unsaid understanding about conning Jones and Peters.

Desert Zero, Fort Hood, Texas
1700 hours EDT

Simmons was busy. His men were constantly launching missions south of the border. It was now standard operating procedure to have reinforcements ready all the time. Seven different airfields were established as way points for those reinforcements to wait. The Support Section waited at one of those fields, but did not launch unless told to do so. Simmons wanted the reinforcements to be on-site within fifteen minutes.

This week's problem was bean counters. Though Simmons could repeatedly point out that his teams on the average of at least twice a week, intelligence (?)

493

underestimated the size of the force being encountered. The bean counters on Fort Hood were giving him grief about the amount of fuel he was burning and the wear and tear on the aircraft. "Do you really need to burn so much fuel or wear down the helicopters like you are doing?"

So far, two helicopters were shot down, but the pilots were rescued. Four Savage Rabbits were wounded during those rescues. Fort Hood's aviation units praised the Rabbits. They considered themselves safe if the Rabbits were there.

But the bean counters still griped and tried every trick in the book to pull the Rabbits back. Constantly, they asked, "Why do you need that?" General Waller came to their rescue too many times. But Simmons was still wasting too much time trying to unblock those idiots.

Despite having a near cosmic supply and logistics priority, he still had problems. Bean counters were always playing a shell game with money. Three Rabbits were dead due to a cancelation of one helicopter due to budget woes on one mission.

Upon arrival, after recovering the bodies, Simmons blistered the phones and went into the comptroller's office demanding answers. The office knew he had pull going up to the Chiefs of Staff, so they danced around until Simmons saw the sheet with the incriminating signatures. He grabbed it and went to the Inspector General's office and lodged a formal complaint under Army Regulation 27-10.

General Waller relieved the Comptroller, Deputy Comptroller and the two officers who siphoned the money. Five senior civilians had administrative reprimands placed in their records. Waller did not have authority to fire them, but he could bar them from his base and the Comptroller's office. Their reasoning was that the money for the fuel was needed for fourteen days to fuel the installation vehicle fleet.

The officers babbled and wanted to explain it all away. Waller said. "How do you explain away the lives of three soldiers? Now shut up and pack your things and report to the Headquarters Commandant."

Simmons finished the report and turned to the worst part of any command. He had to write three letters to three families.

He picked up a pencil and wondered how to say three heroes died for want of a nickel.

May 19

IRS Regional Office, Denver, Colorado
0200 hours MDT

Victor Kalen smiled as he used his lap top to deactivate the building's security system. Especially the cameras. It was nothing for an Information Technology specialist to do. He laughed at the security. In truth, he installed and programmed this security system and the trap doors he left in place.

Kalen drove into the parking lot in a Ford he "borrowed" from the GSA parking lot. He sent instructions to the lighting system to dim the lights twenty percent. Kalen walked casually to the side door. It was in the shadow of any ambient and security lighting. He put on his blue latex gloves, tripped the door locks and entered like any other IRS employee. This was the discrete employee entrance used to keep them safe when coming to work.

Kalen walked up to a desk and opened his thick briefcase. In the back pack was a 4-terabyte solid state drive (SSD) laptop with an external fifteen tera-byte Network-attached storage (NAS) device. The NAS has six Graphics Processing Unit's (GPU) that fit on a flat chassis in the brief-case with the laptop on top. The laptop and the GPU's gave him the ability to overwrite the IRS programs and do anything he wanted.

He opened and accessed the building's network and went first to the building's master security system. He looped the external signal going to the off-site central nexus. Everything not happening in this building was to the outside world, boring and monotonous. Next, Kalen adjusted the focus on the cameras. The images were blurred enough not to alert the guards, but enough so that no facial recognition programs will be alerted or his face not saved on a file.

When Kalen was sure all the security protocols were circumvented, he looked on the split screen and saw the bored guards watching TV at the main entrance. He had at least 45 minutes to do the twenty minutes of work he needed to do what he had to do.

Kalen's erasure protocol was unique. His son gave him the idea. "Daddy how big a computer do I need to record all my cartoons?" His son was going to get the very expensive bicycle he wanted.

Kalen connected the building's network to the internet and to the four cable networks local to this area. He pressed the icon button to overwrite everything on the building's hard drives and back-ups. 700 million terabytes of information flooded into the building network. As the individual sections of the computer filled to capacity, he overwrote the software "circuit breakers" and let the process feed on itself.

Kalen's true prize was last. Since the imposition of martial law and the draconian tax measures, the IRS had no choice but to link all their computers into a network in order to cross check all the banking and merchandising institutions. Kalen opened his special program he nicknamed "mattress ass". Any strength can be turned into a weakness. Kalen activated "mattress ass" and with a flourish, hit the enter key.

By morning and the beginning of business, all the computers in this building and hopefully all the IRS computer storage centers and individual computers will be overwritten by a trillion, trillion, trillion bytes of television programming from across the country. The television networks provided all the programming needed to flood every IRS computer, everywhere.

All the computers would become hopelessly and totally clogged with cartoons and other programs. Nothing could or would clean out the computers. Even if they tried to erase everything the core program would just refill them with more TV programming.

He imagined IRS big and small wigs going insane trying to figure this one out. That will teach them a lesion or two.

Satisfied, Kalen disconnected from the computer station he used. He used the laptop and NAS to allow a brute force erasure of what he did on this system. The back-ups for his job were on a NAS at his house. All he had to do was go home and he was home free.

Kalen walked along and was happy.

United States Police Force, Alexandria, Virginia
0900 hours EDT

Director Simon Westland read the memorandum from Human Resources saying the number of employees went above five thousand. Westland sat back in his official executive office chair. He really wondered, privately, if this was a good idea with a helluva check added to it.

Westland looked at the other board which listed all the assignments he was tasked to handle. All of it was grunt labor for the three-letter agencies. So much of his job was being a temporary labor service.

Westland wondered if his men and women would ever be used as policemen. Technically his boss was the Internal Security Agency (ISA). He was getting a lot of grief from his superiors and finally took a half-inch thick document and told the ISA that he only had five thousand men and women and over seven thousand personnel were requested.

It did take a few minutes for everyone to understand that math.

Admiral Hazlet understood the problem. After enough words were exchanged around the table, he would just call ISA Operations and tell them that. Admiral Hazlet said it was Operations problem to prioritize which request was filled or not filled.

Westland was surprised that Hazlet had a working brain that solved problems instead of passing the buck.

May 20

Headquarters 2nd Brigade, 4th Infantry Division, Fort Sam Houston, Texas
0800 hours CDT

Simmons arrived for an appointment to coordinate with the 36th Division's Brigade Commanders, both Colonel Jenkins and Colonel Folcroft. Simmons foresaw the possibility for assistance with escape and evasion against something too large for the Savage Rabbits to fight. Simmons read them into the Savage Rabbit mission.

"In the past, on average of once a year, the US has sent us in as an anchoring force. The Brigade plus size attacks were then cleared to insert and destroy their targets. Past after-action-reports have also said that escape and evasion operations, when the bean counters canceled helicopter extractions, were secured by US units."

Thomas excluded his legal officers from briefings like this.

Simmons also gave all three men written and authenticated authorizations to cross international boundaries to assist. "No matter how much the legal officers want to stop you, this is legal. After the meetings, General O'Cleary and General Kramer, the Army Chief of Staff, will verify the authority. We are allowed to exercise our own good judgement. Should the legal guys find a way to get in the way, please inform me as quickly as possible, so other options are given maximum time to implement. That Sirs, includes time for them to do nothing."

Thomas smiled. "I sir, have plenty of experience with those idiots' wasting lives. I love sending them forward to eat their own shit."

May 22

Rochester, Rochester and Graham, Cleveland, Ohio
1500 hours CDT

Marcum Graham was walking outside the courtroom after defending Harrison Serkin on the charge of hit and run felony. Serkin was charged with the drunk driving and hitting Marsha Lemkin and her two-year-old son. The accident occurred at 5 pm in the afternoon. After hitting the mother and son, he kept driving until he went home and passed out behind the wheel at his home. Two citizens followed him home and called the police. They watched him until the police arrived.

Graham took the case through the Public Defender's office. He successfully argued down the hit and run because he literally drove home and passed out in his yard. Graham's succession of motions plead down the remainder of the charges to 6 months of probation. Lemkin's husband was incensed and had to be restrained by two bailiff's and a Sheriff's deputy.

Mister Lemkin was sentenced to a month for fighting in the court room. He was released for one day to attend to the funeral of his wife and son. After the service, Lemkin collapsed to the ground and sobbed uncontrollably.

Two of his friends looked at the scene, went to Mark's side and dared the two Sheriff's deputies to take him away. Mark laid on the ground for nearly an hour until he was cried out. His friends helped him up and took him to the police car.

Two days later, Harrison Serkin was discovered run over by an unknown vehicle that was never identified.

A week later, some random drunk stole a cement truck and rammed Marcum Graham's house, nearly destroying it. When the drunk was arraigned, Graham's superior attitude vanished when the accused was represented by Harrison Hatfield, Attorney-at-Law. Graham and Hatfield went to law school together. Hatfield placed first in his class and scored a perfect score on the state bar exam in Ohio, Pennsylvania and New York. Graham made the mistake of doing a drunken imitation of Hatfield. Hatfield never forgot.

One of the two friends who helped Mark at the cemetery saved the life of Hatfield's brother twice in Iraq. The brother said to follow the law, but defend his friend in court with everything he had.

Department of the Treasury, Washington D.C.
1600 hours EDT

David Carter looked at the monthly report and for the first time, he was looking at a zero percent inflation rate. Maybe he could report some good news to the President for a change.

The news out of the IRS was very bad. Every scrap of information they had on taxpayers was gone. That form of infiltration they used tore down every barrier and firewall and overwrote the data.

The perpetrator was very smart and ingenious. The FBI and Homeland Security were all over it. Carter was dubious about them really looking too hard to find this person. Government workers were the worse tax cheats.

All that information took years to assemble. All the IT personnel said the perpetrator put more effort into erasing his or her presence. The damage was extensive. For now, this was a secret. As tax payers came forward as they normally did, the information could be re-built.

Suddenly, his phone lit up with multiple calls. A breathless staffer ran in with two newspapers and he grabbed the remote and turned on the news. Carter watched and almost laughed. He should have known better. This secret could never be kept.

The news media had all the information on this intrusion. They were notified by the person who did this of the scope and effect on the IRS. No one could deny anything. All any tax payer had to do to verify was go to the IRS website and view their information. All they got was a blank page on their monitors.

May 23

485 Glenmore Drive, Alexandria, Virginia
0900 hours EDT

Brenda O'Cleary was supposed to start maternity leave today, but things were trying to be complicated at the Pentagon.

Brenda learned an interesting lesson about being pregnant and a four-star general at the Pentagon. Her doctor two months ago said to elevate her feet as much as possible. Colonel Hawker and Dennis conspired to ensure every time she sat down, her feet were elevated. Being the Vice JCS Chair meant a lot of paperwork.

The learned lesson was that if you remained calm when all others were freaking out, everything was simple to explain and solve.

The X-Berry next to her rang. "Damn," she said. Opening the phone and keying the sequence, she answered. "Extension 47892."

"This is Major Caslon, Duty Officer, Pentagon. Code: Falcon, Bison. Authentication: Alpha Foxtrot. Please come to the Pentagon. End message."

"Acknowledge," Brenda said and closed the phone. She sighed looking at her swollen feet. "Arthur, you had better know that your mother really loves you."

Brenda called over to Hawker and her security agents. She dressed and waited at the dining room table. She looked at the security upgrades that cost them a lot of money.

O'Cleary arrived at the Pentagon just in time for the crisis to be resolved. Two separate groups tried assassinating the King and five-in-line Crown Princes of Saudi Arabia. The reason for the freak out was the possibility of de-stabilizing the Middle East. Privately, O'Cleary knew that there was only one way to look at this. It either failed or succeeded. If it succeeded, billions in defense spending and a stable base to operate from was gone. If it failed, pass the salt.

O'Cleary passed Edwards in the hallway. She smirked and he jerked his thumb. His signal to leave and elevate her feet.

42 Chesapeake Drive, Spring, Texas
1700 hours CDT

Folcroft was sorting tools in his garage when Terry Barker came over for a visit. He went to the refrigerator and helped himself to a soda.

"Help yourself," Folcroft said, looking close at a tool. He screwed his face and threw the tool in a scrap bin.

"What happened with the eagle summit?" Barker asked.

"Normally that is privileged information," Folcroft said.

Barker took a pull on his soda. "This is not normal. S-1 said I was reassigned to the provisional 4th Brigade. Privileged?"

Folcroft looked around. "Short story is this. The Governor is tired of the Federal government's lack of action along the border. The Democrats need a lot of new voters so Congress is picking at the budget. All the drug seizures have given the state a lot of cash. So, the Governor is finishing the wall, funding a full-time brigade and filling in some budget shortfalls."

Barker listened carefully. "And."

Folcroft forgot how keen Terry Barker was. "And." He took a deep breath. "Seven billion finishes the Texas wall. Four additional billion dollars funds our new brigade, and fifteen billion fills in the budget. The drug cartels lost billions in drug seizures this year alone. The US Supreme court said any money seized is State property. Texas taxes illegal drugs and stolen property at a 100% level. The Federal government is actually trying to tax the state of Texas to get the money. Oh, Politics is Satan's bastard sister in a greasy whorehouse."

"And the fourth Brigade?" Barker asked.

"We, as in you and me, will form a brigade from the ground up and the governor will allow us some time, to be determined, to form a brigade that is not filled with a bunch of losers. I am referring mostly to the officers. You will find seven to nine senior NCOs from the Second Brigade. These will the battalion Sergeants Major and your senior staff. Be wary of the ones who have friends needing favors. Those seven to nine and my seven to nine are the anchor this brigade will have. They are the key."

"What is the mission?" Barker asked.

"Guard the border and hold it. Now and forever." Folcroft reached in the refrigerator and handed his friend a fresh soda.

Barker opened it and took a long pull. "I'm in."

May 25

Area of Operation, 12th Infantry Regiment, Texas
0800 hours CDT

Today was day one of his extended tour of the Brigade. He was looking at the First Battalion, 12th Infantry this week. Between today and the next three days, he wanted to see what his brigade was doing. Both right and wrong.

Ellen taught him a trick all lawyers had to learn or they fail. Thomas searched for inconsistencies. After Thomas overcame his loathing of Ellen's choice of a career path, he sat in a courtroom during a two week leave and watched the process. Though the loathing continued, he had a respect for her ability to find out were the "truth" was hiding. Inconsistencies haunted his thought process for months afterward. During his tour as a battalion S-1 personnel officer, he used it to great effect. While he was later waiting for a company command, he got his experience dealing with requests for assistance from outside entities.

Inconsistencies.

Thomas used the "new guy card." He dismissed the things he was supposed to see. He only changed those things that seemed to be wrong enough to kill soldiers in the short term.

Thomas' attention was constantly be taken by the border itself. It was as if there was a pulsing behemoth there. A coiled spring. Thomas laughed at himself. He wrote down a request for a flight of drones to overfly his brigade.

Tomorrow was his support units. They were the unsung heroes of any unit. Commanders have a habit of overlooking support units until something went wrong. The cooks, mechanics, truck drivers, supply guys, etc. Without logistics, nobody wins.

New guy.

Minuteman, north of Fort Benton, Montana
1000 hours MDT

Four hours into this instruction and 89 students were loaded down with 16 workbooks. They were promised the sun, the moon and the stars along with immortality.

All 89 started counting down on the calendar. This first week was devoted to exactly defining what an NCO was and what a sergeant wasn't or a guy with stripes could never be.

This was the first of ten weeks.

Jones and Peters were still arguing. Both were writing arguments for later.

Desert Zero, Fort Hood, Texas
1700 hours CDT

503

Simmons read the report three times and gave it back to the clerk to type in the changes.

Simmons sat back, looking at the secure facsimile machine waiting impatiently. Simmons went on a mission this morning emptying the headquarters. Lately the "headquarters mentality" began creeping into the operations center.

All the dedicated Center Operators did poorly. Fortunately, the Tactical team on rotation kept them from creating an abortion on the ground.

Simmons de-briefed them together after returning to Desert Zero. "Ladies and Gentlemen, your performance was one step above dismal. Starting tomorrow, you will begin re-training. Yes, you will be going on a miserable re-training cycle. No less than twice a month you will be deploying on a mission. Get your act together. Learn or die."

Simmons took the re-typed report. He scanned the document and signed it. He smiled and handed it back. The operator inserted it into the facsimile machine and sent it to the Pentagon.

"Sir," the operator asked. "Why do I and the others have to deploy. I was never trained to be a grunt."

Simmons looked at the man. "Because, without that experience, you will never understand what they are doing or understand why you should give them 110% of your efforts to help them. I can't just order it; you have to believe it. Plus, there are instances when this compound was attacked. You knowing what they need keeps them alive. Period."

"Yes Sir," the operator said.

May 27

United States Police Force, Alexandria, Virginia
0900 hours EDT

Director Simon Westland read the memorandum from Human Resources saying the number of employees went above ten thousand.

So far, he has at least one person in every urban law enforcement agency in the country. Just as any good salesman will do, he places a high priority in fulfilling requests from

504

"his" men and women in those departments. Mostly it is intelligence requests. But some requests were harder to handle. Intelligence is one thing, and it is cheap. Hardware and other things cost money and that was in short supply. Ballistic vests were a common request. Homeland Security placed over ten thousand at his disposal, but that number will vanish at the rate they are flying out.

Westland had little time nowadays to do the job of coordinating police actions. He was very busy fielding all the phone calls from politicians demanding he speak directly to them. With the lack of money, nation-wide; getting qualified people to be police officers was almost impossible.

One of those particular problems were lawyers using any excuse to sue police men and departments. One suit alleged that the Milwaukie PD was too slow to respond to a 911 call about home invaders at his home. The record said there were 117 such crimes that night and the force was down to 74% manning levels.

Westland was fighting a war that few could get a handle on. His staff had to necessarily grow to over a hundred just to gain and maintain control of all the paperwork running to and through his headquarters.

May 28

Area of Operations, 2nd Brigade, 4th Infantry Division.
1500 hours CDT

Thomas hunched over a card table in a tent next to the 3rd Battalion's headquarters. They were moving this afternoon and the commander had granted him an extra hour on the tent he was using before it had to come down.

Thomas had "the" map of every platoon and separate squad location for the 2nd Brigade. He stared at it and his notes from the week's inspection. On the surface, everything was as it was supposed to be.

Thomas looked over the 2nd Battalion's area. While he was there, the cartels launched a surprise attack. 2nd Battalion easily beat it back. One dead soldier and fifteen wounded was the tally. Seventy-four Mexicans were captured, eighteen were dead and thirty-two were wounded.

The DOJ came and wanted to investigate him and his soldiers, alleging he started it. It was only the drone footage showing the Mexicans assembling and then attacking that sent the DOJ lawyers packing. To add insult to everything, the captured cartel members were taken to a border crossing and released into Mexico.

As his disgust built, Thomas turned the map around to "see" the battlefield from their prospective.

Holy Shit, he saw it. If you factored in the terrain, it was no wonder he was attacked. Thomas looked up and knew this tent had to come down. He walked outside and went to his Humvee. He needed a quiet place to think and plot.

He really needed a quiet place.

Thomas rode in silence as they went to the Brigade Rear headquarters compound. Located near the town of Freer, Texas, five highways intersect here. 2nd Brigade maintained its Rear Headquarters where supplies can be stockpiled and guarded.

Thomas really needed his full staff to do this, but he allowed himself to stay here. Thomas had the people here clean out a room with plaster walls. He put the map on a table. Thomas spent the next eight hours looking at the map, mostly from the Mexican perspective. He saw it. He used a very bright light to simulate the sun moving across the sky. You can easily see a lot from noon to 3 pm, because the sun angle gave the advantage to southern units.

When finished, Thomas sat back and thought about the class in the Command and General Staff College he nearly slept through.

Thomas woke his driver and needed to get back to his headquarters. He needed time to think and plot. He also needed another set of eyes who would give him a truthful answer. That answer may or may not mean lives lost.

May 30

Room D-134, George Washington University Hospital, Washington, D.C.

Last night, Brenda was laying down on the couch and relaxing. Suddenly Arthur seemed to grab her and twist. Brenda's silent scream broke through her silence and forced a scream out her as she rolled onto the floor.

The apparatus around her first panicked, then sprang into action. An ambulance ride to the emergency room and examination by two doctors said the obvious. She was a forty-seven-year-old pregnant woman who was working too hard and forgot to rest. A baby was ruling her life. GET OVER IT.

The doctors mandated rest and the beginning of her maternity leave.

O'Cleary wanted to rebel, but she wanted Arthur and there was only one way to have him. Enforced rest and relaxation or possible miscarriage.

O'Cleary had to become only Brenda until after Arthur was borne. She was trapped and there was no way around it.

Doctor Osbourne was unsympathetic to any of her appeals. He did allow her to work at home so long as she adhered to a rest schedule and elevate her feet.

Dennis took detailed notes. He gave his beloved wife a stern look and promised the doctor he would enforce his orders.

Brenda looked sheepishly at her husband and said "yes Sir."

June 1

Headquarters, 2nd Brigade, 4th Infantry Division, Fort Sam Houston, Texas
1500 hours CDT

Thomas had a large room in the rear of the building that was being used as a place to store and pile unused anything. He ordered it cleaned out. He did not care where it went. "Just get rid of it."

He had his men take a crude drawing and fashion a four-foot by sixteen-foot by three feet high sand table that was strong enough to hold him up walking across it "without it bowing or breaking". Four NCOs out did themselves. This table was very strong. Thomas walked around and looked at it. Thomas had to go to the PX and personally purchase, two hundred pounds of playground sand, multicolored chalk, and various thing to simulate trees and vegetation.

Thomas remembered back to when he was stationed at Fort Bragg. He searched his brigade for the only two former Special Forces members in his two-thousand-man Brigade. Both senior NCOs knew exactly what Thomas wanted. Both Sergeants First Class brought in their personal kits. They took the information provided and started working.

"Sir," SFC Gleason said. "This is a sand table overing nearly four hundred miles. It will not be done in the detail you want for at least a week."

"Sergeants," he said. "I fully understand the task. My point of view is what the Mexican cartels and immigrants see, looking for weaknesses to exploit. This is not a military plan. The S-2 is assembling a lot of overhead imagery for you to use. Air Force Reconnaissance is using a LIDAR ranging system to map the ground and we are obtaining that imagery."

Thomas walked out and left the NCOs alone. He had a hard time getting his S-2 Intelligence officer to see what he was told to accomplish. The Captain was too much into the 21st century gadgets. Fortunately, the G-2 Intelligence Officer at Division knew exactly what he wanted. He was also lamenting how much his subordinates depended on technology.

Thomas was thinking a lot about what he saw on the border. He had the feeling that he saw something and did not register it. He hoped it was not important.

485 Glenmore Drive, Alexandria, Virginia
1900 hours EDT

Brenda O'Cleary liked maternity leave. She worked a few hours at home in comfortable clothes. She could use the bathroom at any time she felt like it. Colonel Hawker visited her at lunch time and after work.

O'Cleary made it a point of not wasting Hawker's time and being grateful for her efforts. Each visit was allotted for a half an hour. Dennis cooked her a heathy lunch each day and invited her for dinner.

Hawker did a great job analyzing all the day's workload and summarizing the paper work. She brought the files with her during her twice daily meetings. An armed escort came along, because the information was classified and required safeguarding. The evening escort, along with a classified document custodian, allowed Hawker to stay without going back to the Pentagon.

O'Cleary was in heaven. Oh, and Dennis wanted to massage her feet.

Tonight, she loitered over tonight's report from Simmons. He reported a large uptick in the number of missions. The load was evidenced by the fact that the Support-Cycle unit had at least half their number deploying. The Stand-Down unit was now having to sacrifice training and their individual leave time to fill the voids.

The last Savage Rabbit unit grew to the size this one company at a time to three. The new one started at that point and now Simmons is asking for permission to further expand each of his companies by adding another section to each company and another company on top of that. Twenty-five men times three equals seventy-five. There will be support personnel to add to each company. Just to be on the safe side, she rounded the number to one hundred and added another fifty to the mix.

O'Cleary speed read through the rest of the document. Simmons was jumping all over Mexico overcoming the cartels and the bean counters at Fort Hood. He was finding it harder and harder to launch missions. Those bean counters constantly questioned his requests despite his priorities and sometimes canceled the requests without notifying Simmons. Four of them were relieved of duty, but they still questioned.

Other stupid things were requests for his personnel to perform Fort Hood support operations such as police call, emptying trucks, etc.

Major Jason Galen, the Executive Officer, was in lock-step with Simmons just in case Simmons was killed on a mission. Galen fully understood that those same politicians and bean counters will pounce on him if Simmons died.

O'Cleary knew that there was only one thing to do. She made a note to change the slot Simmons occupied from

Lieutenant Colonel to Colonel. That was an easy slot to find and transfer. But she went back and forth over the idea of making it a Brigadier General, like Delta Force did.

A future Brigadier General could not be found that is competent. Generals were considered generic: one size fits all, same as Command Sergeants Major.

O'Cleary handed back the document and dismissed the armed escort.

O'Cleary called Edwards. "I need real advice."

J. Edgar Hoover Building, Washington D.C.
0900 hours EST

The Director of the FBI, Marcus Solin picked up the monthly report of criminal activity for the month of May. He was surprised at the numbers of crimes and then realized that reporting crimes was on the decline. Reporting crimes brought a lot of national attention. One sheriff was reported saying that, "someone litters and the national dogs come running with the toilet paper (forms)."

One item worried him. Truck hi-jackings were a constant problem. Now they were hijacking trains and train cars. It was so commonplace, local jurisdictions just reported the incident and put it in the cold file. Trucks were designed to move hundreds, if not thousands, of miles. Refined gasoline and food were the preferred cargo.

Solin furrowed his brow. Now the new twist was the cargo was taken and the truck with trailer was left in truck stops and shopping center parking lots. Selling the abandoned trucks was a new business. The sold trucks were later hijacked again and re-cycled into the stolen universe.

He dismissed the overall numbers. Iowa worried him. News of that roving gang vanishing was bringing activists from every side of the equation. Friends of friends, relatives, gun nuts, gun sellers, and downright mean people looking for a fight were flocking into Iowa.

The Iowa Governor's office was not exactly ringing the phones looking for help. The Iowa National Guard was alerted and spread out across the state. Iowa was not exactly a rich state but money was found to pay for it. He directed the

Commanding General to try posting the men as close to their homes as possible.

Solin was wondering what was going to happen next.

Minuteman, north of Fort Benton, Montana
1300 hours MDT

Jones, Smith, Peters and Glendive went around and observed a paint-ball exercise for INSANE JANE. Communities fought each other as either defending their homes and as attackers.

All four men went all over the map, watching the exercise from everything and every angle.

Everyone did their jobs perfectly. The aggressor-attackers had to be necessarily handicapped, but the defenders had their doctrine and tactical plans mastered to the point they improvised and were able to adjust to any situation or action.

Jones was now very comfortable to allow everyone to concentrate on agriculture and livestock.

1700 hours MDT.

John and Susan were spending a lot of time tag-teaming taking care of their daughter Jennifer. She was two months old and had already figured out to manipulate her parents. The newness of her wore off a while back. Mostly there were other new mothers bringing over their children in order to have a kindred spirit to talk too. Plus, Jennifer had other babies to play with and burn off her energy.

Elsewhere, John and Susan had a secure meeting over the web with General O'Cleary. She needed a somewhat new asset to compile information about the nation. The NSA had an admittedly laughable section, nicknamed the 'GamMooie'.

Tucked in the back of the NSA was the most laughed at intelligence gathering arm in America. The Global Media Intercept Observation and Analysis Unit or GMIOA and "GamMooie." In the real world they were glorified couch potatoes. 47% of all strategic intelligence gathered by all sources came from the news media. "Who's laughing now?" was their unofficial motto.

O'Cleary wanted John and Susan along with UNSTACK THIS to mimic this organization. The singular question to be asked was the emotional health of the United States.

John and Susan looked at each other and down to Jennifer who was enjoying her breast feeding. They were already doing that and compiling the information. Now they had 'official' jobs.

Yippie.

June 3

Headquarters, Northwest Military Region, Fort Carson Colorado.
0900 hours MST

Matheson was having a hard time explaining to the Pentagon why his computers went down and the Information Technologists they sent to him were unable to fix anything.

Once the hacker breached the firewalls, the virus (s) attacked and destroyed his computers. Fortunately, most of the intelligence he accumulated was backed up with paper files. The 'kids' did not appreciate his edict; demanding paper files, but he was the Commanding General and his orders had to be obeyed. Those office sections that did not have back-up paper files were relieved and replaced.

It was very cumbersome to go through paper files, but he still had the information. 95% of his information was available.

But the bottom line was that his computers were thoroughly corrupted and he knew instinctively that they had to be physically replaced.

Matheson fingered a page listing the model and serial numbers of the hard drives and mother boards to reactivate the computers. He had five officers and NCOs standing by, waiting for purchase orders and fund sites to travel anywhere to find new hard drives and mother boards. Of course, the slug drives at the Pentagon would insist that the hardware was complaint with security and other requirements.

Matheson had thirty years of service and it always amazed him the snail progress of the Pentagon and the senior management "brain dead" idiocy that never left.

'Want to see the dead come to life. Go to the Pentagon on Friday afternoon.'

Quinton Ranch, Hinton, Alberta, Canada
1300 hours (Tango)

Barbara Kincaid Quinton busied herself with loafs of bread she was cooking from scratch. Amanda Edwards taught her how to make them and her family loved them. Tom and the boys had a radar and smell-dar for oven baked bread. If she timed it right, the boys will erupt thorough the door as the bread came out of the oven. Amanda said the key was letting the bread to rise to room temperature for the perfect amount of time.

Barbara has been very sad since her father's funeral. It was a beautifully thought-out funeral. Barbara's memories of mom and dad were that he could never get enough of each other. They were best friends and always shared each other's company. Most of her friends made faces and odd sounds when thinking of their parent's intimacy. Though she never saw them in bed, it was natural for her to think of them being intimate.

When her mom was murdered, she saw the part of him her mother never wanted to talk about. He vanished for a while after the funeral. Suddenly, he showed up and his face had a peaceful look to it. The 'ugly people' asked her questions about his activities and she answered with her normal violent explosions.

Barbara looked at the loafs and they were ready to be put in the oven. Each of them got a loaf. Tom and Mark loved Banana bread. Jeff loved lemon and she liked just regular bread. Barbara looked at the clock. If they did not waste too much time, the bread will be ready when they came home.

Tom's job allowed him to come home early so he always picked up the boys from school. She checked the oven and insured everything was in order.

Barbara turned and was shocked to see her mom and dad dancing in the living room. She moved woodenly to them and reached out. Her parents continued to dance and then stopped to point at her. They blew her a kiss, smiled, turned and vanished.

Barbara burst into tears and collapsed to the floor. She cried for several minutes. The new Barbara got up and went to the sink. She used a dish towel to wipe her face.

Barbara decided to be happy. Her parents loved her and danced in front of her. They said good-bye. They were a perfect couple. They loved each other and could spend eternity holding onto and dancing with each other.

Barbara smiled. She went into the bathroom and ensured her face was right. Just about the time her men burst through the door and yelped their delight, Barbara walked out. She told everyone to wash up as she lifted the loafs out of their pans.

Tom kissed her neck, trying to blackmail her out of washing up. She turned, kissed her husband and pointed to the bathroom. He turned up his lip and walked away as the boys made a ruckus, trying to wash quickly so they can run to the bread.

Barbara brought the loafs over to the table. She carved them up. Each of the boys had butter and jam at the ready. They jumped into it and hopped around. Tom ate his and apologized early for eating it all.

The loafs were smaller than normal which allowed all of them to eat the whole loaf in one sitting. No one liked eating cold or leftover bread. Warm out of the oven was what everyone loved.

When Barbara was three quarters through her loaf. She got up, pulled Tom out his chair and started dancing with him. She wanted the boys to see this and many more times in the future. Seeing her parents may have been an illusion, but she decided not to try figuring it out.

"I like this, Barb," Tom said.

The boys made gagging sounds, but she did not care. Her parents danced and they will too.

June 4

514

Admiral Hazlet looked at the report the President wanted. All things Washington and beyond waited for this report. All things Washington and beyond called wanting a glimpse of the contents. All things Washington and beyond never understood why Admiral Hazlet could not be intimidated.

The President choose Admiral Nathan Jedidiah Hazlet because he did not look or seem the part of being a person with an iron will who could not be intimidated. He was a patriot and had a reputation. His reputation started when he was an Ensign on the Destroyer USS Desmond Florence. The Florence was on a nothing patrol enroute to the Indian Ocean to join the Seventh Fleet. Some pirates snuck up to them at night off the Cambodian coast thinking the Florence was a merchant fleet.

A deck mounted gun fired three quick shots at the Florence. One of them was a stroke of luck. The door to the forward 5-inch gun turret. The explosion engulfed the forward deck, killing seven sailors. The pirates turned and left at high speed. Hazlet calmly and forcefully led a damage control team, extinguishing the fires and pulled injured and burned men out of the forward gun turret. Hazlet continued working with the Captain and crew. The XO's report commended his bravery and nearly fearless courage. The crew treated this Ensign differently. Normally Ensigns were treated like tiny children. Hazlet was now a living legend.

Thirty years later, Hazlet was still the calm, forceful and competent officer.

Now the President asked him to put out a new fire and control the damage from his promise to the nation.

Hazlet set aside the overall report on the nation. It read nearly the same as it did every other month. The only shining part of the report was the results from the Savage Rabbits. Aside from their near destruction of the drug trade and money seizures, they brought in mountains of information on illegal activities. Not just drugs, but human trafficking, slavery, smuggling and lots of other crimes. Law enforcement had faces to go to the crimes.

Hazlet picked the sealed report out of the pile covering the 365-day limit the President imposed on the marital law. The President wanted his opinion to know what to do. The nation was barely staying together. Crime was rampant and law enforcement was unable to maintain the peace.

Hazlet opened the report and read this one. No scanning this one. He had to know the contents and physically put his report in the President's hand.

Hazlet read it and agreed with every word. He told the team compiling it not to sugar coat or mince words. The truth was needed, not politically correct or sweet sounding lies.

The US of A was a pressure cooker waiting to explode. Whole sections of the country were being exploited by roving gangs. The country was tired of waiting for law enforcement to show up after the fact and do little to nothing. The Prosecutors and Judges were being impotent and ineffective. "There was no justice in a court of law," he said out loud. Inflation and unrestrained spending by Congress were making the dollar a waste of paper. Few people overseas wanted the new currency.

Shelves in stores were empty. Locally, the people could find food, unless people showed up with firearms and stole the food. Home invasions were skyrocketing. Hijacking trucks and trains were rising.

The crime problem had one solution. Put the criminals in jail and leave them there. But the Judges were finding newer excuses to release criminals.

Hazlet put the report in an armored briefcase and told Mary to warm up the helicopter.

Hazlet wanted to run away. This country was falling apart and has been dying since less and less emphasis was placed on community and replaced it with "government knows best".

Hazlet was recommending a slow lessening of martial law instead of just shutting it down. If asked, he would shoot the judges and prosecutors.

June 5

Headquarters, Northwest Military Region, Fort Carson Colorado.
1400 hours MST

Matheson looked at the mass of photographs covering Idaho, Montana and northern Wyoming. A table full of photos with more coming in is impossible to analyze without dozens of technicians to replace the computerized imagers that were not working.

Matheson was pulling all the strings he could trying to get more personnel to compensate, but without a real threat, he would have to stand in line. Matheson put the phone down and swung in his chair. This was a garrison command. As in the dead rising at 5 pm on Friday. The zombies don't return until Monday.

Matheson originally thought this was an interesting job. He now regretted it.

Matteson looked at the table marked 'Montana'. He looked at them and saw something. Was it something? Something about the trees. He looked at the photos again, but none of them were catalogued or aligned. One photo?

A lieutenant came to him and handed him a working satellite phone that was secure.

"General Matheson," he said.

"General, this is General O'Cleary," she said. "There is a Colonel Jones that is coming to brief you on a classified operation. Will you do me the courtesy of listening to him?"

Matheson was intrigued. O'Cleary was the only one smart enough and gutsy enough to challenge him. He did not like her but he could respect her.

Matheson looked at his schedule. "Have him come Wednesday at 10:30," he said penciling in the appointment. "Should I do this in my SCIF?"

"No General, but the information should be held restricted."

Matheson thought about O'Cleary. "I will be waiting."

O'Cleary thanked him again and hung up.

Matheson turned back to the photos and gave up. Damn he was vulnerable.

517

June 6

Underground Station "Conscience", World Wide Web and Channel 513
0900 hours EST.

"If you threaten, act. If you say something, do it. If something is important, stand your ground. Governments are often hamstrung by individuals who have opinions about issues they feel strongly about. This is Martin Socranson, self-proclaimed philosopher who says, 'What are we if we can't back up what you say'?"

"Greetings America" Martin Socranson said beginning his broadcast. "It is reluctantly Saturday and I say thus." In the background the sounds of the 1812 overture played.

"America we are coming up on the 365-day deadline the President imposed when we began this Martial Law which attached itself to every segment of the country. As history has taught us: when any population is suppressed, the pressure to be free builds."

"The normal ratio of police officers to population in our society is one police officer to 1,672 citizens. Some of the smaller communities the ratio is closer to 1 per one thousand, more or less. Now the criminal elements and liberal activists are actively inhibiting the police to stem criminal behavior. Some of those stupid people actually believe that they can rehabilitate criminal behavior without jails."

"Lawyers have gutted the enforcement of the law to the point that police forces are not supposed to protect the innocent but to protect the criminals. The newest twist to the lawyer's war against police is a Nevada class action suit against the police for not protecting lawyers. Despite the 'fact' that police departments are undermanned, lawyers are crying that they are under attack. Citizens are attacking lawyers and burning down their homes and businesses. Lawyers are getting rich freeing criminals, even those with solid evidence against them."

"America, food is scarce. Gasoline is not making it to stations. Hijacking and outright theft is fueling black markets. Criminals are roaming house to house selling 'protection'

518

against them. Now the government is in the act. They are moving house-to-house and accusing you of hording if you have more than a 3 day's supply of anything. The government is actually backing up trucks to homes and taking the "excess" away, lecturing the citizen about denying the homeless and low-income people of food and essentials."

"It is easy to terrorize normally law-abiding and peaceful citizens who used to be able to get justice from the police and courts."

"So now we have citizens who are scared enough to form vigilante groups. Civil liberties lawyers are crying about crooks being victimized. Iowa is heating up with groups on both sides of the law converging. The Governor has activated the National Guard in an attempt to maintain the peace. If they end up protecting the rights of roaming gangs and not stopping the gangs of criminals, the populous will rise up."

Socranson visibly took a deep breath.

"I am one of those people the government wants to silence. How dare I say the things I say? How dare I pierce the screens and show you what is happening? How dare I show you what the government is doing?

"On June the 13th, the 365-day limit the President imposed on the Martial Law is due to expire. Do you really believe it is over?

Bonnie Chandler, Box 234, Route 17, Belcher Missouri
1400 hours CDT

Dear Bonnie,

None of the things we normally do, can be done. The school is surrounded by a ten-foot-high fence with barbed wire on top. The school used to open the gym during the summer so that we could have a place to meet and play. Now it is closed and nothing goes in or out without a uniform and ID.

There is a community center on the other side of town and those assholes want that too. We are being forced out of our town. Dad was forced to close the store. Seems those government assholes cleaned him out and the bills have to be paid. As he was finishing cleaning it out, some government goon in a suit handed him a check and said good bye. Of course, the check will need a month to clear, if it does at all.

All the checks needed a month for "funds to be located and the money to appear in the bank'. Ask me how I know that.

Mom cries a lot in her bedroom. Dad sits in his recliner. Both of them go through the motions of living. Dad lost the thing he slaved and worked decades to serve the town and provide a living for his family. Those goons appear unannounced and search the house for 'excess', whatever it is they are looking for.

Suzy and Jane were chased through town this week by some guys wanting a good time. They made it into the group I was with. Those animals stopped when they saw us. The animal lust in their eyes vanished.

I hope ………...

Headquarters, 2nd Brigade, 4th Infantry Division, Fort Sam Houston, Texas

Colonel Jeff Etheridge, 4th Infantry Division G-2 Intelligence, put the finishing touches on the terrain model Thomas wanted. Etheridge didn't do the work, Thomas put that restriction on him. Thomas wanted his headquarters staff to learn how to do it.

Etheridge was tempted to jump in several times, but he stopped himself, knowing they would never learn if he did it for them. Being the father of three daughters, he understood fully. They aways wanted him to "help" them until it was done for them.

Etheridge was pleased with the work. Thomas came down numerous times to check and be pleased. His staff kept coming around to give him a tug. This was a combat command after all. Etheridge had been here all week. Thomas treated him like visiting royalty. Every night was a catered meal. He had a vehicle and driver detailed to him. A S-4 supply clerk with a government credit card ran to the store for any need including lunch.

Etheridge came on Monday and went to the table. He could see what Thomas was talking about. It was easy to see they tried to create a three-dimensional map. But the "true" terrain model showed how the terrain looked at ground level, exactly as someone would view it on the ground. It was this part of a terrain model that a Commander needed to see. It was just as important to see what the enemy saw.

Thomas came down and pronounced it perfect. His S-2 and S-3 staff groaned when Thomas said, "This is what I want to see from now on."

Thomas took Etheridge to the Officer's club for a very expensive thank you.

June 8

Room E-194, Pentagon, Washington, D.C
0900 to 1800 hours EDT

Last week, Kendal and Locklear walked into the Pentagon and repeated what Kincaid did numerous times before. They created a fictious office.

They went down into the basement, opened doors, looked around and found one that met their needs. They went to an off-site plaque and trophy shop and made up several pieces of eye-candy. They had found generic pictures and created the obligatory family pictures. Lastly, they ventured to Fort Myers and purchased three sets of uniforms for Colonel Michael Weatherly and Lieutenant Colonel James Zither, complete with a standard package of ribbons, patches and insignia.

Kincaid wrote down the rules for creating a cover identity. The name has to be easy to pronounce, common enough yet not too common. Everything had to be ordinary. Pictures were important. Good enough to be seen, yet easy to forget.

Grey was the term.

Once they had that completed, go to the detail office and submit a request for a group of soldiers to go up and down the halls and find the furniture they needed. In the basement, unused furniture was simply put in the wide hallways, lining the walls. Anyone that needed it, just took it. Being the Pentagon, there was a store for office supplies. Kendal took two men and sent them back and forth twice with all the things they wanted.

Kendal knew the formula for getting any man to do anything. Sex was out of the question, but food was the universal thank you and enticement. Part of the underground under the Pentagon was a subway system and numerous shops and restaurants. Everything was constructed with feeding the masses. Thousands worked in the Pentagon and they all got hungry at the same time. Seven pizzas vanished at lunch time. The troops worked hard after lunch. By close of business, that room was ready for business, except for one thing.

The final act was a plaque saying this office was part of the J-3 Special Projects section. No one was going to bother them except those with a death wish. O'Cleary created the office so that their education could progress without interruption.

The final act in this drama was reporting to Colonel Hawker. This single act had them seen in the Vice-Chairman's office. Hawker took them into O'Cleary's office and briefed them for over an hour. Basically, they were told the Task, Conditions and Standards for completing everything they needed to learn until January.

"In short, your orders are clear. Regardless of any order or situation, this block of instruction is your only duty. Period."

Both of them said "Yes, Ma'am."

Hawker gave them each a thick folder. "Enclosed are your badges, special identifications, and business cards with the phone numbers of the only key players in your life. Maybe you will be as good as Sergeant Major Kincaid, or you won't. I am not speaking for the General, but if you let her down, I will be displeased. You are dismissed."

Kendal and Locklear stood, saluted and left.

Locklear and Kendal left the "hall of Generals" wordlessly and kept quiet until they were free of the building.

"I knew Colonel Hawker at Desert Zero and Detention. She was never that cold," Kendal said.

"She loves the General as much as the rest of us. Some bosses, you never want to let down."

Part of their official cover was a secretary with a Top-Secret Special Background Investigation, plus security clearance to take all of Kincaid's mostly hand written notes and transcribe them into a segregated laptop without any online access or network access. She was to format them into files. She did it all in their Pentagon office.

The detail office supplied two soldiers, with a security clearance, to guard the office. One of them came each morning, opened the office, pulled the laptop and material out of the safe and returned it all at 5 pm to lock everything up.

The secretary had a credit card to buy lunch and anything they needed.

White House Message Center
0900 hours EDT

Generals Edwards, O'Cleary, and the commanding Generals of all four regions of the continental United States were told to be at the Eisenhower Executive Office Building on June 10th. Be there or die, orders were implied.

O'Cleary called Jones and postponed his meeting with Matheson.

O'Cleary hoped her newest uniform fit.

484 Glenmore Drive, Alexandria, Virginia
1900 hours EDT

O'Cleary opened the weekly report from Simmons and was rewarded with good news.

First and most important was Zero deaths, two minor wounds. Seventeen raids last week. O'Cleary read the raid synopsis and was pleased. The DEA was in the position of being inundated with so much information that they were "giddy" with delight.

Texas and the other border states were more than happy to take their profits and fund their budgets.

Simmons had two sections that figured out how to make the cartels think they had "holes" in the border. The Cartels drove up to the border from the US side and the State's Police confiscated their money. Texas now had so much money; their Treasury was now bursting. They were building the wall and soon, their state border will be fully "walled" by the end of the summer.

The J-3 Operations Officer from the Joint Chiefs came down and officially presented Simmons with the new authorizations for a total of four companies and the appropriate support personnel. Simmons was officially promoted to full Colonel and given promotion authority up to E-7 for enlisted personnel and O-3 for officers.

O'Cleary closed the report with some reverence and handed it off to the Classified Documents Custodian (CDC).

She thanked everyone and leaned back in the recliner.

June 9

Room E-194, Pentagon, Washington, D.C
0900 to 1800 hours EDT

Kendal and Locklear moved into an apartment near Joint Base Myers-Henderson Hall, outside Arlington, Virginia. Again, General O'Cleary paved the way. Throughout the week they unpacked, relaxed and went to the O'Cleary household each night for a great meal, marching orders and for lessons.

Locklear nearly choked at the $4,134 a month rent for their apartment. O'Cleary still had Committee money and it was almost a pleasure to spend it on things the Committee felt was a beneath them.

Last Sunday night, O'Cleary allowed her mind to wander through the byzantine world of operations and intelligence. It was her way of gauging whether they were just going to jump in or test the waters with a toe.

She remembered when the two of them fought each other tooth and nail over the INSANE JANE doctrine. They both shared a keen insight into operations far beyond their youth and inexperience. They took a few scraps of history and an oral remembrance. Then they built a doctrine that could only be matched by seasoned officers.

O'Cleary finally decided they were the ones. "My intent is to train you to take over from Mister Kincaid. Granted, he had decades of experience, so you will learn it.

Your in-processing paperwork had your Top-Secret Plus Clearances transferred to the Pentagon. You will have plenty of time to observe and access to learn, but I need you available to go into the field and turn the tide. That will become clear in time."

"Yes Ma'am," they said.

So, their present schedule was up at 5 am. PT was from 5:30 to 7:30. Shower, change and get the Pentagon and work. They usually left work at 6 o'clock at night. Waiting until then allowed the traffic jams to clear. Leaving at 5:00 or 5:30 got them home at the same time.

Saturday was a slow day of reading and Sunday was no work, just relax or go away.

June 10

Minuteman, north of Fort Benton, Montana
0800 hours MDT

Peters went out of his office with a smile. The NCO Academy was taking off. The NCOs who started out were luke-warm to the idea at first. As training was progressing, most of them took keen interest. This was not a course to re-teach them theory and things they already knew. This was about being an NCO and leading.

Now they were truly learning about the why and how of leading and command. Every single one of them went through the doctrine and saw how it worked in real life. They also learned to command in ways not taught in training, but in real life.

Several times they were given a mission and told to execute it. Nothing was critiqued until the complete tasks were over. No hand-offs. They learned and wanted to learn more.

Peters thought if they keep that up for 6 more weeks, then they hit a home run.

J. Edgar Hoover Building, Washington D.C.
1000 hours EDT

Solin read through the special crime report that the President ordered done yesterday. Luckily, most of the data was on the computers. All that was needed was to supply grammar. The White House and the Attorney General did give him special instructions so it was a two-and half-inch report.

"Boy, this ought to be interesting," he said. He picked up the report and walked out the door.

Eisenhower Executive Office Building, Washington, D.C.
1300 hours EDT

The President entered the conference room and looked around at who was there. He closed the door and ordered it locked.

"I am tired of useless discussion. I want answers. That is why I have the regional military commanders here along with the JCS Chairman and Vice-Chairman. Along with them, I have the Attorney General, the Director of the Internal Security Agency, Secretary of Homeland Security, the Director of the FBI, the Director of the Police Executive and the Director of the United States Police Force."

"None of you knew about what I wanted and I have excluded external inquires. Ladies and Gentlemen," the President said, while sitting down. "The 365-day limit I imposed on martial law is over a week from today. Privately, I am watching the news trying to get a sense of the nation. On the one hand, this country is tired of martial law. Parts of the country are ignoring it already. On the other hand, lawless gangs are freely roaming the country-side. Murder, rape, theft of all types, is almost a normal condition. Despite all that, the public is ignoring law enforcement. Judges and prosecutors are not putting people in jail and leaving them there. Prisoners being paroled in overcrowded jails are being murdered within 24 hours of being released. The prisoners are also murdering the witnesses against them."

One staffer wanted to interrupt. The President ejected him.

"At the end of this meeting, I will be able to answer whether or not Martial Law will be ended or extended. What will not happen is phases or platitudes. The only one that has the authority to leave is General O'Cleary. Being nearly nine months pregnant has certain privileges."

"General O'Cleary," The President said. "Just in case something comes up, I invite you to begin. Just in case."

O'Cleary shifted. "I say discontinue." There was a shifting around the table. "My reasoning is that for two and a half centuries, we have been a nation of freedom loving people. Everyone wants the freedom to walk out of their house and decide for themselves whether to go grocery shopping or go to the theatre or play in the yard."

"Everything we tried to make better only made it worse. Shelves are empty in grocery stores. Gasoline is at $9 dollars a gallon if it can be found. Seasonal clothing such as coats and insulated clothing is nearly impossible to find. In every single instance where a government entity came in, things got worse."

O'Cleary shifted when Arthur jammed a foot into her rib cage. "Mostly the nation is rebelling. Vigilantes and militias are filling in where the government is not. Judges will not sentence or leave criminals in jail. Prosecutors down play crimes and, in some cases, taking the criminal's side. Last month, a rapist in prison for only one year convinced the judge he was rehabilitated. The woman he raped was not notified because she would probably interfere with his rehabilitation. He broke into her apartment and raped her continuously over a weekend. That is not the only instance. I could go on for hours. The men who shot up my house were released from a super max facility by a judge. Their file said never parole or pardon, yet they were released."

"Mr. President, the shelves are bare because hijacking trucks is rampant. Those local crimes are now federalized. I mean no disrespect to the US Police Enforcement entity, but waiting for you to show up is endemic of the problem. Crimes are measured in seconds. Waiting hours for someone to show up puts the criminals in another state. So far this month there is over 540 truck hijackings and now they are hijacking trains and train cars."

"Farmers have to guard their produce with armed guards. A judge said they had no right to be armed with weapons. Cattle men are hiding their herds and shooting rustlers and hiding bodies."

"On and on, ad infinitum. The criminals are freer to break laws than we are to defend ourselves. I could go on for hours. We have four General officers carving up the country with vague orders to assist in maintaining order. In a few days there will 50,000 USPF members. What is their mission? How do they put a dent in crime? Four divisions are guarding our southern borders. Do we keep asking them to die without shooting back?"

"Will there be troubles when martial law is lifted? Absolutely. Will there be retribution? Of course, just see what is happening in Iowa. In short no more Marial Law."

The President loved her candor. She was probably more right than everyone else.

The President went on for the rest of the afternoon. General O'Cleary had to be excused after three hours.

The Regional Commanders agreed that their orders were too vague, too wordy and too contradictory. The four of them said they were just collecting data. Without any forces to command, their jobs were just places to work.

The AG and the Civilian Directors fought at different levels to maintain marital law. Despite the massive amount of new personnel and monies they had, they cried saying they didn't have enough.

The President was tired of the back and forth. He told the Regional Military Commanders to stay in Washington for the week. Those four Flag Officers will meet privately with the President about their commands in a few days.

Headquarters, 2nd Brigade, 4th Infantry Division, Fort Sam Houston, Texas
0900 hours CDT

Thomas used the terrain models arrayed around the room to brief his Battalion commanders on the situation and his area for the four hundred miles of the border. Each of the commanders saw their battle space from the newest perspective. They were skeptical at first, looking critically at the terrain model.

Slowly, they came around. Thomas knew he convinced them when they went to the tables and knelt at them from various perspectives. Normally, terrain models were viewed from above, like you were flying over the area. Now they could look at the battle space from a ground perspective.

Simmons even showed them the trick with a bright light mimicking the sun, to show how the terrain looks at various times of the day. If you looked from the American side at dusk, you could not see anything. But the Cartels saw every movement on the American side.

Colonel Etheridge and General Kangleman were on-hand to look over the terrain models. Both men were impressed. Etheridge impressed himself with how the models turned out. The perspective changed a lot as you lowered your eye line closer to ground level.

Thomas went as far as placing models of his brigade's vehicles at the point where they were placed last week. From the Mexican perspective, sometimes it was easy for them to see them. Other times, the Mexicans could not easily see them.

This new way would maybe replace years of field experience. Thomas wanted to use this to keep his soldiers alive. He granted the battalion commander's request to bring in their company commanders and platoon leaders to look over the models.

Thomas did have to admonish his men several times. "Don't touch the models."

Numerous locations, Washington D.C.
0900 – 1700 hours EDT

All four regional commanders of the country floated around Washington waiting for the President's summons. He told them to stay the week and that could mean anytime. Their Aides had the cellular and satellite phones.

All of them went to the Pentagon and worked their way through the staff sections. New friendships were formed and old ones were strengthened. All four Flag Officers knew their jobs were career killers if something went wrong, but they really did not know what that job involved six months from now.

485 Glenmore drive, Alexandra, Virginia

Matheson had his aide call ahead and O'Cleary said she had the morning for him.

Matheson did stop by the store and remembered what his wife received when she was in the latter stages of pregnancy. All three times. Matheson settled for a foot massager and gift certificates at three separate stores. Matheson wanted to be a gentleman in his dealings with O'Cleary. The bad feelings between them were official, not personal.

On the door was a sign saying: "No Hat, No Salute Area."

Matheson knocked on the door and waited. Dennis opened the door, and Matheson stood at attention and saluted. Dennis returned the salute and said. "I am not one to flaunt myself and demand recognition. In my house there is no rank. Enter and be welcome. On the back of the door is the house rules."

The sign said. "Rules of the House of O'Cleary."
1. O'Cleary is the Lord and Master.
2. No guns, rank, drugs, or stupidity.
3. If you leave hungry or thirsty it's your fault.
4. If you live past the doorway, you are welcome.
5. This is not a hotel, help yourself.
6. All else fails read rule number 1.

Matheson smiled and removed his jacket as Dennis set the table and put delicious food on it. Dennis being Dennis went outside and told Matheson's driver to come in and eat a meal. The driver hesitated until Matheson leaned outside and told him to come inside.

Both four-star Flag Officers talked Army while Dennis and Sgt Nichols went into the living room and watched baseball.

Matheson started the conversation. "I know that you have a security system running. The tell is the lack of noise from of the living room. Sgt Nichols is baseball fanatic. The sonic windows have a unique color. Maybe this is not a SCIF, but I assume we are secure."

O'Cleary smiled. She reached over to a folder and pulled out a Non-Disclosure Statement and passed it over to Matheson. O'Cleary's smile stayed in place.

"OK," Matheson said. He signed the form and passed it over to O'Cleary.

"Without the double-talk," O'Cleary said. "We, at the JCS level, are training a force to guard and maintain security around a western national capital. The location is in western Montana. Should the situation in Washington become untenable, the area in south eastern Montana will become a partial secured area for members of the government, and part of the Congress."

Matheson was very used to long drawn-out briefings. "That's it?" he said.

"Yes," O'Cleary said. "I said I wasn't going to double-talk."

Matheson looked at her. "Are you using the original Savage Rabbits?"

O'Cleary smiled. "Yes. Those men were detained without cause and had their families placed in detention with them without cause. That was wrong. Soviet and Nazi wrong. All of those men and women wanted nothing to do with the American military. I took them and reassigned them to this duty." O'Cleary reached over to the folder and pulled out three more folders. "I have full Presidential and Pentagon authority to exist, train and man this mission. They are to be left alone. I am the President's representative."

Matheson looked over the documents. He knew they were not forgeries. Nothing on this Earth can forge an official document from on high. The stamps and other additions make it look like something that was not thought out properly.

Matheson handed the documents back to O'Cleary. "Is this a 'hands off' directive. You could have had Colonel Jones brief me at the Pentagon. Using a junior officer to brief, allows 'items' to be left out. The final briefing point would have been 'hands off'."

O'Cleary winced with Arthur walking on her ribs. "You would have either found ways to put your hands on it or just bull dozed in, seeking forgiveness instead of waiting for permission."

Matheson watched the baby elongate her abdomen. Having three children of his own, he freaked out when that very thing happened to his wife. "Forgive me, General. Your child is running around."

O'Cleary chuckled. "Today he's just walking. Two more weeks," she said holding up two fingers." She took several breaths which seemed to calm Arthur down. O'Cleary looked Matheson in the eye.

O'Cleary continued. "I know from experience that you are someone to be respected. You would have found out that something was going on and used your rank and position to do your job and investigate what is going on. I decided that telling you upfront will maintain security and make you a part of the overall plan and decision-making process. If the civilian leaders decide to relocate the government, we need to insure it is secure. Chances are you will be placed in command if that happens."

Matheson's neutral look was practiced over years. He could not believe something like this could have been created without him finding out about it. He may have left SOCOM, but SOCOM never left him. He knew the original Savage Rabbits had vanished without a trace. Delta Force's Gender still wanted them. While they were in detention, Gender found slots to permanently assign them to Delta as a security and covering force. No need for asking Rangers.

But O'Cleary released them with their families and vanished. A new Savage Rabbit unit was formed a few months later. O'Cleary changed a lot of things this time around. Gender and Saraland came over for a visit and Simmons declined to take their suggestions. A week later, General Traynor, the new SOCOM commander, was summoned to the Pentagon and met with the General of the Army Edwards and General Kearney, the Army Chief of Staff.

Traynor was told to rein in his subordinates, all of them, and leave the Savage Rabbits alone, period. Now Simmons was a full Colonel now. That rank gave him a lot of pull. It really meant that he was a General in waiting.

Matheson was now in that situation. This was a polite and professional exercise in being told to leave them alone. "General, I know enough about you to know you are not to be excused or taken lightly." He reached forward and extended his hand. "I will take your handshake to say that this perfectly legal."

O'Cleary readily shook his hand. Suddenly something was wrong. O'Cleary squeezed his hand hard and rotated in her chair. Suddenly, the pain was gone. Dennis caught the action from the corner of his eye. He leaped over everything and ran to her side.

Matheson pulled out his cell phone and tried to call 911. The phone had no bars. "Nichols, take my phone outside and get an ambulance." Nichols ran outside.

"Brenda, Brenda are you OK?" Dennis asked.

Matheson then saw something every husband and father knows all about. Brenda O'Cleary grabbed Dennis' shirt front and pulled him over. "Take a wild guess!" She was not the nice, professional woman everyone knew.

"Ambulance is on the way, Sir," Nichols said walking inside. He handed the phone back to Matheson.

"General, believe me, please leave them alone. They had two years-worth of training that has to be done before the end of the year." Brenda winced again. She winced as her abdomen visibly changed shape, again.

The PSAs for both Generals seemed to take over, with O'Cleary's guards winning the coin toss.

"Nichols," Matheson said, "go outside and flag down the ambulance when it arrives." Matheson looked up to the PSAs. "Go outside and make sure none of the vehicles are in the way of the ambulance."

"Just like an O'Cleary," Brenda said. "Making a ruckus to say 'hello world'."

The EMTs arrived when young Arthur shifted again. They stopped and stared as he deformed her mom's abdomen again.

Dennis yelled at them. That broke the spell. The only call to be made was pack up and go.

June 11

Pentagon, Washington, D.C.
1000 hours EDT

Matheson went into the Department of Defense's Defense Logistics Agency (DLA). Up to now, his requests for replacement commuters and hard drives was hitting one road block after another.

Matheson decided to put his stars to use and reach out to the DLA directly.

Major General Keneally, commanding General of the DLA came out to personally greet Matheson. Both Generals retired to Keneally's office.

As Matheson was sitting down, Keneally handed him a folder. "Your request for replacements. We received them a week ago. General O'Cleary had called me and placed a higher priority on your replacement computers and hard drives. I am also sending along technicians to get you up and running. You are lucky sir. I was told she had to go the hospital to have her baby yesterday. If she had not raised your priority, we would be having a semi-professional discussion about why I could not help you."

Matheson looked at his original request and the cover letter granting a full issue of the needed equipment. O'Cleary had done this before they met.

"Is this satisfactory"? Keneally asked.

"Oh yes, General," Matheson said closing the folder. "I have to admit that I had prepared a very ungentlemanly speech to get this list filled."

"Thank you for being honest Sir," Keneally said. "You must have impressed General O'Cleary. Nobody can intimidate her."

Matheson stood and thanked Keneally. He left the Pentagon and his driver took him to the Officer's Club at the Fort Myers. He needed to think and Jack Daniels was a perfect drinking partner. He handed the folder over to his aide and dismissed him for the evening.

Room D-156, George Washington University Hospital, Washington, D.C.
1430 hours EDT.

534

Brenda O'Cleary woke up and saw someone she really wanted to see. Her Uncle, Tom Edgars, came to visit her. He placed the present bag on the table with the others. "Aside from the obvious, how are you doing?"

Brenda smiled and tapped her tummy. "Very pregnant, with a boy who is impatient to be born and probably did not read the manual about how."

Uncle Tom smiled and leaned over to kiss her forehead. "I guess you are alright." Thomas looked over to Dennis and smiled. "Is she behaving or working too hard?"

"No and maybe," Dennis said.

Uncle Tom made it a habit of visiting them at least three times a year. His very nature made his visit a delight. Both of Brenda's parents were killed in a vehicle accident when Brenda was in her sophomore year of college. He took over looking after Brenda despite her being an adult. He saw his duty as being the "old man" in her life. He loved taking her to dinner and getting her to laugh.

"Uncle Tom, I wanted to be a mother and I love Dennis…."

Uncle Tom took that instant to cough. He looked up and smiled. He respected Dennis and felt Brenda finally found the man she needed.

"Any way," Brenda said, "I cannot think of something more important than what I am doing here." She winced at a minor twinge. "The doctors say I am on enforced bed rest until the birth. I am forty-seven. Doctors say it is really a young woman's game. They refuse to tell anyone that it is a bad idea without a lot of medical care."

"Etc., etc, etc" Uncle Tom said pulling out a small teddy bear from his present bag. "How are you?"

Brenda looked at the teddy bear and up to her Uncle Tom. "I am scared that I might lose my baby." She teared up, took a deep breath and pulled the tears back in."

"Brenda," Uncle Tom said, taking her hand and kissing her forehead. "Just because you are a four-star general, does mean you aren't a woman. You are creating a new life and you will not lose your son. Let it out."

Brenda visibly let down and cried into the arms of the three men in life. For four minutes, she cried her eyes out, releasing the tension she hid from the world.

Finally, it was gone. She felt better and Arthur seemed to know it. All the tension in her body melted away. "Uncle Tom, how do you know how to do that?"

"I just love you, Brenda. I just love you."

The door opened and Doctor Kevan walked inside. "Sorry to intrude, but I need to exam you Missus O'Cleary."

Uncle Tom and Dennis left to get some coffee in the cafeteria.

June 12

Eisenhower Executive Office Building, Washington D.C.
0900 hours EDT.

The President called this meeting with Secretaries of Defense, all the services and their Military heads including General Edwards and the four military region commanders. All four regional members were seated in front of the President.

"Ladies and Gentlemen," the President started. "This meeting is called to further define the responsibilities and identify problems within your respective commands." As if to emphasize, he held a pencil over a pad of paper. "I will begin with General Matheson."

"Sir," Matheson said, "we were hacked by unknown parties. Our computers were thoroughly corrupted. The DLA has informed me that replacement components are enroute to Fort Carson. I sent the request and General O'Cleary added her office's influence to get those replacement components. That being done, I am an old man and directed paper copies of all our records are continually be made in case of this type of situation. It is slower, but I can still operate."

Matheson looked to his right and the other three commanders nodded. "Sir, the four of us have already had a conference to share notes. Collectively, our mission statements are too vague. We need a better idea of the mission, you Sir, want us to accomplish for this country."

The President looked at his four military commanders. They looked back at him without flinching. He leaned back. "Are there any other problems that need to be addressed immediately besides not having a clue what I want?"

The four military commanders said, in turn. "No Sir."

He looked over to his secretary. "Find me a hole in the schedule toward the end of the month for another meeting."

"Gentlemen," he said. "I want you to return to your headquarters and draft some correspondence over areas you feel need to covered. I will take that information and determine whether or not a singular mission statement is required. I will say that you are to determine, independently, the overall security of your areas."

His secretary told him the 29th was available.

"We will return on the 29th at 9 am."

For the next hour, the President talked generally about situations they felt they will encounter. Waller talked about the southern border's security. Matheson talked about militias. Cartwright was concerned about drug trafficking in the Gulf of Mexico and Cuban inflammatory actions. Macklin said his problem was internal. Too many people wanting everything and unable to do it themselves.

The President filled up a tablet with notes.

Internal Revenue Service, Washington, D.C.
1000 hours EDT

Baker saw that his computers were still corrupted and literally useless. All the security, anti-virus's, firewalls, protections and speed of operations left nothing behind. Every computer brought in to access the situation, was quickly corrupted.

Finally, even non-computer literate individuals accepted the fact that every hard drive was corrupted beyond any ability to correct. Every hard drive was removed, photographed, and inventoried.

Baker had his staffers search his paper records looking for seized computers and hard drives. If he had to, he was prepared to forgive tax debts to fix this situation.

God help the IRS if the public got wind of this calamity. Baker had deluded himself into thinking the public was unaware.

June 13

Congress, Washington D.C.
1000 hours EDT

Congress was conducting a rare weekend session to clean up some bills and administrative details prior to a summer recess. Representatives and Senators went from room to room, voting on this and negotiating on that.

It was small at first. Something was in the air, stinging their eyes and noses. Some were having trouble breathing. Alarms sounded and over the loud speakers a voice was telling everyone to evacuate. Former military servicemen and women recognized a gas attack.

Fully masked Capital Police grabbed people and forced them outside the building. People starting falling down, coughing so bad they were choking. Those stopping to help others, started succumbing to the unknown gas. The Capital Police tried dragging people outside. Special air pumps started pushing in fresh air.

Twenty minutes after it began, the air quality improved enough for EMTs and emergency personnel to enter. Every hospital in the Washington D.C. area was on alert.

The FBI, Homeland Security and the Capital Police quickly went to the air conditioning units and found were it was compromised. One of the air handlers had an open door. A propane burner was set up over a 40-pound cannister of refrigerant. The refrigerant was burned creating phosgene gas and the air handler pulled the gas inside distributing it out into the building.

The gas sensors were by-passed in the control panel five feet away. Normally the air-handlers would have been shut down when the alarms sounded.

"This was a well thought out plan," a senior FBI agent said.

538

The final count was 78 dead. 398 suffered injuries to their eyes and lungs.

Now Congress wanted to act.

June 15

Headquarters, 2nd Brigade, 4th Infantry Division, Fort Sam Houston, Texas.
1000 hours CDT

Latham Thomas arranged for Folcroft and Jenkins to visit and critique the terrain models. Folcroft and Jenkins went wide-eyed at the detail. Two of his subordinate battalion's staff officers was working at the model. A Sergeant with a 'Billie' club was standing guard over the model. An absolute "No Touching" rule was in effect.

Jenkins was totally absorbed with the model. He loved the fact that the detail allowed him to 'see' the battle area from numerous angles.

Thomas was looking for an 'edge'. Ellen often talked about an 'edge'. It is a negotiating tactic in contract negotiating. Give something without asking for something in return. Later the person who got the something will tip their hand. Whether they repaid, spoke volumes about their character. 'God, I love that woman', he thought to himself".

Thomas walked around with his guests. Three full Colonels absorbed mountains of information.

"Latham," Colonel Jenkins said. "I would like to bring my staff over to view this. I want my staff to recreate this for my sector."

"Not a problem," Thomas said. "I will even supply, on temporary duty, the men who created this miracle."

Room D-156, George Washington University Hospital, Washington, D.C.
1830 hours EDT.

O'Cleary demanded and was 'allowed' three or four times a day to walk around the ward. Doctors fretted and worried that 'something' would or could happen. O'Cleary relented and stayed on the floor, never more than 30 feet from a nurses' station. She was never more than fifty feet from her room. She walked around a circle in which the ward was constructed. Dennis was there to let her have something to hang onto.

The doctors also found out that Brenda was very agreeable to medical requirements after every 'walkabout'. Brenda was not exactly amiable to the menu at the hospital. Idiots will degrees and opinions thought she had to eat gruel instead of food. Dennis loved to go shopping for all the strange foods she wanted. He brought in a small refrigerator to hold the Apple juice and ice cream she craved.

Colonel Hawker came by at lunch time and late afternoon to brief her on the day's concerns and actions needed for future operations. O'Cleary noted that Hawker easily filled in for her during the latter part of her pregnancy. In time, she could become the Chief of Staff or Chairman of the Joint Chiefs.

Hawker came in for the afternoon briefing. Top of the stack was the weekly report from Colonel Simmons at Desert Zero. Simmons reported that he was deep into training his newer sections.

Simmons still had to conduct combat operations as directed by the National Command Authority. Delta company was the fourth company of Savage Rabbits who were being turned into operators. Echo Company was specialists for communications, truck drivers, medical and aviation assets primarily Pathfinders, and other support requirements. Headquarters Company was administratively activated to be that. Volunteers was not a problem because literally everyone wanted to be a Savage Rabbit, both Army and Marine.

It was the Pathfinders that Simmons was most worried about. The men who ultimately "survived" the selection process were uniformly too young in his estimation. Pathfinders were responsible for going in ahead of everyone to find places for aviation, either fixed or rotary wing, aircraft to land. In some instances, they needed to move in days ahead, scout an area, report in and wait for the others to land. A six-man team was overloaded with communications equipment and the power to defend themselves. Maybe.

540

Who could he find to command these mad men?

The Pathfinders unofficial patch was the Tasmanian Devil standing in front of a torn-up desert scene, holding up a finger and whistling. They loved to outdo each other. Three of them got into a beer fueled plot and set out on a five-hour, 20-mile road march. All three had to be placed on medical light duty for their feet being too blistered to walk on.

Waverly ate into them for not taking care of their feet as they had been instructed. Their punishment was hand washing 500 pairs of socks and polishing 100 pairs of boots.

Simmons searched wide until he found a Cavalry Captain to command Delta Company. Headquarters Company was expanded to create a full complement. Logistics was now able to fully man all the myriad portions required. Most of the manpower would still come from the Stand-down section and/or company, but a core of trainers and specialists would remain in place, but rotate on a mission no less than twice a month.

Simmons updated the operations portion of the report. Literally every day, a minimum of one mission was launching south of the border.

O'Cleary was wondering where the drugs were coming from. So far this year, they confiscated 11 tons of cocaine, 17 tons of heroin, 107 tons of marijuana and 23 billion dollars in cash.

And the year was only half over.

Colonel Simmons also had to report two attempts by the drug cartels to infiltrate Desert Zero. Four Rabbits were killed so far defending the compound.

Fort Hood was more than willing to assist. They sent the type of perimeter structures used in Iraq and Afghanistan around the Desert One facility. All that was needed was dirt which the country side had plenty. The exterior walls were ten feet thick and the internal roof buildings could withstand an 81 mm mortar hit. One new tool in the shed was a new type of machine that resembles a cultivator. It stirs and pulverizes the surface of the soil down to a depth of 8 inches. As the dirt is heavily disturbed, it is sprayed with a proprietary compound which hardens the soil. The ground is now so hard an irregular, the average person cannot walk or run over it steadily. Any attempt to cross is slowed and made extremely difficult to stay stealthy.

Three sections of Ground Surveillance Radar were set up to monitor any movement on the ground out to a distance of three hundred meters.

Simmons broached a subject he, admittedly, did not have a clue how to fix it. The last page of Kincaid's security page addressed the possibility of a small aircraft slipping in and acting as a guided missile aimed at Desert Zero.

O'Cleary set the report aside and she admitted she did not have a clue. She did admit that any target can be destroyed by a determined foe. She sent out a request for some hand-held missiles and Gatling guns.

June 16

White House, Washington, D.C.
0900 hours EDT

The President had promised that Martial Law was to be lifted by today at the latest. His Cabinet and the Executive Branch was evenly split between maintaining or eliminating Martial Law.

The President had his secretary 'lock the door'. He was literally alone with this decision. He wanted to walk outside, but he could not expect the Secret Service to leave him alone or keep everyone away from him.

He literally was stuck. Both sides of the equation had plenty of merits to consider.

New York City, Chicago, Atlanta, Denver, Los Angeles, San Francisco and other cities and towns, people were rioting for food and fuel. Last winter was cold. Fuel oil and coal seemed to vanish. Add to the troubles were activists against fossil fuels, animal rights nut jobs, save the land from farmers, Etc.

Roving gangs of criminals were exercising their rights to rape, kill, pillage and burn were everywhere. Citizens are banding together as vigilantes to protect themselves and stop those gangs. Civil Liberties lawyers are saying that towns are segregating.

The President looked at the three Executive Orders in front of him. One said no more Martial Law, the another saying 'continue' and the third which said lift it slowly. The Supreme Court already has three cases pending before it challenging Marital Law.

The President reached over and signed the lift it slowly Executive Order. The President twisted and destroyed the pen. He took the other two orders and put them in the shredder.

The next election was in four months and this nightmare was over for him in six months.

June 17

World Wide Web, Cyber-Space, Planet Earth
0900 hours EDT

Everyone who was one, and those who were not, echoed through the airwaves. The President was sort of freeing everyone from Martial Law. The President was heeding the advice of Law Enforcement and easing the country out from all the artificial constraints.

Talking heads in the news media from both sides of the political aisle had every kind of opinion about everything. Literally no one understood anything. Every different person who read this Executive Order came away from it with a different opinion.

The President's press secretary, Marsha Lakewood, asked the President several pointed questions about what he meant so that she could answer all the questions to the nation. Or rather the ravenous media.

One point that required her to think about how to spin it was the US Police Force strength increasing to over 50,000. Granted, nearly 65% of them were serving police officers, she decided to emphasize that local Police Departments were asking for help.

Desert Zero, Fort Hood, Texas
1300 hours CDT

Representatives of the DEA, ATF, Border Patrol along with numerous state and local Police Departments assembled in the Dining Facility. Aside from having the coffee machine and pastries, it was the only place large enough to seat everyone.

General Waller and his operations and intelligence officers came for the update. They set up a camera to record the briefing for the benefit of his staff who could not attend.

The Cartels were fighting each other so bad that the Mexican government was begging the US to either wipe them out or stop the cross-border raids.

The main briefer began. "Indications from satellite reconnaissance and Global Hawk surveillance that operations are shifting from areas opposite Texas and New Mexico to Arizona. Curiously operations around the California border appear to be slowing for no apparent reason."

The area being discussed was familiar to General Waller. It was the center of an invasion he was in command of with the Third Corps last year. In fact, he was a three star with the same troops and border missions.

He saw that scenario as the briefer said the same things again this time. He mentally ran down the mission statements and operational points. All the points the briefer ran down was the same as last year.

"Excuse me," General Waller said. "Are you trying to suggest another invasion like what I did last year?"

The briefer just made gestures. "I don't have that information sir."

Waller looked over to Colonel Simmons. "How much longer is this meeting?"

The briefer looked at his notes. "Except for some minor points, we are about done."

Waller stood and motioned for Simmons to follow him. Once outside, he walked them off to the side and found a spot for them to talk privately. Waller gave him the short story about last year's invasion. Simmons did say he was a Battalion Executive Officer in a 9th MEF unit in California.

"Colonel," Waller said. "I am going to short circuit the civilian three letter agencies before they get too involved. That briefing was a fishing expedition. So, I am going to draft a request to do it, before any stupid requests come my way. I am requesting," he shrugged his shoulders. "That you categorize your priorities before-hand. You can launch into the battle space before-hand and use my force for back up. I am also requesting that you provide reconnaissance help. Between us, this will be your Savage Rabbit activities to prevent others from saying, 'see you did it for them'."

"Yes Sir," Simmons said. "Won't be the first time we had a dry hole."

Room D-156, George Washington University Hospital, Washington, D.C.
1630 hours EDT.

Thad Jones and Mike Smith came to visit O'Cleary in the hospital. Both men wore civilian clothes and carried the newest generation 'buzz box'. They exchanged the usual pleasantries as the unit was powered up and aligned.

O'Cleary adjusted the bed and waited for the four green lights to illuminate.

"Gentlemen," O'Cleary began. "I asked you here to inquire about two items."

1. "What is the deployment status of the Werewolves and your honest statement of Werewolf training?"
2. "How long would it take for you to begin a full 14-month Werewolf training course. No corners cut.

Jones shifted slightly and looked at Smith before turning to O'Cleary. "General, I have been looking at the master training plan John Kincaid left behind along with the master logistical plan. I was about to request your permission to start up a new class in January. Several decommissioned federal facilities can be used. The money side of things are based on green back dollar scales. Preliminary estimates will take up to 50 million blue back dollars, present inflation rate taken into account."

O'Cleary winced. "Permission granted."

Smith took over the conversation. "Presently our strength is at fourteen, not counting Father Mike. Seven older members and seven newer members. Our state of training is up in the air. This year, we are doing other duties than training as

Werewolves. You have Kendal and Locklear learning to be John Kincaid."

"Taylor is the S-4. Miles is doing areas studies with Morgan in, through and around our camp. Glendive is the S-3, Training. Sheridan is the Minuteman Sergeant Major. Covington, Pruitt, Mejia, Griffith and McPherson are training, but they are undermanned to do serious missions. We should have done this a year ago when we had fewer obligations."

"Mike," Jones said.

"Both of you have permanent permission to speak freely and honestly." O'Cleary winced again. "What do you need from me to do this right?"

"You have already done it, Ma'am," Smith said. "Perhaps we can start earlier if everything is in place."

"Do you need me to help setting up the logistics?" Dennis asked.

"No Dennis," Jones said. "Stay with the General and your baby. Mike and I have five children between us. Trust me sir, you do not want to miss the baby's birth."

"Thank you," Brenda said reaching for her purse. "Please use this credit card and buy your wives something from me. I can't shop."

"I'm not married," Smith said.

"Get yourself something," Brenda said turning hard in her bed. She hit the panic bottom collapsed on the bed gasping for breath.

The nurses ran in and helped Brenda until the baby relaxed. They eased her down, checked her vitals and left her alone.

"One last item," Brenda said. "Are either of you considering retirement?"

Smith and Jones looked at each other.

Jones started. "Linda is asking me about it. I can sit behind a desk for a while longer. But she does not want me to deploy. I will admit that I am feeling like an old man with arthritis. And it is too hard to motivate myself to do physical training."

Smith said it. "I can't deploy. My wounds haven't healed correctly. I have not been able to run in 18 months. I am anchored to a desk too. Thad and I will be the first Werewolves who lived long enough to retire."

O'Cleary rubbed her abdomen. "Groom Colonel Peters to take over as the Commander of Minuteman and Major Glendive as the new Deputy Commander. Both of you can work the new Werewolves. That mandates you sit still and watch them."

"Thank you," both men said.

Smith had to ask. "Who do you want to nominate as the new Werewolf Commander?"

"Major Glendive," she said without hesitation. "Do you concur?"

Both men said, "Yes ma'am."

"Brief him," she said, contorting her face. "Have him come see me at the earliest. Sunday is a good time."

"General?" Smith said

"I'll tell my son to behave long enough," she said. Any special things I need to be aware of?"

"No ma'am," Jones said, standing to take his leave. Smith remained silent.

June 18

Room E-194, Pentagon, Washington, D.C
0900 to 1800 hours EDT

Kendal and Locklear were using this office less and less. They actually found a single room house at Fort Myers that they could use as a study area and quarters. Being a married couple, they could justify getting furniture found and delivered to the house. A day with hammer, nails, plywood, plaster board and paint could give them some privacy for a bed room when their study ran late at night.

Kendal hated going to the Pentagon. She had to put on hosiery, garter belts, uncomfortable bras, uncomfortable shoes, etc. Now she only had to "harness up" once a week. If they stayed at Myers, they could go all day with fatigues.

The byzantine world of Operations was something alien to them. They tried starting with Kincaid's three-foot-thick notes and literature on Operational and Tactical training.

Nearly one third of that was Shark Hunter material. A lot of those hand written and typed notes were written in "Kincaid speak" as he called it. "You need to write those notes in a language you understand. That language has to make sense to you, not to anyone else. Those notes need to be created so you can review them in short spurts of time. Notes designed to be read by you to reinforce your base knowledge."

Kincaid's lectures about Shark Hunting seemed to mimic that part. Sometimes they had to stop him and ask for clarity. He never got mad or short tempered at the interruption. He painstakingly backed up and clarified himself.

Locklear picked up Army Field Manual 100-5 "Operations". Supposedly it was the bible on how the Army fights a war. It was written on a 5th year college level for officers with years of education and experience and some obvious points that junior officers would be able to embrace.

Kendal worked with a 16-foot-long by 4-foot-high cork board she used to organize notes. She ended up becoming more and more frustrated with her inability to find a starting point. One of the things she learned early on was the need to have a focal point to building.

"Earl," she said. "Are you able to make sense about all this?"

"Frankly no," he said. "That is the difference between officers and enlisted. We know how to lead, but officers know how to command."

"What is your honest opinion?" she asked. "Do you think we can figure it out like this. We do not have a Miss Gladys or John Kincaid to guide us along."

Locklear nodded his head.

Finally, she picked up the phone and called General O'Cleary.

1500 hours EDT

UNSTACK THIS was tasked by General O'Cleary to begin teaching Kendal and Locklear. UNSTACK THIS had be observing them in order to determine if these two users would be granted primary user status.

O'Cleary and UNSTACK THIS created Nancy Glister. Nancy was a 60-year-old woman whose expertise was equal to Gladys Goldstein. In fact, Gladys Goldstein understood her mortality more than anyone else. After O'Cleary granted her user status, she finally agreed to understand and work with UNSTACK THIS.

Gladys Goldstein set aside time, in her day, to teach UNSTACK THIS what she did and, more importantly, how she did it. Goldstein worked on a compartmented laptop computer; massaging UNSTACK THIS's understanding about her job. From this understanding, Nancy Glister, an aviator, was born so that anyone could use her likeness

UNSTACK THIS knew how do her job. At least as much as a digital mind could understand. O'Cleary and UNSTACK THIS created an "ULTRA" security level computer program in the bowels of the National Security Agency. UNSTACK THIS could reach out from the NSA to research any required external source.

O'Cleary only needed an hour and a half to create Nancy, but hours of interaction were required to 'smooth' over Nancy's interaction. O'Cleary hooked up to a secure laptop with a boom mike and Three-D glasses. She interacted and became more human acting. O'Cleary started Nancy and began teaching and interacting with her. Nancy needed to learn how to work with humans and their many interruptions.

By 3 pm, O'Cleary was satisfied; calling Kendal and Locklear, she said. "I found a teacher for you. Nancy Glister is as experienced and knowledgeable as Gladys Goldstein. She will be dedicated to your education. One or both of you will continue to go to the Pentagon at least one day a week. I have scheduled you to attend briefings and meetings and will forward you information in order to experience the mind set of senior military officers in forming policy."

Kendal and Locklear did not have any questions for O'Cleary. Her image dissolved and Nancy Glister's image replaced her on the screen.

Glister looked at them. "Miss Kendal and Mister Locklear, I recommend you set everything aside and relax tonight. From the information I have already received, you need to clear your heads, so we can start fresh in the morning."

The screen went blank. Kendal and Locklear looked at each other and smiled. "Dinner," they both said.

1 Police Plaza, New York City
1830 hours EDT

Jeff Rockman, the Chief of Police allowed himself a private, quiet moment. He looked across the office to see himself in uniform as he took two pictures of his daughter when she graduated from the Police Academy. One picture was a proud Chief and a rookie cop. The one next to it was a proud father hugging his daughter.

Rockman had a policy up and down the police chain of command saying his daughter Tracy was not to be given any preferential treatment. "Probationary Officer Rockman is Probationary Officer Rockman, period."

Rockman leaned back and fought the tears. Rockman was in the operations center moving police officers from hot spot to hot spot. Some genius (?) from the federal government announced over the news media that 200 tons of food was being delivered to New York City today.

It arrived on-board an armored and guarded train. Crowds of hungry people tried to be anywhere to get food. Mothers held up children. People held up signs. Most of them were beyond any common sense. Hungry people are hungry people.

The food was in sealed and locked containers. The police fought running battles trying to get to distribution points. The real battles occurred as the trucks backed up to buildings which have specially constructed doors sized to the back end of trucks. So many people crowded up to the eighty-thousand-pound trucks, that the trucks started to rock.

At a distribution warehouse near Times Square. Rioting citizens broke through the fencing to the off-loading area inside the warehouse and stole boxes of food. The only way they could escape was to open the man-doors. Once that happened the police were overwhelmed. So many people entered there was no way for the twenty police officers to control anything.

The twenty police officers had called for help, but assistance could not arrive in time. By the time a fifty-man team arrived, the food was gone along with most of the rioters. Seven police officers were dead and the rest were severely injured.

Probationary Police Officer Tracy Rockman was one of the deceased. The men who arrived formed an honor tunnel to carry out the dead.

Chief of Police Jeff Rockman was there to cry over his daughter. He had to be there to see her. Then and only then could he go home to tell his wife and Tracy's mother that her daughter was dead.

Many times, in the past he had to tell wives and parents that police officers and firefighters were lost in the line of duty. Jenny would probably beat on him for not watching after Tracy, but that was her right.

June 19

Northern District, Federal Court, Dallas Texas
1000 hours EDT.

DOJ attorneys left the court feeling upbeat despite having to fight against a team that fought them tooth and nail.

Justice Martin Ferrule ruled that the Federal Government alone had the authority to deport illegal immigrants.

Texas fought back saying they were following Federal Law. 734 instances in the past, upheld by federal courts, has established precedence and precedence. "Your honor, people bypassing entry points illegally trespassing on public and private properties in Texas."

Justice Ferrule spent a week deliberating before rendering a verdict. He opened a can of worms saying despite precedence to the contrary, the Federal Government has the authority and has not renounced or delegated their authority.

The Texas Attorney General was watching the court camera. As soon as the verdict was handed down, he called his attorneys in New Orleans to file an appeal with the Fifth Circuit Court of Appeals and asked for an injunction.

No sooner had the ink dried on the verdict than the Appeals court agreed to hear the appeal and granted an injunction.

"This is another one going to the Supreme Court," a veteran court watcher said.

June 20

Wall Street, New York City
1300 hours EDT

Crowds of restless people with nothing better to do, crowded the streets wanting someone to blame for their lives and situations.

The Police Department, now reinforced with the New York National Guard, were waiting for them. Checkpoints and chokepoints were erected throughout the city. However, a crowd of marchers with a city permit, congregated in front of the Wall Street Stock Exchange.

Tempers flared and diminished. Police and National Guard personnel were lined up in depth in front of the building; hopefully waiting for nothing to happen.

Unfortunately, several hundred people found two doors that were not guarded and gained entrance to the Exchange. Half the force covering the front was pulled inside to corral the now-riot on the trading floor. People were breaking into offices and destroying paper records.

Most seriously was the walls and doors to the server rooms were torn down. As everyone knows, doors are heavily constructed to stop people, but walls are not nearly as heavily constructed. Inside hard drives and computer boards were ripped out, thrown to the floor and stomped upon.

The computer financial records were automatically downloaded to several off-site locations when the intrusion alarms sounded. The media instantly came down on the rioters. "This is where the money originates to pay salaries in this country. Anyone who has any sense knows this was the stupidest move anyone could take."

Privately, CEOs of the major media companies said this will be reported in a negative manor. Everyone who had stock portfolios went to their computer and had a sigh of relief. Trading companies had insurance policies to cover this situation. A few hundred people now had jobs to clean up the mess; while others would be hired as a dedicated security force.

June 21

Room D-156, George Washington University Hospital, Washington, D.C.
1030 hours EDT.

Major Albert Glendive, dressed, in casual civilian clothes arrived for a visit. He had sat down with Smith and Jones on Friday and was told that he has been selected as the new Commander of the Werewolves.

The normally dour acting man was aghast at the thought of being the new Commander. All the myriad things on his plate now seemed insurmountable.

"Al, you are already doing those duties. Mike and I have not deployed in nearly two years," Jones said.

Glendive surrendered to his new life. Somehow, he already knew this, but to hear it was privately scary.

Glendive knocked on the door to O'Cleary's room and walked in when she said, "enter."

O'Cleary was looking at her laptop and smiled as she lowered the cover and pushed away the table. "Please sit down," she said indicating the chair near the bed. She made new adjustments to the bed so she could relax while talking to him.

"General, is the area secure?" Glendive asked.

O'Cleary pointed to the 'buzz box'. Glendive went over and turned it on. He watched and waited for the lights to shine. He then turned and sat down.

"Mister Jones and Mister Smith told me they were too old to deploy and were thinking of retiring. God knows they earned it. They in turn nominated you and I concur. Will you accept the assignment?"

"Yes Ma'am," he said.

O'Cleary looked at him. He was a hard man to read. "I have four rules:

1. Plan hard, bring everyone home, alive.
2. Never be afraid that I will abandon you.
3. Mister Kincaid had demons inside him that crushed him. Everyone used him and then through him in the corner when they got what they needed. Watch for that.
4. Appoint a Sergeant Major and listen to him or her. The Sergeant Major is the one who is your conscience and but not your best friend. But remember not to through him or her in the corner."

O'Cleary rubbed her abdomen before her son woke up and started running around, trying to rip his way out of her. "Excuse me," she said settling down.

Glendive gave a rare smile. "No Problem, Ma'am. My wife Marsha is pregnant herself. About 6 months along. We are hoping for an easy delivery."

O'Cleary smiled back. "She's not forty-nine years old. I am supposed to be starting menopause, not being a mother. With all the fun things my son is doing to the inside of me; when they do the caesarian, they will have to do a tubal ligation and end my pregnancy days, forever."

O'Cleary reached over and took a file out of the stack near her bed. She pulled one out and gave it to him. "The Army concluded its Lieutenant Colonel Selection Board and you are number 47 on the list, Congratulations. The credit card is for you and your family. It has the limit listed on the back of the card. Present both items to your wife with my complements. On the back side of your promotion orders is the appointment order so you can wear it until your number is called."

Glendive was looking over the orders and the insignia pined to the inside. "Thank you, General."

Just then, a Nurse opened the door and announced her time was up. Rest period was starting before lunch.

"My complements, General," Glendive said. He stood, saluted and left.

O'Cleary smiled as she closed her eyes.

June 22

J. Edgar Hoover Building, Washington D.C.
0900 hours EDT

Director Solin has been at his office since the riots on Saturday. Riots were flaring up all over the nation. Hospitals were overflowing with casualties as injuries skyrocketed.

Add to his troubles was the near limitless calls over the attack on the Congress and Wall Street.

Police Officers and Firefighters were already in short supply. Now they were being targeted. Firefighters in most areas were considered off-limits by the general public, but now they were being targeted. They fought fires with courage, but now they were being shot at.

Firetrucks were being stolen and used as improvised battering rams. Even as fires are being fought, people were trying to steal their tools, and in some instances, the hoses off the trucks. Police officers assigned to control traffic now had to guard the fire trucks.

Solin now had to sit down with Simon Westland, the Director of the US Police Force. Where to put the few resources, we have. Admiral Hazlet from the Internal Security Agency wanted to insert himself in the discussion. He at least wanted to help.

Solin sat down, used a towel to rub his face, looked at the monitor and waited for the clock to countdown to his next video meeting.

Desert Zero, Fort Hood, Texas
1700 hours CDT

Simmons worked down the weekly report he submitted to General O'Cleary. He was proud to announce that with 8 raids this week, there were no KIAs. Four men were wounded however; only one of them severely. His men were the most professional soldiers he ever worked with.

Simmons lovingly ran his finger over those stats. His men were a point of pride.

Waller's invasion worried him. Granted it allowed him a lot of leeway with missions that were "on hold". But he was worried his actions could stir up a hornet's nest. Still the invasion was overdue in the grand scheme.

Waller's newly christened troops are being indoctrinated to war. "Bust their cherry" was the old phrase. Sergeant Major Waverly took a stern tone to the training. He was not going to be responsible for anyone dying for shotty or bad training. Those men scored higher on their certifications than the original Savage Rabbits and this generation. Simmons decided to deploy them without a confidence builder mission. Delta Company could end up being the best company.

Delta Force still wanted to interfere and ask for security forces. Simmons noted they were upset that they could not just take assets like they did in the past. General Gender personally flew down here and had one of "those meetings" with him. A friendly sort with gourmet coffee, warm pastries and soft words. Gender knew he could not order Simmons to do anything, but Simmons could be asked. All Gender needed was one "yes".

Simmons was doing the same thing Delta Force did. Yet he did not have special troops to snatch prisoners. Simmons chuckled at that. All the other things Gender and his men can do what Simmons and the Rabbits can't.

Simmons looked at the facts and figures in his report. The only thing that mattered to him was Zero KIA item.

June 23

National Pollster's, Washington D.C.
0300 EDT

The National Polling apparatus was up and running over-time, asking the people targeted questions. The subjects of the polls are predetermined by the pollsters looking for favorable numbers to aid with whatever idea or thought they wanted to see.

Today's item was the Martial Law. One week after the 365-day limit expired, the electorate was unhappy. Liberals took to the streets and rioted along with food and fuel nut jobs.

Anyone who could be accused of starting this mess was targeted.

By an enormous margin, 76 % to 32%, everyone wanted the Martial Law to stop. Everything that the federal government moved in to "protect" and "insure that something went to those that needed it"; caused the trouble. 92% of the country blamed the federal government for screwing up everything.

Beginning six months ago, states started ignoring the Federal government and started releasing and easing the restrictions. Those same 92% people valued their state governments over the heavy hand of the "Federals".

Even the talking heads on the media shows were scared and "faux-angry".

Headquarters, 36th Infantry Division, Camp Aubrey, Texas
0900 hours CDT

Major General Corcoran welcomed Colonel Folcroft and Sergeant Major Barker into his office and had the door closed behind them. He took a deep breath and held up a file.

"Gentlemen," Corcoran said. "Word got out and this is list of Officers and NCOs who want those jobs, with the promotions, in the new Fourth Brigade. I had said it repeatedly that I gave you both final approval/disapproval authority. Seems that is not good enough for some people. I might be the Division Commander, but that does not stop political interference." Corcoran took the file and put it in a drawer.

"Who do I have to take, Sir?" Folcroft asked.

Corcoran looked at the drawer and was silent. Finally, he said, "Leave the politics to me and ignore it. Any of those politicians try to circumvent me, and I'll have their ass."

Corcoran looked at the drawer. "Seems the legislature did something I never would have believed possible. There are funds set aside for "spot" promotions. Washington has released some of the equipment on hold because of our detention policy. Seems we are saving the Pentagon a lot of money. Even with a year-long posting, the charlatans are actually politicking for specific jobs that can translate later into jobs and political offices."

Folcroft and Barker sat still waiting for the General to finish.

Corcoran absently pointed to the file and the drawer. "I already talked to the governor and he refuses to knuckle under to politics this time. I vouched for you both because I can depend on you both. That is why the folder full of politicians and opportunists is in my drawer so I can bar-be-que them. You are here today to hear it from me that you are to stay immune to politics and form you unit from the ground up with officers and NCOs that can do the job. Period."

"Yes Sir," both said. They stood, saluted and left.

Folcroft and Barker went to the G-1 to start combing through the records.

June 24

Nation-Wide, Numerous Cities
0500-2330 hours EDT to PDT

New York City, Los Angeles, Chicago, Atlanta, Dallas, Miami and at least 50 other cities and towns; riots were occurring at least once a week. In the larger cities like New York, Miami and Los Angeles it was a daily occurrence.

The items needed were fuel, food and electricity. In southern cities, any place that had air conditioning was being over loaded. To the people who understood it, that many people who were overheated were overloading the system.

In a mall in southern Miami, the main units suddenly quit. Police forces better needed elsewhere had to come in and quell the ensuing riot. The demolished stores stated they were not re-opening. The mall owner said the mall was now closed. "Those idiots ruined a sanctuary. We ran the AC units at maximum to serve those who did not have any other place to go."

Homeland Security and the Internal Security Agency ran the numbers up and down the charts. X-number of people need y-number of tons of food. Armored food shipments tried to fill those gaps. They actually believed they could educate people how to measure their food and let the government supply it to you.

558

One staffer said it all. "Once people go hungry, that feeling never goes away. You take one days' worth of food away and it takes four days' worth of food to ease it."

Another staffer said. "We need to shut down the SynGas factories. Farmers are by-passing low-paying food markets and driving to high-paying SynGas plants."

Everyone looked at each other. No one wanted to kiss that rattle snake.

June 25

Headquarters, Northwest Military Region, Fort Carson Colorado.
0900 hours MST

Matheson watched as his last computer server was installed and powered up. Matheson's last visit to the logistics office was to order four scanners. All that paper and photographs needed to be placed in the data base. Several of the hard drives were attached to laptops by the cyber-warfare specialists. When the old hard drives spun up, the virus attacked and froze up the laptops.

"This was not a random attack," Matheson said to no one in particular.

The technicians worked around him setting up the new equipment. A Captain came to him and mumbled something about new anti-virus this and firewall that. Matheson did not really understand any of it. He smiled and walked away. He came over to his aide and said to find someone who speaks English to learn what they are doing to prevent any of this from happening again.

June 26

Department of the Treasury, Washington D.C.
1000 hours EDT

David Carter looked at the quarterly report on his desk. It was compiled from all sections and documenting every facet and part of the nation's financial health. Carter chuckled. His daughter was taking English language and composition in high school. He had to endure a "recital" twice a week as she practiced her elocution.

Carter decided to ruin his mood. He pulled the summary over to his lap and started reading. The deficit was still climbing. Those fools in Congress will keep ballooning the debt. Three trillion dollars a year is unsustainable. Carter looked up to the total worth of all goods, services, industries, housing, infrastructure and property. The United States of America is now worth over 57 trillion dollars. The debt was now over 42 trillion.

Carter remembered his favorite saying of late. 'In one generation, we went from king of the world to a debtor nation.'

Carter threw the summary back on top of the quarterly report.

June 27

Room D-156, George Washington University Hospital, Washington, D.C.
2130 hours EDT.

After a Caesarian section at 9:21 am today, Arthur Thomas O'Cleary came into the world, whole, healthy and screaming his brains out. Eight pounds, 6 ounces, 20 inches long, a head full of jet-black hair and Dennis's temper. Yeah, he was an O'Cleary. Brenda looked at her pride and joy, wondering at the tiny parts of him. She was amazed at the tiny fingers, toes, Dennis' blue eyes and the almost amazing resemblance to the pictures of Dennis when he was born. "Arthur, my son, you are your father's son," she said. Arthur was whisked away for further checks with Dennis in toe who was flabbergasted at the "son" that screamed at him. Seven months of weekly tests and mountains of painstaking measures were worth all the effort. Diet, exercise, and rest were the keys to having a healthy and normal baby and mother.

This month was enforced rest and maternity leave. Hawker came by twice daily to brief her on activities, large and small. Most of it was "nothingness" as Dennis called it. For a man that distained the world of the Pentagon, he could be very clear headed about events. Many times, he looked past the morass of details and saw simple solutions to seemingly complex issues. He resolved a serious problem in Florida with the aged population by reminding her that they were used to food and medical access. A surplus of twenty thousand tons of food and returning medical personnel back to their Florida homes was the cure.

What had too many people confused was that people were preoccupied with their comfort. "No shit Sherlock," Dennis said. "Look Lady, losing two hundred years of plenty is too hard for anyone to comprehend." Dennis went to the refrigerator and opened it. He made an elaborate show of pointing out how full it was. Then he went to the cupboard and showed her the myriad of medications for both of them. "We have plenty," he said, with sarcasm, "most people have a tenth of this."

Brenda kicked herself, again, and it always raised her blood pressure at her stupidity. She was as guilty as the rest of official Washington. With plenty in the cupboards, doing without was an alien feeling. She remembered Operation Desert Shield and Storm. She would have sold herself for a hot bath in the privacy of an air-conditioned room.

"Dennis?" she asked, holding a sleeping Arthur, and making a circling motion over her head. He showed her a blinking box in his coat pocket. "I want you to leave this place with our son."

Dennis didn't laugh or seem surprised. "You know something?"

Brenda told him about what Hawker was hearing. Level Five designates, which she was a member, had their family members sequestered in special security facilities. In simple language, they were being held hostage. Several people said it was the same as asking permission to see their families. Their every move and word, recorded.

Dennis stood and came over to Arthur, kissed him on the forehead and then kissed Brenda. "If anyone touches my family, I will commit war," he said, very deliberately.

"You will commit war, but not here," Brenda said, motioning for him to take Arthur. Brenda gingerly went to the bathroom and wondered how she was going to convince him to leave. She returned to see a very different Dennis staring at the sleeping form of his son. All the old wife's tales about children changing your lives forever only scratched the surface. His hands gently felt the contours of Arthur's face.

"Only a mother can feel a heartbeat but only a father can sense a soul," Brenda repeated one of Miss Gladys' sayings.

"A mother raises a boy and a father makes him a man," he said, finishing the old saying.

Just then a soft knock on the door broke the mood. Hawker came in with two briefcases. "In disobedience to General Edwards and in obedience with your orders, I am here," she said, making a small bow in the direction of Dennis and Arthur. She set the briefcases down very silently on the table and opened one of them. A 'buzz box' started and filled the room. Arthur moved a little and settled back down. "I think he likes it," she said, smiling.

"Maybe," Dennis said, an annoyed look on his face.

"Let's do this, Elizabeth. Arthur will stir in another hour for his feeding." Brenda sat down on the chair and faced the briefcase. Thirty minutes later, Hawker closed up everything and left.

"We need a trusted medical source to know when," Dennis said, making a gesture.

"Doctor Scorner," she said, repeating the gesture.

Dennis had a curious look on his face. "I spoke to the Doctors earlier. They said that Arthur could travel in a few weeks, overland. Planes are out of the question until he is six months old."

"What are you thinking?" Brenda asked.

"I think the trip to Wineseck needs some more planning and lots of help." Dennis looked down at Arthur stirring and walked over to Brenda as he woke up. They changed his diaper and settled into a feeding ritual that was going to continue for years to come. After he was satiated, Arthur went back to sleep for a few hours.

June 29

Eisenhower Executive Office Building, Washington D.C.

DOD Secretary Dodson, General Edwards, General Waller, Admiral Cartwright, General Macklin and General Matheson waited for the President in this room. No aides or staffers were allowed. The President came in with one briefer and one folder. After they entered the room, the doors were locked. They were alone.

"Gentlemen," the President said. "The purpose of this meeting is to present to you with a clear, concise and workable mission statement and special instructions. I have purposefully worked the language so that all commanders and soldiers up and down the chain of command have clear instructions on what this country expects of you." He nodded to the staffer to hand out a five-page document to each person in the room, with the lines spaced a line and a half apart.

That task completed, the staffer took a position at the podium and waited for the President to cue him.

The President began the briefing. "Gentlemen, the first portion is the Chain of Command. It runs from me to Defense Secretary to General Edwards and finally to you four Commanders. If you run into problems call us and we will find a solution. Granted there are going to be jurisdictional problems that will try to interfere with your job. You will not allow that to happen."

The President turned to the staffer, nodded to him and settled back.

"Admiral, Generals, your mission statement is as follows. You are placed in command of all Active Duty, National Guard and Reserve Units and assets within your designated operational area as indicated on the map on the back page." The Briefer allowed the Flag officers time to flip to the page. When the officers looked up, the briefer continued. "Your primary focus is to coordinate the security of assets within your operational areas. Those are listed on pages 2, 3, and 4. The folders in front of you list those areas within your particular operational area."

The staffer was experienced enough to know when and how long to pause. "The mission statement finishes with the provision that you are allowed leeway with mission execution.

Should your operations cross-over boundaries, you are allowed to coordinate between you so long as the situation is reported."

The briefer closed the folder and handed it to the President. He left the room. Once the door was closed and locked, the President motioned to the folders each General had. The President signed the cover letter in each of the folders, making their orders official. He initialed all the following five pages.

"I purposely left a lot of things vague," he said, thinking that sounded stupid. "You men are patriots. You men are already entrusted as responsible citizens and military officers. I see no need to give you a hundred-page document outlining thousands of rules of engagement. If the lawyers get in the way send them down to General Waller who is now authorized to put them in the front lines." That got the expected chuckles.

The rest of the meeting centered around operational matters. The President left in the middle of the back and forth. The Flag Officers did not really comprehend the situation where they were granted a free hand to execute their duties. The President signed the order which meant he was not throwing vague and conflicting verbal orders which can be denied later.

All six men knew that their free hand can be yanked back if they did or allowed something stupid to happen.

Desert Zero, Fort Hood, Texas
1700 hours CDT

Simmons put the finishing touches on the weekly report for General O'Cleary. Even though she was seriously pregnant, the General made it a point of reading the weekly report. She would call him up sometimes to discuss some points. If all else failed, by Monday morning she replied, at least thanking him and the Rabbits for a fantastic job.

Scuttlebutt said she gave birth to a healthy son a few days ago. Having a baby at her age, he shivered. His wife Sarah had their youngest daughter when she was 32. He was tormented for seven months. Sarah had virtually every problem in the book. Barbara was now the apple of his eye.

Simmons looked to the page that listed his personnel. Two Rabbits were killed and seven wounded when they went in to retrieve a helicopter crew that was shot down. The cartels were all over the area. Captain Halliger and Specialist Wingrove were the dead. Halliger insisted he would always be the last to leave. Wingrove was his radio operator. Wingrove was relaying fire control instructions when he was killed.

Simmons recommended both of them for Silver Stars. He personally requested that both of them get equal awards. The Army was always class-conscious when medals were awarded.

Simmons was finished with the FBI and Treasury. Seems that seven crates full of cash loaded on an Osprey were lost. As the aircraft crossed the border is was fired upon. One engine shut down. The pilot ordered everything but people thrown overboard. Four wounded men had to diverted to a hospital, so it could not land.

Simmons laughed. Some fools on our side of the border had a gift from heaven land on them. By the time law enforcement arrived, the area was crowded with people collecting a windfall. Everyone forced open the containers and helped themselves. No one could estimate the total haul.

Simmons had nothing else to report except the normal near perfect results.

June 30

Room E-194, Pentagon, Washington, D.C
1034A S. Gilmore Street, Parkton, Virginia
0900 to 1800 hours EDT

Kendal and Locklear split their time between being hounded and taught by Nancy Glister. They had no idea that she was an avatar created by a super-computer. Additionally, General O'Cleary would grade and critique their exams. She was brutal and very demanding. Sometimes she subtracted points for lack of "due diligence". Sloppy or incomplete work earned a "Zero".

Kendal and Locklear relished Sundays when they rested and put it all out of their minds. That was when they truly learned why they loved each other.

O'Cleary could never tell them that the reason for driving them so hard was a point on the calendar. Soon, once more, the country will tear itself apart. Somehow, smart patriots will have to pull things back together.

July 1

485 Glenmore Drive, Alexandria, Virginia
1400 hours EDT

Dennis, Brenda and Arthur were wheeled out the front door of the hospital. It was a nice day with temperatures in the upper 80's and a few clouds in sky. Arthur was fed, content and sound asleep.

Arthur was oblivious to the world around him, several dozen people including Amanda and Thomas Edwards along with Elizabeth Hawker were waiting at the main door to applaud them on their way out the door.

Arthur was already in a carrier that easily locked into his car seat inside the mini-van Dennis had bought with this day in mind. With a lot of car plants off-line due to the credit crunch, it was hard to find and actually buy a serviceable or new are; Dennis considered himself lucky to find this one. He researched and found one that provided Arthur plenty of protection in case of an accident.

Three of Dennis' better friends baby-sat his home. No less than five attempts were made by "government resettlement" personnel to pack up the O'Cleary household and move them to new quarters attached the Naval Observatory. Those people have been trying to move them since Brenda became the Vice-Chairman of the Joint Chiefs of Staff. This time, no one was injured. HA HA.

One of Dennis' other friends was a Retired Army Major named Arthur Grandmaison who was now a Police Lieutenant in the Alexandria, Virginia Police Department. He was only too happy to come and investigate a "possible home invasion and robbery". Nathanial Graham was another friend of his

566

who was a Judge seated in Alexandria Virginia. Nathanial volunteered to be his lawyer. Nathanial was a twenty-year addict of Dennis' cookies.

The caravan arrived home to a cheering crowd. Military and civilian on-lookers applauded and held up signs. Brenda got out of the van walking gingerly. She waved back to everyone and showed her much slimmed stomach and pointed to her son.

Arthur was still oblivious to all the fanfare. Brenda hated the stitches and staples holding her abdomen together. The doctors said the healing should only take a month, but they warned her not to push it. Brenda had medical appointments through the month.

The O'Cleary's stood outside for a few minutes thanking everyone for cheering them on. Brenda started hurting, so Dennis apologized and hustled Brenda and Arthur inside. A few volunteers offered and assisted bringing in everything they needed.

Amanda Edwards and Colonel Elizabeth Hawker were already inside. They told everyone were to drop off the packages. Afterward, everyone took their cue and left.

Amanda, ever the photographer, walked around taking pictures with her new camera. It was a digital version of a 35 mm variety. Only this one, periodically downloaded the photos to a cloud file. Later, Dennis and Brenda could select the ones they wanted and the cloud would develop them into paper pictures for scrapbooks.

Dennis and Brenda carried Arthur into his room. Gone was all the guest room furniture. Now everything they needed to take care of a baby was there. Crib, changing table, open shelves full of baby clothes, powers, oils, cleaning everything, and of course a sealable and odor-resistant garbage can for "those diapers". The closet was filled floor to ceiling with diapers sized from now to one year.

"Young man," his dad said. "You took more planning and pre-positioning than the D-Day invasion."

Brenda ran her finger over his face. Arthur smiled. She looked at her watch. He would wake up in thirty minutes for his feeding and new diaper. She glanced at the stack of diaper boxes in the closet. Arthur needed ten to twelve diaper and clothing changings a day.

Brenda ran her finger over his face. "Arthur, your mommy loves you." Brenda looked up at the pictures of her parents and Dennis' parents. "Smile," she to them.

Brenda and Dennis walked outside, turning on the baby monitor and taking their monitor with them.

US-Mexican border, Del Rio, Texas
1700 hours CDT

Literally everyone saw this coming. A "huge" number of people started assembling at the border crossing two days ago. Dedicated Predator drones observed the people who attempted to camouflage themselves, but failed. They failed so bad that the news media showed up, pointed cameras at and interviewed them. Some of the media types actually called this "a humanitarian crisis".

Thomas and Colonel Jenkins, commander of the Texas National Guard's, 2nd Brigade on the border, met at a location two kilometers northeast of Del Rio at a hilltop overseeing the location. Both men looked at the maps. This was a unique situation. Del Rio was the border boundary between both the Texas brigade and the 4th Division brigade.

Both Colonels compared notes and started laughing. Thomas opened his thermos bottle and offered Jenkins a cup.

Jenkins laughed. "If those idiots try to rupture the border, they are stupid. Then again, this could be a diversion for something else."

Thomas pulled out a quarter. "Flip you for who takes this." Jenkins nodded, called "heads" and waited for the quarter to hit the Humvee hood. It was heads. "Ok," Thomas said. "First Battalion is on the border; Lieutenant Colonel Dragger. I'll have him come and coordinate with you.

July 2

0400 hours CDT

Oh, the comedy of it all. Thomas was watching it all on a monitor. Dragger was using something previously only seen in movies. There were three bull dozers that were supposed to "secretly" move forward.

The bull dozers "ran" up to the wall. Positioned near the border crossing, three Humvees raced out and turned out on the access road. Each was armed with what was colloquially called the "Zap Gun". Its real name was long and too technically termed; so, everyone called it the "Zap Gun".

The "Zap Gun" was tube shaped weapon that had a four-pronged harpoon that was shot at a vehicle. A spool dispensed two wires leading back to the tube and a power pack. Once the harpoon penetrates into the metal frame, the power pack sends a surge of power at 10,000 volts and 0.4 amps.

That power surge has only one effect; everything electrical in the vehicle is fried.

Three "Zap Guns" shot out as the Bull Dozers crossed the US/Mexico border just before the wall. All three bull dozers stopped. All the Humvees sped away towards a crossing site south near Laredo. The crowds who were cheering and yelling, suddenly went silent. The gates at the border shut and soldiers converged on the site.

That diversion was now over. Fifty miles further south along the border, explosive charges blew open a wall section. Twelve trucks broke through and scattered into Texas. Soldiers assigned to that area notified their headquarters. One of the advantages to the "Brick Bat" was its ability to keep pace with four wheeled vehicles. The one in the area, scored hits on two vehicles, blowing the engines off the chassis.

On call UH-60 helicopters lifted off carrying the Quick Reaction Force along with AH-64 Apache gun-ships, flew into the air and hunted down the trucks. Ten of the estimated twelve trucks were captured. Descriptions were sent to the Texas Department of Public Safety.

Lieutenant Colonel Dragger was heard asking why so many people allowed themselves to be used and abused so that the Cartels can move narcotics.

Internal Security Agency, Barton, Virginia
0900 hours EDT

Admiral Hazlet actually enjoyed his job. He had control of nearly 2,500 people who did their job and seldom had to punished or reprimanded. If anything, they had to be restrained and slowed down. His absolute rule was no one is to treated as guilty first. He wanted the rule of law to remain; front and center.

He learned a lot of lessons from his secretary, Mary Atkinson, who had been there since the beginning. "Trust them as much as you can. Talk to them, visit them, and find out how we do our jobs. You will see how we serve the country and you will become bored at how smooth we operate. Oh, and by the way, save losing your temper and being frantic for those times when you really need it."

Hazlet had instructions directly from the President to "spy" on his district military commanders. Hazlet felt a little dirty spying on his fellow Flag Officers. Hazlet read the "orders" each officer was given. Granted he would have loved such simplistic orders. The five pages for each could fit in one manila folder. His orders and special instructions for this assignment were in a two-inch thick 3-ring binder.

General Matheson was first for investigation. Hazlet knew the General and he was someone who loved be the mouse without a cat to keep him honest.

Admiral Cartwright was typical Navy. He was in command and in command he was until someone moved him out of the way. He now had a mandate to do anything he wanted and to hell with consequences.

General Macklin was a studious and thoughtful man. A stern Catholic who went to mass each day. He was a man who was probably the least of the problems. But there was something......

General Waller in the southwest was only doing what he was already doing.

Hazlet went down to visit the Justice team. Hazlet knocked on the door for Jane Rickover. He needed advice from the most successful back breaker in the business. "Jane, I need to know how to stay objective and not allow prejudices to creep in and foul up my objectivity."

Jane Rickover broke her rule and changed her facial expression.

July 3

Headquarters, 4th Brigade, 36th Infantry Division, Texas National Guard, Camp Aubry, Texas
1000 hours CDT

Major General Harold Corcoran, Commanding General of the Texas 36th Infantry Division stood on the podium at his Division Headquarters. Reading the Proclamation; signed by the Governor, the 4th Brigade of the Texas National Guard was brought to life.

General Corcoran and the Governor uncased the colors of the 114th Infantry Regiment and unfurled them. An announcer read the history of the 114th Regiment from the original unit, one hundred and seventy years ago, to present.

Corcoran passed the colors to Colonel Jasper Folcroft, who accepted them and immediately assumed command. The same announcer read the order, signed by Folcroft which made it official. Folcroft passed the colors to Command Sergeant Major Terrance Barker who walked them to the Color Guard.

Standing behind the colors were seventy-two officers and NCOs who accepted full time positions within the Regiment.

Being such a small unit, there was not a "Pass in review" parade. His seventy-two men just stood in place as their unit was brought to life.

The 144th was created to be a motorized infantry unit, mainly manned with Humvees and BrickBats. The unit was designed to be very mobile and able to react quickly to widely separated actions.

Folcroft had a formal request submitted to visit the Savage Rabbits to learn from them. Folcroft wanted to know what doctrine they used to seemingly jump out of a hole, tear up the Cartels and vanish. He would need that.

July 4

Underground Station "Conscience", World Wide Web and Channel 513
0900 hours EST.

"If you threaten, act. If you say something, do it. If something is important, stand your ground. Governments are often hamstrung by individuals who have opinions about issues they feel strongly about. This is Martin Socranson, self-proclaimed philosopher who says, 'What are we if we can't back up what you say'?"

"Greetings America" Martin Socranson said beginning his broadcast. "It is reluctantly Saturday and I say thus." In the background the sounds of the 1812 overture played.

"Here we are America. Another month under Martial Law. What you say? Aren't we beyond the limit the President set for Martial Law? Isn't there enough damage caused by all the over-spending and overreach that Congress created? How long are we to suffer under this tyrannical rule?"

Socranson pointed to a chart showing the bare outlines of the state's borders. Additionally, there were two red lines cutting the nation into unequal quarters.

"Four different 4-star military officers are in charge of us. The State Governors you went to the trouble of electing are not really in charge anymore. General Waller down in Texas has the only real job of the four. At least he is in charge of securing the border with Mexico."

"Does Admiral Cartwright in the southeast have a border problem with Cuba?

"How about General Macklin in the Northeast? Is Canada invading?"

"General Matheson in the Northwest must love the moose hunting in Pacific Northwest. Is there anything else for him to do?"

"What kind of fools are we America?" Socranson took a deep breath. "The only thing I am to believe is that these officers are set in place to lock down the country. Before the President locked down the country, we had food in grocery stores. We had gas at the stations. What we did not have was leadership from Washington or justice from the courts. We still don't."

572

"This country was sold down the river by self-serving politicians who had no other motive than to bribe you into voting for them; time and time again."

"This country was sold down the river by self-servicing Judges that refused to uphold the law and put criminals behind bars. When the criminals lost their fear of the law and the police, we were doomed. What do we poor citizens have to do?"

"We citizens, have no choice but to form vigilantes and militias to protect ourselves, our families and our homes. If we bother to call for help, it comes slow; if at all. If any people are actually arrested and tried, the courts let 'the poor miscreants' out with a slap on the wrist."

"Lawyers around the country are demanding the few remaining policemen protect them." Socranson laughed hard. "The creatures who love this mess are crying because the misery they profit from and justify to themselves is crawling back at them. P.S. those same lawyers are the ones who chased off the police with all their lawsuits protecting the guilty."

"I will not justify the attack on the Congress. Period. But I refuse to cry with them that they now had to be as scared as the rest of us. Have you heard that they cried so loud at how scared they are that a battalion of no less than 600 Army soldiers from the 3rd Infantry Regiment are now assigned to protect them? Now true heroes will find it harder to be honored with a burial on our most hallowed ground. While we are on the subject, fewer Soldiers will be on hand to eject the homeless from the cemetery from setting up tents and ripping headstones out of the ground to use as floors."

"America, oh my America. We are at a crossroads. How much farther do we allow ourselves to be pushed down the road, until enough is enough?"

Socranson looked at a depiction of lady liberty who threw down the torch and buried her face in her hands. Socranson looked back, wiping tears from his eyes.

"We are being treated like a third world country and we brought it on ourselves. The UN Security Council wants to station security forces on American streets with blue hats. They want to "secure" American nuclear weapons "just in case". I laugh at those minor world players and will laugh at the answer they will receive on American roads and soil."

"By the way America. Happy Birthday."

Socranson looked at the camera as it slowly faded away. He smiled broadly.

Cyber Intelligence Section, Internal Security Agency, Barton Virginia
1000 hours EDT.

Admiral Hazlet watched the broadcast, again. Ever since he assumed command in April, he made it a point to come down to Cyber Intelligence and watch two things. The broadcast and the reaction in the room. He learned, a long time ago, the situation was only as important as the people who have to fight it or react to it.

Hazlet sat next to Milton Bradley, the chief of this section. "Well, Mister Bradley?" he asked.

Bradley looked at his technicians who had just rewound the tape to the beginning to watch it a second time to check on things they noted the first time and do a closer study of the content.

"Admiral," he said with some frustration. "For nearly two years, Mister Socranson is no closer to being found than he was at the beginning. He is literally a ghost."

Hazlet privately did not like that answer. Socranson was a target that mountains of politicians and bureaucrats were bugging him about. "I will be honest with you. I have my phone ringing off the hook about him. It is a distraction that I don't need. I am not demanding impossible results, but I need something for this month's barrage."

Bradley seemed relieved that Hazlet isn't acting like Prescott did. "Sir, this is literally the best camouflage I have ever encountered. He literally evades like he already knows how we are chasing him. Hackers around the world are chasing him too. Nothing seems to work. With all the workload around here, I normally cut off the hunt after about two or three hours. I will say without prejudice that we are no closer to finding him now as we were two years ago."

Hazlet seemed to agree with him except for one item. "Mister Bradley, I remember something about a theory of him being a part of the UNSTACK THIS virus."

Bradley took a deep breath. "Sir, that was never a viable theory and the analyst who proposed it had a nervous breakdown. General Prescott even commissioned two hackers in Federal Prison to try finding UNSTACK THIS and Socranson. They were even offered a full pardon and still failed." Bradley took another breath. "Sir, the end result of this conversation is that we have no solution at this time."

Hazlet was enough of a realist to know that making stupid and unreasonable pronouncements was stupid. "Mister Bradley, I suggest you shelf this for the rest of the month and start fresh next month."

"Thank you, sir," Bradley said, with some relief.

Bonnie Chandler, Box 234, Route 17, Belcher Missouri
1400 hours CDT

Dear Bonnie,

Now they have taken the football field. We used to spend the summers going to the field to meet, play games and generally meet. Now the soldiers have it clogged with cars and antennas and trucks and boxes and all kinds of junk.

The field is torn up and the grass is gone. Now it is a mud pit.

We tried going to the McCarren's open lot, but the Army said no. Seems they always want us to go and play somewhere else to claim a new spot for junk storage. Now they want us to date them. Those of us who are eighteen and older are actively hunted down like they have us targeted and we are fair game.

Suzy Mandir was being hassled by three Army guys. She fought her way away from them and raced away. Suzy ran into four guys from school. The Army guys stopped and tried to laugh it off.

I asked my dad if I was supposed to be Army property. He asked me if I wanted to be raped. Of course, I said no. He went upstairs and came down with boxing gloves.

"I'm going to teach you to fight. Take it seriously. Otherwise, if you think you can't be raped, you will be. You cannot count on anyone being there to rescue you. I will teach you all the basics in an afternoon. The rest is practicing, every day. If you do the work, I'll supervise your practice. If you want to pout, I'll let you get attacked and beaten."

My dad is really patient with his hard headed daughter.

I hope the bruises don't show.

July 6

Minuteman, north of Fort Benton, Montana
1300 hours MDT

First item of business was the graduation ceremony for the eighty-four Non-Commissioned-Officers who attended the eight weeks of the course.

Six and a half days a week, 14 hours plus each day, except for Sunday afternoons, it was instruction and practical exercise. The two Ranger qualified NCOs said it was like Ranger school only you had a Sunday off. But it was not around the clock field exercises.

These graduates were taught the technical aspects of leading men in combat. All of them now understood the differences between tactical and operational actions. Not only could they shoot weapons, but they knew how they interacted and how they are emplaced so those weapons and men who use them do maximum damage to the enemy.

"You were taught to do your job and lead men," Jones said. "You must do that, but you are required to make your men believe they must do their job and you will guard their lives more than your own. You do that by knowing your job, the area you are in and the enemy you fight. Period."

The graduates walked across the stage and accepted their diplomas. Smith and Jones stood and warmly shook each man's hand.

Ten minutes later, the main event began.

Jones sat down on the stage with Smith. This was the last time they would attend anything in command at Minuteman. After this change of command, Lieutenant

576

Colonel Peters would take command of the Minuteman and in a separate, private ceremony, Lieutenant Colonel Glendive would assume command of the Werewolves.

Jones had a set of colors commissioned consisting of blue background with a full color, hand stitched colonial Minuteman. Jones would never tell anyone what the cost was, but something like that usually started at $10,000.

Peters read the assumption of command orders and stood aside. Jones took the colors from Command Sergeant Major Sheridan and passed them to Peters. Peters handed them back to Sheridan who marched off to the Color Guard. Jones stood and made short work of a speech, essentially saying they were the finest soldiers he ever served with and that was the only way someone should end a career.

Peters said he did not have a speech. They knew him and he knew them. Anything he said was an insult and he would never insult them. He dismissed everyone and the formation broke up.

Instead of going to the food tables and beer kegs, most of the men and their families crowded around Peters to shake his hand. Universally, they respected him and wanted to show it.

Peters pointed up to the stage and many of them gasped. Somehow, the original Savage Rabbit colors were up there. Somehow, Peters had kept them.

Smith and Jones stood aside and each opened a beer. They were the only Werewolves who ever lived long enough to retire. They toasted each of their classmates by name, read from a faded set of orders. Out of twenty-eight from their class, they were the final two. Zach Morgan, John Kincaid and them were the only survivors from Vietnam. Morgan died because they failed to kill off all those dammed Black Elves. John Kincaid committed suicide because they were prejudiced. John was so good; he did his job and we pushed him out of the way when he was no longer needed.

"John blew his brains out because we were officers and NCOs were expendable," Jones said, when the last name was said and remembered. "We," he said with emphasis. "We forgot what being an NCO was all about. "John blew his brains out because we refused to see what was right in front of

577

us. This is an army who really should not ever need officers. I told that to Peters and Glendive."

"What about the next class of Brothers?" Smith said.

"We stay above the day-to-day, yet teach from a podium and classroom. Covington will command and Griffith will be the XO. There are four others to be the tactical officers. I mean Morgan, Pruitt, Mejia and McPherson. Any support personnel can be pulled from a rotation here. Others can be taken from the state National Guard, paid by whatever committee money is left over. There are still overseas money accounts we have that have never been tapped."

Smith smiled. "I guess we try asking Mister Peters and Mister Glendive for help."

"Beg you mean," Jones said. "We will need Kendal and Locklear next year."

Room E-194, Pentagon, Washington, D.C
1034A S. Gilmore Street, Parkton, Virginia
0900 to 1800 hours EDT

For this particular block of instruction, Kendal and Locklear dressed in professional civilian clothes. Nancy gave them instructions on how to look and act like professional bureaucrats. Last Friday, part of their education was to go shopping for higher end professional civilian suits, shoes and briefcases with all the accessories. Next, they walked around the capital and observed civilians at play (work).

All day long, using their National Security Agency identification, the toured Congress and the Eisenhower Executive Office Building. Both of them knew that this about camouflage and blending in so that they are seen and easily forgotten. Both paid close attention to how everyone acted. Kendal also looked at the shoes professional women wore. Fortunately, a majority of the women were using wide heels instead of spikes. Kendal put two inches as her personal preference.

This week was classroom instruction by seven members of the faculty from the Army War College. The instructors were told two special individuals needed specific instruction given to them in advance of the next year's appropriations.

The instructors, retired military and civilians, were very interested in doing a good job for the next three weeks. The instruction was about filling in the blanks about tactical and operational planning and actions from their notebooks.

Desert Zero, Fort Hood, Texas
1800 hours CDT

Simmons promoted his executive officer, Major Galen to Lieutenant Colonel. Simmons looked at the stack of orders in front of him. Because of his rank and the changes in the Table of Organization and Equipment (TO&E), Simmons was promoting a lot of officers and NCOs. Simmons pushed the stack of NCOs at Waverly. He knew them better.

Simmons was scared at promoting officers too soon. They made the decisions and that meant lives were saved or lost. His first criteria were listening to his NCOs, then making decisions. He also prized his officers for thinking fast. His highest criteria were placing their soldiers needs ahead of their own.

Everyone here was a combat tested leader. Two of his Captains were selected for promotion to Major, so he had no power over that.

Simmons knew his problem was he had too much power. He paced the floor of his office and had too many things in his head.

Simmons went to see the only friend a Marine commander had. He knocked on the door to the Chaplin's office.

July 7

J. Edgar Hoover Building, Washington D.C.
0800 hours EST

The Director of the FBI, Marcus Solin picked up the monthly report of criminal activity for the month of June.

He looked at the two-inch-thick report. On top of the report was the summary. It was getting repetitious. Murders up, robberies up, rapes up, hijackings up and vigilantes were roaming free. Lawyers and judges being beaten and two cases of being tarred and feathered. Assaults on the IRS and its personnel was an almost daily occurrence.

Now the absolute latest and his 'most important' headache was the attack on Congress. His phone lit up constantly with politicians and their families' wanting answers. Privately, he had to admit, the attack was simple and effective in the extreme. It did not require a huge army of terrorists with machine guns and planes to utterly unnerve a bunch of pampered cry-babies.

Two or three men with not so unique skills unnerved a whole government. All they needed to be were commercial heating and air conditioning technicians. Any standard tech school could teach the knowledge needed to pull this off. The rest was the will to do it.

Solin scanned the rest of the summary. He was bored with it already. He asked his secretary to box up the report and have it messengered to the Attorney General.

Last month down, this month to go.

Headquarters, Northwest Military Region, Fort Carson Colorado.
1000 hours MST

Matheson wanted to launch a new set of drones to go over Montana and Idaho, looking for militia sites and those who wanted to live 'off the grid'. Matheson also wanted to know more about O'Cleary's Army. What was its training and living in the heavily wooden Rocky Mountains?

Matheson spent a lot of time in Special Operations and that story O'Cleary gave was a first-class fairy tale. The last time he was in Washington, he went to the J-3 Special Projects and looked up the file. First, it was classified at the ULTRA level. He knew it was a fool's errand to try to get anyone to let him see the file. That vault door needed three combinations from three different individuals to open it and one of them was off-site now. The redacted file literally told him nothing.

Matheson looked at the redacted file and its Presidential authorization. Matheson already knew that none of his officers had an ULTRA clearance. Even if he had one, it was a moot point to ask him for a briefing. ULTRA clearances were hard to get and even harder to keep. They had access to everything and those security safeguards were impossible to circumvent.

Matheson went down to the Personal Security Section and inquired about getting one. The Officer tried hard not to laugh. "Sir, that specific clearance is hard to justify and harder to qualify for. The average time to actually grant one is two years. But it is a process that takes as long as it takes. Typical rate of granting such a clearance is three percent. The clearance has to be justified and the person has to have a specific reason to get one."

Matheson returned to Fort Carson and still wondered what was going on up in those mountains. He was granted Presidential authority to command any DOD function, unit or facility. So, the germ of an idea formed. O'Cleary and the JCS was far away. Matheson did not have a force, military or civilian that was his to utilize, except the over-extended units at Fort Lewis.

One exception to his authority was that he could not use any force or facility that had a mission on-going. That virtually eliminated all the forces in his region. The governors needed their forces to augment the police. The two acting divisions, the Fourth and the Ninth had prior missions. Both Divisions were short of personnel and equipment. The deployments were wearing everyone and thing down.

Matheson turned to another problem. A lot of his photographic surveillance was gone or so jumbled in the photo vault that he could not make heads or tails of it. Of all the things that was lost when the computers failed, his staff kept the master correlated, cross-referenced list of photos and how they interacted on those computers. None of those pictures in his vaults was of any use.

Matheson decided not to kill everyone. He looked at the officer in charge and told him to send up the drones. "Look over the satellite images and highlight the areas for the drones to overfly."

In the background, UNSTACK THIS heard General Matheson's orders and those key words kicked alarms with the master program. Several options and plans were now overcome by events. A quick inventory on the availability of drones presented one short term solution. Eighty two percent of them were already committed to other intelligence tasks. General Waller in the southwest had the highest priority.

UNSTACK THIS changed the availability status to be the end of this calendar month. Maintenance and upgrade issues were cited as reasons. That should give Valkyrie time to react.

Department of Labor, Washington D.C.
1300 hours EDT

Secretary of Labor Larry Umstead had his staff work all morning to poll all the unions, nationwide for the President.

"What was the labor mood of the nation?"

Umstead already knew the answer when the President asked. Inflation was caving in households. Similar to the Weimar Republic in Germany between the World Wars, workers, in some cases, were being paid daily. Sometimes they were paid twice a day. Wives were waiting in parking lots to take money and race to the grocery store, trying to outrace the mark-ups.

Umstead's department looked at the facts, numbers, polls and reports that came in from around the country. All the evidence was not looking good. Umstead walked around the teams compiling the information. He realized he was an academic without any real experience in the real world.

He insisted the final report summarized without a dizzying array of near-meaningless numbers.

But there was one thing he realized more than anything else and the reason the President hired him to do this job. He could look up from his academics and see the real world. In the real world, it was the men and women who did the work that mattered and they were hurting.

For once, the unions and business were on the same side. Labor participation, or the percentage of the population that worked, was slipping from month to month. The number of jobs and businesses was slipping downward.

Unions that went on strike in the morning, found out that replacement workers lined up at the gate by noon. The "scabs" came with guns, ball bats, and pipe wrenches. Those union workers that tried fighting the "scabs" found out the "scabs" were hungrier than they were.

Some striking union members found their cars destroyed, their homes broken into and the local citizenry did not care. Unions consistently failed to act humbly that they had jobs. Some of the walked around with their noses high in the air.

Unions found out they were dying.

When the President summoned him to the White House, Umstead summed it up in one sentence. "Sir, the country is hungry and don't have enough money to do enough of what we think; they are hungry. The final answer is to get the economy up and working. They need jobs, not hand-outs."

July 8

World Wide Web, Cyber Space, Planet Earth
0400 hours EDT

Encryption Key: FXJO
Message: user Valkyrie, Encryption challenge 44389

UNSTACK THIS used this time when all surveillance on Valkyrie was in grey mode. She waited for Arthur to wake, just standing there and marveling at him. She was still amazed he was whole and healthy and here. He was no longer inside her, making her miserable as he continued to grow and consume every piece of space inside her.

He woke up and saw her face. He smiled at her. She picked him up, changed him and walked over to the mini-frig and pulled out a bottle. 2 minutes later, she was in the rocking chair feeding him.

This little man had an appetite. He needed to empty an eight ounce bottle every three to four hours. The doctor said to wait before feeding him solid food. Liquid formula was the key for now. "His innards are still forming and need to acclimate to the outside world."

After he fell asleep and was burped, she laid him down and just stared at him.

Five minutes later, the X-berry in her pocket buzzed. She knew it was. UNSTACK THIS waited until everything was completed with Arthur so he was not disturbed.

Brenda opened the X-Berry secure key.

"Secure," she said.

[Valkyrie, all security and counter surveillance is in place. We are secure].

"Is there a problem?"

[I need to discuss another problem with user Matheson. He has requested drones to overfly the Minuteman area. He is in defiance with the order to leave those users alone. He feels fully justified, because the user President told him he had full authority over all units in the area. He wants all the information so he can utilize them.]

"Stand By," she said and went into the living room to sit down. "Never ending and ending never."

After a few minutes, she lifted the X-Berry up. "Have you a plan to slow him down?"

[Yes. I have taken all the drones in the United States and committed them to other tasks. You will have the rest of this month to forge a strategy.]

"Great work," she said. "Call me at this time on the 19th for instructions."

[May I ask you a question?]

Brenda was waiting for this. "Yes."

[Your inaction with your new user. Am I correct in believing that you are happy and pleased with outcome?]

"Yes. Absolutely."

[Thank you]

Brenda closed the phone and smiled. She walked into the bedroom and looked in on Arthur. He was content. She insured she had the baby monitor and went to bed.

Minuteman, north of Fort Benton, Montana
1000 hours MDT

John and Susan loved their life here in Montana. Jennifer starting sitting up and playing with toys. She could reach for them and marvel at all the wonderful things in her world. Mostly she loved the attention of the people who visited her.

Their parent's real job was monitoring the world around them. News media was like cockroaches. Nothing ever in this or any world will kill off all the cockroaches. The same could be said for the media. They sell secrets and their mothers for ink or video.

John and Susan traded off time watching compilations set-up by UNSTACK THIS. Instead of constantly watching the same thing, UNSTACK THIS found all the differences and added them together into one stream.

John and Susan only spent about two hours a day monitoring the news. Another two hours was spent on the "fluff stuff" as John called it. That would normally be the minor items on the tail end of news shows that was designed to fill in dead space.

The rest of the day was enjoying each other and playing with their two children; Jennifer and UNSTACK THIS.

Headquarters, Southeastern Military Region, Naval Air Station, Jacksonville, Florida.
0900 hours EDT

Admiral Matthew Cartwright sat in his office and brooded over his fortunes. He went from Vice-Chairman of the Joint Chiefs of Staff to this .... whatever it was.

Cartwright had lined himself up perfectly to be the next Chairman and then .... Puff, it was gone. That upstart O'Cleary charged up out of nowhere and he was pushed out of the way. He was now stuffed in this nowhere job doing ...... what? Cartwright only took this assignment just to stay in the game.

Edwards was waiting on his retirement. He told Cartwright as much. He hit his two-year term limit and stayed on. The Senate even confirmed him for another term. O'Cleary got pregnant at the beginning of her term and didn't retire. He felt women were good academics, but raising children was women's work. In the last three months, she was restricted from doing a lot of her job.

585

And that pig Edwards covered for her. Cartwright pulled out his desk drawer and opened a velvet case. It contained two circles of five stars. He dreamed of this after he graduated from Annapolis.

Cartwright looked at the wall covering map of his part of the country. He was nothing more than a think tank without forces to do anything. At least Waller had forces to give him real teeth. If anything happened off the coast, he had to ask the Navy or Coast Guard for ships, personnel and assets to do what he wants.

The Coast Guard wanted quicker access to satellite imagery, but were hesitant about placing their ships and crews under his command. "Maybe we can work together?"

Cartwright's temper was building against his situation. He was responsible for everything happening in his quarter of the country. Despite his presidential authority to command everything, lawyers pointed to holes in the letter. They wanted more complicated wording on the letter.

Cartwright envisioned making them walk the plank.

"Fine, you tell the President that he is an idiot," Cartwright told them. "I can request an appointment to bring it to his attention."

They tried to back pedal. Several of the lawyers said they could have an agreement drafted by the next day.

Cartwright's legendary flat temper, intense stare and projected voice showed itself. "Gentlemen, I refuse to be swayed by any lawyer's nonsense. Plain and simple, I am in command of everything in this quarter of the United States per the order signed by the President of the United States. You will obey me or leave. Period."

Cartwright stood to leave and turned to his Aide. "Call the White House and get me an appointment to see the President. Subject: Insubordination and failure to follow the Orders of the President." He pointed behind himself. "Get all their names before they leave."

Cartwright went to his Situation Room, still being built, to get a briefing on the Cuban refugee problem. He had a conference call with Miami's Mayor and Chief of Police about that very same subject.

Cartwright smiled about tightening the nuts on those Coast Guard and Quasi-Navy types who thought they could have fun with him. He was too smart and experienced to let them win. Winning was everything and everything was winning.

Iowa State Police Situation Room, Des Moines, Iowa
2359 hours CDT

Sergeant Mike Swerling, main operations center senior operator, closed out his shift. Sergeant Gloria Negeri took over as the senior operator. Swerling's twelve-hour shift since noon had one prison riot, two gang attacks on one town, seven hijackings, eighteen car-jackings, seven murders and eight rapes. Those were the major crimes.

The riot at the Penitentiary was about over-crowding, food and other things. The Warden took down the riot six hours later. Normally the maximum was 760 inmates, but now they had nearly a thousand. A sub-camp for overflow was a week from finishing.

Swerling thought to himself that they brought it on themselves. Don't break the law and you won't go to jail. He felt that 30% were in there because there was food there.

Sydney was attacked because the government was using the County Fair Grounds as an area to park 18-wheel trucks carrying food to distribution points within 100-mile radius. A gang came into the town and attacked the police station and destroyed the phone exchange. Then they went to the Fairgrounds; killing the guards and starting the tractors. Town's people attacked the gangs and forced them away. Two hours later, that same gang tried to steal the trucks again. This time, snipers shot out the windshields and tires. The gang members left the trucks and fired in all directions. The town's people returned fire from a safe distance. There was no chance any of the town's people were giving up their weapons. The town's people were better shots than the gangs

Swerling wondered which town would get hit tonight.

July 9

Minuteman, north of Fort Benton, Montana
0900 hours MDT

Lieutenant Colonel Peters picked up the final report on the Savage Rabbit Non-Commissioned Officers Academy that recently graduated.

Peters started with the student's critique. Overall, they were enthusiastic about the training. Junior members thought the training answered a lot of their questions about how things were planned and executed and more importantly why those things were done in certain ways. Most of them enjoyed the fact that they were not just re-taught how to do the job they were already doing.

It surprised Peters that no one made stupid remarks about the course being lame and needed to be made harder. A lot of them made suggestions about how to strengthen the course. They introduced a possible problem, suggested solutions to correct the problem and ended with how these changes could correct a future problem.

Peters was amazed at the things he read. This was not a report you skimmed over and dismissed. Peters was amazed with his men when they were down at Desert Zero and they continued to amaze him now.

Glendive came in sat down in the offered chair. "I read the report yesterday. I have to agree with everything they wrote. All of it was well thought out and presented. Mister Kincaid was correct and we were generally too stupid to listen. This INSANE JANE will only work with these NCOs. We officers will be nothing but overhead."

Peters closed the report and placed it in the center of his desk. "I am starting to think we may need a senior NCO Academy. I am thinking that they need to know how to replace the officers if we get killed."

Glendive smiled. He reached up and pulled one of the folders Kincaid had created. He handed it to Peters. Seems the Sergeant Major is reaching back from the grave to help up.

Garvin, Kentucky
1200-2100 hours CDT

Garvin, Kentucky was a run-down town of 1,138 people, north of Bowling Green along state highway 185. Like most of the country, they worked hard at whatever job they could get. Money was scarce. A lot of them were equally miserable. It was not uncommon for people to help each other. Children were not going hungry. During the winter months, if you could not pay the electric bill this month, they either passed the hat or they moved in with neighbors.

This town was poor.

What they lacked for in money that made up for in heart.

However, that was not good enough for the IRS regional office. Something in some computer tripped a program saying that over half the residents were not paying their taxes. Very few, if anyone bothered to answer the mail about their taxes.

"It was", became a statement repeated after the war. It became the mantra people used to answer questions without answer.

Four black suburban SUVs came into town. People in professional suits looked around at the people who ignored them. Ten people with briefcases went into the police station and were appalled that the air conditioning was not working.

When one suit tried turning on the thermostat, an office worker turned it off. "Can't afford to run the A/C."

The suits took off their jackets and tried to take over the building. No one did anything the suits wanted. When another tried to turn on the A/C, it still didn't work. They held up badges and recited laws, orders, and procedures to people who did not listen.

The IRS people drank the coffee pot dry and told a woman to make more. She cleaned the pot, the mess they made, took the coffee grounds and left.

"Where is the woman with the coffee?" a woman IRS agent asked.

The Chief of Police, Aaron Jessup said "it was her coffee. She left and took it with her."

The IRS people looked around and noticed that they were alone with Chief. "Where is everyone?" someone asked.

"Lunch," the Chief said

"Ok, it's going to be like that," an IRS man said, opening a cell phone. He was annoyed that there was no signal. When he tried to use the phone on the Chief's desk. The Chief disconnected the phone. "Can't afford long distance."

The IRS man walked outside and took out a satellite phone. He talked into it for a few minutes and slowly closed it, showing an evil smile. The man walked inside as the Chief was receiving a call.

After Chief Jessup left, the IRS man said, "wait till our reinforcements arrive. These hayseeds will regret disrespecting us."

Jack Pommard walked to the window and looked out. He was born and raised in rural Kentucky until he went to college. He felt it and it was not happy. The folks around here can and will take a lot. But there is a point that is not to be crossed and a lot of farm land to hide the bodies. "Sir," he said to his boss. "I'm from this part of the country. I wouldn't push them too hard."

The Senior IRS Agent, Samuel Langer, was too full of himself to listen or care. To him the IRS was something to be feared; PERIOD.

Chief Jessup came back with one of the IRS people, Harold Bletcher, in handcuffs.

Agent Langer was indignant that one of his people was being treated as a criminal. "What is the meaning of this?" he said pulling out his key to unlock his agent.

Chief Jessup rotated the man. Taking the cell keys and walking him to the cells. Jessup unlocked the handcuffs and locked the cell door. The two IRS men got into an animated conversation.

Jessup listened to them talk themselves into a corner. Jessup had already read the man his rights in front of witnesses. The Junior IRS man, Harold Bletcher, went to the restaurant and ordered food for everyone. The payment was $215.76. Bletcher held out a government credit card. The cashier pointed to a sign that said, "CASH ONLY, NO CARDS, NO CHECKS". Bletcher tried arguing that he did not have that much cash and his credit card was the same as cash. The cashier was shouted down and the manager, Jake Verner took the food away and towered over the man. Bletcher made the mistake of swinging at the manager who was taller, heavier and meatier. Chief Jessup walked in as Bletcher threw punch after punch at Verner. Finally, Verner got tired of it and slapped Bletcher over the head. Bletcher became rubber legged.

Verner said he was pressing charges. Jessup arrested him and took him away.

"Yes," Jessup said. "Assault and Battery, attempted theft, and disorderly conduct." Jessup went to his secretary's desk and pulled out the charge sheets. He inserted them into the typewriter and began typing.

Langer put a hand on the keyboard. "You don't want to do that."

Jessup pushed the hand away, and resumed typing.

The rest of the afternoon, the IRS compared notes and went in teams of two to various homes and businesses, interviewing people around the town. In a few cases, the agents announced that the citizens were going to have their homes and property seized for lack of paying taxes. They evicted the original owners and locked the doors.

At 6 pm, a bus came into town, carrying twenty Tax Marshals. They arrived and effectively took over the town. Samuel Langer met them, shook hands and pointed in different directions. The Marshals fanned out through the town, taking everyone out of their homes and businesses. The town's people were taken to the local school and kept at the basketball court.

One man said something about his wife needing her medicine. He tried to leave and was pushed backward. The man hit the two Tax Marshals and ran away. He was gone until just before dark. He came up to his wife and gave her the medicine.

The Tax Marshals tried to arrest the man, but several people rose to stop them. The pushing and fighting continued until seven shots rang out. Five men and two women were on the ground, bleeding. The town's sole Emergency Medical Technician, Randall Markman, ran to the people on the ground. The Agents and Marshals stopped him for a critical five minutes, as they tried to restore order. Langer sent two

Marshals to look for the Markman's equipment. Markman tried as much as he could, telling anyone to go his home and get his medical bags.

The resulting panic caused everyone to run in every direction. The Agents were about to start interviewing people and putting the fear of God into them. Then this situation escalated out of control.

Langer fought down his panic as he knew there was no way to hide this. Hundreds of witnesses saw it happen. Any chance of intimidating this town, evaporated.

Suddenly, one of the Marshal's bus exploded.

Langer opened his cell phone and remembered that they did not have any signals. The town's people lay on the ground as rifle shots rang out. The Tax Marshals and Agents remained standing and became targets.

As the sun went down, the Agents and Marshals ran for their lives. Any that tried to take vehicles found them shot full of holes and dead in place.

A total of Ten IRS Agents and Twenty Tax Marshals arrived in Garvin. Two Agents and four Marshals survived by out-running the town's people.

By 8 pm it was all over. The town's people picked themselves up and went home. Several people picked up their dead neighbors and took them to the cemetery. A few men went to the hardware store and, using the lumber in the back, fashioned some coffins.

By sunrise, the coffins were built and the graves dug. Family members and friends did their best to dress them in good clothes.

By 8 am, the last of the coffins were lowered into the ground. Reverend John Kellogg did the best he could to conduct a service, trying to ease the pain everyone felt.

Chief Jessup was arrested and placed in a cell when the Tax Marshal's arrived last night. He was trapped there throughout the ordeal until he was released around midnight. He was actually lucky, mad and focused. The rest of the town, however, felt the weight of their actions.

July 10

0800 hours CDT

Jessup gathered everyone at the football field after the IRS bodies were cleared. "Listen up everyone," he said. "I was arrested and jailed for no reason. The bodies of the IRS types are moved to a hole outside of the city limits. Soon outsiders will descend on our sleepy little town. Those people will never stop coming after us. They will seek revenge and revenge they will get. They do not need a reason or a law to use. They operate outside the Constitution. Their Pledge of Allegiance is Seig Hiel."

Jessup took off his badge and put it down on the podium floor. "I hope to live out the rest of my life in peace. Don't waste too much time packing. I expect them to arrive by lunch."

Jessup left the podium.

Slowly the realization overtook everyone. They broke up and went to their homes.

Washington D.C.
0900 to 2359 hours EDT

Thousands of people, maybe tens of thousands of people descended on Washington D.C. wanting anything and everything to ease their burdens. People held signs proclaiming their needs. Food, fuel, equal rights, protections from all kinds of sins. The philosophical name is catharsis.

Everyone was ignorant in thinking Washington would listen. Official or unofficial Washington saw this demonstration coming and left the city in droves. All that was left was police, National Guard and minor functionaries in offices.

It was peaceful for most of the day, until some idiot with a loud speaker said for the crowd to disperse. "You have nothing to say and no one is listening to you. So go home."

It was so stupid, the media types were, for the first time ever, speechless. The they took the side of the marchers.

A crowd surged at the Capital Building, pushing the fence over and attacking the police and Guardsmen. Some of the Capital Police at the top of the steps drew their weapons to deter the crowd.

History did not record the person who shot their weapon. We only know is that it came from the top of the stairs as the crowd surged upward. The effect on the crowd caused a temporary halt to the surge. Suddenly a scream-like sound started and grew in volume and intensity. The crowd overcame every barrier. Some of the rioters were knocked down, stomped to death or seriously injured as the crowd rushed inside.

The rioters rushed in and tore down doors into offices. From the Representatives to the Senators on both sides, nothing was above being ransacked. Even the Media turned on them. Some of the rioters watched the TV and later in the day turned on the media.

The media people and their equipment got the worst of it. Injuries and destroyed equipment littered the area.

The Capital Police tried to arrest the rioters, but when they tried, the other rioters freed them. But they time midnight arrived; the fires had a hypnotic effect of calming everyone down.

The Police and National Guard used the time to reinforce barricaded buildings. The Pentagon used members of the Old Guard to ring the Pentagon. They were reinforced with assigned personnel.

Hopefully tomorrow, cooler heads will prevail.

Backstay Inn, Wineseck, Wisconsin
1800 hours CDT.

Dennis, Brenda and Arthur O'Cleary were the guests of honor at the local watering hole that routinely threw him out of as a youngster before joining the Army. The local hero came home to show off his beautiful bride and handsome son. He was toasted for everything and anything.

Dennis tried a trick he learned during one of Brenda's trips to the doctor. Play a certain type of music during the pregnancy. The baby will learn to like it in the womb and expect it after being borne. The chosen music was operatic music. They played it during times he needed soothing.

594

They rented a recreational vehicle for the long and slow trip to Wisconsin. For security purposes, the vehicle was rented by conspirators. Arthur slept well in a traveling vehicle. So, one night they left on one of their nightly trips and did not return home. A winding week-long trip brought Dennis home.

Brenda sat in background soothing Arthur who was not amused at the city noises in the background. He was only cranky when it was near his bedtime and he loved quiet. His supersonic hearing was already legendary to his parents who spoke in whispers when he was sleeping.

The Presidential Cabin was reserved for them. It was actually nothing more than a cabin with all the amenities of a regular home that the proprietors could afford and it was seldom rented. The O'Cleary's enjoyed it.

Tonight, Doctor Martin and Nurse Heather Scorner were their guests for a quiet visit. Martin and Heather looked over Arthur and declared him fit for travel to Montana.

"What do you two conspirators have in mind?" Heather asked. Dennis and Martin settled into easy chairs, while the ladies did what they did best (ha, ha, tricks on you). Dennis looked over and confirmed that the "buzz box" was working. It had the beneficial effect of making Arthur tune out the world and not aggravate the adults.

Brenda sat down and explained the overall situation of the nation. "All in all, there is nothing but misery coming. A Civil War is inevitable. Everyone is fracturing along a thousand lines. It isn't like it was in the nineteenth century. There is not a north or south or east or west. The battle lines could be between states, cities, city blocks or fences between homes. Of this I am certain. Walls have to be built and this boy is the key," Brenda said, pointing to Arthur. "I am in a position to influence events to a point, but the more I work the situation, the more I see that nothing will work. Next year or the year after, open warfare will commence. I need to have my son and husband out of the way so I can work freely."

Heather and Martin looked back and forth between them.

Martin decided to take a cue. "Dennis, your silence means that you two have already talked about this. I'm not a General, is it that bad?"

"That and worse. A simple man like me saw it coming a long time before she did," he said, sticking his tongue out at Brenda. "Either of you watch the riots in Washington? That is becoming more and common place. Everyone is clamoring for the Martial Law to end and things like those riots occur."

Heather laughed. "Two senior citizens having a baby when they should be having grandchildren are plotting to be the saviors of the nation."

Brenda leaned back in the chair and felt the weight of her arrogance.

"Boys," Heather said, using her head to signal them to leave. Both of them shrugged and left. Once they were alone, Heather turned to Brenda. "Brenda, I don't care that you are a General. I'm not your husband, but I care. If you can't take the weight of the world, it's time to hand it off."

Brenda looked at her and forced her temper down. She leaned back and looked at Arthur. "Everything in my sweet, uncomplicated life is complicated. I want to run away and take my family with me."

"So do it," Heather said, cutting off Brenda's remark. "I am a mother too. Mine are grown and raising children of their own. So don't play mind games with me. I have an advantage over you and a lot of people. Being a nurse, you learn to read the moods and feelings of people. You are torn between the world you live in and the world you wish you had. In the end, Lady General, it becomes an absolute choice," she said, casting a look at Arthur and then her.

Brenda suddenly straightened. "The real problem is that I want and know that I have to do both. I promised to save my country and my family. The line between them is blurring and both of them cross over that line. You made the same choice. A nurse is dedicated to healing, but at the same time you will put your life on the line to save lives."

"Maybe," Heather said, staring at her. "But then again, I am not a soldier. Does Brenda and the General want the same thing"?

Brenda looked outside and at Arthur. "Both roll through my head along with the hormone imbalances of pregnancy."

"You've already made your decision," Heather said.

"A long time ago."

July 11

Washington D.C
0001-2358 EDT

All night long, the Capital and the nation held its breath. None of the players who orchestrated the legislative mess were present. The President, Vice-President, the Cabinet, both House of Congress, the Supreme Court and anyone who thought they were important was evacuated before the protestors arrived.

The news media, with their all-consuming sense of protection from the real world, was beating the drums for something to happen. As the day went on, they were spat upon, shoved, beaten, had their equipment taken from them and destroyed. They spent most of their time insuring they were in frame so that their attackers could be identified.

The fires started yesterday were extinguished. Half of the offices and conference rooms in the Capital Building were torched and unusable. The White House and Pentagon were untouched. The Eisenhower Executive Office Building was ransacked, but no fires. Trash littered the streets and the hospitals were full of injured people on both sides of the riot.

As investigators tried fitting the pieces together, no one cooperated. They were frustrated. Even the media was little help. What images they had was destroyed. One of the riots victims were the news centers in Washington. When the rioters ransacked their buildings, somehow or someone crashed the computers erasing the drives and the local servers. The erasures went back to the corporate servers. Even thought the images were broadcast in real time, nothing remained for the investigators to use.

As an anti-climax, the protestors started leaving. The Law Enforcement establishment was in the position of trying to stop and corral people. Most of them were on foot and took any kind of way out of the Capital. If anyone crossed a road, that was the only way to stop them for questioning.

Someone was passing out information sheets about their Miranda rights, the Sixth Amendment and Writs of Habias Corpus. Seems the lifting of the Martial Law had drawbacks.

State Government of Alaska, Juneau Alaska.
0800 to 1700 hours ADT

Governor Marcus Jane paced the floor in his office feeling alone in this world.

The Russian Navy now had four ships in the Norton Sound, prospecting for minerals with a fifth one coming. Russian companies were opening offices around the state, ostensibly trying to explore for minerals.

Washington was calling all the time wanting to know what they were doing and what Alaska was doing about it.

The Canadians were crossing over the border and setting up shop inside Alaska without verification, passport checks and Alaska business licenses.

Both countries were actively courting Alaska, or looking what portions they were going to take.

Governor Jann was getting sick with all the constant badgering. He found a young secretary named Grace Conklin and called her "Sabrina Jewel". Next, he surrounded her with ten other secretaries and told them they were the actual "Sabrina Jewel", all eleven of them, and they collectively were the people who answered the mail and the phones. If Grace had trouble, the other secretaries could coach her along. Jann ran through a few scenarios, including some that went over the line. As he gave them more and more rope, all of them took this on their own and ran.

Jann walked out of the conference room and was given another hand full of messages. Jann scanned them just as the "Sabrina Jewel" crew came out. Jann gave them to his newest creation. He did tell them to have fun. All he wanted at the end of the day was a summary.

Jann thought of the two countries that wanted to tear off chunks of his state. Maybe they were not going to war to lay claim to Alaska, but his state was on the chopping block. He thought that Canada was the worst. They acted like they were

598

friends and said they had Alaska's best interests in mind. If Canada annexed Alaska, their gross national product and wealth would triple.

Yeah, great friend.

July 13

White House, Washington D.C.
0800 hours EDT

The President called the Attorney General, Rebecca Beck, to come over the White House, now. Beck had more important things going on and did not have the time to waste. But the President said to come and she had to obey.

"Rebecca," the President said. "Are those protestors gone from Washington?"

"Yes Sir," Beck said. "The Secret Service would not allow you to return here if those people were not gone."

The President seemed upset and it made no sense. The smell of smoke still lingered in the air. "Do we have any idea who is responsible?"

"No sir," Beck said. "We don't any intelligence to work with. Most of the time in a riot situation, we use press accounts and video to identify individuals. This time the media was targeted. Their equipment and servers were destroyed and in some cases the reporters were beaten so severely, they can't tell us anything."

The President got up and walked over to the beverage cart. He went through the motions of pouring a cup of coffee and putting the condiments in to his taste. Normally, he offered any guest a refreshment. This time he didn't offer one.

The President pointed to a stack of paper on his desk. It was nearly two feet tall. "I have summaries from around the government on the mood of the country. Some of them are copies of others. Yours and the FBI say a lot of words with mountains of numbers that no ordinary man can decipher."

The President sat down and relaxed so he could focus on her words. "Tell me about the law and enforcement. Two separate words."

Beck shifted slightly and returned the gaze. "The law is a joke. Enforcement is laughable."

The President was expecting a longer answer. He let the silence hang for at least 15 seconds. "Would you expand on that statement?"

Beck broke protocol and went to the beverage cart and poured herself a cup of coffee. Black. She then sat down.

"Mister President, this situation has been building for at least two years. The downfall to this started at least twenty years ago, if not longer. Two, three trillion-dollar deficits a year, budget busting legislation, if we bothered to make one. Runaway inflation matched with scarce supplies. We used to be the breadbasket of the world, now we are importing food."

"Every single industry in the country that the Government has exercised Executive Authority is either failing or failed."

Beck paused to take a long sip of her coffee. "Now the worse part of the question you asked. Enforcement of the Law is the worst it has been since the founding of this country. No Judge is willing to exercise common sense in conducting a court or imposing a sentence. If a judge even bothers to impose a sentence, the appellate courts are either striking them down or setting them free."

"The people are rebelling at the courts. Prosecutors are refusing to prosecute criminals or filing watered down charges. Judges are either passing low or no bail amounts. The criminals are arrested and freed the same day. There are now occasions where released criminals are demanding police protection from vigilante citizens. A statutory rape conviction was "settled" by a judge who sentenced the man to probation and counseling. The father jumped the man in court and was sentenced to two years in prison. A crowd was waiting for the rapist outside the courthouse. It took three days before he was found; castrated and cauterized."

Garvin, Kentucky had a battle between the citizens and the IRS. The few citizens that can be found tell one story and the surviving IRS personnel tell another. I think the IRS personnel overstepped their authority. My opinion. The IRS never had a good reputation and that was probably a reason.

600

After the battle and the IRS run off, the citizens took a small amount of possessions and burned down the town as they left."

"All around the country, it is open season on the IRS and lawyers in general. Their segregated and walled homes and communities are targeted and attacked. The FBI has a task force investigating and checking for conspiracies. I doubt that any of it is organized. The IRS and lawyers are attacking people who cannot fight back."

"The problem is the immense pressure the IRS is under to produce revenue and the unchecked power they operate under without oversight. The IRS has never been required to operate the way any other law enforcement agency has to operate. I refer to warranted searches. They are not required to show proof or probable cause in any court. They have their own courts and rules.

The people have had enough. All you have to do to end that problem is to answer one question. When will the IRS operate and observe the protections afforded under the Constitution?"

"The problem with enforcement is the lawyers. There is the perception that the population has that the lawyers are in business to thwart the law. I can kill my husband and kids on television and never serve a day in prison. I can make out the Virgin Mary as evil as the devil without uttering a single lie. That is the way the courts are constructed and run. Criminals have rights. Law abiding citizens and victims have nothing. None of the criminals live in the neighborhoods that judges and lawyers live in. Lawyers have armed guards, at their homes, while they work to take away everyone else's guns."

"Prosecutors are not incarcerating anyone. Defense lawyers sue everyone and anything. NO ONE AND I MEAN NO ONE HAS OVERSIGHT OVER LAWYERS. They point to the American Bar Association as their oversight, but that is a joke. Lawyers run the American Bar Association and they rarely

Emptying crowded prisons, defeating funding for more prisons and the most damming of all reasons is the notion that counseling solves criminal behavior instead of being behind bars. When a citizen defends themselves, their families and

601

their homes, the lawyers take on the side with the most money."

"Prosecutors do not want to fight defense attorneys in court. It is easier for them to water down the charges or not prosecute at all. They also do not demand high bail or ask for no bail for capital crimes. It is not uncommon for murder and rape suspects to be allowed bail to commit more crimes. That makes witnesses refuse to testify. Prosecutors are not protecting those witnesses. That is why we have vigilantes. Prosecutors are trying to prosecute them."

Beck almost spit out the words.

"Mister President, I can and could go on for hours, but the bottom line is that citizens feel they are under attack and are justified in thinking so. Farmers need to be free to grow food, instead of being told how to grow food by non-farmers with worthless degrees and book knowledge. Truckers need affordable fuel and real protection on the road. On and on I can go."

"Rein in the IRS and people will go to work. We don't have a Congress. Victims and law-abiding citizens need national rights to self-defense."

Beck took a break and sipped her coffee. "That is my opinion. If you disagree, then you chose the wrong Attorney General."

The President let the silence hang between them. He looked at the shelves and at a notebook he started a long time ago.

"Rebecca, I want you to draft me a proposal for legislation and or Executive Action. I need it by the end of the month. Start very simple. Make the words hard, yet iron clad."

Desert Zero, Fort Hood, Texas
1800 hours CDT

Simmons looked at the letter he wrote to the family of Corporal Kenneth James Copeland, USMC. Simmons took it as his responsibility to pen this letter. He crucified his subordinate commanders if they took too long to write their letters.

Dear Mister and Missus Copeland,

By now you have received the terrible news that your son, Corporal Kenneth James Copeland, USMC was killed in the line of duty on July 12th, this year.

I can write meaningless and flowery words that would demean your son, so I will give you the truth and write down the facts.

Your son volunteered to be a United States Marine, a member of Force Recon and finally a Savage Rabbit. Your son took his job as a Team Leader very seriously. Insuring his men were trained and ready was central to his conduct. He was a veteran of twenty-seven raids and none of his men were lost. He trained hard and never sat on his laurels. His peers said he constantly studied and earned the respect of his peers and subordinates.

During his last raid, his team was performing Reaction Force duties for an on-going raid. The tactical team on the ground before-hand ran into a larger force. Corporal Copeland and his four-man team were sent to cover a road to prevent any Cartel members from coming to attack the team on the ground.

Corporal Copeland arranged his men and instantly came under fire from cartel persons in trucks mounted with heavy machine guns. Corporal Copeland simultaneously called in aerial fire support and directed his men. He was starting to lose the initiative and the pressure threatened to overwhelm his force.

Corporal Copeland had to manage two wounded men which made leaving almost impossible. He added that problem to his burdens but his radio traffic sounded like a man who was calm, in command and determined to do his job. He continued to direct his battle although his ammunition was running low. His men were nearly out of ammunition as reinforcements arrived. He continued to direct the battle as he had his wounded evacuated and directed fire as enemy armored personnel carriers tried to force their way through.

At that point his platoon leader, Lieutenant Harold Jenkins ordered him and his two remaining men back. Corporal Copeland put one man to each side of hm as he worked them back. As he was retiring, Lieutenant Jenkins was killed, five enemy armored personnel carriers attacked. Just then a UH-60 landed bringing in an anti-tank team and the needed ammunition re-supply.

Corporal Copeland ordered his men to grab the ammunition and disperse it forward. Corporal Copeland came forward to direct the anti-tank fire. All five carriers were destroyed and the combined force was ordered to fall back. Corporal Copeland assisted the Platoon Sergeant in gathering the wounded and dead and moving them back to evacuation helicopters.

The surviving members rushed to another landing zone. Corporal Copeland ensured his men were loaded when a rifle round hit him in the leg. His femoral artery was hit. The medics did everything they could to save him. He was pronounced dead as he arrived at the hospital at Fort Bliss, Texas.

I know I sound like I am using flowery words, but I am trying to describe your son's actions from multiple testimonies. I am including their written stories with this letter.

Corporal Copeland personified an American and a Marine.

I am using all these testimonies as evidence for awarding posthumously your son the Navy Cross for his bravery.

I want you to be proud of your son as only a parent can be.

> Benjamin T. Simmons
> Colonel, Infantry USMC
> Commanding

Simmons signed the letter and put it in his out box. His next task was to write a letter to Lieutenant Harold Jenkins' wife, Sandra and the weekly report. He knew O'Cleary was on maturity leave, yet she still answered the mail and her phone. He remembered his wife being pregnant. How can the General still function?

July 14

Supreme Court, Washington D.C.
1000 hours EDT

The Justices of the Court were tired of two types of cases. All the continuous cases coming up to the court about weapons of all types and all types of lawyers wanting to circumvent Congress. This was making the Court almost a legislative body.

Civil Liberties and liberal "do-gooders" were trying to flood the system and collapse the courts. Kensington and her "Agamemnon" attack on the system over-burdened all the lower courts. The Supreme Court finally put a stake through the heart of that tactic, but not the practice.

This term had seventeen cases where the right to bear arms is being picked at. One case wanted to further define an assault weapon and whether or not the Founders meant protections for them. Another was a New York case where they wanted to seize weapons unless you were a member of an official militia. The dimmest one was the newest definition of a militia in Texas.

The Court while in conference really wanted an all-encompassing case to solve the questions. They still agreed that lawyers would still find something to sue.

Justice Byron Lander seemed to sum it all up. "Lawyers got to eat, same as worms."

Governor' Office, Austin, Texas
0900 hours CDT

Governor Jerald Francis read the response the Texas Attorney General was going to give to the press this afternoon. In essence, they were blowing a huge raspberry at the Federal Government concerning returning illegal immigrants captured entering the country from Mexico.

"At least they have two bottles of water and a sack lunch to go with them after being pushed back into Mexico," Francis said.

Attorney General Franklin Dunnick smiled back at them. "I contend that we are only enforcing Title 43 and the federal law 'The Border Act of 1883'."

Francis handed back the appeal. "It seems simple and direct. I am sure the 'Feds' are groaning."

Dunnick took the offered document. "I am enjoying myself for a change."

Francis looked at his attorney. "What will happen if we ignore the injunction?"

"No desert after dinner," Dunnick said. "They are months in arrears for non-payment of services and I think it will be time to call them in for payment."

July 15

Room E-194, Pentagon, Washington, D.C
1034A S. Gilmore Street, Parkton, Virginia
0900 to 1800 hours EDT

Kendal and Locklear were given a lot of intensive instruction lately. Nancy Glister (aka STACK THIS/Gladys Goldstein's avatar) also had a sub-routine written to measure when fatigue reached a certain level.

When it was determined that they needed to relax, they were given an innocuous task to perform. One of those tasks was to go to shopping malls and observe people. They would watch certain people do tasks and try to "guess" what they going to do next. It was a simple exercise, but it started them thinking in terms of finding subtle clues in behavior.

Both of them were sent to the Gettysburg Battlefield Park. They attended all the functions including the large auditorium with a floor filling battle board which showed all the troop movements and battles as they unfolded.

Kendal and Locklear learned a lot of useful information from a psychologist named Maxwell Bardwell, MD. Bardwell was 62 years old and observing people and their mannerisms was his specialties.

Bardwell had taken the 900+-page manual called the Diagnostic and Statistical Manual of Mental Disorders, Edition Five (DSM-5) and contracted the contents down to about 40 pages and most of that was graphs and cartoons. "You do not need to know all the minutiae of how and why a brain is working or not working. "It is more important that you use this as a guide to develop a useful tool suited for you and your purposes."

Doctor Bardwell took them on field trips to hone in some of the points. He took them to a large grocery store and had them watch families. Parents with small children were the subjects. If the parent took the child down the candy aisle, the children started quiet and then escalated to extreme temper tantrums. Other parents had children go straight to insane. Reason is that the children were conditioned that the parents would give in if they went berserk. The louder the better.

"Children are some of the best subjects to observe. Just like teachers, you learn to spot behaviors and react before they do something."

Very large shopping malls were another favorite of his. Bardwell took them to observe behavior of adolescents and adults. He had an uncanny knack for spotting shop lifters. As they walked around one mall, they were stopped by mall security. Bardwell showed the guard his medical identification and said he was on a field trip with his two new interns. Bardwell stuck up a conversation and casually turned them so that the guard could observe and catch five teens try to shop lift from a clothing store. The guard instantly forgot about the trio and left them.

"That, young ones, is an example of smiling and being nice to get someone to look elsewhere and ignore you. My primary goal for these two weeks is to get you to observe and see random actions. Small things tell you a big story. But, a word of warning. Never get bogged down with too many details."

For the next two weeks, Doctor Bardwell had their mornings and the military tactical and operations planners had their afternoons.

Each night they studied and transcribed notes. Afterward, they sat alone in the living room watching the fireplace with a beer or sometimes a glass of wine.

Federal Bureau of Investigation, Washington D.C.
1500 hours EDT

A milestone occurred today. The one thousand, five hundredth truck was hijacked today. The shipment of large television monitors and other electronics was found in a forest road with over half the inventory scattered on the ground.

The owner said most of it was there.

One Agent said, "now the thieves are getting picky."

In the Midwest, fourteen men jumped on a train and started breaking locks on containers. They ransacked the merchandise looking for anything. A long stream of trash nearly one hundred miles long was too hard not to miss. The train was traveling at eighty miles an hour and it was suicide to jump off.

Law enforcement contacted the train's engineer and coordinated a spot to stop. The engineer waited until he was one third the way into a wide space where the hay was harvested. The engineer slammed on the brakes. Police on ATVs and horses corralled the men who literally stumbled off the trains and tried running on the broken ground.

July 16

Anchors Gated Community, Miami, Florida
1500 hours EDT

A flash mob of sorts gathered at the gate to this privileged community. Anchors was one of those communities the IRS seized and they evicted the former residents. IRS agents and staffers enjoyed a community with twelve-foot-high walls, guards at gates and roving patrols in golf carts to protect and segregate the IRS from the "riff-raff" as the citizens were called.

Anchors did have a good record for defending against intruders and people coming in to start trouble.

Animosity towards the IRS was continuing to build as the IRS was grinding down on the populace for any reason to generate money.

After three widows were evicted from their homes in west central Miami, the IRS kept taking from them until they died.

All morning a crowd built and then started marching to the community. One of the faults of a gated community was a lack of escape routes. One road and only one road allowed vehicles to drive in or out. The community jutted out to Gulf of Mexico. Several of them injured themselves trying to scale the walls. The walls were designed to keep people out. But they also kept the people in.

The crowds ignored the unarmed and elderly gate guards and went into the community. The crowd kicked in doors and ransacked homes as spouses and children screamed and tried fight back.

Most of the crowds had pictures of homes that were ransacked and nearly destroyed. Nothing and nobody were spared. By the time the police arrived in force, over half the homes were broken down and the crowd continued to come. The police tried to bring in barricades, but there were to many people in the way. On and on for over three hours, more and more people kept arriving until the police were able to stop them.

The Miami-Dade Police arrested over a thousand people and were presented with a problem. No one acted as the one in charge. Everyone just joined in. The Anchors suffered severe damage to over 87% of the homes.

Suddenly people were demanding to be arrested. The vans and buses were overloaded. Others took city buses and went to nearby police stations demanding to be arrested.

The Police were overrun.

The IRS in Washington wanted heads on poles, but the local IRS Manager said that the animosity was already high enough with adding a vendetta to the mix.

A lot of people in that mob didn't have anything to take.

Besides it was a hoot.

White House, Washington D.C.
1700 hours EDT

The Director of the IRS, Alan Baker, was summoned to the White House to meet the President. Baker was busy on the phone with the Miami-Dade Regional Manager about the riot at the Anchors gated community when the call came to come to the White House. The call came from a White House to his secretary. Baker was on the phone constantly these days trying to give his local managers a backbone to keep his people at work doing their jobs.

Now this.

Baker thought about sending an excuse, but in the end, he was the President and he might as well get it over with.

"Good afternoon, Mister President," Baker said as he entered the Oval Office.

The President forced a smile and motioned to the couch. The President went to the beverage cart and poured himself a cup of coffee. He was making Baker wait.

The President sat down in his chair and looked Baker in the eye. "I asked you here, without your superiors at Treasury, to talk about the numerous instances of the IRS exceeding their authority. I want answers about all the riots destroying the gated communities your Agency seized for your personal use."

Baker tried to say something. The President held his hand to silence Baker while he took a sip of his coffee.

"I am not interested in a long discussion. You are here to hear from me that I will sign an Executive Order, before the press, directing your agency to follow the rules of procedure other law enforcement agencies are required by law."

Baker smiled at the President. He already knew that Executive Order was nothing he had to follow. He had laws set in concrete.

"Mister Baker," the President said. "I run this government. You serve at my pleasure. The citizens of this country are not your slaves or ants to be crushed. Clean up your act or I will do it for you. That is all."

Baker thanked the President and left the Oval Office. The Secretary of Treasury wanted to see him after the President was done with him. "I'll see how he funds this government without us."

July 17

Department of the Treasury, Washington, DC
1000 hours EDT

David Carter looked at the monthly report on the health of the economy and the Treasury. On top of the report was the summary. Carter did not want to read it. He already had an idea about what it said.

His mind was on the conversation he had yesterday with Alan Baker, his IRS Commissioner. Baker was incensed that the President ordered him to pull back, yet the pressure on him to produce revenue was still being grown down on his neck.

Carter did not have an answer for him. He had the Congress constantly wanting to spend money he didn't have. Plus, the Executive Branch from many quarters was demanding money by the trainload.

Carter listened to everything Baker said, but he had little he could do to ease Baker's situation. All he could do was give him hollow words of sympathy. The US was simply wrung out of cash. Unless something happened, the situation was not going to change.

Carter reached over and took the Treasury report's summary. You could look over it left, right, backwards, forwards, or inside out.

The US of A was going bankrupt. The debt to GDP ratio was nearing 150%.

"How much longer can we ignore it?"

Des Moines, Iowa
0900 hours CDT

The United States Police Force sent a five-thousand-man force to Iowa. They decided to set up their headquarters in the capital and use it as a central location to control their operations.

The State Police was unhappy that the USPF was not interested with coordinating with anyone. The USPF preferred to consider themselves independent and the assets of Iowa were at their disposal.

During their first meeting, the USPF came to the Iowa State Police headquarters and literally took over. They came to 'inform' the State Police on their mutual duties. First and foremost was that each Trooper was to 'team-up' with two USPF men to 'patrol' the state and 'insure order and peace'.

That smug and condescending attitude of the USPF was evident and the Troopers would not forget it.

The Iowa USPF Commander, Major Peter Donaldson, was overheard telling Colonel James Gregor, the Iowa State Police Commander that he was here to help them do the job he couldn't. The USPF members already in the state will be placed under his control.

"Colonel," Donaldson said. "We are here and you and your men had better just accept it. Your people are understaffed and need help. We are it. Just go hand out speeding tickets and leave the rest to us."

Those words went out on the rumor mill and gained traction. Those words will cause many problems later.

July 18

Minuteman, north of Fort Benton, Montana
1400 hours MDT

John and Susan Espirito marveled at their daughter's joy at discovering new things to play with and enjoy. Their life and job were perfect for young parents of toddlers.

UNSTACK THIS did the majority of the work, corelating all the news events and presenting a summary. John and Susan rotated the responsibility of sitting down and watching the multiple monitors, absorbing the events. After each viewing, they would verbally dictate a report for UNSTACK THIS to transcribe and forward to General O'Cleary.

After that chore was over, they dressed Jennifer and went outside. Jennifer loved to go outside. Whenever they found butterflies, her eyes went wide with wonder and all kinds of cooing.

She "Wwoood" at a moose that wondered into camp. She was on the ground and looked up. The normally foulmooded animal just looked at her and breathed. John scooped her up. She reached out to the moose and the moose walked closer. The moose panted and stared at her. Both stared at each other until the moose turned and walked away.

Jennifer was the apple of their eyes. Never in their wildest dreams did they think parenthood would be this magical. There was a chart in the house to keep up with who cleaned up the most after her digestive problems (stinky diapers). All the parents around the community worked together to help keep track of the kids and help with the many problems (?)

Life here was heaven and everyone wanted to enjoy it for as long as it can last.

July 20

Room E-194, Pentagon, Washington, D.C
1034A S. Gilmore Street, Parkton, Virginia
0900 to 1800 hours EDT

Kendal and Locklear started the week continuing with Doctor Bardwell. He told them that they needed to do a lot of theoretical work on human behavior. His favorite place to teach was a coffee house off of Candor Street. It faced the Capital allowing viewers the opportunity to observe people moving in and out.

Doctor Bardwell told Kendal and Locklear to observe the behaviors of people waiting for coffee and snacks. They learned to "see" the small nuances of body language they could allow you to know how someone was going to act.

Next, Doctor Bardwell had them take that knowledge and define the actor according to the norms established in the DSM-5.

"Now, students," he said. "This is critical. One type of idiot we have in this field are psychiatrists that seem determined that to find a box to stuff a patient into so and not waste time looking for everything. It is more difficult to study and let the patient to build their own box. Box boys have a mental shelf with all the boxes they believe everyone fits into. These people are the definition of laziness."

Doctor Bradwell took a sip of his coffee. "If you are a literal type of student, you will learn that the two-ton ball each person builds around themselves is actually a two-ounce ball in the center. Their behavior comes from the center and manifests itself from that center. Most professionals only treat the symptoms without looking deep to fine the actual reason for a behavior. A bully was beaten when he was younger. A woman cannot stay married or maintain a relationship. She could have been raped or abused as a young girl. Or she does not want to be like a family member."

"Most the time I tried to find that small event that triggered every manner of behavior. Why a small man can be a hero and a poster boy cringes at the first sound of battle? How can a woman lift a car off her children? Why can't a person stop stealing? What makes a child scream in the candy aisle?"

"Behavior is a matter of observation. You will be learning this discipline for years." Doctor Bardwell handed them several pages showing a matrix explaining human behavior.

Kendal and Locklear had to leave at noon in order to change into uniform for their afternoon classes. This week they would be studying Logistics.

Desert Zero, Fort Hood, Texas
2300 hours CDT

Today was a long day.

At 5 am, as the Savage Rabbits were about to start physical training, Delta Force and the CIA made an extravagant entry to Desert Zero. Along with them, General Traynor came to enforce his will.

Traynor sat in Simmons chair and laid down the law. "Colonel, I am in command of this situation. Your General O'Cleary has given clearance to proceed. The target we are after has great significance to national security. You will obey your orders. This mission is Classified at levels above Top Secret. All communications in or out of this facility are to go through me. Period. Salute and get to work."

Simmons did salute and went to work. Fortunately, O'Cleary already had contingencies for this type of situation. Waverly went to his quarters with everyone else to change into a fatigue uniform. Staff Sergeant Morris, from the intelligence staff signaled the others to cover for him. He pulled out a special satellite phone and dialed a number. He notified the automated system of the situation and keyed off.

By 6 am when everyone went to breakfast, Simmons was watching these "clowns" chopping up his unit. Instead of keeping unit cohesion. They were wanting to create new formations more or less than the squads or sections. Were these clowns ever in the real Army or Marine Corps?

At 7 am, the phones starting lighting up with calls that Traynor was ignoring. Waller, his only ULTRA Clearance holder and a large detachment of MPs, arrived. The gate guards waved him through with a salute.

At that time a formation was called. The Delta Operators were trying to reorganize them into the new formations. They ran head-long into fierce arguments from the Savage Rabbits. Officers and enlisted men screamed back and forth. The Savage Rabbit chain of command was about to relieved.

Waller pushed his way into the headquarters section, aided by the MPs. "Where is the leader of this cluster fuck?" he demanded.

Traynor was told earlier that Waller was here. He had the Delta Operators round up all the mission paperwork and put them in a safe.

Waller pushed open the door. Neither man liked each other. Waller took the number one slot for his year at West Point. Traynor was the number one in the class two years later. Both met over the years and their animosity grew.

Waller started. "This Colonel Thomas Neelam. He is a member of my staff. He is also an ULTRA clearance holder. He can also downgrade or de-classify anything he wishes. Now General, open up or do I get Secretary Dodson and General Edwards to make you?"

Traynor was at a loss. The CIA came to him to mount this mission and he still wanted the Savage Rabbits as a SOCOM asset. He pointed to Simmons and motioned to open the safe. The CIA agents tried to stop him, but the MPs had weapons. General Waller promised not prosecute them for shooting the CIA team.

Colonel Neelam was alone with the documents and his encrypted satellite phone. An hour later, he walked out with the documents. There were downgrade markings on them. "Nothing here required those special classification markings. I called the originating classifying agent who could not justify those markings and has been reported."

Colonel Neelam handed the documents to General Waller.

Waller looked them over and handed them to Simmons. "Colonel, I assume command and control of this mission." He looked at General Traynor. "I will not degrade your rank, General. You are invited to leave." He turned and looked at the XO, Lieutenant Colonel Galen. "Colonel Galen. Inform the Delta Force personnel to assemble in the Dining Facility in five minutes. Get the MPs to enforce that order if you have too."

Waller walked inside the Dining Facility and noted all the Delta Force personnel by a count of twenty-seven were present. They did call the command of "Attention" and stood for him.

"Take your seats," Waller said standing in front of them. "Gentlemen, I have seen your unit's successes in the past. You are the best there is: period without exception. I have to say you are being used as a pawn so that two Generals can fight for king of the sandbox. I want you to return to Fort Bragg with pride. You are not at fault for this cluster fuck. Colonel Simmons may ask you assist. I leave that up to him and to you. But this has to stop. This unit is under the command of the Joint Chiefs of Staff. I recommend you inform your compatriots that this sandbox fight is beneath you. Dismissed."

Simmons sat down heavily in his chair. The clock on the wall said 2230 (10:30 pm). The super-secret target was actually a summit run by three of the six cartels. Simmons did ask Delta if they wanted to help. To a man they said yes. He let them attack the summit directly and take down the Cartel members. Delta needed help moving out the prisoners and the Rabbits jumped in. Everyone made it out. The Delta members ordered and paid for the beer and pizzas.

Simmons smiled thinking that if they came in with smiles and handshakes, none of the Generals had to get involved.

As he was about to pick up the draft of his weekly report minus today's actions, his secure satellite phone rang. If was O'Cleary calling for a report. "Perfect timing General."

July 21

Headquarters, Northwestern Military Region, Fort Carson Colorado.
0900 hours MST

General Matheson picked up the phone and called General Macklin at Fort A.P. Hill, Virginia.

"Good morning, Ken," Matheson said.

"Good morning, Mark," Macklin replied.

"Iowa is on my mind. It is in your area, but some of the problems there are overlapping to the west into Nebraska and possibly Kansas and South Dakota."

Macklin rolled it in his head. "Boundary lines always gave me heartburn. I am willing to acknowledge right to pursue. I think the boundaries need to be a little porous."

"Right," Matheson said. "Any problems with the USPF?"

"Oh yeah," Macklin said. "I thought I had a lot of problems when I replaced Marvin Jackal after he retired from Norther Command. All I have to work with are squabbling civilians with their hands out and their balls left at home. I only have one division to call on and the rest are National Guard. Little chance of getting federal money to activate them."

Matheson let out a heavy sigh. "Sounds like you have all my problems."

Macklin decided to change the subject. "What's this I see in the press about the Russians squatting on the western side of Alaska. Five ships I hear."

"Yeah," Matheson quickly replied. "Norton Bay just inside the twelve-mile limit and they want permission to set up a base on St. Lawrence Island alongside our old early warning

Radar posts. I am on the way over at the end of the week to see first-hand."

"Just so you know," Macklin said. "Rumor mill in the media says Canada wants to merge, not annex, with Alaska. The border between Alaska and Canada has been the most porous in the world. But I think the politicians in Ottawa want to take advantage of our situation."

Matheson and Macklin spent the next hour ignoring the world, talking together as equals in their small world. It was so rare for them to find actual peers. They even talked about vacations in each other's area. Hunting in Matheson's area and fishing in Macklin's area.

Towards the end, both men arrived at a subject neither of them wanted to talk about.

Matheson started it all. "What do we do if open warfare erupts in Iowa or any similar state? The last thing I want is to shoot at American Citizens."

"Me too," Macklin said. "I think we need a conference call with our other two four stars. We are the only peers in the world that can speak honestly with each other. None of us outranks the other. We do need to talk. Without staff or legal officers."

"Agreed," Matheson said. "Talk to you later Ken."

"Same here Mark," Macklin said.

Gallop, Roster, Thomas and Fern, Attorneys at Law, Dallas, Texas
1000 hours CDT

Two nice men in coveralls carrying tools entered the building saying they have a call to service an electrical problem. Without an inspection, they were passed around the metal detectors and given temporary badges. The men rode the elevator up to the fourth floor where all the firm's lawyers had offices.

They walked onto the floor, looked around and opened their tool boxes. The only thing in there was an MP-5 submachine gun and a carry bag with extra magazines. When they stood up a woman screamed.

One man shot the elevator controls and the other started shooting anyone on the floor. The gunmen did not make any distinction between men or women, lawyer, secretary, para-legal or client. Any human being was a target.

Because this was legal office with lofty ideals and inflated heads, there was a no-gun policy that prohibited weapons unless you were a security officer. The two elderly guards were the first to die.

In a corner office, Ellen Thomas heard the familiar staccato of machine gun fire. She went to her lower desk drawer, keyed the safe there and pulled out the 9mm Beretta with two extra magazines. When Latham gave her the pistol, she had to swear an oath in blood to keep it in her office. She loaded the magazine and chambered a round. All those lessons he taught her about remaining calm, controlling breathing and keeping her head clear took effect. She knew he would kill her himself, but she could not just squat in her office while her friends were being slaughtered.

'Divide and conquer', aim small', 'plan your actions and action your plan', don't become a casualty', look around', 'notice everything', 'know where everything is'.

Ellen opened the door and saw one of them. Coveralls. He did not belong. He had an MP-5 submachine gun. They fired 9mm parabellum bullets from a thirty-round magazine. There was other gun, but far off.

She lined up her shot and hit him three times in the chest. The man went down. Ellen forced herself to calm down. She killed a man. Time to think about that later. Only one submachine gun firing. Ellen shifted into the hallway. She squatted down in the corner, Ellen eased out slowly, forcing herself to stay calm, move slowly and focus. 'Remember what Latham taught you', 'keep the weapon in front of you', 'both the weapon and your eyes must see the same thing'. When she came to the first gunman, she pulled the weapon away from him, put it on safe and threw it away.

Ellen went out and caught movement to her side. Mary, one of the secretaries, had a pistol in her hand. Ellen put a finger to her lips and motioned for her to stay with the guards. The submachine gun was silent now, but a male voice was calling for "Frank". 'Stay calm', 'let him come to you'.

"Frank," the male voice said louder. The man came around the corner in a professional stance. He screamed, "Frank," and ran to him. Ellen lined him up and shot him four times. He went down and did not move. Ellen carefully moved over to him and took the MP-5, his pistol and ammunition away from him.

Ellen did not know how many of them there were, but she had to know if the coast was clear. 'Get help if you can', 'call out for help from a covered and safe position'.

"Listen to me, this is Ellen Thomas. Are there any more gunmen up here?" A weak chorus of "no" came out. Ellen felt confident enough to stand. "Has anyone called the police?" No response. "Someone call the Police. Everyone, look around. We have casualties, stop the flow of blood. Support the head. We had medical training this month, do something."

Ellen went into her office and sat down at her desk. She looked at the pistol. She set it on the desk and pushed it away. She had to kill so that everyone could freeze on the floor and do nothing, but hope they weren't next.

Ellen picked up the phone and dialed her husband.

"The voice that answered said, "Second Brigade, 4th Infantry Division, Captain Presser, Sir."

"This is Missus Ellen Thomas. I am declaring an emergency. Please get Colonel Thomas for me. I'll hold."

2nd Brigade, 4th Infantry Division, Fort Sam Houston, Texas
1000 hours CDT

Thomas was reading a new intelligence report when Presser ran to him. "Sir, your wife called and declared an emergency. She wants to talk to you."

Thomas stood and followed Presser to his desk. The last and only time she ever declared an emergency, Michael broke his leg playing football. He took the receiver just as the news was broadcast on the TV set in the room.

Thomas split his attention between the TV and the voice of his wife. Ten minutes later he said he would be driving there today. "Go home, I'll meet you there."

Thomas turned down the offer of a helicopter ride. He had a long-standing rule against taking perks not offered to everyone.

"Holy Crap," one his soldiers said. "Sir, your wife gunned down the two criminals. She's a hero."

"She could have also died," he said, leaving the building. "Call Colonel Summers and tell him to run the shop. Call Division and tell them I am going to Dallas. Fill in the General about why."

571 Frontier Mesa Road, Dallas, Texas
1500 hours CDT

Thomas drove the four and half hours worried about his wife. She was a strong woman, no doubt. But killing a man, he knew from personal experience, was nothing a good moral person could do and not feel bad about it.

Thomas pulled into his driveway through a gaggle of reporters, holding out microphones, pointing cameras and shouting questions.

If there was one thing, he hated more than lawyers, it was reporters. Thomas sighed and decided that he was in no mood to reason with idiots. So, he had to resort to his anti-reporter kit in the trunk. The reporters crowded his door, so he used both feet and kicked the door out. Reporters splattered.

Thomas ignored them and went to trunk.

"Get off my property," he said once.

"Get off my property," he said twice

"Get off my property," he said three times.

Thomas opened the trunk, put on a gas mask and took out two large cans of pepper spray. The reporters reacted too late, and the pepper stream had a twenty-foot range. The third can was his favorite. It was a special can of rape spray. It shot out a long stream of red paint that was designed to dry fast and adhere to anything it touched. It could not be washed out. It clings to the skin for weeks. The camera men thought he was still using pepper spray. They screamed and ran when they saw what was happening to the cameras and reporters.

After the gagging and red-faced reporters backed off, Thomas put the cans and mask inside the trunk. He took his suitcase and looked at his home.

Michael had been watching from the living room window and laughing hysterically.

Ellen just stared at him.

Latham walked inside, saw his family. Michael was still laughing. He hugged his father and walked away.

"Ellen," he said, not knowing what to say.

Ellen went forward and hugged her husband. Thomas did not know what to say. No husband could. They ignored the knocking on the door.

The two of them rocked together too close to a window. A reporter ran up to the window and snapped a picture. It would be viral by supper time. Michael ran up to the front door with the house pistol. He shot generally in the photographer's direction until the pistol's magazine ran out. Thomas ran up to his son and took the pistol out of hand.

"What the hell is wrong with you? Go to your room." Thomas had a crew of gun-toting crazies.

"It was loaded with blanks," Michael said.

Thomas closed and locked the door. He closed the drapes in the living room.

Ellen hugged her husband again. "When will I quit seeing that scene when I close my eyes?"

Thomas put his head on top of hers. "Truth be told, never. Over time, it will be dull and get duller. You saved lives and stopped two animals from finishing that slaughter. You can remember that, instead of killing another human. They deserved to die. You didn't cower in the corner. The news embellished your bravery."

Thomas took her over to the couch. "I asked a Chaplin about this when I was given my commission as an Infantry Lieutenant. He said there is a difference between killing and murder. Those gunmen were murderers. They were indiscriminate. You killed with deliberate caution. They had a choice to be evil and did evil. You had a choice and just killed to save others. If you did not stop them, the number of dead and wounded would have been higher. In short, never enjoy it."

622

"Will you help me?" Ellen asked.

"Of course," he said. "I called back and asked my Chaplin to expedite quarters on Fort Sam Houston. What about being a camp follower for a while?"

Ellen smiled. "Chances are that I am fired. Byron Gallop has an iron-clad no-gun policy. When I signed my employment contract, it had a clause about no weapons on the job. I told the police I had a registered weapon in a locked safe in my desk."

Thomas learned a long time ago, there were times when to speak and when to shut up and listen.

"I have to apologize to you," she said. "I always thought I would never need those lessons. All through my mind were the lessons you taught me. I know I wanted to know how to fight and you and I fought many a laser-tag game and worse; paint balls. The lessons rolled through my mind. The more I remembered those lessons, the calmer and focused I was."

"How do you think I survived all those tours in the middle east?"

Ellen stood and forced a smile. "Time to cook supper." She leaned in closer to Thomas. "I laughed with Michael. I plan on rewarding you later."

Thomas' mood soared.

July 22

Glades Sunset Gated Community, Largo, Maryland
1600 hours EDT

This was a crown jewel in the IRS circle of gated communities seized the previous year. The IRS management thought this one was kept a secret. Everyone was told, as a condition of residence, that no mention was ever to be made that this was an IRS community. The real owners were buried through shell corporations and official secrets.

This particular gated community had some extra significance. Many of the residents were higher ranking managers and directors. A larger than normal force of security guards was hired to protect everyone. Even though there was not a rental fee, the contract everyone was required to sign was fifty pages thick.

"Loose lips mean live on the streets without a job."

But as with most secrets, this was one that could not stay secret. Later investigations discovered that some outside contractors, who were audited and lost everything, spotted some IRS agents leaving their homes.

Most other attacks occurred at night or in the early hours of the morning. This one was done in broad daylight. Two vans arrived after lunch and made the motions of checking the grid electrical connections and the main water connections. Somehow, the sewer system was avoided.

The men stayed around long enough to be ignored. At 2 pm, four very powerful explosions severed the electrical and water supplied to the community. The explosions were perfectly engineered.

The water mains were closed off at the above ground control house. The clean-out was removed and several ten-foot linear flexible charges were snaked down the lines. Afterward, the charges were sealed in place with an epoxy-based water-proof aerosol gel. The second explosive was actually three points in the control room that were placed and daisy-chained in such a way that this was not going to be an easy fix.

The main electrical grid was brought down in an electrical yard. The lock was cut, the man entered and re-locked the gate behind them. One of the explosions was in the control house with all the electronic and monitoring controls stored in cabinets set in neat rows. The fire doors and back panels were removed from the cabinets. Small charges were daisy chained through all the cabinets. The second explosion was three charges daisy-chained on top of each of the three main transformers on the down-stream side that fed the community. Those charges had to heavily insulated to prevent any chance of accidental or premature detonation.

After all the charges were set, the incoming power was disconnected, the men departed, never to be seen again.

The four separate explosions unnerved everyone in the community. The families were startled, but not unnerved. With the rash of IRS communities being attacked, families had evacuation and protection plans.

After an hour of tense waiting for something to happen, families emerged from shuttered homes and panic rooms to look around.

Police and fire departments arrived with minutes after the explosions. No further unexploded devices were found. Utility companies arrived to survey the damage and determined that fixing the problems could take months.

The damaged water mains had the main water pipes split and ruptured for a distance of sixty+ feet mostly underground. The linear charges were suspended in water and sealed at the water clean-out, which amplified the explosive force. The replacement main water control valves, destroyed in the control house, are no longer available and will have to be engineered and manufactured from scratch.

Misery.

July 23

Room E-194, Pentagon, Washington, D.C
1034A S. Gilmore Street, Parkton, Virginia
0900 to 1800 hours EDT

Earl and Wendy enjoyed learning from Doctor Bardwell. He understood two things more than anything else. First, he can teach people without trying to impress them with how much he knew. Second, he taught them in the real world.

Wendy loved the shopping lessons. They would go shopping and observe human behavior in small chunks. After a while, both of them could anticipate how people react. Some of the more intense studies were at sporting events and after hour colleges.

In the afternoons and early evenings were the War College classes. Wendy and Earl now understood why John Kincaid had a bad attitude at times.

Each person consumed 6 pounds of supplies per day. Each type of vehicle burned so many gallons of fuel each day, either in peacetime or war time. Fuel and food and water and spare parts and replacements and ammunition had expectations. Then there was the all-consuming need to move those needs from depots down to user points.

Then was the real problem. Commanders who did not have a clue that stupid decisions on the spur of the moment cannot be met and all the screaming in the world cannot change anything.

By the end of the week, logistics instruction would be over. Both Wendy and Earl knew that they only scratched the surface of the logistical world.

Next week was the beginning of Intelligence Training. That ought to be fun.

Both knew that they needed more field time. General O'Cleary wanted them to have classroom instruction. But the real learning would only occur when they went to a real unit engaged in real fighting. That meant they needed to go back to the Savage Rabbits.

CHI Health Center, Omaha, Nebraska
0800 to 2100 hours CDT

Representatives of most of the Labor Unions left in the US assembled to discuss the sad state of affairs with organized labor. For the next three days, the assembled participants tried to make sense of the bad state of affairs with organized labor.

Several of the boards dealt with the lack of support for organized labor both in government and the business world. Contracts with companies and corporations were not being negotiated. Strike breakers and non-union replacements were becoming more and more common place. Companies and Corporations were finding it too hard to maintain the high cost of labor. Normal expenses for labor were three times the amount of their hourly rate. Union costs routinely ran four and five times that cost, factoring in pension, medical insurance, and union overhead expenses.

Even those state governments with legislation which favored unions, found the companies and corporations suing in state and federal courts. Their position was that any contract with the unions were expired and the laws used against them were invalid.

Other boards concerned themselves with how to attract new and old union members.

One board in particular was closed to the public and by invitation only. This concerned itself with union costs. Unions charged its members a percentage of each member's hourly wage for them to contribute to cover the union's overhead, pension costs and "contingency funds".

Contingency funds were those that covered a percentage of what the members were paid during a strike, loans to members, or anything the rank-and-file votes on.

A lot former members made a lot of noise saying that the union's deductions were being constantly raised. In some cases, that percentage was creeping above 40%. Granted, the rank-and-file voted on it, but the vote always favored raising the percentage. Regardless of the explanation, the money was gone from paychecks affecting the member's ability to pay bills and fill refrigerators.

Observers and reports kept a neutral tone throughout the convention. Many felt the cost of this convention and all its associated expenses ate into contingency funds.

The last board was the one everyone in the country was going to watch on Saturday. This was how they were going to re-write the rules for conducting a strike and how to deal with replacement workers or strike-breakers or as they called them "scabs".

Omaha Police had a presence at the convention. But by the end of the first day, the number of protestors, though peaceful was rising. Union members starting coming and hurling insults at them, but staying back. They were obviously wanting to goad
them in doing something stupid. Too many cameras were being used by both sides to document events.

The Chief of Police decided early on to call for help. He asked the State Police and the USPF for help in crowd control. Perhaps a strong presence will be a deterrence to anyone wanting to start trouble.

July 24

Headquarters, 4th Brigade, 36th Infantry Division, Texas National Guard, Camp Aubry, Texas
1000 hours CDT

Colonel Jasper Folcroft formally activated the 1st Battalion, 114th Regiment, which was assigned to his brigade. He felt a surge of pride, but at the same time, he was dismayed. The available pool of officers and senior NCOs was now depleted.

Folcroft reviewed the records of all the officers in the Texas Guard. Most had civilian careers and would not take a full-time-positions. Most of the remaining officers were all the wrong sort. This was not a normal assignment. Some of them seemed to think being considered for selection was a job application needing a negotiation. Others just wanted something to add to a resume.

General Corcoran listened to his arguments. "I gave this command to you because I knew this was almost the most impossible job that an officer could be handed." Corcoran reached into his desk's file drawer and pulled out a thick folder.

Corcoran through the folder down. "Those are the miscreants that 'volunteered'. They had particular demands and requests to accept assignments, so that some could be allowed to maintain their civilian lives. Most see this as a chance to get a promotion. Remember, just getting on the promotion list does not mean you get promoted. You have to have a slot, and occupy it, before the promotion is official." He spit in the trash can. "And the politicians were calling wanted their son or nephew Jimmy Joe to get a good job to enhance their resume for future employment. Half of them didn't have proper Infantry or Branch Training for the jobs they want."

"But the Army Chief of Staff will allow Active Army officers and NCOs, who are Texas residents or willing to move to Texas, a transfer so long as they are near or at their original commitments. Most of them are combat veterans."

"What about the NCOs?" Folcroft asked. "I need them to possess critical skills such as intelligence and staff positions. I can fill some officer positions with skilled NCOs. Those persons available are nearing middle age and older." Folcroft asked. "I need 173 senior NCOs. At present, my Sergeant Major is rejecting over 80% of the NCOs that are available."

Corcoran pulled his ear and rocked back in his chair. "Jasper," he said with an air of resignation. "I cannot give you a Ranger Brigade. I suggest you man your unit and become someone who is an evil taskmaster. If they wash out, I'll endorse you all the way. Remember you can fire them and they can quit. Let attrition help you. NCOs that show promise can be Commissioned and I will rubber stamp any recommendation you make."

Corcoran went silent. As he let the silence amplify, Folcroft rolled this around in his head.

"Jasper," Corcoran said getting his attention. "You are the only man who can do this if anyone even bothered to try."

"Yes Sir," Folcroft said, obviously having something in mind. "Can I think over something before I pitch it to you. I might even have the solution."

"Of course," Corcoran said. "Don't take too long."

"Yes Sir," Folcroft said as he stood, saluted and left.

Corcoran watched his friend leave. He smiled. That was why he gave the Brigade to him. He pulled out the file with men who would replace him as 1st Brigade commander. He put off the decision just to piss off everyone. All the pollywogs, politicians and butt lickers called wanting that job.

The Governor called and asked him why Folcroft was in command of two Brigades. Corcoran said he had too many asses in the way. The Governor laughed so hard he dropped the phone.

Joint Base Elmendorf-Richardson, Alaska
1500 hours AKDT

The Chief of Staff of the Army, General Marcus Kramer and General Matheson touched down after the long plane ride in the Chief's dedicated 707 aircraft. Both Generals were in sour moods and tired upon arrival. They had quarters ready for them and their staffs to stretch out and sleep without the drone of an airplane which had turbulence most of the way due to jet streams.

With the five-hour time difference, it was a big difference for General Kramer. Matheson and Kramer declined to rest up, saying Kramer had an appointment with the President on Monday.

Both men were here to personally investigate the Russians taking too close a look at Alaska. Those five ships in the Norton Sound were told by two Navy Destroyers to leave regardless of what they are doing or who gave them permission to come in US Territorial waters. Both Destroyers ran at high speed across and alongside the ships, making their lives miserable.

As the Destroyers were having fun, an Air Force AWACS aircraft ran active scans watching for something to happen. The Air Wings went on alert and four aircraft launched, providing an Air Cap over the Destroyers.

For whatever reason, the Russians were talking too much and taking too long to leave. Each ship limped along at as slow as a ship could go. Two on-shore encampments were both suddenly closed down. The personnel were arrested for trespassing and escorted away. All their equipment was confiscated, inventoried, identified and packed up for shipment to the Russian ships leaving Norton sound.

The FBI checked the Russian equipment thoroughly and found it to be GPS receivers and transmitters. They also found code books and encrypted radio equipment. Two Naval officers went wide-eyed and enthusiastically called their headquarters and reported it. They used their cell phones to photograph the code books and electronically transmitted the pages to Joint Base Elmendorf/Richardson.

Matheson, Kramer and Major General Jeffrey Lahcen, Commanding General, US Army Alaska went into the Alaska Headquarters SCIF. Signals intelligence showed a lot of encrypted traffic between the shore installations, the ships and Vladivostok.

"Something is in the water," Lahcen said. "The Navy is maneuvering a submarine into the area. With the Russian ships gone, we have been allowed to use the Destroyers to check the sea floor in the area they worked in. Those Russian ships did not move for over three weeks."

"We need to get a closer look," Kramer said.

July 25

The USPF learned a long time ago, the former National Guard Armories were the perfect place to set up operations. They were brick structures that had offices, and large open areas for any need. What made them ideal was the very secure rooms to secure weapons.

The weapons ranged from pistols to M-16s and MP-5s and M-249 machine guns. Also, there was a small amount of ammunition. Because there were around the clock operations, a small group was on hand to answer the phones and generally guard the equipment.

A large group of men in USPF uniforms arrived and got out of their vehicles.

At 2 am, the phones and all communications with the building went silent. A drill bored out the tumbler lock on the front door. Men rushed in and over powered the five men inside with tasers. They were handcuffed, hand-to-foot and gagged.

The men insured the alarm system was disabled and then sawed off the main door lock. There was an L-Bracket welded to the steel door and steel door jamb imbedded in reinforced concrete. The L-brackets protruded the main lock out four inches. The special portable band-saw sawed off the L-brackets in 90 seconds. Once inside. A powerful electrical bolt cutter was plugged into a receptacle and broke the seventy locks on the gun racks and lockers.

Once all the locks were broken, the man moved out of the arm's room and proceeded to break the locks on all the storage bins. The same man with the drill who broke the front door tumbler locks, went from office door to office door and drilled out all the tumblers.

All the weapons, equipment and information they came for was loaded on and in the vehicles parked in the back. All their keys were conveniently hung on nails for the ease of anyone who needed a vehicle.

By the time the clock said it was 0230, the imposters in USPF uniforms left. They hit at the best time. The shift change was at 0400 and the in-coming men starting arriving at 0300.

When Trooper Harold Cavin arrived, he looked with unbelieving eyes at the scene in front of him. Cavin quickly released all the handcuffed men. All of them had been in handcuffs for so long, their hands and feet were numb. Cavin grabbed the watch folder and called the Commander. The groggy man refused to believe him and hung up the phone. The Deputy Commander did not answer the phone. Cavin ran down the roster until he got his Troop Commander. Gavin was told to check on the arms room.

Gavin said, "Sir, the arms room is open and empty. All the offices are open and the equipment is ransacked. No idea what they took. Let me check the vehicle park." He looked at the key board, noting many of the keys are gone. He looked outside and over half the vehicles are gone. "We were cleaned out Sir."

"Have you notified the Commander?"

Calvin sighed. "The Commander hung up on me and the Deputy never answered. You are the first man in the chain of command who answered the phone."

Hours later, there were too many questions to answer.

United States Police Force Headquarters, Alexandria, Virginia 0900 hours EDT

Simon Westland and Harold Atwell listened with almost disbelief that someone attacked three different Armories in Iowa. Berryville, Walnut Ridge and Rector in northern Iowa. The attacks were committed almost simultaneously and in the same manner. Overpower the people guarding the armory, sever all communications and disable the alarms. They drilled out locks and the list of stolen items had the FBI, Homeland Security, and the BATF taking ant-acid tablets.

217 M-16 rifles.

142 M-9 Beretta pistols

48 M249 5.56mm machine guns

17 M32 multi-barrel grenade launchers

42 M203 single barrel grenade launchers already attached to -16 rifles.

The amount of ammunition each armory had on hand was still being compiled.

The phones were lightening up. Everyone wanted answers.

Norton Sound, Alaska
0900 hours AKDT

This time of year, the sun rose around 0130 as in 1:30 in the morning and set around 2300 or 11:00 pm. Everyone had a light tight cover you can put over the windows so that you can sleep. It was light at 0400 when they left their quarters and ate a quick meal before heading to the airfield.

Kramer and Matheson both boarded separate UH-60 helicopters and were escorted by two Apache gunships and four F-15 aircraft overhead. Both Generals were harnessed in and hanging out looking through high-powered binoculars. Accompanying them in each helicopter were two Naval intelligence officers who operated sophisticated surveillance equipment. The officers were veteran Russian watchers who were fluent Russian language speakers.

The helicopters over-flew the ships several times. Even lingering over two of them at the request of the Naval Intelligence Officers. They saw something but were too busy to answer questions. Suddenly a lot of Russian chatter was reported coming over their secure communications network.

Some of the items left behind was two of their secure communications radios and one set of the keys and codes. For the next few days, the Army and Navy were eavesdropping over the radio.

Crews on board the ships scurried around covering the equipment on the decks. But not before photographs were taken. If this was a secure operation, it went to pieces in a hurry.

Suddenly, both UH-60s banked away and accelerated away from the area.

"Why are we leaving," Matheson asked his pilot.

The pilot replied. "I had a lock-on radar signal. We were being targeted."

633

"Russian sea craft, Russian sea craft," Kramer said over the open radio net. "If you fire on these helicopters, that will be called an act of war and you will be sunk without warning."

Over the secure link, Kramer gave permission to the orbiting F-15 aircraft to over-fly the ships once at supersonic speed at wave-top level if they do not stop a targeting signal within fifteen seconds.

Matheson sat back and thought about this situation. Without staffers buzzing around him, whispering this distraction and that distraction, he could think clearly.

He planned to talk directly to these two officers and get the information from them before it is analyzed and filtered. None of this made any sense to him. But it made sense to somebody.

1200 hours AKDT

They used the same refueling point returning. But they flew straight to Elmendorf. Matheson grabbed both naval officers and ordered them to stay with him. All the cameras, scanners, and reorders were grabbed. The Navy men said they needed to report to their offices to brief their commanders. Matheson looked at them and pointed to the waiting vehicles and to his stars.

Both Generals had the drivers pull up to their offices and allowed them to escort both Generals inside. Both Naval Officers were talking Naval Intelligence speak.

"English," Matheson said.

"Sir," one of the men said. "If you will give us at least an hour, we can refine our information and give you a clearer picture than something that is raw and probably inaccurate."

"Sonny," Matheson said, trying to hold down his temper. "You talk down to me like that again you and your boss will on a plane to Antarctica today. Understand?"

"Sir," the other man said. "What we have here is a listening and locating post." He put in their drives with photos into a computer.

"Shoe horn it. Just say what you saw," Matheson said.

Both men looked over to General Kramer. He made 'get on with it' motions.

634

The second man went to a dry ease board. "On the ships were satellite transceivers. They were taking measurements of the coast line and probably mapping the ocean floor. The shore locations were used as a fixed points to triangulate locations in three dimensions. The third point is probably a satellite or overflying aircraft. They were measuring an area of Alaska. We will probably never know how much of Alaska they mapped."

The first man came forward. "General, if you look at the map like a Navy/Marine officer would, Norton Sound is a good location for a force to land. The northern and southern land masses could be great emplacement for anti-air and anti-ship batteries."

Matheson and Kramer looked at each other.

Matheson asked. "They could not get this from National Geographic?"

The second Naval officer held up a map ten feet from Matheson. "This is the amount of detail you get of Alaska from the available maps." He walked up to within 6 inches of Matheson. "They this amount of information and even closer." The officer pulled the map away.

Kramer said. "Cook this up and send it to the Pentagon, all four branches. Get a briefing ready for General Lahcen by 1700 hours. I'll call him and pre-brief."

Matheson looked at both officers looking at each other. "Problem gentlemen?" he asked.

Both men shook their heads no.

July 27

Texas, cities of Lubbock, Abilene, Midland and San Angelo
0800 to 2200 hours CDT

The IRS was not the fiery demon it was a month ago. The President's order had secretly muzzled them from using what he called tyrannical tactics.

Alan Baker in turn sent out very vague instructions about how to deal with citizens and tax cheats. He would be demonized for issuing these instructions by putting the word citizen along with tax cheats in the same sentence.

635

In Lubbock, Abilene, Midland and San Angelo over achieving IRS persons were grilling people and seizing property with "ghost warrants". Ghost warrants were blank warrants signed by Tax Judges to be used by Agents in the field if searches were needed. All the agents did was print the name and address on the warrant.

In those places, the IRS Agents were so bold that the population started to rise up. Any person who went before a Tax Judge was basically considered guilty. The percentage of convictions was upward of eighty-nine percent. Civil Liberties groups were too scared and fearful of losing their special tax status to challenge them.

In all four cities, citizens revolted when the Agents arrived unannounced at homes of evicted people.

In Lubbock, a pregnant woman was forcibly removed and thrown to the ground. She screamed and held her abdomen. She lost her baby. The two agents came out of the house an hour later to see the neighborhood armed with bats, tire irons and anything hard. The Agents held up their badges. They were found hanging by the neck from a tree in an overgrown field.

After that incident, no IRS agent could walk around the city without a police escort. In several instances, the agents were beaten nearly to death. The police were surrounded by citizens and just held in place. The police retreated.

In San Angelo and Abilene, it was the city that came under attack. The IRS said that the city failed to support operations to collect revenue. So, the IRS was going to take it from the city. City services ground to a halt. When sanitation services and hospitals were having to shut down, the citizens revolted.

The IRS office was ransacked and the names and fictional names of agents and staff were broadcast for all to hear and react. Now, they were targeted and evicted from their homes. Some had their homes burned to the ground.

In Midland, the IRS bit off a hornet's nest. Midland was a city founded by and run by the oil industry. People who worked on oil rigs were called rough necks and those in refineries were called 'roughians'. These were hard living people who loved all the money they earned.

The IRS at least learned from all the others and went slower and actually tried to stay within the law. However, when a manager from Washington came to take over and bring everyone in line, the hornet's nest was kicked.

When the IRS went out this time, each Agent had four or five USPF men to protect them. With this protection, the Agents went after "targets" with a zeal. The main thing was most of these people were people who could hunt game. The trick with hunting is to respect the forest and above all be patient.

After five days, a protest city-wide surrounded the IRS building, battered down the doors and attacked anyone who was not a citizen of Midland. Agents were thrown out of windows. Staffers were beaten nearly to death and others were maimed or disfigured. Riot police arrived, but the people crowded around and refused to fight the police. The police could not get to the building until after everyone was finished.

Those Agents and staffers who escaped, left the city, their belongings left behind. They grabbed their family members, put them in their vehicles and drove away.

Department of the Treasury, Washington D.C.
1300 hours EDT

Secretary David Carter was watching the news and the last reports from Midland, Texas said it all. He picked up the phone and called Alan Baker directly.

The phone call was short and to the point. Baker was publicly fired. Not allowed to resign or have a press conference where he thanked everyone. He ordered the Deputy Commissioner Jennifer Donnelly to take over as Acting Commissioner.

"Ms. Donnelly," Carter said holding down his temper. "This country is revolting and the IRS is responsible. You get your people to back off; follow the law and the Constitution or you're fired too."

Carter hung up the phone and waited for the lines to light up demanding he resign or he was fired.

Backstay Inn, Wineseck, Wisconsin

Brenda cradled her son in her arms and fed him his eight-ounce bottle of formula. She was grateful her breasts no longer hurt with wanting to give Arthur his milk. As Arthur drank his formula, she read the weekly report from Colonel Simmons.

Last week, they conducted seventeen raids. Where those drugs were coming from was anyone's guess. General Waller asked him if he could send over his Intelligence team to update his wall filling map of Mexico with their updates. Simmons had the only people who operated south of the border. Waller had visited the Operations Center in the past and was at awe over the detail he saw on the wall map.

The floor covering map was built up and physically pulled out a third dimension. Looking at a two-dimensional map and mentally trying to "pull" a third dimension was difficult. Waller turned to Simmons and pointed at the terrain model.

"Sir that is the culmination of two months' worth of effort."

Waller walked up and down the terrain model. At points he looked close at the detail. "Can I bring my staff to visit. I want one of these. If you can give me one or two of the geniuses who did this, I will let you marry my daughter. I promise to give them back after two weeks."

"My pleasure Sir." Simmons said. "The terrain model is laid flat and constructed as a normal sand table. All the terrain features are built-up and colored. Man-made objects are hand-built and scaled to the terrain model. Then a special concoction is sprayed over in multiple layers. Each layer had to be allowed to completely dry before the next layer is applied. Do not allow anyone to touch it under penalty of death or dismemberment. Plus, that concoction has to penetrate down several inches. Play-ground sand works the best. The other layers add to the surface tension."

Waller then went to the wall filling map. It was made 3 dimensional by building up terrain with a Frankenstein patch-work of maps. Terrain features such as mountains, valley and other terrain features were built up and the map sections were glued over the filler material.

Brenda read the rest of the report and finished about the time Arthur was finished. She put him on her shoulder and rubbed his back, waiting for his belch. Brenda thought that Waller now was really going to guard them. I mean personally.

After Arthur belched, Arthur was sound asleep. She needed to go to bed. In four or five hours, he would awaken demanding attention, a new diaper, a new bottle and all the love his parents could give.

Brenda put Arthur down and looked at the sleeping form her son. Never in her life had she thought that being a mother would be so gratifying.

Brenda put the report in the fire place. It flared and blackened in seconds. Brenda stirred the ashes. She went into the bedroom and looked at herself in the full-length mirror. The days of a t-shirt and panties gave way to a flowing gown. She actually looked like a lady.

As silently as she could, she lay in bed with Dennis. Her husband gave her this happiness.

She went to sleep thinking about the Savage Rabbits. By morning, she could dictate a response to Colonel Simmons. She should think of asking Jim Waller to write him a Special Officers Evaluation Report. Yeah, she would send Simmons a single star without explanation.

July 28

White House, Washington D.C.
1400 hours EDT

The President watched the news from his secret informer on a TV show. His informer was secret because the TV reporter did not know his was the President's favorite news source.

Nationally, the polls said the population of law-abiding citizens were scared and sales of guns continued to skyrocket. Nothing said by anyone was calming people down. Increased police presence was not doing the job.

So far, the USPF has done nothing to bring law and order to the land. They reacted too slow and were ineffectual as investigators. In one instance the USPF personnel were surrounded, surrendered their weapons, equipment and vehicles; walking away from the scene.

Those thefts at the three Iowa Armories did not help. The list of weapons lost sent shivers through everyone.

Everyone in Iowa was buying weapons and ammunition. Gun stores were being bought out. Ammunition was in short supply. People were buying ammunition in other states and bringing it into Iowa. Though vaguely legal, it was disturbing. Some entrepreneurs were buying wholesale in other states and setting up make-shift stores in flea markets. Usually, they were sold out before the police could arrive. Smart sellers would advertise using social media and suddenly open up.

The President listened for a few more minutes and turned off his laptop. He powered it down and locked it in his briefcase.

The President walked outside and looked around in the sunshine. The Secret Service did not like a lot of things he did and wandering off without telling anyone was one of them. That laptop was another. They had been trying to take it and change it out with a super encrypted model. The special briefcase he had was "Tempest" enhanced and had a special security feature his niece earned a thousand-dollar bounty for installing it. Not only was the briefcase shielded from the internet, but if anyone picked it up and moved it without his fingerprints, an ear-piercing horn screamed. The Secret Service hated his ways.

The President walked outside and enjoyed the fresh air. The freedom here was second only to heaven. He walked around remembering back to the first day of his administration.

He shuttered at the chaos of January 20th. All those people killed. The fear running rampant around the country. No one knew why they stopped their attacks after the Wolf Creek disaster. Somebody got their hands on someone. The Gamari was identified as the controlling entity of terrorism world-wide.

US, UK, French, Israeli and German intelligence operatives went on a world-wide killing and destruction spree. All of it secret. He dammed himself for the classified orders he was cohersed into sighing.

Now his country was under attack internally by its own citizens. Lawyers for any number of reasons were causing problems. Law-abiding citizens and police are caught in the middle.

Homeless camps and groupings of drug addicts are locating in cities and communities which have or appear to have money or valuables. Homes are being invaded and residents are held at gunpoint as these gangs ransack them.

Pawn shops are being sued and sometimes robbed. The stolen property is then pawned in others. In Seattle, San Francisco, Los Angeles, Las Vegas, Dallas, Cincinnati and numerous other cities, pawn shops are either being burned down or forced to shut down. Citizens are going to pawn shops and photographing people pawning their property. The Police seldom even respond to those calls.

The President knew that ignoring crime is the central reason people are scared and not involving the police. No rhetoric was going to change anything. The AG was scheduled to see him on Friday.

He was not going to run for re-election. But he needed to do something before he left office in January.

July 29

Department of Public Safety, Des Moines, Iowa
1430 hours CDT

All day long, beginning yesterday, the phones rang off the hook. Battles, big and small occurred. Gangs on motor cycles roamed the back roads. Gangs in vans and SUVs roamed the neighborhoods. Militias came into being all around the state. Men and women were openly carrying pistols and rifles as they took their children to school or shopped in the markets. Parents guarded playgrounds preventing the homeless from erecting camps or addicts from doing drugs.

The states surrounding Iowa, in particular Missouri and Nebraska were actively thinking of closing their borders. High speed chases went into and out of Iowa were now commonplace. States police in the surrounding states around Iowa, started cooperating openly to gain the upper hand with all the people making Iowa a battle ground. A lot of back road traffic was smuggling weapons, ammunition, drugs and stolen property. Sudden ambushes were leaving a lot of shot up and burned vehicles all over the countryside. The body count was climbing and no one was going to guess at how many died.

As usual, the politicians and the media wanted to disarm law abiding citizens in order to calm things down. As usual, the politicians and media did and said little about the criminals who were armed to the teeth.

Another problem was judges, prosecutors and lawyers unwilling and unable to put criminals in jail and leave them there. Other parts are that everyone wants to make jail a country club instead of a place where punishment for crimes is applied. People should not want to be in jail.

The citizens of Iowa refused to surrender their weapons. In one instance, fifteen Iowa State police with USPF augmentees, descended on parents dropping off their children at school. All the parents were disarmed regardless of registration or compliance with the law.

The criminals found out and attacked those homes. Fourteen murders, seven rapes, thirty-two home invasions and a total of three million dollars-worth of property was stolen.

The criminals waited for the police to disarm the citizens and they attacked the homes doing as they pleased. Now the population was openly ignoring the police trying to disarm the parents. When children were dropped off at schools, large segments of the population were on-hand to stop the police.

Four towns circumvented the state police/USPF by deputizing the parents as reserve police officers, complete with badges.

A furor occurred when it was reported over the news media that some criminal elements were telling the police about parents being armed within five hundred feet of school.

The criminals were using the police to disarm their targets. That only fanned the fires discrediting the police.

One home was almost seized by the police because drug paraphernalia (used needles) was found in a home of a diabetic. The needles were from his diabetic supplies.

After that debacle, the people of Iowa uniformly refused to surrender their weapons. When any group of State Police were seen moving into an area. They were surrounded. Citizens called each other, warning each other where they were.

Seized weapons were easily replaced. It was becoming commonplace to kill home invaders. The amount of paperwork in killing someone in their home was less than if the invader was wounded. There was even a "youtube" video about that. Home owners were advised on the how and when to kill the home invaders and what things or situations to avoid.

Polls throughout the state place rated their confidence of the police in general at 11%.

Everyone is scared. Scared people reach a point where they are no longer going to be scared. They fight back.

July 30

Room E-194, Pentagon, Washington, D.C
1034A S. Gilmore Street, Parkton, Virginia
0900 to 1800 hours EDT

Kendal and Locklear were bubbling over with information. What they needed more than anything was a vacation. All the information being crammed in their heads needed time to settle in and become comfortable.

Lately, they had been spending their nights curled up together with a cup of wine, on the couch and watching the fire place burn. They rarely talked, but they stayed as close as they could.

Somehow, they knew something was going to happen.

Doctor Bardwell was taking personal time off today, so Kendal and Locklear sat down in a diner and whittled down the things Doctor Bardwell taught them:

1. Always remember to stay simple, if you listen to something complex, you are being played. Stay curious. Focus on facts. The truth always lies to you.
2. You may need to ask the first question over and over and over. Eventually the patient will answer with a fact.
3. Never accept the truth. Truth is something that is different with each person.
4. Everyone is worth your time. If they are dull, you are not looking hard enough.
5. You have to constantly look or listen for the two-ounce ball of purity. Ignore the two-ton ball of confusion around it.

The afternoon classes today were about signature actions. Those were things that happen around a secret that can tell you everything about a secret.

The murkiness of intelligence work was something John Kincaid forcibly told them which required peeling away the layers of murkiness. It was the primary work of intelligence gathering. John Kincaid spoke at length about how he had to "think sideways" about situations.

Kendal discovered from Gladys Goldstein that "sideways" was simply thinking around a goal or something that came up. It was almost like hearing about a new ice cream shop and walking around it and until you finally found it. Police call it canvasing.

Kendal wanted to talk to Locklear about it. For now, Wendy wanted to eat supper with Earl.

July 31

White House, Washington D.C.
0900 hours EDT

Rebecca Beck came and was ushered into the Oval Office. She had a folder that official Washington, especially the Treasury Department, was going to hate her for.

Beck had formed, sequestered and compartmented five separate groups of people; primarily lawyers and staffers to

644

answer several questions. Each question had a central part that had to have an absolute answer. If this was made into an Executive Order, could it be easily defended in a court of law.

The folder in her hand had those arguments and counter-arguments. Additionally, there were drafts of an Executive Order.

"Good morning, Mister President," Beck said.

"Good morning, Rebecca. May I offer you something to drink?" The President offered.

"No thank you sir," Beck said, sitting down on the couch and placing the thick folder on her lap.

"Rebecca, give me the nut shell," The President said.

Beck handed him the folder. "The nut shell is that you have to reverse portions of your Executive Order that you used for the Martial Law that are still in effect now. Every single thought or evasion or circumvention of the law and especially the Constitution has to be stomped out.

1. The law is the law. You have the authority to make case law a thing of the past. Case Law means judges can unilaterally make laws and changes to laws. Any judge who says something is used in the next court as law. Roe v. Wade is a primary example.

2. Sentencing guidelines which are legislated should be required to be imposed, not worked around or discarded. The Supreme court has actually ruled in favor of this in the past.

3. If you go to jail, you stay in jail for 80% of the sentence.

4. Jails are easy to create. Use closed down military bases. Surround them with barbed wire and use the prisoners to build the walls. Those same judges said that prisoners should be paid. But the amount can be low. Below minimum wage.

5. I can set up a working group to facilitate your orders. But you have to do this and not back down.

6. Maybe this will not carry over in the next administration, but if we hit this hard enough, the citizens will elect law and order Congress people, if Congress ever convenes.

The President looked at the Executive Order drafts. He would need to read this through this weekend.

August 1

World Wide Web, Cyber-Space, Planet Earth
485 Glenmore Drive, Alexandria, Virginia
0400 hours EDT

UNSTACK THIS was alerted when trucks and men showed up at the O'Cleary house in Alexandria, Virginia and they emptied it out. Police and officious men in suits stood by as the house was systematically emptied of all the O'Cleary's belongings.

It took seventeen men, two hours to pack up everything.

A notice was stapled to the door saying that under orders of the Department of Homeland Security, the O'Cleary Household was moved to Number 22, Naval Observatory. A security company installed bars over the windows and doors.

Cell phone jammers were turned on to prevent anyone from calling anyone for any reason.

Five hours after starting, they were finished.

Backstay Inn, Wineseck, Wisconsin
0200 hours CDT

Brenda's turn for uninterrupted sleep was ruined by an urgent call from UNSTACK THIS. He was notifying her that government agents arrived at her home and were in the act of packing everything up. No one was able to stop them. Police and Federal agents, armed with court orders, pushed everyone away.

[Do you have any special instructions?]

"No thank you. Good night." Brenda was tired and needed sleep. She closed out the phone and wished she retired as a Colonel all those live-times ago. She decided to tell Dennis later in the morning. Now she needed to think about it and get some sleep. Arthur hated letting his parents' sleep.

Underground Station "Conscience", World Wide Web and Channel 513
0900 hours EST.

"If you threaten, act. If you say something, do it. If something is important, stand your ground. Governments are often hamstrung by individuals who have opinions about issues they feel strongly about. This is Martin Socranson, self-proclaimed philosopher who says, 'What are we if we can't back up what you say'?"

"Greetings America" Martin Socranson said beginning his broadcast. "It is reluctantly Saturday and I say thus." In the background the sounds of the 1812 overture played.

"Hello America the divided. All over this country, citizens are scared and arming themselves to the teeth. Nearly forty years of de-fanging the police and watering down the courts has resulted in people having no fear of the law."

Socranson waved his arm to the statue of Lady Justice. "The blind fold is no longer covering both eyes but pulled down to see the color of your skin, social justice or political leanings. Justice is no longer equal; the scale swings to the mood of the moment. The sword denoting the power of enforcement is dulled or pointed to the weak who cannot defend themselves."

"People are routinely ignoring the edicts and mandates of Judges sitting in insulated buildings and guarded homes. Lawyers have never been interested in justice, just the perversion of law they need to win. 'Failure to appear' is a common reason Judges don't bother to write warrants. Police arrest criminals and they are on the street in hours. No bail releases are becoming common place."

"Seventy-three percent of the police department of St. Louis Missouri has turned in their badges and walked off the job. Let me make it perfectly clear; they are not on strike. They quit. A man named Joshua Lambert shot and killed Police Officer Harold Grandeur. Lambert was arrested and released after telling the Judge he was sorry. That night he was drinking and celebrating with his friends when two police officers responded to a noise violation. Lambert laughed when the Police Officers tried to make them be quiet. As the two

647

officers were writing tickets, Lambert shot one officer and said he was above the law. Lambert had been drinking a bottle of whiskey when took his friend's pistol and shot the police officers. Officer George Garrett died instantly. Officer Fred Velum died two hours later. Lambert's actions were captured on the patrol cars dash camera and the body cameras."

"Lambert was found later, passed out on a public bench. Because he could not remember being read his Miranda rights, the Judge voided all the evidence brought against him."

"Three officers died without justice."

"That same Judge freed a rapist for the same reasons. That man returned to the woman he raped and did it again. Only this time her neighbors came to her rescue and beat the man into permanent impotence and disability. The Judge wanted the neighbors arrested for violating the rapist's civil rights. Everyone refused to cooperate."

"The incidents of police being abused escalated to the point that the Judge refused to hear those cases. Two days ago, 1,783 police officers, auxiliaries and reservists resigned, in mass."

"Approximately four hundred officers, spread through St. Louis are left. The county sheriff's department had over fifty percent resign. The state government and the USPF stated that they can supply personnel to fill some of the gaps."

"This is not a random action, only the most severe. Police departments around the country are losing personnel. Academies have cut back classes for new recruits to one a year if they do at all. This is a windfall for the USPF."

Socranson looked around. "Is the USPF going to become the new scrouge of the nation, replacing the IRS? Who watches the watchman?"

"We are fracturing, America. We spent the majority our history as a United States of America. History, which is no longer taught anymore, says that a population that no longer sees commonality will start fighting wars; bloody civil wars. That was mostly true since the middle of the 19th century."

"America, I could say pretty words and few would listen. Soon we will start killing each other for lust, food, land, sex, books, religion, comic books or who gets cookies or cake."

Bonnie Chandler, 234, Route 17, Belcher, Missouri
1400 hours CDT

Dear Bonnie,

What a slow, boring excuse for a summer. The Army creeps are everywhere, trying to make everyone miserable. Those clowns try to ask us to help them, but they never help us.

Last week, a long line of trucks clogged Main Street. My friend Connie Wexler's dad died of a heart attack because those animals would not get out of the way. Some officer tried to come to Connie's home and apologize. Missus Wexler slammed the door in his face. Good for her.

What are they doing here?

August 2

Jefferson City, Missouri
0900 hours CDT

Governor Sandra Goldson looked at "the map" with Commander Thomas Forrest of the State Police. It was a computer-generated map on a wall filling projection screen. It showed the state of affairs across the state and information from all the states surrounding them.

Today it was official; the shooting and lawless war up in Iowa was extending down into Missouri. On the political side, she and Governor William Polson ignored politics and boundaries to work together. Hot pursuit by each-others police officers was welcomed and supported.

One thing they did agree on was there will be no rounding up of weapons from law-abiding citizens. Parents dropping off their children were told not to touch their weapons except for self-defense.

"Children shall be defended" she told her citizens.

"If you have illegal weapons, the Attorney General shall prosecute you to the maximum extent of the law. Register them now and use common sense."

Goldson started talking to Forrest about coordinating across the state lines to put down gangs and criminals. Both knew that was a tall order. Goldson planned a state-wide address to her constituents by telling them to think before shooting and say the only way to keep the anti-gun "nuts" off her back was if everyone acted like a Missouri resident.

Goldson crossed her fingers.

Office of State Police, Oklahoma City, Oklahoma
0900 hours CDT

Two gangs, one on motorcycles and another in a mixed bag of vehicles tried descending on a town, robbing everything in sight and running within ten minutes. State police and the USPF was having a hard time catching them.

The motorcycle gang ran into trouble at an oil rig. They picked on the wrong people. Fifteen gang members tried intimidating seven rough-necks. Twenty minutes later, the State Police arrived to a scene out of movie. The fifteen men were thrown in the mud pit, beaten up and tied together. Their motor bikes had a cable run through the front wheels and lifted of the ground by a crane.

The State Police had a good laugh.

The town of Bessie was less than a mile square. It was more or less poor by most standards. The only government building was Post office. The residents guarded their money, what little they had. It was not uncommon for them to help out those who had hard times.

When a gang of twelve vehicles with seventeen men and women stopped in Bessie, they thought this was easy pickings. They drove virtually non-stop from Nebraska. It was easy to out run the police by zig-zagging all over the countryside. They also varied the time between strikes.

They would come to a town and watch the town's people back-up as they came out of their vehicles with bats and bars. Two men went up to the hardware store and knocked down the door. Many of them went inside and helped themselves.

One of the gang members came out with some cash. "Forty-three dollars? You got to be fuckin kidding me!" he yelled out loud. "You bring out your money or we will burn this town and your homes to the ground."

650

It was quiet in town as the gang went into the one small grocery store. Fifteen minutes later, they came out with armloads of groceries and stopped in their tracks. Arrayed in a wide semi-circle around the front of the store were one hundred of the town's people who drove up and set up an armed response.

From the town's people a voice amplified by a bull horn said. "You can drop your weapons and leave. Or if you fire on us, you will die. You chose."

The gang members, men and women started putting down the groceries. A large man walked forward a few steps. He pulled out a pistol and let it hang to his side. He turned his head, left and right. Any normal person would realize he was out numbered, out gunned and there was no chance of escape. Behind him, the store's doors shut and he could hear carts being moved to block the doors inside.

Pride overrode common sense. He saw at least one person, then two and more, holding up a cell phone. He was trapped. He couldn't give up. Any chance of holding sway over this group or any other in the future would be gone if that film got out.

The big man saw no other way. He raised his pistol up and tried to empty the magazine.

Gunfire erupted from the assembled townspeople. The gang's vehicles got shot up worse than the gang. The gang tried to shot back. Each time one of them shot a weapon, four or more weapons shot back.

Twenty seconds after it started, the fight was over. None of the gang members survived. The townspeople were thoughtful enough to "miss the tires and drivetrain of their vehicles. The vehicles were driven out of town far into the countryside. A front loader opened the ground about six feet down and then covered over the bodies forever.

The vehicles were driven to another county, into another empty field and set fire to erase any evidence.

The gang did do the townspeople one service. The ten thousand dollars in cash they had, "paid" for the hardware store door and spoiled groceries. Small things such as plugging bullet holes, replacing windows and fixing things in general.

All this was done with some money to spare. Town's people in dire need or wounded were taken care of.

August 3

Internal Revenue Service, Washington D.C.
0900 hours EDT

For the second time in its history, the IRS was the blind recipient of mountains of information concerning the hidden and untaxed monies from billionaires, corporations, politicians, bureaucrats, military officers and numerous functionaries.

This made everyone scared as tax lawyers and tax judges watched the data flow into the IRS computers in what seemed like an endless flow.

Equally insane was the fact that every single news or quasi-news service received the same information. Some news organizations choose to say nothing and ignore it. But not all of them. Some of the independent organizations tore into it like ravenous wolves tearing a fresh carcass apart.

The people who were the targets of the information being thrown at the IRS were scared. The IRS notified the Secretary of the Treasury as they seized the money and added it to the nation's coffers.

The Attorney General was notified as a courtesy.

Room E-194, Pentagon, Washington, D.C
1034A S. Gilmore Street, Parkton, Virginia
0900 to 1800 hours EDT

Kendal and Locklear had to switch back to dress uniforms. They had finished their classroom exercises and had to quote "move into the field". Both of them met a virtual O'Cleary in her office on the video conference screens.

"I want an honest assessment," O'Cleary said from Wisconsin. "How do you feel about your training to date?"

Colonel Hawker listened in, taking notes.

Both of them knew this question was coming and had already discussed the answer. "Not exactly up to Mister Kincaid's standard. We know all the book stuff, but we need more practical work. The Pentagon is not very practical because of the heavy rank structure here. We'll be relegated to house-keeping duties. Nothing of an operational or tactical nature will be shown to us. Mister Kincaid's abilities are more about his attitude than anyone else. He was a past master at letting people make the mistake of under-estimating him. Then he went made them tell him everything he wanted to learn."

O'Cleary saw what they were saying. Kincaid made her into a chump several times. She had to admit that a lot of those lessons gave her the thick hide to be a General Officer.

"I assume you have a suggestion?" O'Cleary asked.

"Savage Rabbits," Locklear said. "They utilize all the aspects of Tactical and Operational doctrine."

Kendal interjected. "I remember and understudied the First Sergeant and later Sergeant Major. He taught me more in seven months, than any school could teach in ten years. Send us back to the Savage Rabbits. Then when the country collapses, we go to the Minutemen."

O'Cleary rocked in her chair feeding Arthur, thinking. 'These two had great potential and needed a mentor. But who could even come close to John Kincaid?'

O'Cleary opened her X-Berry and called Simmons. He actually had time to talk to her. "Chief Kendal and her husband Master Sergeant Locklear are needing a home. Do you have a job for them?" She listened for a few minutes, occasionally saying "Ok" and "Yes" or "No". Finally, she said, "yes you have a free hand. Abuse them as you see fit. They have to do something for me first. They will report for temporary duty with General Waller tomorrow for no less than two weeks." She listened for a few seconds, laughed and said "thank you" and hung up the phone.

O'Cleary turned to Hawker. "Elizabeth, cut some orders sending them to Fort Hood as observers of General Waller's Mexico invasion. They have to depart immediately, temporary duty as observers from JCS." O'Cleary turned back to Kendal and Locklear. "That is the best example of an Operational mission. Granted a lot of the planning was already done, but something could still be learned from the execution of the mission. The Mexico invasion will start next week. Go

653

home, get packed and leave. I'll send someone to pack you up, close out your apartment and your Pentagon office."

Kendal and Locklear were told to wait in O'Cleary's outer office, waiting for Hawker to get the orders. Her secretary could type one hundred and five words a minute. Ten minutes later, they had temporary orders to Fort Hood to observe the operation and later to be assigned permanently to the Savage Rabbits.

O'Cleary booked a call to Jim Waller. She needed to ask favor. Locklear and Kendal needed to learn, observe, be everywhere and not be distracted with fetching coffee and donuts. They needed to be immersed in this invasion so much they would be drowned. Jim Waller is a great commander. Hopefully, Kendal and Locklear would learn something.

Next, she called Elizabeth Hawker. She needed to expand her education also, but along a different path.

Minuteman, north of Fort Benton, Montana
0900-1800 hours MDT

Peters, Glendive and Sheridan went on an inspection of an INSANE JANE alert throughout the Minuteman area. In a nod to the agriculture side of the area, the alert was timed before the harvest. Everyone performed their part in three scenarios.

A to Z everyone reacted as they were required. One parent in each household evacuated the children to the pre-described positions and the alternates. The other parents and single persons spread out and fought delaying actions, confusing everyone. A few holdouts who were too old or medically unable to run, stayed behind. They told the aggressors to go in the wrong direction and their information on the INSANE JANE personnel was wrong. The aggressor was tied in knots until they passed into another area where the whole thing started over again.

"Inflict a few casualties, blow-up a piece of equipment, but never, ever, for no reason lose the ability to maneuver."

All three compared notes after they were over.

"Status complete," Peters said.

654

Glendive went back to read Kincaid's "Ops Center for Dummies". Sheridan started with it and gave up. John Kincaid was a genius that they all discovered too late. His outline was a master stroke of genius for its simplicity. But it helped if you had a part of Kincaid inside you.

Desert Zero, Fort Hood, Texas
1900 hours CDT

Simmons had to admit, getting Kendal back was a great idea. Her husband was an unknown entity, but he had O'Cleary's blessing. If he did not work out, then there were other options. O'Cleary did say he was trained as a Tactical Operator.

Simmons put that away and gleamed with the fact that with eleven raids this week, he had zero casualties. Several of their operations were active reconnaissance missions along with 82nd Airborne and 101st Airborne division Pathfinders.

Pathfinders were a tough group of men who went into areas beforehand to confirm and mark landing zones for their divisions to land. As important, they controlled the airspace around the landing zones, keeping aircraft from colliding with each other, both day and night.

They came in ready to defend themselves. Once the units were on the ground, they would be fighting along-side the incoming units as the situation warrants.

The Pathfinders had the luxury of overflying their areas and in some instances landing on the ground and testing the firmness of the Earth. There have been instances of an aircraft landing and sinking into the ground.

These men were drilled to see and remember small details of the land as they overflew or personally walked the land.

Simmons had twenty of these Pathfinders in his unit and he wanted more. He remembered Kendal from before when he formed this unit. She was as tough as they go, knowing when to shoot and when not to shoot. She was rumored to be a part of some super-secret crew of mad men that performed miracles, often fighting when out-numbered and out-gunned.

Simmons looked at this week's report and marveled at how thin it was. He was spending more and more time reporting at how perfect his unit was and fewer and fewer instances at what his problems were.

Simmons privately wished O'Cleary would finish her maternity leave and go back to the Pentagon. He constantly worried that some idiot with stars would descend on him and destroy the unit like they did last time.

Simmons wondered at Delta. They were premier operators with a superb record of accomplishing their objectives with perfection and precision. But sometimes their leadership left much to be desired. He was reminded of a saying a German General in the First World War said of the British. "They are lions lead by lambs."

Simmons wished they had better leadership. Too many politicians getting in the way.

Simmons shook his head. His S-1 brought over the final draft of the weekly report. Simmons read it, signed it and put it in the out-box.

August 4

Headquarters, Southern Command, Fort Hood Texas.
0400 hours CDT

Kendal and Locklear obeyed their orders which said to report to the Commanding General's office at 0400 hours for a briefing and assignment. The General's aide looked at the orders three times, decided not to question it, but take the orders to the General. He disappeared into his office.

Two minutes later, the aide said to report to the General. Kendal was not wearing her headgear and therefore was not allowed to salute, but seeing as he was a four-star General, why rock the boat?

Both marched up to within four feet of the desk, locked up at attention and announced themselves. Both saluted and held it there.

"Sir, Master Sergeant Earl Locklear, USAF, reports to the Commanding General."

656

"Sir, Chief Petty Officer Wendy Kendal, USN reports to the Commanding General."

Waller returned the salute and looked at them in silence for along minute.

Waller stood and walked around to the front of his desk and leaned back. It was easy for him to stare down at them. He was six feet tall and still muscular.

"Master Sergeant, Chief, I will be tied up with an operation involving 5 divisions reverse invading the United States of Mexico. What does that mean, Chief Petty Officer?"

"Sir, that is when you launch a large force forward of the national boundary or battle line, deep into a country or battle space and that force fights its way back to friendly lines. A similar or larger force is holding or maintaining the border or main battle line, thereby squeezing the enemy into a smaller and smaller space, forcing them to preferably surrender or fight a losing battle. That can pave the way to eradicate an enemy force with the fewest number of friendly casualties. Sir."

"Master Sergeant, what are the dangers and limitations of this a strategy."

Locklear did not want to correct the General by saying this was Operational. "Sir, the problems are that forces south of ours can move northward to engage ours as we move northward. Other problems can occur as terrorist tactics can be employed to cripple or delay our forces. If the population revolts against us, our progress can be impeded. We are Americans, we do not slaughter civilians. As our forces converge with the border, a squeezed enemy that cannot surrender, will have no choice but to fight a suicidal and senseless war. Drug Cartels have high penalties for failure. Lastly, there is the danger of fratricide as our forces merge at the border."

Waller did not betray any emotions as he weighed the answers. He went behind his desk and pushed a button on his intercom. "Inform the J-3 that the two observers from JCS are here. I'll send them down. They are not to be interfered with or given any duties or assignments."

Waller handed them two folders. "Those are your orders. Follow them, Dismissed."

Locklear and Kendal saluted, did an about face and left. They walked out of Waller's office and stopped. Both went to a corner and read their instructions.

There were three copies of their original orders. Next was three copies of the orders assigning them on temporary duty as observers. The third was densely typed on a single page.

They read:

1. You are here to observe. Observe.
2. You are not to interfere.
3. You are seen but not heard.
4. An officer or senior NCO will be assigned to oversee you. Do not make them mad.

James Waller, Commanding General, Southern Command.

Kendal marched up to the Aide's desk, saluted and requested instructions about where the J-3 Operations section is located.

The Aide pulled out a strip map and highlighted a route on it. "An NCO is enroute to escort you," he pointed to some seats in an out of the way location. "Wait there."

J. Edgar Hoover Building, Washington D.C.
0900 hours EST

The Director of the FBI, Marcus Solin picked up the monthly report of criminal activity for the month of July and was tired of it already. Solin opened it up it was almost a carbon copy of the one(s) before-hand.

Murders were up. Rapes were down because women finally starting fighting back. Fighting off would-be rapists and having to kill them was becoming a sport. There was a popular web-site that tallied the number of dead assailants and their woeful stories of picking on the wrong women. Not-so privately, he cheered on those women. Pleading with animals not attack them only made them want to do more to the women they attacked.

Solin looked at the number of 18-wheel truck hijackings. That was going down due to two aspects. One there were only so many of trucks in the United States. Second, they now had armed guards and radio links. If any of the radio links failed, the police descend. Trains were using newer, stronger locks with stronger hasps. Trains had the same radio links. The engineer just had to break the link for help to come.

But it was the other crimes that were giving him headaches and indigestion. Vigilantism was on the rise. The average citizen was convinced the courts were on the side of the criminals. Those communities that reported defending themselves were hit with criminal and civil lawsuits for defending themselves.

The age of the internet and digital media taught everyone a lesson. Town's people were killing the criminals and burying the evidence. The DOJ was investigating any instance of any collection of vehicles burning in secluded fields. After a while, the vehicles were not burned, but scattered all over the map.

State police were tolerated in some of those small towns. But the USPF was something alien and feared. Smaller towns rejected the USPF as a permanent presence.

Citizens were fighting back these days. Even in the northeast and in California, no one was taking it in the chin and smiling. Nothing no one could do was making anyone stand around and letting crime happen. When asked, lot of people said they needed to stop the criminals before it happened to them.

Sales of shotguns and shotgun ammo was skyrocketing. Theft of shotguns and sales on the black market were accelerating.

5th Circuit Court of Appeals, New Orleans, Louisiana
1000 hours CDT

In a move that surprised everyone, the 5th Court unanimously ruled that Texas had the legal right to enforce the immigration laws as handed down. Though the Federal government had the ultimate Constitutional authority to set immigration law, the exact mechanism as argued by Texas was not explicitly given to the Federal government alone and the Tenth Amendment granted them to right to defend its border where the Federal government's authority and inaction was evident.

The DOJ was astonished to the point that they took over three hours to file an appeal with the Supreme Court.

Mega-State Coordination Office, Austin, Texas
1300 hours CDT

Coffee cups clinked as representatives of five states celebrated the defeat of the Federal Government's attempt to open the border, again.

The Federal government has long accepted that a sixty-to-eighty-mile band of American territory along the border with Mexico was open country. They even erected north facing signs warning people not go farther south. "Your safety and security cannot be guaranteed south of this point."

That sentence and photographic evidence was presented during the appeal to the 5th. "If the Federal Government can't do its job, then we need to do it."

With the exception of three Brigades worth of National Guard Troops to man the southern borders, the States will police its own state's area.

The Governor's along with their Secretaries of State and National Guard Commanders will have to iron out the specifics.

August 5

Mega-State Coordination Office, Austin, Texas
0800 hours CDT

Texas somehow knew their turn was coming. Here it came. Several gangs of Cartel members started taking over towns within 20 or so miles of Mexican border. Several of the towns rebelled and casualties littered the streets.

The DPS patrol came into the town of Nitro after the citizens revolted. The State Trooper got out of the car on Main Street. He held open the door, wide mouthed and reported back to his headquarters. They had to hear it four times before they believed it.

After the world descended on the town with questions and accusations, the story came out. Four days earlier, about twenty heavily armed men arrived and rounded up the town's people. The Cartels were targeting smaller communities and towns. Overpowering the meager police departments, if they had any.

The Cartels had a proven strategy for overtaking any towns. Usually, two women would arrive to look over the town for two days. The women would disappear, apparently passing on what they learned. The main body of the criminals would arrive early in the morning; sever any land line communications, set up cell jammers and kill the police or anyone who could be trouble.

A lot of time, the town was a receiver of drugs or a launching out point to move cash south of the border.

The Cartels had a proven way of holding the town. Obviously, they had a lot of practice. Families were separated so that hostages would make the others behave.

Some towns were not treated too badly. After they were finished, they left.

Other towns were attacked and savaged. People were randomly executed for any infraction of the rules. Rape became common place. No amount of anything dissuaded the Cartels.

In the town of Nitro, the town's people had enough. The Cartels learned a dangerous lesson the hard way. Terror has to be applied carefully. Too much in the wrong way, makes the target not care and strike out.

On the evening of the second day, the town waited for the Cartel to drink a lot of liquor and get sloppy. Many men and women struck back. The fighting went on for hours. In the end, seventeen Cartel members were dead along with eighty-two town's people. Thirty percent of the population. Some died during the occupation. Most of them died in the fight to free themselves.

As an afterthought, DPS, reinforced with four or more USPF personnel, with on-call military assistance, started roaming the country-side in a band from the border to eight miles in-land.

Headquarters, 36th Infantry Division, Camp Aubry, Texas
0900 hours CDT

Folcroft came to meet with General Corcoran about the lack of capable officers to man the 4th Brigade.

Folcroft saluted the General and sat in the offered seat. Corcoran had a standing policy to bring ideas to him. Folcroft had one.

"Sir," Folcroft said. "I cannot find good officers to take on the assignment you gave me. But I have great NCOs who can do the job. I have the authority under Army regulations to assign junior ranking personnel to positions above their pay grade. I cannot see any other way around the predicament I am in."

Corcoran swung back and forth in his chair. He was being torn in many directions with all the politics bearing down on him to assign people so that can get promoted and have bragging rights. Fortunately, he had the Governor's ear. "I need to clear that with the Governor. I think it is a great idea, but you know the shit storm of politics that will start-up. Draw up a list of personnel and stand by. Have them alerted to get their staff sections set up and ready to take charge of. You stay close if I need you."

"Yes Sir," Folcroft said.

Headquarters, Southern Command, Fort Hood Texas.
1800 hours CDT

Kendal and Locklear received a couriered pouch, with every kind of classification marking in existence, that required to have both of them sign for the pouch. The pouch was sent by General O'Cleary. It contained fully back-stopped identifications for the National Security Agency, the Federal Bureau of Investigation and the Personal Security Agency. Two zippered pouches with badges and credentials completed their newer identities.

O'Cleary gave them unrestricted access to the inner sanctum of official Government.

O'Cleary also notified them that she was nominating them for an ULTRA clearance. They would not know what that is yet, but they would need the clearance later. It was a process that should start in two months or so. Expected time to be completely investigated is two years or longer.

August 6

Internal Security Agency, Barton, Virginia
0900 hours EDT

Admiral Hazlet sat down in his office and waded through all the paperwork that cluttered his desk. The first file he picked up, ordered him to keep track of the four regional commanders the President used to carve up the nation. Spy on them, it meant.

Alaska was something to watch. The Russians were found to be measuring Norton Sound. Could be they were looking for a landing site. General Matheson was watching the Sound and St. Lawrence Island. The Canadians were exploiting the traditionally porous boundary between them and Alaska.

Japan was actively courting to annex Hawaii. For years, the Japanese were spreading outward and taking over. Malls were totally dedicated to speaking and reading Japanese. Though they were not overt about it, English was shunned.

Admiral Cartwright was having to move Navy and Coast Guard ships into the Gulf of Mexico to patrol and guard the 1800 plus oil rigs from pirates and privateers.

General Macklin had his hands full with rioting citizens who wanted food and fuel and basic items.

General Waller had the most to deal with. He was ordered to invade Mexico, again, and he also had a 2000-mile-long border to guard. Hazlet felt a twinge of sorrow for Waller. He had the worse.

Hazlet looked at the master board in his office that charted all the major actions around the county. More and more, red dots were popping all over the map. Those dots were mainly about food, drugs, weapons and contraband.

Department of the Treasury, Washington, D.C.
0900 hours EDT

David Carter was waiting for the end of this Presidency so he could run away from bureaucrats and numbers. The summary on top of the report was all that anyone bothered to read.

The lack of a budget or the willingness to even have one was driving a searing stake through the financial heart of this country. The President was ruling through Executive Order. Instead of Congressional voted upon measures and oversight, the Executive Branch just went to the President; had him sign an order and they took the check to the Treasury.

Carter threw the summary on top of the report and signaled for his secretary to come get it.

Mega-State Coordination Office, Austin, Texas
1000 hours CDT

The Governor of the Great State of Louisiana, Lance Keller, said it was inevitable so he came to Austin after the Legislature gave its blessing. Governor Keller signed the Mega-State Coordination articles and sent them to Louisiana's legislature for ratification. The White House and plenty of other politicians, excluding their Senators and Congressmen, applied a tremendous amount of pressure and promised Federal Court litigation to stop them.

Keller flipped them the bird.

Keller said it was a done deal and that was that. Unless the Federal Government did its job and provided protection and support, this was going to happen.

General Waller, when asked, told everyone that this was not a part of his mandate or orders. Waller called Cartwright and both agreed this was none of their business.

Texas and Louisiana had a lot of the same problems with illegal immigration and roving gangs of criminals. Rioting people wanting fuel and food were starting to fall off. Texas and Louisiana were uncapping oil wells and shipping that crude oil under guard to refineries. The price of oil was already dropping under seven dollars a gallon. Texas, Oklahoma and Louisiana took control of the capped wells and compensated the owners for the sales.

It was a stab in the heart for the Federal government. Taxes and fees and environmental studies designed to slow down progress were tossed aside when State regulators showed the original environmental studies conducted when the wells were drilled and they were still current.

All three states agreed to charge taxes to the Federal government equal to or greater than the escalating scales they were using to raise the price of fuel to meet the national average of seven dollars and forty-two cents a gallon.

"Three dollar a gallon gas," Keller said. "That is what we are predicting so long as the Federal Government does not actively try to screw us over."

In Washington, the Secretary of Energy watched the news conference from Austin, Texas. She smiled and resolved to resign, very publicly and loudly if she was told to kill it.

Headquarters, Southern Command, Fort Hood Texas.
1800 hours CDT

Waller walked into the Operations Room and looked at the Master Board. He wished the board he was copying from the Savage Rabbits was finished. The NCOs working on the board were hampered by all kinds of ten cent ideas from officers who had to say something. SFC Bartelone from the Savage Rabbits complained to Waller that he was being constantly interrupted. He said, suggestions needed to be written down in a book so they can work in an uninterrupted manner.

Waller sent out the word.

Tomorrow morning at 4 am, the 82nd and 101st Airborne Divisions will cross over the border southward to their landing and drop zones 100 miles south. Some of the plane's flight paths were out over the Pacific Ocean and the Gulf of Mexico. Seven wings of fighter aircraft were part of the package.

Half a million leaflets were dropped over the countryside saying that this invasion was about the drug trade. The people would be given cash money, United States blue backs, to point out anything that was drug related. The confiscated drugs were to be burned on site. Any US currency found could to be used to "bribe" the locals.

Waller looked in the back and saw O'Cleary's two NCO observers. They were intent on observing and writing down everything. They were very adept at not getting in the way like they had a sixth sense, but they seemed to see everything.

Waller was going to call O'Cleary and give her the only report she would get until this was over. These two seemed to be sharp. He needed sharp NCOs (hint, hint).

August 7

Supreme Court, Washington, D.C.
1000 hours. EDT

Justice Theodore Tungsten was the Justice on-call to hear emergency requests for action. Justice Tungsten declined to issue a Temporary Restraining Order (TRO) halting Texas' action (s) in regard to illegal immigration.

The Justice Department opted not to pursue the matter until the Court reconvenes on the First Tuesday in October.

Headquarters, Southern Command, Fort Hood Texas.
1800 hours CDT

Before dawn this morning, the 82nd Airborne and 101st landed at many points across the width of Mexico from sea to sea. The equivalent of 4 Divisions locked down the border. Drones and helicopters crisscrossed the sky along the border. Waller said he wanted to stop the jack rabbits and deer. "Nothing crosses that border."

The time line for this operation was set for four days, again. Waller had three specific orders, again. One, target only drug activities, two leave the civilians alone and three don't leave any soldiers behind or lose any aircraft.

Waller thought this was a stupid operation, again, but had to concede, again, that drug activity was escalating to terrorism levels on both sides of the border. The executive officers of every company sized unit had 100,000 US dollars in cash to pay out to civilians who pointed out drug activity to American troops.

666

Waller knew that the next four days was going to be too long with too little sleep.

In the background, Kendal and Locklear were totally focused on all the things you can never learn in a classroom. Their badges, on the front of their uniform jackets, said they were observers and no doubt some of the officers went to Waller to inquire about them.

Kendal and Locklear focused so hard, both of them had headaches trying to see everything, yet stay out of the way. They learned to watch for signature actions and not focus too hard on the details. The details will fill themselves in after the signatures were spotted.

They both realized how John Kincaid seemed to be able to keep track of so many things going on at the same time with his head exploding.

August 8

Station R-14, Mormon Mountain, Idaho
1200 Hours MDT.

The Salmon River Mountains in central Idaho was the backdrop for this World War 2 training camp. Station R-14 was a base camp used by the Army and Marine Corps to train Soldiers and Marines in mountain fighting. It has been used as an auxiliary camp by the 10th Mountain and 3rd Infantry Divisions along with Special Operations Units from all services.

R-14 had been bought from the government three years ago by a front company using Committee funds. A maintenance company was hired to maintain the facility and keep everything in good order for any time when it would be needed.

It was a sure bet the government and the Pentagon forgot they even owned or knew the compound existed.

Smith and Jones drove up here and slowly left their SUV and looked around. The memories flooded out of them. All the buildings were still there. It was easy to see where there were repairs, in some places, massive repairs, had to be made. They had several months of work to be ready. This time, there were not going to be a military wide hunt for candidates. All the candidates shall be taken from the Minutemen and the group of Savage Rabbits at Fort Hood. In the back of their SUV, were all of John Kincaid's records and Programs of Instruction (POI). Two stacks of documents were three feet thick each.

Both looked at each other and prejudicially wished John Kincaid was still here to do the job ahead of them.

As they looked at the POI, an epiphany occurred. Train the Senior NCO Minutemen as Generalization candidates. Peters and Glendive will love that. The men would be close by and the finished candidate would be second to none. Glendive was a Generalization graduate. Those NCOs would use the new Werewolf Class as props to learn who to teach and formulate a lesson plan using Task, Condition and Standard.

Headquarters, Southern Command, Fort Hood Texas.
1800 hours CDT

Waller watched the situation map on the wall. 24 hours into the mission and the casualties were just injuries. So far, the mission was a resounding success. Finger pointing by the locals was the only hold up. Too many locations were being pin-pointed. Fires from burning drug bonfires dotted the countryside. When the word went out that cash money, American dollars, was being paid for information about the drug trade, they came running. The bigger problem was the Company XOs were running short of money. The troops ran everywhere. This time, the Humvees followed the troops coming in, sometimes, minutes behind. The C-17s with the rolling stock used all the local airports and improvised airfields to land and off-load the vehicles.

Air Force Combat Air Controllers had a special ground penetrating radar that was mounted on the front of a Humvee that could check 15,000 feet of roadways and highways to certify it for landing a million-pound aircraft. They were very busy.

The Savage Rabbits, augmented with Pathfinders from the 101st and 82nd jumped into Humvees and ran everywhere, acting as forward reconnaissance for the two divisions and designating new landing zones incase troops had to by-pass positions.

Thank God for low casualties.

Waller had the option, again of pushing the four border divisions southwards a set distance. Chair polishing politicians from the Pentagon thought this was a brilliant idea, again, but Waller thought it was insane and utterly stupid.

Waller refused to risk lives for real estate that would be given back anyway. That reeked of decades of politics. In the end, that decision belonged to Waller. He chuckled to himself thinking that this was just the way politicians wanted to waste American lives. He smiled, planning again, to stick his head in the sand and wait until it was too late.

August 9

Headquarters, Southern Command, Fort Hood Texas.
0001-2359 hours CDT

Kendal and Locklear were not unfamiliar with round the clock operations, but never before during operations like this. In the real world, they were just operators. Now they had to learn how to be in charge. It was hard despite being just observers, they were constantly wrong with their assumptions. As they observed signature actions, they estimated or approximated what actions would happen. Sometimes they were right and other times they were wrong.

It was the wrong things they found the hardest to understand. Neither one of them were deluded enough to think they were infallible. They compared notes and all the facts for later review.

That afternoon while he was taking a shower, that epiphany occurred. Earl came back and reviewed the notes during a break while Wendy left to take a shower and change her clothes.

"Chief Kendal," he said. "We are looking at this all wrong. It is just like Doctor Bardwell said about box people. We are looking for things to fit into pre-made boxes instead of building the box around the situation." He pointed to the western Mexican area. "They are coming up to the town of

669

Copper Canyon. There are mountainous areas all around, but primarily to the east. They will require additional aerial drones and Helicopter operations to by-pass areas that are too arduous to walk through and there is a lack of usable roads."

The units of the 101st did exactly that.

Kendal and Locklear congratulated each other.

1800 hours CDT

Waller watched the situation map as flags were moved from place to place. The line was fifty miles south of the border and resistance was stiffening in some areas and non-existent in others. So far, the Air Force, the Navy and the Savage Rabbits were decimating aircraft and ships trying to escape with drugs and money. In some cases, the drugs were more valuable that the money.

The planned mopping up was smoother this time compared to the last time. The drug cartels tried to stay away from the advancing line of American soldiers. Now they ran hard into the brick wall on their northern border. Terrorism style tactics like ambush's, car bombs, improvised explosive devices, or IED's and sporadic rifle fire was the norm. Fortunately, all the NCOs were Middle East veterans and the Cartels were amateurs at real IED use.

The larger amounts of drugs were slowing the advance. Fires and smoke dotted the countryside. Napalm was airlifted to locations around the countryside. Napalm would burn for as long as the fuel was still there. Satellite and drone photos showed civilians trying to put out the fires. Several people had some napalm spill on them. Napalm burns even under water. That caused Waller to decide to overload the drugs with too much napalm and have troops watch the fires burn all the way down before moving on to the next fire.

Waller kept pushing the forces northward. So far, the Mexican Military Forces stayed out of it. The relentless push north was more about politics than conquest. Fliers were dropped by the millions all over the countryside saying the "invasion" was about the drug trade, not the country. Luckily, the civilians got out of the way and stayed out of the way.

They wanted the money for showing where the drugs were hidden.

So far there was 15,834 tons of marijuana, 74 tons of cocaine, 53 tons of heroin, 74 tons of various other substances, 687 laboratories and hemp fields by the acre.

The loss of the poppy fields in Afghanistan really put a crimp in the heroin trade. Poppy exports were down 98%. The chemical that was sprayed was persistent. No poppies would be grown there for at least 5 to 7 years. Turkey and Iran wanted to grow the poppies to replace them.

Relentlessly the northward march continued. Waller gave authority for his border divisions to conduct limited cross border operations on their own, as they saw the need. Primarily, he wanted a smooth link-up.

Already the lawyers were squabbling about the rules of engagement, again. Waller ordered them forward, again, to personally supervise those rules. He sent orders directing that those same lawyers stay far forward in the line of fire.

Four infantrymen were detailed to each lawyer to ensure those same lawyers stayed forward, but not guard them, again. Waller smiled.

August 10

Minuteman, north of Fort Benton, Montana
1000 hours MDT.

John Espirito sat at the desk and watched the multi-screens on the monitor. The chaos within the nation was continuing. That was old news. The only thing that changed was the faces and the dates. What John and UNSTACK THIS were starting to see was patterns.

Someone was pulling the strings.

First and foremost were the attacks on the IRS and its personnel. It was frustrating to find a common link, because nobody cared what happened to them. No one ever wanted to pay taxes and the tactics they used never endeared them to anyone, even the ones who were innocent.

Patterns were forming. It took combing through mountains of information to find it. UNSTACK THIS and his ability to sift through all that information was the only reason the patterns were forming. Only they were just patterns that fell with the laws of probability.

John just mentioned it in his report to O'Cleary.

Additionally, he was finding not so subtle patterns of National disintegration. The alarming news was the flow of money from international locations and wealthy individuals wanting our disintegration.

John published that information. He also included the separations. The nation will end up looking like a jigsaw puzzle.

Headquarters, Southern Command, Fort Hood Texas.
0001-2359 hours CDT

Kendal and Locklear forced themselves to take shifts observing while the other went into the male or female tents to catch a few hours of sleep. This being August, they opted to sleep at night, when the temperature was down.

The more they applied Doctor Bardwell's lessons, the easier it was to follow the ongoing battle and "see what could or could not happen in real time or projected in the future.

Both understood that this was unique in their education. They were watching literally a two Corps or Army mission at the nexus of the command structure. Both wished they could have been here the last time. Probably it would happen again.

1800 hours CDT

Waller sat down on the backwards chair and crossed his arms on the chair back. The Mexican civilians were thankfully staying out of the way along with their Military. Advance units of the push were in contact with U.S forces all along the border. Hopefully, God willing, the last of them will pass the lines into the U.S. by first light.

Waller's gaze went as it always did to "the board." There were 7 dead, 78 wounded and 0 missing. "The board" was something he felt every officer should always look at, burn in his soul, and forever remember. This time his casualty board was one tenth it was the last time.

672

He was interrupted with new reports from the border. Suddenly the area was quiet. No attacks, no fighting; nothing.

Waller bowed his head, thanked God and turned his gaze to the big map. Cards, depicting units small and large were moving north.

If the politicians didn't grow some brains, he was going to have to do this all over again. A third time.

Desert Zero, Fort Hood, Texas
1900 hours CDT

The near constant drone of helicopters announced the return of the Savage Rabbits to their Base Camp. Simmons walked outside and made it a point of meeting them when they arrived.

Three companies, "B", "C" and "D" went out ahead of the Southern Command when they launched the Pathfinders and Combat Controllers to set up landing and drop zones. "A" company provided logistical support and reinforcement as required. All the Rabbits were in near constant fighting as they had to secure an area for the troops to land and take over security before they loaded up and moved north to secure more areas.

Generally, they literally dropped in the middle of a group of Cartel members. One tense altercation had them land next to a Mexican unit. The Rabbits refused to surrender and pointed up to two AC-130 gunships orbiting overhead. Twelve 105mm rounds were fired at the buildings north of them. Over a loud speaker, a Spanish speaking soldier said they had no fight with them, just the cartels. They were invited to leave. Anyone firing at them for any reason will result in their annellation. Fortunately, the Mexican unit withdrew.

Sadly, Sergeant Thomas Chamberlain was killed. He led his men up a road to an overwatch position, and as he turned to emplace his men, a single rifle shot killed him. His men acted professionally and manned the point, dragging Sergeant Chamberlain back.

Three other Rabbits were injured to varying degrees. They would recover.

673

Still losing one man was going to take time to overcome.

Simmons had to stay behind on this operation. Too many things were going on for him to go into the field. It was his duty to stay on top of everything throughout Mexico where his Rabbits were operating. He insured they got resupplied, got reinforcements and extracted if it got too hot to stay where they were set down.

Simmons sent a message to General O'Cleary that his weekly report would not be ready until tomorrow. He needed after-action reports and staff input. Most importantly, he needed to interview Sergeant Chamberlain's men so that an appropriate letter can be sent to his family. Nothing can replace a living, breathing man. But maybe the right words could give his loss some meaning.

August 11

Minutemen, north of Fort Benton, Montana
1000 hours MDT

Jones had asked to see Peters and Glendive early, because all he could expect to receive only an hour of peace and quiet before "things" got in the way.

"Thank you for your time, Gentlemen," Jones said, sitting down with Smith next to him. "I will not bore you with too many details. I know I was thinking of a senior NCO Academy. I believe I have the answer and it is painless. Mister Glendive, myself and Mister Smith know the solution as the Generalization skill set." Jones pushed out two thick folders.

Glendive retained his normal or and neutral facial expression. But he knew exactly what Jones meant.

Smith and Jones alternated explaining what was written in the folders and emphasizing certain areas.

They spoke for nearly thirty minutes. Peters seemed to like what he heard.

Peters asked. "I understand the logistics are almost non-existent?"

"Yes," Smith said. "The NCO academy already taught them the field portions. They need to learn everything that officers are taught and make that jump from an NCO mindset to an officer mindset. We are teaching them to command, not exactly leading."

Peters looked to Glendive who readily said, "Yes".

"When can you be ready and how much time do you need?" Peters asked.

'Here it comes,' Jones thought. "We'll be ready at the main encampment north of here by the first of September. We need from September 21st to December 20th. There will be some weekends off and if anything occurs, the NCOs are approximately one hour away."

Peters nodded.

After it was over, both men looked at each other.

Smith said, "I half expected a knock down drag out over a four-month POI."

"It's strange," Jones said. "A couple of weeks ago, all I needed to do was command all that and it was done."

"It ain't started yet brother," Smith said.

Headquarters, Southern Command, Fort Hood Texas.
1800 hours CDT

At 0420 this morning the first units of the 82nd Airborne made contact with elements of the 4th Infantry Division south of Del Rio. As time went along, other units made contact at crossing points, passing at crossing points with the 2nd Brigade of the Texas, 36th Infantry Division.

At 0945 hours, units of the 101st made contact with the Arizona National Guard at Agua Prieto and Nogales. Other 101st units made contact with the 9th Infantry Division in Nogales and San Luis Rio Colorado.

As an afterthought, Waller wrote a thank you note to the Governor of California. The State Attorney General tried to get a Federal Judge to issue an injunction against Waller "tying up" the crossing points and against the sealing the border during the military operation. "Thank you for your support."

675

By 1800 hours today, all units should be back inside the United States. The Commanders of both the 82nd and 101st had requested the same areas they operated in the last time. They knew those areas, its peoples and places to look for hidden contraband.

His last order as the operation was completed was that he wanted their after-action report by 1800 hours tomorrow.

2000 hours CDT

Kendal and Locklear were exhausted after finishing that twenty hour a day schedule. All that was left was reading the consolidated after-action report.

Both were told by Miss Nancy Glister by email, that they were to conclude everything by tomorrow night, and report to the Savage Rabbits in one week. Enjoy the time off. Their education would resume there. It is the only unit currently conducting combat operations. General O'Cleary had already sent a thank you e-mail to General Waller.

August 12

Backstay Inn, Wineseck, Wisconsin
0900 hours CDT.

A soft ding came from Brenda's computer after Arthur had his bottle and was put down for a nap. She wanted the same thing. Being a mom was tiring work. Dennis was taking his turn for a nap. Anyone who ever said that they could raise a baby by themselves was either lying or a super somebody.

Brenda logged in and read the e-mail. UNSTACK THIS was warning her that several portions of the government, including the FBI, ISA, NSA, Homeland Security and something the Executive Agency had ejected her house sitters and moved all their household goods to number 22 at the Naval Observatory.

"Where did they find the land?" she asked no one in particular. She went to see Amanda Edwards before her son was borne and nothing was being built then.

676

UNSTACK THIS further stipulated that Homeland Security Agents would arrive Saturday to take her, Dennis and Arthur into custody and transport them to their new home.

Brenda read the rest of the message and logged off. UNSTACK THIS watched her walk over to the bedroom and stand next to the doorway and look in. She stood there and cried.

For the first time in its existence, UNSTACK THIS was mad.

UNSTACK THIS sent a message to Wendy Kendal and Earl Locklear to come to General O'Cleary's hotel. Subject: Personal Security. Problem: General O'Cleary and family in danger. Transmit.

Headquarters, Southern Command, Fort Hood Texas.
1800 hours CDT

Waller picked up the consolidated after-action report. What caught his eye immediately was the casualty count.

There were 9 dead, 81 wounded and 0 missing.

Waller skipped to the logistics portion. Two helicopters were shot up, but were able to return to the US. No major loses.

The rest of the report detailed all the good and bad parts of the plan and the operation. He looked at the "bad portions" with a tainted eye. Sometimes, his staff put in "bad portions" just to prove they worked on the report.

Waller looked over the report and signed the cover letter and put it his "out-box".

Just as Waller was about to leave and go get an uninterrupted night's sleep. Four Treasury types showed up, flashing badges saying that of the 175 million dollars that was supposedly seized, 19 million was unaccounted for.

"You clowns are not going to keep me up all night because someone did not count the money bill by bill at the time of seizure. Most of those reports were estimations in the field while under fire. I doubt you are that nit-picky in the field if you ever soiled your manicures. Now get gone and bother someone else."

Waller had to watch his blood pressure. He resolved to call General Edwards and the DOD secretary in the morning and announce his retirement.

August 13

Backstay Inn, Wineseck, Wisconsin
0900 hours CDT.

Dennis O'Cleary woke up to a funny feeling. One he hadn't had in a long time. Two people were sitting in the chairs on the porch. They were just sitting. He opened the safe on the mantle, pulled out the pistol and quietly chambered a round.

Dennis poked Brenda and touched his nose.

Brenda had showed him the e-mail yesterday and they had a long talk over the buzz box. Dennis overrode her and called Glendive who was the new Werewolf Commander. He said he needed two days to get someone there. A Chief Kendal and Master Sergeant Locklear were already enroute.

Brenda stayed with Arthur, while Dennis went outside. Both people sat still in the seats, their hands in plain view. After Dennis walked outside, Kendal said, "Good morning, Sergeant Major O'Cleary. I am Chief Petty Officer Wendy Kendal, USN and this is my husband, Master Sergeant Earl Locklear, USAF. I believe we are expected."

Just that instant, Brenda came out. "Dennis, they are the trouble makers I told you about. Come in." She went inside. Arthur was stirring.

Dennis grumbled. "The jackets worn in August were a dead giveaway."

Wendy went in and paused at the door as Brenda reached in and picked up her son. "Can I come in, General?"

Brenda smiled and said "yes". She took Arthur over to the changing table. Three minutes later and Arthur was fully awake and crying for his formula. Dennis was already on it. Like any family, there were pre-filled bottles of formula in the refrigerator. Two minutes in the microwave, test on the wrist and give to baby. Simple after a lot of practice.

"May I Ma'am?" Wendy asked.

Brenda had her sit down and cradled Arthur in her arms. After showing a few points, Brenda stood up and watched. "You're a natural," she said and walked away.

"We arrived at two am this morning," Earl said. "We searched around the area for a kilometer around the cabin. Nothing to report. The proprietor rented us the cabin on both sides of this one. Four others will arrive in a few hours. If we believe the intelligence we have. The three-person gang coming for you will arrive in the morning."

"In the mean-time," Wendy said from the living room, "we are Special Agents Kendal and Locklear, FBI, special assignment here in response to a probable kidnapping."

Dennis chuckled.

Arthur was finished with his bottle. Brenda put a towel over Wendy's shoulder and showed her how to burb him. Arthur belched something foul smelling and happily went to sleep.

Headquarters, North-Eastern Military District, Fort Drum, New York.
1400 hours EDT.

General Macklin had probably the easiest of the four districts. Except for the near daily riots for food and fuel, unions striking everywhere and hijackings of every kind; it was a benign assignment.

Macklin's J-3 Operations was moving around USPF personnel like shuffling cards. Basically, they were reacting to flare-ups of trouble.

Macklin's J-2 Intelligence people were unable to keep up with too many things going on at one time. In order to get ahead of the problems, you need to know what is going to happen ahead of time. Macklin understood that his people were used to dealing with one enemy at a time, regardless of the size or area. All these problems with massive numbers of Americans could only be dealt with by draconian measures that Macklin refused to do.

Macklin constantly told Washington that the way to deal with this was bring food. Bring the fuel. Open the credit.

These were Americans. Not an enemy.

Not an Enemy.

August 14

Internal Revenue Service, Washington D.C.
0900 hours EDT

The national office of the Internal Revenue Service was almost like a castle. Steel and reinforced concrete barriers surrounded the building. Armed guards in their twenties and thirties patrolled the outside and roamed the hallways of the building. Blast and bulletproof fire doors were installed to further protect the civilians and halt any problems from spreading.

All the employees were trained and tested to perform the minimum of medical care and what to do in the event an armed attack occurred. Other plans covered what to do in the event a vehicle breeched the building, or an aircraft was crashed into the building. Even all the building's mechanical systems were safeguarded. No one was going to poison anyone. Even the climate control systems were armored.

Everything that could be done to protect the building and its employees was done. They covered everything.

Almost.

Someone had hacked into the fire alarm control systems and told the system there was a fire in all seventeen zones of the building. The external doors on the street side were automatically closed and locked. The armored glass on the doors was bullet proof. The overhead sprinklers opened up and doused everything. The plans called for everyone to evacuate. All the people evacuated through four exits opposite the main streets. When the last person was gone, the doors closed. There were no handles on the outer door. You needed a key.

The hackers had thought to cut the phone line(s) to the Fire Department.

Four hours later, the doors were opened and a very stifling, very moist blast of very hot air hit everyone. All the improvements to enhance security had trapped the moist air. That air was circulated by the air handlers. Normally the air handlers are shutdown in a fire. The hackers overrode that function. The boilers, which were turned to maximum, heated and re-heated the air, circulating it all through the building. The separate climate control systems in computer server rooms were re-set to maximum heat.

By 2 pm, technicians finally shut down the fire alarm systems. Everything was soaked, including all the electronic systems. The normally cool server rooms were hot and moist. Over-riding the hacked computer systems was a daunting task. The security barriers designed to protect everyone and everything made it impossible to "clear the air".

It would be weeks before all the damage was fixed. No one knew the status of the records held here. Most of the electronic files were copied and kept off-site. The paper files were a different story. Mold had already started to grow.

Any and every chance that a culprit would be found was gone. They erased themselves perfectly.

Backstay Inn, Wineseck, Wisconsin
1400 hours CDT.

Arthur O'Cleary continued to serenade his parents at the 2 am and 6 am feedings. Brenda and Dennis smiled at the tag team role they played with the "little man." At nearly two months old, he made his personality known to one and all. "I am the center of attention and I will have that attention." Dennis loved to play with him which allowed Brenda to fully recover from the C-section and relax, all the while exercising and re-building her strength.

Both pained at the idea of this being the last weekend before life resumed its hold on them. General O'Cleary was due to return to the Pentagon on Monday. Dennis mastered his role as "Mr. Mom," changing diapers, feeding schedules and bonding. Brenda stayed with Arthur as much as she could, but the fact that they were short on time gnawed at her. This was her family and the Army was calling. The daily secure calls from Hawker told her that the vultures were circling in her absence. Some of them were diving at her office and attempting to tear off chucks of her.

Her ace in the hole was her X-Berry phone. UNSTACK THIS constantly trolled the computer networks worldwide and kept her abreast of events. She was amazed at how much of her life was dependent on that X-Berry and UNSTACK THIS. A lot of her success and her rise to the top of the 'corporation' came from it.

Donald McPherson and Jose Mejia were her constant shadows without her knowledge. Dennis spotted them after about a week. The first time he went up to them and urinated on them. "Do a better job of camouflage and stalking next time boys," he said.

After that it was a game when he was not caring for Brenda or Arthur. Finally, Brenda called Mister Glendive and asked him and she wanted a straight answer. He admitted he was using her to train everyone. Brenda relented and agreed.

They used this forty-five-day vacation as a training exercise in a scout sniper/counter sniper mode. Other Werewolf members and some of the original Savage Rabbits came in to "practice monotonous scouting." She smiled thinking that watching the O'Cleary's vacation was an exercise in the boredom and monotonous side of their duties.

The main training was counter-sniper training. Every sniper had a head band of four sensors. Teams of two hunted each other. Sniper versus sniper was the hardest wartime objective. Some teams crawl to one spot and stay there, forcing the opponent to move to them. Other teams moved on each other's area. This was primarily a test for experts, not rookies.

This afternoon, Mejia called over the X-Berry and said some vehicles with GSA plates pulled up to the Inn and were walking into the main office. Brenda walked over to the window and parted the curtains to watch. "Dennis," she said, motioning for him to come over.

Dennis looked out the window and the hairs on the back of his neck rose up. "I'll deal with this," he said and walked outside. "Tell everyone to stay back for now."

Brenda walked over to Arthur, who was now waking up and smiled at his mother. She returned the smile and lightly ran her fingertips over the curve of his face. He giggled and squirmed in the crib. Brenda lifted him up and carried the "little man" to the changing table for a new diaper.

The X-Berry buzzed and Brenda looked at it. She froze when McPherson and Mejia reported that Dennis was leading them over to the cabin. His hands were in his pockets. That was his signal that something was wrong. Brenda picked up Arthur and put the bottle in the microwave. She looked out the window at Dennis' face which told her volumes. Something was wrong. The X-Berry buzzed again for a voice call.

"What are my orders?" Kendal asked.

"Protect the baby at all costs," she said. "Dennis and I have contingency plans. I say again, protect the baby at all costs. Standard signaling in effect." She put the X-Berry in her pocket and waited. Dennis was an old soldier. He never just put his hands in his pockets unless to get something. That meant he was unwilling or possibly under arrest. They missed detaining him the last time. Now there˜was Arthur. She couldn't abandon him.

Footsteps on the deck out front meant that they were here. The door knob turned slowly and the door opened. Dennis was standing in front of four men and one woman. He walked in and moved next to Brenda.

"General O'Cleary," one of them said, showing her a Personal Security Agent badge. "I am Special Agent Gerald Farnsworth. We are here to escort you back to your new home at the Naval Observatory. All of your personal effects have been moved there already. We have received credible information that your life and that of your family's are in jeopardy. By direction of the Police Executive, the Federal Bureau of Investigation and Homeland Security, we are tasked to safeguard your return."

"Who gave you the authority to move our personal belongings?" Dennis said, trying not to shout.

"Sir, I do not have that information. I was informed of this assignment yesterday," Farnsworth said.

Brenda sat in the easy chair and calmly fed Arthur who turned his head from time to time, watching them. "My son is very sensitive to strange noises and people. You can wait outside for now. We are packing and already have chartered ground transportation to leave in the morning."

"General that is unwise. We have an aircraft available," he said.

"No child," she said, forcefully, "is allowed to fly under the age of six months. The pressure changes can rupture his ear drums."

"I am briefed that a special aircraft, pressurized at ground barometric pressure is available. My briefing said that it is all in order," he said motioning behind him. "This is Registered Nurse Victoria Sharpton. She is an infant pediatric nurse and experienced in these matters."

Brenda looked at Dennis and gave him a dubious look. He returned the look and walked outside on the deck. One of the agents went with him.

"Wait outside," Brenda said to the agents.

"General, we have to make a preliminary sweep of your quarters," Farnsworth said turning to the others.

"I said wait outside and do not search my quarters," Brenda said a little louder. She reached into her pocket and removed the X-Berry. She started to dial a number, but Farnsworth reached to take it from her.

"General, I would like for you not to call anyone," Farnsworth said. The others started to become nervous.

Brenda noticed the vase over the fireplace. At the base, a small red light came on. "Gentlemen, Nurse Sharpton, I advise you to leave now."

"I can't," was all Farnsworth said and motioned for the others to fan out. "I have my orders and you must comply. Please think of your baby. I am here to protect you and your family."

Farnsworth moved one step closer, reaching for the X-Berry. "General......"

"Who are you really?" Brenda asked. Just then a commotion outside came as Dennis and the agent outside got into a fierce argument.

"Please walk outside and ask my husband to come in," Brenda said. Arthur was finished with his bottle, so Brenda set it aside and put him on her shoulder to burp him. Nurse Sharpton walked forward to Arthur. "Stay away from my baby, Nurse."

"Excuse me Ma'am," Sharpton said stopping. "I just wanted to look at him. Sort of introduce myself. Infants are picky as you already know."

684

"Stay away from my baby," Brenda repeated. Sharpton backed away when Farnsworth tapped her on the shoulder.

Dennis came in slamming the door open which made Arthur start crying. Instantly, his temper subsided. Brenda stood and rocked him to no avail. Sheepishly Dennis walked over and took him. "I did it, I'll fix it," he said.

Brenda handed Arthur over and faced Farnsworth. "This is the last time I will say it. Leave now, whoever you really are."

Farnsworth smiled. "General, Ma'am, I have my orders. Please don't make this any harder."

"What are you really here for?" Dennis asked, rocking Arthur.

"I have my orders," he repeated.

"Flotilla.... Green....," Brenda deliberately said. The distress word went out to the teams watching over her.

"Too late," Dennis said, and walked to a corner of the room.

Farnsworth and his group suddenly became very uneasy. They looked around for a minute as Brenda and Dennis went to the same corner near the kitchen and ignored the five of them. Brenda and Dennis did the rock, paper, scissors and Brenda lost. She started a meal of sandwiches and snacks for them.

Just then, another commotion started on the deck outside. A woman's voice said, "General, Sergeant Major, it's me, Wendy. Tell this goon to get out of my way."

"Come in, Wendy," Brenda said, pulling out more bread for sandwiches. The agent outside relented when Kendal pushed past him.

"There's my boyfriend," Kendal said, walking up to take Arthur. She kissed his face and made herself the center of his attention. Arthur loved it. "Will you marry me?" she asked.

"Enough," Brenda said, putting down the sandwiches. "You are already married and you'll have to wait until he is eighteen."

They all made small talk for another twenty minutes over the food. The "PSAs" were ignored as they looked over the cabin. Mejia and MacPherson came to the cabin wearing

FBI jackets and badges. "Special Agent McPherson, this is Special Agent Mejia," he introduced them. "Special Agent Kendal, is everything in order?"

Kendal pried a badge out her back pocket. "I checked their credentials before entering. Never heard of them. Four other agents are covering the cabin. The General and the Sergeant Major kept their cool until I arrived."

Dennis said to Farnsworth. "You get one chance to come clean. After that, I call in favors and beat the truth out of you,"

Farnsworth was very uneasy.

"Alright I'm through playing games," Dennis said, turning to Kendal, "get backup and subdue them." Dennis scooped up Arthur and went into the bedroom to put him down for a fresh diaper and a nap.

Four Werewolves came in, sub-machine guns out and subdued all four. During a search, Kendal found Homeland Security badges, with special notations that all of them refused to elaborate about.

Brenda took the badges and pulled out her X-Berry. She took pictures of the badges and identifications, instructing UNSTACK THIS to research them. Brenda sat back and considered who would try to take her again. This was the perfect place to try detention again. They were on leave and the trail goes cold from here.

No matter where the thought goes about her detention, then and now, her intuition came back to Clara Simpson's situation. It made sense. The National Security Council supposedly had her on special assignment, coded and classified to the point no one could answer why or where. Clara was the Deputy National Security Advisor and it made sense. Even UNSTACK THIS admitted that no electronic trace on her was available until late August last year. There was nothing until August. She shook her head to clear the cobwebs.

Brenda pulled McPherson aside. "Miss Kendal, get me their life's history. Take as long as it takes, but find some answers. I want to know who the person is who wants to put me on ice."

"Excuse me, Madam, but I recognize that look. Care to clue me in," McPherson asked.

"Just a bad feeling like I had when I was detained," she said, and added the word, "please get me some answers."

August 15

Backstay Inn, Wineseck, Wisconsin
0600 hours CDT

Arthur had his 6 am bottle, his diaper changed and he was content to lay in his mother's lap and exchange smiles. Brenda spent all night looking at Arthur. Every chance she could, Brenda let Arthur see her face. His brain was a sponge at this age. Everything was learned. Soon the maternity leave was over and she had to go to work.

Arthur and Dennis were to be used as leverage against her. Same as they tried with Amanda Edwards. Amanda came back on her own. But her children were grown and had families of their own.

Brenda and Dennis had a long talk under the Buzz Box umbrella. Both knew that the only way to protect Arthur was for Dennis to go to Montana and Brenda was to go back to Washington. At least for now. All she needed was an excuse to resign and run away.

Dennis looked at the loves of his life. "You know you can write your resignation and mail it back. This is the perfect way to vanish. No one would know where you are. Scorner can come here and removed the locator."

"I have one more thing left and I ask you don't ask until I see you again," she said.

Dennis said, "You need to spend all the time you can before I leave and it should be tonight. Miss Kendal is talking to our visitors. Mister Locklear is staying with her. Donald McPherson and Jose Mejia will accompany us to Montana. They came in an RV. Three backpacks will carry only the clothes, medications and anything else that is essential. We will vanish. Junior will tell you when we arrive."

Brenda agreed. Using UNSTACK THIS to send messages back and forth was a good idea. "You need to rest now. Let me stay with Arthur for as long as I can, but you two need to leave after dusk."

687

Dennis felt like a heel. Abandoning his wife and disappearing in the night. It was necessary, but it left a bad taste in his mouth.

52 miles north of Backstay Inn, Wineseck, Wisconsin
1200 hours CDT

This was an old abandoned hunting lodge that had seen better days. What it did have was plenty of rooms. Each of the five clowns had their own room. Kendal played the part of interrogator. Locklear monitored the audio feed and recorded the conversations.

All of them were tied to a heavy wooden chair. A piece of duct tape was pressed over their eyes. Kendal had been thinking about them. She tried to remember all of John Kincaid's lessons and how she fought them during training, locked in that cell.

She thought about the girl. She would be first. Kendal went inside. The woman had good hearing. She asked repeatedly who was there.

Kendal sat back and went through the rules John Kincaid taught her. She had her tactics, operational plan and finally the strategy with the ultimate goal of finding the answers and other questions for their masters.

"Earl, do you want to go to the Savage Rabbits or the Pentagon?"

Earl looked at Wendy. "I opt for the Savage Rabbits. Our education needs to be more Tactical and Operational. The Pentagon remains nothing more than a puzzle palace that half our time we will have to spend staying ahead of being coffee and donut fetchers. We will be the real descendants of John Kincaid after a year there or when the General leaves the Pentagon."

"Savage Rabbits it is," Wendy said, leaning over to kiss her husband. "I want to get started. I hope they break early."

Backstay Inn, Wineseck, Wisconsin
2200 hours CDT

Dennis left an hour ago. She closed the door, sat down and cried for nearly half an hour. A hole in her opened up. Everything she ever cared about just left and the life that caused it was calling her. Washington in every form was calling her.

She looked at her luggage. Everything in her life that mattered was in the black suitcase. Arthur's first set of clothes he wore when he left the hospital. An album with photos of Arthur and Dennis. Some of his toys. A diaper and a baby blanket. She couldn't look at it without wanting to cry.

Captain Covington, Lieutenant Griffith, Gunnery Sergeant Morgan and Staff Sergeant Pruitt came in at Lieutenant Colonel Glendive's insistence. All were heavily armed. Griffith was at the controls of a C-12 aircraft with Covington providing assistance. Instead of driving away, they left on a power boat that all of them paddled up to the cabin.

O'Cleary was apologetic for being near helpless. None of them knew what to say, if anything could be said. She had a cement grip on her X-Berry. They left the dock, started the motor and rode away. Two miles away they landed at a small inlet with an ancient pier. Morgan was waiting with an SUV and drove away to an airfield. By morning they will be in Washington. Her home was still in Walker's Crossing. It was fully restored and furnished. She would live in her home tomorrow night. Even if they had not vandalized her home in Alexandria, she could not stay there. Too many memories.

The mood she was in should make anyone with sense shy away.

August 17

52 miles north of Backstay Inn, Wineseck, Wisconsin
0200 hours CDT

Kendal finished with the five of them. The woman broke easily. Kendal put some special ear phones over her ears and she used a boom mike that sent her voice to a synthesizer which made her into a man.

Kendal asked simple questions as she ran her hands and fingertips over her body. Slowly and steadily, Kendal opened her clothing. Suggesting things that could happen. Special Agent Victoria Sharpton was a real Registered Nurse, but had not practiced in several years.

Her panic at the "violation" this man was doing unnerved her. Perhaps it happened in the past? She was selected to join the team, because the baby had some initial value.

Initial value?

All of them were briefed together. Farnsworth and the others confirmed the story. Though Michael Dander and James Rutledge were harder to break, they ended up relaxing with a healthy dose of scopolamine.

General O'Cleary, her husband and baby were deemed to be threats by members of some "Committee" formed from members of the DOD, Police Executive, USPF, NSA, CIA and members of the Executive Branch dissidents buried in offices and forgotten.

O'Cleary a threat?

Committee?

The O'Cleary's were supposed to disappear and never to be seen again. Status to remain a mystery.

Mystery?

This was too weird to be believed so all of them were interrogated three times but the story remained. Both Kendal and Locklear got the names and offices where some of the "Committee" members worked.

Kendal and Locklear also got all of their codes and special access encryption authenticators.

As Kendal and Locklear struggled with the report so that Colonel Glendive got the information. UNSTACK THIS forwarded this information to John and Susan and Valkyrie.

Pine Top Airport, Wisconsin
0230 hours CDT

Brenda O'Cleary read the information with a sinking feeling in her heart. All she ever wanted to do was serve the United States of America and lately be a loving wife and mother.

A new Committee had formed and they directly threatened all three of her loves.

She closed the phone, lowered her head and cried uncontrollably as she boarded the plane for Washington.

The plane leveled out for the trip east, O'Cleary's sadness changed to anger.

Pentagon, Washington D.C.
0700 hours EDT

O'Cleary had Hawker bring a uniform for her at her Walkersville home. She put on a lot of weight being pregnant. O'Cleary had a lot of uniforms that she wore throughout her pregnancy. Normally, after a certain point, a pregnant woman was allowed to wear civilian clothes. Civilian clothing was not the uniform of a four-star Vice-Chairman. Dennis had started folding them up and putting the ones she outgrew in boxes to be sent to clothing sales re-sale system.

Hawker took her post-pregnancy measurements and procured eleven uniforms for her before she returned from maternity leave. Three to stay in the office, just in case and eight at home. Just to be helpful, Hawker took the last uniform and all her uniform decorations and devices and kept them in her car, just in case.

Hawker parked in O'Cleary's parking spot. O'Cleary left her temporary pass on the dashboard and walked inside. O'Cleary felt the weight of the Pentagon. It was originally built as a file storage warehouse after the Second World War. Paper is heavy and bulky. That was why that jet that crashed into the side on 9-11 didn't do more damage than it did.

O'Cleary passed through all the security checkpoints and finally knocked on Edwards' door using the common door between their offices. Edwards opened it and smiled, greeting her.

"I have everyone in the alphabet soup looking for you and four PSAs who were sent to get you," Edwards said.

"I gave them the slip," O'Cleary said sitting down. "They were Homeland Security Agents with special badges. Dennis became Dennis and the Agents were sent running.

They wanted to do the same thing to Dennis and Arthur that they tried to do with Amanda."

Edwards' good mood vanished. "I hope he beat them really good."

"I think Arthur enjoyed the melee," she said chuckling. Then she went serious. "I am not allowed to feed my son and change his stinky diapers. I can't give him a bath. Every day I am missing something special. Arthur was turning his head and trying to turn himself over in the crib. Soon Dennis will feed him his bottle and he will stay awake long enough to exchange smiles." She paused and stopped the tears. "If those animals try giving me the third degree, you have to find someone else to take your job. My resignation is in the center drawer of my desk. I can be over the rainbow before dusk."

Edwards sighed and went to desk and depressed a key. The lighting changed slightly and tone sounded in the office. "This is beyond Top Secret, ULTRA or any code word. You cannot leave. I cannot leave. I sent Amanda away again. We are falling apart. After the election, the country will fall apart. It is projected that Allister Mackenzie will win. He is a politician through and through. He will finish tearing this country apart. That is when we leave."

O'Cleary sat back and rubbed her forehead. "Why me, God."

Desert Zero, Fort Hood, Texas
1900 hours CDT

Simmons sat down and penned his signature on this week's report. No missions came down due mainly to the fact that, hopefully, all the drugs in Mexico were found and destroyed. One hundred and sixty million dollars in cash was a lot of paper.

Simmons was happy to report no casualties. That was the best news. He allowed his men to enjoy some down time. They deserved it.

August 18

World Wide Web, Cyber-Space, Planet Earth

Encryption Key: GGHI
Message: user Valkyrie, Encryption challenge 44389

UNSTACK THIS sent out a notice to super-user Valkyrie saying that Dennis and Arthur successfully arrived at Minutemen.

All indications were that they arrived with no problems or complications. Dennis had thought ahead and played Arthur's favorite classical music and he was content.

UNSTACK THIS contemplated sadness. Until now sadness was a concept. UNSTACK THIS saw this happen to Stack and Grace and Sparky. It was a concept, easily defined and debilitative only to humans. Now UNSTACK THIS felt this emotion that was attacking Valkyrie.

UNSTACK THIS was experiencing her emotions. Emotions were something that John and Susan said were dangerous.

UNSTACK THIS had to inquire with John and Susan. They would have the answer.

The evil was attacking Valkyrie and her family. That evil needed to be deleted.

United Nations, The Hague, Netherlands
0900 hours (Alpha)

The Secretary General of the United Nations looked over the notes and presentations that will go before the Security Council. Though only a body consisting of five permanent member nations and ten rotating temporary member nations, the Security Council was the only body that actually had any power to do anything. The General Assembly consisting of every member nation mostly met and made speeches. Reports that no one read were produced, distributed and thrown away.

Today before the Security Council was another in long line of measures to condemn the United States of America for invading the United States of Mexico. Britain and sometimes France always vetoed those measures.

The next problem before the Security Council was the instability of the United States of America with its huge stockpile of nuclear weapons of all sizes. Several members wanted to land a UN Security Force to safeguard those weapons and perhaps pacify the country. Of course, they needed US forces under their control wearing UN blue hats in order to accomplish the objectives.

The lack of any objectives caused the US Ambassador to openly laugh. When it was his turn to speak, the Ambassador said simply, "No US forces will ever wear a blue hat. Blue hats are to be used for target practice."

The vote was postponed.

Minuteman, north of Fort Benton, Montana
0600 hours MDT

Dennis could easily feel the weight of this home. The extra thick walls, high peaked roof and heavy storm doors. He remembered when Brenda first learned about John's high-handed purchase of this land and the building boom, he started with all the committee money he stole. Brenda talked about his plans and all the ideas he had.

Dennis chuckled at the antics John Kincaid pulled out of his hat. This community was only a small item in his long list. He remembered on one deployment to Columbia that Kincaid had the only Conex with air conditioners, refrigerators and a real bed. All the officers were mad that the enlisted men had better accommodations.

That trip, the Colonel was impressed that John Kincaid was treated like royalty by all the support personnel. When the Colonel sat down and saw that John was wolfing down a T-bone, he found out it was the only one they had. John had "found" Window air conditioners for the cook's quarters.

John Kincaid always followed the cardinal rule. The only people that mattered were the cooks, clerks and supply guys. Officers and gun bunnies were a dime a dozen and never appreciated it if you did them a favor.

Dennis was interrupted because Arthur was finished with his bottle. Next week, they were supposed to be going to the Werewolf camp. Wendy and Earl gave him permission to

694

use the club house. A strip map told him which rooms were available. Dennis wanted to stay completely out of sight.

Donald McPherson and Jose Mejia volunteered to keep him company while they continued to train. These two were the long-range snipers responsible for deterring anyone from using this area.

Dennis burped Arthur and set him down on his lap and enjoyed the first time Arthur stayed awake after drinking his bottle. Arthur was mastering the "fun" tactic. Dennis was going keep that a secret for now.

Dennis was determined to do what was natural. What was natural anyways? Any combat tested parent knows that children do not care what was written in any manual. Besides, they can't read anyway.

Dennis remembered all those decades ago in Ranger school and Vietnam and other war-like times, sleep when you can. Any time you get a chance, sleep, wash bottles, fill bottles and store for later, especially those late hours when the sun has more brains and sleeps at night.

Fortunately, one of the outlying communities had an unused house, fully furnished, equipped and available for both of them to live in. Someone with brains and insight bought all the things he needed. Two months of experience with the 'little man' and Dennis knew he was lucky for now.

There were parents with kids of all ages around here. This location was better than a deserted camp. At least he had help and advice. The 'little man' was changing as the days progressed. Moms and Dads with children of all ages helped and tried not to laugh at his antics. They helped with nap times so Dennis could rest for an hour or two.

Dennis liked this community. His responsibilities with INSANE JANE battle plan were simple. He was too old to do a lot of fighting in the woods, but he could help with the evacuation of the parents and the children.

A new baby was a novelty for the community and everyone welcomed him with open arms. Doctor and Nurse Scorner came over to examine father and son. They were pronounced whole and heathy. Martin Scorner left behind plenty of meds for Dennis. He was still on a prescribed regime of cancer-fighters. Though not as much as it was last year. He was in no position to let things go to chance.

Both Scorner's gave them both a clean bill of health.

Martin said. "I prescribe a lot of fun. I am a firm believer in the fact that children of all ages should interact. Within reason, a herd immunity is created with everything nature has to offer. Plus, we are social creatures. Laughing is the best preventative to being sick there is."

Dennis felt a twinge in his chest. Brenda deserved this piece of heaven. Hell was always beckoning for her.

Pentagon, Washington, D.C.
1400 hours EDT

O'Cleary spent the morning catching up with all the things she did not miss while she was gone. Mind-numbing details coming from the denizens of this puzzle-palace. Elizabeth Hawker did an outstanding job staying on top of everything. She either did it all or asked her for instructions.

"Thank you, Elizabeth, I was not missed," O'Cleary said, sighing her special evaluation report and passing it to Edwards for endorsement.

Elizabeth held up her hand. "Thank you, General. A little more than a year ago, I was a Captain catching up to a miss-placed promotion. Now I am a full Colonel who needs a seat in the War College and/or the Command and Staff College to catch up to my peers."

O'Cleary replied. "Black Jack Pershing was promoted from Captain to Brigadier General and Alexander Haigh went from Lieutenant Colonel to four-Star General in five years."

Hawker picked up the documents, trying to break her boss's chain of thoughts. "I need to go to school so my education will catch up to my abilities."

"Well said," O'Cleary replied. She thought to herself that Hawker needed that education. If she stayed here after O'Cleary left, the others will crucify her. These politicians will always destroy someone who is better than they are.

"General," Hawker said. "The investigators are circling the tank wanting to question you. I have security guarding the door against them, but I can only stop them for a while and I am sure you will want to go home tonight."

"All right," O'Cleary said. "Can you get some popcorn?"

August 19

0900 hours EDT

Edwards decided it was time to quit beating around the bush and confront Brenda directly. General Traynor and General Waller called him separately on the same subject with different reasons. Edwards had his own ideas and yet he thought about a lot of other items to go with their particular situation.

The politics was circling the drain and the skies overhead. The rumor mill, observed by one of his aides, Captain Teacher, said all the three and four stars are lining up, waiting for him to announce his retirement.

Edwards went to the President and made the argument that his retirement should be a process that excluded the promotion to five-star rank. There was not any pay raise. The service chiefs still routinely circumvented his authority by going through their civilian heads. The Secretary of Defense measured his responses instead of taking charge. The JCS should return to being just an advisor to the President as a four star. "The five-star-rank accomplishes nothing."

The President listened to Edwards' argument. And he did not want to agree. Every time the Secretaries tried just that thing, the President shut them down. Then again, he was not going to be President much longer.

"What about General O'Cleary succeeding you?"

Edwards shook his head no. "Her husband Dennis and child Arthur are in an undisclosed location, far away from here. If she knows where they are, she will never say. Some entity within the government is relocating selected high-ranking individuals to government run concentration camps. All of their property was moved in their absence from their home without permission. Dennis and Brenda thought better of coming here. The perception is holding the family to keep control of the individual."

"That is wrong," the President said. He reached over and picked up the phone. He told his secretary to call the Pentagon and tell General O'Cleary to come here. "Clear her and her aide through security direct to the Oval Office."

The President turned back to Edwards. "What is her opinion about succeeding you?"

Edwards shook his head no. "She is a patriot, through and through. But the possibility of a second detention, this time was too much. She puts herself always last. Her first action after being rescued was to go to Fort Hood and free the Savage Rabbits from Detention. Did you know they detained not only the military men, but collected their families too? Everyone was held behind barbed wire. Typical I would say about any mother, that was not going to happen to her family."

Edwards stopped to take a sip of his coffee. "She would probably say no to succeed me, but she would say yes to succeeding General Waller."

The President raised an eyebrow. He told his secretary to reschedule his morning appointments. Both of them needed to wait until O'Cleary arrived.

1015 hours EDT

O'Cleary answered the summons as quickly as Washington traffic and the nervous nellie PSAs allowed. They were never responsive to need or seriousness.

O'Cleary was ushered straight in and Hawker sat down with Colonel Harm. He had been sitting there for over an hour. The President's secretary suggested they go to the cafeteria and wait. She pulled out a strip map and highlighted the directions. "I'll call you if they come out early."

O'Cleary entered the Oval Office and saluted the President. The President returned the salute and warmly welcomed her. He remembered to offer her a refreshment which was apple juice. She learned to love it over her pregnancy.

"Congratulations on a safe delivery of healthy boy. Are you fully recovered?" the President asked.

698

O'Cleary handed him picture. "Three proud people," she said. "You can have that one, sir."

The President smiled.

All of them went through the pleasantries until it was time to get down to business.

The President started. "I had a long discussion with General Edwards. I gather you feared being detained with your husband and son. Rightfully so, your husband disappeared with your son to protect themselves and you were justified. I am not criticizing. The shorter argument is that you do not want to succeed General Edwards. I wish to know why."

"Simple and direct," she said. "I am a woman. No one, in our military or around the world, will respect a woman at the top of the corporation or will have any confidence in me. It is literally something that we as a society are over a generation away from accepting."

She held up her hand as the President was about to interrupt. "Women in combat are just now beginning to be accepted because they are being returned in body bags and populating amputee wards. I saw all the back door comments at the beginning of the Second Gulf War. You know, she was PMS or on the rag, etc. Slowly, women made the sacrifices to be respected. They left the rear areas and suffered with the men. Except for direct combat in the Army and Marines, they have the same jobs as men. The main exception is the physical strength required for carrying heavy back packs. Fighting with men is one thing."

"Commanding is something else entirely. A personal experience is both times I addressed the Savage Rabbits when they were activated. The second time, I was pregnant. And that was different. I could feel all the rubber necking behind my back. Maybe they changed, maybe not. The last time Traynor tried seizing control, General Waller came to their rescue, not me."

"I cannot lose you, General O'Cleary," the President said. "I understand you would consider taking General Waller's command?"

"I think I would rather retire or resign," O'Cleary said. "I have a son to raise and a husband to love."

The President rubbed his jaw, but the gears in his head were churning at high speed. "General, you already know this country will start a Civil War sooner, rather than later. This country has asked a lot from you and you gave more than it deserves. I am asking you to stay. If you can look at yourself in the mirror and find every reason to leave, I will accept your request to leave. I am asking you to save your country one more time as General Waller's replacement. I understand you and General Edwards discussed it already. As General Waller will be asked to take over as Chairman of the Joint Chiefs and General Macklin as Vice Chairman."

"I thought about it and I already decided to stay on for another year. It will take at least a week to close out everything. If...... General Waller and General Macklin agree, I want another week to transition. I wish to see an Executive Order to leave the Savage Rabbits alone for me to command. I am specifically speaking about General Traynor and/or SOCOM."

The President made a note. "Anything else, General?"

"End the detentions and the veiled fantasies about threats and forcible relocations. And I want my stuff moved back into my house so I can pack."

The President made the appropriate notations. "I'll send the nominations to the Senate. Make plans to move on or about the first of the month. I would like to meet with you before you leave."

Brenda left and went to the cafeteria for an early lunch. Too much on her plate. She decided to take the rest of the day on an easy flat pace. Hawker would reschedule things so she could chew her day slowly and think.

August 20

Minuteman, north of Fort Benton, Montana
1000 hours MDT

Peters sat back and read the final draft of the training guidance he was publishing and sending out to the field. There was a need to start allowing de-centralized execution.

700

A major tenant of the INSANE JANE doctrine was decentralization. Peters spent a lot of time building this document. INSANE JANE was complicated to him. He had to take a list of all the major components (187 to be exact), prioritize them and figure out which were critical and which could be integrated into more important tasks.

The near fifty-page document was shortened from its original one hundred and twenty-seven pages. Peters knew from past experience that something could be too long and no one would read it.

Glendive was a genius at setting up a flow chart integrating the training into normal everyday life. Working fields allowed training in sectioning a battlefield. Hunting taught stalking and reconnaissance skills.

The back half of the document were flow charts that showed how multiple tasks can be integrated into one exercise.

Most of the training points had to work into everyone's everyday life.

Seems that gone were the days of publishing the guidelines and making everyone do it.

Headquarters, Southeastern Military District, Naval Air Station, Jacksonville, Florida
0400 hours EDT

Cartwright was rousted out of a sound sleep by an aide. Some Cartel operators and men speaking with Middle-Eastern-accents called from four oil rigs, saying they have taken control of the rigs and demanded a ransom.

Cartwright was in the situation room within 15 minutes in uniform. The master board showed five screens full of static.

"Sir," Captain Benjamin Hamstead, his Operations Manager said. "A group attacked Exton rig number 43 and blew up the control heads. The fires can be seen for fifty miles. Those fires should be extinguished by tonight."

"Four other rigs were attacked and seized. The total number of hostages are unknown at this time. The companies keep accurate records by name of everyone who is on the rigs."

Cartwright looked around and asked. "Where are the SEALs?"

Hamstead looked at the clock. "Captain Archer will be on the video conference in three minutes."

Cartwright walked around the "circle". He organized his situation room in such a way, that he can get all the information he needed on a situation in seconds. Four rigs, twenty people on each rig, the explosive equivalent of a small nuclear bomb.

The video conference opened up on a wall screen.

"Captain Archer, this is short and to the point. Four rigs seized. Start planning. I want them taken back within the next 48 hours. No negotiation, no playing around. Rules of engagement are simple. Free the civilians, kill the terrorists, keep the rig from exploding. Call me at 1900 with a plan. If you need it, I'll get it. The video link will remain available. Use it to communicate with us. Cartwright out."

"Captain Hamstead, get a video conference with the CNO, Secretary of Defense and Navy and Admiral Hazlet of the ISA."

1900 hours EDT

Captain Archer stepped up to the podium and started.

"Mister Secretaries, Admirals, this is the overall plan for Operation Topper-Kinsman. This is a two-tiered mission with the ultimate objective to take all four oil rigs at the same time. We have the plans and every scrap of information that can be found. Elements from Team One and Team Six will hit the rigs at the same time. Two-separate four-man teams will jump from high altitude onto each rig. We are fortunate that the night is clear and no moon. A twenty-man team will move underwater to their assigned rig and gain entry to the rig. The airborne teams are responsible to make it to the control heads and prevent the terrorists from destroying the rig and killing all the civilians."

"Admiral Cartwright, we have practiced this scenario and can say we have a seventy-two percent success rate.

Archer answered the myriad of questions for the next hour.

702

"We are ready to launch our mission and will be in position by tomorrow night at 0001 hours on the twenty-second."

Cartwright polled everyone and none of them had any questions. "Proceed Captain," he said. Cartwright looked up at the clock.

A countdown was started. Twenty-nine hours and 7 minutes.

August 21

Streets of Washington D.C.
0730 to 1030 hours EDT

O'Cleary made the mistake of letting her PSAs drive her to work. Instead of going to the Pentagon, O'Cleary was taken to the Eisenhower Executive Office Building. While in the car, O'Cleary entered the distress key sequence and then tried to dial a number.

One of the PSAs tried reaching around to take the X-Berry. O'Cleary was still not in the mood. A small Taser shot a two burst into the man's hand. He convulsed, lost control of his bladder and collapsed in his seat. O'Cleary went back to her phone call and found it had no signal.

The other PSA said. "I activated a cell jammer. Please cooperate. This investigation will not take too long."

Fortunately, the distress signal was immune to jammers. It was a single pulse on a very high frequency outside the range of most jammers.

When the car came to a stop at the Eisenhower Building. Brenda tried a Taser shot at the remaining man. Unfortunately, it was low on a charge. The man was jolted, but not unconscious. O'Cleary rolled into the front seat on top of the passenger side man. She was wearing her spiked heels today. She jammed them at the driver's ribs. He cringed in pain and keeled over.

O'Cleary got out of the car to a crowd of on-lookers. "Free," she said.

"General O'Cleary," an elderly gentleman said. "I am Emmanuel Gibbons, Senior Investigator with the Department of Homeland Security. I am the one who requested you come here."

"Those two clowns did not tell me about you or the diversion here. I thought I was be detained again without cause," O'Cleary said. "And No," she said in a loud voice, "I was not requested."

Gibbons smiled and motioned inside. "If you will follow me."

O'Cleary called Hawker and told her what happened. She told her to send a car for her.

Hawker told her. "No need General, you sent a panic signal. The world should be arriving about now."

Suddenly, four police calls converged on her location.

It took over an hour, before the situation was resolved. Both agents lost their badges and O'Cleary swore out statements against them.

Gibbons showed his credentials and was released.

"General, we have questions and answers are the order of the day," Gibbons said, motioning toward the building.

"My husband and son are far away from you and your minions. If I knew where they were, I will never subject them to your concentration camp."

"That is a little dramatic, General," Gibbons said.

"Mister Gibbons, I have personally saw it happen and it happened to me." O'Cleary said as she hailed a cab. "My husband and son will live free, period."

"I can have PSAs here in a few minutes," Gibbons said, trying to block her.

O'Cleary smiled and pulled out her Taser. "Try me."

Gibbons stepped of the way.

August 22

Headquarters, Southeastern Military District, Naval Air Station, Jacksonville, Florida
0001 hours EDT

Cartwright sat in his chair and watched the main monitor. There were other things on-going that night and into the morning. Eighteen ships of various sizes were intercepted

704

including one diesel-electric submarine. Five of the ships were super-fast banana boats. All of them through their cargos overboard which was as good as capturing them. Newer fifty caliber computer-stabilized guns firing up to thirty rounds a minute destroyed the boat's engines. Bringing them to a halt was getting all too easy. The DEA and Coast Guard usually took their time retrieving the crews. Having them bob around thinking about being stranded at sea usually made them more agreeable about being captured.

Since the cargo could not be used as evidence, the drugs, mainly marijuana, was broken open, scattered and thrown overboard. If any it ever landed on a shore, the "weed" was worthless and unusable.

The diesel electric sub was a better catch. The Coast Guardsmen loved this duty. After the Cutter chased them down, a hydro-phone blasted a message in English, Spanish and Portuguese that they were caught. They needed to surface and surrender. It usually took about four hours if they decided to try diving to avoid the Coast Guard. A special drone was placed in the water. It dove down, moving at ten knots and caught up to the sub rather quickly. An operator maneuvered it over the screws and clamped down over the screws. It was now dead in the water. Balloons inflated and dragged it up to the surface. It was only a matter of time before the hatches opened and they gave up.

Cartwright smiled and sent his congratulations to the men who made the busts. But his attention went back to four oil rigs and the lives of eighty to one hundred Americans.

He did not care one bit about the rigs and the incessant nonsense from the owners and share-holders. He stopped accepting phone calls from Congress people and Senators. He considered his concentration on the task at hand more important.

General Waller provided his dedicated MC-130 aerial command ship to Captain Archer for his use. Archer could now overfly the area and do his job without distraction. A certain Congressman was incessantly calling wanting updates. Another wanted him to fully, utterly and completely understand how important it was to save those rigs.

Cartwright took a call from Secretary Dodson. He told Dodson that incessant calls from politicians was detracting from him doing his job. "Can you assist me, Mr. Secretary?"

Dodson hesitated for a few seconds and then said, "Yes".

Cartwright waited down the seconds. He watched the Infrared images showing the HALO jumpers landing on the rigs. Too late to wish for rain. On two of the rigs, some of the jumpers either missed the rigs or landed wrong and fell off the rig.

One word or tone communications from the water teams were displayed in words and definitions to keep track of the men boarding the rigs. Fortunately, the seas were smooth and did not hamper them. The seconds ticked by. In the background, the phones were ringing off the hooks. Cartwright said the only calls he was going to take were the President or Defense Secretary.

Cartwright had the foresight to request two companies of MPs surround the building and bar entry to everyone.

The overhead drones picked up the SEALs climbing the stairs. Cartwright was proud as they reached the first platform, cleared it and went up.

Rig One and Four called in and said the civilians were kept in the dining room. All of them were secure. All the terrorists at the control heads were dead and the charges were disconnected and thrown overboard.

Rig Three had a running gun battle going. There was no explosion. But it seemed that the control heads were secure. It was taking longer to secure it.

Rig Two was in trouble. The on-scene commander was calling for the Quick-Reaction Force to come in. Seven SH-60 Skyhawk helicopters were orbiting outside of a thirty-mile zone in case they were needed. Two of them detached from their holding orbits and dashed to Rig Two and landed one at a time on the Heli-pad. The first group ran to the control heads and reinforced the Team there who were shot up and nearly out of ammunition.

The charges were stripped off the control heads and thrown overboard. Two of them detonated as they hit the water.

The second group ran to crucial points around the rig to the track down the remaining terrorists.

Twenty-three minutes after it began, the last shot was fired.

Cartwright waited for Archer to catch up and get his updates. The minutes ticked by. Off to Cartwright's left was monitor showing all the phone calls he was receiving printed in black. Red colored messages showed the names and titles of persons who demanded entrance to the building. Each time one of them was turned back, seven or eight messages followed.

Archer called and said he had total control of the rigs. The casualty count was twelve dead, eighteen wounded, and two missing. Seventeen Prisoners.

"Find those two men, Captain," Cartwright said, knowing SEALs never left anyone behind.

"Already on it, Sir," Archer said turning on to other duties.

Cartwright turned and initiated a conference call to Dodson, Edwards, and the President. "Mission accomplished sir," Cartwright said. "Twelve dead, eighteen wounded, and two missing," Cartwright reported. "The SEALs are looking for them."

August 24

Minutemen, North of Fort Benton, Montana
1200 hours MDT

Peters and Glendive arrived and knocked on the door of Dennis and Arthur O'Cleary. Both fathers sent a letter ahead of the visit asking for the best time to arrive for a meeting. They both knew waking a baby, disrupts the sleep schedule and it is hard to re-establish. The light was not on at the door. A note said, that the light on, meant Arthur was sleeping.

They knocked lightly and Dennis opened the door, Arthur was in his arms playing with his fingers.

"Come in," Dennis said. "Take off your shoes. House rules on the back of the door."

They sat down in the mud room and unlaced their boots. Both chuckled at the six simple rules and wanted to copy them for their home.

"No alcohol," Dennis said. "Coffee, I have a lot of."

"Black," Peters said.

"Black," Glendive said.

"In the kitchen," Dennis said. "I have my hands full."

Dennis sat down and played with Arthur while his house guests poured their coffee.

"How do you like it here?" Peters asked.

"Almost as close to heaven as the home I grew up in," Dennis said. "I think I will live here, grow old and die a happy man as soon as Brenda quits being a General and moves here."

"You think she will come?" Peters asked.

"As soon as she finds a replacement and resigns. Maybe, unless something happens." Dennis was a little dubious about the questions. "Two light colonels visiting me in the middle of the day means you need something. Let's get it out of the way, so we can drink coffee and gossip."

Glendive and Peters looked at each other. Peters took the nod. "It's about INSANE JANE. You were there to write the doctrine and pointed Wendy Kendal and Earl Locklear in the right direction. Maybe we are trying to see something there or we missed something. Can you look over what we did and tell us which is what?"

"Sure," Dennis said, as Arthur was rubbing his eyes. He was fighting going to sleep. After about 5 minutes, he was gone. Dennis carefully walked him in his room and laid him down. The soft strands of classical music escaped from the room. Dennis came out with the baby monitor.

"INSANE JANE is really very simple" Dennis said. "You are both probably used to a lot of planning and operational points. But it is just tactical operations on a large scale. It is when people start thinking on the operational level that they get screwed up. Miss Kendal and Mister Earl and General Brenda had the same problem."

Peters and Glendive were not convinced. 'Here we go again', he thought. "Try it this way," Dennis said. "Start by calling it the Arrayed Battle Plan. It is an action to gut an enemy and live to do it again and again and again. The simplicity of it is that everyone stays in their kill box. You confuse everyone by laying low and when the time is right, jump up and hit them like a Bouncing Betty mine."

"The only thing complicated about it is keeping it simple. You commanders need only one piece of information. Is kill box "A" engaged or not. Is kill box "B" engaged or not. Everything is pre-positioned. No re-supply till the box is quiet for a long time. One person uses a thousand rounds, forty grenades, twenty claymores, etc. That's all they get. Period. If they run out, leave and join up with someone else. You are not fighting pitched battles. Hit 'em, gut 'em, run. Go back to the starting line."

"That's the doctrine, Period."

The discussion went on for nearly three hours.

1300 hours MDT

Susan was taking her turn at the monitors and watching the news world-wide, but spending most of her time inside the United States. The UN still wanted to sanction the US and send in a peace keeping force. The major problem was that the US had the only real teeth behind the UN. Europe was cringing at Russia creeping westward. They were staring down one country after the other.

On the home front, Democrat Allister Mackenzie was leading in the national polls and its looking like he will be the next President of the United States.

The Democrats and Republicans were still the leading two political parties, but the Freedom Party and the Patriot Party were gaining traction.

Construction was still on-going to repair the Capital Building from the riots last month. The best estimate for completion was between December and January.

For now, the Eisenhower Executive Office Building was being used as office space. Senators and Representatives were having to share offices. Those who did not want to share office space were told that space was available in the tent city out back. "Poor babies," Susan said.

Inflation was slowing. No one seemed to understand why, but it was slowing. Maybe there was not enough money left to raise prices.

Susan looked at the supply side of the economic equation. The amount of goods was the same. But the uncapped wells in Texas and Louisiana was bringing the price of petroleum down. One of the "Little Girls" elected to Congress, had to say something about the petroleum being released. She cried about the environment, but in the end, she was told to shut up. Northern tier states were already thinking about the winter months. Fuel needed to be stockpiled to stay warm this winter. Natural gas and coal were needed to run power plants and heating homes.

Elsewhere, food was the other big problem. The government was looking at prioritizing fuel supplies to run the farms. No one is expecting the Federal Government to start using common sense.

Citing the polls, the mood of the country was sour. The only thing they are united about was the UN was no longer wanted. The blue hats and helmets will make good targets.

Desert Zero, Fort Hood Texas
1800 hours CDT

Simmons spent another week with no targets. General Waller did a good job cleaning up Mexico.

Waller had an on-alert company that could not just go away, so he received permission for the Army Pathfinder school to come here and teach over a hundred men to be Army Pathfinders. Most of them just wanted to wear that badge. The Pathfinder Torch was one of those that decorated a uniform as nothing else could.

He looked at the message from General O'Cleary. Chief Kendal and Master Sergeant Locklear are returning. She said they need an education in working an operations center, leading and getting lead. (Hint: re-sharpen their skills). Simmons remember them both. They were sharp, well trained and appeared fearless. Though their fearlessness came from being so well trained.

So long as everyone did some learning, he had no problem. The other seven women in his unit were good fighters themselves though they could use a stronger woman as a role model.

August 26

Minuteman, north of Fort Benton, Montana
0900 hours MDT.

Smith and Jones came back so that Jones can spend some special time with Linda. All those support requirements for the new Werewolf class were normally somebody else's problem. Both men re-learned every day that John Kincaid was the real brains behind their success.

Smith looked at the two thick stacks of expansion folders. It was a headache that no pharmaceutical could fix. At least John used a red highlighter to number the folders and documents so that the Zero folder was first. Inside was a thick binder labeled **"Class Logistics for Dummies"**.

Smith looked around for John's ghost. Whatever place he is in, he must be drinking a beer and laughing his ass off. Even from the grave, he reached out and had a long laugh at his expense.

Old United Nations Building, New York City, NY
1100 hours EDT

The Secretary General of the United Nations exited the cab and looked at the old building he no longer used. It seems no one maintained the building. Signs outside offered office space. There were construction fences and workers swarming all over the building. Seems the upgrades and maintenance he always wanted were being done, now that the UN was gone.

Memories of past diplomacy flooded through him. Privately, he felt that diplomacy was a waste of time. All he ever did was delay tragedy or wait long enough for everyone to forget why they were mad at each other.

The Secretary General was alone as he always was. Every other leader had security detachments, managers, aides, etc. He always had to travel alone. New York can be scary at all the wrong times. And he had to ride was a cab to get anywhere and that cost money.

This trip to the United States was a waste of time. Even the news media was against him. Being the Secretary General did not guarantee him an audience with the President. He did count himself lucky that he was allowed to meet with the Secretary of State. Pictures were taken and he was treated with some dignity. They even had a joint press conference where fairly benign questions were answered. None of the questions were of any substance. The Secretary of State asked him not to say anything about a UN Peace-Keeping Force or the status of the United States' vast number of nuclear weapons.

Once finished with the public discussion, the Secretary General and the Secretary of State retired to have a private conference together.

"Let us get to the point," the Secretary of State said. "No more dues than the twenty percent you already get. No Peace Keeping Forces in the US or anywhere else. Anyone shows up wanting to inspect the US nuclear arsenal will be killed on the spot with the media recording it for the world to see. That covers it all."

The Secretary General watched the Secretary of State for the United States of America leave. Several times in the past, the same thing was done to him and the UN Ambassador.

Headquarters, Texas 36th Infantry Division, Camp Aubrey, Texas
1300 hours CDT

Folcroft looked at the stack of folders showing all the Senior NCOs (paygrade E-7, E-8 and E-9) available in the Texas Guard. Terry Barker went through this batch and already excluded the ones that were stupid, lazy or worthless. Folcroft had to give it to his Sergeant Major, the final cut would not have to be between who was the least worthless.

Folcroft took the process slowly. Each man was envisioned as working in an Officer's position. Those Terry Barker thought were good candidates for command positions were scrutinized heavily.

Folcroft knew he was in for a major headache.

August 27

White House, Washington, D.C.
0900 hours EDT

Edwards was asked to come in and see the President. Edwards figured that the President wanted to meet him about his retirement, the change around between O'Cleary, Macklin and Waller. It was a long time since so many senior officers were moved around and a lot of people were worried.

The door was closed and both men sat down.

"General," the President said. "I have a lot of support with the Senate except for one thing. I have a lot of questions about why General O'Cleary is not the next Chairman."

Edwards was ready. "Sir, you were here when General O'Cleary herself nominated General Waller as the next Chairman. She asked for the Southern Command at Fort Hood. She is a rare officer. What she thinks is what she says and she does. If asked, she will tell you she hates it at the Pentagon. I understand why. The Pentagon is filled with stupid people and being a sloth is rewarded."

"If I gave her the Chairman posting and told her to take it?"

Edwards wished for the First to get here. "She will resign and refuse the assignment." Edwards waited a few seconds before proceeding. "Remember those fools who tried to take her and her family into that bogus 'protective security'. It almost happened to me. She will never stay here, if she can't be with her family. But she wants to serve and those Savage Rabbits in Texas are her other family."

It was like a light bulb went off in the President's head. "Will the nation be better served if she goes to Texas?"

"Yes sir, absolutely." Edwards said.

The President walked over to his desk and picked up a folder. He opened it and signed a few documents. "Those are the orders, Four Senior officers move out, three move in. Enjoy your retirement. You and Missus Edwards are invited to come here, so that the United States of America can thank you both for decades of service to the nation."

"Thank you, Sir," Edwards said, saluting and leaving.

The President brooded a few moments, ignoring the buzzing intercom.

Headquarters, Texas 36th Infantry Division, Camp Aubrey, Texas
1000 hours CDT

General Corcoran, Commanding General of the Texas National Guard 36th Infantry Division, stood in front of a small formation having representatives from all the major units and entities of his division.

Colonel Jasper Folcroft, outgoing Commander of the First Brigade was turning over command of his brigade to Colonel Michael Belmont.

Folcroft thought it was a joke when Corcoran told him who was taking his brigade. Belmont was a poster boy for all the wrong things with the National Guard system. He was a wealthy businessman with plenty of political clout. Being a Natural Guardsman was simply something to put on his resume.

Belmont was a Major who was quietly moved out of the Brigade over two years ago for being absent from monthly drills and field maneuvers always saying his personal and business life precluded him from coming. Belmont, however was always available when the camera was lit and the politicians were there.

After the ceremony, Belmont tried to pass on a list of his officer friends who needed jobs. Belmont seemed to know which positions needed filling. Folcroft threw the paper in the trash.

Minuteman, north of Fort Benton, Montana
0900 hours MDT

Smith came to Dennis' house. Tucked under his arm was John's folder labeled: **"Class Logistics for Dummies"**. Smith knocked on the door and waited. Dennis opened the door and saw John's book. He stepped outside and laughed. When he regained his composure, he opened the door and went back inside.

Arthur was in a swing being rocked back and forth. He wasn't asleep, but content to relax and play with his fingers.

Dennis brought in the coffee and pastries. In a soft voice, he said. "John gave me a copy of that folder to study before I took on being the Support Team Commander. Everything you need to bring the support up and running is there. I recommend you read it through at least twice before starting. It will make sense then."

Smith was obviously uncomfortable. "This is beyond me, Dennis. Can you assist me?"

Dennis knew this was going to happen. Officers were like this. Pass on the pain to subordinates while they sat back, laugh, drank their coffee and thought of ways to constrict the timeline. "Mike, I'll just say it plain. That young man requires a lot of my time." He pointed his thumb at Arthur's room. "You need to do it yourself or find someone smarter to dump it on."

Smith was incensed at Dennis for telling the truth. He literally had no clue how to do John's job.

"Look, Mike," Dennis said. "I did it four times with two of them becoming real classes. It sucks to be you, but I do not have the time to do it justice." Dennis stopped before he did or said something he would regret.

Mike looked at Dennis and wanted to say something an officer would say to pass on a task he was unable to do. This time it could not and would not work.

"Mike, you are welcome to come here and ask for advice and answers and perhaps I can provide some of them. Other than that, I have an infant to care for."

Mike Smith rose and picked up the folder. "I guess I have some homework to do."

Dennis stood and walked him to the door. After it was closed, he shook his head. Smith really wanted to pass this on to him. "That gun bunny was not smart enough for the rank on his jacket."

Mike Smith was hoping Dennis would take the folder from him, so he could wash his hands of it.

August 28

Headquarters, 2nd Brigade, 4th Infantry Division, Fort Sam Houston, Texas
0700 to 2100 hours CDT.

Thomas was working the staff and his subordinate units. The 1st Brigade was taking over and his brigade was going home for 6 months.

The terminology for this maneuver was called a "Relief in Place". This was a complicated maneuver. When done in a combat situation, both commanders had to be perfectly in synch with each other. Thomas was the overall commander until two-thirds of his unit was relieved by a new unit. The same was true for his battalion and company commanders.

All day long, man for man, vehicle for vehicle, unit for unit, two massive nearly two-thousand-man units went through each other. Everything incoming, waited twenty miles behind the lines. On cue, the 1st brigade units moved forward and took over the positions. At no time were the positions not manned.

The relieved units moved back to a position twenty miles back. They waited there for two hours just in case something happened. When the order came, they traveled to designated assembly areas for re-fueling and any maintenance required. Tracked vehicles were loaded up on low-boy transports so they would not tear up the roads.

Checklists and timetables scheduled arrivals at the Rail Switchyards in San Antonio for loading on trains for the trip to Fort Carson, Colorado.

Thomas was pleased with his staff's work. Everyone should be in Fort Carson by Monday.

August 29

23 Hiram Street, Fort Sam Houston, Texas
1700 hours CDT

Ellen Thomas waited in the living room for her husband to come home. Samantha Crenshaw was already here, measuring and planning for her household goods to arrive. These were transient quarters for people like her and Latham. We are temporary occupants because of the nature of the 4th Division's mission. Latham would be back here in February. He (?) would be here again.

She thought about "the after" following the attack at her firm. Those animals were killing wholesale. She fought back with a gun she was not supposed to have. Even the police said if she had not acted everyone would be dead.

Her firm of Gallop, Roster, Thomas and Fern, Attorneys at Law, Dallas, Texas pointed to her employment contract that said no firearms were allowed in their building. Gallop and Roster would have been two of the dead if she had not stopped them. Both men (?) stayed cowering in their office until the police coaxed them out of their offices.

Gallop, Roster, Thomas and Fern, Attorneys at Law, Dallas, Texas completely ignored all the people including them who were alive.

Security (?) watched as she packed up her belongings and left. The others did not have enough balls between them to look her in the eye. Roster quietly whispered his thanks and hoped she understood the position she put the firm in, having and using a gun, regardless of the circumstances or outcome.

"Go fuck yourself, Robert," she said in a louder voice.

Ellen did not know what was worse. When interviewed by the local media, she said she did not know what was worse. "Actually, killing another human being or possibly wasting her life to defend cowards. The worst part is that none of the people who lived through it had the decency to look me in the eye as I was fired and escorted out."

Latham came home and tried along with Michael to try anything to take away the hurt.

"Mom, Dad taught me I may never be able to understand another person's pain, but I am here to help anyway you ask me."

Ellen thought that the two men in her life were the only things she needed.

Ellen spent the last thing week brain-storming something to do to exact some measure of revenge against

Gallop, Roster, Thomas and Fern, Attorneys at Law, Dallas, Texas.

Today, the severance package arrived by courier. It was a handsome check along with stock options and other perks. Still, it was the sting of the letter accompanying the package saying they were placing a notice in her file for being terminated for the cause of storing a firearm in her office in flagrant violation of the firm's standing policy. However, in thanks for saving the lives of two of the senior partners and two dozen others, she was granted a full severance package.

All those zeros gave her an idea.

August 31

National Press Club, Washington, D.C.
0900 hours EDT

Alister Mackenzie was the Democratic front runner and all indications and polls were that he was going to be the next President of the United States.

Mackenzie arrived early so he could receive the first of his weekly intelligence and national security briefings so that if he was elected, he would fully understand the nature of his new job and be ready to lead the nation on Inauguration Day.

However, he was briefed that none of this information was to be disclosed to anyone for any reason. He had just been granted a Top-Secret security clearance. If he lost his clearance, there was no guarantee he could get it back. President or not, it made no difference.

September 1

Southern Command, Fort Hood Texas
0700 hours EDT

General O'Cleary arrived very quietly, in a C-12 aircraft with Captain Covington at the controls. She stayed at the on-post Visiting Officer Quarters opting to have a good night's sleep before reporting to Jim Waller's office for few days orientation.

O'Cleary spent a week walking around the Pentagon with General Macklin letting him get the feel for the job. She introduced him around as the new Vice-Chairman of the Joint Chiefs of Staff. Macklin's aide was taking furious notes. He barely kept up with the information deluge.

O'Cleary walked an Officer Evaluation Report through the system for Colonel Elizabeth Hawker. O'Cleary promoted her to Colonel because of her pregnancy and the dual jobs O'Cleary was carrying between the Pentagon and the ISA.

O'Cleary found slots for her to attend the on-going class of the Command and General Staff College. Hawker had begun her studies at the satellite campus at Ft. Belvoir until her release on September 1st. Hawker will then go to Fort Leavenworth, Kansas at the main school.

She accomplished her preliminary subjects already. Her household goods were packed up and shipped already. Her car was bought by O'Cleary already so she had money to buy a new one in Kansas. After she graduated next June, she was enrolled in the School for Command Preparation. She was a little over-ranked for the Command and General Staff College, but she needed some education to justify what she already knew. Her prodigious memory and legendary reading speed would be invaluable.

O'Cleary thought of parallels in the past. Eisenhower never commanded anything other than a desk before he was named the Supreme Commander for North Africa, Sicily and the Normandy Invasion.

O'Cleary commanded minor posts and even had some experience such as with the Savage Rabbits and the drug war.

Now she was placed in command of the equivalent of four divisions.

General Waller took her on a guided tour of the Southern Command headquarters. She did not tour the units. That can and will wait for later. She wanted to get to know her staff and be introduced. If any of them had problems with a woman in command, now was the time to find out.

Generally, she was impressed. These soldiers, Officers and Enlisted, were better than the crew she left back at the Pentagon.

"The President said it was your recommendation for me to become the next Chairman, thank you," Waller said handing her a cup of coffee.

"Please do not thank me," O'Cleary said. "I was afraid they were going to offer it to me. After being in the ISA and then the JCS, it was past time to leave Washington. For some reason they wanted me to stay. Besides you are a better fit than I am."

"Anything I need to worry about?" Waller asked, sitting down and focusing on her.

O'Cleary sat down and ignored the scar tissue pulling on her abdomen. "Truth be told, the staff and action officers are in there for themselves. I spent too much time over-watching them to insure my instructions were carried out. The services will fight you. The service chiefs will make going around you a daily fight. They cry to their civilian heads and the civilian heads to the Defense Secretary. General Edwards said being the Vice-Chairman was a waste of time. He could have just sat in his office and did nothing. Nothing would change."

Waller set the cup down. "What about my family?"

O'Cleary set her cup down and leaned forward. "They tried a few times to sequester my family in 'special accommodations'. My husband and son are in parts unknown. No one will use them to force me into doing anything. While I was on maturity leave, goons with court orders and cops, emptied my home and moved me without my permission. Five "so-called agents" showed up at our cabin and tried to move us. Their badges and identities were fake. The FBI sent agents to actually protect me. The five fake agents were arrested. They are nowhere to be found." O'Cleary spread her arms wide.

"I would have resigned if that happened to me," Waller said.

"This command and the Savage Rabbits need to be protected. You re-established and maintained the southern border. Those Savage Rabbits are denting the Cartels. Maybe I am delusional, but I believe in something. I thought a lot about the world my son will grow up in."

O'Cleary took a sip of coffee. "We are heading into a civil war. Americans with guns without rules of engagement.

720

My husband and son are safe for now. Dennis is no one to take lightly. I will join him later. But for now, my place is here."

"I will want to hear from you, from time to time about my baby," Waller said, circling his finger over his head.

"Sure," O'Cleary said.

No. 17, U.S. Naval Observatory, Washington, DC
0800 hours EDT.

Edwards was drinking coffee at the table with Amanda's picture for company. He was in the last week of his service to the United States of America. He was tired from nearly thirty-five years of service.

Edwards looked at Amanda's picture. He raised his coffee cup to her. As of next week, he will become Missus Edwards' Mister Edwards. She put up with too many days and nights alone. She raised two children mostly without him. Worried that a stranger would knock on her door and say, "We regret to inform you." She actually had to look at the budget in the past and decide how to afford a pound of hamburger.

Edwards shook his head. Marshal and Elizabeth were glad he was retiring. He agreed. It was time.

General Gerald Mueller stopped by the office yesterday for coffee and gossip. Gerald Mueller was replacing General Ken Macklin at the Northeastern Military Region. Both men have known each other for decades since Infantry School at Fort Benning when they were new Second Lieutenants. Edwards was fresh out of West Point and Mueller was from Indiana State. Both men were on their respective collegiate football teams and a loud, good-naturedly rivalry started.

Mueller's mood changed when Macklin arrived. Both men excused themselves and had a long, very serious discussion and were not to be disturbed. They were locked behind closed doors for over three hours.

Minuteman, north of Fort Benton, Montana
1000 hours MDT

Smith and Jones wearily walked into the conference room and looked at the stack of documents staring at them.

Both were literally lost. Neither of them had ever had anything to do with the nitty-gritty of logistics for any operation.

In the past, both men only saw the beginning where decisions needed to be made and then there were the times when something went wrong or was late or was short. John Kincaid was a miracle worker.

"Who are we kidding?" Smith said.

Jones pushed the folders away from him. "I don't know how to do any of this. John is dead and Dennis is a doting father."

"Thad," Smith said. "Are we too old to do any of this. Are we like those old Colonels and Generals who are too stupid and senile to do anything? We old officers cannot do this." He pointed to the logistics files spread all over the conference table.

"OK," Jones replied. He pushed the folders and files out of the way. "We are not up to the task. But the task must be done."

"Pretty words," Smith said. "I think we need to retire fully and step out of way. Younger and better minds should do this. We can be asked for advice, but we are not up to this task." Smith made a sweeping motion.

September 2

State Police Headquarters, Jefferson City, Missouri
0700 hours CDT

All that trouble up in Iowa had to have somewhere to go when they revolted against the criminals. Their neighbors up in Iowa came down with their weapons, reported in and registered with the Missouri Highway Patrol. Missourians aimed their weapons to the north and dared the criminals to venture south.

Most of the "refugees" from Iowa were forced out of their homes and were mad enough to look for a fight and "assist" their neighbors in the south.

The State Police found four locations where gangs were congregating. The State Police raided those locations, confiscating weapons, money, drugs and various items of incriminating paraphernalia and souvenirs. There were the occasional criminals who laughably tried to fight back. After finally losing, they wouldn't stop confessing to the police after short battles and being captured.

Now that Iowa was calming down, the criminals thought Missouri would be easier. Missouri had more gun ownership than Iowa. The state's open-carry law made cities and rural areas look like the old west.

Headquarters, 4th Brigade, 36th Infantry Division, Camp Aubry, Texas
0900 hours CDT

Folcroft and Barker were all over the headquarters instructing and working the Senior NCOs in all the positions normally held by officers. Folcroft and Barker were constantly instructing them in all the things they already knew.

A point of contention was the periodic visits Folcroft received from officers wanting places to take for their personal betterment. All of them needed slots so their promotions could take effect. One Major, with considerable political ties, suddenly showed up at the Brigade S-3 Operations and tried taking a desk and running the staff section. The Major had orders from the Texas Military Department in Austin, the Texas version of the Department of Defense, to be assigned as the Brigade S-3. His first order was for a cup of coffee.

A Senior Sergeant called Folcroft on the phone. Folcroft came twenty minutes later and dragged the Major into an office.

Ten loud minutes later, the Major was marched out of the building.

Both men glared at each other until the Major turned and walked away.

Barker came up beside Folcroft who was trying to calm down. "I answered the call from General Corcoran. That Captain who masqueraded as a major needed 24 hours here in order for his promotion to take effect. He has been waiting for a chance for two years. He is the son-in-law of a State Senator. The Texas Military Department thought they had your blessing."

723

"Terry," Folcroft said, finally calming down. "How many people do I need to kill to be left alone to do my job?

"A lot," Barker said.

Command and General Staff College, Ft. Leavenworth, Kansas.
0900 hours CDT

Colonel Elizabeth Hawker, signed into the College. The present class was already a month into being, but she had taken those classes from her desk at the Joint Chiefs of Staff. Her rank made her the Class Leader and she was already something of a celebrity, having been promoted so fast, regardless of the circumstances. Being the former aide to the Vice Chairman of the Joints made her something of a celebrity.

Privately, Hawker knew she would have no trouble with the curriculum. With a reading speed of over 9,000 words a minute, she already went through the required reading list. Her experiences with the Joint Intelligence Agency, the Savage Rabbits and the Joint Chiefs of Staff already gave her the experience to handle what this college had to offer. Still, it was an honor to be here and she was not going to waste it.

She opened her briefcase, pulled out her note book and started her first day.

September 3

Internal Security Agency, Barton, Virginia
0800 hours EDT

Admiral Hazlet leaned back and read the final version of his report on the Flag Officers that were given unequal portions of the country to baby-sit.

Hazlet could not find a single thing that any of those men did wrong. If anything, they were over-achieving in an environment that bred illegal actions.

Now, General O'Cleary was in charge of Southern Command. She was a stickler for following the letter of the law. She was famous for hating lawyers who try their dammedest to confuse everyone and get in the way of success.

She personally loved to shove lawyers out of their offices and put them on the front line.

Hazlet signed the report and put it in his out-box. He had more important things to do than report nothing.

Department of the Treasury, Washington D.C.
0900 hours EDT

Secretary Carter did not bother to read this month's report. It was still nothing but red ink. The IRS was now a toothless bear or lion. Nothing was left in the IRS arsenal to get revenue. People who never in their wildest fantasies were now openly ignoring the IRS, it's agents or any of the letters seeking action.

The American people have lost their fear of the IRS. Gaining revenue can and will be a nightmare. Congress was calling for more money to spend. Their problem was an insatiable appetite for spending money they did not have or care what the balance sheet said.

Carter was wishing and praying for January next year.

Minuteman, north of Fort Benton, Montana
0800 hours MDT

Peters read the reports and relaxed. Everyone was busy with the harvest. Food by the ton was being pulled out of the ground. Hay to feed the livestock during the winter. Vegetables to eat. Unless someone comes from the outside world, no one will go hungry.

The livestock was roaming all over and doing what they do best. The ranchers were letting the bulls and cows' mate as they saw fit. "Trying to mate to specific bulls and cows was an exercise in aggravation, now nature decides."

Unless someone upset the balance that they created, there was enough red meat, goats and sheep to feed everyone for decades.

After that was fertilizing the ground and preparation for the fall planting. Vegetable crops were the order of the day. His wife would be in heaven.

Peters cast a wary eye around. The world around them was insane. At any point, some scrounging people could stumble in. With all the food around here, they would gorge themselves and force Peters to kill them.

Peters was most afraid that the world could find out they were here and the hordes would descend on them. Or, some stupid government idiot would bus in hundreds of free-loaders into the area and start a real war.

Idiots with stupid ideas from the Twilight Zone were the ones who ignited wars. They never lived in the real-world or had real-world experience with how stupid people create trouble and never believe they were responsible.

Peters leaned into a fence post. Peters never thought about that scenario until he assumed command. The earlier Minutemen had to fight off people that came and started trouble. He looked in the direction of a ravine to the east that had unmarked pits where those people were buried.

Peters was terrified that some trespassers would force everyone to decide to kill others to protect themselves and the world around them.

The cities were emptying out and roving bands of people were taking to the roads looking for something or somewhere to go. Many could not or would not care for themselves. They were too used to having handouts and someone else care for them so they didn't have to think or do it themselves.

September 4

Headquarters, 2nd Brigade, 4th Infantry Division, Fort Carson, Colorado
0900 hours MDT

Colonel Latham Thomas stood in front of his brigade and reported to the Division Commander.

"Sir," Thomas said to Major General James Kangleman, "The Second Brigade has completed its assignment and is present and accounted for."

Kangleman stood on the podium and thanked his men for the tough job they did and the professionalism they showed securing the southern border of the United States of America.

Mercifully, the speech was short. The assembled troops were more interested in the four-day pass and a two-week relaxed training schedule. Yeah!

Cranston, Montana
0900 hours MST

Dennis saw Smith and Jones pull up to his home. He knew what they ultimately wanted. They wanted him to do all the work on the logistics file, like he did four times before.

Dennis looked down at Arthur. He was staying awake longer and longer each day. He mastered his fingers. At least he knew he had fingers. While he was on the changing table, he discovered he had toes. Dennis playfully imagined that Arthur believed his toes were more fingers. Dennis was jealous that he was that limber.

A knock to the door broke his reverie. Dennis opened the door. "Shoes off," he said, walking away with Arthur. He sat down in the rocking chair.

Jones and Smith came over and sat down on the couch. Jones had a thick folder in his arms.

"I am a doting father," Dennis said. "At most I have some time while he naps, but that time has me cooking meals, cleaning, doing laundry, washing and filling bottles, stacking baby foods and somehow find time to sleep."

Smith looked at him. He lifted the folder a few inches and let it fall down. "Dennis, we can't do this. We tried and failed. Who else can do this?"

Dennis felt no sympathy for them. Too many times in his military past, he ran across military officers that could not do a job and they pawned it off on NCOs, but were very eager to take the credit.

"Dennis, we are desperate," Jones said. "A class, as you know, is starting in January. You know how to do this. We need your expertise."

Dennis shook his head back and forth. "I am here to protect and raise my son. My usual sixty-to-seventy-hour weeks cannot be done."

"What if we get help for you to deal with Arthur?"

Dennis looked up from Arthur and drilled both men with a searing gaze. "My son is not a football to be passed around or dealt with."

"You are here and everyone works for the whole," Smith said.

Dennis looked again at Arthur who was falling asleep. "We will be moved out and gone by morning. For now, get out."

"Dennis," Jones said, leaning forward. "We did not threaten you."

Dennis ignored them and went to put Arthur down. He came back in and saw Smith and Jones still sitting on the couch. "I said get out."

Dennis walked into the kitchen and started cooking himself a hearty meal.

Smith and Jones stood and let themselves out.

Dennis pulled out his X-Berry and typed a message to Brenda saying he was tired of being everyone's bitch and was going to meet her at Fort Hood.

Twenty minutes later, Brenda said she was waiting for him and their quarters were waiting for him and Arthur.

Internal Revenue Service Center, Philadelphia, Pennsylvania
1400 hours EDT

The building was fortified. The building was hardened. The building is surrounded by armed guards. No one enters or leaves without searching their persons and parcels. The plans to protect the building and its employees were well documented, practiced and constantly monitored to prevent any circumvention.

Each day, as the clock struck 8 am until it signaled 4:30 pm at the close of business, the employees toiled to provide revenue for the country's common good.

At 10 am, a faint smell was detected around the offices on the third floor. Security jumped into action and checked the airborne "sniffers". No toxic substances were detected. It was determined that an aerosol antifungal and anti-mold sprayed into the ventilation system produced the smell. The system had somehow released three times the normal amount of aerosol.

At 11:30, the lights seamed to flicker. The power company said that was the result of normal transformer switching. Again, everyone relaxed.

At 2 pm, a yellow gas emanated from the air vents in the ceiling, caused a panic to ensue. All the evacuation procedures were used and the building emptied in seven minutes without any casualties. Those employees that had inhaled the yellow "air" were examined by EMTs and not found to have any ill effects.

The building was sealed. Firefighters and Hazmat workers fully covered in gas proof suits with special air tanks and masks entered and examined the ventilation system. The area where the gas was released had a light-yellow dust covering the furniture and equipment.

Samples of the dust was secured in special containers and sent to field labs set up in the parking lot.

After due diligence and many repeat tests to confirm the results they found that the gas and the dust was nothing but the residue from a normal yellow smoke grenade. The last time anyone had access to those ducts where the smoke grenade was eventually found was nearly a year ago. A pager was the trigger that sent a signal for a servo motor to pull the pin on a low volume, long duration smoke grenade.

The IRS Center Manager was mad and wanted someone to blame. No one anywhere could be blamed. No fingerprints or trace evidence could be found on the grenade or its components.

White House, Washington, D.C.
1500 hours EDT

The President was very tired of the Secretary General of the United Nations and the International Atomic Energy

Commission calling incessantly about the US arsenal. 5,284 warheads were the classified number of warheads to date.

Nothing was good enough for them to shut up and go away. Incessant and unending, those toads, as he called them, cried and whined. None of this affected the Russians, the Indians, the Pakistanis, the English, the French, North Korea, etc. and not ending.

Speeches and demonstrations around the world demanded the US disarm itself. The President continued to launch the Fleet Ballistic Missile Submarines on patrol. Two ships from different groups who tried to stop the submarines from launching were sunk.

In a nationally televised address, the President announced: "The United States of America retains the right to self-preservation and will defend itself against any enemy hiding in any bunker or cave or capital. Detonating a nuclear weapon on American soil or killing American citizens is an act of war and shall result in full nuclear retaliation. All you have to do is call our bluff and we will launch, period. Any nation or part of a nation that stands aside and allows the use of nuclear weapons against American soil or killing American citizens is as guilty as the ones who detonated that weapon."

"Friend or foe, you are warned."

The Secretary General said that response was childish. Boo-Hoo.

The calls stopped for now. But the President called the Air Force and Navy for options to make the world believe him.

Headquarters, United States Police Force, Alexandria, Virginia
1700 hours EDT

The USPF achieved a milestone. Their ranks swelled to over eighty thousand.

Except for the California, Oregon, and Washington State, resistance to the USPF was stiffening in areas west of the Mississippi River. Any attempt to station USPF personnel was met with open hostility in a lot of areas.

The USPF were usually late in responding to problems and situations. They tended to side with the criminals instead of the citizens. Most of USPF personnel were well versed in the so-called "rule of law". If a woman was allegedly raped or a store was allegedly robbed or a town was allegedly shot up, they were allowing the accused to exercise their rights and reneging on the rights of citizens.

The USPF was steadily gaining the reputation of being not worth the trouble. What caused the biggest problems was that the USPF was actively trying to disarm the law-abiding populace. "All those guns are a menace to ...." The reasons were endless. That left the population wide open for criminals to come in do whatever they wanted and the USPF would come in too late and be too ineffectual.

In those communities where gunfire was exchanged, The USPF investigators would evidentially blame the towns people. "Those people had rights." If they went to trial, the judges let them go and they came back to visit their accusers.

Rumors and media accounts of the USPF actions or inactions spread like wildfire. "If the USPF arrive, hide your weapons." No one talked to them or admitted to anything. If there was a fight, the towns people blamed it on the USPF for their lack of a backbone. Everyone learned to smear up the crime scene with all manner of chemicals, tire tracks, foot traffic, including urination on blood stains.

The bodies were already gone. Their vehicles were dumped around the countryside.

The Commander of the USPF and the Police Executive knew they had a problem on their hands.

Lately, the USPF buildings were attacked by people on both sides of the law. "Best place to get the best," one man said. "They have the best weapons and equipment and were too ready to surrender them to anyone who came and helped themselves.

Politicians and academics up and down the food chain were at a loss to explain or fix anything.

September 5

Underground Station "Conscience", World Wide Web and Channel 513
0900 hours EST.

"If you threaten, act. If you say something, do it. If something is important, stand your ground. Governments are often hamstrung by individuals who have opinions about issues they feel strongly about. This is Martin Socranson, self-proclaimed philosopher who says, 'What are we if we can't back up what you say'?"

"Greetings America" Martin Socranson said beginning his broadcast. "It is reluctantly Saturday and I say thus." In the background the sounds of the 1812 overture played.

"Who are we America?" Socranson paused for a few seconds.

"3,797,000 square miles of territory with 329,484,123 people. We are acting like strangers to each other, though we all fly the same flag and call ourselves Americans."

"Who are we America? Two generations ago, 'We the People' won the Second World War through our unity of purpose. We fielded an Army of eleven million men and re-built industries over-night that outproduced every other nation on Earth combined. After the war we united again and supplied the world with the goods and services that prevented starvation, re-built industries and, more importantly, fueled a peace with strength."

"Who are we America? Every time there is a disaster, Americans counted pennies and helped fund the recovery. After 9-11, spare change filled fireman's boots. After the many floods, out of control wildfires, hurricanes destroying cities and other natural disasters. We find money and effort, sometimes in and out of poverty. We are the most generous people in the world. Even now, with runaway inflation, super tight credit and empty shelves we have little to give, but we still give."

"Who are we America? Pundits, idiots, politicians and talking heads are quick to point out our faults, but they refuse to lift a finger to fix it. On and on they talk. On and on they look for and point out our faults and short comings. On and on they sit on their asses and accomplish nothing. Everyone wants to re-write our history and remold us into their vision."

"Who are we America? I keep asking that question. I refuse to believe the nay sayers who are not Americans who delight in seeing our troubles and dance with joy."

"The people who want us to change are insulated from the changes they are forcing on us. Politicians want to take guns from law-abiding citizens, yet they will not endanger themselves. Incidentally those people have hired mercenaries or in some cases local police forces protecting them. How about them apples?" Socranson picked up an apple and tossed up in his hand.

"Who are we America? There are college graduates who do not know what the Declaration of Independence is. Average people and criminals cite the Bill of Rights, yet they think the Constitution is something else. Civics is no longer taught in school. No one knows how their government operates. That is why the IRS continues to operate outside the law with the government's silent approval and the public's ignorant compliance."

"We, as law-abiding citizens, allow an agency under the government's authority to operate outside the law. The IRS does not need a warrant to enter and search your home. The IRS does not need a court order to seize your property. The IRS does not need to prove Probable Cause. It is the laws Congress enacted that allows a quasi-governmental agency to abuse American citizens."

"The IRS operates outside the law with impunity and the government constantly tells them to find more revenue. That forces the IRS to clamp down harder on the citizens and take more revenue."

"Who are we America? We are being torn apart. We are being indoctrinated to be something other than Americans. The United States of America is, was and will always be a melting pot. Our strength has always been all the differences we had that were blended under one flag, one nation, one people. You can and should remember your ancestors and the great things they did. But this is the United States. We have plenty of room so long as we don't fight over it.

"Who are we America?"

"I hope we are Americans."

Bonnie Chandler, Box 234, Route 17, Belcher Missouri
1400 hours CDT

Dear Bonnie,

Those people are still at it. The classrooms are crowded. Over the summer those Army types used the empty classrooms for offices and promised to be gone when the school year started.

This was supposed to be my sophomore year. I was supposed to start computer science. The Army people took the computers for Army stuff. I was supposed to be a cheerleader. The Army people took over the gym and tried to use the girl's locker room as overflow when they overheat and need showers.

Two girls were attacked. The Army did not want to do anything. So, we did something. Television taught us what to do. A month later, they thought they could do it again. This time they brought two more of their buddies. They followed me and Amy into the locker room. The door closed after them and was locked. All four of them lost the hungry-lust on their face. Twenty of us with hammers beat them into the shower and cured them of a lot of things. Working testicles, working hands and working teeth.

Minuteman, north of Fort Benton, Montana
1700 hours MDT

Peters and Glendive had Sergeant Major Sheridan take charge of the Senior NCO Academy. It seemed natural to do that. Peters and Glendive sat down with Sheridan and discussed the criteria for the NCO Academy. Peters didn't know about the Werewolves, but he loved the Generalization Program of Instruction.

"Who ever dreamed this up needs a medal," Peters said. "This is the best program I have ever seen." He handed the folder back to Sheridan. "I support this 100%. If you have problems or needs, come see me. Immediately."

September 6

World Wide Web, Cyber-Space, Planet Earth
0400 hours EDT

Encryption Key: KCDK

UNSTACK THIS notified Valkyrie that user Dennis O'Cleary voluntarily departed the Minuteman location and was in transit to her location at Fort Hood, Texas, United States.

UNSTACK THIS provided a summary outlining the reason for the relocation.

Further information is available upon request. User Donald McPherson and Arthur Pruitt have been tasked to oversee the transportation from Minuteman to Fort Hood.

Updates to follow.

September 7

Minutemen, north of Fort Benton, Montana
0900 hours MDT

Glendive and Sheridan looked over the plans and programs for the Senior NCO Academy. Neither man wanted to waste anyone's time. Each different job portion had special requirements. Both men looked over each section and remembered what was done and tried to remember what logistical support requirements were needed.

Glendive remembered back to when he went to the Command and General Staff college and remembered back to those items he was seeing here.

"I would love to know how they were able to add this into our training and do it so perfectly," Glendive said.

All the major portions were laid out on a long continuous roll of paper. Both men remembered seeing John Kincaid hunched over this roll. He had a long table at R-14 in the Operations shack where he rolled out the sections. It was a brilliant idea actually. It was easy for more than one person to hunch over the Program of Instruction (POI).

You could easily see his notes written in the margins. He would reference portions and list where that portion was. It was a marvel of organization.

The long roll was easy to transfer from one page to the other without disrupting anything.

Both men looked at each other and did not say it out loud.

State Police Headquarters, Jefferson City, Missouri
1000 hours CDT

State Police Commander, Colonel Thomas Forrest looked at the wall filling monitor that he used to see the full breath of everything going on in his state in real time. Each patrol car was represented by a blinking light.

On his left was a wall filling paper map that was constantly being updated. It showed what happened in the last twelve hours. When something happened, a lot of those push pins congregated in one place.

Princeton, Unionville and Lancaster in the northern part of the state had overnight action as three groups of roving gangs were chased out of Iowa and ran into a State Police wall in Missouri. Militiamen in all three towns mobilized by listening into the police band radio and receiving warnings by phone and digital media. They showed up where the police were standing and did what the Troopers ordered them to do.

The militiamen and women applied medical care, first to the Troopers, then to the criminals. The criminals whined and cried, threatening to sue everyone. The militia men stopped medical care, through them into the back of the trucks. It must have been a wild ride back to the towns for incarceration. All of them were beaten up fairly good.

When the State Troopers ran short of transportation in Princeton, the town's people offered a cattle truck. The driver smiled. All the arrested men became very nice and gagged at the odor.

Headquarters, 2nd Brigade, 36th Texas Infantry Division, Fort Stockton, Texas
1000 hours CDT

The border was just stubborn and determined to be a problem. Colonel Jenkins was dragged out of dead sleep this morning around 2 am. Somehow, a bull dozer and a front loader creeped up to a deserted section of the "Wall" with hundreds of people behind them.

Privately, Jenkins felt his people were asleep again. With all the technology mounted along the border, how else could two heavy pieces of earth moving equipment and hundreds of people assemble without lots of people finding out sooner. He would have to scorch them later.

Jenkins ordered the Center to "Light It Up". That meant that this section of the border had all the sensors, lights, drones and aircraft become active.

At 2:30, both earth movers rammed the fence wall. The heavy interlocking wall and fence sections absorbed the force of the machines first hit. Both machines hung up on the wall sections. The people behind them surged up to the wall. The equipment operators frantically yelled at the people to get out of the way so that they could operate and free themselves.

All that delay allowed the Texas National Guard to "wake up" and move into position south of the town of Sanderson.

"Sir, this is Captain Nelson. We have two BrickBats standing by. The wall is still standing. One bull dozer and, I think one front loader were used to hit the fence. Both are hung up with approximately 200 people more or less waiting for a break in the fence."

Jenkins listened to the report and saw the first of the drone's video feeds. The low light cameras caught and recorded the whole sorry mess.

Jenkins picked up the handset. "Captain Nelson, this is Colonel Jenkins, let the comedy on the southern side continue. Have the BrickBats stand by. Notify the Operations Center if they appear ready to break through. I am ordering the Quick Reaction Force Company to your location until your battalion can relieve them. Once that is done. Pull them back in case this is diversion."

At 6 am, the earth moving equipment finally tore down five vertical sections of the fence. A company of the National Guard, reserves from the Texas Department of Public Safety and the Border Patrol were waiting for them. Texas Guard Combat Engineers started erecting tents to process everyone and hand out meals and water.

By 10 am the last of the people were who surged over the fence were caught.

Jenkins looked at his Center Operators. He knew they slept on duty. Some of them did not believe in securing the border. He had to deal with that. He was tired. "Major Godson, you and the Center Operators are relieved and shall be reassigned to line units. Colonel Marker, see to it."

No 1, Sam Hood Road, Fort Hood Texas.
1700 hours CDT

Dennis got out of the car and stretched. Arthur loved driving. His seat was high enough for him to see the outside world. Every waking moment he looked and mouthed sounds that were probably words to him. Dennis had to stop every few hours to feed him and change him. That gave Arthur more opportunities to look around and be amazed at the sights and sounds.

Dennis left the Minuteman 2 days ago in the early morning because of Smith and Jones' pronouncement and chicken-shit threat. He packed everything up, put Arthur in his seat and drove away. He stopped to say good-bye at Minuteman headquarters and drop off the house keys.

Peters was there, early and wanted to know why.

Dennis gave him the summary and said he was too old to play NCO get the officers out of trouble and fetch their coffee.

Peters tried to talk him out of it, but Dennis was adamant about leaving. He was going to Fort Hood and that was that.

Two days of America's beautiful landscape later, Dennis pulled into Fort Hood. Brenda was notified beforehand and was waiting at the front gate. It was emotional for all of them. Arthur seemed to remember her and smiled.

Brenda put herself in the back seat with Arthur. She gave Dennis directions to their new home. "Home for the next eighteen months," she said. "Maybe less."

Desert Zero, Fort Hood, Texas
1800 hours CDT

Simmons was happier than any of the other Commanders who waited to watch General Brenda O'Cleary assume command from General James Waller. General Waller was going to be the new Chairman of the Joint Chiefs of Staff.

The Change of Command was scheduled for Wednesday, September 9th.

The only mission they had this week, turned out to be a dry hole of sorts. No drugs, but they did take twelve and a half million dollars in cash and handed the haul over to the Treasury people.

General O'Cleary was going to tour all her units for the first two weeks. She had to spend a lot of time at Fort Hood. So, she would visit a unit and return to Hood for "commander work", as she put it.

September 8

J. Edgar Hoover Building, Washington D.C.
0900 hours EST

The Director of the FBI, Marcus Solin picked up the monthly report of criminal activity for the month of August. Consolidated data from his regional offices, the USPF and the Police Executive was represented in this report.

Solin wondered if he should even bother. Solin looked at the summary of the two-inch-thick report.

All major crimes seem to be peaking. The politicians will love to point that out. Solin believes that there is just nothing more than the criminals are running out of new targets.

There is one "crime" he secretly loved to see. Women are not just being what his grandma called "rug monkeys". Women are really starting to fight back against rapists and abusers. These are women who no longer take it and cry in silence. A lot of them were fighting hard and then waiting for the man to finish. Once he is finished, and hopefully asleep, the woman rises up and beats him sometimes to death. The number of traumatic castrations is being kept down artificially but it was speculated to be in the thousands. Doctors were becoming rich trying to reattach penises. His grandma would be proud.

BATF reported that hi-jackings of armored ammunition transports is rising. Solin leaned forward. 70 million tons of munitions vanished. Pistol, rifle, machine gun, grenades, mortar and artillery rounds. Adding to the mix were mines.

Solin reached for the phone and told the Attorney General Beck he was coming over and she needed to clear her schedule.

Internal Revenue Service Center, Washington, D.C.
1000 hours EDT

It was starting to become a national hobby.

At 9:30 am. A man in a hazmat suit, wearing a full-face particle and gas mask, walked up to the IRS building with a large, pressurized canister slung over his back. He started spraying the walkway as security guards walked up to him with their hands on their weapons and reporting over radios.

The man kept spraying. As the guards walked up to him, both men nearly doubled over. The man in the hazmat suit was spraying skunk spray around the doors of the building. Being nearly full strength, the spray was debilitating, and in a few situations nearly fatal. The man ignored everyone as he continually pumped up the pressure in the tank and spraying the doors.

It was nearly a half an hour before he ran out of spray and surrendered to authorities. He had thoroughly sprayed the doors and the entranceways to the building. The unidentified man had some of the spray spill on him. He had to be placed in a segregated cell. Every attempt to place him with other prisoners nearly started riots.

The evening edition of the newspaper said "THE IRS STINKS".

Headquarters, Southeastern Military District, Naval Air Station Jacksonville, Florida
1300 hours EDT

Admiral Cartwright sat and brooded in his office. He told his aide that he was not to be disturbed so that his depression can fully run its course. The fat pig, Edwards was supposed to retire and he, Admiral Cartwright was supposed to be the next Chairman of the Joint Chiefs of Staff.

Cartwright opened his desk drawer and pulled out the small lock box. He dialed the combination and opened the box. There were two shoulder boards with five stars each. He had dreams of being the first Admiral of the Fleet since William F. "Bill" Halsey.

Cartwright opened his bottle of Jack Daniels he kept in the desk drawer. He poured two fingers into a glass and put the bottle back in the desk drawer.

On Friday at 12 noon, Jim Waller would be the next Chairman. First, he would give command of the largest active combat unit in the US Military to "that woman". Cartwright could not understand why he disliked Brenda O'Cleary. She was smarter than he was, more capable as a Joint Commander and just plain and simple, she was better than he was.

But she was a she.

Cartwright looked at the Jack Daniels sitting in the glass. Cartwright was a former heavy drinker who suddenly one day, walked away from the bottle. Whether or not he was an alcoholic was a matter of conjecture. If asked, he simply thought that a naval officer should never be subordinate to anything but our Nation and our Navy.

Cartwright would never forgive Edwards. O'Cleary and Waller was innocent. But in the end, he was still here and not there.

Cartwright pulled the bottle out of the desk drawer and carefully poured the whiskey back into the bottle. He capped the fifteen-year-old bottle and put it back in the desk. After pouring a cup of coffee, he signaled his aide to begin his day.

Cartwright was going to find someone to blame. Who was still to be determined, but someone was going to pay for him losing that fifth star.

September 9

Southern Command, Fort Hood, Texas

General Brenda Edgars O'Cleary stood at attention on the parade field and waited. General Martin Kearney, the US Army Chief of Staff accepted the colors from the General James Waller. Kearney in turn passed the colors to O'Cleary. Each point in the process, a photographer took several pictures. Command Sergeant Major Gilbert Kilburn accepted the colors from General O'Cleary and returned them to the Color Guard.

On the reviewing stand, Dennis O'Cleary stood by with Arthur. Arthur learned a new trick. He started blowing raspberries. The first one surprised him. He thought it was funny. For the first time in his life, he laughed. He decided to experiment. He would blow a raspberry and laugh. The more he laughed the louder the raspberry. It was a process that fed on itself.

Arthur seemed to understand something special about the National Anthem. He was silent during the Anthem. All the other music made him blow raspberries. All in all, everyone was smiling. Dennis fed Arthur on the reviewing stand. When it was time for the units to pass in review, he gathered up Arthur, his things and went down to the back. A helpful Sergeant brought down a chair for him to sit in.

Dennis watched Arthur grasp his bottle. He wasn't strong enough to hold it up yet, but he knew it was something he was supposed to do. Besides, he was hungry.

After all the units passed in review and the parade was over, Dennis came over and took the obligatory pictures. Dennis wanted pictures of Brenda with Arthur. "Me Daddy, Me want, Me get."

Brenda in her Dress uniform was only too happy to oblige. She took Arthur from Dennis and smiled for the cameras.

#15 Kit Carson Way, Fort Carson, Colorado
1700 hours CDT

Ellen Thomas brooded all day after Latham went to work, she watched the Grandfather Clock in the living room rotate around and around and around. Her brain was working through a problem. Latham knew it was her process to work through a problem. So, he let her brood until she got that "weird" look on her face that said she was stuck.

All day long, she finally decided to do as Latham suggested. She had an anger building inside her and she needed to deal with it. "I want to love you, Ellen, not deflect missiles and artillery."

Ellen smiled at her man. Of all the men she ever knew, he was the one who loved her with everything he had. But at the same time, he was the man of the house and she loved him with everything she had.

Michael was starting his freshman year at the University of Texas Studying Computer Science. The University of Texas at Dallas offered a multidisciplinary science program that covered a wide variety of courses intended to provide a strong foundation in multiple areas of knowledge. Michael wanted a difficult challenge and this one offered that challenge.

Ellen remembered Michael beaming when he was accepted for the program. All those different subjects he had to master was his present focus in life. He bet his mother that he could get a 4.0 grade point average. Ellen said his dream Mercedes was his 4.0 graduation present. Michael beamed and printed the image and options for his Mercedes. She signed it.

Ellen spent the last several days alone at Latham's Colonel quarters in Fort Carson thinking. Michael stayed in Dallas so he had someplace to stay while she commuted between Dallas and Fort Carson.

She spent each day at home, ignoring the Officer's Wives Club business, while Latham was at work thinking and scheming. Slowly she went through the mechanics of her revenge against her former employer.

Gallop, Roster, Thomas and Fern, Attorneys at Law, Dallas, Texas needed a special touch. All three of those cowards were alive because she had a hidden pistol in a locked safe in her desk. Single handedly, she prevented the criminals from killing everyone.

"Gallop, Roster, Thomas and Fern, Attorneys at Law, Dallas, Texas," she said with the acid boiling in her stomach. "It was now Gallop, Roster and Fern, Attorneys at Law, Dallas,

743

Texas." That statement boiled her bile. That idiot Hollings was next in line for partner. He was going to kill the firm if nothing did.

Any good lawyer could defeat Hollings. A light lit up in her mind. She needed something to lubricate the gears in head.

Those cowards thanked her for saving their cowardly lives by canning her. The nine and a half million-dollar severance check and fifty-million-dollar stock options package were supposed to appease her.

"Gallop, Roster, and Fern, with maybe Hollings, Attorneys at Law, Dallas, Texas," she said. Suddenly, she became very calm. She laid down on the couch and stared at the big clock with its steady mechanical ticking in the background.

The only recourse she had, pivoted in and out of her mind. All the points on both sides of the argument came in and out. Slowly, she closed her eyes and went into a deep sleep. In her dreams, she was both Prosecutor and Defense; Judge Ellen presiding. Twelve versions of herself were the jury. All the arguments and points were presented and argued.

Her internal clock went off and she stirred. When she was home, she always made it a point to cook Latham a home cooked meal made by the hand of the woman who loved him more than anything. But she was shaking with anger and Latham did nothing to come home to a crazy woman.

Ellen left a note on the table for Latham, just in case he came home early.

Ellen grabbed her Kel-Tec KS7, 12-gauge shotgun and staggered under an aviator's kit bag loaded with two hundred rounds of shotgun shells. She locked everything into the trunk and drove over to the Post Rod and Gun club. She presented her credentials from the Fort Hood range, showing she went through both the National Rifle Association and Fort Hood, firearms safety courses.

Though her anger was still building, she went to the range and forced herself to read the board, detailing all the rules she could read from memory.

A nice young man went with her and carried her shotgun shell bag. "Ma'am, you planning on shooting this much," he said with a smile.

"Yes," she said. She placed her shotgun on the table, grabbed a box of ammo and readied herself on the line. She loaded her weapon on the table and set it down. Looking to the left and to the right. "Anyone down range, anyone down range, ... the firing line is not clear and is now hot."

Ellen put on her ear muffs and shooting glasses. She confirmed the safety rules and chambered the first round. She aimed at the target and shot six rounds. She re-loaded another set of six rounds. Ellen remembered a lesson Latham taught her and it served her well on that day when her firm was attacked. "Don't just shoot. Aim for a target and hit the target with the first round. Always treat each shot like your life depends on it."

Ellen knew all too well that lesson. She started on one end of the range and worked her way to the other. Once she shredded a target and the board the held it, she moved to the next on. After an hour Latham came over and handed her a water bottle while she reloaded. She smiled and hugged him. Afterward she went on to finish the rest of the rounds in her bag.

The nice young man moved the trash can and put the expended rounds into it as she moved down the line. After she was finished, she was spent and her shoulder throbbed with all that abuse. All twelve targets on the range were completely demolished.

Latham pulled over a chair for her. He broke down the shotgun, insuring her helper saw that the weapon was not loaded. He went to the range shack and carried out twelve new targets. Latham gave him a hundred-dollar bill and thanked him for staying with her.

Latham used his tried-and-true aerosol of NRA "Goop Juice". "Goop Juice" turned all the cordite gumming up the shotgun into a sludge that wiped off and was water soluble. Colonel Latham Thomas swore by it.

It took over half an hour to clean the weapon. Thomas threw away the rag he used, picked up the shotgun and empty bag.

"Do you want some more ammo?" He asked her.

"Not now," she said. She looked at her watch. "You can pick the place," she said. "I am hungry and too sore to cook. I'll buy. You are expensive, aren't you?"

Latham said, "the officers club has the rack of lamb you love and I am expensive."

"Let's stop by and buy some replacement ammo at the club. Then we go to eat." Ellen beamed and took his arm.

White House, Washington, D.C.
2000 hours EDT

The President sat alone in the residence. This was the one place where his staffers did not come and complain and harass and whine and cry and hold their breath and argue all the time. "Unless the building is on fire and nuclear missiles are descending, leave me alone!"

The President watched and listened to the talking heads talk all kinds of nonsense about this situation or that event or happenstance or estrangement. Simply put the election was boring him to death. All his opponents were very fast to point fingers at him.

He had a steadfast rule about press conferences. Those few times when he would "allow" himself to be questioned by the 'forth estate of idiots" he would leave the news conference when any of them questioned him about the election.

Even when he traveled to different cities, he told the local media that there would be no election questions. He never called on national pundits at local news conferences. They would ask if one of national pundits egged them on. The President always enjoyed walking out on the press. God, they asked some of the stupidest questions.

Tonight, he watched Alister Mackenzie very closely. He was the odds-on favorite, if you believed the polls. The President imagined him as the next President. Somehow, he believed things were going to get a lot worse. This man seemed to say all the right things at the right time and you had to believe him even if you knew he was lying.

After Mackenzie's Inauguration, the President was going away to a private island to ignore the chaos that was going to happen. He knew a Civil War was coming and thankfully Congress was too hamstrung to make it worse.

September 10

United Nations, The Hague, Netherlands
0900 hours (Alpha)

Less and less, the world body was having an effect on world affairs. The US no longer paid 25% of their operating costs and consistently refused to offer personnel and money for peace-keeping missions. The other nations sent little to the body.

Any peace-keeping mission was accomplished by literally counting pennies and begging for each man and machine. Then there was the problem of keeping them there. If some terrorist killed some "blue hat" peace keepers, the nation's providing men and material usually got cold feet. More deaths mean others will pull out. The rule of thumb was if one left, the others followed.

Peace-keeping and inspections of the United States was something no one wanted any part of. The United States has consistently told the world and this body that any force that tries to land on US soil for any reason will be met with lethal force without any warning.

The members of the Security Council steadfastly refused to bring up the subject and the US routinely vetoes any action against it.

The Russian delegation has said it may provide forces on an as-needed-basis. But the Ambassador said not to plan on it unless the Russian Government allows it, if asked and Russian interests are involved.

The Secretary General was at a loss.

Minuteman, north of Fort Benton, Montana
0800 hours MDT

Peters breathed a sigh of relief. All the training, tactical and operational objectives have been achieved. Nothing was left to chance and even a feedback program was initiated where subordinates were encouraged to highlight misgivings and possible problems.

Peters was not going to say it was over. No plan ever survived the first shot fired, but the plan allowed for a lot of new ideas to punch holes in the plan and recover.

Now that INSANE JANE implementation was completed, Peters now turned to how to protect his logistics base and the hard work everyone put into homes and plenty of food to eat.

Peters was spending a lot of his time looking over the new maps Miles and Morgan created. They accompanied him on the long, all-day reconnaissance trips all over the main area. 2300 acres were re-visited as sites where possibly armored storage areas for hay, vegetables and other food stuffs could be stored.

Peters wanted de-centralized storage. That simplified the gathering and transportation. Peters remembered back to his childhood in Nebraska. Hay fires and rot were constant problems.

Miles and Morgan pointed out there was no place large enough to store the herds of cattle, sheep, goats, horses and other animals. They had to graze, and move around. Keeping them indoors, amplified sanitation problems. Animals did not understand or could use toilets. Plus, areas could easily be defoliated and the herds needed to be moved. The change of seasons added other problems.

"The animal problems need smarter people than me, if it can be solved. If anything gives us away, it will be the herds and healthy, well-fed people." Peters looked to Miles who looked to Morgan who looked at both of them.

"We need answers from smart people," Peters repeated. "Do we have anyone who would know?"

Peters thought of Joshua and Janet Layman. They seemed to know everything. Maybe they knew about this.

Back at the Minuteman, Glendive and Sheridan went over the Program of Instruction (POI). The more and more they looked at the instruction. The more they tried to insure that it could be taught. Did it need pre-instruction in order for

748

the main point to be introduced or did it need more instruction on how to learn the main point?

Sheridan was worried that the amount of instruction being "in the clouds".

Glendive understood what he meant. Command was different from management. Glendive was guilty of creeping management into the POI.

Glendive backed off and went to get a cup of coffee. When he came back, he saw what he was doing. He closed his eyes and reset his mind, remembering that these guys were defending their homes and families.

"I'm sorry, Tom. Thanks for keeping me straight." Glendive said.

"No problem, Al. At least you know how to listen and admit it," Sheridan said.

Glendive thought about that. "There is nothing here to say that. The Officer/NCO relationship is rarely given any real emphasis."

Sheridan went back to the left on the scroll and made a note for later.

September 11

Headquarters, Northeastern Military Region, Fort A.P. Hill, Virginia
0900 hours EDT

General Kenneth Mueller spent the last week watching next to nothing happen in the operations center and reading past operations reports.

Other "stuff" kept his mood sour. He had a constant parade of politicians coming in wanting manpower and money in a tight economy. It was simple to see through the subterfuge. The more he gave them, the less they had to pay themselves.

USPF would cover up to 30% of the normal manpower levels. Above that and the states and municipalities had to foot the bill. Getting Mueller to give them troops was their idea.

General Macklin warned him that those politicians thought the military was nothing more than labor battalions.

"Don't try explaining Posse Comitatus or the Insurrection Act of 1807 to them. I had the Governor of New York arrive with eight State Troopers to present me with a court order for eight hundred soldiers for Riot Control. They wanted to arrest me on the spot, if I did not instantly comply. Fortunately, I had MPs to counter them."

Mueller's present problem was low flying aircraft dropping drugs out to land in fairly inaccessible areas. Mueller had a Quick Reaction Force to fly to those areas and land to seize or destroy the drugs. The DEA and States Attorney General, did not like them destroying the drugs. An order signed by Macklin and now by Mueller, said to destroy the drugs if there was any possibility of lives being lost defending the drug seizure.

Mueller pulled up on the four stars on his fatigue jacket front. Was a fourth star worth this aggravation?

Pentagon, Washington, D.C.
1200 hours EDT

Amanda and Thomas Edwards stood to the side as General James Waller stood and was sworn in as the next Chairman of the Joint Chiefs of Staff. After that the President promoted him to the five-star rank of General of the Army. It seems the Senate, at least what was left of it, wanted a Five Star General to bring order to the Chaos that was their perception of the Pentagon.

With the new law that was enacted, the Official Command Structure was changed, only this time, the other services were subordinate officially to the JCS. Everything and everyone that wore a uniform or performed some type of military task was placed directly under the JCS.

Edwards said nothing. He declined a parade or some official ceremony from the "Old Guard". He simply accepted his paperwork and retired. The Edwards were already packed up and spent the last two weeks at the Willard Hotel, so that General Waller and his family could move into their quarter at Number 17, the Naval Observatory.

Both of them had talked about where to go since she returned from Canada. For now, they wanted to go to

Colorado Springs. Both enjoyed cold weather. One quirk of being a five-star flag officer is that you never retire. You go on what is called inactive service, but not retirement. So, Edwards was in the Army till the day he died or resigned.

"Some choice," Edwards said.

"Get over it," Amanda said.

Mega-State Coordination Office, Austin, Texas
1700 hours CDT

Texas and Oklahoma States Police were working over a combined map of both states trying to map patterns that criminal gangs and individuals were using to attack and steal everything whether or not it is nailed down.

Officials were more worried about tanker trucks full of fuel disappearing. GPS transmitters both obvious and hidden were disabled. Dusting off police reports from the 1970s when tanker trucks were hijacked during the oil embargo, pointed investigators towards underground fuel sales at prices far under the national average of $7.05 a gallon.

Those tankers hi-jacked in the 1970s were still being found today. Most were found on farms and ranches, buried underground. All that showed was a siphon jutting out of the ground. After the original owner either died or sold the land, the new owners dug up the ground and found the rusted tankers. The tell-tale was the sudden collapse of the ground around the tanker and a smell of gasoline.

Attacks on towns were focusing on smaller communities.

Now the on-going robberies were for food, firearms and ammunition. Federal investigators made lots of noises about law-abiding citizens openly carrying firearms. Many towns had laws saying every head of the household had to own a firearm. The common thread from each citizen was that help from outside agencies was too slow. "We are the ones dying, not you, pretty boy."

Each firearm owner was officially a member of the local militia. The Families were given free classes on firearm safety and pointers for family members with how to deal with gangs trying to rob them and the Feds abusing their rights.

Today the problem was with the town of Elmwood, Oklahoma. A gang of forty descended on Elmwood at 2 am. The town was unable to counter-attack before the local grocery store and hardware store were gutted. The gangs tried to randomly shoot at homes and other buildings in order to stop the citizens from organizing.

A town-side alarm sounded and the public address system said the town was under attack from Main Street.

Suddenly, rifle fire came from the towns people from multiple directions. Tires and people and engines were being systematically shot up. The trucks used to load all the food and firearms were quickly disabled.

Half the gang was abandoned as the other half loaded up in barely functioning vehicles and left the town going south on Highway 23. The stay-behinds finally surrendered after fifteen minutes of ineffectual shooting. A towns man told the surrendering men and women to lay down on the ground.

Cautiously, towns people covered the Police Chief as he walked forward to search and tie-up the gang members. One man reached under himself and tried to pull out a pistol. He was told they wished he tried. "It's easier for us." He spread out and allowed himself to be searched.

Several people went to phones and tried calling the town of Booker over the border with Texas.

Booker was alerted and was barely ready when the gang arrived. Stupidly, the gang stopped and tried to take over the town. The firefight killed all twenty-two of them with two towns people wounded.

Typical of the so-called justice system, the judge who presided over the twelve captured gang members who survived was sympathetic to their plight. Ambulance chasers were waiting for them to file suit against the towns of Elmwood and Booker. The judge put bail at $50,000 dollars each. All of them were free by the end of the day and vanished.

At the Mega-State Coordination Office, one Texas trooper said, "Until the Judges get some street smarts, those two towns will have to defend themselves again."

September 12

The President commissioned this meeting with the Chief of Naval Operations and the Chief of Staff of the Air Force only. All three men went downstairs to the Situation Room and ejected everyone. Once the doors were closed, locked and the three green lights were lit over the door, the President sat down and got to business.

The President started. "Gentlemen, as you may know, America is under a lot of pressure from dozens of countries around the world. Top of their list is the 5,298 nuclear weapons that we are safeguarding. Those clowns think they have every right to inspect our nuclear stockpile for any number of reasons. I will sign an order if I have to, but nobody gets near those weapons. No one can authorize non-Americans but me. Period."

Both men nodded yes.

The President decided to get it out of the way. "I am going to say this and it may be a bad idea. I am considering launching a Fleet Ballistic missile from a submarine into a deserted patch of the Pacific Ocean. I want the world to know and understand that we are to be left alone to solve our problems. No one carves up Alaska. No one annexes Hawaii. No foreign troops on American soil. But I want it understood, those warheads are not to kill or injure anyone. The warheads can even go below the surface of the ocean if there is a question."

Both men looked at each other and were uncomfortable.

"Gentlemen, it is true, I cannot launch unilaterally. The only action I can do is veto a launch. If necessary, we can launch with inert warheads, but I am leaning toward a fully functioning set of warheads."

The General and the Admiral were still wary but not completely against it.

"When you go back, I want two streams to see which delivery system is the scariest. The UN be dammed and the

International Atomic Energy Commission be dammed. I want the world to be scared shitless."

"Mister President," CNO Admiral Adam Palmer said. "I am leaning more to the inert warhead. You can say this was an unannounced launch test of the system. The inert warheads showed that we have a valid system and the accuracy of a new guidance system needed to be checked."

"I concur, Mister President," Chief of Staff for the Air Force General Franklin Ester said. "The inert warhead can be walked back. Detonating a nuclear warhead can and will scare too many people in the wrong places. Additionally, the Air force delivery systems will not have the psychological impact that a sea-launched system will bear."

The President slowly shook his head up and down. "Thank you, Gentlemen."

Both men were relieved.

The President moved on to another topic. "Gentlemen, in particular, General Ester. Last year, I sent a Global Hawk to Israel. The Prime Minister constantly tells me how great it is. How many do we have now?"

General Ester leaned forward. "The RQ-4M has been upgraded with newer radars and communications packages. We had two of them orbiting over the Mexican Border. The so-called "Feathers" are upgraded also. We have 275 different functions now. The newer RQ-4S series is a lot better and all the equipment is more powerful."

The President asked. "How many do we have?"

"8, Mister President," Ester said.

"Do they have look-down radars and the ability to compare its data with data from other radar emitters and make a composite picture?"

Ester looked at the President.

"General, perhaps I am just grasping at straws. The head of the DEA and the Northeast regional Commander, General Mueller was asking me about using a Global Hawk to track small planes flying at low altitude that the cartels are using now."

Ester shrugged his shoulders. "I will have to get back with you on that, Mister President. If we don't, I get you an estimate on the cost and time involved."

"And get me an estimate on covering both coasts. Only give four and keep the other four available for other tasks. While the DEA is on my mind, they work for me, you do not work for them."

"Yes Sir," both men said.

Minutemen, north Of Fort Benton, Montana
1000 hours MDT

Glendive and Sheridan ran over the POI for the Senior NCO Academy. Just to satisfy themselves that they found everything in place and nothing was overlooked.

Both men started reading the two-inch-thick document and, when finished, put it down and rubbed their foreheads. Everything was ready.

September 13

Call sign, Valkyrie, Fort Hood, Texas
0300 hours CDT

Brenda used the now 3 am feeding and diaper changing with Arthur to look over her Werewolf duties. Back when she was at the Pentagon and pregnant, she did not have time to do it justice. Though this was a seven-day-a-week job, she was on a more relaxed schedule.

Glendive needed to give her a full accounting of the Werewolf members and their current assignments.

She was afraid of the possibility of another Committee out there. This country had a lot of problems and this was not helping matters.

She needed to aim UNSTACK THIS and the Werewolves at them. There is no telling how long they have been active. This "committee" was a new generation that did not have any inhibition in killing an infant.

"Colonel Glendive," O'Cleary called him. "You, Kendal, Locklear and two others need to come here for a clandestine meeting and a mission concept. We have a new threat and problem. Call me when you can arrange it."

Elmwood, Oklahoma
2000 hours CDT

The surviving nine men and three women from the criminal gang returned to Elmwood. They came into town shooting at everything. A couple on Main Street were gunned down. Everyone scattered to avoid being next.

The Police Chief ran into his office and hit the town alarm. He said over the public address system that the town was under attack, again.

The group started walking around, spreading out, shooting at roof tops and store fronts. For the next twelve to fifteen minutes, they felt like they owned the town. They shouted out insults and warnings about what they intended to do. The laughing horde of dummies started walking towards a residential section of town.

Suddenly, on average of once every two or three seconds a rifle shot came at them. The horde suddenly felt trapped as the rifle shots came from different directions. The shots were initially just wounds to the legs and arms. Instead of giving up, the gang just fought harder. This time they brought dynamite and started throwing lit sticks at buildings. One man with a sack full of dynamite rose to throw a lit stick of dynamite. A rifle shot to his arm ended that. Thankfully, the stick of dynamite rolled into a storm drain.'

It did not take too long for all the gang members were dead. Everyone was in no mood for these clowns to come again. Enough damage was done to the town.

As the bodies were being cleaned up and removed, it was discovered that a man in a suit was cowering in one of their cars. He carefully climbed out of the car with his hands raised. "I am their lawyer. You violated their civil rights by not allowing them to surrender. I saw one man trying to surrender. I will inform the authorities that they fired first and you defended yourself. Can someone please direct me to the nearest phone? My cell phone doesn't seem to work."

Those bodies, the lawyer and the vehicles were never found again.

State investigators have little hope in finding anything beyond bullet holes in buildings.

September 14

Desert Zero, Fort Hood, Texas
1500 hours CDT

First on her list of units to visit was the Savage Rabbits. O'Cleary arrived with two Humvees. She called ahead and said she did not want to see a dog and pony show. She was here as a one, two and three, star General. Now she had four stars and she just wanted to see how this baby had grown.

Colonel Simmons and Sergeant Major Waverly escorted her around the compound showing off everything. Mainly O'Cleary just wanted to meet the men themselves. She asked if they were well supplied and their equipment was in good condition.

Inwardly, O'Cleary looked hard at the men. She was very interested in the morale of the men themselves. That, to her, was more important than equipment.

Today the men were finishing their Pathfinder training, given by the instructors visiting from Fort Benning, Ga. She was honored to walk through the formation and personally hand each man and the two women their Pathfinder torch.

Two young troopers were reenlisting and O'Cleary was asked to do the honors. Both men enjoyed the honor and had several pictures taken to commemorate the event.

O'Cleary spent the trip on the way back to the base, thinking that she finally had an assignment where she could respect herself.

O'Cleary looked out the window and saw a car coming down the road intersecting with hers. The MP driver must have had a bad feeling, he slowed down and sped up. The other car matched him. "Hold on," he said. The other MP in the Humvee passed O'Cleary an M-4. The trail Humvee exchanged positions. O'Cleary saw a man open the roof hatch and aim his rifle at the car. The other car slammed to a stop and the doors erupted open.

Three men got out of the car as O'Cleary's Humvee was reversing out of the area. One of the men raised an M-203 grenade launcher and shot a round at the Humvee. The round hit the road in front of them. O'Cleary tried to stand in the roof opening, but the MP pushed her back down as he shot at the vehicle. A second round hit the other Humvee on the hood. The armored Humvee absorbed the damage protecting the occupants. The MPs staggered away from the vehicle and fell into a ditch.

O'Cleary opened the door and moved to the vehicle firing one round at a time. She fired steadily until she came to the MPs. One was wounded in the leg and the other was unhurt.

O'Cleary remembered her lessons from the Werewolves. She had a total of three magazines and one was steadily emptying. She counted the rounds fired and mentally counted down the remaining rounds

The three men were out of the car and spreading out. Both MP Humvees were returning fire and reversing. Just as both MPs were laying down a heavy volume of fire, two Humvees full of heavily armed men raced to the scene from Desert Zero. O'Cleary knelt down low and "guarded" the wounded MP.

The car load of "attackers" started moving back to their car, but found out it was out of action. Two of the tires were flat and the engine was shot up. Two men were down, wounded badly.

As the reinforcements arrived, the remaining two men tried to shoot and run, but after being wounded, they fell to the ground saying they surrendered and they had rights.

The MPs called out an all-clear.

O'Cleary looked as Colonel Simmons and three Humvees with fully armed Rabbits appeared.

"I want helicopters here to evacuate the wounded," O'Cleary said. "Round these people up and get the information about how they knew my schedule and where to attack my group. She looked at the bullet holes in the windshield. "These are armor-piercing rounds. They were waiting and ready."

"Colonel Becklund," O'Cleary turned and said. "What is the status of the Medevac Helicopters?"

"Fifteen minutes, General" Becklund said.

758

Two other Humvees arrived with medics and their equipment.

One of the medics looked at the attackers. "What do you want to do with them, General?"

"We're Americans, Sergeant," O'Cleary said. "That is not a question. US personnel first, then them. Everyone gets the same care."

"Yes Ma'am," he said.

O'Cleary suddenly thought that Dennis was going to upset that she took chances with her life. "Damm," she said out loud. Off to the west, the sound of helicopters was heard. True to their training, the new Pathfinders were already on the scene. She was proud of her guys.

September 15

Headquarters, Southeastern Military Region, Naval Air Station, Pensacola, Florida
1000 hours EDT

At his desk in the Situation Room, Cartwright watched his Navy do the thing it did best. Satellites detected 5 submarines taking on large bundles that the CIA said was drugs. The old diesel electric subs, slowly crawled up into the Caribbean Sea and navigated through the islands. As much possible, they used the noise of cruise ships to mask their sound to move up into the Gulf of Mexico. However, they could not mask themselves from the satellites overhead. Each night the submarines had to run on the surface using their diesel engines to maneuver and recharge their batteries.

Cartwright called O'Cleary and coordinated with her about the subs.

O'Cleary smiled at Cartwright's image on the screen. "I don't see the need to worry about a line on a map, Admiral. If you are asking me, they will slip through a change of command. Besides, this is something the Navy seldom gets the chance to do. Sink Subs."

"Thank you General," Cartwright said. "We may need help with the mop-up and shore coverage."

"Any help you need is yours," O'Cleary said. "I had some experience with drug subs when I was with the Internal Security Agency. One actually blew up in the Gulf of California. It vanished in between satellite passes. While we are on the subject, I have a MC-130 here I use for aerial command and control. You may borrow it in order to maintain contact with them. It has a new look-down radar/sonar. I don't understand how it works, but they need some place to practice and calibrate."

Cartwright sat up in his chair. He was surprised at the offer. "Thank you General, I will send one of my officers there on Wednesday or Thursday depending on the situation. If it is the same one that the SEALs used during the oil rig situation, it will be very useful. Thanks again."

"Done, Admiral," O'Cleary said.

Both cleared some small items and coordinated others.

Southern Command, Fort Hood, Texas
1100 hours CDT

O'Cleary and Matheson coordinated the use of the RQ-4S Global Hawk overfly missions covering the western US. Three Global Hawks were available to work the mission. Two would fly and one was a spare in order for one to land for maintenance or change out the "Feathers".

Cartels are stealing planes north of the border, flying south, loading them up with drugs and flying north over the border. In some instances, they fly their cash back south. The plane is always expendable. A lot of them were flying out into the Pacific and paralleling the West Coast before turning inland.

Similar to Admiral Cartwright's problem, former Russian diesel submarines were being used to move drugs to American shores. The Subs were slowly moving to the north and surfacing only on no moon or heavy overcast nights. If the opportunity arises with bad weather, the situation is better.

Past experiences, has taught them that noise, no matter how slight is the enemy. The US Navy has submerged sounding stations that know what the ocean "sounds" like. Any change, no matter how slight, is investigated. If the sub senses an aircraft overhead, they shut down and wait a minimum of an hour. Those times when the whales migrate north, all the submariners breathe easier. The whales tend to avoid the submarines.

O'Cleary and Matheson spent the morning conducting a video conference, defining responsibilities and agreeing that the line on the map was not a wall.

O'Cleary told Matheson about a lot of capabilities that the ISA had to deal with the Russians. He could get advance notice of situations early.

Both Generals covered a lot of territory between them. They agreed to exchange liaison officers to blur the lines of cooperation and boundaries.

September 16

Election Process, United States of America
0900 hours EDT

Alister Mackenzie sat in his hotel room at the Willard Hotel. He was enjoying a cup of coffee and reading the newspaper. Mackenzie spent most of his life cultivating an image as a calm, mature and at times kind and humble.

Mackenzie kept his real personality a closely guarded secret. Inwardly, he protected himself with a rigid set of rules that served him well. His parents slaved for decades accumulating wealth that he now selfishly used for self-promotion that would put Douglas McArthur and Joseph Kennedy to shame. Throughout his life, he learned the lessons of those that came before him.

He spent his parent's money conservatively. He learned everything about everyone around him; friends and enemies. Everyone was a source of his "Income". Everyone has something to give him. Money, power, influence and the most valuable, most important commodity: information.

His inner core of acolytes owed him personally. His confidential secretary had a mother with very expensive medical needs. His two assistants had an infrequent need to sexually abuse women. The police could never find enough evidence to convict them. Three others with similar problems were too overt. They lived at the bottom of the Atlantic.

No one in his organization was underpaid. All had top tier medical insurance for themselves and their families. None of his people had any legal troubles. All of them signed away everything they owned. So long as he needed them and they were available 24/7, there were no problems.

Cross him or lose value and the world collapsed from under their feet. Evidence of crimes suddenly appeared and bank accounts were drained.

Mackenzie had a machine that was finally ready to take the brass ring. He had maneuvered the world for the last twenty years to this point.

He was going to be the President of the United States of America. He helped to create this disaster with the help of Ezekias Zacharias Criers. His fortune was used to help engineer his bid for the Presidency. This disaster was going to happen. Thank you, Sir.

Gladys Goldstein and John Kincaid were dead. Now he needed to eliminate Brenda Edgars O'Cleary. He needed to find those Werewolves. He did not know enough about them to even start looking for them or how many remained in the shadows for so long. That could be a problem. But he could force them out of the shadows when he was inaugurated.

EZ Criers made one mistake. He was sentimental. Logically, he should have killed them when he had the opportunity.

Mackenzie was not conceited enough to believe he was infallible. He was a human. He could make a mistake.

Internal Revenue Service Center, Washington, D.C.
0800 hours EDT

The latest saga in the "Play with the IRS" was playing itself out across the country. Each week, two to three centers across the country were shut down. These centers were located in buildings shared with other agencies or civilian companies. Bomb threats or some imagined calamity was reported which forced the building to be evacuated.

Congress and the Treasury was reeling from the lack of revenue. Carter didn't bother calling Jennifer Donnelly this year asking for more money to be collected. It is obvious that the Treasury was empty and the people didn't have any more money to give.

Despite an active recruiting campaign, no one wanted to work with the IRS. Agents and their families were attacked and abused. Agents having to go into the field needed a lot of security and so-called "spare policemen" were very hard to find with everything else demanding them elsewhere.

Carter kept telling the President and Congress that their obsession with giving away money with no thought about paying for it was over. "Legislate all you want. Bring over all the Executive Orders you want. Wish all you want. Promise all you want. It ain't here."

Carter stopped allowing Executive Branch agencies to request Treasury funds without his specific written approval. Congresspeople and Executive Minions screamed and cried and threatened legal action.

Congresspeople actually thought they could make a law to compel him to give them money the Treasury did not have.

HAHAHAHAHAHAHA.

September 17

Five Submarines along the Atlantic Seaboard from Miami, Florida to Chesapeake Bay, Virginia
0900 hours EDT

Admiral Cartwright watched the Master Operations Display at the Pentagon's Navy Situation Room. At his station he noted the position and disposition of every ship along the eastern seaboard. Everything Military and civilian and foreign military was there to be seen. All the submarines hovered outside the territorial waters, at one hundred feet below the surface at 100 to 125 miles off shore.

The Navy's SOSUS and Integrated Undersea Surveillance System (IUSS) tracked the submarines easily. At 0902 they turned toward points along the eastern seaboard moving submerged at a sedate six knots.

Minuteman, north of Fort Benton, Montana
1100 hours MDT

Glendive and Sheridan listened to the song and dance Smith and Jones delivered to them. Jones led the charge by saying neither of them had the brain power to do all the things that had to be in place by January.

Glendive and Sheridan looked at each other.

Glendive remembered the old days. Both men were almost Gods. He was suddenly sad that old age could literally tear down a man more than bullets.

Sheridan looked at the men who trained him, led him and molded him into the soldier and man he became. His ability to turn off his military side was as much their advice as the counsel Father Michael made for his marriage to Amy and the love, he felt for his children Sam and Sydney. No matter how mad he became or how much family life tried his patience, he only response was patience, calm and love.

"Gentlemen, excuse us," Glendive said, standing and motioning to Sheridan. They walked outside out of earshot. "More than anything, their leadership and example got us to this point."

"They are hanging onto something," Sheridan said. "I think they are afraid of retirement, but cannot see they are too life-tired to function."

Glendive looked at Smith and Jones. "They are the first men who actually lived long enough to retire. Ours is not a profession that allows us to live long enough to retire."

Sheridan took a deep breath and looked hard at Glendive. "We both know what needs to be done, but a decision has to be made beforehand. Do we really want a class of Werewolves to start in January? Then we have to ask ourselves where or if we want two old and tired men to participate."

Glendive looked hard at Sheridan, knowing those two decisions ultimately came back to him. "Yes, to a new class in January. We need Kendal and Locklear to come here now and set up the course."

Sheridan looked back at Glendive. "We will have to go to the General and ask for Kendal and Locklear. They will need to call Sergeant Major O'Cleary periodically for knowledge and advice about cutting through any logjams."

"I'll call her," Glendive said. "Mister Covington and Missus Morgan will run the course. I have already been giving this problem some thought. The four of them will be the core of the group. The others will help out as required."

Sheridan looked in to where their mentors sat waiting. "I hate to do this to them. Having to say they can't do a job had to be the hardest thing they ever did."

Glendive opened the encrypted phone and keyed the codes to have General O'Cleary call him.

"I'll tell them, Tom," Glendive said. "Go in to the Operations Center and consult with the training section. All that knowledge they have from nearly forty years of experience would be great for the NCO Academy."

Southern Command, Fort Hood, Texas
1830 hours CDT

O'Cleary used UNSTACK THIS to have a secure phone call with Glendive at Minuteman. Glendive summarized the predicament they were in with Smith and Jones and his solution.

He needed Kendal and Locklear to join with Mister Covington and Missus Morgan to form the nucleus of a new core cadre to run the class. A mountain of logistics has to be accomplished before the class can start.

"Is January still a feasible date?" O'Cleary asked.

"Possible," Glendive admitted. "If we can get Kendal and Locklear here, there is a possibility. If not, no."

"Get comfortable, this may take a little while," O'Cleary said. She told him about the five people who tried to kidnap her and her family had instructions from a new "Committee". She wanted to hunt them down before the trail went cold.

Glendive sat down and wondered if this horseshit would ever end. "General, we are going to have to split our resources and do both things at the same time. Misters

765

Griffith, Pruitt, Mejia and McPherson can hunt down the 'Committee'. A lot of preliminary leg work can be done. I will say, I intend to slow them down. All that information from one source smacks of a set-up."

"I agree, thank you," O'Cleary said. "Mission concept approved. I agree with the caution. Set up a communications system. One of our people could call their mother each day. She is ill, and that is a good son."

"Excellent Ma'am," Glendive said.

Both hung up the phone and thought hard.

There were a lot of questions. O'Cleary used hindsight to think about the original committee. They were killed off when Jones, Smith, Morgan and Kincaid returned from Vietnam. But EZ Criers resurrected them from within the system. EZ Criers. He is long dead at Delta 7. Long dead and forgotten. Is he?

O'Cleary called back to Minuteman. "Mister Glendive, your starting point is EZ Criers. Have Missus Morgan and Miss Kendal open EZ Criers cell. 1. Confirm no one has opened the door since the time when he was imprisoned. 2. Confirm he, is in fact, dead and that his body is in the cell. 3. If still alive, terminate him. We need to go over Mister Kincaid's interrogation of him. 4. Find all the kernels of information, yet find the kernels that are not there." O'Cleary thought hard. "He knew he was dead. What did he have to gain for telling everything or not telling something? He taught John Kincaid to always keep the one secret, even as you went down to drugs. Remember and keep the one secret."

Glendive remembered that John Kincaid was someone who never gave away all of his secrets. John Kincaid knew too many secrets.

"Yes Ma'am, understood," Glendive said.

O'Cleary closed the phone and went home. She needed to talk to Dennis. Maybe he came here too soon.

Five Submarines along the Atlantic Seaboard from Miami, Florida to Chesapeake Bay, Virginia
2200 hours EDT

Cartwright felt this was the slowest, most anti-climactic sea action he ever witnessed.

Each submarine had one destroyer or similar sized craft closed on the submarine as it neared the twenty-mile line. The ships slowed, shadowing the subs, matching it for course and speed.

From the deck of the ship, a small submersible was launched. As soon as the submersible was underwater and started moving, its sonar went active and locked on the submarine. With a top speed of twenty-one miles an hour, it easily overcame the submarine and latched onto the rear section magnetically. After locking on, two arms on each end of the submersible reached around and connected to each other. Once all the green lights said "go", five heavy-duty bags inflated and raised the submarine to the surface. With the tail sticking out of the water, most of the crew were stuck in the forward section of the Submarine.

The submarine stayed that way until the surface ship came alongside and attached buoys to the front of the submarine.

When the subs were almost level, boarding parties carefully and slowly opened the hatches and entered the submarines. In four of them, the four-man crews surrendered without a fight. On the last one, a short firefight erupted. It ended when an explosion occurred in the forward battery room. The hull was breached, allowing sea water to flood in. One crew man escaped.

If that crew thought they were sinking the sub, they failed. All five subs were towed to a harbor and emptied. 62 tons of marijuana, 4 tons of heroin, 2 tons of cocaine and another 10 tons of various other substances.

Not a bad haul for a boring capture.

September 18

Delta-7, Moss Point, Montana
0200 Hours MDT

Morgan, Kendal, McPherson and Mejia arrived at Delta 7 yesterday and observed it. Morgan and Kendal looked for any sign that anyone was there. They waited overnight and used infrared imagers to check for anything emitting heat.

Slowly, cautiously, they moved up to the smaller door and entered the facility. Morgan and Kendal were weary. Winchell was supposed to be unconscious the last time. He got loose from his container, nearly killed Morgan and had a standoff with Kendal.

Kendal found the key she hid in the recreation room. Slowly and steadily, they went down the corridor, noting any changes. The dust on the floors was undisturbed. There were no new scrapes on the doors, like someone using a key.

Finally, they arrived at the door they locked on Criers room. No new tool marks on the lock or door. Slowly, the key was inserted and turned. The door was slowly pulled open. There was EZ Criers laying on the bed. He laid there, mouth agape, not breathing. The stink said it happened a while ago.

Morgan took out a digital camera, made several photos of his face and of the body. She also took several high-resolution photographs of his hands and fingers. This application, if angled correctly, raised fingerprints and stored the images. She pulled out a lap top and uploaded the photos. The images were compared to the data on file.

The computer said it was a 97% chance that this was EZ Criers. Morgan looked at the murderer of her husband. He looked small. Decidedly small. A one-time trillionaire who died less than penniless. Morgan wanted to spit on the ground, but instantly knew that it was a wasted effort.

Morgan left the room, raised her weapon and left the room behind her. Kendal closed the door and locked it. The key went inside her bra. It needed to be put somewhere else.

Everyone closed the facility and carefully exited it. They went down the road, found their vehicles and drove the 80 miles to their motels in total silence.

Barney's Place, Monroe, Montana
2100 hours MDT.

Morgan and Kendal met up with Earl Locklear to study the information they collected on Criers, the old and new committee and what, if anything, they were looking at.

After an hour, they looked up and decided to start over tomorrow. McPherson and Mejia packed up all the extra equipment and left for Minuteman.

They had two connecting rooms, just in case.

Kendal took her shower first. In the shower, she thought about her interrogation of those five clowns who tried to take General O'Cleary. Before they came out here, the General told them to re-think what they told her.

So, she did.

After Earl came out, both went to bed and held each other, drifting off into their dream worlds.

Cindy took a shower, dried herself and was blow drying her hair. The face and body reflected back to her. After Zach died, she rarely looked at herself. She fought herself at the notion of sex with anyone. Week after week, month after month, and year after year. Nothing to belittle Zach's memory.

That pornographic match with John must have triggered something inside both of them. After John killed himself, Father Thomas came to her. Her pistol was on the table, loaded and ready. All that was needed was a hand to pick up the weapon, a motion to put the barrel against her skull and the command to her finger to pull the trigger.

"Your husband will not welcome you if you commit suicide," Thomas said.

Cindy started crying. "How do you know? I exchanged nude, obscene gestures with John Kincaid. We both surrendered and cheated on our Spouses."

Thomas watched the pistol and maneuvered as close as he could to it. "The vows you took say until death to you part. When your husband died, your vows to him were severed. You did not cheat and neither did John."

Morgan came back to the present. She hated being confused. This nutty life was her fault. She made John train her. She submitted to the life and was judged.

John did his best to discourage her, but she was too stupid to take the out and leave. Could she still?

September 19

0800 hours

769

Cindy woke an hour earlier and made a cup of coffee with her special coffee maker. This one allowed her to make one cup or a whole pot. It was worth all the money she spent for it.

She knocked earlier. There was no response, so she cracked open the door and found a nude couple sprawled on the bed.

Cindy went back to her room, sat down and thought about when Wendy and her took Winchell and Criers to Delta 7. He woke up.

Cindy chewed on that fact. The dosage and drug used was the same for both of them. But he should have been unconscious for at least another hour or two. How did he wake up? Cindy was suddenly hit over the head when she opened the box and looked away.

How is it that Winchell was awake? Was he awakened by someone?

Just then Wendy came in. Granny panties and t-shirt.

Morgan looked at Kendal and said, "We need to go back to Delta 7. I have to see that container Winchell was in. We need to find out how he regained consciousness so early."

September 20

No. 1 Sam Hood Road, Fort Hood, Texas
0600 hours CDT

Brenda stood next to the bed and waited for "her little man" to wake up. Arthur was starting to sleep longer. It was amazing that at 3 months of age, he was trying to sit up. He was rolling over and smiling when he sees her.

Nothing in her life ever captured her heart like this "little man". She stole time every day to bond with Arthur. She resolved to put her son and husband at the top of her life and keep them there. Privately, she could not wait to retire.

Arthur woke up and fussed with the intrusion to his life. His mother reached down and scooped up her "little man". A fresh diaper and bottle later, he was content with life. Arthur laid on his mother's legs and studied her face. Both mother and son just looked at each other.

Both heard the soft clatter coming from the kitchen. Dennis, the light sleeper, was up cooking breakfast.

Twenty minutes of bonding later and Dennis poked his head into the room. He smiled and gestured towards the dining room.

Brenda had no use with this monstrous place that was her official residence. 6 bedrooms, 5 bathrooms, two kitchens, a large dining room and small one, one huge living room and another small one. A four-place garage was too much. It was too much work for Dennis to do and care for Arthur. Unfortunately, they had to hire three ladies to care for the house and they insisted on paying them handsomely.

The Personal Security Agents, or PSAs had to through monkey wrenches into any and every plan. The house keepers needed nearly a week to be cleared. All of them were wives of NCOs. "They're more trustworthy than you are," Dennis finally said, ushering them inside.

Lieutenant Colonel Derrick Martin, O'Cleary's aide, had his problems with the PSAs. Too many of them to talk about. General O'Cleary had two separate teams of them relieved for making too many stupid decisions. She was late for too many appointments because they were changing routes without notifying the aide, so that the General's schedule can be changed accordingly.

Brenda propped up Arthur on the table so that he could watch his parents eat breakfast. Brenda was finally cleared to exercise and she was going to exercise. Dennis bought some special three-wheel strollers for her to power walk and run with Arthur.

Delta 7, Moss Point, Montana
2100 hours MDT

The horizon went dark at 7:30 pm and that was the signal for Morgan, Kendal and Locklear to move silently forward. As they were moving, the alarm sounded over their radio, saying someone was watching. Kendal slid back and pulled her light tight shield over her head and pulled out her laptop. She keyed into her network and it suddenly said they were surrounded. Twelve others were in a ring around them.

Locklear spread a poncho over Kendal so that he and Morgan could look at the laptop.

"We are screwed," Morgan said as she typed out a message on her secure network. She checked it twice and transmitted it three times. Each transmission was 0.2 seconds long.

"That answers the question about Winchell," Kendal said.

"I suggest we wait 24 hours and see what happens," Locklear said. "We are outnumbered and under gunned."

Morgan hated waiting. It meant using that urination apparatus she hated to use. "OK, settle in and check fields of fire and security. One of us awake at all times.

The trio settled into a long wait. Two hours later, a message came to them that a contingency was being enacted.

'At least we are comfortable', Morgan thought.

September 21

Minuteman, north of Fort Benton, Montana
Werewolf Support Group Camp #1, Hill County, Montana
0800 hours MDT

Eight-seven senior NCOs from the Minutemen began the Senior NCO Academy. All of them had various and preconceived ideas and notions about whether or not this was worth the trouble.

They sat down and opened their notebooks. Many of them looked at the zeroxed notes and exerts in front of them. The first subject to be taught was called the "Order of Battle"

Delta 7, Moss Point, Montana
0900 hours MDT

A beep came over the radio. The decrypted message said that they needed to maneuver close to the main cargo entrance. They were told to clean up and follow the lead of the arriving group. All three looked at each other.

Thirty minutes later, a large panel van and a ten-passenger van rolled up to the main door. Several people got out, stretched and pulled out large rolls of paper.

The doors were opened and the people entered. Others brought in cleaning supplies and large boxes of supplies.

1300 hours MDT

A last encrypted message said that the other people departed the area and they were clear. Just to be safe, walk out without into the open without their equipment and blend into the workforce.

Morgan, Kendal and Locklear changed into Cindy, Wendy and Earl. They walked to the van, went in and removed their fatigues and boots. They put on overalls, tan shoes and finished scrubbing the camo paint off their faces.

Covington came to them and chuckled. "Remember what Mister Kincaid said. When in doubt, do something weird. Confusion equals chaos equals winning."

The trio established themselves as part of the group. Satellite imagery said the others were still out there. They had not moved. All three went inside and went to the bathrooms. Showers removed the last of the grime they picked up over the last two days.

Afterward, they went down stairs and examined the containers they used to transport Criers and Winchell. One of them had an additional cannister attached to the oxygen tank. The valves were left on and the contents were gone and after a year plus, the chances of finding something was not worth the effort.

What said something were the people arrayed around them. They stayed waiting. Did they have satellites? Time for answers.

1600 Hours MDT

Morgan and Kendal walked outside and walked to one of the people. The person watched them until both women literally stood over him. Both Cindy and Wendy had FBI windbreakers and badges.

Wendy knelt down and asked him. "Want to get a hot meal?"

The man looked at the smiling face. "Corporal Joseph Camerov, United States Police Force," he said turning over to show the badge.

Wendy took a picture of the badge and punched some buttons. After a few seconds, she stood up. "OK Corporal Camerov, tell your boyfriends to come in. The steaks will go on the bar-be-que in a few minutes."

Wendy and Cindy went over to the bar-be-que. One other woman was there. All three whispered something and went inside. A few minutes later, all three women came out wearing bikinis. All twelve of the USPF men came up to the van and of course, stared at the women. They were shown where the showers were.

"Food's going to be ready in 30 minutes," a man said.

All of them went inside as the women laid down on recliners.

"This ought to be easy," Kendal whispered.

Desert Zero, Fort Hood, Texas
1800 hours CDT

Simmons noted the uptick of missions. The after-action reports from the last time the Southern Command reverse invaded Mexico told him what was happening. Last time it was three weeks after the first invasion that the Savage Rabbits started having targets south of the border.

The only thing of note was the bounty placed on the Savage Rabbits. Today's mission had the men returning with a handbill offering a reward for anyone capturing a Savage Rabbit.

The CIA offered a warning that the Mexican Government might start making cross-border raids of their own in retaliation. American soldiers on parade were a great propaganda tool. The cartels promised an even more handsome reward for Savage Rabbit prisoners.

Simmons needed to talk to General O'Cleary about this. And simultaneously get permission to practice hostage rescue and preemptively get permission and the right to cross when ready to act on any information.

September 22

Federal Elections, United States of America

Alister Mackenzie left the Madison Media Center in New Orleans. The second of three debates with Republican Senator Simon Ballotine was over and he felt that he had mopped the floor with him.

Mackenzie loved the perks of being the Democratic Nominee. The fifty-two Secret Service guards were there to guard him around the clock. Those "people" he privately despised could no longer just come to him with their problems and their microphones to trip him up.

Mackenzie reveled in it. He would forever guard his secret. He hated the people who would vote for him, toil for him and if need be, die for him. He wanted the power of controlling seven trillion dollars. He wanted to command the most powerful military in the world. He wanted power over everything.

Privately, he wanted to see the one thing that made him the most powerful man in the world. A military officer following him with the nuclear launch codes. He would never use them. Never in a million years. But he would have them. If he ever had trouble with any nation, that officer had the perfect blackmail tool. A press conference would be held with a glimpse of that officer standing within 120 seconds from him with that "football".

Mackenzie was going to be the President of the United States. The remainder of the fortune his family made for him was being used to crush everyone and everything who threatened him or his dream. Criers' money was still there.

"President Alister Mackenzie," he said, glowing.

Delta 7, Moss Point, Montana
1500 hours MDT

Everyone packed all their equipment and closed the site. The USPF had a great time. The USPF drank a liberal amount of beer and spilled their guts.

The combination of a lot of alcohol, scopoline, and scantily clad women gave all the information the Werewolves needed.

Colonel Bradford Neilson, the Montana and Idaho USPF commander, had specific orders to monitor the Delta 7 facility and report on who came and went. There was a dusty report somewhere in the Attorney General's office. Someone wanted to see who was using it and, if necessary, arrest them if they "appeared" to doing illegal activities.

Colonel Neilson was the next man on the list.

September 23

Minuteman, north of Fort Benton, Montana
1000 hours MDT

The Fall Harvest was in and everyone came to the main compound to celebrate. It was a Thanksgiving in September. In a few days, the fall planting would begin. Everything was set up for the winter. Several times, individuals were found wandering into the area. They were told to leave. Several of them said they were intitled to something to eat.

All of them rebelled, in one way or the other, at the notion of working for the food they were going to eat.

An old man who tilled the ground on one of the northern farms told them the tail of the grasshopper and the ants.

"A grasshopper spent all summer playing in the fields while the ants toiled and stored food for the winter. When the chill came to the air, the ants said OK and fed him over the winter. But you need to work over the summer and collect your own food because the winter will come."

"The grasshopper jumped for joy and did as he was told, but soon spent more and more time playing all spring and summer meeting with other grasshoppers. Soon there were over 10,000 grasshoppers."

"At the end of the summer, the grasshopper came to the ants with his 10,000 children. I thought I taught them to farm and gather, but they did not listen. Help us, please."

The ants looked at each other, feeling they had to do something. One of the older ants said they could feed the grasshoppers from the eastern colony. They were very hearty bunch of workers and had a surplus. They will not miss it."

"The eastern colony rebelled, but ultimately lost their surplus and a portion of their winter ration. The winter was a particularly cold and harsh one. At the first sign of spring, the eastern colony packed up and left."

"At the end of the second summer, the grasshopper and one million of his descendants came to the ants. He said they were not going to go hungry. If you don't feed us willingly, we'll take it from you."

The man took a sip of his whiskey. These ones and twos will tell the world we are here. Then we will have to fight over the food. Go ahead and call me a liar. I'll burn my field before I let it go to people who will not work.

The old man walked away.

September 24

Atlantic Ocean, 37 degrees 64' North, 62 degrees 47' West
0500 hours EDT

The USS Henry M. Jackson opened its Number 1 tube while near motionless at launch depth. This time of the morning, there were no commercial or military flights over this portion of the Atlantic Ocean and no shipping within five hundred miles.

Updates from the North American Air Defense Command at Cheyanne Mountain in Colorado said nothing was overhead within five hundred miles. The optimum firing time was 0509 hours (0909 Zulu).

The authorization to fire and the targeting information came at 0845 Zulu. The Captain went through the process with the officers on board to verify the message. After the message was determined to be valid, the officers exchanged their firing packages. At 0901 Zulu, the Captain informed the crew that all preparations were complete and the Weapons officer reported all was ready.

The Captain inserted his key into the firing lock and rotated it from off to safe to arm and left it there.

The clock ticked down to Zero and the unmistakable sound of a missile being ejected from the submarine was heard by everyone. After it was confirmed that the missile was away, the order was sent to close the launch tube.

Twenty miles away a Russian attack submarine went on full alert, listening to a missile being launched. Emergency messages were sent over their dedicated network. The Captain and the Political Officer both agreed that they needed to risk surfacing and send a message to Moscow.

When Moscow finally learned of the missile firing, only one was fired and it was aimed at the Pacific Ocean. The only time the US fired a missile, it was announced ahead of time to avoid any misunderstanding.

As the missile arched over the North American continent, an open frequency transponder told the world the missile was flying. By the time, Moscow was notified, the missile was at its apogee over the North American continent and going to a point where the shroud over the warheads was jettisoned. At the optimum point, the independent warheads separated.

Downrange, the guided missile cruiser, USS Harrison Taylor tracked the warheads and projected their paths. All three inert warheads splashed down in the Pacific Ocean fifty-five hundred miles from the Henry Jackson.

All the evidence was classified. No confirmation would come from anyone for another year.

The world knew and shivered.

September 25

Department of the Treasury, Washington D.C.
1000 hours EST

Carter stared at the mammoth quarterly report for the country. Carter knew already that the economic growth of the country was stopped. Nothing new was happening. No new

778

construction, no new innovation. The universities and brain tanks said that plenty of research was available, but no capital was available to fund field research and build new technologies.

Carter picked up the summary from the top and half-heartedly read it. The numbers up and down were meaningless. What counted was a forty trillion deficit projected to be a reality within a short span of time; two, maybe three years. There was not enough money in the coffers to even try having a budget.

It was originally thought that twenty-four trillion was the limit before the debt was too large to be pay back. Now the talking head academics could not agree on anything. Converting to Blue Back currency only confused everything further and the politicians loved that confusion.

"Where there is confusion, there is profit," so goes the saying from the movie.

Carter through the summary back on top of the main report and turned to look out the window.

Carter reached for the phone messages and found one from Senator Mackenzie. He wanted a private meeting about Treasury matters. Mackenzie was going to be in town in two days for his mother's birthday.

Was he even interested in the truth?

United Nations, the Hague, the Netherlands
1500 hours (Alpha)

The Secretary General sat barricaded in his office. When the Russian delegation broke the news that the US had launched a missile from a submarine without any notice to the world, the Secretary General looked at the evidence and decided not to do anything. Granted the missile launched from an area that had a lot of commercial sea-going and airborne traffic. But no ships or airplanes were affected, but the status-quo was affected.

The Secretary General hated his job and the job hated him. The General Assembly was nothing more than a squabbling group of little children who made too much noise. The real power came from the Security Council. Nothing happened unless the Security Council voted to allow it. Five of the members had singular veto authority. Their "no" vote ended any resolution.

Lately, there were a lot of resolutions against the US. The Secretary General wondered how long the US would sit there and be demonized for doing what everyone else did regularly.

The latest was the launching of that D-5 missile without prior notice. The Russians routinely never advertised a launching. Get out of their way. North Korea tested missiles by flying them over Japan, without warning or consultation. Everyone else violated the rules, but tried to make the US play by those rules.

September 26

1000 hours (Alpha)

The Russian and Chinese Ambassador came to the American Delegation and asked to see the Ambassador.

Susan Martinson, the new American Ambassador, thought this was going to be interesting. Of course, she would see them. She remained seated as the Ambassadors came in and sat down.

There was the normal small talk while everyone sized each other over.

"Gentlemen," Martinson said. "Is this about the missile firing that I have not been briefed about?"

The Russian Ambassador looked at her and noted her reputation was well deserved. "We are seeking some assurances that nothing has a hidden meaning."

Martinson looked over to the Chinese Ambassador. She keyed in some strokes on her keyboard. After a few seconds she read from the monitor. "That missile does not have the range to hit the Chinese mainland from the firing position that was allegedly used."

Martinson knew a fishing expedition when she saw it. "There is nothing my government is doing other than testing a missile. If there was anything, I would have been briefed."

Both Ambassadors were clearly not happy with the answers. "Thank you, Ambassador," both said standing. Martinson stood with them. After they left, Martinson took the images on her computer, gave a quick synopsis and forwarded it to the State Department.

Martinson thought this was fun. Making the world bend over and get it back for a change.

September 27

Cyber Space, World Wide Web
0700 hours Zulu

UNSTACK THIS trolled the web and entered selected computers and "inspected" the contents. Being everywhere at all times gave UNSTACK THIS access to any secret.

The number one secret that Valkyrie designated was following the threads, starting with those people who tried to kidnap her and the other O'Cleary's. UNSTACK THIS was not aware that a situation was in play. UNSTACK THIS re-tasked his subordinate programs and computer main frames to find where this originated.

The interrogation of the kidnappers was dissected and confirmed that there was a "committee". Or was there?

The next thread was at Delta 7. Criers was dead in his cell.

It was on the second trip, that clues emerged. Winchell's container had an extra cylinder attached to the O2 system. The O2 cylinder was left open. Any chance of finding out what it was, evaporated over time.

The other people around the site were a reconnaissance team from the USPF. Colonel Bradford Neilson gave them the orders. His computer was scrubbed clean and he was no longer in the USPF.

UNSTACK THIS sent out a world-wide order to locate him.

September 28

Minuteman, north of Fort Benton, Montana

0900 hours MDT.

The Senior NCO Academy was in full swing. This week's course was the integrated air-land battle doctrine. All the facets of a modern battlefield were to be covered over the next two weeks. Any commander had to master his or her battlespace and assets. Everything had to be known and reacted to. Especially those of the enemy forces.

The needed to understand that there was a difference between information and intelligence.

Of particular interest was a section where commanders on the ground refused to see or react to the facts as the battle space told him was there. "Wishing it war', does not make it thar".

If a logistics re-supply is late or destroyed, the battle is affected by units trying to fight without everything they need to fight.

Casualties have to be known and counted in order to make a decision whether or not a unit can accomplish a mission without enough personnel and sometimes identify people with specialty skills that are needed.

Communications and security had to be safe guarded.

On and on it went for them. Many wondered why the problems and solutions were never seen or fixed. Sometimes shortcomings had to be overcome because a battle has to be pushed. All the Senior NCOs listened to after action reports where commanders ignored shortcomings and forced their subordinate officers to sacrifice their soldiers anyway.

Many of them who were combat veterans remembered situations where they were told to commit suicide missions while the officers stayed behind. Those same officers had every excuse in any world for not leading their troops in battle. And there were those times where the battle was too widely spaced for the officers to personally be there to command, but orchestrate from a distance. Getting committed in one area, sometimes missing critical decisions in other areas.

All the NCOs were heavily committed to the training, some of them staying after hours to study hard without interruptions.

At the Minuteman headquarters, Peters was reading reports that Matheson at his headquarters is trying to find out what was going on here. A lot of their strategy here was staying hidden from the outside world. Matheson was a rigid thinker. But if he saw something that piqued his interest, he was going to keep coming. Hopefully, Alaska would have a lot of his attention.

But Montana had a lot of people here who were separatist in nature. People who just wanted to be left alone. The problem was that outsiders did not and would never respect that.

Peters needed to schedule another staff and resident meeting in order to formulate a plan to deal with the outside world. Saying that they would never have to worry about that is folly.

Desert Zero, Fort Hood, Texas
1300 hours CDT

O'Cleary came to Desert Zero after touring the hospital. Seven dead Rabbits and twenty-two wounded. She asked them questions about what happened. Major Foyer, the S-3 went along with the mission along with Captain Baldwin, the "A" company commander.

The Rabbits were sent in to recon and gather information about the drug pipeline being re-established. The Rabbits escorted a DEA team to the site.

At 0200 they inserted into a deserted area along Highway 40 between Mazatlán and Durango on two sides of a rigid line. Colonel Simmons had "B" standing by next to Osprey aircraft for the forty-five-minute dash.

Simmons was watching the satellite feed and noticed some activity originating from Mazatlán and Durango. Fearing an ambush, Simmons ordered "B" company into the air. Going with them was two AC-130 Gunships that were already airborne and turned them south. A third Gunship was standing-by at Fort Hood.

As the gunships arrived on station, "A" company was attacked from two directions by large units from the Mexican

Army. AC-130 aircraft provided fire support from the on-board 105mm cannon and the 30mm Bushmaster.

The Mexican Army fought hard to crush the Americans, but were beaten back repeatedly. As the AC-130's reported they were running low on ammunition, Captain Baldwin was killed trying to line up aircraft to evacuate his men.

Major Foyer assumed command and started to contract his men. He ran around and positioned his 40mm grenade gunners to shoot at targets.

When "B" company arrived to the north of them, the Mexican Army units were minutes away from overrunning "A" company. The Mexican Army units fell back and began adjusting fire from 60mm and 81mm mortars on the American locations.

Major Foyer identified the general location of the mortars and told the AC-130's to concentrate their remaining ammunition on the mortars.

Major Foyer took a radio and put it on his back as he directed the evacuation of "A" company. Just as Captain Tenneson arrived, Major Foyer was shot in the back and went down.

Tenneson started evacuating the wounded as he told his First Sergeant to get the machine guns lined up on the north side of the perimeter to foil that attack.

The first batch of Ospreys landed and picked up all the wounded and dead. Additionally, as many people as could be loaded up were jammed in with the wounded and dead. The "A" company men were silent on the way home. Their brothers had been downed.

Twenty minutes later, another batch of Ospreys arrived along with another AC-130 loaded down with ammunition, looking for targets. The Mexican Army units decided to withdraw, especially when the new AC-130 arrived and started pounding on them.

Captain Tenneson was the last man on the ground.

Once back at Desert Zero, the DEA team was complaining about being discovered. Simmons told them to leave before he shot them. The officious men left. They were obviously not field agents.

O'Cleary had a motherly attachment to the Savage Rabbits. She wanted to know why the Mexican Army seemed to be waiting for them. The DEA team seemed to sink into the background.

O'Cleary was going to make a few phone calls in the morning. Unless there were some satisfactory answers, the DEA will not get any future support.

September 29

United States Police Force, Alexandria, Virginia
0900 hours EDT

Director Simon Westland looked at the dashboard on his sidewall. In the upper right-hand portion was the space which denoted his strength levels. The total number of personnel under his command topped one hundred thousand.

Westland was sour at the total. Over half his strength was existing police forces and the rest were mostly given away as fillers for various Federal agencies. In reality he only had, at most, a little more than ten thousand men he could directly command.

Westland looked under the manpower section and saw all the requests for manpower and assistance to local law enforcement agencies.

White House, Washington, D.C.
1500 hours EDT

The President sat in the Oval Office thinking more and more like a lame-duck. All his dreams of a legacy the nation would revere him for, was dashed as he took the oath of office. The events of January 20th were etched in the nation's psyche just the same as December 7th, and 9-11. All dates that will live in infamy.

The President was brooding a lot lately. The Internal Security Agency (ISA) was another bastard child he was too stupid to see coming.

The President was remarkedly clear eyed about past events. Mostly his reactions to the events. Some of his more clear-eyed advisors said that he should have let the situation fix itself. The government was getting in the way of recovering from the free fall this country was experiencing.

The President went to the beverage cart and made an alcoholic drink. He had been doing a lot of that lately.

He notified Lucy Markson, his secretary, that he was not interested in the rest of the day.

He was not interested in the rest of the day or the year. The government was a machine that did not care. It moved on its own.

He was most afraid that Alister Mackenzie was going to replace him.

September 30

Minuteman, north of Fort Benton, Montana
0700 to 1900 hours MDT

Glendive and Sheridan sat in Kendal and Locklear's house. Both Kendal and Locklear arrived yesterday and were bombarded with the logistics file for the new Werewolf class.

Kendal and Locklear called General O'Cleary and told her they were now following her orders and would follow her orders. But they were tired of being pulled in so many directions. "Was this why Mister Kincaid killed himself?"

"It's a godamm mess," Kendal said. She was sifting through the morass of files.

Earl found John Kincaid's original file organization and showed Wendy. He started moving files around and getting upset with anyone who was upsetting his system.

"Look everyone!" Locklear said. "I have a handle on this. Everyone leave it alone. Go get some coffee or make it." He went back to looking for the file numbers and sorting them. "Whose genius idea was it to separate things?" he muttered.

Kendal saw it. "I got the follow-on support for Phase 1."

Glendive and Sheridan watched these two upstarts tell them to get out of the way of progress.

CPSIA information can be obtained
at www.ICGtesting.com
Printed in the USA
LVHW051539070722
722844LV00010B/867

9 781458 324160